W9-BAG-510

From the day I was introduced to the "Worlds of the Crystal Moon" I was enthralled. When you've been in the business as long as I have, it doesn't take long to recognize real talent and a writer gifted with that rare ability to create a compelling world that not only entertains, but profoundly touches the heart, mind and soul. The Worlds of The Crystal Moon is such a story. I implore all of you to enter and explore this powerful and magical story which will stir and inspire your imagination for generations to come.

Richard Hatch (Apollo – Battlestar Galactica)
Actor, Writer, Director and Producer

Thanks to the Worlds of the Crystal Moon Artists

Todd Sheridan - Cover
sheridan.todd@gmail.com

Kathleen Stone - Black & White Illustrations
kathleen@kastone-illustrations.com

Daniel Vest - 3D Color Illustrations
dvestzeus@hotmail.com

Cindy Fletcher - cinfl37@yahoo.com

View high-def maps of the Worlds of the Crystal Moon at
www.worldsofthecrystalmoon.com

Phillip "Big Dog" Jones' Facebook fan page:
www.facebook.com/worldsofthecrystalmoon

Principal Editor: William Zavatchin - **wjzavatchin@msn.com**

Special Thanks: To the fans of the Worlds of the Crystal Moon, your feedback was invaluable while creating this final edition. Your input was a blessing.

I am dedicating this book to my sons: Christopher and Chase

This printing was done by:
Worzalla Publishing Co., Stevens Point, WI • 866-523-7737

Athena's Jewelry Armoire - created by: RJ the Leather Guy, www.rjleatherguy.com
Athena's Poem on page 518, written by: Joanne Hill, oceanseleven1242@yahoo.com

Library of Congress Cataloging-in-Publication Data
First published in 2010 under ISBN — 978-0-9816423-3-8

Crystal Moon, Magic of Luvelles

ISBN: 978-0-9816423-3-8

5 1 6 9 5

9 780981 642338

Second Edition
Appropriate for readers of advanced
seasons 13 and older.

Printed in the United States of America
10 9 8 7 6 5 4 3

Published by: Shapeshift Productions, LLC

George and Kepler

Payne

Sam and Shalee
In the Royal Garden of Brandor

Boyafed *(Boy-a-fed)*
Leader of the Order

Lord Dowd
Leader of the White Army

Athena Nailer

The Head Master's Island
Brayson Id's Home

Gregory Id
White Chancellor of Luvelles

Marcus Id
Dark Chancellor of Luvelles

Strongbear

Kesdelain *(Kes-de-lane)*
Troll King of Trollcom

Mosley
Night Terror Wolf

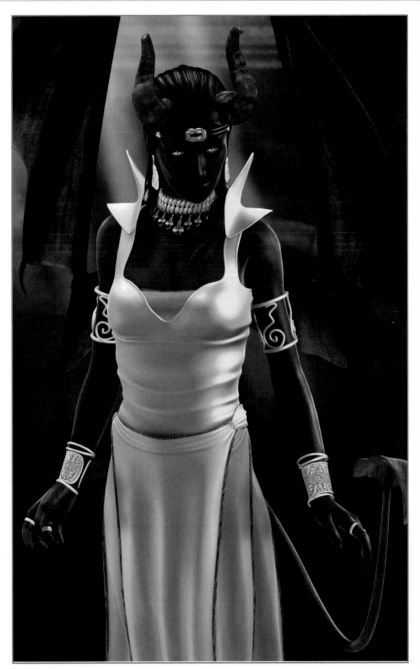

Sharvesa *(Shar-**vay**-sa)*
Demon Queen of Dragonia

Lasidious
The Mischievous One

Mountains of Oraness *(Or-a-**ness**)*
Home of The Source

The Dome of Helmep's Temple
The City of Inspiration

Bryana – *The Seer*
Brayson Id - *Head Master of Luvelles*

Western Luvelles
Lands of Kerkinn

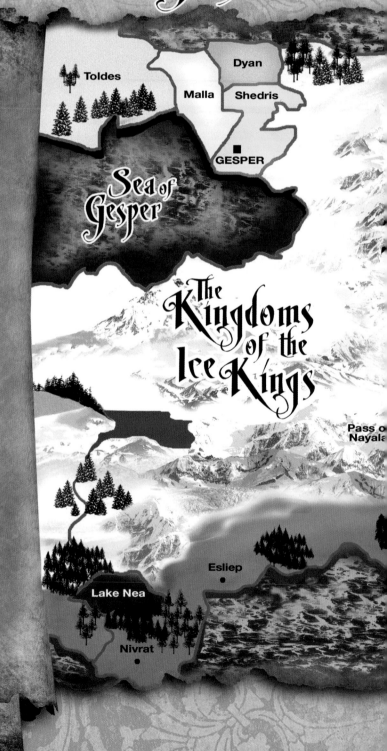

Northern Grayham

Toldes

Dyan

Malla **Shedris**

■ **GESPER**

Sea of Gesper

The Kingdoms of the Ice Kings

Pass o Nayala

Esliep

Lake Nea

Nivrat

Southern Grayham

Temple of the Gods

Springs of Grayham

Temple Platform

Griffin Cliffs

Griffin Falls

Siren's Song

Blood River

War

Lake Blood

Dark Forest

Pool of Sorro

Ocean of Maroepa

Neutral Territory

Latsky Divide

Angel

Angel's Crossing

River of Death

Enchanted Forest

Minotaur Hills

Champion

Latsky River

Bear Clan

Zandra

Scorpion Island

Zander River

Poison River

Lake Zandra

Cottle

Lake Cottle

Kingdom of Serpents

Snake River

Serpent city

Cartosam

Glossary

Dawn
The moment when the sun rises just above the horizon.

Morning
Period of the day between Dawn and Early Bailem.

Early Bailem
When the sun has reached the halfway point between the horizon and its highest point in the sky, the Peak of Bailem.

Peak of Bailem
The moment when the sun has reached its highest point.

Late Bailem
The moment when the sun has passed the Peak of Bailem and taken a position halfway between the Peak of Bailem and when the sun disappears behind the horizon.

Evening
The moments between Late Bailem and when the sun is about to disappear behind the horizon.

Night
The moments after the sun has disappeared behind the horizon until it once again rises and becomes Dawn.

Midnight
An estimated series of moments that is said to be in the middle of the night.

———————————— SEASON or SEASONS ————————————
There are different uses for the words *season* and *seasons*.

Season
The common meaning referring to winter, spring, summer, and fall.

Seasons
People can refer to their ages by using the term *season* or *seasons*. For example: if someone was born during a winter season, he or she would become another season older once they reach the following winter. They are said to be so many winter seasons old.

Table of Contents

Grogger's Swamp
Western Luvelles

Soul to Soul

Fellow Soul...

...I am pleased to see you have decided to join me for the second of many stories. When last we visited the Worlds of the Crystal Moon, you were left with many unanswered questions. As we move forward, I offer a word of warning. This story is not for the fainthearted. It requires a mind with an ardent wit, one which has the ability to follow the manipulations of the gods and those involved in the events which inspired the telling of this story.

Even I, your spirited bard, have found the revelations which have been said to be fact, disturbing. I have struggled to determine the truth—if such a thing still exists.

I beg you. Give me your undivided attention. I hope you enjoy my recollections.

Your friend, and fellow soul inside the Book of Immortality,
Phillip **"Big Dog"** Jones

The City of Brandor
Just After Dawn

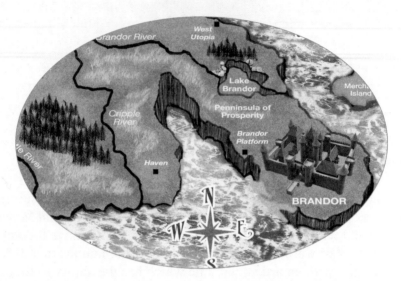

As the queen entered the throne room, the king sheathed his blessed blade, then extended a hand to each of his guards to help them from the cold stones of the castle floor. Once they had been dismissed from training, Sam moved to look out the stone-framed window to catch his breath.

The cobblestone streets leading away from Brandor's castle were quiet. Despite the silence, the smell of greggled hash and eggs could be savored as the aroma escaped the kitchen window below and made its way to the king's nose.

Sam smiled as he turned from the window and gave Shalee a good morning kiss. "Hello, beautiful," he said as he brushed the queen's cheek.

Before Shalee could respond, a familiar voice called out. "My King...My Queen," Michael said as the last limping guard passed him on his way out. The general hurried across the throne room and took a knee at the base of the steps leading to their thrones.

Michael was a strong, bold man and held the position of General Absolute in Brandor's army. He wore his best chain armor, and a black cape had been draped across his back. The Crest of Brandor was positioned at the cape's center.

"Speak, Michael," Sam said as he walked from the window. He ascended the stairs and stood next to his throne. The king was large, or at least considered large for a human, but was small in stature compared to the barbarians of the north. Sam's brown hair and brown eyes complemented a handsome face which rested atop a 6'4", 275-pound, well-defined frame.

"The news I bring is good, My King. The army's advance on Bloodvain is promising. The barbarians are surrendering as news of Senchae's death spreads. There are those who've chosen to fight, but their numbers are scattered. They are disorganized, with no real battle plan. They have proven to be no match for our forces. It's only a matter of moments before all of Southern Grayham lives in service to your crown, Sire."

Sam motioned to one of the servants to bring him a mug of ale. "Have the two missing pieces of the crystal been found?"

"No. We have searched everywhere and continue to search. It's as if Seth's underground kingdom is never ending. The serpent had no knowledge George hid the crystals there." A smile appeared on Michael's face. "There is other news."

"I'm listening."

"In an effort to show his willingness to cooperate, Seth has led the army to a shaft full of coin."

"Why would he have a shaft full of coin? I can think of no reason why his species would have use for it."

Michael grinned. "Seth's race has always sold their poison and various forms of plant life, which grow in the marsh, to Merchant Island. They do this to keep us 'two-legs' from crossing their borders. For them, it's not about the coin, it's about being left alone. For thousands of seasons they've been throwing their profits into this pit. I've ordered the spoils to be brought to Brandor. But, I fear we don't have the means to hold it."

Pushing his hands through his hair, Sam began to chuckle. "There are some things on Grayham I'll never get used to. Calling a bunch of snakes a race...how strange is that? But, no matter. Too much coin is what I consider a pleasant problem. I'll order new vaults constructed. How many do you think we'll need?"

Again, Michael grinned. "I would say another twenty-five or so, but you may want to make them twice as large."

Sam placed his free hand on the back of his throne. "Holy garesh! There's that much?" He took another drink of ale. "If this is the case, our kingdom will never lack for anything. We'll be able to enhance not only Brandor, but the rest of the kingdom as well."

The king motioned for Michael to stand. Moving to look out the window to the city below, Sam sighed as he watched the everyday man walk across the meticulously placed stones of the streets. Their pain would soon be over.

Their loved ones would be able to return and life would move forward in peace.

Sam enjoyed a deep breath of Grayham's crisp, clean air as a gentle breeze found its way through the stone-framed opening and onto his face. "Finally…some good news." He turned to look at Michael. "The coin will be a blessing."

After looking at Shalee, Sam pointed toward the street and continued to address his general. "I was worried there would be further bloodshed before the barbarians surrendered. The families of our men will be happy to know it's only a matter of moments before their loved ones return. I imagine there's enough coin to reward each man for his service?"

"There is more than enough to reward every man in each legion for a hundred lives lived, My King."

Sam shook his head. "It's hard to envision that much coin. I look forward to seeing the mounds myself."

"But, what about George?" Shalee interrupted, wanting answers of her own.

As always, the queen was stunning, her fashion impeccable. Her soft blue gown accented her natural glow, courtesy of her pregnancy. She stood from her throne and pushed her blonde hair behind her shoulders. After taking Precious into her hand, she tapped the staff's butt end on the floor and looked at the general through a pair of beautiful blue eyes.

"The coin sounds great and all, General, but for heaven's sake, do ya know where George is? Does anyone know where Kepler is? How 'bout his brothers for that matta'? They're enemies ta our way of life. We need ta find 'em to keep 'em from hurtin' anyone else. This doggone war was their creation in the first place."

Michael's mood changed as his report of the kingdom's newfound fortune was overshadowed by George and Kepler's disappearance. "My Queen, I have assigned 500 men to hunt Kepler and his brothers. I have assigned another 200 to do nothing but search for George. It's only a matter of moments before their flesh meets the chains of our dungeon."

Shalee moved next to Sam and took hold of his arm. "Michael, I want ta make sure everythin' is peaceful before our baby is born." She touched her stomach. "I don't want any child of mine bein' born into a world with this kinda hate existin' in it. 200 men aren't enough to fight George's power."

"I understand. I'll double the numbers." Michael turned to Sam. "What other orders would you give, My King?"

Sam motioned for the servants and his guard to clear the room. Once they were alone, he continued. "Michael, let's talk as friends for a moment."

"What's on your mind?"

"You know I've commanded the members of the Senate to come to Brandor. I want to discuss how we should proceed before giving further orders. I've called on the Senate because we need the members of our government to go into the Barbarian Kingdom and spread word we wish to live with them in peace. They'll need to take an offering for each of the barbarian nobles. Their royal families are to remain esteemed."

Michael's face showed his disdain. "You want us to treat them as royalty? Sam, this is outrageous. I don't think Senchae would have done the same for our nobles."

"Exactly. That's why it's important for our actions to show otherwise. I want all barbarians to be apprised of our respect for their people. I want to meet with their nobles to determine who among them would be the best choices to offer positions as new members of the Senate. I plan to select ten and will give each their own seat within the courts of Brandor. It's important the barbarian people are represented within a united Southern Grayham."

Michael stood in silence. Shalee could see the confusion on his face. "What's got ya all boggled, Michael? Why so quiet?"

"I don't like the thought of barbarians polluting our Senate. The senators will have much to say about this. I'm sure your ideas won't be welcomed with open arms."

The king rubbed the scruff on his chin. "Pollute: a harsh word for people we don't understand. Let me ask you something, Michael. If you were a barbarian and you hated the people of the south, not to mention the fact you were taught to hate us since childhood, wouldn't you loathe us further if your people were left out of the day-to-day functions of a government forced down your throat? Think about it. How would you feel? Don't you think you would find it easier to accept the changes in your life if you had a voice within this new government?"

After spending a while pondering his king's opinion, Michael responded. "Your logic makes sense. I agree with what you've said. I don't like it, but I agree. It will take many moments for my mind to adjust. It will take many more moments for the men of our army to understand. But, they trust you. The Senate will not be so trusting."

"Don't worry 'bout them," Shalee responded. "After Sam reminds the Senate it was the gods' decision for us ta come into this world and create a peaceful empire, they'll see things our way. Besides, we're still at war until

Sam declares otherwise. Sam can do as he pleases. The Senate will have no choice but ta comply."

Michael patted Sam on the shoulder. "I do hope you handle this matter with greater tact than our queen has just suggested."

Sam laughed as he pulled Shalee close. "Our queen is spirited. I'm sure I'll figure something out before I address the Senate."

Michael sighed. "I often forget the two of you have such powerful friends backing your positions. Not many men have the gods on their side." The general bowed to his queen. "Please forgive…I don't understand how the mind of a woman from Earth works. I still find myself getting used to you."

Shalee moved to Michael and gave him a hug, followed by a quick wink. "There's no forgiveness necessary. Goodness-gracious, it's not just a woman from Earth the men from Grayham don't understand. Women are pretty much the same here as they were there. As all good women do, we keep our men guessin'. You know, keep ya wonderin' if you'll eva' figure us out."

Michael gave a half-hearted smile and, because of his discomfort, changed the tone of the meeting. "As for me, My King, you have my full support. I agree it's best to give the barbarians a voice. I believe this will work to change their perception that the people of Brandor are nothing more than common swine."

"Let's hope you're right, General. Let me know when you've found George and Kepler."

"Yes, My King."

Three Days Later
Griffin Falls

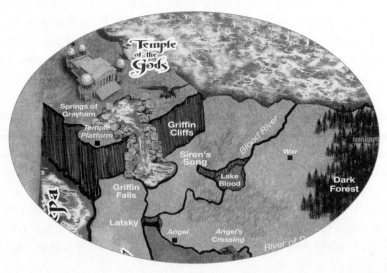

After asking Shalee for a scroll in which to teleport, Sam took four of his men into the royal garden and ordered them to teleport to the Temple of the Gods. When the queen asked why, all the king would say was he had a surprise for her.

With Late Bailem approaching, Sam and Shalee are now sitting at a small wooden table close to the edge of the Griffin's Platform which overlooks Southern Grayham. Cooked hen is on the menu and the royal chef is there to serve them.

Sam watched a smile appear on his queen's face as their meal was uncovered. "I'm glad you like it. Your ability to teleport has its uses. We haven't had many moments to ourselves since our arrival on this world. I want you to understand how much I love you." Sam motioned for Shalee to look at the area surrounding them. "I couldn't think of any place more romantic."

"Well, aren't *you* a peach. This was a lovely idea. You've outdone yourself."

Shalee stood from her chair and moved to her king, holding his eyes with her gaze. She leaned over. The passion she felt could be seen as she prepared to thank him. The men standing guard at the edges of the platform turned their backs, but the royal chef simply smiled and moved to a better position to enjoy the romance filling the moments.

The queen's lips were soft and tasted like melon, her tongue accenting the mood. Sam's heart melted as she nibbled his bottom lip and the top of his right ear. He trembled and forgot everything around him. When Shalee moved back, she once again held his eyes with hers until she settled into her seat.

The chef could not contain his excitement. "Well done, My Queen," he shouted. "Bravo! It's nice to know My King and his bride share a love so divine."

Shalee blushed. Sam turned and gave the chef a look. "Thomas, don't you have something better to do with your moments?"

"My apologies, Sire. I shall fetch some wine."

As Sam watched Thomas move to the far side of the platform, he marveled at the gigantic doors of the temple beyond the pools which bubbled to the surface across the plateau. He could remember how he felt the first moment he saw their massive hinges. Each door was nearly 95 feet tall and arched toward each other at the top. He remembered thinking how heavy they must be. At almost two meters thick, he had imagined the sound they would make if one of them was to slam into the wall.

Shalee lifted her glass from the table and sauntered to the railing overlooking the falls fed by the natural springs. The water fell over 7,000 feet to the land below. The view across the steppe was breathtaking. Many beautiful flowers as well as other vegetation, she had grown accustomed to since their arrival on Grayham, bloomed around the pools. The scene was glorious and set the mood for an evening of romance with her regal husband.

After dinner, Sam had his men clear the table and teleport to Brandor, Once they were gone, Sam moved to the edge of the platform and rang a large bell. "I have a surprise for you. I know you don't remember our first ride with Soresym since you were asleep. You know...the day you threw your fit."

"I rememba' my fit. I regret missin' that experience."

"Well, now you'll have the chance to make up for it."

Shalee smiled and pushed up against him. "Just take a look at ya, Sam Goodrich. Who would have eva' guessed ya had a romantic bone inside that delicious body of yours?"

Sam remembered Shalee's exact words when she found out they would need to ride the griffin to get to Brandor. Shalee had shouted at Mosley, *"If you think I'm gonna ride some giant whateva' it is, you got anotha' think comin'. I'm not about ta get on some creepy, flyin' thingy. I don't know how ta ride stuff like that. Do they bite? Goodness-gracious, I bet they bite. Oh, my gosh, do they smell?"*

Mosley had become sick of Shalee's ranting. The wolf breathed on her face and her body slumped onto the same platform where they now stood. The wolf said, *"She will sleep for a while. I am sure she will be far more pleasant after she has had the chance to adjust. Are all the women from your Earth like her?"*

Sam had smiled at the wolf and responded by saying, *"Only the ones worth keeping. I have to admit, I find her attractive. I like her sassiness. She'll grow on you, Mosley. She's just stressed right now, that's all. Ever since I got here, so many things have seemed familiar. She's from Texas and I know I've never met her before, but even she seems familiar. I would have told her, but that would have been kind of creepy. Just trust me on this, Mosley, you'll like her. I just know it."*

"I hope you're right."

Sam's thoughts returned to the present. He grinned at the pleasant feeling of the memory and pulled Shalee close. He was kissing her when Soresym crested the cliff's ledge. The king reacted, grabbing the railing surrounding the platform as the massive wings of the griffin stirred the evening air. As Soresym's majestic form lowered to the landing platform, Shalee couldn't contain her excitement. She ran to the griffin and stroked his feather-covered neck.

"Well, aren't ya just a sight. It's good ta see ya, Soresym. I think of ya often."

"And, I you, young one."

"Thank you for doing this for me, Soresym," Sam said as he approached. "I cannot express how much I appreciate you."

"You're welcome, King of Brandor."

Sam lifted Shalee onto the griffin's back, then climbed up. He tied his queen in with the heavy leather straps attached to the saddle's padded surface, then pulled her close. The beast walked to the edge of the platform with his head held high and wings spread. Shalee lifted her arms into the air and screamed as the griffin folded his wings and jumped from the cliff's ledge.

Soresym kept his wings folded as the ground approached, waiting until the last possible moment before allowing the wind to funnel beneath his feathers. They swooped to a position just above the mist of the falls. The rush and the coolness of the spray was refreshing.

Shalee shouted, "Oohhh, my goodness-gracious, Sam! This is the best date eva'!"

Sam reached around her waist and pulled her closer. He looked across the countryside as it passed. After a while, he leaned in and put his mouth to the queen's ear. "I love you."

After tasting his lips, Shalee responded, "I love ya, too, ya big lug."

Meanwhile, Western Luvelles
The Dark Chancellor's Tower-palace

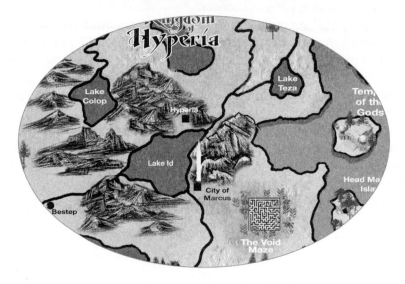

The Dark Chancellor, Marcus Id, stormed into the highest level of his tower-palace. He threw his black cape, marked with the order's symbol, and watched it fly across the room. Despite the chancellor's desire for the cape to hit the wall, the cloth refused to be abused and adjusted its course, peacefully hanging itself on a hook near the door.

Marcus grunted his disappointment. His brown eyes were cold. Tension filled his lanky limbs beneath the confines of his golden shirt. His long brownish-black hair fell across his elven features as he shouted at the top of his lungs, "My brother's self-righteous attitude is becoming tiresome!"

After a moment of silence, Marcus realized he was yelling at an empty room. He grunted again before lighting his pipe. "Gage, get in here before I have you skinned!"

Another few moments passed before a dark brown badger, covered in a short, fitted, red robe entered the room walking erect. He ignored the chancellor's threat and tapped his tiny wooden cane on the cold stones of the tower-palace floor, taking his own sweet moments. "Would you stop shouting? Just relax, will you? Stick to the plan. Your actions will accomplish nothing."

"Careful, goswig. Watch your tongue. I'm not in the mood."

"Watch my tongue? Who are you jesting? You're always in a mood. You created me to fight with you. It's my obligation to tell you when you're being ridiculous. If memory serves me right, and it always does, you created me to speak my mind, or rather, our mind, when you have these idiotic fits. You know you're acting rash or I wouldn't feel the need to bring it to your attention."

Marcus slammed his boney hand on the stone table resting at the center of the room. The table was large and sat within his dismal bedroom chamber. The stone's surface held many chiseled markings which represented the ways of dark magic. "Then, you know what I'm thinking," Marcus barked as the smoke from his pipe drifted past the anger in his eyes.

Gage's furry face cringed. He hurried across the floor—a task hard for a badger to do while walking on his hind legs—and jumped onto the table. The badger pounded the butt of his cane against its stone surface.

"It's too early to kill your brothers...either of them, no matter how strong your desire. You don't have the power."

"Bah! Gregory is no match. I could kill him with little trouble. I should destroy his precious city of glass while I'm at it. Why someone would want to live in a glass palace is beyond me. His goodness binds my bowels."

Gage growled, then looked up at the petrified wooden rafters spanning the length of the room. "Would you stop? We both know it isn't Gregory you fear. You cower to the Head Master."

Marcus snapped his head around and stormed toward the window. He took a long, deep breath and looked down at the roof of the Order's temple which surrounded his tower below. Taking a moment to admire the gloom of a city which he had named after himself, he responded. "I cower to no one, not even Brayson. I could defeat him."

Gage gave Marcus a look.

Seeing the badger's expression, Marcus turned and glared at the cloud covered sky. "So, what if I am afraid of Brayson? I don't need you pointing it out to me. Besides, my power has grown. Perhaps, it's the right moment to challenge him."

The badger growled as he sat on the table's stone surface and started tracing the etched markings with a claw. "You must wait. If you're wrong about your ability to defeat Brayson, you'll be dead, and for what? Because you have no patience. The Head Master hasn't taken a new Mystic Learner in over twenty seasons. You must wait for this to happen. I'm sure it will be soon."

"How can you be so sure? Brayson doesn't seem to be in a hurry to find another student. How am I going to get my hands on his spell? Without it, I can't open the chest that holds the key."

◆═╬═◆

Marcus thought back to a confrontation he had with Brayson's last Mystic Learner. Hettolyn, a young halfling, was making his way to Brayson's shrine after receiving the secret spell from the Head Master. The shrine, located on the southern end of the Head Master's Island, served the most important purpose on Luvelles.

Marcus had stopped Hettolyn just prior to his arrival. The shrine housed a locked chest and the spell Hettolyn had memorized was the only magic that would open it. The key unlocking the way to The Source was inside.

"Where do you think you're going, boy?" the Dark Chancellor asked, appearing in front of Hettolyn.

"You startled me! Who are you, sir?"

"Who doesn't matter. You and I have something to discuss."

"I see," the young halfling responded. *"Then, I suppose it doesn't matter what I'm doing here, or where I'm going, if it doesn't matter who you are."*

Marcus laughed. *"You're right. It doesn't matter. It's what you have that matters. And, what you have, you're going to give to me."*

Marcus remembered the fear in Hettolyn's eyes as he lifted his hand and bound the halfling with his magic.

"Please, let me go! I have nothing of value, sir. I have nothing other than the clothes on my back."

"Sir? How could you not know who I am, boy?"

"I do not know your face. You have the wrong man. You must be waiting for someone else."

"What's your name, boy?"

"I am called Hettolyn, from Equality."

"Ha! Equality is a city full of weak minds. Are you also weak, Hettolyn? Is your mind strong enough to resist my advance?"

"I believe I'm strong. Why do you bind me?"

"How about if we find out how strong you are? Today...you're going to recite the spell my brother gave you to unlock his precious chest. Or, today... you're going to die if I don't lay my hands on the key."

"I have no idea what you're speaking about. I have a family. Please... they need me."

"Don't lie to me! I know you seek the key resting inside your Master's chest. You seek your chance to meet with The Source. You wish to look into the Eye of Magic. I think we both know I have the right man."

"As I have said, I don't know anything about these things!"

"Hmpf! We shall see." Marcus lifted his hands.

The Halfling had proven to be unforthcoming. He gave his life to protect Brayson's secret spell, and the Dark Chancellor destroyed the evidence.

Marcus shook his head. "Brayson's spell is the gateway to my desires. Once I have it, I can get the key and gain access to The Source. Only then will I be able to rule Luvelles."

Gage showed his sharp teeth, picked up his cane and once again tapped it against the table. His tone was firm as he snarled. "The key is worth the wait. Controlling this world means everything to you. Only The Source can give you the power you seek, and without it, you'll be unable to kill Brayson."

"I already know this, goswig!"

"Then, why speak of it?"

"Because waiting while my brother basks in his glory is killing me! Brayson is so pompous. I want to rip that arrogant smile from his face and feed it to the krape lords. It's absurd he remains neutral in all things. How could someone avoid choosing a side. At least Gregory's vexatious mind has chosen to wallow in tender-heartedness."

Gage shook his head. "Your impatience solves nothing. It won't be long and Brayson will have a new Mystic Learner."

Marcus relit his pipe. After a long drag, he held the smoke within his lungs, then exhaled over an expanded series of moments. He chuckled as he rolled his hands around one another. "Yes...and he'll give this fool the spell. As always, the spell will only be able to be spoken once before it's forgotten. All I need to do is force this doomed spirit to speak the words. Once I have them, I can get past Brayson's magic and gain access to the key."

"You're right," Gage snapped, "but you might want to maintain your composure when the moment presents itself. You should wait until the student recites the spell before you kill him."

"Your babbling is testing my patience, goswig! I already know this." Marcus took another drag from his pipe.

"Your mind's affliction will subside. Once you've spoken with The Source, you'll be all powerful...without rival."

The goswig swallowed hard at the thought of his words and shook his furry head in disgust, careful not to allow Marcus to see his disapproval. He would have continued to dwell on his dislike for Marcus' repulsive ways, but he became distracted after capturing another thought from Marcus' mind. The thought was ridiculous. The badger had to laugh.

"What's so funny?" Marcus sneered.

After collecting his composure, Gage responded. "I find it humorous you call your brother pompous when you were thinking you're the only brother vain enough to name a city after yourself. You cast stones in the wrong direction."

"Careful, goswig, you're walking on thin ice."

Gage shrugged. "Don't become unbalanced. You thought it."

Marcus gave the goswig a look of warning and pointed a bony finger in the badger's direction.

"Okay," the badger recoiled.

Gage watched as Marcus left the room. The badger sighed, then thought, *My duties as your goswig are becoming taxing. There's much hate in your heart. Marcus, you make my head hurt.*

The Village of Floren
Kebble's Kettle

George Nailer rushed into his room, his blue eyes full of anxiety. The day had come to leave Kebble's inn. "Athena! Athena! Where are you?" Shutting the door, the mage scanned the empty room. "We need to hurry. This is the day we've been waiting for."

"Honey, just relax," Athena responded from behind the washroom door. "I'll be ready in a moment. Besides, you don't want to look over-anxious. You said so yourself."

Athena's light-blue eyes carried a sense of joy. Her belly was beginning to show the life the couple had created on Grayham. She could only smile as she brushed her long blonde hair with an ivory handled brush while gazing in the mirror.

"I know what I said," George huffed, "but that doesn't change the fact I am anxious and want to get going. We've been stuck here at this damn inn for far too long. It's about time that piece of garesh sent word for us to come see him."

Athena poked her head out the door. "George Nailer, you watch that mouth of yours! You know I hate it when you speak so foul. And, there you go again, using that word 'time.' You know there is no such thing."

"Bah," George whispered, careful not to allow Athena to hear. "Yes, dear. I'm sure I meant to say, I'm glad the *moment* has arrived for the Head Master to send for us. We're supposed to meet with him to find out where the family's new homes are."

Athena looked back into the mirror. She knew it was hard for her husband to change his habits after a life filled with such nasty language. Taking a deep breath, she continued to brush her hair. "I know. You're right. I agree. I'm also glad the moment has come, but the family has enjoyed our stay here. Kebble has been more than pleasant. I thank the gods you had enough coin to keep us sheltered for so long. I can't imagine what my family would have done if you didn't have the means."

"The gods had nothing to do with it," George boasted as he shifted from one foot to another. His wealth had come at Amar's expense. It was Lasidious who had convinced the Head Master to give him the dead mage's riches.

"Coin isn't an issue," George continued. "I've told you more than once. You need to stop worrying. I'm ready to move on and get settled. This inn has been an okay place to crash, but I think we need to have our own space. I want to get past this damn pit stop."

Athena looked out from behind the door. "What's a pit stop? I'm sure we haven't crashed into anything. Some of the things you say are odd. There are moments when I have trouble understanding how you talk. The people from your Earth must have been strange." She laid down her brush. "Mother said you confused her the other day. She said you spoke of how much you missed your car and metal beasts called planes. I've been meaning to ask you about them."

Rolling his eyes, George sat on the edge of the bed and threw himself back with a flop. "Babe, you're killing me. It's nothing worth talking about. Don't worry about it. Just hurry up so we can get going. I'm sure you look stunning. Can we go now?"

"Yes, but this doesn't mean I won't ask later."

"Well, later is better." He stood up, moved into the washroom and pulled her close. "I love you."

She smiled and lowered her head against his chest, her favorite spot. "I love you, too. I'll be ready in a moment. I want to look beautiful for you."

As they left the inn, they said goodbye to Kebble. As always, the short, plump elf lifted his pipe into the air and bid them farewell. "Be careful. Come back in one piece," he joked. His rosy cheeks and yellowish smoke stained mustache complemented his jovial smile.

As the couple exited, Kepler was napping on the front porch. The demon stood and stretched, his massive form spanning the porch's width as his muscles rippled beneath his black coat. The top of the cat's back was as tall as George and his weight bent the wooden planks where his paws rested.

"Where're we off to?" the demon questioned with a yawn. As the weight of his paws cleared the porch, the building's life source replenished the area where it had been displaced.

George marveled as the color returned to the planks. *I'll never get used to living in buildings that are alive,* he thought.

After leading Athena down the steps, the mage placed his hand on the demon's neck. "The Head Master has sent for us. We're supposed to meet him at his school at the center of the village."

"Finally, some action. Let's get going. I hope he has a task worthy of my prowess. If I spend another moment lying on that porch, I'll lose my mind."

George nodded. "I agree, big guy. I'm sure things are about to change."

Now...fellow soul...just a quick reminder to bring you up to speed. The village of Floren has been the family's home for the last 115 Peaks of Bailem. After their arrival on Luvelles, George and Kepler have maintained a low profile. This was necessary to stay out of the spotlight since the Collective has no idea where they are—except Lasidious and Celestria.

After George killed the witches Celestria stayed with during her pregnancy, there has been no need to use magic. George retrieved Lasidious' newborn son from the witches' home and has been playing uncle ever since.

Susanne, Athena's sister, has done a wonderful job adapting to motherhood, despite the fact she has never given birth. A vision has been implanted in Susanne's mind. She believes, with her whole heart, she is a mother, though she does not realize she is a mother to a son of gods.

The rest of Athena's family has also been given this vision to create the same belief. There is no doubt in anyone's mind that Susanne is the child's mother. The façade worked.

George has given Lasidious and Celestria's son the name Garrin. Garrin's birth broke the most sacred rule within the Book of Immortality—a rule created by the gods to avoid a power struggle between those of the Collective. The rule forbids two gods from having a child, and Gabriel, the Book of Immortality, is in charge of enforcing this rule.

Lasidious, staying true to form and doing what the Mischievous One does best, found a way to break this rule with his lover, Celestria. The conception and birth of their son had been planned for more than 14,000 seasons, and special precautions were taken to keep the Book of Immortality from knowing of the child's birth.

A being born of two gods could possess the ability to control the Book of Immortality. Gabriel would no longer be able to protect the gods from one another. Instead, the Book would forced to serve. Chaos would be the result. All that remains: George must hide Garrin's existence from the Collective until the baby is old enough to command his power.

The theft of the Crystal Moon was brilliant. Hiding two of its pieces provided a beautiful distraction which has kept the gods busy and the beings of Southern Grayham at war.

Lasidious' created a pact with George: a promise to retrieve his daughter's soul from the Book and allow her to live again. The Mischievous One has used this promise to motivate the ex-Earthling. Though Lasidious has shown George a way to attain large amounts of power, this level of power has been attained by many on Luvelles. Further attention to George's growth is necessary to achieve the Mischievous One's goals.

The Village of Floren is an area of highly concentrated magic. The air smells of it. The strongest of all who command the arts—both white and dark—come to Floren to begin their training. But, true to the nature of these conflicted paths, they part ways once their training is complete.

The Head Master's school is only for those with exceptional power—power like George stole from Amar. Few are allowed to attend Brayson's school, and fewer are allowed to train under the Head Master's supervision.

It isn't uncommon for a student to become injured while trying to command too much power. As a result, Floren has some of the finest healers on all the worlds. Healers are given passage to Luvelles from the world of Harvestom by the Head Master to keep his students alive.

So, enough telling. Let's get back to the story.

It wasn't long before George stood with Athena and Kepler at the base of the Head Master's school. The building was invisible to the naked eye. If it had not been for a note delivered to Kebble's Kettle with specific directions and detailed instructions, George would have never known they had arrived.

Words to a spell had been scribed on the parchment. They were written in the Elven language, and without Kebble's help, George would not have been able to pronounce any of them to reveal the entrance. The mage spoke with a forceful tongue. *"Aa'menle nauva calen ar'ta hwesta e'ale'quenle,"* which meant—*May thy paths be green and the breeze on thy backs.*

Athena squealed when the door appeared. The mage reached out to open it. "Hmpf, just another freaky thing. I wish I could say I'm surprised, but not much surprises me any longer." George motioned for Athena to enter. "After you, my dear." Once she was inside, he looked at Kepler. "Get your furry ass in there."

Kepler growled, "There are days you look like a morsel."

"A morsel? I taste like garesh. Don't get your hairy panties in a bunch. I'm just kidding, buddy."

The demon sauntered in without responding.

"Geesh, tough crowd," George snickered.

Once the door shut, the entrance vanished to the outside world. The inside of the school was capacious. A circular staircase stretched upward for what seemed to be forever. Bookcases full of endless knowledge lined every wall and stretched upward just as far. The furniture was made of dark, heavy stone. Symbols had been chiseled into their surfaces and were filled with gold. Each symbol had a unique meaning, but each represented the paths of white and dark magic in their own way. The floor throughout the tower changed color. The green glow faded and was replaced by a bright yellow. It was as if a source of light had been placed beneath to shine through.

"Everything is so beautiful," Athena marveled as she watched many pairings of fairies carry assorted tomes from one shelf to another. "It looks as if they are reorganizing. Look, George! Look how many it takes to carry that big book. I bet there are at least seven of them."

George was still fascinated with the floor. He bent over to see if the light created warmth, but before he had the chance to touch it, a silver sphere, no bigger than two fists, appeared and hovered in front of them.

"Looks like they know we're here," Kepler snarled.

"Holy crap. I feel like we just stepped onto the set of Phantasm," George said as he studied the sphere. "Maybe, it will lead us to the Head Master."

"Say something to it," the demon replied. "See if it responds. I don't have a good feeling about this...this...thing."

Athena tugged at George's robe. "I agree with Kepler. Something isn't right. Let's leave. We can come back when someone is here to greet us."

George rolled his eyes. He put on a smile. "Babe, don't worry. I'm sure everything will be just..."

George was unable to finish his sentence. Small electric shocks burst from the ball. Kepler roared as the first of these charges hit his nose. George threw up a wall of force to protect them, but the ball moved through the invisible barrier as if it was not there. Once again, the ball took the offensive.

Athena was hit. She cried out, begging George to protect her. George lifted his hands. Fire erupted from the mage's fingertips, pushing the ball backward. The sphere absorbed the magic, then used the power against him, redirecting the fire at George's face. It cut through the air at a high rate of speed. George barely managed to get out of the way.

The books resting on the shelves behind him exploded from the intensity of the impact. The force knocked the trio across the room. As they landed, the floor changed to the color red. George and the now unconscious Athena slid to a stop. But, Kepler was not so fortunate. He took the brunt of the explosion and stopped sliding after hitting his head against the edge of a heavy stone table near the spiral staircase.

The jaguar let out a hellish roar. The sound was deafening. Chills ran down George's spine as he heard the demon's cry. The mage jumped to his feet and shouted to capture the sphere's attention.

Again, the sphere shot its charges. George was hit in the leg. Pissed off, he screamed, "Take this, you S.O.B!" The mage blasted the ball with hundreds of magical arrows which sent the sphere crashing into a bookcase located at the far side of the room. The severity of the collision sent pieces—of not only the shelf, but the books as well—flying in every direction. George used a wall of force to keep Athena from being hit again, but his act of heroism left him vulnerable. The edge of a heavy book's binding caught him on the temple. Dazed, he fell to the floor and struggled to stay alert. A moment later, the silver menace lifted from the floor and resumed its offensive.

Kepler growled as he stood. His head had suffered a gash and his black coat was singed. He could feel the blood running down his skin as he looked to the mage. "We can't take much more of this!"

George was unable to respond. Knowing it was up to him, the giant cat launched into the air. As he came down, the demon hit the sphere with his right paw. The ball bounced and rolled across the now purple-colored floor. The light reflected off the sphere's shiny surface. A metallic clanking pierced the air.

Kepler followed. Covering the distance, he pounced onto his enemy, putting all of his weight on top of the sphere to hold it down. He turned to yell, "George, get over..."

Suddenly, the demon-cat roared in pain, unable to finish his plea for help. He pulled his massive paw clear of the ball's surface. Blood poured from the end of three silver spikes which remained embedded. Kepler's roar reverberated throughout the tower with such force that three tomes fell free from the highest shelves and landed with a thud.

The smack of the books against the floor helped to clear George's mind. As he regained his composure, the floor turned blue. The mage grabbed the nearest bookshelf and used it as a crutch to maintain his balance. As he did, he saw Athena lying motionless behind the wall of force. His anger turned to hatred for his enemy. Finding the ball, he shouted for Kepler to move clear. The giant cat limped away, leaving a trail of black demon blood to stain the floor as it completed its cycle and returned to green.

Before George could take the offensive, the sphere retracted its large needles and moved to hover just outside the invisible wall protecting Athena. Waking from the pain, Athena screamed as another electrical charge passed through her pocket of protection and hit her belly. Seeing this, George's emotions took over and fueled his power to a level he had never experienced.

Kepler, sensing George's use of magic was going to be dangerous, leapt skyward. With his massive claws, he ripped into the spiral staircase and hung suspended. Twisting his head around, the demon watched as George lifted his hands to release his wickedness. The anger the mage felt, knowing his wife and unborn baby were in danger, added to the magic's velocity. A powerful wave erupted from George's fingertips. The force of the gush consumed the tower's lower level.

The torrential force pushed the ball backward, smashing it against the bookshelves. The orb sunk to the now yellow-colored floor which illuminated the water with an eerie glow as it sloshed. The wave not only stopped the ball, but pushed the heavy stone table beyond Athena's bubble of protection.

Once the water settled, it was chest high. Beneath the surface, the damaged sphere exploded, sending a powerful fountain of water and debris skyward. Kepler was the one to suffer. Besides becoming drenched, the demon was clubbed with many of the heavy tomes and, as a result, was knocked clear of the staircase. The cat landed with a walloping splash.

George lowered his pocket of protection and pushed through the refuse to get to Athena. He submerged and, to his delight, found his beautiful wife sitting well-protected within her bubble of force. He gave Athena a wink and stood to check on Kepler. The jaguar looked miserable, as all wet pussycats look.

Again, the mage lifted his hand, but in the direction of the door and used his magic to open it. The water siphoned out of the school and gushed down the stairs, away from the tower. Once George was certain there would be no other threats, he released Athena from her barrier.

From high above, a male voice called out, "Well done...ha, ha, ha...well done, George!" A figure in a red robe began his descent. He did not use the spiral staircase, but rather floated toward them. The man removed his hood. George could see he had short brown hair and a goatee. He appeared to be an older man, maybe 55 or 60 seasons, with elven features, something George had become accustomed to since the family's arrival on Luvelles. George could only imagine how old this guy actually was, since other elves—elves that also looked his age—were hundreds of seasons old.

"A good first lesson. You handled yourself well. Amar said you would be a worthy Mystic Learner. I'm sure you can understand my desire to see for myself."

George trudged through what was left of the watery mess, now ankle-high with a blue glow. He pushed Athena's hair clear of her face to make sure she was okay before responding. "Who the hell are you?" he shouted.

"I don't know of this hell you speak of, but you know who I am."

"My wife is pregnant, you son of a..."

"Now, now, now, let's not be hasty, George. You're assuming I didn't know she was pregnant. I know plenty. I would never challenge you with something strong enough to do real damage to you or your wife...well, to your wife anyway. The sphere knew to use weaker magic on Athena. The charges were not strong enough to damage her or the baby.

"The orb's stronger magic was directed toward you...and Kepler, of course. In fact, it was your power that did the damage. Looking back, maybe I should have taken away the sphere's ability to deflect your fire. I was concerned when the explosion from the blast knocked Athena unconscious. I'll need to remember this for later encounters. Look at my bookshelves. They're a mess. I do hope you're okay, Athena."

Athena stayed quiet, but Kepler didn't hesitate to jump into the conversation after pulling the last spike free of his paw with his teeth. "Don't forget me! I'm sure your concern is not limited. I'm bleeding. My paw is riddled with holes and the back of my head throbs."

Brayson laughed. "I'm sure you won't bleed out before I can stop the flow. I don't think I've ever seen a beast your size cry so."

Kepler growled, but Brayson ignored the cat's threat. "Let's retire to my office, shall we?" He waved his hand and the group began to float upward.

Athena squealed as her feet left the floor. Brayson took hold of her arm. "Relax, young one. There's nothing to fear. My name is Brayson Id."

George watched the distance between them and the floor expand. "Brayson, I'm sure I should feel like it's a pleasure, but you're going to have to forgive my lack of enthusiasm."

The Head Master frowned, "I told Athena my name is Brayson. I did not say you could use it, George. You will call me Master Id."

"I'll what? You must be out of your freaking mind if you think..."

Before the mage could finish, George began to fall toward the floor. As he fell, he screamed, "Master, Master!" His descent stopped and once again, George began to lift toward the others.

"Ha! Now, that was primal," Kepler said with a sinister grin. "George, you should've seen your face. It was a moment I won't soon forget." A drop of blood fell from the giant cat's paw and passed George before landing in what was left of the water covering the now yellow-colored floor.

George snapped, "Don't forget, Kep...I may not be able to fight off the Master here, but I can give you a look to match Kroger's."

The demon stopped laughing. The idea of being turned to stone wasn't pleasing. He whispered to the others, "What a trobletted soul."

Everyone laughed, except Athena. She had never seen George command the power he had used to defeat the silver sphere. His power bothered her and she would need to speak with him, but now was not the right moment. She put on a strong face and joined the conversation. "Honey, you're so cute when you're angry."

George had to smile. Athena always had a way of softening his mood, no matter how disgruntled he became.

When they approached the ceiling, the group passed through it and appeared in the Head Master's office. In awe, they moved to the windows.

"I can see everything from here," Athena said. "It's all so beautiful. This building must be tall. I can see the mountains below us. Honey, look, it's the island the Merchant Angels left us on. I had no idea Western Luvelles was so beautiful."

Brayson responded. "Very good, Athena. Your sense of direction is impeccable, but you're not in my school any longer. My office floats high above the lands of Western Luvelles and is invisible to those who live below. Only a few know of its existence. When you leave this place, you'll remember everything you've seen, but will be unable to speak of your experience. This spell is how I ensure my secret stays safe. Only those I invite may return."

Athena pointed toward the water. "What's beyond the ocean?"

Brayson smiled, enjoying her curiosity. "Good question. Allow me to tell you more about our world. There are four large areas of land which are populated. I'm responsible for keeping in touch with their leaders. Western Luvelles is divided into two territories. We call these territories The Lands of Kerkinn. Eastern Luvelles, which I'm sure you can imagine by the name, lies far to the east. The territories which make up Eastern Luvelles are called Doridelven. Doridelven is an area known for abusing slaves, and its leaders have been fighting one another for many, many seasons. Eastern Luvelles is mostly populated by Halflings, but there is one race who lives there, known as wood elves, who have a unique ability."

Athena was intrigued. "What kind of ability, and how does it affect their lives?"

Brayson pulled a book from one of the heavy wooden shelves which held many ancient tomes. After ruffling through the pages, he handed it to Athena. "Wood elves have the ability to take the form of different animals. Usually, their personality determines what kind of animal they shift into. This special race of elf is able to use the senses of their animal form, even while walking as men. I would have to say this would be how their ability affects their lives. Now, as a whole, wood elves are known for producing some of the finest students of healing. I've sent more than one to Harvestom to train with the High Priestess."

George looked over Athena's shoulder. "This ability to shift is intriguing, and something I want to learn more about. Is their ability to change magical or natural?"

"This ability is magical. It's a magic no other elf has been able to master...not even myself. Though my magic is far stronger than theirs, I cannot comprehend this special power. They have managed to keep this secret well-guarded and it is only passed down within their race."

Skimming the tome further, George turned the page and thought, *The power to shift could give me an advantage. Maybe, I'll have to eat another heart someday.*

Brayson changed the subject. "There are two other large land masses. The first lies far to the south. This area is called the Unmarked Territory and has been unmapped due to the savagery of the people who live there. Over the seasons, every man who has tried to study the area has perished. No one even tries any longer. Perhaps, when my days have passed as Head Master, I will map this area myself since I have the power to avoid a similar fate.

"The final area is located far to the north. This area is called Desolation, and a small population lives there, maybe a few thousand or so. They have adapted to the intense cold and keep to themselves, causing no harm to anyone. This land has been mapped, but there's really nothing of interest other than the animals which roam the area."

It was easy to see George's excitement. "This world is incredible. I must learn everything I can while I'm here. Tell us more. I can't wait to learn. And, I love your office, by the way. How do I get this kind of power? I want an office like this of my own."

Brayson smiled. "Your enthusiasm is encouraging. Come. Take a look."

The Head Master waved his hand. One of the windows began to zoom in on some of the farther areas of the land below, acting as a large telescope of sorts while Brayson took the moments necessary to point out many places of interest. "As I have said, Western Luvelles is called The Lands of Kerkinn, and there are two kingdoms which exist within it."

The window settled on one of the many cities.

"Look here...this is the city of Marcus, my brother's city of shadows, which he has named after himself. The lake just west of his city is called

Lake Id. It would take a man 63 Peaks to make this journey by foot if he were to begin from the entrance of my school."

Athena grabbed George's arm. "We should travel there someday."

Brayson chuckled. "To visit would be a bad idea, Athena. Allow me to explain. My brother is the Chancellor of Dark Magic. I would suggest you stay away from him at all costs. He doesn't take to outsiders. He hates even himself. His city is located in the Kingdom of Hyperia. There isn't much about this kingdom which is appealing to men with goodness in their hearts. All the lands within the Western Territory are under the rule of King Gedlin Hyperia, but my brother rules even him, through fear. But, enough of this. I find it depressing to speak about. Let's change the subject, shall we?"

Brayson adjusted the window's angle to another area. "Just to the north of Lake Id is the city of Hyperia. If you look to the east, there is a large strait which divides both kingdoms. The Eastern Territory is controlled by the King of Lavan, Heltgone Lavan. And, this territory is called the Kingdom of Lavan. If you're thinking this is not an original appellation, I agree. Kings tend to be vain.

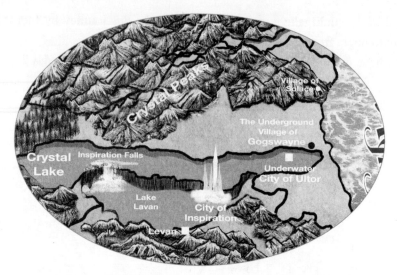

"Within this kingdom lives my youngest brother, Gregory, and he is the Chancellor of White Magic, or all magic considered good or neutral in nature. Both kings, and my brothers, answer to me. I'm sure you understand; with great power comes great responsibility, George."

"I do, Master Id."

George hated the way the name sounded as it left his tongue. He thought to himself, *It won't be long before you're calling me Master...you piece of garesh.* He filed the thought in the back of his mind. "So, what else can you tell us?"

"As I was saying, Marcus is the chancellor of all those who command dark magic. He is the brother whom many fear. If it were up to Marcus, every living thing would answer to him or perish. He isn't the one you want to befriend."

Marcus sounds like my kind of guy, George thought. *Maybe I'll have to look into this some more.*

Once again, Brayson redirected the group's attention. "Allow me to show you the finest city on Western Luvelles."

Brayson moved his hand and the window on the east side of the room zoomed in across the world. "Now, you can see the city of my youngest brother. Look closely." The window zoomed in further with another wave. "Gregory calls this his City of Inspiration. It's made of solid glass. The glass has been magically altered and protected from damage. It has been colored many different ways to give the people their privacy, but more importantly, the color gives the depth necessary to outline the edges of the buildings. We wouldn't want the inhabitants to be running into clear walls, now would we?"

Athena giggled, "I suppose not. That would be terrible. Your brother's city is so beautiful. I would love to visit." She hesitated. "I hate to be rude, but where is my family to live?"

Brayson smiled. "You're a woman who gets to the point, I see. Come here, young lady." The Head Master walked to one of the other windows and waved his hand. "Do you see the island north of the one the Merchant Angels left you on?"

"I do," Athena replied, with George looking over her shoulder.

"This is my island." Again, he waved his hand and the window zoomed in on its northern shore. "If you look, you'll see I've prepared a home for each of you and your family's individual needs."

Athena gave Brayson a hug. "Thank you, Master Id. My family will be very happy there, I'm sure."

"I'm glad you like them. Please, call me Brayson."

George rolled his eyes and turned to look out the window. Kepler hid his smile, but enjoyed every moment of George's irritation.

Brayson moved to the center of the room. "In the morning, I'll take your family there. This will be where you'll stay until George's training is complete. Few have had the privilege of training under my supervision. George, if you hadn't come so highly recommended by Amar, you wouldn't have been given this privilege. I'll see you bright and early, before Early Bailem. Athena, make sure George has a full belly and a pack full of food. These rations will need to last for a while. You won't be seeing much of your husband. Let's hope he won't miss anything important."

Athena responded. "I'm fine with this…as long as he's there when I need him for the baby."

"I wouldn't worry. I'll keep an eye on you and help if anything unexpected happens."

George tried to interject. "Why can't..."

Before the mage could finish, Brayson waved his hand. The next thing the group knew, they were standing on the ground outside the school, without Brayson.

"Damn it, this guy is going to drive me crazy," George snapped.

Athena winked at Kepler and started walking. "Let's go, boys."

Kepler thought a moment as they began walking toward the inn. The giant cat hobbled from his wounds. "At least the bleeding has stopped. I thought Brayson was going to give me something to help. I left blood on his floor. I hope the stain is a constant reminder of the moments he has spent in the presence of the Master of the Hunt."

"Yeah, yeah, yeah, blah, blah, blah...could you be more full of yourself? I'm going to puke. Besides, the stain on his damn floor serves the chump right. I hope that's just the beginning of the damage."

Athena slapped George on the arm. "George Nailer, stop speaking so foul."

"Yes, dear."

After walking a bit, Kepler thought of something that perplexed him. "George...why does Brayson think Amar visited him? How could he have done this when you..."

George cut him off. "Kep, buddy, maybe we could save this conversation for later. I'm sure you'll agree it's too long of a story and maybe something we could chat about after we've started our journey."

The demon understood and dropped the subject.

"You boys sure know how to keep a secret," Athena said, poking George playfully as she walked beside him. "Perhaps, you should allow me in on some of your boy talk."

George looked at Kepler, then at Athena. "Nope, I think we'll just leave it as guy stuff."

"Suit yourself." Athena's brows furrowed.

Meanwhile, Western Luvelles
Shade Hollow

"Payne...the moments have come," the Mischievous One said after appearing inside a large cave full of bat-like creatures. Icy blue stalactites hung from the ceiling above a deep pool of fresh water. Light found its way into the cave, despite this particular spot being hidden deep within the ground. It reflected off the pool's surface and shimmered against the cave's walls.

Payne, on the other hand, was not one of the bat-like creatures. He was a fairy-demon—the only fairy-demon in existence. Each moment a bat approached his meal, the demon side of Payne snatched it up, bit its head off, then spit it on the ground.

"Go away! Eating," Payne growled, not knowing or, perhaps not understanding, the being in front of him was a "so-called" god.

"The human I told you about is on Luvelles. Are you ready to find some new friends? I know how important this is to you. You do want to have friends...right, Payne?"

Payne's red face lifted with his mouth full of shredded throat from a female elf. "Now? You want Payne go now?" The fairy-demon growled and began to pout. "I want eat because…because…um…it took forever."

"What took forever, Payne?"

"Errrr, for her to be...uh...uh, the right heat...yeah, the right heat. Payne eat now. She good now. Won't taste good again. Gotta eat now."

"Are you saying that her temperature is just right and she won't taste this good if you eat her later?"

"Yeah. You leave. Payne eat."

Lasidious smiled inside and took a deep breath. Payne was important and he was too young to argue with. He needed to be patient with the fairy-demon. "By all means, continue eating. I would hate to ruin your dinner. I can wait a while longer."

"Don't watch. Don't like that."

Lasidious turned, then moved to stand next to the pool. "I will wait over here. You continue eating, but you need to get going."

Now...fellow soul...let me tell you a little bit about Payne. The birth of Payne was a successful manipulation, or better yet, a suggestion planted by Lasidious into the mind of Payne's father just over four seasons ago.

The fairy-demon is solid red from head to toe. His mother, Sharvesa, a carver demon, is the Queen of Demons on the world of Dragonia. Payne has taken after his mother, for the most part, when it comes to his looks. Tiny horns rest on his forehead. Claw-like hands, both razor-sharp, serve him well when killing. He has a whip-like tail that ends in a fine point. The little fairy-demon has many of Sharvesa's natural abilities but, Payne is an outcast, unable to live amongst the other demons of a pure bloodline, thanks to his father. Payne's white wings serve as a reminder to Sharvesa's subjects that he is an abomination to their race.

To satisfy a desire placed in his mind by Lasidious, Defondel, the Fairy King of Luvelles, set out on a quest to create a new race of fairies. After arriving on the demon queen's world, Defondel found Sharvesa. He used his magic to cast a powerful spell on the demon queen, and while Payne's mother lay in slumber, Defondel took advantage of her. The fairy's four-inch frame disappeared inside the queen as he crawled around within her. It didn't take long. When the fairy king slid out onto the cave's floor, Payne's mother was pregnant.

The demon world would have killed Payne if not for his mother's decision to send him to be raised by his father—a decision made only after the queen requested to visit Luvelles and was denied. Sharvesa's anger toward Defondel was evident when speaking with the Head Master. Brayson turned down the demon queen's request, knowing vengeance would have been the sole reason for her presence on his world.

In order to cause the fairy king discomfort and spare herself the irritation of raising an unwanted child, Sharvesa sent Payne with the Merchant Angels to live with his father. This decision—one also manipulated by Lasidious—was a welcome suggestion and acted upon. The choice avoided a sure death for her mutt of a son. Payne would have been devoured by the demon world. Sharvesa's subjects, though loyal to their queen, would not allow an impure demon-fairy-midget to live amongst them as a constant reminder of the disgrace they felt by his miserable existence.

Payne's small body, compliments of his tiny father, functioned without imperfection. Although only three feet tall, he looks like a miniature body-builder with wings and possesses the agility of a gazelle. He keeps his budding horns sharp. The youthfulness of his face reminds Defondel of a red demon-cherub.

For a while, Payne was accepted by the fairy king's people. But, because of his differences, he was misunderstood. His demon half loves mischief. Before his segregation from his father's kind, there were many occasions when Payne would fly around the fairy kingdom dusting the armies of his father with their own magical powders stolen from the fairy army's armory. He would sit back and laugh at the intoxicating effects the fairy dust had. The sight of the male fairies kissing one another in a drunken state never seemed to get old. Payne was warned by the council that such acts were not welcome. The fairy council explained the safety of all fairies was in jeopardy when the army is unable to perform its duties. Finally, at two seasons old, Payne was asked to leave and live in a cave which rests at the center of Shade Hollow. He has lived the last full season of his life alone and must fend for himself.

Since Payne's natural immunities are many, the magic of the fairy army was not strong enough to force him out. King Defondel was left with no choice but to uphold the council's wishes and banish his son to a life of solitude. Payne's heart was crushed, but he obeyed his father and left the Fairy Kingdom without incident. This life of solitude was something Lasidious hoped would happen when he began his plotting of the fairy-demon's creation.

Fellow soul...there's much for you to learn about Payne, but I have done enough telling. Let's get back to the story.

"Have you considered my proposal?" Lasidious inquired after giving the fairy-demon the moments to eat.

"Yep."

"What have you decided?"

"Payne don't know. Seems okay. Payne don't know."

The god rolled his eyes. "Why are you hesitating?"

Payne ripped into the belly of the female elf. After a moment, he pulled out a handful of her intestines—his favorite part. He cleared away the fat and began to eat. Lasidious turned up his nose in disgust. He never imagined the manipulation of Payne's birth would turn out to be so foul.

"Listen to me, Payne. If you want to get out of this cave, it would be wise for you to befriend this human."

"'Befriend?' What that mean?"

Lasidious took a deep breath. He had to remind himself he was dealing with a child. "It means to become his friend."

"So, say that, that...um...that way then."

"Payne, focus. You're getting sidetracked. Okay?"

"Fine! Ebbish nay! You say them big words...not Payne."

"Payne, listen to me. Try to focus. This human will be seeking power. If you're at his side, those who hurt you will have no choice but to bow to you."

The fairy-demon growled as if confused. "Don't need bowing. Payne like fun. Payne want friends." He fumbled to keep the last of the intestinal delicacy from running down his chin as he continued. "Ummmm...the human, the human get Payne?"

"No, if you want to travel with him, you'll need to seek him out in the village of Floren. You can find this man at Kebble's Kettle. It's the only inn in that village."

"What 'inn' mean?"

Lasidious rolled his eyes again. "It's a place where people pay to sleep. Many people stay there and they can eat there, too."

"Eat! Payne like to eat. Why not sleep on ground? What 'pay' mean?"

"They pay coin to sleep because most humans don't like to sleep on the ground!"

"What 'coin?'"

"You'll see what many things are, including coin, as you travel with this human. You'll learn and can ask this human your questions."

"The human feed Payne?"

"Yes, he'll feed you...but not elves. This is your decision. Only you can decide if you want to go. But, if you want to have friends, I would go and find this man. His name is George, and he travels with a large black cat named Kepler. I would imagine you'll find Kepler to be helpful in learning the ways of your mother. Kepler is also demon. Maybe, with training, you can become powerful, strong enough to go back to your mother's world, and punish those who forced her to send you away."

"Payne no angry. Maybe Payne make them like Payne a lot. Do you think...um, Payne mean...they might like Payne, a bunch?"

"Of course they would, but you would need to travel with this human first."

"The human do for Payne, so Payne do this? How...um...how make friends with him?"

"He will help if you listen. Have I ever lied to you? I've been your friend for over a season. Don't you trust me? I want you to tell this human you have been sent to be his goswig."

"What a 'goswig?'"

Lasidious took another deep breath. "A goswig is a creature who assists his master and does whatever the master asks. Goswigs come in all shapes and sizes. Some have natural and magical abilities, much like you, Payne. It's an honor to be a goswig. Very few beings are chosen to be one."

"Honor...what 'honor?'"

"It's a good thing. It means you're special."

"But, Payne want a friend. Does Payne gots to be goswig? Does Payne gots to do stuff he says for Payne to do?"

"You don't have to do anything you don't want to. But, this is the only way for you to meet friends. This human will accept you no matter what happens, no matter what you do."

"All Payne do...is um...what do Payne say again?"

"Pay attention or you'll mess this up. And, stop talking about yourself in third person. It sounds ridiculous."

"What 'third person' mean?"

"Bah! Never mind. You need to tell this human you've been sent to be his goswig."

"Okay. Goswig. Got it. And, Payne gotta do what he say. Got it. You promise him be Payne's friend?"

Lasidious forced the smile to remain on his face. "I promise. Do you have any other questions before I continue?"

"Payne no remember your name. Tell Payne."

"My name is, Friend," Lasidious said, forcing another patient smile that showed his teeth. "Payne, you won't see me again after this. The human you'll be looking for goes by the name, George Nailer. I'll show you where to teleport."

"George Nailer. Silly name. Payne make fun with name. Payne see no human before."

"No, no, no. You're to be his goswig, remember? Goswigs don't make fun of their masters. Goswigs call the one they serve, Master."

"Master...yuck. Payne no want to say that. Payne want be friends. I like George gooder."

"It's better, Payne," Lasidious snapped, his patience having run its course. "You like the name...George...better. That's how you say it. You really need to listen when people talk. You need to learn how to speak with intelligence."

"Ebbish nay! Don't be mad to Payne."

"Ugggh! Do you want friends or not?"

"Yes." The fairy-demon lowered his red head the way any child does when scolded. He kicked a small rock. "Payne want friends."

"Then, maybe you should choose to call George, Master. If you don't, he may not want you around. It's up to you. I personally don't care any longer."

"Ummm...all right...fine, ebbish nay...stop yelling to Payne. I hate his name. It's stupid, stupid, stupid, stupid. He better feed Payne gooder!"

"I'm sure he will feed you well, but you better get going." Lasidious touched the fairy-demon's head and gave him the vision of Kebble's Kettle. "This is the inn I told you about, and this is what George looks like."

"Yuck! Human ugly!"

"Payne, focus. The jaguar's name is Kepler and here's how the cat looks. You best get going."

"Kepler. I like. Him have red eyes. That's shev. Nice kitty."

Lasidious had to smile. He knew Kepler hated the word 'kitty.' This meeting was going to be fun to watch. "Shev? Payne, your whole body is red. How can Kepler's eyes be shev?"

"Payne don't know. Just 'cuz. Well...ummm...yeah, just 'cuz...Payne guess."

Lasidious' patience was gone. "Just be good to George. You want him to like you. If George likes you, you'll have a new friend and good food."

"Yes...um...Payne want George..."

"His name is Master! Concentrate, Payne, or you'll mess this up!"

"Ummm...yeah...uhh, yeah, yeah...Master to like Payne. Food...good. Payne go to George. Payne mean, to Master. Thanks, Friend."

"You're welcome, Payne." The God of Mischief vanished.

Payne devoured a few more mouthfuls of elf before disappearing.

A Whole Lotta Glass

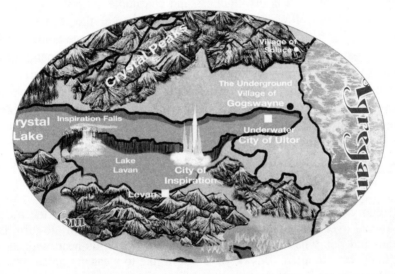

Gregory Id stood from his bed and walked across the transparent floor of his bedroom chamber. As always, he enjoyed the sight of the torrent water as it rushed beneath the glass under his feet. "A glorious morning," he said as he closed his eyes and listened.

Now...fellow soul...allow me to tell you about Gregory and his city of Inspiration. One of Luvelles' wonders, Inspiration is a city created by the White Chancellor's magic. Every structure, no matter how large or small, is made of glass and Gregory's bedroom chamber, located on the lowest level of a 200 foot tall shimmering tower-palace, is no exception.

To provide privacy, an array of color permeates the walls to keep wandering eyes out. It is this color which adds to the city's perfection. If there is a flaw to be seen, it will not be discovered by the naked eye.

Crystal Lake is Western Luvelles' largest body of water. It sits high above Gregory's city. The area it covers is vast—so vast, it could have been named a sea. The clear water cascades down the steep cliffs to the north, then works its way underground toward the city. After rushing beneath Gregory's tower-palace, it surfaces and flows through a crystal moat before continuing to Lake Lavan.

Gregory is an elf of average height. He is known for his strong will and charisma. His long hair is sandy-brown and covers his pointed ears. Deep blue eyes accent his smooth complexion. He is beloved throughout the Kingdom of Lavan. It is his kindness and charitable uses of magic which have served him well while creating a relationship with the people.

On many occasions, Gregory has used his power to create homes for the less fortunate—the less fortunate being those who cannot command magic. Though Luvelles is mostly populated by elves, halflings, and spirits, it is not a magical world in its entirety, despite the magical nature of these races. Even though the air in some areas smells of magic, not everyone is able to summon its uses.

Fellow soul...I would suggest that is enough telling from this babbling bard. Shall I push forward?

Gregory looked at his naked body as he stood in front of the mirror. He looked over his shoulder to make sure he was alone, only to turn back around and flex what little muscle he had. He shook his head with disappointment and shouted, "Mykklyn, I would like to wear my green robe today. Please bring it, and my yellow belt."

"Who would have ever guessed?" a graceful lioness responded while entering the room. "You are predictable." The goswig growled, as if annoyed. "I'll have them brought to you. It gets old. Watching you wear the same attire is far from inspiring. There are moments when I find it difficult to believe you were the one who created this striking city full of beautiful colors. How could you dress in such drab?" The lioness turned to leave the room.

Gregory stopped her. "Mykklyn...on second thought, let's change it up a bit. How about I wear my green robe and my black belt?"

"May the gods be praised...a black belt. You best be careful. You're stretching your boundaries with this decision. You might find yourself venturing too far out onto a thin limb." The lioness shook her head. "Green and black it is. One of these days I'm not going to allow you to dress yourself. Why don't you run around without clothes on? At least this would be a change, and far less boring."

Mykklyn growled as she left the room. It wasn't long before she returned. A servant entered behind her with the chancellor's clothes. "Shall I have your normal prepared for breakfast?" The lioness jumped onto the glass table and lowered her heavy, golden fur-covered body into a comfortable position. She began to move one of her sharp claws along the symbols of white magic etched into the table's surface. "Perhaps, we should try something new. Perhaps, a bergan egg, with greggle hash, corgan blood steak and some poppel bread would be perfect."

"No, no, no. I'll have my usual. Why must we do this every morning? I have enough to worry about." Gregory turned toward the mirror and adjusted his belt.

The lioness snorted at the chancellor's vexatious response. "We do this because you're boring. I'm trying to fix you. You have a perfect eye for beauty when it comes to this city, but you're nothing more than sad when it pertains to matters of dress. You should be setting a precedent. But, you're predictable. Even your diet is predictable. It's tiresome. Eating the same thing every day is farcical. You're broken and you don't even know it."

Gregory's forehead tightened. "Just bring my oats and let's get the day going. I have to meet with my brothers at the Peak of Bailem and there are things I must do before I go."

Mykklyn jumped from the table. "I'll fetch your breakfast, Your Boringness." The lioness vanished.

Gregory sighed, "That goswig is going to drive me crazy."

Meanwhile, the Village of Floren
Kebble's Kettle

Mary kept her eyes focused on the teleportation platform as she approached. The dark-haired, hazel-eyed woman had been summoned to the front desk of Kebble's inn to retrieve another gift. She still has no clue where they are coming from, but someone has their eye on her.

As Mary opened the box, she smiled. It was perfect—a beautiful, light blue sundress and, as always, just her size. This made fifteen dresses she had received since the family's arrival on Luvelles.

The stay at the inn had been pleasant for the most part, but she was glad the moment had arrived to move on. Mary had not ventured past the front porch of Kebble's establishment due to her son-in-law's request. George had said it wasn't safe to go out until he had been informed the moment was right. The air within the village smelled strange and something as simple as sitting on the porch made her nervous. It was also strange the sky had a purple haze and further, it was odd to see her homeworld of Grayham crossing the sky and disappearing behind the horizon.

The family had become restless waiting for this day, and a change of environment was welcome. Countless individuals of questionable character had checked into the inn over the past 115 Peaks. Many of these individuals traveled with different forms of intimidating looking beasts.

Mary hurried back to her room. She put on the new dress and stood in front of the mirror in the washroom to bask in the glow of how it made her feel. It was not long before she was interrupted by George, knocking on her door.

"Mother," the mage shouted through the heavy wood. "We need to get going. Are you packed? I hope you're ready to go."

"I am. Come in and carry my bag."

George opened the door. "Ahhh, now that's just the sweetest thing, another new dress," he chided with a hint of sarcasm. "You look stunning. I think someone is trying to get on your good side. I wonder when you'll meet this person."

Mary moved close and whispered in his ear like a child, "I don't know, but I hope he's handsome."

"Who said it's a man?" George joked.

Mary turned up her nose. "I would never!"

Amused at her response, the mage winked. As they left the room, George headed toward the teleportation platform, but Mary hesitated and took a few moments to lean over the balcony's wooden railing. This would be the last chance she would have to look at the dining area and the bar below.

She had never become accustomed to how the walls and this railing felt. From a distance, Kebble's inn looked to be made of many normal types of building material, but once a person drew near, they could see the inn was alive.

As Mary passed her hand across the railing's surface, she could feel the tiny hairs which tickled her palm. The heart of the organic structure could be felt as a pulse shot through the railing like some sort of artery. She pulled her hand away and thought, *How unsettling.*

Many nights she had watched the diverse characteristics of Kebble's patrons from this very spot, and on one occasion she had seen something that scared her—a man had died. The cause of his death remained unexplained. It was as if nobody cared. The gentleman was expendable, as if he had no importance—almost as if he had been expected to die. One moment, the man was laughing and the next, he was burning from the inside out. She would never forget his cries as his body reduced to a pile of ash.

Everyone had continued eating, not bothering to give his remains anything more than a casual glance. Kebble was the only one who seemed to care. She didn't know if it was because he was a good man, or if his actions had more to do with the fact that it was his inn and there was just another mess to clean up. Despite her confusion about the short elf's rationale that night, she had made friends with Kebble and would miss him.

Mary took one final mental snapshot of the place before making her way to the teleportation platform. As she stood on it, she disappeared from the fourth floor and reappeared near the front desk. "Goodbye, Kebble. I don't know if we'll see one another again. You've been a gracious host."

The chubby, rosy-cheeked elf removed his pipe and kissed the top of her hand before bidding her farewell. "I shall miss you, Mary."

"And, I you...you've been wonderful. I do hope this isn't the last series of moments we shall see each other. I haven't made other friends since our arrival."

Kebble smiled, then winked. "Ohhhh, I think you're about to meet someone special, and I'm sure this won't be our last conversation. I want details of your adventures when we meet next."

"My, my, I do hope you're right. I could use someone special in my life. I promise to keep you informed. Goodbye, Kebble."

"Goodbye, my lady."

❖⟨⟨•⟩⟩❖

Payne was enjoying the morning sun as it fell across the village. Sitting on top of Kebble's roof, the fairy-demon lifted his face into the air and absorbed its warmth, all while bouncing one of his legs. He was anxious. Waiting for George to exit the building was hard. But, as usual, the fairy-demon had created company.

Payne had torn off one of his fingers and allowed it to morph into a small rabbit. The animal had a perfect cottontail and gray fur. It twitched its pudgy nose and began to speak. "Would you stop shaking your leg? The human will come out soon."

"Payne know...um...Payne know. Stupid rabbit," the fairy-demon growled.

"Who're you calling stupid, idiot?"

"Payne no idiot."

"You're the one bouncing your leg all over the place."

"So?"

"So, relax. This George will come out."

"No say relax. Payne not need relax. Shut up! Ebbish nay!"

The bunny scratched the back of one of its long ears. "I'll say whatever I want."

"No."

"Yes, I will. And, you are an idiot."

"No, no, no! No...Payne not...um...not an idiot...you make Payne mad."

The rabbit pretended to shiver in fright. "Forgive me. Whatever will I do? I best run and hide. The mighty fairy-demon is angry."

Payne ground his teeth, "Stop...or...Payne...Payne..."

The rabbit turned, lifted onto his back legs and raised his front paws in defiance. "Payne will what?"

"Payne do this." Payne grabbed the animal and lifted it toward his mouth.

"What're you doing?"

"Eating. Ebbish nay. And, you think Payne stupid."

"If you eat me, you'll lose a finger."

"Oh...um...yeah...Payne forgot. Then...then...Payne will..."

"Shut up! You'll do nothing. I have grown bored with you. Goodbye." The rabbit began to melt away and once again attached itself to Payne's hand.

The fairy-demon growled, "Stupid finger!"

Not long afterward, George and Athena's family exited the inn. Payne was now more nervous than ever. He whispered to himself, "Great. Can't talk...can't talk to human. Too many. Too many to talk. Those other ones... oh, too many with the human. Not good. Payne go. Got to go. Go home."

A voice from behind the fairy-demon spoke—a voice from someone Payne couldn't see, but recognized. "Yes, you can, Payne. You can talk to George. It'll be okay."

"Who there?" the demon said, turning, ready to bite. "Is that you, Friend?"

"It's okay, Payne. You can do this. Go down there and say hello."

The fairy-demon shouted with excitement. "Payne not go! Payne scared! Can't go nowheres! Payne not talk to human!"

"I think you will. You have been discovered. Look below."

George looked up as the fairy-demon looked down. "Hey Kep, what the hell is that?"

"I have no idea, but it's small...ugly, too."

"Eeeek," Athena squealed. "George, what is that?"

Now, the whole family was looking.

"Is it dangerous?" Mary shrieked.

"Beats me. Kepler, are you sure you haven't seen anything like it before?"

"No, nothing quite like that. I would remember. It appears to be some sort of demon, but why so tiny? I have no clue. It's odd. If you ask me, it's an ugly little thing."

Payne yelled at the invisible voice. "Now look...you made Payne...errr, um...they know! Human know!" Payne reached out to feel the air, but found nothing. "Hello...um...voice...you there? Pssst, hey voice...you there? Can you hear Payne?" The fairy demon shouted. "Great...hearing stuff!"

Payne turned back around and looked at George. After seeing the look on

George's face, he snapped, "What? Human never seen no one talk before?"

Kepler laughed, then lowered to the ground. He answered before George had the chance. "We have, in fact, but nothing as odd as you."

"Odd...me...um, Payne no odd. Who you calling odd...furball? And, Payne not nothing. Me Payne. Me Payne!"

The jaguar stood and began to walk away. "Clearly. You are definitely odd, and you're right. You are a pain, a pain in my ass."

Athena glared at the demon-cat. "Kepler, I told you not to speak with such vulgarity. You're starting to sound like George."

The jaguar was not interested in being chastised. "Yes, Athena." Kepler began to walk away from the group, but Payne was not finished with him.

The fairy-demon teleported onto Kepler's back, then grabbed the cat's ears with his claws and hung on. "Payne not odd! Payne bite. Payne bite furball."

The giant cat began to shake, trying to hurl the fairy-demon off, but when Kepler moved, Payne dug his claws in deeper to keep from being thrown. "Kitty, no get Payne off. Kitty fun. Friend say Payne like kitty."

Kepler roared. "George, get this damn thing off me!"

It took a moment for the mage to stop laughing and wave his hand. Kepler and Payne froze. George walked over to the tiny annoyance and plucked him from Kepler's back. He moved away before releasing the giant jaguar. Once the demon-cat could move, he began to walk toward Payne, growling.

"Stay there, Kep," George commanded.

"Why? He'll make a great meal. Let his bones break within my jaws. I despise being called a kitty."

"Back off and give me a moment, will you?" George's mind was working fast. He wanted to know more before he let Kepler at him. He lifted Payne in front of his face. "What are you, and what's your name? Don't lie to me, or I'll feed you to the furball."

"Not funny, George," Kepler growled.

Smiling, the mage waved his free hand to release Payne's mouth. "Speak, and be quick about it."

"Me, Payne. Payne...um...um, fairy-demon."

Kepler growled. "There's no such thing. He lies."

"There is so!"

"No, there is not," Kepler snarled.

"Is so!" Payne shouted louder.

"No, there isn't!" Kepler roared.

The mage lifted his voice. "Hey! You two are acting like dumbasses."

Kepler's eyes flashed a burning red. "George, who are you going to listen to, me, or this thing?"

"Payne not a thing. Payne fairy-demon. Payne mother queen...Queen of Demon on...on...errr, um...Payne forget."

"Ha," the demon snarled. "There is only one Queen of Demons, and she lives on another world. I doubt your mother is the demon queen on Dragonia."

"That it...that it. Dragonia. Payne mother...the queen."

"You lie."

"No lie. Payne swear."

Kepler growled and his eyes began to glow an even deeper red. "And, your father? What of him? I suppose he's a king?"

"Yes...um, he...he Fairy King. He here."

Kepler licked his chops. "George, he lies. Let me eat him. I don't have the moments to waste on this foolishness. His stench fouls the air of this territory."

Payne showed his pointed teeth. "Then...then...why do Payne got fairy wings...stupid?"

Kepler began to respond, but George spoke over him. "Stop this! Let's take a look...shall we?" The mage turned Payne's little red figure over and examined his wings."

Susanne—pretty, but not fabulous-looking—jumped into the conversation. "Hang on a moment." She turned and handed baby Garrin to Mary, who was still dwelling on the fact that George had used magic to control the situation.

Susanne moved to take a closer look. "George, they do look like fairy wings. I've seen them in drawings, but I never thought I'd see a pair. Maybe this little...whatever he is, is telling the truth."

George looked beyond Susanne and took note of the stunned look on Mary's face. He was glad he had informed the family he could command magic. As he studied the rest of the group, he could see how shocked they were by its use, despite this knowledge.

After a moment, George said, "Athena, maybe you could help them find a way to close their mouths. We wouldn't want bugs to take up residence."

Athena's brow furrowed. "What did you expect? I told you they haven't seen magic used before. Go about your business and give me a moment."

As Athena turned to address the family, she had to smile. She had thought about this moment and what it would be like for them. She remembered what it was like to experience the fear of seeing magic for the first moment. When George teleported with her in his arms on their wedding night, she was frightened. She understood the anxiety her family was feeling. At this moment, her strength was necessary to ease their minds.

George turned his attention back to Susanne. "I'm inclined to think he's telling the truth." He touched Payne's wings. "What did you say your name was?"

"Payne. Ebbish nay."

"Ebbish nay? What the hell does that mean?"

Kepler growled. "He speaks in demon tongue. If I were to translate it in terms you would understand, ebbish nay means, duh, or gee whiz in your English."

George chuckled. "I like that. Ebbish nay, he says. Now, that's pretty damn funny. Payne, tell me why I should stop the big kitty from eating you."

Again, Kepler growled. "George, you test my patience."

"Well, ebbish nay!" The mage grinned, "You know I love you, buddy." Again, he lifted the fairy-demon in front of his face and waited for Payne's response.

"'Cuz...um...'cuz Friend said Payne be goswig to Master," Payne was anxious to find a way out of the trouble he was in. He hated being frozen and the idea he couldn't teleport while in this condition ate at him.

"Goswig? And, why would I want you to be my goswig? What makes you think I'm your master?"

"Friend said come. Friend said Payne got to call human, Master. Friend said Payne got to do stuff human say, and...um...Payne got to be...um... gooder, Payne guess."

George looked at Kepler. He sat Payne down and lowered to the ground beside him, pushing his new tunic into a more comfortable position. "You said your friend sent you? Who is your friend?"

"Yes...Payne friend."

"You're driving me freaking crazy. Stop speaking about yourself in third person. If you must, it's Payne's friend, not Payne friend. I want you to say, Payne's friend sent you."

"Um...errr...Payne's friend sent Payne."

George slapped his own forehead. "What's your friend's name?"

"Payne told you," the fairy-demon snapped. "Friend."

"No, you said your friend sent you. I want to know his name."

"Him name Friend."

"Friend? What the hell are you talking about? What's his name?"

"Friend!"

George shook his head. "You're saying your friend sent you, I get that. Now, what's his name?"

Payne groaned, "Him name Friend."

"Yes, I know he's your friend, but I'm asking for his name, not your relationship?"

"Grrrrrrr, him name Friend."

"Friend...really, it's just Friend? He's got to have a name."

The fairy-demon growled and snapped back. "Him name Friend. Please no make Payne say it no more. Payne friend name...um...Friend. Friend told Payne to come. He say human be gooder to Payne."

George thought a moment. He knew he was missing something. None of this made sense. He would allow Payne to tag along until he could figure the little guy out. He could make a decision on what to do with him later. The mage turned to look at Kepler. "Come with me."

The two walked away from the group. George was the first to speak. "Something tells me we should take this thing with us until we know more. If he turns out to be useless, you can eat him, okay?"

"I hate this idea. This little freak is going to be a pain in my furry black ass. I won't be responsible if he comes up missing."

"Look, I understand how you feel. I'll tell him he needs to chill. I'll tell him he's got to act right. I'll tell him to stay away from you. I'll tell him..."

"George, stop." Kepler grinned as a jaguar would. "You're not really going to do the tell him, tell him, tell him, tell him thing again, are you? You sound like a fool."

"Shut up, will you? Look, I just need you to look at the bigger picture. Someone has sent him to be my goswig. Why...I don't know, but it's happened. I think I have an idea who, but I'm not sure it's wise to say it out loud. Come here." George leaned over and whispered in Kepler's ear.

"Really? Why would he send this...this, whatever it is?"

"Hell if I know. When I talk with him, I'll ask. For now, we need to tolerate the little guy until I know for sure. I'm asking you to be patient. I think the fairy-demon could come in handy if I'm right about who sent him."

"This isn't part of our agreement, George, and you know it." Kepler turned and made his way back to Payne. "I suggest you stay away from my ears. Touch them again and I'll have you for dinner."

"Okay, kitty."

"And, don't call me kitty!"

"Okay, furball."

"Or furball, or anything else you find amusing or clever. You will call me Kepler, and only Kepler."

"Why pissy...kitty?"

Kepler let out a hellacious roar. Athena's entire family backed away. Baby Garrin woke from his sleep and began to cry. Kepler lowered his mouth around Payne's head and was about to chomp, but George froze him.

George stomped his foot against the ground. "You have got to be freaking kidding me," the mage shouted as he walked over and pulled Payne from under the demon-cat's jaws. He lifted the fairy-demon in front of his face. "If I were you, I would do as he says or I'll freeze you again and allow him to tear you apart. You may have been sent to be my goswig, but you will call me Master, and the jaguar, Kepler. Do we have an understanding?"

Payne rolled his eyes. "Payne do. Will Master feed Payne gooder?"

"I will feed you well, but you must eat what the rest of us eat. I'm not a restaurant."

"Restaurant? What 'restaurant' mean?"

"Never mind. You'll eat what we eat, got it?"

"Do Master eat elves? Elves tasty...um...small girl ones, mmmmm. Payne kill them. Payne like part that holds brown stuff. Down here." The demon pointed to his abdomen.

George looked at Kepler, then back at Payne. "You mean you like to eat their garesh? That's nasty. That's just sick and wrong. How could you be any more repulsive?" He shook his head. "You'll eat what we eat. Don't even think about putting something in your mouth unless you ask me first. Do you understand? And, stop calling yourself by your name. You sound stupid."

George did not listen to anything else Payne had to say. He was fighting his need to vomit. He would need to pay close attention to their new companion—killing elves was not a good idea. He released his magic and began to walk with the family toward the Head Master's school. "Let's go. Mary, let me have Garrin. I'll calm him down."

On his way past the fairy-demon, Kepler thumped Payne on the head with the backside of his large paw and sent the little guy flying into the side of Kebble's inn. It took a while, but once Payne collected his bearings, he shook off the cobwebs and flew to catch up with the group.

Meanwhile, Head Master Brayson's Floating Office

"Amar, it's good to see you, my friend," Brayson said, hugging his old Mystic Learner.

"You also, Master," Lasidious responded, disguised as the deceased mage. The Mischievous One was dressed in a black robe and his hair was long and gray, just as Amar's had been.

"Master, I have sent Payne to George. The fairy-demon will make a fine goswig. I know this is abnormal, and I know it was not my place to do so, but I think they will be good for each other. I ask your forgiveness."

Brayson frowned. "Why would you do this? I planned on giving George a goswig this morning. This crosses the boundaries of our friendship."

"Please forgive me, Master. I have traveled with this human. He's one of the few who can handle such a powerful goswig. He is the only one who can tolerate Payne's immaturity. This is the perfect chance for Payne to get out of his cave and become useful."

Brayson walked around his office for a long series of moments before waving his hand across one of the magical windows. It did not take long for the portal to zoom in on George's position. As he watched the mage's family walk toward the school, Brayson continued. "Amar, you're going out of your way to help this human. I want to know why."

Lasidious moved toward the window and took a look. "I see much of myself in him. He's going to be strong. George doesn't understand how he can do the things he does, but yet he does them. He does them naturally, without words or a staff. I find this fascinating. I think with your guidance, he could stand before The Source. George is loyal to those he chooses as friends. He could prove helpful when Marcus becomes more of an annoyance than he already is."

The Head Master turned to look into Amar's eyes. "How do you know of the struggles between us?"

"Let's just say I pay attention. You're my friend and I would do anything to help. It's clear your brother is becoming more agitated as the days pass. He carries a tremendous anger in his heart, though I don't know why."

"I didn't know you paid such close attention to the happenings of Luvelles. I assumed you were content to live with your brother on Grayham. How is your brother?"

"He is well, and I make it my business to pay attention. We are friends, are we not?" Lasidious looked out the window and pushed his hair behind his ears as Amar would have done. "It looks as if Payne has found George. Perhaps, you should trust me on this. Allow them to stay together. I know I should've come to you first, but I didn't have the moments necessary. If I had waited, you would've assigned him a different goswig. I will mind my place in the future."

"I don't know that this is a good idea." Brayson sat in his chair. "Perhaps, you're right. After all, you do know him better than I. Do nothing further without my knowledge. I'll allow Payne to stay with George. This is an odd pairing, to say the least. Your decision better be the right one."

"I'm right, but if I'm proven wrong, it will serve to remind me why you are the Head Master and I am not."

Brayson pulled Amar close and put an arm across his shoulders. "Flattery will get you everywhere. Now, get going before George arrives. The things I let my favorite Mystic Learner get away with...it's criminal. Keep in touch. I'll keep you informed of things."

"Until then, Master." With that said, the Mischievous One vanished.

Brayson watched as the family arrived at the base of his invisible school. With a wave of his hand, one of the windows of his office adjusted as the magic manipulated the vision. The faces of the family appeared and with another quick motion, the portal adjusted further and zoomed in on Mary's face, leaving a soft glow about her head as if she were some kind of angel.

"Your beauty is beyond compare," Brayson whispered as he gazed at her image. "I have looked forward to this day. I find myself suddenly nervous. You must have been molded by the goddess herself to possess such grace."

***

"Finally, we're here," George said as he stopped the family at the base of the invisible tower.

Mary gave a quizzical look. "What do you mean? There's nothing here."

"I know. That's what's so great about this place. Just watch and see. This is really cool, so watch closely. Man, I love this world." The mage began to speak the words that would reveal the front door. Before he could finish, Brayson appeared next to him.

Astonished, Mary was the first to react. "Oh my, you startled me, sir. The use of magic on this world is overwhelming. It doesn't feel normal and is somewhat perturbing."

"I would not worry yourself with such concerns, Mary," Brayson responded. "I welcome you to my school of magic. You'll become familiar with the uses of magic soon enough. This world is where The Source resides. Where I'm about to take your family, you'll experience different uses of magic. Many creatures living near you will use different forms of the arts on a daily basis."

Mary replied, "I see no school. All I see is a field. Who are you, and how do you know my name, sir?"

"I know many things, Mary. You will see my school in a moment. My name is Brayson Id. I am the Head Master of the lands of Luvelles. It's a pleasure to meet you. I have looked forward to this day for quite a while. I see you're wearing the dress I sent you."

Mary gasped, "You're the one who sent me this dress?" It was hard for her to fight back the smile. "Do you always keep a woman waiting? I've wondered on many occasions about who was sending me these wonderful gifts. You should be punished for making me wait so."

Brayson reached out and lifted her hand to kiss the top of it, watching Mary's eyes as she trembled with excitement. His goatee tickled her skin, and his blue eyes delivered the message of his affections. "You're absolutely right. I should be tortured for my abuse."

"Yes, yes you should, sir," she giggled. This was the first moment she had been flirted with in many seasons, and to say it was hard for her to hold back her excitement would be an understatement.

Brayson's smile was full of charm as he spoke in the language of the Elves. *"Khila amin, voronwer!"*

"Oh my, I don't know what you said, but it sounded charming."

"I said, follow me, lovely one."

The remark was a welcomed advance. Mary would file the compliment in the back of her mind as unforgettable. "You know all the right things to say to make a lady smile, Mr. Id. Lead the way."

The family stood in silence as glances were exchanged between them. It was as if Brayson and Mary had forgotten they were present. They simply stood in awe as Brayson continued. "It will be wonderful to have such beauty on my island. I've been watching you and have done so since your arrival on Merchant Island. I can't recall seeing such grace in any other woman."

Watching Mary smile, Brayson changed the subject. "I have prepared many homes for your family. I hope you like them."

"I shall be sure to let you know if I approve." She winked and put her arm through Brayson's.

Grinning, Brayson moved his hand through the air in a big circle. The door to the school appeared, and after enjoying the shock on Mary's face, he guided the speechless woman inside with the rest of the family in tow.

It only took a moment for Mary's shock to disappear. A big smile crossed her face as she looked over her shoulder at Athena and Susanne. Her girls giggled as they watched their mother disappear inside.

George and Kepler remained outside while Payne stayed close to Athena and entered with the others.

"Well, that's just great!" George sighed. "He just put the moves on my mother-in-law. Damn, Kep, this guy is smooth. You know she's gonna fall for him. He looks like Tom Selleck, for hell's sake. You've got to be kidding me. This clown and his red power-robe are oozing with charm. I want to puke. He's been sending her dresses this entire series of moments. If this isn't a conflict of interest, I don't know what is."

Kepler looked down at him. "What do you mean? Why is this so bad? Who is Tom Selleck?"

"Other than being my favorite private eye on one of my favorite shows on Earth, just forget who Tom Selleck is. If Brayson butters Mary up, how could I ta..." The mage thought twice before finishing his sentence. He whispered into Kepler's ear.

The demon cat's red eyes lit up. "Aahhhh, I see your point. We'll have to cross that river when we arrive at its shore. Oh, and by the way, you called him Brayson. It's Master Id to you, Mr. Mystic Learner."

"Shut up before I make a statue out of you."

"That's not funny, George."

The mage grinned and gave his large feline friend a hug around the neck.

"Okay, George, you can stop now. I hate it when you act so disgustingly nice. It's not natural for me to be seen this way."

After a short pause to enjoy the demon's discomfort, George continued. "I don't like how this looks. Let's keep our eyes open for a way to stop this. We can't have Brayson getting close to Mary. If he gets too close to her, then he's too close to us." They entered the school and shut the door. It vanished from the rest of the world.

Mary walked about the room. The details of the school's design captured her fancy, especially the spiraling staircase. The destruction created by George's fight with the sphere was gone, as if it had never happened. Everything was normal.

"My, my, Mr. Id, I've never seen such a place."

"Mary, please call me Brayson."

George rolled his eyes. "Great, everyone gets to call him Brayson, but me."

"Oh, honey," Athena said as she took his arms and pulled them about her waist. She kissed the end of his nose. "You're forgetting you're here to learn. He must have a reason for you to call him Master."

"Yeah, it's to piss me off."

"Stop that," she said with a touch of harshness. "You might want to change your attitude. Make me proud."

George had to smile. He pulled his wife close. After some moments passed, Brayson gathered everyone into a tight group and teleported them to the northern shore of his personal island. "This is where you'll be living until the completion of George's training."

The family's faces expressed their delight. Eleven structures had been created and formed a perfect circle. The four children who were old enough to play ran toward the mound of large rocks at the community's center and began a game of capture the tyrant, jumping from stone to stone.

Brayson spoke. "It appears the children like it. I trust you all will enjoy your stay here." The Head Master found the mage's eyes. "George, Amar explained your tastes when I met with him. I have to admit, it took many, many moments to understand how the details should look. He said it would remind you of Earth. I quizzed him on how he knew such things, but all he said was that I should speak with you. I would very much like to know about your Earth. I hope you find this place to your liking."

George scanned the area. It looked like a nice, family-friendly subdivision. It felt like he was back on Earth. Granted, there were no roads, sidewalks, or fancy landscapes, but the homes did have style: rock-covered exterior walls, good lines, and heavy wooden doors.

George rubbed the scruff on his chin. "So, Amar was the one who told you I would like this?"

"He did. I trust you find everything acceptable."

"You've outdone yourself, Master Id. You have given me a taste of my old home. Thank you."

"You're more than welcome." Brayson cleared his throat. "We have much to discuss. We will begin your training this evening. Meet me in my office by Late Bailem. You may bring Kepler and Payne. Amar informed me he sent Payne to be your goswig. I do hope you can handle him once you've finished the bonding ritual."

Payne tugged on Brayson's robe. Once he had everyone's attention, he showed all his fairy-demon teeth. "Payne goswig?"

Brayson laughed, then reached down to pick Payne up. "Not yet, Payne, but you will be soon. You'll need to listen to your master."

"Um...master...um…ahhh…George, Payne master?"

"Yes, Payne, it's George."

George knew now his suspicions were correct. Lasidious had been plotting, and with the way current events were unfolding, they all seemed to be in his favor. He appreciated the god's gestures, but wondered when he would be able to speak with him.

George interrupted the moment shared by Payne and Master Id. "I'm sure I'll find out soon enough if I can handle Payne, but what type of goswig do you have, Master Id, and where is it?"

Brayson spoke with pride. "My goswig is a phoenix. He's the most powerful goswig on Luvelles. The power of a phoenix lies within its feathers. His crimson colored feathers are coveted by kings. He is a marvelous creature. I keep him someplace safe. You'll meet him one of these days, George, if you manage to go through the trials."

"What trials are you talking about, and what is this bonding ritual you referred to?"

"We can discuss this later tonight." Without saying another word, Brayson walked over to Mary and took her by the arm. "Allow me to guide you to your new home, my lady. I have added something special, just for you... something I hope you'll use often. You may contact me whenever you want. I do hope we'll become well-acquainted."

Mary's hazel eyes accented her blushing cheeks. She moved her dark hair clear of her face. "You know how to treat a woman. I hope for this as well."

Brayson smiled and guided her to the front door. After showing her how to use the mirror, he kissed the top of her hand. *"Tenna' ento lye omenta."* Brayson vanished.

Mary turned to the rest of the family, who had followed out of curiosity. "This magic thing is kind of sexy. I don't know what he said, but it was beautiful, I'm sure."

George whispered into Kepler's ear as the commotion of the family grew. "This isn't looking good. I have a gut feeling this is going to be a huge problem."

Payne appeared on Kepler's back. "Let's eat!"
Kepler growled. "Get off me, freak!"

The Head Master's Island
Brayson's Home

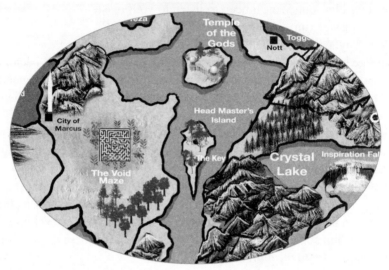

The Peak of Bailem is approaching. Brayson is waiting for his brothers to arrive. His home is hidden within a wooded area near the center of his island. From the outside, the home appears to be nothing more than a massive mound of boulders. Plants grow between the many cracks and, like his school, the door remains invisible to the outside world.

Once inside, Brayson's dwelling appears to have no walls, but they are there. A powerful illusion provides the perfect atmosphere. His mound of boulders have been hollowed at its center, but Brayson's furniture looks as if it sits in the open of the forest. The trees cast shadows across the home's floor which, in reality, is a smoothed rock. Subtle key points define the boundaries of the magic's illusion hiding the walls. Only Brayson, and a race of beings called kedgles, know where to look to avoid running into them.

The kedgles are fascinating creatures—only eight inches tall. They have a human head with human eyes, a mouse-like nose with whiskers, a tiny human torso, elf ears, and a full head of hair. The rest of their body from the waist down resembles a large tarantula. Wings are attached to the top of their spidery back. The kedgles are a magical race, proficient in creating illusions.

Brayson was waiting at his table when the door opened. "Hello, brother," Marcus said as he moved across the room, the smoke from his pipe trailing behind him. "I see you're still living inside this miserable mound of rocks. I'll never understand why you insist on such a simple existence."

"There are many things you'll never understand, Marcus. You spend far too many of your moments thinking about trivial things. I much prefer this over the darkness of your city."

Marcus leaned over the table and lowered his pipe, his brown eyes filled with disgust beneath his long hair. "How typical! You'll never change. You think you're better than me."

"No, just more pleasant."

Before anything else could be said, Gregory entered. "Gentlemen, how are we today?" He vanished, only to reappear in the seat next to Brayson.

Marcus grunted, then took a seat. Brayson leaned back in his chair and smiled. "I'm well, Gregory, and yourself?"

"Busy. I've been working on a set of plans to build a bridge across Lake Lavan. It will connect the shores of Inspiration to the shores of Lavan. The king and I have been working on this idea for over a season. We're about ready to break ground."

"You're pathetic," Marcus snapped. "Why do you feel the need to connect your precious city to Lavan? Why share it with a people who can't command the simplest uses of magic? They're beneath you, brother. They are mere halflings. How could you associate with those of impure blood?"

Brayson shook his head. "You'll never get it. It's hard to believe we come from the same mother. How you ever became so angry we'll never know."

Marcus wanted to curse their mother. He knew he did not share this half of their bloodline. Either his brothers did not know this, or they had forgotten what they heard as children. Their father's blood was their only common thread. To divulge this forgotten secret would serve to hurt his future plans. Any edge the belief they were of the same bloodline might give—was worth keeping.

Brayson studied Marcus' countenance. "You asked for this meeting. Why are we here? I don't have all day to listen to your negativity. Get on with it."

Welcome to the first edition of

The Luvelles Gazette

When you want an update about your favorite characters

Lasidious and Celestria are inside their home beneath the Peaks of Angels on the god world, Ancients Sovereign. They are discussing the next part of their plan. The moment to call for a meeting of the gods is at hand. The next piece of the Crystal Moon will be hidden.

Brayson, Gregory and Marcus are still inside Brayson's home. The conversation has become heated and from the look of things, it may prove to be a useless gathering.

Payne is with Kepler. George has requested they talk. Kepler, although reluctant, has agreed and is trying to find a way to tolerate the fairy-demon.

Susanne and Athena are in Susanne's new home. Susanne is feeding baby Garrin, but he won't stop crying. Athena is doing everything she can to help her sister find a way to soothe the child.

Mary is anxious to use her mirror to contact Brayson. The only obstacle stopping her is the short amount of moments it has been since his departure.

Sam Goodrich, King of Brandor, and his queen, Shalee, are discussing what to do with Kepler's brothers on the World of Grayham. Sam's army has hunted them down and brought the beasts to Brandor in two large cages.

Southern Grayham has changed over the past 115 Peaks of Bailem. There are two major issues to deal with. The first is the queen's health. Nearing the end of her second trimester, Shalee has started to bleed sporadically. The city's best healers have been summoned to keep an eye on their queen until she delivers.

The second issue is the reactions the king will face when attending the meeting he has called for with the Senate. Sam must explain his decision to allow ten barbarians to join the Senate as members of a reformed government. He must convince them that these barbarians must have a voice to vote on the laws governing the kingdom's daily operations. Sam will need to leave Shalee and head to Brandor's version of a courthouse.

Mosley has been using many of his moments to watch Sam and Shalee. The wolf is invisible to those within Sam's castle and has been listening in on their conversations to get an idea of how expected events may unfold.

On Ancients Sovereign the others of the Collective have watched to see how the Kingdom of Brandor will change. Brandor's army has defeated the barbarians of the north and is now in control of all Southern Grayham. Brandor, as or-dered by Sam, has continued to spare barbarian lives as they surrender and swear their allegiance to his crown.

Thank you for reading the Luvelles Gazette

Bitter Memories
The World of Grayham
Brandor's Royal Court

Sam has taken the position as head of Brandor's legislative session. The Senate's chamber is wide, large enough for 120 members. Stadium-style seating surrounds a stage which has been covered with a red, woven rug. Positioned at the rug's center is a rectangular table made of dark wood. A single chair rests at the table's head. It is from the opposing sides of this table that legislators present their arguments.

The leader of the Senate, Tenarkin Kois, who is also a judge, has been moved from his normal seat at the table's head and asked to join the others to make room for the king's throne. Until Sam declares the war is over, Tenarkin will not be allowed to reclaim his seat.

As the door to the chamber bearing Brandor's symbol was closed, Sam stood from his throne and moved to the far side of the table. He removed Kael from his sheath and commanded the sword to burst into flame. Once Sam had everyone's attention, he addressed the group. "I have called you here to inform you of changes I'm going to implement in the Senate. They will be made common practice before I declare an end to the war. Each of you will be required to adjust your beliefs. If you argue, you will be removed from your position, and I will appoint a wiser man to take your seat. I am not asking for your approval, nor will I allow dissention."

Mosley watched from within his invisible cover as the murmurs of the senators filled the room. Not a single soul dared object. The tone Sam had used in his delivery set the mood of the meeting. The king grabbed the end of Kael's fiery blade. He lifted both arms and placed the sword against the back of his neck. The men in the chamber watched in awe as their king remained unburned.

"I will be adding ten members to the body of this Senate. These men will not be your normal representatives. They will be barbarian nobles." He took Kael from behind his head and pointed the blade in the direction of the senators. "Does any man wish to voice an objection? If so, speak now, and I will fill your seat with another barbarian."

After a long period of silence, Sam continued. "This change will happen with or without your support. I suggest you wrap your minds around this new idea. This kingdom will find harmony and you, you, you, and the rest of you, will make this happen. Does everyone understand?"

Brayson's Home
The Meeting Continues

"You had your chance to speak with The Source, Marcus. I gave it to you more than a hundred seasons ago. If you had been considered worthy, you would've been given the chance to look into the Eye. It's good the dragon didn't find you worthy. The Eye would have swallowed your soul. You'd be dead!"

"What a pile of garesh! I've grown stronger, brother...almost as strong as you. Even without looking into the Eye, I have become the chancellor of the dark arts. I'm sure The Source would find me worthy now." Marcus took a puff of his pipe and blew it in Brayson's direction.

Brayson waved his hand and stood from the table to avoid the smoke. Grabbing his glass, he took a drink. "I don't doubt your abilities. I'm sure the dragon would allow you to look into the Eye. But, you have a problem, dear brother. It's my job to determine who sees the Ancient One. Frankly, the hate in your heart sickens me. If I allow you to stand before him and the beast allows you to look into the Eye, and you live, who knows what kind of pain the people would suffer."

Marcus pointed his boney finger in Brayson's direction. "Careful, brother, it's not for you to monitor what I do."

"You're right. Monitoring your actions isn't my concern, until it becomes a problem for the well being of many. It's my job to determine who stands before The Source. You won't be getting another chance. You would abuse this power."

Gregory spoke before Marcus had the chance to explode. "I agree with Brayson. You would become a threat if given the chance. Your heart is full of darkness, and for the life of me, I can't figure out why."

"Imbecile! Who cares what you can't understand? I don't owe you an explanation for my actions. You should watch yourself, Gregory. You aren't strong enough to oppose me. I would hate to suffer the reality of looking down at your corpse."

Brayson had enough. "And, you aren't strong enough to make threats of this nature in my presence! You should leave. If you aspire to hurt Gregory, you'll deal with me. I'll kill you myself if you cross that line."

"Ha! You don't have it in you. I could defeat you. My power rivals your own."

Brayson's face turned cold. His blue eyes darkened as he leaned across the table toward Marcus. "I would not test my resolve."

"We will see, my brother. Someday...we will see." Marcus vanished.

After a moment of silence, Gregory spoke. "Should I be worried? He makes me nervous."

Brayson put his hand to his chin. "I'm scared for your wellbeing. I need to think. We need to figure out what he's up to. If he were to stand before the Eye, he would receive the knowledge to destroy us all. I can't allow him to meet with the Ancient One. He has overcome his weakness. The reason The Source rejected him no longer exists."

Gregory moved to stand near the hearth of the cold fireplace. He leaned over and touched the bottom log. A strong fire began to burn. Turning back to Brayson, he sighed. "Exactly what is the key to getting past The Source? Tell me the secret."

"Doubt. You must not have doubt. You must believe you are worthy, or The Source won't allow you to pass."

"After all these seasons, I've never figured this out. It's disturbing to know I was held back because of doubt. I wish I would've known."

"As do I."

"What should we do?"

Brayson fidgeted with his goatee as he pondered the situation. "We need to figure out what Marcus is planning. This is a matter of urgency. I'll come to you when I know more. Until then, I want you to wear my amulet."

The Head Master opened a small chest sitting on a bookshelf. He removed the amulet and waved his hand across it. The diamond shaped stone burned bright green within its leather strapped setting. "Put this on. It will protect you until I can determine a proper course of action."

Brayson clapped his hands. Three kedgles approached, their spider legs making clicking sounds as they hurried across the illusion of the forest floor.

He bent down, picked one up, and placed it in the palm of his hand. "Hepplesif, my friend, I need your assistance."

The kedgle twitched his mouse-like nose and listened with his tiny elf-ears as Brayson continued. "I need 100 of your kind to go with my brother. You will take-up residence in his palace. Your illusions could prove useful. This would be temporary. Speak with your king and tell him I need his approval."

Hepplesif spread his wings, then responded as he lifted to a hovering position above Brayson's palm. "What shall I tell the king you're offering in return?"

"What would he want?"

The kedgle lifted his tiny hand to his chin. "Maybe a case of Froslip."

Brayson took a step back. "Hepplesif...you ask too much. You know how hard it is to acquire this ale from Harvestom. I had to make many promises before it was brought by the Merchant Angels. It is the rarest ale on all the worlds."

The kedgle lowered to the table. "Perhaps, a bottle would do. And, I would require a mug for myself since it is I who must deliver the message."

"Ha, ha, ha...my friend, you drive a hard bargain. Tell your king, a bottle is his, and I will give you two mugs, but they will be mugs of your own size. Agreed?"

"You know me too well. I would have chosen one of your mugs. It would have lasted much longer."

"Like you said, I know you too well. Please hurry. Find your king." Brayson opened the door and let the kedgles fly out.

Gregory lowered the crystal to his chest. "Thank you, brother. You're a good man and a better leader." They embraced, then Gregory vanished.

The City of Brandor
Sam's Throne Room

Sam stood from his throne. After asking everyone to leave, he turned to speak with Shalee. "How are you feeling?"

"I'm okay, I guess, but the spottin' won't stop. I'm scared for the baby. These cramps are killin' me. This has been goin' on for ova' six days now, and it isn't gettin' any betta'."

"Dang it, Shalee! On how many different occasions do I need to tell you to lie down? You don't listen to me. It's not like I'm a doctor or anything. God forbid you pay attention."

"For heaven's sake, Sammy-kins, stop barkin' at me. I don't need the stress."

Sam softened his approach. "You're right, but you should be lying down. Michael will be here soon with Kepler's brothers. I will question the jaguars, then dispose of them. I'll fill you in when it's over."

"No, Sam. I want ta see this. I want ta hear their answers for m'self. I've been doin' a lotta thinkin'. There's gotta be a way ta convince the jaguars ta live in peace. There's been enough bloodshed. Besides, Kepler was their ring leader. Without him, they're just big pussycats."

"You can't be serious. The cats must die."

"No, Sam, no. There's been enough killin'. All we need ta know is where Kepler is and George shouldn't be far away."

Near the throne room window, Mosley was listening to their conversation with his wolf ears lifted high, invisible to the mortals.

The king rubbed his hand softly across his queen's face. "You can't possibly expect me to allow the cats to live."

"The jaguars are smart. Our army has proven they can be captured. The cats will agree ta live in peace. Ya need ta show compassion. Make the cats an ally."

Sam smiled, "If I promise to let them live, will you lie down and get some rest? I can get the information we want without risking your health. I promise to tell you everything. I love you. The baby needs you to take it easy right now."

Shalee thought a moment. She couldn't understand why she was having so many problems. Mosley told her that Bassorine had chosen her to be Sam's mate. The wolf said she was perfect for childbearing. He further stated that Bassorine had met with the gods of Earth and this was one of the requests he asked of them before her soul had been sent to join with her fetus. But now, the blood and cramping suggested otherwise.

"I think I'll lie down afta' all. Wake me when you're done." The king kissed her forehead, then summoned three healers to escort their queen from the throne room.

Not long after, Michael entered. "Sire, the demon cats are outside. What would you have me do with them?"

"Take them away from the castle. Take them beyond the garden. I want privacy. Don't allow the people to follow. Keep the cats in their cages. I want to question them myself."

After checking on Shalee, Sam cut through the royal garden to where the cats were being held. He didn't waste any of his moments. "What are your names, demons?"

Koffler laughed, then mocked Sam. "What are your names, demons? What are your names? What are your names? We're not going to tell you anything, human." The demon flashed his eyes and growled.

Sam shook his head and remained calm. "I will offer one of you a chance at freedom in return for the information I'm after."

Koffler laughed again, but Keller, with a mind equal to Kepler's, took a different approach. "My name is Keller. This is Koffler."

Koffler became angered. "What are you doing? He is..."

"Shut up," Keller growled. The cat turned to look at Sam. "What guarantee do I have you'll spare my existence once I've given you the information you seek? What will keep your army from hunting me?"

Sam moved close to the cage, but stayed far enough away to avoid the demon-cat's powerful claws. He held up his sword. "I don't need you to tell me anything. I'm asking you to tell me what I want to know. I could always have my men torture you. Once you're near death, I'll touch this sword to your shoulder and you'll be forced to give me the information I'm after. Which would you prefer?"

Koffler shouted, "Don't tell. He'll destroy..."

"Shut up, idiot!" He turned back to Sam. "And, how will your sword fetch this information? Your blade will not penetrate my coat."

Michael spoke. "My King, the mens' swords were useless. Their arrows bounced from the demons' bodies. They were captured with nets. But, I'm sure these beasts have never seen a sword of the gods. Perhaps, you should test Kael on his flesh."

Keller lowered to his belly. "I have no desire to tempt fate. I'll tell you what you want to know, King of Brandor. Killing me is impossible. I'm already dead, but I suspect you know my weakness, and my destruction would be inevitable."

"Don't do it," Koffler roared. The demon threw himself against the side of his cage to make his point.

Sam walked over to Koffler's mobile prison. "You have exceeded your usefulness. Allow me to demonstrate my knowledge of your weakness."

The king commanded Kael to bring forth his fire. Once this had been done, he spoke the words of power to extend the length of the blade as he pointed the tip in the jaguar's direction. The demon cried out as the sword skewered his undead heart. The men surrounding the oversized wagons backed away as the sword's heat intensified. Keller was forced to move to the far side of his cage. It didn't take long before Koffler was reduced to nothing more than a pile of ash.

The king commanded the blade to go cold, then redirected his attention to his General Absolute. "Michael, say nothing of the cat's death to our queen. If asked, the beasts have returned to their pass and have agreed to live in peace. See to it the men keep their mouths shut. Remind them that I will remember their faces."

"As you wish, Sire."

Sam found the eyes of every man present before directing his attention to Keller. "I assume you're ready to talk?"

"I am. Will you allow me to walk out of this city unharmed? Do I have your word you won't send your army after me once I've gone? Agree to this pact and I will tell you all you want to know."

"You have my word. My army will not come for you. Once you are past the city gates, you are on your own. Are we agreed?"

"Agreed."

"Where is Kepler? Is George with him?"

"And, if I tell you this, I'm free to go?"

"I will open your cage myself. I'll escort you to the city's gates to ensure your safety. Beyond that, you're on your own. My army will not set foot outside this city in pursuit."

Keller studied Sam's face. After a moment of silence, the cat spoke. "My brother left with George. They went to Luvelles. They traveled with the Merchant Angels. I haven't seen them since."

Sam looked deep into the demon's eyes. "Come to the edge of the cage. If you're telling the truth, the sword will confirm it, and you'll be freed."

Keller moved toward Sam. Once Kael was placed against the jaguar's shoulder, Sam spoke. "Say everything you told me again, demon."

"My brother and George left together. They are no longer on this world. They went to Luvelles."

Kael's blade began to pulse with a soft light. "He's telling the truth, Sam, but this creature's heart is dark, and he could become an issue if you let him live."

Keller took a defensive posture and growled. "You gave your word!"

Sam moved to the end of the cage. "A promise is a promise." Sam looked into the demon's glowing eyes. "When I open this door, I expect you to be on your best behavior. Don't doubt my ability with this sword. You'll stay with me until we get to the city gates. If you make one false move, I'll separate your coat from the rest of your body and use your hide as my bedcover."

The demon rolled his eyes. "You don't need to be so dramatic. I will do as you command. I have not dominated territories by being witless."

As Sam and the giant cat walked through the streets of Brandor with the army in tow, the people darted inside the closest building. Little kids peered over the ledges of window sills to capture a glimpse. Mothers closed their wooden shutters as if these flimsy barriers would stop the demon's weight if it chose to attack.

As they arrived at the gate, Sam ordered his men to open it since Keller's body would not fit through its smaller opening. As the heavy wood was pushed back, Sam turned to the demon and commanded Kael's flame. "You should run. I want you out of my sight."

Without a word, the jaguar bolted. A moment later, Sam asked Michael to bring his bow. The general did as instructed. Michael removed the weapon from the king's mount and tossed it through the air.

Sam held the bow to his side. "General, if memory serves me right, I promised the army would not set foot outside the city's gates."

"Yes, Sire, you're correct."

"I also said...once he gets past the gates, he's on his own."

"Right again, My King."

"But, I did not say I wouldn't kill him myself. I wonder if my arrows will pierce his coat?"

"I also would like to know this answer. Here's to good shooting, Sire."

Sam raised his Bow of Accuracy. Five arrows with burning tips were made ready and handed to him one by one. The king waited until the jaguar was almost out of sight. He shot the arrows without pause, then waited. Moments later, the demon tumbled head over heels.

"General, it appears I've kept my word. But, the cat has somehow managed to perish. Who would have ever guessed that a tragedy such as this would happen to our feline friend? I find it rather convenient that burning hot arrows would fall from the sky and pierce the heart of our undead ally. I'm heartbroken. But, I would hate to see his coat go to waste. You deserve to have a new bedcover. Say nothing of this to our queen, and enjoy the warmth while bedding your woman."

"My King, as always, your sarcasm is amusing. I will tell our queen the cats have promised to allow our people to sojourn through their pass." Michael signaled his men to follow him. "The men will hold their tongues."

One of the castle handmaidens rushed up on horseback, shouting as she approached. "Sire...the queen! The queen is screaming and the baby..."

Before the servant could finish, Sam ordered the general to hand him the reins of his mount. He threw his weight on top of the beast and directed the ghostly, now-tamed, water mist mare toward the castle.

The Hidden God World
of Ancients Sovereign
Beneath the Peaks of Angels

Lasidious walked up behind his seductive lover. After pushing her hair clear, he leaned over and kissed the nape of her neck. "Brayson has allowed George to keep Payne as his goswig." He kissed the side of her neck and enjoyed the softness of her skin against his lips. "You look beautiful, as always, love."

Celestria was sitting at the large stone table of their home. The goddess had recently redecorated with bright yellow accents which contrasted against the dark walls. Every vase was filled with an array of color and a small lantern, sitting at the center of the table, filled the room with a soft light and the smell of evergreen. The goddess had been staring into the green flames of their fireplace when Lasidious entered.

Celestria leaned her head back and allowed Lasidious to kiss her lips. It was his charm that won her heart over 14,000 seasons ago. She stood and moved into Lasidious' arms. Her every curve and gesture was flawless. Her voice—angelic—was sweet and soft to the ear. She was worthy of the title, Goddess.

"How did our baby look, my pet? Did you see him?" Celestria leaned in and nibbled on Lasidious' ear. The god trembled as the wetness of her tongue left its mark.

Lasidious struggled to focus, but somehow, he managed to answer her question. "I did. Garrin is loved. He cried when Kepler roared, but he's well. He was just startled."

Celestria caressed his chin as she responded. "We need to be careful. Garrin must grow before he can command the power necessary to control the Book. We cannot afford a mistake."

"Which is why I have been working to create tension between the brothers. Marcus' anger is becoming stronger by the day. His dreams are becoming nightmares. All he thinks about is how much he hates his siblings."

Celestria cupped the god's face. "Your mind amazes me, my sweet. How you ever thought to plant the seeds of resentment all those seasons ago is beyond imagination. I would have loved to see Marcus' face when he heard his mother's rejection. I can only imagine how it stung. I so enjoy his pain. If you push Marcus, he will start a war. This should keep the eyes of the Collective off our son."

Lasidious lifted Celestria into his arms. He spun with her, then set her down, only to kiss her once more. "I don't need to push him further. Marcus has decided to go after his brother's position as Head Master. He just needs to figure out how. The great thing is...Marcus is standing in George's way, and George will stop at nothing to get his daughter's soul out of the Book. All I need to do is give George some simple guidance, and he'll do the rest."

"When does he meet with Brayson again?"

"I don't know, but I'm sure it will happen soon. George will go through the bonding ritual with Payne, and if he survives, the fairy-demon should be able to help George when the moment arrives that he is needed."

"What of the others? They are talking. They want to know when you will reveal the location of the next piece of the Crystal Moon."

Lasidious smiled, took Celestria by the hand, and guided her toward their bedroom. "I will call a meeting of the gods tomorrow. I'll meet with the Book of Immortality before I do. But first, a little fun is in order." The deity shut the door as he pulled Celestria close.

Marcus Id's Dark Tower-palace

Gage kept his distance as Marcus threw most everything he could get his hands on around the bedroom chamber of his dark tower-palace. Books, scrolls, quills, chairs, and even his pillows now lay scattered across the cold floor. The badger was feeling a whirlwind of emotions as the chancellor's mind screamed with unorganized thoughts. It was clear Marcus was hurting. He sucked on the tip of his pipe as if he wished to pull the tobacco through it. His heart was not only full of hate, but also full of a tremendous, agonizing sorrow. All Gage could piece together were small bits of Marcus' past. After many moments, the chancellor settled down. His exhaustion consumed him and sleep followed not long after.

The goswig walked over to the side of the bed and jumped up. He lowered into a seated position on the mattress, put his small wooden cane to his side, then took a deep breath. What he was about to do was forbidden, but he had to know the reason Marcus acted the way he did. He began to search his master's memories. Something had to be the cause of all this hate, resentment, and fear.

Gage closed his eyes. The memories presented themselves in a vision—a vision as clear as if he had been there.

"Mother, mother," a young boy's voice, full of excitement, shouted as he entered the school of magic. Gage recognized the boy and the school. The boy was a memory of the past, a young Brayson Id who looked no older than 13 seasons. The school was under the care of the boy's father, Hedron, the Head Master whom Brayson would replace as an adult. A moment later, another boy ran in, but this child was younger by nearly four seasons. The badger also recognized this child. It was Gregory.

"I'll be right down," a stout female voice shouted. "Stay on the rug and off the floor...it's just been polished." A heavy woman began making her decent down the spiral staircase. She was an elf with a rounded face and clearly out of shape. Her outfit, although nice, did not hide her weight. She waddled as she walked. Her face was broken out, and scarred because of it.

Gage looked for Marcus, assuming he must be nearby. When he did not see him, he noticed a small crack in the door leading outside to the village. He moved to take a look, passing through the door as if it were not there. On the other side was the child, about 11 seasons old. He was waiting, crouched, ready to jump out and yell. His ear was pressed against the door close to the crack, listening for his brothers' footsteps and heard the conversation inside.

"Mother, Gregory cast his first spell today," Brayson shouted.

"Yeah, I turned a frog into a mouse. It was neat."

"That's wonderful. Your father will be proud. I'll tell him, once he has finished the lesson with his new Mystic Learner. I'm proud of you, too, Gregory."

"Thanks! Where's Marcus? I've got to show him."

What Gage heard come out of Helen's mouth was unbelievable. "On how many occasions have I told you boys to stay away from Marcus? He's a mistake your father made with the local whore. You two need to stick together. Marcus isn't worth your love. He's an abomination, an ugly little thing that won't go away."

"But, mom," both boys said, almost at the same moment.

"No, no, no! I'll hear nothing of this. You stay away from Marcus. I pray to Mieonus that tragedy will find him and take him from this world."

Gage watched Marcus lower his head and walk down the village road. He could feel the rejection and pain the boy felt.

The vision began to fade. A moment later, the badger found himself in a different memory.

Marcus, still only 11 seasons old, crept into his father's bedroom. The Head Master was not home, but Helen, now nothing more than another fat corgan he hated, lay sleeping beneath a quilted cover. The badger could feel the boy's anger as he approached the bed.

Helen's words were playing over and over in his mind as her snoring filled the night. *On how many occasions have I told you boys to stay away from Marcus? He's a mistake your father made with the local whore. You two need to stick together. Marcus isn't worth your love. He's an abomination, an ugly little thing that won't go away. I pray to Mieonus that tragedy will find him and take him from this world.*

Gage watched as Marcus lifted the cover, careful not to wake Helen. The boy pulled a cossenger from his pack. The snake was the deadliest reptile on Luvelles. Once bitten, the venom would kill its victim in a short series of moments.

The badger desperately wanted to cry out for Marcus to stop, but this was only a memory. The past could not be changed and Marcus could not hear him no matter how loud he screamed for his attention. All he could do was watch. It was only a matter of moments before the bite would happen. When it did, Marcus covered Helen's mouth so she couldn't scream. The boy looked into her eyes until she was lifeless. Gage's heart ached for Marcus as the boy put the snake back into his pack.

"I hate you, too," was all the child said before leaving the room.

Many other memories filled with pain entered Marcus' mind as Gage sat next to the chancellor's sleeping figure. After a while, another specific memory surfaced.

The children were in the Head Master's office, but now, all three boys had grown into adult, elf men. They were standing in front of their father.

Hedron spoke. "Brayson, the moment has come for you to visit The Source...you too, Gregory. Let's see if what I've taught you has sunk into your brains."

"Am I going, father?" Marcus asked. "I'm ready. I can make you proud."

"You won't. Only your brothers are ready."

"But, I can do everything they can. I'm better than they are, and my magic is stronger."

Hedron waved his hand across the top of Brayson and Gregory's heads. Once the brothers had vanished, the Head Master responded. "You're not ready. Something isn't right with you, boy. Until you figure it out, I cannot send you to speak with The Source."

"But..."

"But nothing! You're not ready. We'll continue your training tomorrow. Now, fetch my dinner."

Gage could not believe how cold Hedron had been. It was as if he viewed the young man as an irritation, not a son.

The vision faded and after a moment, another memory surfaced.

It was many seasons later and again it was a vision of the Head Master's office. Marcus didn't stand before Hedron. He stood before Brayson, the new Head Master. Gregory was not present.

"I don't know what to say, Marcus. I can't help you anymore. I allowed you to speak with The Source. It's not my fault you were found lacking and denied the opportunity to look into the Eye."

"It is your fault. You knew I wouldn't be allowed to pass. You could've told me the secret. All you had to do was tell me how to get past The Source."

"Why would I do that, Marcus? That's not how it works, and you know it. It wouldn't be much of a test if I told you the answer. Some things need to remain sacred."

"Of everyone, brother, I thought you would be the last person on Luvelles to hold me back. You could've helped me. You're the Head Master.

You can do whatever you want. Tell me the secret and allow me to speak with The Source again."

"No! You had your chance. I won't give you another. There are things you must learn before you deserve the power you seek. The only person holding you back...is you."

The memory faded.

Gage lifted from his seated position and stood on the bed. He looked at Marcus and thought, *Master, you are a mountain waiting to erupt. I'm sorry, but I don't wish to be in your presence when this happens. I'm not strong enough to share your hate. When you wake, I will be gone. I must get away, far enough to avoid sharing your thoughts. I hope you find happiness.*

The badger vanished.

The Luvelles Gazette

When you want an update about your favorite characters

Lasidious plans to meet with the Book of Immortality in the morning. He will address various topics and set a meeting of the gods.

Celestria plans to visit Grogger's Swamp to secure a hiding place for the third piece of the Crystal Moon.

Head Master Brayson will meet with George. There is much to discuss about taking on the responsibility of a goswig. Other matters of George's training are also necessary subjects of conversation.

George is with Kepler and Payne. He is going over a few last moment instructions before teleporting their group to Brayson's floating office.

Athena and Susanne are inside Susanne's new home. Garrin will not stop crying. They are finding it hard to comfort him. Both women feel the addition of Payne to George's little group is an odd one, but Athena was quick to point out her husband's tendency to pick strange companions. The conversation turned to the absence of Maldwin, the rat.

Mary has stopped on many occasions to stand in front of the mirror Brayson gave her. She can't stop looking at herself. She has felt desired ever since the Head Master's advance. This is the tenth dress she has tried on of the fifteen given to her. She wants to look perfect before she activates the mirror to summon Brayson.

Sam is making his way back to Shalee in the city of Brandor on Southern Grayham. The situation is grim.

Mosley plans to go to Luvelles. He wants to see for himself what George and Kepler are up to.

Gregory is inside his glass palace. The confrontation with Marcus has left him on edge. He appreciates the amulet Brayson has given him for protection, but he is still increasing the security within his tower. He hopes the Kedgle King will accept Brayson's offer of Froslip in exchange for their help.

Marcus is still sleeping inside his tower-palace.

Gage has left Marcus' palace. He has teleported to the far west side of Crystal Lake, located in the Kingdom of Lavan. The badger is hoping to find a temporary place of refuge there. To do this, he must seek permission from a race of beings called Ultorians.

Thank you for reading the Luvelles Gazette

Sam Junior
The Head Master's Island

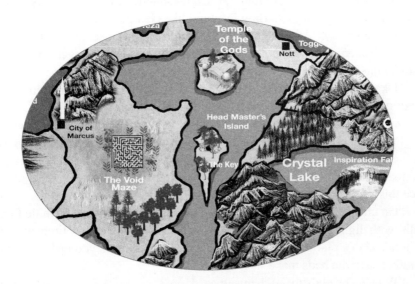

The homes Brayson provided the family were sturdy. A luxurious combination of natural colors, throw rugs, and magical lamps had been placed throughout each structure, which at the moment of George's departure from Earth were considered in style. The furniture was elegant and, to George's surprise, Lasidious had done a thorough job of describing his tastes. The wood looked as if it had been stained, something he had not seen until now, but was just another fascinating use of magic. Compared to Grayham, the class and style of living on Luvelles had proven to be far more enjoyable.

"He left the rat on Grayham," Athena said as she bounded down the stairs toward Susanne's food closet in hopes of finding something to settle Garrin. When she opened the door, she was blasted by a burst of cold air. Many frozen items rested on hardwood shelves.

Athena shut the door. "Brrrr." She shouted up the stairs, "I have not asked George about Maldwin lately! I don't know if we'll see the rat again! Is there another food closet in this house?"

"Not that I know of," Susanne's voice echoed. "Mother said her food closet changes. She was excited about it, but changed the subject when she put on another dress."

"What do you mean? It changes?"

"I don't know! I didn't get into it with her! Garrin started to cry and needed to be changed! I swear, this child must be full to the top of his head! It's like he never stops gareshing!"

"You don't have to be so foul," Athena responded as Susanne walked into the room. "Now, *you're* starting to sound like George. I swear that man rubs off on everybody." Athena grabbed the handle of the closet door and opened it. The frozen food was gone and the temperature had changed. Now, she saw grains, rice, and other nonperishable items. She shut the door.

"Okay, this isn't normal," she whispered to herself. "I don't think I'll ever get used to magic. I wonder what else is in here?"

Again, she opened the door and peeked in. Through the crack, she could feel the temperature had dropped, but it was not cold enough to freeze anything. Now, there were bergan eggs, corgan milk, greggle hash, hogswayne (fatback), and many forms of fruit and vegetables. "Susanne, you've got to see this! Your food closet is the most amazing thing I've ever seen."

"Go check out the washroom. Say the word illuminate. The whole thing fills with light, just like it did at Kebble's inn. I never get tired of that. There's also a platform near the front door that teleports you upstairs. And, mother says the beds make themselves."

"What? The beds make themselves? How?"

"How am I supposed to know? Magic, I guess."

"I hope our clothes will do the same."

"Wouldn't that be nice."

The sun warmed the front porch of George's new home. The smell of the rain lingered as George shook his finger. "Damn it, Payne, you need to listen! If you're going to be my goswig, you've got to pay attention. That's all I need you to do."

"George pick on Payne."

Kepler rolled his eyes. "No one's picking on you, freak. Shut up and do what you're told. You're supposed to call him, Master." Kepler glared at

George. His eyes flashed. "We have become jesters, not territorial forces. We have digressed since the freak's arrival."

Before George could say anything, Payne disappeared. "Where did he go?" Kepler questioned, scanning.

"Hell if I know."

Suddenly, the giant jaguar cried out. Payne had reappeared, grabbed the tip of the undead cat's tail and bit hard. The look on Kepler's face was classic. George laughed, despite the fairy-demon's disregard for his former instructions.

"Get this damn thing off me, George!"

Payne released his bite and flew away, but Kepler was not finished. His massive paw swiped through the air, aiming at Payne's head.

"You missed! Kitty too slow! Too fat!"

Kepler roared. Athena heard it from inside Susanne's house. The jaguar began to chase Payne around the clearing at the center of the community of homes. Payne was enjoying the excitement, but Kepler was dead set on killing him. "Come here, you little freak!"

"Try catch Payne...kitty!"

"Be still so I can bash your head in!"

Kepler was adjusting to the quick changes in Payne's direction. His muscles rippled under his dark coat as he moved as fast as he could, but it was not fast enough.

George tried to get their attention, but as hard as he was laughing, the words took a moment to form. "We've got to go guys. Hey! Hey! Hey! Dang it! We've got to get going!"

Athena walked up behind him. "I think the whole family heard Kepler. The baby's crying again. What's with those two?"

"Payne bit his tail. Kepler's pissed."

"I thought you were going to have a talk with them?"

"I did, but I don't think it sunk in. Kepler called Payne a freak and it was on. I swear to you, Kepler is going to kill him."

Athena shook her head. "I'm glad I'm not in your boots. I don't think I'd have enough patience to put up with them. But, you can't let Kepler hurt Payne. He's just a baby. How do you think you acted at three seasons?"

"I know...I know. I find this humorous, to tell you the truth, but I need to put a leash on Payne. I don't understand what a goswig does, but I'm sure it'll require better behavior than this. I'm going to need your help with him."

Nothing else could be said before Payne flew over and stopped next to the side of George's new home. He taunted the jaguar as he waited in front of the stone-covered wall.

"Come, kitty...come get Payne. Fat kitty! Slow kitty!"

"Bad idea, Kep..." George shouted, unable to finish his sentence before the jaguar launched. He watched as the giant cat stretched out, zeroing in on the fairy-demon's position—ignoring the stone-covered wall. Just before impact, Payne vanished. George scowled as Kepler smashed face first into the granite.

"Oh, my! Go see if he's okay, George." Athena shouted, "Payne, you come over here...right now! You will take a seat on the porch steps! Don't you dare move a muscle! You do as I say! Right now!"

George watched as Payne did as he was told, the little guy held his head low as he settled on the steps. Once the fairy-demon's wings rested against his back, George turned to look at Kepler's motionless form. "I think it's a bad idea to walk up on a jaguar when his pride is hurt. I don't think he wants to be asked if he's okay."

Athena squeezed George's arm. "But, he's not moving."

"I know. Let's give him a bit."

After a moment, Payne began to antagonize Kepler from the steps. "La, la, la, Payne bet kitty won't call Payne freak no more!"

George pointed. "Don't say anything else. If he's dead, I'm going to kill you myself."

"But..."

"Not another word!"

Slowly, George approached the giant cat. "Kep, you okay?"

"Ugggggh...ohhhh...my head. I hate that little freak."

"You scared me," Athena said as she shoved past George. "Let me have a look at you." She squatted near his jaw and used the bottom of her dress to wipe off his nose. "You'll be okay. You have a nasty cut, but it's nothing some healing mud won't fix. Between your ears and your face, you're going to look frightful for a few days."

George studied the wall. "Kep, look at the hole you put in my house. It's a close call, but I'm pretty sure the house won."

"Not funny, George. Do you see me laughing? I'm not laughing, am I? I hate that little freak."

"I get it, I get it. You don't like him."

"No! You don't get it. He's going to drive me insane. Take me back to Grayham if you're going to allow him to stay. I could be lying in my pass without this irritation. I could be eating people in peace."

George was caught off guard. He didn't expect Kepler to react this way. He had a decision to make—it was either Payne or Kepler, and he needed to choose now. "I'll tell Payne to go. Your friendship is more important to me than he is. Just give me a moment, okay?"

"Fine. I'll be inside with Athena." The giant cat brushed past George, nearly knocking him over, then strolled past Payne without as much as a single glance. The door of the home slammed behind him. Payne cringed.

George took a knee beside the fairy-demon. "I'm sorry, but I've got to say this. I don't want you around any longer. I can't afford to have a goswig that doesn't listen. You need to leave."

"Payne no go. Payne be really, really, really gooder. I like here...um and...Athena gooder to Payne."

"I understand, little guy, but you don't listen and you're creating problems. I'm sorry, but you have to go. Goodbye." George shook his head and went inside.

Payne stood on the steps and stared at the heavy wooden door. Tears began to flow from the corners of his eyes. An agonizing series of moments passed before he lowered his head, then vanished.

George and Kepler appeared in Brayson's office a little while later. The left side of Kepler's head was swollen. The brown healing mud Athena had administered stuck out like a sore thumb on his thick, black fur.

"What happened to you?" Brayson asked as he stood from his desk. He closed a large, heavily bound book and walked across the room.

Kepler responded with a grunt and moved to a comfortable spot to lie down.

"A wall hit him," George responded.

"What do you mean?"

"It's a long story. Don't ask."

"Where's Payne?"

"I told him to go home. He's more trouble than he's worth."

Brayson sighed. "Too bad. I'm not surprised you couldn't handle him. He could have been an asset to your growth. He could have been the strongest goswig on Luvelles. But, if you're unable to control him, it's best you found out now."

George rolled his eyes. "Yeah, right. I could've handled him. The problem wasn't me. It was the relationship between Payne and Kepler. I was put in a position of choosing, so I chose the one I knew I could count on."

Brayson thought a moment as he looked out the window to the land below. "Loyalty is important. But, if you are able to handle Payne, then Kepler needs to try harder. As I have said, the fairy-demon could be useful."

Kepler snarled. "I can't stand the little freak. Power or not, I won't travel with him."

Brayson smiled. "When you met George, did you like him at first?"

"No, not at first, but he was much easier to stomach."

Brayson nodded in a fatherly manner. "I'm sure he was, but look at you now. Your relationship has grown, and now, two friends have appeared before me, choosing each other's friendship over any other. If you take the moments necessary, perhaps, just perhaps, you could find a similar relationship with Payne."

"I doubt it," Kepler sneered.

The Head Master moved over to the jaguar and looked at his face. Kepler winced as Brayson touched a sore spot, then went to a bookcase at the center of the room and removed a small vial. Opening the lid, he motioned for the cat to open his mouth. He poured a drop of the potion under Kepler's massive tongue. It was only a short series of moments before the swelling began to reduce. Brayson watched as the last cut on the jaguar's face mended. "I trust that feels better?"

"Yes...much. Thank you."

George spread Kepler's fur to study the cat's skin. "There's no scar. I've never seen anything like this. He healed in a matter of moments. How's this possible?"

Master Id handed George a different vial. "The healers in Floren are the best at what they do. You'll find no stronger magical cures than what they possess. If you have a pulse, they can fix you. I want you to keep this vial with you. It's not as powerful as what I've given Kepler, but it will do the job. It will take longer for its effects to work. The vial I possess is rare and I don't wish to part with it. You will need something to keep Kepler healthy. You'll need it...because I'm not going to allow you to abandon Payne."

"What?" Kepler growled. The demon stood. "I said I won't travel with that little freak."

Brayson looked Kepler in the eyes and moved within inches of the deadly beast's snout. He spoke with authority. "You are going to find a way to get along with Payne. This conversation is over and the matter is settled."

Kepler tried to object, but found his ability to argue was gone, thanks to Brayson's power. The giant cat could only watch as Brayson waved his hand across one of the windows. "Seek Payne," he commanded. A moment later, the window zoomed in on the fairy-demon's position. He was sitting on top of George's house, waiting for the mage to come out. "George, take a look."

George moved to the window. "I can't believe it. Kep, come look at this. The little bastard hasn't left."

Brayson waved his hand to release his magic, allowing the cat to speak. "So what? Just give him enough moments and he'll go away. That's what freaks do."

Brayson moved across the room and took a seat behind his desk. After putting his feet up, he looked at Kepler. "You need to change your attitude. You're not getting out of this. You're going to learn to work together."

Kepler snorted his disdain. "Easy for you to say. You're not the one getting your ears ripped off. He hasn't taken a bite out of *your* tail, which, by the way, I could use another drop of that potion."

Brayson administered the elixir. It wasn't long before Kepler's tail mended. "George, I want you to leave Kepler with me. Go home and allow Payne back in your good graces."

George hesitated, looked at the demon-cat, then shrugged his shoulders as if he had no say in the matter. "Okay...but, he might not be willing to come back with me."

Brayson looked out the window and waved his hand. Payne's face came into focus. "Look at him. I'm sure he'd like another chance. He has lived alone for the last season of his life. He's young. You need to be a mentor. Kepler will adjust."

Again, Kepler growled, "And, if I refuse?" The cat lowered to the floor with a smug look on his face.

Brayson moved to stand beside the cat. He pulled back the top of the demon's ear and whispered into its opening. "I have not given you that option. I'm sure we understand one another."

Kepler didn't respond as he watched Brayson. Instead, he rolled over and closed his eyes. It was pointless to object.

George was impressed at how Brayson handled the situation. He was also glad he could explore the use of Payne's skills. The Head Master had given him the perfect place to put blame. When it came to having the fairy-demon around, he would be able to point the finger at Brayson whenever Payne pissed Kepler off. It was perfect.

When George appeared outside his home, he had a plan.

"George!" Payne shouted from the rooftop. "Um...Payne mean, Master!"

The mage ignored the call and continued up the stairs as if he heard nothing. Again, Payne shouted, and again, George ignored him. The mage pushed open the large wooden door and called out, "Babe, I'm home!"

Before George could shut the door and take another step, the fairy-demon appeared in front of him, his wings flapping like a hummingbird as he hovered. George acted surprised. "Payne, what are you doing? I thought I told you to get lost."

"Payne be gooder. Payne stay. Payne be bad no more."

"You won't be good. You ignored me when I asked you to get along with Kepler. How can I trust you?"

"No, Payne really, really, really, really, really promise to do gooder. Payne be gooder."

Athena walked up. She was a welcome sight. George knew she had a soft spot for Payne and she understood the child's mind. Though Payne was not your normal child, she would still treat him the way she would any young one, and this meant giving him a second chance. George knew he could use this to his advantage.

"I thought you were meeting with Brayson." Athena said, kissing him on the cheek. "Miss me?"

"Always. I am meeting with Brayson, or rather, I was. I had to come home for a bit." George didn't want Athena to quiz him further, so he redirected the conversation toward Payne. "He's asking me to give him a second chance. Do you think I should? I don't think he'll behave."

"Oh, oh, oh...Payne be so gooder. Payne promise. Payne really, really be gooder."

"Ahhh, honey, he's sorry." Athena turned to look at Payne. "Will you try hard to do as you're told?"

"Payne promise, promise, promise!" A big smile appeared.

George chuckled inside. He knew what his wife would say next and he'd be able to use this as leverage to control Payne. All he needed to do was play out his role a little longer and Payne would do everything he said.

Athena reached out and pulled Payne into her arms. The fairy-demon stopped his wings and allowed her to cradle him. "George, you should give him another chance."

"I don't know. I don't think he'll behave. Maybe, I should think about it for a while."

Payne looked to Athena for help. He nestled into her to gain favor. While his eyes were on hers, he gave his best forgive me look.

Athena looked up at George. He winked so she would play along. Athena understood what he wanted. She raised her voice and barked out a command. "I said, give Payne another chance. I don't want to hear another word about this. Payne, you'll behave, and George, you'll allow him to stay with you. Do you two understand me?"

Payne lowered his head, not liking the scolding. "Okay...ebbish nay."

George winked. "Yeah! Ebbish nay! Gosh, you're so bossy." He could not have been happier with Athena's performance. He looked at Payne, then back at Athena. "I will do as you say. We better get going." The mage touched the fairy-demon on the forehead. Both of them disappeared.

From the window of Mary's home, Brayson looked through the open door of George's home as he watched the pair vanish. A smile crossed his face as he shut the blind. "Mary, I must go. It has been a pleasure to see you. I'm glad you used the mirror to call me." He lifted her hand and kissed the top of it. "It seems my moments have run out. I must get back to my office. I would like to see you again. I will take you someplace special."

Mary sighed. "I would like that."

Brayson kissed her cheek and spoke in the language of the elves. *"Vanim-le sila tiri."*

"Oh my, that sounded glorious. What did you say?"

"I said, 'Your beauty shines bright.'" Brayson vanished.

Mary giggled, "I'm going to like this magic thing." She retired to her room.

Southern Grayham
Sam and Shalee's Bedroom Chamber

Sam rode his mist mare as fast as it could carry him to the castle. His problems with Kepler's brothers were over and now he knew where George was hiding, but the news paled in comparison to what he was about to find out as he walked through the door of his bedroom chamber.

Seeing the situation was grim, the king adjusted his mindset and prepared to use the medical knowledge he had acquired on Earth. He sat on the edge of the bed to assess the situation.

Shalee was pale, fatigued, her forehead cold to the touch, eyes bloodshot and full of tears. "Shalee, I need you to tell me what you're feeling. I need you to explain everything that's happened since I left."

The queen pulled back the covers. Her voice was weak. "It's the baby."

Sam moved to the end of the bed. As he looked between her legs, it took every ounce of strength to hold back the heartache. The infant had been expelled, and the baby's skin was blue from the lack of oxygen within the womb. Sam, Jr. was motionless—lying lifeless in his own afterbirth. Shalee had been near the end of her second trimester. The baby looked to be nearly three pounds. Every finger and toe was accounted for, but unable to grab hold of Sam's finger. The king ordered everyone to leave the room.

Without a word, he gathered a clean cloth and spread it on the corner of the bed. He lifted the baby and placed him at its center. He folded the edges to cover the body. Sam moved to the center of the room and placed his life-less son on the table.

Moving to the edge of the bed, Sam gathered his wife into his arms. He held her close to provide a safe place to grieve. After many moments passed, Sam pulled back. "Shalee, we need to get you cleaned up. There are things we need to do to prevent further complications. I need to check inside you to see if all the afterbirth has passed. I'll put padding in place to absorb the drainage."

Shalee pulled on the collar of his shirt. "Sam, I'm so sorry. I'm so very sorry. I know I let ya down."

"No, you didn't. This kind of thing can happen to any woman. We'll get through this, I promise. But first, we need to get you cleaned up."

Shalee nodded. Sam took charge of the situation. It was not long before the queen was sleeping, exhaustion overwhelming her.

With the situation in hand, tears began to roll down Sam's face.

Western Luvelles
Brayson's Office in the Sky

When George appeared inside the Head Master's office, Kepler was sleeping. There was no sign of Master Id.

"Kep, where's Brayson?"

The demon opened his eyes and yawned. "I don't know. Who cares. We were talking about Payne when Brayson excused himself, then vanished. I see you brought the freak with you."

Payne looked at George. He wanted to fight with the cat, but did not want to get in trouble.

"Well, that's just great," George snapped, ignoring Kepler's comment. "I bet he went to see Mary. Damn it, Kep, this isn't good."

"What's not good?" Brayson responded, after appearing behind the mage.

George whirled around. "How long have you been standing there?"

"Long enough to hear something isn't good. What are we talking about?"

"Oh, it's nothing I can't handle." George changed the subject. "So, what are we supposed to do? You said something about beginning my training. You were going to explain how to bond with a goswig. What did you mean by that?"

Brayson moved to sit at his desk. It was made of a heavy wood and carved across its front was an image of a dragon—The Source. He opened a giant book which sat on its top. "George, come here a moment. Bring Payne with you. I want you to see this."

George did as he was told. As he looked down, the images on the book's pages began to shimmer across the tattered pieces of parchment. "This is fascinating. I've never seen anything that looked so ancient. I don't understand the Elven language. How can I read it?"

"It won't matter. Concentrate."

George began to focus, but his lack of comprehension frustrated him. "Master Id, what does this phrase mean?"

Brayson leaned over and took a look. "It is a phrase of power." He explained some of the phonetics of the Elven language. "Try to sound it out. You can do it."

The challenge was intriguing. George wanted to understand the power the book possessed. He began to sound out the phrase. *"Uuma ma' ten' rashwe, ta tuluva a' lle."* The magic within the book began to stir. A swirling mist emanated from its pages and surrounded George and Payne. It wasn't long before the pairing was sucked in, vanishing inside the book as the misty trail followed. The tome slammed shut. A new story of bonding had begun.

Kepler jumped to his paws and growled at Brayson. "What have you done?"

Brayson leaned back in his chair. "Calm yourself, Kepler. Everything will be okay, providing George is able to find a way back. The book is taking them on a journey. The phrase meant, 'Don't look for trouble, it will come to you.'"

"What do you mean...providing he can find a way back? What kind of trouble is he in?"

"George and Payne must take this journey together. If they don't work with one another, they could end up lost or dead. This is how he will learn to bond with Payne."

"What do you mean, lost, and why would he perish?"

"I mean, they may never return. The trials are dangerous."

The demon-cat scoffed, "Athena isn't going to like the sound of this."

Brayson smiled. "Athena doesn't need to know unless George fails. Agreed?

"Bah! I suppose."

A Forbidden Fruit

Southern Grayham
Sam's Throne Room

Sam spent most of the night watching over Shalee after she fell asleep. The king lifted the cloth which held the expired life of his infant son and sought solitude within the confines of his throne room.

As Sam cradled the child, tormented tears rolled down his face. He would never know the joy of Sam Jr.'s company. He was empty, his heart ached, and he trembled with every breath. With his whole heart, he wished to trade his life for the opportunity to give Shalee the chance to know their son.

The memories of everything lost began to flood his mind. He missed Earth, his family, Helga and BJ—especially BJ—and he could only imagine how much the people of his kingdom missed the thousands of men who were lost in the war.

Sitting on his throne, Sam put his legs together and laid the baby on his lap. He peeled back the layers of the blanket hiding the infant's tiny form. It only took a glance for the king to lose what was left of his composure. He began to wail.

The World of Luvelles
Northwestern Hyperia
Grogger's Swamp

Celestria appeared in the middle of Grogger's Swamp. It was a miserable place—cold, dark, and murky. The air smelled putrid. The goddess levitated above the moss-covered water and watched as the back of a large creature skimmed its surface.

The swamp was full of many forms of reptiles, amphibians, insects and birds—most of which had been deformed or altered by magic, then discarded to live the rest of their days in misery.

A large bird with reversed wings flew past. Its long neck was rolled under its body to see where it was going, since it flew tail first. The goddess shook her head at the ridiculous concept that some powerful wizard would waste his moments on such childish manipulations.

The swamp covered a tremendous area of Northwestern Luvelles and had become a magical garbage dump of sorts. These were the experiments of those who sought to strengthen their control of the dark arts.

Now...fellow soul...this territory is the home of Grogger, a fifty foot tall, seventy-five foot wide shapple toad. In general, shapple toads are not a threat. Normally, they are small, about the size of a man's fist. They eat bugs and hop away from anything larger than themselves. Once an insect has been swallowed, it is digested over a series of days.

Grogger, on the other hand, is not your normal shapple toad. He has been transformed by the darkest of magic—magic commanded by Marcus Id. The chancellor has performed many experiments on this beast. As a result, the enormous shapple toad now rules the swamp.

Once inside the Grogger's belly, his prey remains alive and is digested over a period of 10 seasons. Many brave men and other forms of life reside within Grogger's stomach. When a victim is added, the toad's size expands. Allow me to get back to the story.

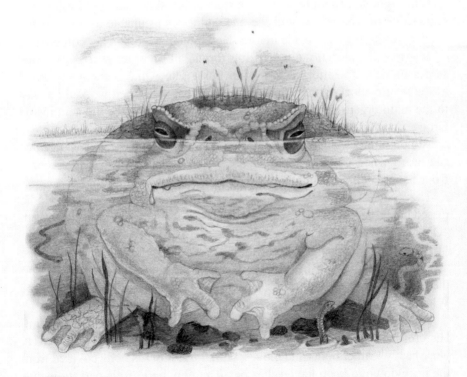

Celestria understood the digestive traits of the acid inside Grogger's belly. This beast was perfect for the plan she and Lasidious had decided to implement over 100 seasons ago. She had been the one to implant the desire to manipulate Grogger in Marcus' mind. The chancellor's lust for power was strong and it didn't take much before he took action.

Now, all Celestria had to do was encourage Grogger to swallow her. It had to be the beast's decision. This was critical—the goddess needed to ensure the rules of free will were obeyed within the Book's pages.

As it turned out, getting inside the beast would not be an issue. The ground shook as Grogger surprised Celestria, landing behind the goddess. The murky water splashed everywhere, saturating her gown. Grogger's mouth opened and the screams of the trapped souls within his belly could be heard. His tongue lashed out and pulled her in.

The goddess could not move. The sheer number of bodies inside the toad's belly had been compacted. She expanded her invisible barrier of protection, then lifted her hand to command the darkness to dissipate.

With light and room to work, she studied her surroundings. Despite the knowledge of what she would see, the goddess was unable to fight off the need to vomit. It took a while before she was able to collect her composure.

Many of the partially digested life forms, all of which were in various stages of decomposition, oozed with puss. The white moisture bubbled as the magic attacked the outermost extremities first, then worked its way to the main organs. Arms, legs, fingers, and toes sizzled as the acid inside Grogger's belly systematically devoured them.

Although alive, none of Grogger's victims were coherent. The screams she heard when Grogger's mouth opened to pull her in must have come from a source other than the sixty motionless figures in front of her.

The goddess removed a piece of toe from the hem of her gown. She tossed it beyond the barrier and into the mound of bodies. Again, she puked. "Oh, my love, our plan is not worth the suffering these beings must bear."

After summoning fresh water to appear in the palms of her hands, she swished it around inside her mouth to remove the vomit's aftertaste. She spit the water to the floor of Grogger's stomach, then focused. "Who to choose? Who to choose?"

Pressed against the wall of her barrier was an elf, dressed for the hunt. His crossbow had been damaged from the force of Grogger's tongue. He wore heavy leather boots and gloves, with the rest of his body covered from the neck down to keep the leeches out. The only part of his person uncovered was his head. Because of the way the magic acid worked, the only damage suffered was to his long blond hair, and even then, just the ends were damaged.

"His capture must have been recent," the goddess whispered as she extended her field of force to pull him inside. She touched his shoulder. "Hello. Hello. Can you hear me?" The elf didn't move. She waved her hand to clear the air of the stench. "Sir, wake up."

After many moments, the hunter opened his eyes. His voice was weak. "Where am I?"

"You're inside the beast-toad," Celestria replied with a soft voice. "We are trapped. How do you feel?"

"I suffer."

"I can imagine. The beast's tongue carries a force with it. What is your name, hunter?"

"I am called Geylyn Jesthrene...from Hyperia." The elf tried to sit up, but pain shot through his chest. "I must've broken something. It appears we are doomed."

"What brought you to the swamp?"

"I came to win the respect of my family. I had no idea the beast had grown so. It appears I have done nothing but assist his growth. What a fool I was to think a miserable crossbow could kill him."

"What happened?" Unconcerned, Celestria allowed her mind to wander, thinking of future plans while Geylyn babbled on.

"The beast surprised me. My mount was spooked and threw me to the ground. I should have known I was in trouble. Krapes are known for sensing danger. I thought I was standing in front of a large, moss-covered hill when suddenly it opened. The beast's tongue was the last thing I saw. I should've paid attention to the warning signs."

Now...fellow soul...for those of you who don't know, krapes are the mounts for those on Luvelles who are unable to command magic. Their appearance is strange. They are hairy, with a large portion of their body resembling the shape of an oversized kangaroo. Their arms resemble those of an ape. A long, heavy tail extends behind them for balance, with a large mass at the end which they use for protection. The head of the krape looks reptilian—similar to a raptor's, but with three eyes. This third eye rests on the back of their head, helping them avoid an attack from behind. It is virtually impossible to surprise one of these creatures.

Krapes are not carnivorous, despite what their sharp teeth would suggest.

Their diet consists of fruits, grains, and many forms of tree bark. Their teeth are used as a weapon when in battle. An untamed krape stores food inside a large pouch which covers its abdomen, but once domesticated, this pouch is used to carry their rider's goods. The saddle of the rider is placed on the beast's back, close to the krape's haunches. A krape can cover a large distance in a short amount of moments, running like a raptor or hopping like a kangaroo. Fully grown, the beasts are nearly twelve feet tall.

Celestria placed her hands on Geylyn's head. Four ribs were cracked from the force of Grogger's tongue. "You should not feel bad about misjudging the shapple's size. From the looks of it, many have underestimated the beast. I am sure you did not expect a toad to be so large and so well camouflaged."

The elf began to laugh, but stopped to grab his side.

"Your ribs are broken. I can mend them if you would like."

Geylyn looked into her eyes, "I would welcome the relief, even if it's only a temporary reprieve before I pass. Are you a healer?"

"You could say that."

"I'm sorry. Where are my manners? What is your name, my lady?"

The goddess healed his wounds as she responded. "You may have heard of me. My name is Celestria."

Geylyn knew the name. He moved to his knees and bowed. "I didn't know your face. I'm sorry for my ignorance, Goddess. I wouldn't have expected you to be in the stomach of a giant beast."

"It is quite all right. Given your current situation, I will extend my forgiveness. How would you like to earn your freedom?"

"I'd wish for the opportunity."

"Geylyn, I need your help."

"I don't understand. Why have you chosen me? My family's prayers are heard by Alistar."

"I do not need your worship to care about your well being. You are a creature of the gods. My eyes look upon you as a cherished being."

Geylyn smiled. "My service to Alistar must be misplaced. He doesn't appear to care about the situation I find myself in."

Celestria cradled the hunter's face. She would use Geylyn's comment to her advantage. "My love for you is why I have come to this miserable place. You do not deserve to meet such an end, or be ignored by your god. Your life should be celebrated, as I celebrate it. However...it is against the rules of the gods for me to remove you from this fate, but there is a way I can save you. It is up to you to choose to help me save your life. You will feel no pain, nor will you smell the stench of this place while you wait. If you choose to live in service to me, I will leave you with enough food to keep you satisfied until help arrives."

Geylyn lowered his head. "What would you ask of me?"

Ancients Sovereign
The Hall of Judgment

Lasidious addressed the gods. "I have called you here to establish the rules for retrieving the third piece of the Crystal Moon."

"Where is Celestria?" Mosley interrupted, taking note of the goddess' absence.

"She is coming. Don't worry yourself about such things, Mosley. We have much to discuss about the continuation of our game. The third piece of the Crystal Moon has been hidden."

Yaloom responded. "Our game? We haven't played this game for many days now." He stood and adjusted his burgundy shirt. As he did, his rings, filled with assorted gems, contrasted against the shirt's cloth. He moved to a more powerful position behind his chair and placed his hands on its back. "You haven't given us any information about the next piece of the crystal's whereabouts for more than 100 Peaks."

Of all the gods in the room, Lasidious hated Yaloom most. "As always, you have managed to annoy me, Yaloom. But, despite your aggravating attributes, your team managed to capture the first two pieces of the Crystal Moon necessary to win the game. If you manage to retrieve this third piece, the worlds will fall under evil's control."

Mosley stopped licking himself long enough to interject again. "I would imagine this conversation will include the location of the crystal?"

Lasidious looked at the wolf and winked. "It may. I haven't decided yet, my friend. First, we need to discuss the rules."

The Book of Immortality floated over, then lowered to the large marble table. He carried a mug of freshly-squeezed nasha—a drink created from the fruit harvested from the gods' orchards.

Now...fellow soul...allow me to explain what nasha is. This pear shaped fruit only exists on Ancients Sovereign. It is from the Collective's version of the Tree of Life—similar to the one used by the gods of Earth when populating that world. The fruit has the ability to resurrect the dead.

Gabriel took a drink and swished the liquid around inside his rosy cheeks. "It's your game, Lasidious. I, for one, would love to hear the rules you wish to lay out."

"As would I," Mosley affirmed.

Lasidious took a deep breath. "I was about to say, each team needs to pick a being to go after this third piece of crystal. This being can be anyone on the lower two worlds, but they cannot be one of the three brothers in control of Luvelles. There's no need to start another war over the crystal's whereabouts."

The Mischievous One leaned back and put his feet on the table. "Of course, we need to live by the laws within Gabriel's pages and observe the sacred right that all mortals have free will. Other than that, there are no more rules. You now have the moments necessary to determine your choice. I will call another meeting to divulge the crystal's location."

"Why not tell us now?" Yaloom snapped.

Mosley shook his furry head. "Because you want him to. He thinks you are an idiot. He is doing this to toy with you. Be patient. We will know the crystal's location soon enough."

Lasidious watched Yaloom sit in a huff. The Mischievous One looked at the rest of the gods. "Are there any questions?"

"Yes," Yaloom barked. "What of the first two pieces of crystal? The ones George collected on Grayham. Where is George, and why haven't the pieces been put back inside the temple on Grayham?"

"George is on Luvelles," Mosley interjected. "So is Kepler."

"And, how do you know this?" Yaloom retorted as he turned his attention to the wolf. "How could George be on Luvelles?"

Mosley snorted his disdain for the god's ignorance. "George is a clever leader of his own pack. Perhaps, you should ask Lasidious the same question."

Yaloom redirected his stare. Lasidious crossed his feet, leaned back in his chair, and put his hands behind his head. "I have no idea. You might want to ask George that question. Better yet, ask Brayson Id. I had nothing to do with it. I didn't know he was on Luvelles. I've been looking for him since the war on Grayham began. Mosley, are you sure that's where he is?"

Yaloom rolled his eyes and listened to the wolf's response. "I heard Sam question Kepler's brothers before he killed them. I heard Keller tell Sam George and Kepler left for Luvelles and caught a ride with the Merchant Angels."

Lasidious continued his ruse. "I wonder how he made this happen? Perhaps, one of us should speak with the Head Master."

"I will speak with Brayson," Gabriel responded.

Lasidious leaned forward and clapped his hands. "Then, it's settled. Meanwhile, are there any questions regarding the retrieval of the third piece of the Crystal Moon?"

"Seems simple enough," Mieonus replied. She stood and adjusted her bosom to a more ample position within her royal purple gown.

Alistar also stood, "I just want to confirm what you've said. We can choose anyone, as long as it's not one of the brothers, or anyone from Harvestom, Trollcom or Dragonia."

"That's what I said, you can only choose from the lower two worlds and you cannot choose the brothers."

"Anyone else we want? No matter what?"

"Yes, no matter what."

Alistar looked at Mosley. "Are you thinking what I'm thinking?"

"I am. We need to take a trip to Brandor. But, we should give it a day or two. Shalee has miscarried her pup, or rather, her infant son."

"Oh, that's wonderful," Mieonus cheered. "She has so much potential. To be bothered by something as trivial as motherhood would slow her progression. It's the best thing for her, really."

Mosley growled as he lowered to the floor, "I disagree."

The goddess smiled. "Let's not let our differences of opinion spoil my moment. I wish to savor the thought of her pain." Mosley shook his head in disgust.

A moment later, Celestria appeared in front of the group. "It's done. The third piece of crystal has been hidden." The goddess had cleaned the moss and filth of the swamp from her dress—all, except a small spot on the bottom, toward the back. From where she appeared, only Mosley noticed. The wolf lifted from the floor and walked past her. As he did, his keen sense of smell took note of the unique aroma. The wolf nodded his head and the spot disappeared.

Mosley rose and put his front paws on the edge of the table. "Lasidious, I will be waiting for your disclosure of the crystal's location. I request those on my team meet with me at my home. We have planning to do. Celestria, as always, it was nice to see you. Perhaps, we will have more of a chance to speak later." With that, Mosley vanished.

"He did not give me the chance to respond." Celestria chuckled and took a seat. "How are the rest of you doing?"

All the members of the wolf's team acknowledged her presence, then vanished. Yaloom's team was all that was left.

Lasidious looked at Yaloom. "I can't believe Mieonus would allow you to take control of your team again. Your last display of leadership was void of any form of real thought. I have no doubt you'll waste this opportunity. Vexatious is as vexatious does."

Yaloom grumbled, "Hmpf, I can handle this with ease. You underestimate my ability."

"I doubt it. Face it, Yaloom, you're an idiot. I would venture to guess you're dumbfounded. Your team has no idea who they will choose. But, this doesn't surprise me. I would've expected as much, considering your inability to lead your team to an informed decision. I'm sure you'll..."

Yaloom cut him off. "Lasidious, you've made this an easy choice. We shall choose George, your pet creation."

As soon as Yaloom finished speaking, the Book of Immortality lifted from the table and sent a brutal wave of power into the God of Greed's chest. The deity was thrown backward and smashed into the thick marble wall. His body hit so hard, his spine cracked as he fell to the floor.

Gabriel floated overtop of Yaloom and relieved the screaming god's pain. Once his cries subsided, the Book spoke. "Your words have broken the Rule of Fromalla. You are now a mortal man. You can no longer stay on Ancients Sovereign. This will be the last series of moments your eyes bear witness to the glory of this world." Yaloom began to sob. He realized what he had done.

The others were astounded and confused. They began to shout questions at the Book. Mieonus, on the other hand, knew full well the promise Yaloom had made. She was present in the theatre of Brandor the day Sam killed Double D.

It was on that day that Lasidious, Mosley, Yaloom and the goddess entered the pact of Fromalla. Lasidious had admitted, it was because of his manipulations that George was able to find his power.

Now...fellow soul...in case you have forgotten, Fromalla is a rule, or rather a law, created by the gods and written in the pages of the Book of Immortality to govern them. It was created due to the overwhelming lack of trust growing within the Collective after the God Wars. Though they fought together, a battle of a new kind started once the wars were over. Each deity needed followers to increase their power when the worlds were populated. While building this group of worshippers, the gods would share each other's secrets within the Collective to undermine each other's campaign.

It was Bassorine, the late God of War, who called a meeting where he suggested they vote to pass the Rule of Fromalla. The law was long and covered most any angle, but it basically meant: if two or more gods shared a secret under Fromalla, they could not divulge this secret to the others without penalty of being made mortal.

The Book of Immortality was made responsible for enforcing this rule. It does not matter if the slip of information is subtle or accidental—the rule is clear: information shared under the Rule of Fromalla is sacred.

Mieonus held her hand up to silence the rest of her team, "There's nothing for us to question. I was there when Fromalla was invoked. Yaloom has broken our sacred law. As we all know, the Book felt this betrayal as soon as the rule was broken. I'll lead our team from now on. Let's meet at Yaloom's old home. I am claiming it as my own."

She turned her attention to the fallen god. "No offense, but I'm not sad to see you go. You did us a favor. We no longer have to deal with your incompetence. I'm so going to enjoy my new home. I have always envied the way the water runs through it. Now, it is mine."

Yaloom screamed, "This isn't over! I'll have my revenge!"

Lasidious walked over, leaned down and smiled. His eyes turned red and his teeth to fine points. He hissed with an evil that made those in the room tremble. "Oh, but it is over! You have lived more than 930,000 seasons. In a few days, you'll be nothing more than a pile of dust. No one will remember your name once those who serve you find out about your fall from grace. I will personally see to it that every trace of your existence is removed from the worlds."

Lasidious stood and took Celestria's hand. The last thing the Mischievous One heard before teleporting home was Yaloom's scream.

Mieonus dismissed herself, "I trust I will see the rest of you at my new home." She vanished, leaving behind an echo of laughter. Moments later, the rest of Mieonus' team disappeared without saying goodbye.

The Book of Immortality looked down at the fallen god. "How you could have made such a stupid mistake is beyond me. Where would you like to live out the rest of your days? I would choose wisely. Your days are short. According to the laws within my pages, you are granted one final request. What will it be?"

Yaloom thought for a long series of moments. A smile crossed his face. "I still have a significant amount of power, despite being stripped of my immortality. I also have my memories. I may no longer be a god, but I can divulge secrets which will effect the balance of power without recourse. I'm no longer required to observe your laws of free will. I may not be able to have my vengence in this life, but I can steal my soul from your pages and seek revenge in another."

The Book lowered to a height level with Yaloom's eyes. "I assure you, once I have your soul, it will remain within my binding. You have not answered my question. What is your final request?"

"I would like you to harness what is left of my power and my memories. Put them into a vial in the form of a potion. I wish to be taken to Sam's throne room in Brandor and left with this vial in my hand."

The Book frowned. "Yet again, the Collective has failed to implement laws to govern another matter of great significance."

Yaloom's eyes darkened as his smile spread. "Yes, but the law states you must grant my final request as long as I do not ask for the return of my immortality. You must give this to me, and you cannot tell the others what I've done."

Gabriel sighed. "Brandor, as you wish."

The World of Luvelles
The Kingdom of Lavan
Just East of Crystal Lake

Gage stood on a hillside, looking down at the village he hoped to make his new home. The badger was nervous and sick to his stomach. He knew without the permission of the ultorians, he would not be able to take up residency here. He would make his descent to the shores of Crystal Lake at nightfall when they would leave their underwater city to come ashore.

Now...fellow soul...allow me to tell you about the goswigs' village. It is a place with an unknown name, a refuge known only to goswigs. Many of its inhabitants have run away to escape the abuse of their master, while others simply need a place to live after their master's death. Magic keeps the village's entrance hidden and only goswigs can see it.

As Gage looked at the village, there appeared to be no movement. It was as if it had been abandoned. *Am I in the right location?* the badger wondered as he tapped his cane against a rock near his foot. *I'm sure the ultorian leaders will have knowledge of my exact location. I hope I have not made a mistake.*

Ancients Sovereign
Lasidious and Celestria's Home

"Do you think Mosley saw the stain on your dress?" Lasidious questioned as he sat near the green flames of their cube shaped fireplace.

Celestria took a seat in her lover's lap, "It appears the residue on my dress is gone. I was not the one to remove it. I would guess he saw our clue and got rid of it before the others noticed. I am sure he knows the crystal is somewhere inside Grogger's Swamp."

Lasidious smiled and removed a flower from the vase sitting on the stone table and caressed Celestria's cheek with it. After a soft kiss was exchanged, he responded. "You've got to love that wolf. He's perceptive. But, can you believe Yaloom's idiocy? How could he make such a mistake? I knew he wasn't the cleverest of minds, but to be made mortal over something as trivial as a poor choice of words, is ridiculous."

The goddess purred as she bit the top of his ear. "Yaloom wanted to use your creation against you, my love. He wanted to rub George in your face to get a reaction. It appears you were under his skin more than you estimated. Now, we can forget about this part of our plan. I am glad it is over. It is just one more piece of our grand design to fall in line."

Celestria glowed in her enjoyment of Yaloom's demise as she continued. "I know we spoke of getting rid of him, but I never imagined it would happen without working for it. I just love it when they do our dirty work for us, my sweet."

Lasidious could only smile. "As you know, Gabriel won't be able to draw from either Yaloom or Bassorine's power when the moment comes to stand against us. Whoever the Book chooses to replace Yaloom will be far weaker. This bodes well for us. We have only one more inconvenience to purge. Are we still in agreement that with him out of the way, we will be able to draw from Garrin's power to hold the book under our control?"

"We are."

"Then, we just need to give Garrin the moments necessary to mature."

"Yes, it will be delightful to watch his power develop."

Lasidious enjoyed the thought. He took a deep breath, then chuckled. "Another matter of discussion. I believe Mosley will convince Shalee to go after the crystal. I'm glad her power has grown so quickly. This is an unexpected twist we can use to our advantage."

"Agreed. Let us plow the road before her feet. I am sure she will follow it to the crystal. Do you think you can convince her to abandon her morality?" The goddess moved to stand before the green flames of their fireplace, then rolled her hands over top of one another. "I do hope she chooses a darker path."

Lasidious tapped his fingers against the table. "Shalee is bitter after the loss of her child. She is vulnerable. There's no better series of moments to tempt the mortal than now." The Mischievous One changed the subject. "Did you find someone to hold the crystal for us...someone who will be grateful?"

Celestria oozed. "Oh yes! And, he's gorgeous, my pet. His name is Geylyn Jesthrene. He is a hunter from Hyperia. Geylyn was quite debonair and handled himself like a true gentleman...even inside Grogger's belly. He addressed me in a proper manner. I gave him the crystal and fixed his wonderful head of hair."

"Your lust for this mortal is not shared by me."

Celestria moved to her mischievous lover and kissed him. "Your jealousy makes my loins moist, my sweet."

"Hmpf! I bet! Let's change the subject." Lasidious stood from his chair and moved across the room. "I imagine Mieonus will choose George to go after the crystal. When she is unable to find him, she'll come looking for us. I think we should implement the next part of our plan."

Celestria closed the gap between them, then rubbed her hands across Lasidious' face, "I agree. But first, you have business to attend to." The goddess took him by the hand. With her free arm, she used her power to clear the table, then encouraged her lover to lie on its surface. She spoke with a seductive voice as she opened the front of his robe. "You have nothing to be jealous of, my pet. My heart yearns only for you."

"It better."

"Oh…it does." Her tongue found his.

The City of Brandor
Sam's Throne Room

When the Book of Immortality appeared in Sam's throne room with Yaloom, the king was asleep. Sam's head rested against the padding of his royal chair—the lifeless body of his miscarried son still in his arms.

Yaloom whispered. "Thank you, Gabriel. This is perfect. Though losing my godliness was unexpected, I can still control my fate. It won't be long before I'm nothing more than another soul within your pages. I am sure you'll give me good dreams as I wait to be reborn."

The Book didn't respond. Instead, Gabriel vanished.

Yaloom shrugged. "Guess not. No matter. I have other ideas."

Yaloom moved across the room and sat next to Sam. He was careful not to startle the king. "Sam, wake up. We need to talk, King of Brandor."

Sam's eyes were bloodshot as he struggled to open them. It took a short series of moments to collect his bearings. He knew the god's face from pictures he had seen in the royal library. He lifted from his throne, then sat Sam Jr. on its soft cushion. Without looking at the deity, he spoke. "I'm in no mood to visit with gods, Yaloom."

"I understand your pain, but I have come to help."

Sam's right eyebrow lifted. He turned to face his visitor. "Exactly how do you intend to help?"

Yaloom opened his hand and revealed the vial. "I have been stripped of my godhood. This vial contains what was left of my power and my memories. If you were to give this to your queen, she could use it to save your baby."

Sam could only stare at the liquid inside the glass. It glowed light blue and was intoxicating to look upon. He stood fixated for what seemed to be forever before Yaloom snapped his fingers. "Sam, are you paying attention?"

"I am. I'm just tired. If I give this liquid to Shalee, you're saying she can use it to give our son life?"

"In a manner of speaking. The liquid could assist your queen in gaining the power necessary to teleport to the hidden god world. Someday, after she meets with The Source on Luvelles, she'll be able to make the journey to Ancients Sovereign. She can pick the fruit from the nasha tree. Then, as parents, you could extract the juice from this forbidden fruit and use it to retrieve your son's soul from the Book of Immortality."

Sam took a step back, then sat on the steps leading to his throne. "Are you saying my boy could live a normal life?"

"I am, but there are a few unknowns."

"And, these unknowns are?"

"I have no way of knowing how Shalee will react to the potion. I do know it won't kill her, but I do not know how long it will take before my memories will fill her mind or when she'll feel the benefit of my power. It could happen within a single moment or it could take several seasons. All I know is, it will eventually happen."

"Okay, okay, hold on a moment. Are you saying, this potion will give her the ability to teleport between worlds? Are you saying, she will have the knowledge of the gods?"

Yaloom shook his head. "I am saying, her mind will need to open to my memories. Only then, will she possess the knowledge to teleport between worlds. But, to do so, she must be able to summon magic's ultimate power. Shalee must become god-like and learn to harness the power within my essence. Only then, will she be able to look upon Ancients Sovereign. Only then, can she pick the fruit of the nasha tree."

Yaloom stood, looked down at the king, then smiled. "Without my potion, Shalee will never develop the power to retrieve your son's soul." He lifted the vial and held it between two fingers. The light from the throne room's window enhanced the potion's glow as he extended it in Sam's direction. "Without this elixir, your son will remain lifeless."

Sam thought long and hard. He walked to the window and looked across the city. He smirked as two young boys chased each other down the street leading to the arena. Once the boys were specks in the distance, he turned to face Yaloom. "I know I will live long enough to see the day my son's soul is returned. I have acquired a unicorn's horn. I have been using it each night to receive the benefit of an extended life."

A frown appeared on Sam's face. "But, what of my son's body? It could be dust by the moment Shalee gains the power to steal his soul from the Book. What then? How will my boy benefit from the fruit's juice after he has wasted away?"

Yaloom put his hand on Sam's shoulder. "The condition of your baby's corpse won't matter. Keep your son's body protected from the elements. When the day comes you have the nasha in your hand, pour its juice over his remains. The power of the fruit will do the rest."

"Okay, okay. Hold on. I need a moment to wrap my mind around this. Are you saying, his soul will return to his body...no matter what condition his remains are in...and, he will live again?"

"Your child's soul will be released from the Book of Immortality and it will return to his body. This is the power the fruit possesses. After all, this is why the gods chose to make nasha forbidden. We kept it from the worlds. Your son will know his father. He'll live as if nothing ever happened, as if he never was expelled. He'll possess the knowledge of the gods—minus their power, of course—but, he will have power of his own."

Sam rubbed the scruff on his chin. "Why would you do this, Yaloom? There must be something in it for you."

Yaloom nodded. "This conversation must remain a secret. The knowledge of our exchange must not be shared with Mosley or any of the others within the Collective. Will you agree to this?"

Sam thought a moment. "I won't say anything, nor will Shalee. But, my question was, why are you doing this?"

Yaloom sighed. "I am dying, Sam. I would ask a favor in return for my vial. I would ask your wife to retrieve a second nasha from the tree. Use its juice on my remains. Please...care for my body as you would your son's. I wish to live again."

Yaloom took a long deep breath. "There is one side effect of the fruit. I will be reduced to nothing more than a helpless baby. I ask to be given to a good family, one of a royal bloodline. Save half of the liquid in this vial and give it to me when I become of age. If you agree to my conditions, I'll surrender all that I am to you. All your queen will need to do is drink her share of the liquid."

Sam pushed his hands through his hair and began to pace. A long series of moments passed before he responded. "I will speak with Shalee. You have my word on this. If she chooses not to undertake this task, I'll return your potion."

Yaloom knew he had nothing to lose. He was dying whether Sam convinced the queen to drink the liquid or not. He surrendered the vial. "I cannot imagine a mother refusing to save her son. But, if she does, drink the potion yourself. Perhaps, you can find a way to save us."

Yaloom placed his hand on Sam's shoulder. "You've proven to be a wise king. Where do you want me when I pass? I don't have many moments left, maybe a few days at most. I can feel my body changing. I imagine by morning, I will be showing signs of death."

Sam called for one of his servants. He ordered the boy to take Yaloom to the castle's guest quarters. "Bring the kingdom's finest casket to his room."

Sam turned to face Yaloom. "When the moment comes, crawl inside the casket and shut the lid. Until then, my servants will give you anything you ask. If everything you have said is true and this potion saves my son's life, I'll do everything you've requested. I will swear this: The queen and I will raise you as our own once you have been reborn. I will save your half of the liquid and give it to you once you're old enough. Let's hope Shalee agrees."

The Luvelles Gazette

When you want an update about your favorite characters

Gage is sitting on the shore of Crystal Lake. He can only hope the ultorians will allow him to live with the other goswigs.

Head Master Brayson is meeting with the Kedgle King. The creature of illusion has agreed to send one hundred of his subjects to protect Gregory for as long as they are needed. In return, the king wants an additional bottle of the rare froslip ale from Harvestom to be delivered to Gregory's glass palace. Brayson has agreed, knowing full-well it is because of Hepplesif the extra bottle has become a condition of their service. Hepplesif will be in charge of the kedgles dispatched for this mission.

George and Payne are lost inside the Book of Bonding sitting on the Head Master's desk. They are wandering in circles. The trees within the fog look the same no matter where they turn.

Athena and Susanne are helping Mary decorate her new home. Garrin is sleeping as the women discuss Brayson's charm.

Kepler is lying on one of the large rocks at the center of the clearing separating the family's new homes. The children were forced to find a different spot to play after the demon-cat interrupted another game of capture the tyrant. Kepler is frustrated that he can do nothing to help George finish the bonding process with Payne.

Sam is with Shalee. He is explaining everything Yaloom spoke of regarding the forbidden fruit located on the hidden god world. Something about Shalee doesn't seem quite right. She is agitated and seems to be upset with everything Sam says. The king is also a bit touchy. The death of their baby is putting a tremendous amount of stress on their relationship.

Mosley plans to go to Brandor, but not until he has given Sam and Shalee the space necessary to deal with their loss. The wolf has no idea Yaloom is in Brandor.

During his team's last meeting, the gods concluded they would have the upper hand since Mosley knows where the third piece of the Crystal Moon has been hidden. They have agreed the stain on Celestria's dress was a clue meant to give their team an advantage. They assume the answer to the crystal's whereabouts will present itself upon Shalee's arrival at the swamp.

Sam will need to request his queen be given a temporary right of passage by the Head Master. She can use it to capture a ride with the Merchant Angels.

Gregory is inside his glass palace. He has increased security and is waiting for the kedgles to arrive.

Marcus has been storming around his dark tower-palace. The chancellor's fit began when his pipe tobacco ran out, and he realized Gage is missing. Gage was responsible for keeping his tobacco stocked. Marcus has killed three servants because of their lack of knowledge of the goswig's whereabouts.

Thank you for reading the Luvelles Gazette

Kiayasis Methelborn

The Shores of Crystal Lake

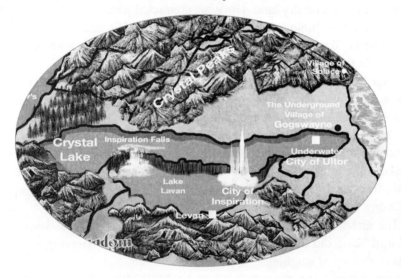

Gage stood on the lake's shore as the sun set to the west. He could see the water change as night swallowed the day. The worlds of Grayham and Harvestom raced one another as they disappeared beyond opposing horizons, north and south.

The change in the water was not what the badger expected. Sure, the lake went dark from the absence of light, but something marvelous happened. The lake's surface began to glow in places. Angelic, soft blue lights skimmed the surface, then dissipated as they returned to the depths. It wasn't long before a combination of illuminations glided through the water at a rapid pace. As the number of figures increased, so did their brilliance, lighting the lake's surface and the beach with a heavenly feel.

Now...fellow soul...allow me to tell you about the ultorians. As a race, they look somewhat transparent. Their internal organs are visible while beneath the water. Their bodies are shaped like humans, but with giant water wings which allow them to glide under the lake's surface. As their numbers increase, so does the intensity of the glow which radiates from their bodies. But, when they come ashore, these incredible beings take on a new form.

Gage watched as the water began to stir not far off shore. A single figure emerged and worked its way toward him. The ultorian's form changed with each step it took on dry land. His wings retracted within the confines of his back, leaving no biological sign they ever existed. His skin began to radiate with a tremendous heat as it turned into a prism of color. Steam rose into the bite of the night air as the water on his body evaporated.

Gage kept his eyes fixed on the ultorian as he walked across the pebbled beach. With each step, a trail of bright white, gelatinous goo, squished out of the back of his heels, staining the small stones and surrounding sand.

The badger listened as the creature tried to communicate in a language he couldn't understand. The phonetics of his speech sounded like a series of clicks, some longer than others, but all high-pitched and somewhat painful to his furry ears. "I'm sorry. I don't understand," Gage said, bowing in case the being was of a royal bloodline.

The ultorian began to make a motion as if he was about to vomit. The colorful being did this over and over before Gage understood this was the creature's way of laughing.

Gage's smile lacked conviction as he spoke. "You're not royalty, are you? I'm not sure if you can understand, but I seek a new home. Can you help?"

The ultorian turned and lifted his hand toward the water. Ultrasonic waves resonated from his palm and disturbed the lake's surface. It wasn't long before another, smaller ultorian emerged and hurried across the beach to stand beside him. This being's face was more childlike, his colors not as bright as his predecessor's, and he failed to leave a gooey trail as he approached.

After an awkward silence, the smaller ultorian spoke. "My name is Syse. This is my friend, Swill. Who are you?"

"Oh good," Gage exhaled, then took in a relaxing breath. "You can understand me."

"I do. You have ignored my question. Who are you?"

"My name is Gage. I seek refuge."

"Are you goswig?"

"I am. I have lived in service to Marcus Id for many, many seasons."

Syse shook his head in a negative manner. "You will need to speak with King Ultor. Unfortunately, considering your circumstances, I will not be able to authorize your asylum."

"Is it because I was created and not born of a natural mother?"

"No. How you were born is of no consequence. I cannot say anything further. You will speak with our king. Only he can give you the permission you seek."

Swill began to speak in a series of high pitched clicks. Syse turned to face the water, giving the attention Swill's mannerisms commanded. Swill's speech sharpened, and the rapid clicking sounds increased. It was as if they were filled with urgency.

Without explantion, Syse rushed into the water and dove beneath the lake's surface. Swill stomped his foot. Goo squirted from his heel and land-ed next to Gage's paw. The ultorian sent another wave of ultrasonic pulses toward the water, as if he had an afterthought.

After a moment of silence, Swill turned and lifted the badger from the ground. He began to walk down the beach and into the water. As the lake deepened, Gage squirmed, "Ummm, Swill, I can't breathe under there. Swill! SWILL!"

Meanwhile, the Outskirts of the City of Marcus

Kiayasis Methelborn set the necessary ingredients on the table. Ever since he can remember, he has helped his mother create the same magical elixir every 20 Peaks of Bailem. Today, as always, Gwen is being difficult. Refusing to drink her potion has become common place, and Kiayasis, just as he has always done, will try to remain loving and understanding.

"Yes, mother, I know you're unhappy. Why must you fight me so?"

A shallow voice responded from the shadows across the room of a run-down home. "I hate myself. I don't want to live."

"You don't mean that, mother. You're just depressed. You'll feel better in a few moments."

"I'll never feel better. I'm hideous. I'm disgusting. Everyone hates me. They look at me as if I am an outcast." She shouted in the Elven language. *"Amin delotha amin Thanga yassen templa!"*

Kiayasis frowned. "Stop that. You know you're not cursed."

"They all hate me!" A cup filled with water flew from the shadows and broke against the wall. The water doused the sconce and the room went dark.

Kiayasis lifted his hand and allowed his magic to fill his palm with the light necessary to replace the sconce's wick. Once lit, he allowed the magic to dissipate. He watched as the flame flickered as he lowered the glass around it. "No one thinks ill of you, mother. Now, stop throwing your fit, and drink your elixir."

Kiayasis siphoned the liquid from the kettle above the fire, then put the necessary dose into a small vial. All Gwen needed to do was swallow the liquid and watch as the scars covering the majority of her body melted away.

Now...fellow soul...for as long as the potion lasted, Gwen was stunning. Her long brunette hair, brown eyes, olive skin, and gentle curves turned every male elf's head. But, as the potion loses its effect, Gwen hides her appearance for 3 Peaks until her body can withstand another dose. During this period of moments, Gwen is a miserable reminder of an experiment gone bad.

At 12 seasons, Gwen snuck into her father's laboratory and began to play with magic she didn't understand. Before anyone could stop her, she had concocted a deadly combination of components which exploded, destroying the lab and nearly took her life. Her instinct was the only thing to save her. She saw the reaction of the components and dove for cover. The large wooden table her father worked on saved her from the blast's devastation. The intense heat left a lasting reminder of that day. Gwen feels that her face, not to mention the rest of her body, is grotesque and monstrous looking.

Kiayasis, now 120 seasons old, has strong features. His eyes are blue, hair is straight, flowing, long, and black. He stands over six feet tall, is well-built, and is almost as strong as his father. He is charismatic and charming. He lives alone at the center of Marcus' city, but returns home to the city's outskirts to let his mother know she is loved during her moments of struggle.

Gwen's home is a shambles. She, like many others, is considered to be one of the city's rejects. A large wall separates Gwen's class from a higher class of people living inside the walls who have the ability to harness the power of the dark arts.

Only elves of a pure bloodline are allowed to reside within Marcus' walls, but bloodline alone isn't enough to gain residency. Along with the ability to command the dark arts, an elf must possess wealth. Many of the people living near Gwen, although of a pure bloodline, are without magical abilities and are forced to live in poverty. As a result, they are treated as irritations and given jobs considered less than desirable.

Gwen never married. She had tried to find a companion, but each relationship ended because of the depression she experienced when the potion wore off. Her longest relationship was just under a season, a union which produced the joy of her life—Kiayasis.

Her baby's father, Boyafed, was a powerful man, and still is to this very day. Boyafed is the leader of the Order which circles the Dark Chancellor's tower-palace and rests on a hill at the city's center. He is also charismatic, charming, strong, and handsome, like his son. These are just a few of his many delicious traits Gwen fell in love with.

It was the best season of Gwen's life, but her happiness was short-lived. Boyafed realized how taxing it was going to be to live with Gwen, and dealing with her ongoing depression wasn't a task he cared to undertake. He took Gwen outside the city's walls and left her with enough coin to pay for the home she lives in. This was Boyafed's way of ensuring she had a safe place to give birth and raise their child. Although Boyafed did not remain a part of Gwen's life, he remained a part of his son's and visited often.

Kiayasis, despite his mother's inability to use magic, benefited from Boyafed's biological contribution. As a result, he commands strong magic. For the last 20 seasons, he has lived near his father, training, and praying to the God of Death, Hosseff, to become a dark paladin.

<hr />

"Mother, drink your elixir. You'll feel beautiful again. I hate seeing you like this."

Gwen kept her head lowered and remained huddled in the corner.

"Mother, stop sulking. Let me help you up." Kiayasis leaned down and, as he had done on many occasions, lifted Gwen and carried her to a chair near the kitchen table. As he sat her down, the wood creaked beneath her weight.

"Open your mouth and drink. You know it will make you feel better. Please, don't make me force it down your throat."

Gwen lifted her head as Kiayasis poured the elixir into her mouth. It only took a moment for the magic to take effect. Her skin began to clear, and the scars peeled away and fell to the floor. Once again, Gwen was beautiful.

Kiayasis smiled. "See, you look wonderful." He lifted a mirror and, as he always did, ensured she could see the potion's benefit.

As always, Gwen acted surprised by the transformation. She smiled. "I'm pretty. I'm beautiful. Do you think I'm beautiful, Kiayasis?"

"You have always been beautiful to me, mother."

"Ohhhh, my boy, you're so good to me. You can never leave me. I need you, Kiayasis. Your father is keeping you from me. I don't think I can stand another day without you."

"I miss you, too, mother. My training is almost at an end. I have enjoyed getting to know my father."

"I can't be without you." Gwen pulled away and turned her back.

"Don't act like that, mother. I have always been there for you."

"It's not the same. Your father has taken you from me. I want you to come home. I demand you come home! I won't spend another day without you!"

"You have said the same thing for 20 seasons. You know I love you."

"Loving me is not enough! You will return home!"

Kiayasis reached out, turned Gwen around and pulled her close. "Would you ask me to give up everything I have worked for? Would you hold me back?"

Tears ran down Gwen's face. "Your father has turned you against me. Your love for me has dwindled."

"Nonsense, mother. I will always love you."

Gwen's mood swings were a source of contention. Kiayasis knew he would never be free to live his own life. She would always command his attention. She would ruin whatever chance he might have at finding lasting enjoyment.

Again, Gwen pulled away. "If you love me, you'll come home. Stay with me. Don't go back to your father's army."

Kiayasis put on a smile and took a long, relaxing, deep breath. "Come here, mother. I will stay with you. You're right. I should not leave you alone."

"Oh, my baby, do you mean it? Thank you. I knew my boy would choose me." She rushed into his arms.

Kiayasis held his smile until her head rested below his chin. He caressed her back with his left hand as he reached behind his own with his right. His hand grasped the bone-handle of his dagger, a blade known only to the Order, as he continued to speak. "Mother, you don't have to worry any longer. I'll come home to you. I've always been here to remove your pain. You're right. I love you more than anything."

Careful to keep Gwen's head tucked under his chin, tears ran down his cheeks. "You mean everything to me. You have always been beautiful to me. I can stop your torment."

Without hesitation, Kiayasis plunged his blade deep into her gut, then lifted it to ensure a quick death. As he reached around his mother's head, he pulled Gwen's face into his chest to smother her cry. It did not take long for the last bit of air to escape her limp form which remained standing only because of his will to keep her erect. With one gentle swoop, Kiayasis lifted her into his arms and carried her lifeless figure into the bedroom.

Kiayasis laid Gwen's head on the pillow, adjusting the rest of her body to a peaceful position. Slowly, he pulled the blade free, then placed the covers over her shoulders to tuck her in. He took a seat on the bed. "See, mother, now you'll always be beautiful. Your scars will never reappear. I can't care for you any longer. May your soul find the peace it seeks with Hosseff."

Wiping the tears from his face, Kiayasis rose and smoothed the blanket. He sighed as he closed the door to her room. As he left the house, he bolted the door and began walking toward the city's gates.

It was not more than a few moments before the magic hiding Gwen's scars began to fade. Kiayasis was wrong. Her beauty faded as her soul left to find its home within the Book of Immortality's pages. Gwen would be found as a hideous reminder of a once gentle soul. She would be forgotten.

The Temple of the Order

"Lord Hosseff, to what do I owe this pleasure?" Boyafed, the leader of the Dark Order of Holy Paladins, said as he dropped to one knee before his god.

"Stand up, Boyafed. We have much to discuss. Walk with me."

The temple of the Order encircles Marcus Id's tower-palace. White granite hallways have been polished to a fine sheen and are lined with tall, red, demonic statues with black wings and thick horns. Some have wings folded while others remain widespread. Their faces look as if they are calling for battle. Each holds a torch which casts an eerie glow.

Boyafed wears all black, except for a gold shirt. His cape carries the Order's symbol at its center—a gold altar representing the Order's belief in sacrifice to Hosseff. Boyafed's eyes are dark brown, his hair is short, and his rock jaw complements his strong frame.

Boyafed lowered his head in reverence. "My Lord, how may I be of service?"

Hosseff stopped to look out the temple window which sat above the rest of the city. The only building higher than the temple is Marcus' tower, which stands hundreds of feet taller at its highest point. The entire city rests beneath the shadows cast by heavy gray clouds which never dissipate. They hover in one spot thanks to Marcus Id's magic, and this depressive atmosphere is why the city became known by its second name, The City of Shadows.

Hosseff's face materialized when in the direct light of the torches. He looked human and his hood hid the fact his ears were not elven. As he walked with Boyafed toward the shadows, his appearance changed. His face vanished and his hands turned hazy.

The god's voice sounded like a windy whisper. "I seek an escort to guide a human woman from Merchant Island to the swamplands of Grogger. She will arrive from Grayham. I'm not here to order this done, but I would appreciate your assistance, Boyafed. I know your son, Kiayasis, has completed his training and will be given his first assignment as an official member of the Order at Early Bailem on the morrow."

"Yes, My Lord, he's strong and will make a fine addition to our numbers. He will make his first sacrifice in your name in the morning. Would you like me to send Kiayasis to retrieve this woman and act as her guide?"

"I'm sure he'll do a fine job. This woman seeks something within the swamp. She must enter alone while Kiayasis waits."

Hosseff put his wispy hand on Boyafed's shoulder. "The woman's name is Shalee. She is powerful...a sorceress who wields magic strong enough to command your respect. Kiayasis will need to make his way to Merchant Island, and wait for her arrival."

"My son lives to serve you, My Lord."

Hosseff moved back into the direct light of the torch. Once again, his features solidified. He returned his hand to Boyafed's shoulder. "You're the foundation of this Order. You have made me proud for over 400 seasons. I'm sure you'll continue this tradition."

"Thank you, My Lord." The Order leader bowed to one knee.

Hosseff lifted Boyafed from the floor. "There's something else I wish to discuss, something of grave importance."

Meanwhile, Southern Grayham
Brandor's Castle

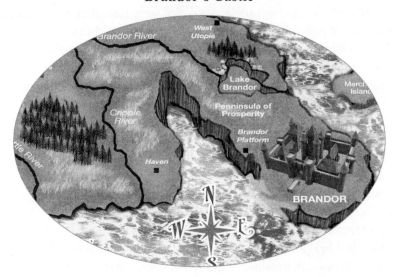

Shalee threw her legs over the side of the bed and motioned for Sam to back off. "For heaven's sake, I'm not gonna ask ya again, Sam. You've been naggin' me all night. I said I'll drink the doggone potion when I'm ready."

Sam moved to the fireplace and took a seat on the hearth to allow the fire to warm his back. "Shalee, why can't you just drink it already? Are you not hearing me? Yaloom said it will give us the chance to save our baby. Don't you want this? Don't you want to be a mother?"

"I'm sick of listenin' ta ya. I'm fixin ta go crazy."

"Then go crazy after you drink the potion, and I'll shut up. What's wrong with you? This is our baby we're talking about."

"Just give me the damn thing! I'll drink it, but ya betta' stop badgerin' me! You're pissin' me off!"

The queen stomped across the room, snatched the potion from Sam's hand, then returned to her seat on the bed. She tilted her head back, slammed the liquid down her throat, then chucked the empty bottle across the room. It smashed against the rock chimney above Sam's head. Sam ducked as it shattered. As the glass fell around him, he thought, *Dang, I'm glad I divided the potion into two vials.*

Shalee grimaced. "Yuck!" The aftertaste tore at the queen's taste buds. "That was awful...almost as awful as our shallow relationship."

Sam looked up. "Okay, okay, hold on a moment. Where the hell did that come from? Talk about left field. How could you say something so mean?"

"Don't act like ya don't understand. We were rushed into this marriage. How could we possibly love one anotha' in such a short time."

"It's not time, it's amount of moments, Shalee. You know that."

"Ya need ta eat a slice of shut up before I put this Texas foot up your ass. Ya know what I meant. Whetha' these stupid people understand time or not has nothin' ta do with this argument. Don't be messin' with me. And, you know what else…I won't stand…"

Shalee stopped talking. She doubled over and pushed her hands against her stomach. As she did, she fell to the floor. Sam rushed to pick her up, then laid her on the bed. Before her head hit the pillow, she was out cold.

"Shalee! Shalee! Come on…wake up!" He pushed her blonde hair clear of her face. "Wake up!"

Sam examined her. The queen's heart rate was elevated, her pupils unresponsive, and her skin felt feverish. He darted out of the room and moments later, pushed through the door of Yaloom's guest quarters. "Why did Shalee pass out after drinking your potion? What's wrong with her?"

The fallen god's appearance had changed. He looked like an old man nearing death as he struggled to stand from his chair. "What did you expect? Your wife's body needs the moments necessary to adjust to her new power. She'll be fine, I assure you. It will be hard for her mind to absorb the information my memories contain. As I told you, she may not be able to use her new abilities at first, but she will come to understand them. I don't know when this will happen. Try not to worry. I would not have given you the potion if she wasn't strong enough to handle its effects."

Sam took a deep breath. "You look like garesh. You might want to consider sleeping inside your casket tonight. From the looks of it, I doubt you'll wake up. No offense, of course."

Yaloom tried to laugh, but instead, he began to cough up blood. It took him a moment to settle down. "No offense taken. I will do that. The coffin looks comfortable. I hope the next series of moments in which my eyes look upon you, they'll be through the eyes of a baby."

"I have given you my word."

"Then, it appears everything is in order, King of Brandor, or should I say, dad." Yaloom struggled to pat Sam on the shoulder.

"I don't think you should call me that. Please, don't say it again. I would rather be spared this title until my son lives."

"I understand. We shall save it for later then. I think I'll retire now. Will you have someone watch me through the night, and seal me inside once I pass?"

"I will. Until later, then?"

"Yes. Until later...Sam."

The king turned to leave. As he approached the door, Yaloom called to him. "Wait."

Sam turned around. "Yes?"

"Thank you. You're a good man, and a better king. Southern Grayham has needed a man like you for many, many seasons. Your wife will succeed. She is strong. I wouldn't worry about the outcome of your son's future."

"I hope you're right, Yaloom. I hope you're right." The king lowered his head and left the room.

Yaloom sighed, then whispered, "I also hope I'm right. With everything that's left of me, I hope I'm right."

Head Master Brayson's Desk
Inside the Book of Bonding

George continued to walk through the fog while Payne flew beside him. The haze covered George from his waist down and was so thick it was impossible to see the ground.

As George studied the looming trees, he reached out and used his magic to scorch the bark of the one closest to him. He rubbed his hand across the mark, then looked at Payne. "I feel like I'm inside some kind of Thriller video. This place is creeping me the hell out."

Payne tilted his head. "What 'Thriller' mean?"

George rolled his eyes. "Nothing. Let's just keep going. Something's got to give pretty soon."

The forest stretched high into the air and became so dense they could not see the sky. All they had seen since their arrival was gloom. It wasn't long before they came upon a tree which bore George's mark. The mage reached out and rubbed his hand across it. "We're going in freaking circles. Nothing about this place makes any sense. Where are we? This must have something to do with Brayson. I just know I'm going to have to kick that S.O.B.'s ass."

Payne gave George another confused look. "What 'S.O.B.' mean?"

"Damn it, Payne, you don't know crap, do you? Just forget about it." George whirled around and threw up his arms in frustration. "Look at this place. It's miserable. We need to find our way out of here or we're going to starve to death."

Payne scratched the top of his head. "Master, use magic."

"To do what? We're in a forest, for hell's sake."

The fairy-demon's brow furrowed. "What 'hell' mean?"

George rolled his eyes and thought, *I should just shoot myself in the damn head.* "Just forget about it. How do you want me to use my magic? What do you have in mind?"

"To find the way...um...gotta find a way."

"And, exactly how would I do that?"

"Payne don't know. You master."

"Bah! How can I find a way when..." George hesitated. After a few moments of studying his surroundings, he raised his hands in front of him, placed his palms together, then motioned for the fog to part. The haze began to split, following his hands as he separated them. The ground beneath was revealed. "Damn! There's nothing here. Maybe, I should try again."

George took a quarter turn to the right and repeated the process. Again, the ground bared itself and again, there was nothing. "Damn!"

"Master say damn, bunches."

George growled, "What do you care? You sound like Athena. Shut up, will you?"

"Master mean to Payne."

George shook his head and lifted his hands for his third try. As he separated them, a path was revealed. "That's weird. We've been walking forever, yet the path begins where my feet touch the ground. What are the odds of that happening? I wonder if magic has something to do with it?"

Payne lowered to the ground and touched the path. "It lives."

"What do you mean...'it lives?'"

"Um...it breathes...you know, like Payne...like Master. He want Master to find it."

"What do you mean, 'he?' And, stop talking about us in third person. You're driving me nuts."

"Ebbish nay. Grouchy Master." Payne lowered his ear to the ground. "His name...um, um...Payne mean...um...the, the, the..."

"The path, Payne, the path. It's called a path."

Payne growled with frustration. "The path name, Follow."

"What? The path has a name?"

"Yes."

"Well, that's the most absurd thing I've ever heard. A path named Follow. You've got to be kidding me. I'm not even sure what to say. At least we're getting somewhere. I wonder where Follow will lead us. My hell...I can't believe I'm referring to a path as a person. So, let's follow Follow's path." George shook his head. "Holy hell, that was confusing."

"Master act stupider."

"Shut up, Payne. Let me think." George pondered a moment, then chuckled. "Now that I think about it, it's kind of humorous. Hey, Payne, ask Follow..."

As George turned to look for the fairy-demon, he was shocked to see that Payne had already started down the path. "Dang it, Payne, wait for me. It's bad enough I have to follow Follow, without following you, too. You should follow me and I will follow Follow." George chuckled, again. *Wow, now that was a mouthful. I amuse myself. Damn, I'm good.*

What was left of the haze had vanished and everything was now in plain sight. As they followed along Follow, the flowers hidden by the fog were now following them. The plants were aware of their presence. They paid attention to the duo's movements as if they were stalking them. The flowers' stigmas acted as eyes, staring the pair down as their stems adjusted their red-petaled bodies for the perfect line of sight.

"What are these things, some kind of creepy tulip creatures or something? I feel like they're sizing us up for something," George said with a touch of anxiety.

Payne lowered next to one. He snatched the flower out of the ground and shoved it in his mouth. "Creepy tulip creature taste good to Payne."

The earth beneath the rest of the flowers began to shift. One by one, leg-like roots emerged as the rest of their bodies pulled free of the ground. They began to surround George, as if preparing for attack. At the base of their petals, tiny mouths opened exposing razor sharp teeth. Their stigmas split in two and transformed into a real pair of eyes. Long, leafy arms peeled away from their stems and turned claw-like.

"Payne, get over here! Right now!"

Payne did as instructed. George grabbed the fairy-demon by the leg and teleported down the path. When they reappeared, he shouted, "Follow me!"

They rushed down the path as the tulip creatures scurried after, their petals falling to the forest floor as they gave chase. But, Follow's path was about to end. George did not see the large hole open in front of them since he was looking over his shoulder to see the distance between them and their botanical bandits. Payne watched as George fell into the darkness. Without hesitation, the fairy-demon folded his wings and dove into the hole to catch up.

You're Proud of Me?
Inside the Book of Bonding

Payne's demon eyes were able to see his surroundings as he fell through the darkness of the shaft. The end of their fall was fast approaching and Payne knew he didn't have many moments to react. He was working to keep his body streamlined to catch up with George, but the mage was too far ahead.

Payne shouted, "Master, teleport!" But, he could not understand George's response.

The rock floor was only a few hundred feet away. Payne's eyes searched for a place to land. He teleported to the bottom and allowed his body to erupt in flames. He burned bright, hoping to shed enough light on the area to define the terrain. The water on the shaft's floor was ankle-deep. The flames enveloping the fairy-demon's body tore into the pool's surface as the water began to hiss. All Payne could do was hope his actions were enough. It was up to George to save himself.

Less than two feet remained before impact. Payne covered his eyes and listened for the splat he knew George would make. After a moment, the fairy-demon peeked through his fiery claws. George was standing in one of the few dry spots on the hole's floor, far enough away to avoid the heat of Payne's body.

Payne began to dance while singing out loud, pleased his plan had worked. As he did, each step he took caused a searing sound as the water found his scorching footsteps. Small clouds of steam rose into the air. "Master so safe...Master so safe. Payne save him...Payne save him. You need Payne...you need Payne. Ha, ha, ha...you need Payne. Payne so gooder... Payne so gooder. Na, la, la...Payne so gooder. Yeah!"

Payne stuck out his tongue and blew slobbery, fiery spit in George's direction, all of which evaporated as it moved through the air.

George, though shaken from his fall, began to laugh, careful to keep his distance from the demon's flame. "Yes, you saved me, Payne. I'm proud of you. I didn't think fast enough. I'd be dead right now if it weren't for you. I couldn't see anything until you lit the area. I'm impressed."

The fairy-demon stopped his celebration. "Master proud of Payne?" The fire encompassing his body dissipated as his black eyes began to shed tears which evaporated as they rolled down his skin. "Payne never hear no one say that to Payne before."

With a wave of his arm, George commanded the darkness to depart. He summoned a breeze to cool the area. As the heat faded, the mage approached his little companion. "You should be told when you do something good. You made me proud."

"Neat. Payne hungry." True to form, the child's attention span had moved on to something else.

"Speaking of eating, your eating habits got us into this mess in the first place. I thought we agreed you would eat what I eat. And, stop talking in third person."

"Nope. Payne no agree. Payne just listen to Master order. Payne never do no agreeing. Why Master not teleport...um...you know...to the top...uhh, the big hole?"

George rolled his eyes at the fairy-demon's attempt to change the direction of the conversation. "I tried, but my power wasn't strong enough. I think we were meant to fall down here. Something stopped me from teleporting to the surface."

"Um...now what to do, Master?"

The Underwater City of Ultor

Swill carried Gage far beneath the surface of Crystal Lake. He protected the badger by using his angelic water wings to create a pocket of air. They were approaching a beautiful reef of freshwater coral with vibrant colors.

The ultorian was heading toward a reef with no sign of slowing. Gage was nervous. He had never been under water, let alone move so quickly beneath it. He was unable to do anything. His magic was not working within Swill's barrier. All he could do was watch.

A pair of sea snakes emerged from their holes. They moved in a large circular pattern, seeming to indicate where Swill needed to go. The reef was nearly upon them, but the ultorian did not change the speed of his approach. Gage balled up and closed his eyes. When the impact with the coral never came, he opened them just enough to peek. The reef appeared to be far away, but they had not moved. Their bodies had shrunk and were continuing to shrink. The sea snakes were also in their same position, but now they appeared to be Titans of this watery underworld.

The smaller they became, the farther away the coral shelf seemed to get. Gage didn't realize it, but he was now no larger than a grain of sand, and the shrinking was not about to stop. Eventually, their approach narrowed to a specific part of the reef, and the coral's pores became gigantic openings, welcoming their microscopic bodies to swim inside. Gage had never seen such magic, and his body was struggling with the change. It wasn't long before his badger eyes closed as he faded into unconsciousness.

Now...fellow soul...allow me to tell you about the Ultorian King's Kingdom. The ultorians number nearly 31,000,000. They occupy a magically protected area of coral totaling two square inches within the depths of Crystal Lake. This lake is the largest body of freshwater on Luvelles. Covering over 210,000 square miles, it should have been called a sea. The lake has served as the ultorians' home since their creation by the gods over 9,000 seasons ago.

When Gage awoke, he was lying on a floor. It took a moment, but he was able to collect himself to study his surroundings. He was in some sort of barrier which held back the water. The floor beneath his paws was porous, sponge-like, and alive. Beyond his bubble, the ultorians' radiant forms could be seen swimming past.

The amount of traffic swimming around his location suggested Gage had been placed in the middle of a heavily populated area. It was as if he was on display. From within the midst of this organized chaos, a familiar face appeared.

It was Syse. He swam up to the bubble, settled on the coral floor, then walked through the barrier's gelatinous wall. Once inside, his form began to change. His skin became hot and the water covering his figure evaporated. Before retracting his wings within the confines of his body, he fanned the area to cool the bubble, then finished his transformation. His skin settled into a soft blend of yellows, oranges, and reds.

"I see you have awakened," Syse said as he sat on the floor and lifted his hand toward the bubble's roof. A series of ultrasonic waves shot from his palm and penetrated the barrier. Once he was sure his message had been delivered, he addressed Gage again. "I have sent word you are awake. Our king will be joining you. We were warned you may seek refuge. I'm sorry, but I had no other choice than to bring you here."

Gage clinched his cane with both paws. "What do you mean, you were warned?"

"Chancellor Id told us you might come. Beyond this, I cannot speak further until King Ultor arrives."

"Am I to be returned to Marcus?"

"This is not for me to decide. The king will determine what is to become of you."

Gage closed his eyes. He tried to teleport, but nothing happened.

Syse sighed. "Your magic is not strong enough to escape. I understand your fear, but our king is a gracious leader. He will listen to you before making a decision."

"This isn't how I imagined my journey would end. I only wanted to find a peaceful existence."

"You will know your fate soon enough."

Mary's Home
The Next Day

Brayson appeared on Mary's doorstep just after Early Bailem. Though he was not expected, he knocked, then waited for her to answer. When Mary opened the door she was still wearing her nightgown, and her hair was a mess. Seeing who was on the other side, she slammed it shut.

She shouted through the heavy wood. "I look awful! I thought you were one of the kids. I don't want you to see me this way."

Brayson had to fight off his desire to laugh. "I seem to remember making you a promise to take you someplace special. I'm sorry for disturbing you, but I assure you it is okay to let me in. I'll ignore the fact you aren't ready for the day."

Mary placed her forehead against the door. "Mr. Id, I need to do my hair. I would love to see you, but I must remind you that a woman needs notice. You'll just have to come back."

Brayson waved his hand across the door. "Mary, please look into the mirror I gave you. I'm sure you look stunning. All you need to do is change."

Waiting for Mary's reaction, Brayson stood in silence with his pointed ear pressed against the wooden barrier. He heard her gasp. A moment later, the door opened. In her excitement, Mary disregarded the fact she was still in her nightgown.

"How did you do that? My hair is perfect."

"Magic, my dear. Magic."

Mary took him by the hand and pulled him into the doorway. She gave him a quick kiss on the cheek. "You stay right here. I'll go up and change." Thrilled with her new look, she jumped onto the teleportation platform near the front door and reappeared in her bedroom—leaving the most powerful and influential elf on Luvelles standing in her doorway.

The Castle of Brandor
Sam's Throne Room

"No, Mosley," Sam shouted as he stood from his throne. "How often do I have to say it? I don't want Shalee going to Luvelles." His eyes moved off the wolf and onto Alistar. "She miscarried! Our relationship is suffering! We need the moments necessary to fix it before she goes tromping off to some other world. Shalee isn't her normal self right now. Everything I do is wrong. The gods need to settle this matter on their own. We need to be left alone."

The wolf-god sighed. "Sam, I understand your pain and your concerns about the stress on your relationship. I also understand your anger about the baby. But..."

Sam interrupted. "You're damn right I'm angry about the baby! I'm also angry because the gods destroyed everything I loved! We did what the gods asked of us. I fought in the arenas of Grayham. I found a way to become a king, and for what...only to lose the Crystal Moon's pieces to George. I have united all of Southern Grayham under one throne and there is peace. But, that's not good enough for the Collective, is it? God forbid they give us the moments we need to move past the problems facing us.

"Shalee believes our relationship is shallow. She feels we were rushed into things, and the sad part about it, I happen to agree. But, I'm not willing to sacrifice what's left of our relationship so she can hunt down your crystal.

"It amazes me how foolish the gods were when they created your laws. The idea that Bassorine could not fix this mess because of some ridiculous rule within the Book of Immortality's pages...what a joke. How could gods be such idiots?"

Mosley and Alistar waited as Sam continued his rant. "Now, I find my-self mourning the loss of my son, and while I'm doing this, you come to me and tell me Shalee is needed on Luvelles. We haven't even had the chance to grieve." Sam pointed his finger at Alistar. "I know how the Book of Im-mortality works. I also know you can't make Shalee go. I won't allow it, and there's nothing you can do about it. I'm tired of the games. Shalee is in no condition to tromp off on some expedition."

Alistar's response would have to wait. Shalee walked into the room, as-sisted by a team of healers. She was groggy and still recovering from the effects of consuming Yaloom's potion. She gave Sam a nasty glance, then looked at Mosley and forced a smile. "Did I hear y'all talkin' 'bout me?"

Sam moved to her side. "It was nothing, sweetheart. Why are you out of bed? You should be resting."

The queen ignored Sam. Mosley and Alistar could feel the tension and moved to greet her. Mosley spoke first. "Hello, Shalee, it is good to see you are up and moving about."

"Agreed," Alistar added. He removed a leaf from a pocket inside his robe and handed it to Shalee. "I brought this for you. It is from Ancients Sover-eign. Chew on it, and it will assist in your recovery. You'll feel as good as new by morning. I'm sorry for your pain."

"What the hell?" Sam shouted. "We don't want to hear you're sorry. We want our son back!"

Shalee took a seat on her throne. "Shut up, Sam! Will ya just shut up? There's no reason ta yell at everyone."

Sam tried to calm himself as he replied, but failed. "I know I shouldn't yell. But dang it...Mosley and Alistar are here to ask you to go to Luvelles. They want you to go after the third piece of the Crystal Moon. We did what the gods asked of us once already, and look where it's gotten us. I've killed many men, and so have you, for that matter. Earth is destroyed and we man-aged to lose both crystals to George. And, if that's not enough...our son is dead. What have we received in return for doing their dirty work? Not a damn thing, that's what. Yeah, we live in this castle, but that doesn't replace our son. That doesn't replace our families. I can't handle this any longer. At least they could give us our baby back."

Shalee began to cry. Sam realized how his tone must have sounded, and as all men do who know they have been idiots, tried to console her.

"No! Don't ya dare touch me. Ya need ta leave me alone. I don't want ta hear anotha' word from ya. I won't stay here while ya resent me for our son's death!"

"I'm not resenting you."

"Yes, ya are! I know ya think I let ya down. Ya think my magic is ta blame for the loss of our baby. Ya aren't mad at the gods. You're mad at me. You're disgusted with me. Maybe, I need ta go. I need ta get outta here for a while." Shalee looked at Mosley. "I will go ta Luvelles."

The wolf-god did not have a chance to respond. Sam became enraged. "Hell, no you won't! You're not going anywhere! You can't go unless I request permission from the Head Master, and I won't do that! You belong here with me!"

"Don't ya dare yell at me like that, mister! Your attitude is chappin' my ass. I belong where I say I belong, not where ya think I belong. I need a break. If ya won't get permission from the Head Master, then I'll leave and find a place ta be alone. I need ta get away from ya. I can't handle your judgmental eyes. The way ya look at me makes me feel like a failure."

"What a crock of garesh! The way I look at you, my ass. All I've done since the miscarriage is take care of you. I don't have a problem with you at all. You act like you're the only one hurting. I have feelings too, you know. You're acting like a witch. Oh wait, what am I thinking, you are one!"

"I'm not a witch! I'm a sorceress!"

Sam rolled his eyes. "Yeah, big difference. You're the only one judging around here. I am not judging you for the loss of our baby."

"Don't lie ta me! Don't ya dare lie ta me, Sam Goodrich! I'll use Precious ta turn ya inside out."

"So, now you're going to use your magic on me. Nice touch, Shalee."

Shalee scowled. "I know ya blame me for everythin' that's happened. I'm goin' ta Luvelles whether ya like it or not. If ya won't get approval, then I'll give ya my crown. You can find a new queen, for all I care."

"What? I don't want anyone else. You can't walk out on me. You're my queen!"

Shalee gave Sam a disgusted look. "Yeah, right! You loathe me. I don't care about bein' your queen. It's not like this relationship eva' had a chance. Are ya goin' ta get the Head Master's permission, or shall I give ya this crown right now? I won't spend anotha' night here with ya if ya don't let me go."

"Dang it, Shalee, I don't loathe you, nor do I want you to go. But, hey...

if you want to leave me...if you want to run out on us...hell, I'll make it happen. You can kiss my royal ass. Maybe with some luck, you'll get it through your thick head that I don't blame you for anything. Take your time apart. Just remember this...I'll always love you, no matter what, no matter how hard it is to do it. And, if you don't believe me, you can kiss my ass again for thinking otherwise!" Sam turned and headed out the door.

Shalee called after him. "Just get the approval, Sam! I'll decide what's best for me from here on out...YA BIG JERK!" She turned to leave out the opposite door. "Mosley, come with me! Alistar, I don't want ta speak with ya. Go away," she shouted as she stormed out an opposing door with the healers in tow.

Mosley turned to Alistar, nodded, then followed Shalee. But, before the wolf could leave the room, Sam came back to make one final comment. "So help me, Mosley, if she so much as suffers a single scratch, I'll find a way to pay the gods back for your manipulations. You have taken enough from us already. Don't make me figure out a way to destroy every last one of you, because I won't rest until I do!"

Mosley shook his head. "Sam, it seems you have forgotten I am your friend. I want to save you, not hurt you. Shalee is the only one I trust to go after this piece of the Crystal Moon. This is bigger than you. This is bigger than your marriage. It is even bigger than the death of your son."

"Nothing's bigger than the death of my son...NOTHING!"

"Perhaps, Shalee is right. The two of you need a break."

"Who are you to tell us we need a break?"

With a motion of his snout, Mosley bound the king's mouth. Sam lifted from the floor and floated into a seated position on his throne. Mosley followed, put his paws on Sam's knees, then rose up. The wolf growled as he leaned in. "You should watch your tongue, Sam. I value our friendship, but not your condescending tone. Do not mistake your ability to lead Brandor's pack with your ability to argue with a god. I will not be spoken to in the manner you have addressed me. Has my message fallen on open ears?"

Sam glared at the wolf. Mosley snorted his irritation with the human's demeanor. He lowered to the floor, then pulled back. "Shalee can save many lives. I am only doing what needs to be done to save billions. I am sure you will see through your anger soon enough. We will speak then. I care for you Sam. I always will. I am sure Shalee will find a way to overcome her depression. She will come back to your den once she has secured the crystal's third piece." With his point made, Mosley released his bond on Sam's mouth.

The king leaned forward. "Get out of my face. You're just like the rest of the gods."

Undeterred, Mosley trotted from the room. Alistar moved to stand beside the king, then reached into his robe. "Sam, this is a piece of fepple root. I want you to brew this in some water, and drink it. It will settle your nerves and allow you to think straight."

"Hmpf! Whatever!" Sam snatched the plant from the god's thin hands and left without saying a word.

Alistar's soft brown eyes turned cold as he watched Sam leave. He whispered beneath his breath as he rubbed his hands together with satisfaction. "Well, that was fun. Everything is coming together rather nicely."

Shalee sat on the edge of the bed. Mosley entered the chamber with caution. The queen didn't waste any of her moments. She looked into the wolf's green eyes. "Ya told me Bassorine asked the gods of Earth ta bless me. Ya said I was given the perfect body for childbearin'."

To protect their conversation, the deity created an invisible barrier before responding. "He did. And, you were."

"Then, why did I lose the baby?"

"Your body is struggling to keep up with the growth of your magic, Shalee. The fetus was unable to handle the strain. Once you have had the moments necessary to adjust, you will be able to have a cub without problems. You have not yet commanded magic for one full season. I was concerned this would happen when I learned of your pregnancy."

"Why didn't ya say somethin' ta me? You're supposed ta be my friend, Mosley."

"I think you know I am your friend, Shalee. What would have changed if I had said something? You still would have been pregnant. If I had told you of my concern, it would have only served to cause unnecessary stress. I was hoping I was wrong and you would carry the child to term. I am sorry for your loss. I really am."

"Then, Sam was right. It is because of my magic that I lost our child."

"Did Sam actually say this to you?"

"Not in those words, but I can see it in his eyes." She took a deep breath. "I want ta go ta Luvelles. I need a break. It may have been a mistake for us ta have gotten togetha' in the first place. We should've neva' gotten married."

Mosley jumped onto the bed, then laid down next to her. "You do not mean that."

"Ohhhhhhh, I do. Did ya hear him? It's all my fault. He hates me. He only says he loves me because I'm the last thing in his life which reminds him of Earth. I can see right through his pile of garesh."

"I did not hear him say that, Shalee." Mosley nudged Shalee with the tip of his nose. "Sam loves you."

The queen rubbed the top of the wolf's head. "Of course ya heard what ya wanted ta hear. You're a male." Shalee stood and walked to the window. "Ya don't need ta pretend Sam wants me. Let's change the subject. This is depressin'. I don't wanna talk 'bout him."

Shalee turned and sat on the sill. "I know ya need me ta go afta' your crystal. I hate this place and I'm ready ta help."

"Okay, but I am sure you will look back on this day and feel differently."

"I don't think so. Anyway...why do ya want *me* ta go ta Luvelles? Isn't there anyone on that world who could go afta' the crystal?"

"Yes, but I trust you. It could be dangerous. In fact, I am sure it will be. But, with the way your power has advanced, I think it will be a good diversion if you were to undertake this journey. I have faith in you."

"I'm not so sure I believe in your faith in me."

Mosley growled. "Are you really going to treat our friendship this way, Shalee?"

Shalee walked across the room and crawled under the bed's cover. She started to cry. "Goodness-gracious, I know you're right. I'm bein' too hard on ya, Mosley. You're not the one I'm mad at. I just feel so unwanted. I can't bear the thought of Sam lookin' down his nose at me. His eyes are full of disgust. Maybe, I'll stay on Luvelles and neva' come back."

Mosley scratched at the back of his neck. "I am sure those are nothing more than emotional words. Your feelings will change."

The wolf's words angered Shalee. "Stop tellin' me how I'm gonna feel. Stop tryin' ta make it betta'. I can't believe how stupid males are. Just shut up and listen. That's all ya need ta do. You're supposed ta be a god. Why don't ya know when ta listen?"

Mosley didn't respond. He simply sat there and waited for her to finish. After a moment of continued male-bashing, Shalee stood from the bed and put the leaf Alistar gave her between her teeth. While chewing, she continued. "I'll go ta Luvelles. I'm done with Sam. I doubt our love was eva' real in the first place. He won't even miss me."

Shalee waited for Mosley's response, but when the wolf just sat there and a reply never came, she snapped. "For heaven's sake! Men are just so...so... ewwwwww!"

The Temple of the Dark Order

Now...fellow soul...allow me to tell you about the Order's beliefs and the great hall where the dark council makes sacrifices to Hosseff. At the head of this great hall stands a sixty foot tall statue of the God of Death. Hosseff's arms are lowered with his palms facing outward.

At Hosseff's feet sits a golden stone altar. It is nine feet long and half as wide. The altar serves three purposes. First, it is the symbol of the Order. Second, it is the only place to offer sacrifices to Hosseff. And third, all dark paladins are laid on top of it after the moment of their passing to symbolize their completion of service to their god.

Two demon statues hang suspended from the end of Hosseff's hands. They hang upside down with their clawed feet holding onto the god's fingers. Their arms reach toward the altar as if they are waiting to receive a sacrifice.

Two elevated platforms, filled with the seats of council members, run along the wall of the great hall on opposite sides of Hosseff's altar. The council consists of forty elves who have retired from the army. They are strong in the ways of dark magic and skilled with the Order's blessed blades.

The chamber is large, able to hold two legions, each totalling 3,000 men. The room is lit with a hundred torches and their flames reflect off the polished, white marble floor. Between where the legions stand and the altar, the leader of the Order must take his place on a circular platform to govern the council's meetings.

Boyafed, leader of the Order, stood on top of his circular pedestal to address the council. Behind him, the first legion of his dark paladin army, along with those in training, had fallen into twenty columned formations. Seven elf men, with brass chalices placed before them, knelt around the base of Boyafed's platform with their heads bowed.

Boyafed lifted his head toward Hosseff's statue and held his arms high. "Today we honor you, Hosseff!"

The gathering responded, shouting. "Our Lord, the wise and mighty Hosseff!" They stomped their right foot once at the completion of their praise.

Again, Boyafed spoke to the statue of Hosseff. "Today, the men before me shall become your holy servants. They shall don the black plate of your army and deliver judgment to any who oppose you."

Again the ranks shouted, "Our Lord, the wise and mighty Hosseff," then stomped their right foot.

Boyafed turned to face the first legion. "These seven brave men have completed their training and have earned the right to be called brother."

The ranks shouted, "Hail, brothers!"

Boyafed pulled his bone-handled dagger from its sheath and held it high. "Today, these men will spread their blood across Hosseff's altar. Their blood will be cherished by our lord. He will take them in as his own children and bless them with his Call of Death. They shall become Holy Paladins of the Dark Order."

Everyone shouted, "Blessed are the children of Hosseff!"

Boyafed lowered from his platform. With his dagger, he cut into the left palm of each man's hand. "Brothers, allow your life to flow into your chalice. Give Hosseff a taste of the man who serves him." He turned to the statue and lifted his arms. "Lord Hosseff, accept the blood of these men as a token of their faith in you."

As Kiayasis Methelborn and his graduating brothers watched the blood flow from their hands, the hall filled with another shout of praise for Hosseff. The men wrapped their hands and moved to stand beside the golden altar.

The seven emptied their chalices across the altar, then shouted, "Lord Hosseff, my blood is your blood! My service is promised within this offering! I pledge my life to you! Blessed are the children of Hosseff!"

The hall shouted, "Blessed are the children of Hosseff," then stomped their right foot.

Once the ceremony was complete and the hall stood empty, Boyafed pulled Kiayasis aside. They stood near the golden altar. "You look strong, Kiayasis. The Order's armor suits you."

"I have longed for this day, father. I want to make you proud."

"And, I am proud. Follow me. I have something for you. Something I've given no other."

Boyafed led Kiayasis to a teleportation platform hidden behind Hosseff's statue. When they reappeared, they were standing outside the city in an area without a population. The Order's stables spanned before them. Covering 24 acres, they were like no other on Luvelles.

Except for the earthen floor and wooden ceiling made of logs harvested from the Petrified Forest, the structures were constructed out of dark marble. Each stall was over 40 feet wide and twice as deep. On either side of every stall's entrance, burnt red demon statues with black wings rested in a seated position. Each demon had six arms, two legs and was thirty feet tall.

Their arms were outstretched and their hands acted as hinges, grasping an iron gate. Each stall was capable of holding only one of the dark paladin's mounts.

After opening one of the stalls, Boyafed looked up and pointed to a krape lord. The beast held a partially eaten corgan in its hand. Amidst the bones crunching in its mouth, Boyafed looked at Kiayasis. "Most men must earn a mount of this caliber, but you are not most men. You are my son. This is my gift to you. I've had this animal groomed since birth over ten seasons ago. He has not matured, yet he stands over 35 feet."

"I had no idea you had such faith in me."

"I have always had faith in you. After all, you're my son. I never expected any less. You're a Methelborn. All Methelborns are strong."

Now...fellow soul...the mounts of the dark paladins are relatives of the krapes, though they are much bigger. Krape lords can grow to a height between thirty and forty feet, which is eight to eighteen feet taller than their cousins. They can carry a saddle large enough to hold three adult elves. Their tail splits at its end, and a large poisonous dart protrudes from its center which can be used as a projectile.

Krape lords have large wings and are hairless. Their head looks more like a dragon's than a raptor's. They also have a large pouch across their abdomen which they use to carry their rider's possessions. When fully loaded with armor, food, weapons and passengers, the krape lords are forced to become giant land runners and possess incredible speed. They use their wings to assist while clearing holes or large gaps in the terrain. But, when the beast is free of excess weight, it can carry a single rider, and fly with grace.

Krape lords use ape-like arms to throw heavy objects. The biggest difference between them and their cousins, krape lords are carnivorous. Their diet consists of corgan meat. On average, they eat two of these 4,000 pound cow-like creatures every 3 Peaks of Bailem.

Kiayasis stood in front of his new mount. "Father, he's majestic."

Boyafed smiled. "I'm glad you approve. He has been named Joss. He has been trained well and is responsive to every command you have learned while in training. He will serve you better than any other mount within our stable."

"I couldn't ask for anything more. Thank you." Kiayasis stood in awe for a moment before changing the subject. "I was told you have an assignment for me."

Boyafed grabbed hold of Joss' reigns and commanded the beast to follow them out of the stable. The krape lord snorted, then did as instructed. Boyafed handed the reigns to Kiayasis. "I want you to go to Merchant Island. Your orders come directly from Hosseff. He has informed me that a woman from Grayham will be arriving soon. You are to take her to Grogger's Swamp. Once there, you will allow her to go in alone."

"What of her safety? The toad will devour her."

"Hosseff has commanded that she be allowed to go in alone. It's not our place to question our lord."

"I'm sorry, father, I meant no disrespect."

"No disrespect has been shown. Besides, this woman is a powerful sorceress. She'll be fine. There's something else I must tell you, something which will please Hosseff."

"What is it?"

Boyafed put his arm around Kiayasis and led him away from the stable with Joss in tow as they finished their conversation.

Lord Dowd
The Underwater City of Ultor

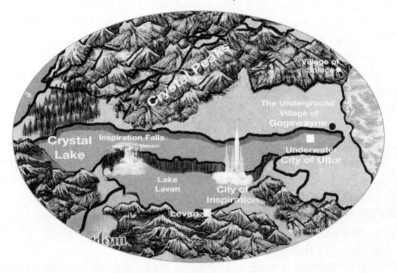

Gage tapped his cane against the gelatinous wall of his underwater barrier and growled. The ultorian children staring at him spread their wings and disappeared into the masses. They just kept coming, swimming up to his bubble and staring at him as if he was some sort of sideshow. Growling seemed to scare them off.

Syse had been called away and Gage's patience was running thin. He was stuck, and all he could do was wait. When King Ultor finally arrived, those who swam past the barrier stopped to acknowledge their beloved leader.

Just as Syse had done, the king used his wings to cool the area as his skin heated up and changed into a rainbow of colors. The king's size was imposing.

Gage marveled as he watched the king's transformation. Despite Ultor's dominant appearance, he remembered his discussion with Syse. The king was still unimaginably small, because just outside Gage's bubble, there were over 300,000 of Ultor's subjects swimming inside a single pore within a small section of coral. Not only that, but another 30,700,000 ultorians occupied the rest of the pores within this two inch square coral kingdom and yet, there seemed to be plenty of room.

King Ultor lowered to one knee, level with the badger's eyes, as his wings retracted into his back. "Why have you come, goswig? You have betrayed your master. Explain your actions."

Gage swallowed hard. "Sire, I seek refuge. My master is an angry man. His hate consumes him, and his thoughts echo throughout my mind. They cause me great distress. I beg you...please, don't send me back."

"Your master told me this day might come. How can I oppose the will of Marcus? To do so would bring suffering to my people. I can appreciate your desire for inner peace, but your presence puts my kind in danger."

Gage lowered his head. He knew Ultor was right. "Sire, I'm sorry for putting you in this position. I'm ready to be returned to my master and face his punishment."

The king could see the distress in Gage's eyes. His heart reached out. "You said your master's thoughts echo in your mind. Please explain."

"My master's thoughts are mine to share when he is near. I've come to you in hopes of escaping this torment. His hate is overwhelming. His pain is my pain. I cannot take it anymore. If it is your intention to send me back, please allow me to die here. I would consider this a merciful death."

Ultor thought a moment. "Does your master share your mind?"

"No, Sire. My thoughts are mine alone."

"Are you claiming you have traveled to the far side of Luvelles to escape his mind?"

"I am."

"This is good. There may be a way to allow you to take refuge with the goswigs. Without you at his side, Marcus will not be able to visit the inner dwelling of my kingdom. You have been with him too long. The loss of your companionship had to weaken even his magic."

Ultor stood and moved to look out the barrier. He watched many of his subjects swim by before turning back to Gage. "No one can know of your service to Marcus. If you agree to this, you can stay."

Gage's furry face gleamed. "Sire, I can become a ghost to my past, you'll see. Thank you."

"You are most welcome. If the day comes you sense your master's thoughts, you must teleport away from the others. You must go into hiding.

I cannot allow Marcus to have the knowledge that I have gone against his wishes. But, I cannot return you to him in good conscience. I know of Marcus Id's ruthlessness."

"I won't fail you, Sire."

Ultor lifted his head and shouted a series of high-pitched clicking sounds. It wasn't long before Swill appeared, along with Syse. With Gage protected, they began their ascent to the shore of Crystal Lake.

The Mountains of Oraness

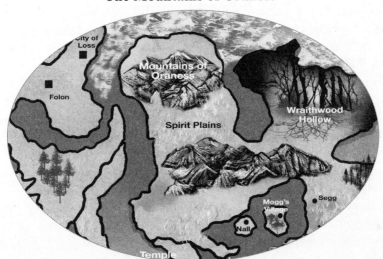

Brayson appeared with Mary at his side within the Mountains of Oraness. Before them, a pool of water with fire burning across its surface, produced an uncomfortable heat which could be felt from where they stood, some 40 feet away.

The pool was surrounded. Cliffs shot up from its edges and created an enclosure which swallowed its perimeter. To the far side, opposite of their position, was an entrance to a cave. There was no way around the flames to get to its opening. The mountains were too steep. The spot where they stood was the only place Brayson could have teleported them without being burned.

"This place is special to me," Brayson said. "I've never brought a woman here. Come to think of it, I have never brought anyone here."

Speechless, Mary studied her surroundings. Brayson smiled as he enjoyed her expressions. "I can see you're pleased. Have you ever seen anything like this?"

Mary collected her thoughts. "Never. How are such things possible? How can fire burn on top of water?"

"The fire doesn't burn on the water. The fire exists because of the creature at the pool's center. It burns as a result of the beast's need to be comforted by the flames. The water isn't affected by the heat. This is powerful magic. This is home to my goswig."

"Your goswig? What kind of goswig would bathe in flames?"

"Take my hand, and I'll show you. Do you remember me telling George I had a phoenix?" Mary took hold, but her feet remained planted. "It's safe. You will be alright, I assure you." Though still apprehensive, she allowed Brayson to guide her into the flames and across the top of the water.

Mary looked down. "Why are we not being burned? Why are we not sinking? How can this be?"

"I think you know the answer to your questions."

As they approached the center of the pool, the fire began to dissipate. They now stood on a small island located at the pool's center. Sitting on top of a stone perch was a small, crimson-yellow bird. A thin layer of flame enveloped its body. Brayson's feathered goswig was no taller than twelve inches.

Mary leaned into Brayson. "It's beautiful."

"I agree. *He* is beautiful." Brayson spoke to the phoenix. "Fisgig, I would like you to meet someone special. This is Mary."

The phoenix responded. *"Hej, de yameso yorkamenta."*

"She doesn't speak your language, my friend. You're going to have to lower yourself to our level to speak with us."

Fisgig sighed. "If I must. I was wondering when I would meet you, Mary. You're every bit as beautiful as Master Id said. It's nice to put a face to the name."

Mary enjoyed the goswig's compliment. "Thank you, Fisgig." She was unsure how to act. Being around magic made her feel alive, yet frightened. But, she wanted to see what Brayson Id was all about, and she was willing to push the boundaries of her comfort zone to do it.

Brayson reached down to take the flaming bird on his hand. "Fisgig is preparing to burn himself to death."

Mary's eyes widened. "What? Why would he do such a thing?"

Brayson laughed. "Perhaps, I should explain. With each death, Fisgig is able to command greater power. This is the end of his fifth life. When he emerges from his ashes four mornings from now, he'll be stronger."

"So, are you saying this is normal? His death is necessary?"

"It is the natural cycle of a phoenix. I also benefit from his rebirth. My power will increase."

"Why does his rebirth affect you?" Mary asked.

"We are bonded and share a foundation of magic. During his absence, I'll be vulnerable. After I take you home, I'll return and wait until Fisgig rises again. I've never told this to anyone. I'm entrusting you with my most sacred secret. This is the kind of trust I wish to have with you."

Mary didn't know what to say. No one had ever wanted this kind of relationship with her, sharing thoughts, feelings, and trust. Brayson took her hand and lifted it to set the phoenix on it.

Mary pulled her arm away. "I don't wish to be burned."

"Nor do I wish to burn you," Fisgig responded. "I can control my flame. You'll be safe. It wasn't Master Id who protected you while you walked through the flames above the pool...it was me. Allow me to sit on your hand."

Mary felt uneasy, but there was something in Fisgig's tone which sounded truthful. She reached out, willing her hand not to tremble.

Brayson changed the subject as Mary took the phoenix on her finger. The bird felt light, and she didn't feel the heat from his flame. She sighed with relief.

Brayson pointed to the opening in the cliffs. "The cave is the home of The Source. No one, but us, knows its true location."

Mary rubbed Fisgig's neck as she responded. "And, what exactly is this true location?"

"My apologies. I failed to consider your newness to this world. You're within the Mountains of Oraness. I send my students here when the moment comes for them to seek the gift."

"What gift?"

"The gift of power...magic's ultimate power."

Mary thought a moment. "If you send your students here, then how is it that we are the only three who know where The Source is located? And, what is this Source, anyway?"

"The mountains are protected. A man cannot teleport into this area unless he possesses the knowledge given by the Head Master. It's a nice title to have, and it has its perks. The knowledge of The Source's location is passed down from one Head Master to another. As I said, the mountains surrounding this area are protected to keep curious minds from climbing them and revealing the true location of The Source's home.

"When my students come here, they must use a teleportation platform within The Source's temple, located inside the Void Maze. The maze is far from here and isn't simple to navigate. The maze is torturous. A man could become lost for days before finding its center, or a way back out. It would take a man nearly 100 Peaks to walk from the base of these mountains to the maze. Not to mention, the boat ride necessary to cross the Straits of Ebarna.

"The Source is an ancient dragon said to be the source of all magic, but this isn't the case. The Source is the protector of the Eye of Magic and has been for ages."

"How old is The Source?" Mary cut in. "How ancient is this dragon?"

Brayson thought a bit before responding. "All I can say is, The Source has seen the creation, and the destruction of many worlds."

"You said he protects the Eye of Magic. What does he protect it from?"

Brayson smiled. "I like your inquisitive nature. I can see how talking to you would keep me on my toes."

Mary winked. "I would rather you like me for my wit, not just my good looks." She held out her hand and allowed Fisgig to return to his perch.

Brayson enjoyed her confidence. "To answer your question, The Source protects the Eye from men. In order for a man to look into the Eye, he must prove himself worthy to pass The Source. If deemed so, the Eye will invite this aspiring mage to look into it. Many men have been swallowed by the Eye and lost forever. Their souls are spit into the darkness beyond our worlds and left to find their way to the gods."

"That's horrible," Mary responded. "Why would someone want to look into the Eye if they could be killed? And, are men the only ones allowed to look into the Eye? What about women? Don't you consider women good enough?" She put her hands on her hips and waited for the answer.

"Power is the reason men look into the Eye." Brayson took note of Mary's body language. He removed Fisgig from his perch and set the bird on his shoulder. "To answer your question regarding women...I've never met a woman who has been ready to meet The Source. I have nothing against women seeking power. In fact, I welcome the day this happens. Until then, I can only speak of what has transpired."

Mary pondered his answer. "I'm glad you're open to the idea. I admire strong women. I hope to know a woman like this someday."

"As do I." Brayson found Mary's eyes. He held her hands in his. "I see much strength in you, Mary. I also see a delightful wit and an ability to enjoy the moment. I watched from the bar at Kebble's inn as you and your daughters made your family laugh."

Mary slapped his arm. "You mean to tell me you were at the inn and never said hello? Why?"

"I had to work up the nerve. I needed to figure out how to approach you. The dresses were intended to buy me the moments necessary to accomplish this. Please forgive me."

Mary giggled. "There is no forgiveness necessary. I find your vulnerability flattering." After giving another wink, she changed the subject. "You were going to tell me about the men who seek the power of the Eye."

Brayson took a deep breath. "Many men seek power, but this search for power causes doubt. A man may succeed and convince The Source he is worthy to pass, but it's not The Source he should fear. In fact, The Source has been known to allow a man to pass without questioning him.

"It's the Eye he should be afraid of. When a man is invited by the Eye to look into it, it sees his doubt. It hates doubt. It devours this weakness and, like I said, it swallows him and spits his soul out.

"Only those who believe they are ready to receive the Eye's gift survive. These men are granted power far beyond their comprehension. They spend the rest of their lives as scholars of the arts trying to understand how to use this power. They strive to become immortal...god-like...but, to my knowledge, no one has managed to attain this level of glory prior to passing."

Mary's brow furrowed. "And, is this your goal? Do you wish to become god-like? Do you desire to have so much power that you would forget to live your life and instead, search for it?"

Brayson smiled. "I do enjoy your directness. I have no desire to become god-like. Furthermore, I enjoy living everyday to its fullest. If I had been so focused on attaining greater power, I would not have noticed you, now would I?"

Again, Mary slapped at his arm, but now, there was a satisfied twinkle in her eyes. "Good answer, Mr. Id. There just might be hope for you and me." Taking his hand, she gave it a squeeze. "Tell me more about you."

Brayson cleared his throat. "I am the last man to look into the Eye and survive. Before me, it was my father. He was 1,200 seasons when he passed."

Removing Fisgig from his shoulder and returning the phoenix to his perch, Brayson continued. "There have been twelve men over the last 10,000 seasons who have passed this ultimate test. 2,764 men have tried and lost their lives in search of this ultimate power."

Brayson could see the look of shock on Mary's face. "Are you okay? You look as if you have concerns."

"Well, of course she does," Fisgig responded. "You would, too, if the situation was reversed. It's alright, Mary. Ask anything you wish."

"I have so many questions, I'm not sure where to start. Is George going to look into the Eye?"

Brayson smiled. "This is nothing to worry about right now. If the day comes when he's ready, I will tell you. But, for now, how would you like to meet your first dragon?"

Mary's smile widened. "Dragon? Me...meet a dragon?"

Brayson's Desk
Inside the Book of Bonding

George sat in frustration, careful to avoid the water surrounding his dry spot at the bottom of the hole. Trying to figure a way out was exhausting. Payne had tried to fly to the surface of the shaft, but some unseen force would not let him pass.

"I don't know what to do," George barked as he threw a small stone against the shaft's wall. "This place is pissing me off." George looked at a skull, partially covered by water. "I don't want to end up like that bastard."

Payne tilted his head. "What 'bastard' mean?"

"Forget it." George stood and adjusted his tunic. He grunted. "I feel freaking filthy. I need a damn bath." His ragged appearance was a far cry from the Gucci persona he sported on Earth.

Again, Payne tilted his head. "What 'bath' mean?"

George glared at Payne. "Shut up, will you? Don't say anything else. I need to figure a way out of here."

Payne growled, "Ebbish nay!" The fairy-demon flew up and sat on a heavy root which protruded from the wall. "Payne, no like Master."

"Blah, blah, blah, whatever."

Many moments passed before George made a conscious decision to stop feeling sorry for himself. He refocused on the task at hand. "Payne, get down here. We must be missing something. Why can't we teleport out of this damn hole? There are no openings for us to go through. I wonder what Brayson would do in a situation like this?"

"Sleep." Payne lowered to George's side.

"Sleep? What the hell are you talking about? Brayson wouldn't do that. Are you even paying attention? What does sleep have to do with what I asked?"

"Master tired. Master sleep. Sleep make Master think gooder."

"I don't need sleep. We need to find a way out of here or we'll starve to death. We've got to focus. There's got to be a way out."

George thought long and hard as he scanned his surroundings. "Didn't Brayson say he had a phoenix? Doesn't a phoenix command fire? They did in the movies I watched. Maybe fire would work on these roots."

"What 'movies' mean?"

George rolled his eyes. "You're freaking killing me. Just let me focus, will you?"

"Ebbish nay. Master grouchy to Payne."

The mage shook his head, then took another look around. His eyes settled on a gathering of thick roots protruding from the base of the shaft's wall. "I wonder how they managed to grow this deep?" He walked over, grabbed the roots and pulled, but they wouldn't budge. "Screw me! This sucks!"

Payne flew over and sat on the roots above George's head. "What 'screw' mean?"

"Nothing, and don't repeat it in front of Athena. She doesn't like it when we talk that way, so forget I said anything. Now, let me think."

George backed up and rubbed his chin. "Those freaky flowers freaked out when you pulled one of them out of the ground. Maybe the plants connected to these roots will freak out and pull their roots to the surface. Maybe they'll…" He stopped. "Payne, get behind me."

Once the fairy-demon was out of the way, the mage lifted his hands. A wave of fire torched the area. The roots retracted and, as they did, a small crack appeared in the wall near the floor of the shaft.

George boasted. "I knew there had to be a way out!"

"Again," Payne shouted. "Again, Master!"

George did and the crack widened further. George put his hands on his hips. "This looks promising. Payne, take a look at this. There's a cave on the other side, but the crack is still too small to fit through. Stand back, let me try again."

George kept at it until the hole was large enough for them to pass. Satisfied with his results, he put his hands on his hips. "Payne, fly through before it closes."

Payne did as he was told. Once George was through, the wall shut behind them. A long, well-lit cave stretched into the distance with no end in sight. The light seemed to come from within the walls. They looked as if they were glowing.

George took a deep breath. "Well, this is freaking eerie. I don't like this one bit. Something tells me we're not out of trouble. I have a bad feeling about this joint."

"What 'freaking' mean?"

"It means I'm scared."

"Payne not scared." The fairy-demon pushed out his chest as he hovered above the floor.

"That's because you're brave."

"Yes, Payne brave."

"That's good. We may need your bravery. At least this place is a change of scenery."

"What 'scenery' mean?"

"I swear to the gods, Payne, I'm going to make you study a freaking dictionary."

"Ebbish nay. Be nice to Payne. Payne save you. What 'dictionary' mean?"

"Payne!"

"Okay!"

Suddenly, a loud scream echoed off the walls of the cave. It sounded like a frightened woman.

George ran toward the noise with Payne flying behind. *I can't believe I'm doing this,* he thought. *Only idiots run toward danger.* As he ran, the screams grew louder. *I'm going to freaking regret this, I just know it.*

It took 400 footsteps before the cave ended. George passed through the threshold of a large room made out of shaped stones in which an old woman had been left hanging by her arms. The shackles around her wrists were connected to opposing ends of a chain which had been pulled through an iron hoop attached to the ceiling.

Suspended high above a banquet table covered with food, her dress had been shredded and beneath the mess, claw marks ran down her calves. Blood dripped from the end of her foot and fell into a wooden pot which had been placed at the table's end.

The pain on the woman's face was evident as she looked down at George. After struggling to get her breath, she warned, "You must run!"

Before George could respond, four large creatures appeared, one in each corner of the room. They began to crawl along the ceiling toward the woman. The figures were dark, without faces, and covered with hair. Their claws ripped into the stones and with every step, the rubble fell to the floor and broke apart.

George thought to himself, *That's just great...a bunch of pissed off Cousin Its. Could this world get any more messed up?* He lifted his hands and without hesitation, sent his magic flying. Thousands of needles filled the air in two directions. As expected, an equal number of creatures fell lifeless to the floor and landed with a thud.

Again, George shot his needles, but when they made contact with the two that remained, nothing happened. The needles bounced off as the creatures turned their attention toward their new visitors.

Again, the woman shouted. "You must run! They'll kill you! You can't save me! Run!"

Payne did not wait for George to give a command. He teleported next to one of the beasts and used his claws to cut the creature free from its grip. Only three of its four claws released, but Payne adjusted his assault and took a bite out of the leg attached to the fourth claw. The squeal the menace made as it fell the sixty feet to the floor before landing on its head was unnerving.

George unsheathed his sword as he ran toward the beast. He buried the blade deep within the center of the animal's mass, then turned to find the final beast.

As the creature scurried down the wall, Payne attacked, but found his claws were no longer able to cause damage. The next thing the fairy-demon knew, he was being clubbed across his tiny face. He was knocked across the room and landed on the table. His fall was softened by a cooked bird sitting at the table's center, but the impact was severe enough to leave him dazed.

The beast finished its descent. As its claws found the floor, the woman screamed again for George to make his retreat. The creature began to creep toward the mage. As it did, the three previously killed vanished, then reappeared by its side.

Again, the woman shouted, "You must run! Save yourself! You cannot kill them!"

George heard something in the woman's voice. She sounded too desperate. His seasons of deception triggered his internal alarm. *Something's not right,* he thought. *Why would she tell me to run? Why isn't she begging me to save her? This is a con. There's no way she's in trouble. This is a set-up... and she's the bait.*

The beasts had surrounded him. George had to make a choice. Run or fight, but one or the other had to be done—and done now.

The beasts leapt toward George, but before they could seize him, he teleported to the end of the table where the large wooden pot sat. The mage lifted his hands. A pulverizing blast of wind shot from his fingertips. It hit the woman with such a force she hit the ceiling over fifteen feet above her and was knocked unconscious.

The chains around her wrists had coiled on her way up. As she fell toward the floor, her arms took the brunt of the pressure. The chains snapped against her weight, ripping her arms off at the elbows. She tumbled head over heels before her head smashed against the floor. Her skull cracked, leaving the brain exposed.

George was forced to redirect his attention. From the corner of his eye, he saw the creatures hurl themselves into the air. He wasn't fast enough. He teleported, but only after a claw tore open a nasty gash across his right shoulder. He reappeared at the opposite end of the table. With his good arm, he aimed for the woman's exposed brain and sent needles flying. They penetrated the soft tissue. The magic's effect was instantaneous. The beasts disappeared in an explosion of smoke.

The woman's body began to expand. Something was causing pressure to build from inside. George teleported, grabbed Payne, then threw up a wall of force. The woman exploded, filling the room with a green, poisonous gas. They would be forced to stay inside the barrier until the air cleared.

Marcus Id's Dark Tower-palace

Boyafed was sitting on Marcus' throne. He was tapping his foot against the edge of the chair's base as Marcus entered the room.

"This better be important," Marcus snapped as he watched the Order's leader lean back to a more comfortable position. The chancellor cringed. "I see you've made yourself at home."

Boyafed smiled. "Your throne suits me."

Marcus hated Boyafed's nerve, but he would not allow Boyafed to see his irritation. "Have you found Gage?"

"No, but I have other news."

"And, this news is?"

Boyafed stood, brushed past Marcus, then retrieved a piece of parchment from his back pant pocket. He tossed it to the chancellor.

"What's this?" Marcus growled as he opened the document. A smile appeared. "Boyafed, my good man, this is, indeed, pleasant news. Are you sure of this information?"

"I am. Your brother has taken a new Mystic Learner. My spies have since lost sight of him, but he does exist."

Marcus began to pace. "This is wonderful. But, the absence of my goswig is a matter I must remedy first. I want your best men looking for Gage. Have your son lead the search. This would make a fine first assignment."

"I cannot, nor would I waste his moments on such nonsense."

"What? Why?"

"Lord Hosseff requested Kiayasis be sent to Merchant Island to escort a woman from Grayham. She needs to go to Grogger's Swamp. She has business there, and furthermore, it's not my problem that you can't keep your goswig under control. I will send others to look for your pet."

Marcus hated his tone, but said nothing of it. "Lord Hosseff was here? Why wasn't I told? Why didn't you send for me?"

"I came to you as soon as I carried out our lord's instructions. Besides, Hosseff did not ask for you. He came seeking my company. I have many men who are capable of finding Gage. Kiayasis has already left."

"You should remember who runs this city, Boyafed. You speak to me as if you have forgotten your place."

Boyafed chuckled. "I haven't forgotten who created this city. Perhaps, you have lost sight of who commands the army you claim to be in charge of. My men respect you only because they follow my orders. It would be wise for you to remember...I am the only reason you have your illusion of control."

It took everything within Marcus to stay calm. "I'll remember that." The chancellor changed the subject. "Why would Hosseff want Kiayasis to escort this woman to Grogger's Swamp?"

"Does why really matter? Our god has spoken." Boyafed plucked the parchment from Marcus' hand, crumpled it up, then threw it across the room into the cold fireplace. He started to leave. "I haven't eaten. Perhaps, we could speak of other matters over a nice corgan steak and some cold ale."

"A pleasant idea. I'm hungry, now that I think about it. We have plans to make. With my brother taking a new Mystic Learner, an opportunity will present itself. I'll meet you in the dining hall in a few moments. I need to put away a few things first."

"Until then." The dark paladin left the room.

As Boyafed left, Marcus whispered. "Soon, you'll be forced to watch your tongue. When that day comes, you'll bow before me or die. I would prefer the latter." Marcus teleported.

Gregory Id's Glass Palace
The Next Day

Gregory called for the leader of his white paladin army to come to a meeting. He was waiting for Lord Dowd to arrive when Mykklyn entered his bedroom chamber. The goswig's paws thumped against the glass floor as she jaunted across it while looking at the rushing water passing beneath.

The lioness spoke. "Dowd has arrived. He is waiting for you in the throne room."

Gregory looked in his mirror and adjusted his green robe. "Please tell him I'll be there in a moment."

"As you wish." The goswig vanished.

Now...fellow soul...allow me to tell you about Lord Dowd and his army. He is the leader of the white paladins and hails from a strong elven family which has lived in service to many White Chancellors for over 6,000 seasons. Dowd is by far the strongest leader the Paladins of Light have ever served. He is large, powerful, and diplomatic. His short, dark hair accents a strong jaw, and his presence demands respect. He exudes confidence, and his men follow him without waiver.

Dowd's men number 21,000, with another 3,000 in training. The white army serves two gods: Keylom—God of Peace, and Helmep—God of Healing. Both deities are glorified amongst their ranks and Dowd sees to it that no man beneath him falls away from their path to glory.

The army is not in existence for the purpose of attaining stature. For this reason, it was not given a specific name on the day of its creation. The Paladins of Light was the name given by the people 8,000 seasons ago. This name was given after the Order attacked. The white army chased the darkness out of their kingdom. With the darkness gone, they became known as the Paladins of Light.

"Lord Dowd, thank you for coming," Gregory said after appearing on his throne.

"Chancellor," Dowd responded. He lowered his head in respect. "How may I be of service?"

"I fear Marcus has become more of an irritation than he normally is. Recently, he has made threats against my safety. I would appreciate it if you would send your spies to gather information on what's to come. For now, the Head Master has offered to help. He has provided additional security. I would like you to meet Hepplesif." Gregory pointed up.

Hepplesif's wings fluttered across his spidery back as he descended from one of the glass beams spanning the room. He twitched his mouse-like nose and settled on the floor a few paces from Dowd.

The leader of the white army watched in amazement as Hepplesif's legs began clicking on the glass floor. "And, what are you?"

Gregory was the one to answer. "Hepplesif is a kedgle. Their king has been kind enough to send 100 of their kind to assist in the protection of the palace."

Dowd was intrigued. He had heard of the kedgles, but had never seen one. He studied Hepplesif's body. After a moment of staring, Hepplesif spoke. "Lord Dowd, this introduction has become uncomfortable. I understand your curiosity, but perhaps, we could get to the matters at hand?"

"By all means, I'm sorry. I didn't mean to be rude."

"Understandable. I felt the same way the first moment I saw one of your kind. You look just as odd to me as I must to you."

"I can imagine." Dowd turned his attention to Gregory, "What is the kedgles' role to be?"

Gregory stood from his throne. The chair was made of opaque, white glass. Thick cushions, both red, had been mounted to the seat's surface and back. The throne sat at the center of a large circular area which was transparent, without imperfection. The throne looked as if it was hovering—sitting on nothing. A man could look through this spot and see Gregory's library. Just as they did in Brayson's school, countless fairies flew back and forth adjusting the books and scrolls from shelf to shelf.

The rest of the throne room floor, though glass, looked and felt like stone. As Gregory responded to Dowd's question, he walked toward the window, "The kedgles will use illusion to create confusion if the palace is attacked by my brother's army. These illusions will give your men an advantage."

Dowd thought a moment. He turned to look at Hepplesif. "These illusions will only affect our enemy. Is this what I'm hearing?"

"You are correct."

"Then, what do you need from me?"

Hepplesif's legs clicked on the glass as he moved to a better position for conversation. He climbed up the side of Gregory's throne and stopped on its arm. "It's best I know what my allies and my enemies will look like. I need to know how they will be dressed. My kind will keep your men from seeing our illusions. The Dark Chancellor's men will appear confused. This should help to defeat Marcus' soldiers."

"Sounds positive." Dowd removed his cape and breastplate, then motioned for a servant to take it from him. After fanning the collar of his shirt to cool himself, he continued. "My men will wear silver, with white markings. Some will wear plate, others will prefer chain. If they aren't wearing armor, they will be wearing a cape. As you saw, it's black, with a white trim. The symbol of our army...the Turtle Elf of Healing...sits at its center.

"As far as the Order, their men wear only black plate, and black capes with gold accents. Their symbol is a golden altar which rests on both shoulders and their capes. You will have no trouble picking them out of a crowd."

Hepplesif looked at Gregory. "Chancellor, it seems as if everything is under control. I will speak with you during some other series of moments. I must speak with the others to ensure they understand what has been discussed."

The kedgle turned to face the white army leader. "Lord Dowd, *Saesa omentien lle. I'narr en gothrim glinuva nuin I'anor!*"

"It was good to meet you as well, Hepplesif. I also hope the sun finds their bones inviting."

Hepplesif flew out of the room. Once gone, Gregory addressed Dowd. "Please keep me updated. I would like to know when your spies have gathered intelligence about my brother's intentions."

"Tenna' ento lye omenta, Chancellor."

"Until then, Lord Dowd."

Gregory and Dowd left the room. A figure emerged from the shadows. It was Marcus. "Well, well...my little brother has a plan. You're smarter than you look, Gregory. But, you're not smart enough." The Dark Chancellor vanished.

The Mountains of Oraness

Brayson looked down at Fisgig's ashes. The phoenix had burned himself to death the night before. Now, it was only a matter of waiting for the bird to rise again.

***

Now...fellow soul...when Brayson took Fisgig as his goswig, he was warned by his father, Hedron—the Head Master before him—of the dangers he would face during the series of moments encompassing the phoenix's death. Despite this danger, Hedron allowed Brayson to make the final choice, a decision his father gave no other Mystic Learner. Brayson chose Fisgig because the phoenix possessed more power than any other creature on Luvelles. Since then, there has been one creature born with the potential to command power stronger than Fisgig's.

***

As Brayson entered The Source's cave, he was dwelling on the relationship between George and Payne. It wasn't long before he was standing in front of The Source. He could not see the beast, since the dragon chose to remain invisible, but he knew he was there. Brayson lowered to one knee. *"Yaaraer...quel re, nae saian luume'!"*

A voice responded from the nothingness. "Hello, Brayson. You're right, it has been too long since we last looked upon each other. I bid you good day, as well. To what do I owe this pleasure?"

Brayson's eyes widened as the dragon appeared. A smile crossed his face as the expanse of the cavern was filled with the beast's form. "Ancient One, I have come to stay while my goswig prepares to be reborn. I have taken a new Mystic Learner. Perhaps, you'll meet him when the moment is right. His skills are advanced for someone who hasn't received training. It's as if he has been blessed by the gods."

"Is this being mortal?"

"He is."

"Intriguing. I will speak with the gods to see if their manipulations have touched his soul. What else can you tell me of the happenings on Luvelles?"

Brayson sat on the floor and crossed his legs. "The woman I introduced you to has stolen a piece of my heart. I don't seem to be able to keep her at bay. I worry she'll be a distraction. I need your advice."

"Ahh. Love can be tricky. Take a seat. Let's discuss this matter further."

The Underground Village of Gogswayne

Gage awoke. He lifted his head from the soft pillow he was lying on. As his eyes focused, he noticed an odd-looking creature staring down at him. Its lower portion looked like a snake. This portion merged with a torso which completed its upper portion. The back of its torso had wings which allowed it to hover in one spot. Two muscular arms, covered with scales, were attached to two claws at their ends. The creature's head appeared as any man's. He had brown hair, dark eyes and the pointed ears of an elf. Every now and then, a slithering tongue shot out of his mouth as a snake's would.

Gage rubbed his eyes against his forearm and took a second look. "Where am I?" he said with a groggy voice.

"What a shame. He doesn't know where he is," the creature hissed, then flew out of the quaint little home without saying another word. The beast retrieved a log which rested near a group of trees. Once back inside, he threw the log onto the fire and moved to a position far enough away from the badger to allow room for good conversation.

"You don't know where you are. I figured as much." His tongue shot out of his mouth. "It's a shame. Everyone forgets. Coming back from King Ultor's kingdom is hard on the body. You're exhausted from the transition your body had to make. We have all been through it. You will be tired for a few more Peaks before you begin to feel normal."

Gage thought a moment. "I remember. I remember shrinking and meeting with the king. The last thing I remember is being carried to the surface, but not much else. My name is Gage."

"Syse and Swill told me before they left. Syse informed me you spoke with King Ultor himself. You should feel honored. I can't think of another goswig who has spoken with him other than Strongbear. Usually, we meet with his second in command. I'm sure your story will be one to tell the others."

Gage stood. His limbs felt feeble. It took most of his strength to remain upright. He stretched. "Where am I?"

"You're in Gogswayne. You'll see everything once you're rested."

"What's your name? And, what are you? How many others of us are there?"

"Where are my manners?" The creature chuckled. "My name is Gallrum. I am a serwin."

"I have heard of your kind." Tired, Gage lowered his head onto the pillow. "But, I have never met one of you."

"Then, it is my honor to be your first." The serwin bowed. "To answer your other question...there are nearly 1,000 of us living in Gogswayne. You, my friend, just increased our village's population to 998. There will be a celebration when we hit an even 1,000."

Gage thought to himself, *So, the village does have a name after all.*

The furniture in Gallrum's home was quaint, made of wood, and the bedding beneath the pillow the badger had been lying on looked as if someone had taken the moments necessary to quilt it. This place was much more pleasant than Marcus Id's dark tower-palace.

Gallrum commented as Gage looked at the craftsmanship of the blanket. "Strongbear is the one who makes such things. He is a master craftsman."

"What? A male made this?"

"Yes...he's talented, don't you think?"

"Is he a little...well, you know, on the sensitive side?"

Gallrum began to laugh. "Strongbear hates it when someone makes that assumption. It would be a shame if you said that to anyone else around here."

"I'm sorry. I just assumed."

"I wouldn't assume much while living in Gogswayne. Strongbear is always sewing something. He provides most everyone in our little village something he has quilted at one moment or another. He's the owner of the finest establishment which serves the best quaggle in town."

"Quaggle?" Gage responded. "What's that?"

Gallrum gasped. "It's a shame you don't know. Quaggle is the finest meal a goswig can eat. You'll just have to see for yourself."

"I look forward to it." Gage thought back to what he had learned of the goswigs' village. "You said the village is called Gogswayne. I thought this was a place with no name."

"As I have already said, I wouldn't assume much while living here."

"What else can you tell me?"

Gallrum flew over to a small table. He reached down and lifted a bound book from its surface with his talons. He tossed it across the room, but Gage failed to catch it. Gallrum shook his head, "What a shame." He retrieved the book and handed it to the badger. "Inside this book you'll find a record of everyone who lives here. I'll give you the moments necessary to study it. You need to rest. I'll take you into the village once you have recovered."

Gage fluffed the pillow, then lowered his head. "I am feeling tired. Thank you, Gallrum. I look forward to meeting the others."

The Luvelles Gazette

When you want an update about your favorite characters

Lasidious and Celestria are inside their home beneath the Peaks of Angels on Ancients Sovereign. They plan to stay away from the others of the Collective until the moment is right to reveal the exact location of the third piece of the Crystal Moon.

Head Master Brayson is still inside The Source's cave. He has spoken at length with the ancient dragon and is now speaking with the one king of Southern Grayham through a pool filled with molten lava. Sam's image is shimmering within the fiery liquid as he informs Brayson of his queen's desire to visit Luvelles. Brayson keeps wiping the sweat from his brow due to the heat, and judging by the way the conversation is going, Shalee will be given a Right of Passage to Luvelles.

George and Payne are still inside the Book of Bonding on the Head Master's desk. They are hungry, but George is unsure if it is safe to eat the food from the banquet table since the room was filled with poisonous gas.

Kepler rounded up a number of swassel gophers. He happened to cross paths with them while roaming the woods around the family's new homes. The demon-jaguar asked the gophers to dig him a lair beneath the large rocks located at the community's center.

Athena, Susanne, and Mary are visiting inside Mary's home. Baby Garrin has finished cutting his first tooth, and he seems happier. Athena and Susanne are enjoying the adventures of Mary's first date with Brayson.

Shalee has arrived on Grayham's Merchant Island. She plans to teleport back to Brandor once she has familiarized herself with the area. Once Sam informs her of her Right of Passage given by the Head Master, she will teleport back to Merchant Island, and catch a ride to Luvelles with the Merchant Angels.

Mosley is with the gods on his team. They have agreed, Mosley will inform Shalee of everything she needs to know about Grogger's Swamp. The wolf plans to have this conversation while keeping Shalee company inside the Merchant Angels' container. The gods believe the answer to the crystal's whereabouts will present itself once she arrives at the swamp.

Mieonus is with her team of gods. They have been looking for George. They intend to use him to go after the crystal. Since the mage cannot be found, the gods have decided to speak with Lasidious to get an idea of where George might be.

Gregory is with the King of Lavan. They have agreed to break ground on the new bridge between their cities. It has been decided, the supports for the bridge will be made of stone, while the undercarriage (substructure), traveled pathway (roadbed), and the upper-carriage (superstructure) will be made of glass in three colors to give the bridge ample definition.

Marcus is meeting with Boyafed. He has a mission for the leader of the Order, but worries the friction in their relationship may create an obstacle which he must overcome. He hates the idea that Boyafed doesn't respect his authority.

Gage is still sleeping. His strength is increasing, but he is not ready to be up and about. Strongbear has called for a meeting of the goswigs. The large brown bear will announce Gage's arrival.

Lord Dowd met with four of his finest Paladins of Light. He has dispatched them to spy on Marcus and the leader of the Order. The men are to return once they understand the intentions of their enemies.

Yaloom has been sealed inside his casket and placed within Brandor's royal crypt. Sam has ensured the ex-god's body was well-preserved. He will keep Yaloom there until Shalee is able to retrieve the nasha fruit from the hidden god world.

Kiayasis has arrived on Luvelles' Merchant Island. He intends to wait for Shalee's arrival, then carry out his orders. Since he was the only one riding Joss, the krape lord was able to fly the distance. Once loaded with the queen and her belongings, flight will no longer be possible. They will have to travel by land to Grogger's Swamp.

Hepplesif is with his battalion of kedgles. The tiny commander is working on the best way to protect Gregory's palace and other key areas of the city.

Thank you for reading the Luvelles Gazette

Quaggle

5 Peaks of Bailem Have Passed
The Merchant Island of Luvelles

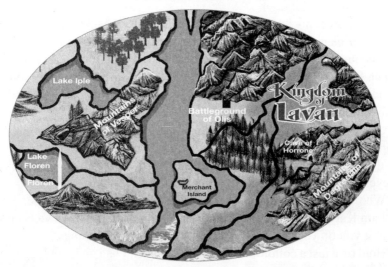

Shalee stepped out of her transport container and took her first look at the Merchant Island of Luvelles. The place was busy, crawling with many rugged-looking elves as they loaded and unloaded containers which were much larger than the one she had just stepped from.

Since becoming a queen, she had learned how each world shared many forms of merchandise between them. It was this sophisticated flow of trade between planets which fueled each world's economy, no matter how barbaric their cultures seemed.

Mosley had visited Shalee during her trip and discussed the dangers of Grogger's Swamp. She now knew where she had to go. It was just prior to the Merchant Angels placing her on the island that Mosley vanished. She had to sit in the darkness until morning and wait for the docking crew to arrive.

While she waited, her thoughts dwelt on Sam. She wanted nothing to do with a man who was judgmental and blamed her for the loss of their baby. Many tears had run down her cheeks since Mosley's departure and now—as if out of nowhere—a man had walked up and claimed to be there to help her.

"Your Majesty," Kiayasis said as he bowed on one knee and lowered his head. "I'm here to assist you with your journey to the swamplands."

Shalee knew she looked horrid and worn out from the trip. Her clothes smelled of her own waste. There had been no provisions inside the container to relieve herself. She had been forced to let it flow.

Shalee studied her visitor. She was unprepared for the surprise and felt embarrassed, not to mention appalled, by her smell. Her outfit was wrinkled from sleeping on the floor.

Kiayasis kept his head lowered as Shalee walked back into the container to grab her bags. She decided to change and pulled the door shut, careful to leave enough of a crack to shed the light she needed to choose something fresher. She dabbed a few drops of Strallise perfume on her neck to cover her odor. Now, she smelled like berries with a dash of pee—a wonderful combination for a first impression.

After grabbing Precious, she threw her bags over her shoulder and stepped out of the container. She studied her escort from head to toe. He was dressed in black pants and a gold shirt. His hair was long and black and his eyes were lowered so she couldn't see them.

"Who are you?" she questioned, wishing she could run and hide.

"I am Kiayasis, a third sergeant in the Order, My Lady. I have been sent to assist you on your journey. Allow me to collect your things."

"Hold on a just a cotton-pickin' minute, mister. I had no knowledge you'd be comin'."

"My apologies, Your Majesty. I have no knowledge what a 'cotton-pickin' minute' means. Do you wish me to go? Shall I leave?"

"It means, give me a moment...please."

Kiayasis shrugged. "As you wish." His shoulders were fit and gave form to the Order's black cape.

"Who sent you?" Shalee inquired as she lowered her bags beside him.

"I have been sent by the Head Master. He has commanded that I take you to your desitination and see to it you arrive safely."

Shalee sighed. "Well now, what an unexpected surprise. I had no idea you'd be comin'. I must tell Brayson how much I appreciate his generosity when I see him."

"May I stand, My Lady?"

Shalee studied Kiayasis. He had a soothing voice. She would allow the escort. "Yes, yes, by all means. Stand up, and let's find me a place ta bathe and get some rest. My crate wasn't comfortable, and I could use a good night's sleep...and a nice hot soakin' bath."

Kiayasis smiled and looked up. As he did, Shalee took note of his blue eyes. They were stunning, what she considered dreamy, and his facial features were perfect. She was so absorbed as she looked him over, she barely heard him speak. "Allow me to call my mount." Kiayasis turned and gave a sharp whistle.

Shalee snapped out of her lapse of concentration and found something new to marvel at. Joss emerged from behind a group of crates. The krape lord kept his wings folded and approached, using only his hind legs. "Goodness-gracious, what's that thing?"

"Don't be alarmed, Your Majesty. This 'thing' has a name. He is called Joss. He will be our ride to the swamplands of Grogger. He is tame. Allow me to have your hand, and I'll introduce you properly."

"I'm not so sure 'bout this. He looks a lil' mean. I would hate for him ta think I always smell so nasty."

Kiayasis looked Shalee in the eyes. "My Lady, I assure you it's safe. He doesn't care how bad you smell. I'm here to protect you, not allow Joss to devour you." He gave a charming smile. "Besides, I have told him queens taste sour."

For a brief moment, Shalee enjoyed Kiayasis' charm. She allowed him to take her hand. The dark paladin lifted her arm into the air and presented her palm. *"Joss, vara tel' Seldarine!"*

"What did you say?" Shalee questioned as she watched Joss lower his head to sniff her hand.

Kiayasis patted Joss on his snout. "I told him to protect you...and ignore the foul smell."

"Well, that was rude. It's not like I could..."

Kiayasis laughed and stopped her before she could finish. "I was just being clever, Your Majesty. I didn't really say that. I only told him to protect you. I hope you like to jest, My Lady." Again, Kiayasis smiled.

"Was that the language of the elves you were speakin'? I've had ta study some of it, but only enough ta get by."

Kiayasis nodded. *"Ta na...Arwenamin."*

"And, what does that mean?"

"I said, 'It was, My Lady.'"

Shalee was going to enjoy Kiayasis' company—and his blue eyes. Kiayasis took her bags and put them inside Joss' pouch. The hair inside acted as a cushion, protecting Joss from being injured when objects shifted. With his large arms, Joss adjusted the weight's distribution until he felt comfortable. Between Kiayasis' armor, his weapons, their food, and Shalee's bags, Joss was carrying more than a full load.

Kiayasis commanded the krape lord to lower to the ground. "My Lady, your foot. Allow me to give you your first lesson on how to mount a beast of this nature. It may take a few tries, but I assure you, it gets easier."

"I'm sure it does. He's so huge. Are ya sure 'bout this?"

"Your Majesty, everything will be alright. If you don't like riding Joss, I can carry you myself, but you have to promise to bathe." Again Kiayasis' smile widened.

Shalee slapped Kiayasis on the arm. "Are ya thick headed? A woman doesn't want ta hear that she smells. I'm sure I'll be just fine ridin' on Joss. I'm not as fragile as I look. And, please, call me Shalee. I'm sure you'll enjoy the way I smell once I've cleaned up."

Kiayasis' smile faded. "I cannot address you by name, Your Highness. To do so would be to disgrace your crown."

Shalee leaned in. "Callin' me by name can't be any worse than tellin' me I smell. Besides, who's gonna know? I most certainly don't plan on tellin' anybody. Consider it an order, and then you'll have ta."

"I will consider it, Your Majesty. We best get going. It will take many moments to get to an inn. The one on Merchant Island is full, but they will allow you to bathe before we cross the Ebarna Strait. We will head to the ferry once you've cleaned up. There's a small village on the other side with an inn fit for a crown. You'll be able to rest there."

The Queen of Southern Grayham held tight to Kiayasis as they departed. She enjoyed how he felt. She would have felt guilty for enjoying this pleasure, but her anger toward Sam welcomed the diversion. At least with Kiayasis, she was being viewed as a woman—not a failure.

Marcus Id's Dark Tower-palace

Boyafed entered Marcus' throne room. Just like the rest of the chancellor's palace, the room smelled of Marcus' nasty habit. The smoke lingered and caused Boyafed to feel ill.

Many symbols of dark magic had been carved into the palace's stone walls, and the heavy pieces of wooden furniture made from trees taken from Wraithwood Hollow had been placed throughout.

"What do you want, Marcus?" the Order leader snapped as he stopped in front of the chancellor's throne.

Marcus bit down on his pipe, annoyed at the way Boyafed spoke. Before turning from a large table at the far side of the room to acknowledge the paladin's presence, he forced a smile to cover his mood. "I have news. I overheard my brother speaking with Lord Dowd. He has sent spies to live among us. You may want to look for new faces within your ranks. They seek to gather information of a possible attack."

Boyafed's brow furrowed. "Why would they seek this information? I have no intention of sending the army to attack your brother's city. Our forces are well matched, and to attack without reason would be a senseless loss of life."

Marcus sat on the edge of the table. "I agree. But, why would Gregory send spies? I would think you would want to deal with these imposters. Perhaps, Gregory intends to give you a reason to attack."

Boyafed crossed his arms, then moved to the throne and took a seat. "How were you in a position to overhear such a conversation? What reason could you have to spy on your brother in the first place?"

Marcus snapped. "I don't presume to know everything you do, Boyafed! How and why I do things or come across information is my business. Perhaps, you should concentrate on getting rid of the intruders, and spend less of your moments scrutinizing my affairs."

The leader of the Order stood from the throne and moved close. His eyes grew cold, and his fist tightened as he leaned in. "If I were you, I would speak only to those who fear you in the manner you have just spoken to me. I won't allow harsh words to escape your lips again when they are directed toward me. Now, answer the question. I'm in no mood for games. Do we have an understanding?"

Marcus was dying inside, debating whether to challenge Boyafed's advance. After a moment of biting his tongue, he responded. "I was at a meeting with my brothers. Gregory spoke as if he plans to march against us. His bravery is growing. He is tightening the security around his palace. If you don't believe me, send someone to check it out."

The chancellor gnawed on the end of his pipe as he continued. "After hearing Gregory speak, I chose to spy on him. I teleported into his throne room and listened from the shadows. He is sending spies, and I thought it best to tell you. I wanted to give you the chance to prepare the army."

Boyafed backed away. "I'll send five men to gather intelligence. What else can you tell me?"

"The kedgle king has sent one hundred of his kind to help Gregory protect his city."

"Why?"

"They are planning to use illusion on your men while Dowd's forces strike them down. Dowd himself explained to the kedgle commander what your army would be wearing. They plan to attack only those who wear the Order's regalia. You'll need a strategy to combat this magic."

Boyafed lowered to the steps leading to Marcus' throne. After a bit, he looked up. "I know of these creatures. Getting past the kedgle's magic seems simple enough. We may be forced to attack your brother's city after all."

Marcus smiled within, then feigned his concern by putting his hand to his chin as if in thought. "Hmmmm…perhaps, you're going about this the wrong way. Perhaps, a smaller strike without a large confrontation would be appropriate?"

Boyafed stood, removed his dagger from its sheath, and tapped the flat of the blade against the palm of his hand. "Agreed. A few men would be able to dispose of the kedgles. Once they're dead, their king won't be so willing to send reinforcements. The men could leave, then I will return with the army when I'm prepared to launch a full assault.

"With the size of the kedgles, I would imagine they are housed in a large room. It would be best to dispose of them at the same moment. I will send two additonal men to gather the intelligence we need to formulate a proper plan."

Marcus lifted his pipe and took a drag. "How will you deal with the spies in your ranks?"

Boyafed turned and headed for the door. He responded without looking back. "Don't worry about it. I've got it under control."

Once the paladin leader was gone, Marcus sat on his throne. He looked at the door and grinned. *That went better than expected.*

Brayson's Desk
Inside the Book of Bonding

A few days have passed since George and Payne's confrontation. They decided to take their chances and partake of the feast they stumbled upon after killing the old woman and her beast protectors. The food on the banquet table had proven to be a blessing in disguise, and it was safe to eat after George summoned water to wash off the residue the poisonous gas left behind.

There seemed to be no specific reason for the table, or the food, to have been there. Despite the puzzle, their need to eat outweighed their need to understand. George made sure they grabbed everything they could and stuffed it into a purple tablecloth. He threw it over his shoulder and waited for something bad to happen, but nothing did.

Since then, they followed a winding corridor which led them back to the surface. They are beyond the outskirts of the forest they appeared in and are walking toward a mountain range. The landscape is changing as they follow a creek fueled by the snow melting on top of the mountains.

As they walk, the appearance of the terrain is changing. The vegetation is becoming scarce and scorch marks darken the earth around them. As they crest a large mound, two boulders can be seen sitting at the center of a circular clearing next to a small statue resting on a pedestal riddled with cracks.

The stone replica was Payne's height and looked exactly like the little guy, right down to his fairy wings and horns. Even the new scratch across the side of Payne's face had been chiseled into it.

Payne flew over to his gray-colored counterpart and hovered next to it. "It's Payne. Neat! Let's eat." Yet again, the fairy-demon's attention span failed to focus on something bigger than his stomach.

George played with the growth of his beard while he studied their surroundings. His body odor was making it hard to concentrate. "Something is telling me this isn't good, Payne."

"Why? Payne like Payne. Payne is me...like Payne."

"Yes, you do like him, buddy, but this isn't right. I think we're in trouble."

"Why?"

"I don't know, but something tells me this isn't where we want to be."

A voice from behind responded. "Our instinct has always served us right, George."

George whirled around to face this new presence. "Now, I know this is bad. Two of me can't be a good thing. There's only room in the universe for one perfection," George responded as he moved to examine his alternate self. "What are you? Who are you? Why are you? What do you want and why do you look like me? Damn! I look like hell."

"I am you...or rather, we are your opposites," he responded while pointing at the statue. As George and Payne turned around, Payne's opposite became animated—its color changed from stone gray to the normal red of Payne's appearance.

"Payne don't like Payne no more, Master. That Payne bad." The fairy-demon moved next to George and hovered beside him. "Payne hate Payne now."

George's duplicate self continued. "This is your final test. You won't be able to leave this place of bonding and return to Luvelles until I have decided you're ready."

The duplicate George lifted his hands. A wave of force knocked George and Payne across the clearing. They landed on the back side of the large mound circling the clearing's circumference.

George shook out the cobwebs and peeked over the top of the hill. "That piece of garesh just jacked us up. I knew this was going to suck." George lifted from the ground and released his magic. Fire covered his alternate self, only to be defended by a bubble of protection.

"Take that...you garesh piece sort of Master," Payne shouted, then followed the insult with an attack of his own. The fairy-demon teleported behind his duplicate self and grabbed it. He ripped into its shoulder with his claw and carried it skyward.

The fight was on.

Ancients Sovereign
The Hall of Judgment

Mieonus, Goddess of Hate, called for a meeting with Lasidious and Celestria, asking them to come to Gabriel's hall. The Book of Immortality was present. As they sat around the heavy stone table, Mieonus was the first to speak. "Lasidious, I thought George was on Luvelles." Mieonus pushed her long dark hair behind her ears and adjusted her elegant white gown as she waited for a response.

"He is. Why would you waste our moments by bringing us here to discuss this?"

Mieonus leaned forward and played with the Book's golden stand as she responded. "Because I have been unable to find him. Is this some sort of a trick you've decided to play?"

Lasidious grinned. "No, Mieonus, there is no trick. You must think beyond what your simple mind is able to comprehend. Mosley was the one who said George was on Luvelles, not me. Knowing the wolf the way I do, I don't think Mosley would lie."

Mieonus stomped the heel of her shoe against the hall's floor. "Then, why can't I sense his presence? I should be able to, now that I know where he is."

Celestria spoke up. "George is inside the Book of Bonding on Head Master Brayson's desk. I would not worry about it. We do not intend to share the location of the crystal's whereabouts until George has had a chance to find his way out. We understand you deserve the chance to manipulate George into going after the third piece of the Crystal Moon. Perhaps, you should relax."

Mieonus pushed her chair back and stood from the table. "Well then, it sounds as if everything is under control. I shall visit with the Head Master and see what I can learn." Mieonus nodded in the Book's direction. "Gabriel, as always, it's good to see you. I'll speak with you later." The goddess vanished.

Gabriel floated across the table and lowered his heavy binding to its surface in front of Lasidious. "You're playing with the gods as if they are puppets. In my opinion, this game you've chosen to play is a diversion for something bigger. I don't know what it is yet, but I intend to find out."

Lasidious was about to respond, but before he could, Mosley appeared. The wolf moved to the head of the table and addressed the Mischievous One. "I would like to speak under the Rule of Fromalla. I would like to have this conversation within the confines of your home, Lasidious. I would like to have the benefit of a conversation without interruption."

The Book floated over to the wolf. "Am I to be part of this conversation?"

"I am sorry, Gabriel, but I wish to speak with Lasidious and Celestria alone."

The Book grunted and floated out of the hall. After a moment, Mosley continued. "If you agree, I will meet you in your home." Celestria looked at her lover, and after another moment of exchanged glances, they agreed, then vanished. Mosley followed.

Once everyone arrived, they sat around the table near the green flames of the gods' fireplace, which cast an eerie glow, setting the mood. Mosley turned one of the chairs into a platform and jumped on top of it and lowered to his haunches. Celestria lit some of the candles she had placed about the home earlier that day as Lasidious waved his hand. A feast appeared before them.

The Mischievous One leaned back, put his feet on the table, then crossed his arms. "Mosley, I have to admit, I'm curious. What could be so important it would require the Rule of Fromalla to be invoked before we could speak?"

Mosley jumped down from his platform and began to pace. "Shalee is on her way to Grogger's Swamp. Something unexpected has happened… something which causes my mind concern. The leader of the Order has sent his son, Kiayasis, to escort Shalee. I was on Merchant Island when Kiayasis introduced himself. He told Shalee the Head Master sent him, but I know this to be a lie. He was sent by Boyafed. My question is...why? Why would the Order care about a sorceress from Grayham? I spoke with Hosseff to see if he had anything to do with it, but it was clear he had no idea what I was talking about. After I left, I came to the conclusion it was you. You were the one who made this happen. I know I'm right, so level with me."

Celestria smiled and stood from the table. She walked over to Mosley, lowered next to the wolf and rubbed the fur on top of his head. "Why is Shalee going to Grogger's Swamp? What could possibly be there that she would want...or even find remotely interesting?"

Mosley sighed. He looked her in the eye. "I know you intentionally left the clue on your gown for me to find regarding the crystal's whereabouts. I smelled its scent. You must give me credit. I have led many packs throughout my seasons. I know Lasidious was the one who convinced Boyafed to send Kiayasis."

The wolf moved past Celestria and jumped back onto the platform. He looked at Lasidious. "We have had an understanding, though it remains unspoken. I have given you the respect you deserve by coming to you first. In return, I would ask you give me the same. I have invoked the Rule of Fromalla to ensure your secret stays safe. Level with me, and let me in on the reason for this manipulation."

Lasidious chuckled as he stood from the table. "Mosley, of all the gods I like you the most. You're perceptive and relentless. I did ask Boyafed to send Kiayasis. I figured you would choose Shalee to go after the crystal, and you're right, we did leave a clue on Celestria's gown."

Mosley sat back and scratched his neck. "Why would you want to help me?"

"Because, my friend, your team needs to capture this piece of the crystal in order to keep our game going. If Mieonus' team captures this third piece, the Book of Immortality will require me to surrender the Crystal Moon to the Temple of the Gods. Evil will rule for eternity. I am not naïve, Mosley. I know there must be a balance between good and evil. This is how things should be. I want this piece of the crystal to be captured by your team."

Again, Mosley jumped from his platform and began to pace. "Why would you send Kiayasis to provide Shalee an escort? His heart is dark, and he serves Hosseff."

Lasidious looked at Celestria. "Would you care to answer this one?"

Celestria lowered her glass of wine to the table. "We sent Kiayasis because the Order is feared. Kiayasis' presence will ensure Shalee makes it safely to her destination. We all know Luvelles is full of magic stronger than she commands. She is traveling through the Kingdom of Hyperia, and as we all know, this is where much of the darkness on Luvelles resides. Beyond what help we've already given Shalee, your precious sorceress can find her own way home to Grayham, after she captures the crystal. If she stumbles across someone who would harm her, then so be it."

Mosley put his paws on the edge of the table, then rose up. He snatched a piece of rare meat off a plate and swallowed it before responding. "It seems my questions have been answered, but something is still not right. I have not figured out what it is yet, but I am sure the answer will present itself during some other moment. I am sure we will speak again. Thank you." The wolf vanished.

Celestria glared at Lasidious and began to shout a wave of questions. "Do you think Mosley and the Book are putting the pieces of our plan together? Do you think they know we are stalling? Are we losing our advantage? Do they know about our baby?"

The Mischievous One pulled Celestria close and pushed her hair clear of her face. He kissed her with tenderness, then spoke in a soft voice. "If they knew anything, we would be dead. They can suspect all they want. The Book can do nothing unless it has evidence we've broken our laws. Our baby is safe and we're still alive. All we need to do it stay the course. Soon, our baby will be old enough to command his power. Garrin will take control of Gabriel with our help. Then, there will be nothing to worry about. It doesn't matter what they suspect. By the moment they put it all together, it will be too late."

The goddess cupped his face. She kissed him and traced his lips with her tongue. "Your confidence is intoxicating. Perhaps, you should demonstrate more of it."

Lasidious lifted her from the floor. "Perhaps, I will."

Their lips met again, soft at first, then the pressure built as their heartbeats rose. Lasidious pinned his lover against a wall and...well...the rest will be left to the imagination.

A New Day on Luvelles
The Village of Gogswayne

Gage awoke and stretched his furry body. The badger jumped down from his resting spot, then reached up to grab his cane from the top of the bed. Since meeting Gallrum, Gage has had more than one conversation with the serwin about Gogswayne. The badger's body has had the moments necessary to recoup, and he is now strong enough to venture out of Gallrum's home.

Now...fellow soul...allow me to tell you about Gallrum and the master he abandoned. As you know, a serwin is the name of Gallrum's race. But, what you don't know, their race occupies the forest of Shade Hollow. As a child, Gallrum was taken from his village and bonded to the wizard, Balecut. Like many of the occupants of Gogswayne, Gallrum left Balecut and sought refuge to escape abuse.

Despite the goswig's absence, Balecut is still considered one of the most powerful wizards on Luvelles, third only to Brayson and Marcus. Gregory is also more powerful than Balecut, but the White Chancellor chose the path of a warlock and commands a different form of the arts. The absence of Gallrum has kept Balecut from growing stronger.

Unlike every other morning, Gage was alone. Gallrum was nowhere to be found in his quaint little home. Gage took a deep breath and opened the door. He was surprised by what he saw as he leaned against his cane. If he had not known they were underground, he would have sworn the village had been built on the surface. The magic here had to be strong. It appeared as if the village had its own sun. Plants grew, trees blossomed, and a gentle breeze passed through their branches. The earth was wet. It had just rained, and the patchy gray clouds which floated by seemed to move along as any normal cloud would.

Gallrum's home was located at the end of a well-traveled pathway. On either side of the path there were many storefronts. Gage adjusted his robe and began to walk. The structures appeared to be similar to Gallrum's, though many were much larger, and sold most anything he could think of—flowers, furniture, food, elixirs, and many other items.

"You must be Gage," a voice called out.

The badger redirected his attention. A large brown bear was approaching. "I am. You must be Strongbear. Gallrum told me all about you."

"I trust it was all pleasant?"

"Most of it." Gage grinned so the bear would know he was jesting.

"Wonderful." Strongbear tossed an item he had quilted. "I made you a blanket. I make everyone something when they arrive. I was hoping you'd be out and about today. I trust you're feeling better."

"I am."

"Recovering after visiting the ultorian's city can be difficult. Come with me. I'll feed you."

"I don't know that I feel up to moving around that much. Maybe I'll stop here and eat with you tomorrow."

Strongbear lifted Gage from the ground. "I'll just carry you. So, are you with me or against me on this?"

The badger had no idea how to respond. "Ummm...I'm with you, I think."

The chubby bear grabbed his belly with his free paw and chuckled. His belly jiggled as he did. "You're going to make a fine addition to Gogswayne. Let's get you some food. What-da-ya say? Are you with me or against me?"

"Ummm...I thought I stated I was with you."

"Oh yeah, I forgot. So, you're with me, then. How grand." The bear scratched the top of his head as if lost in thought.

Gage could see Strongbear was trying to determine if he remembered the badger saying he was with him. Gage cleared his throat to get the bear's attention. "Since you're carrying me, food does sound delightful. Gallrum told me about your diner. He said you have the finest quaggle a goswig could eat. What is quaggle?"

Strongbear's belly jiggled as he chuckled again. "I wouldn't listen to Gallrum's idea of fine dining. A serwin considers corgan flies an acceptable meal. Quaggle is an assortment of eyeballs which I pluck from fish before I serve them to my patrons. It takes me nearly 2 Peaks to gather enough eyes to fill a single plate. I have never told Gallrum he is the only one I serve this meal. He tells everyone how great my quaggle is. The occupants of Gogswayne just allow him to have this fantasy. I'll feed you something far more pleasant."

Gage smiled. "Something more pleasant sounds wonderful."

Strongbear laughed as he began to trot down the path. "I have lived in our underground village for over 600 seasons, and although I didn't intend to do so, the population has a tendency to look to me for guidance."

"Let me guess...they're all with you," Gage jested, seizing the opportunity to poke fun.

Again, the bear laughed. "That's exactly right. I suppose it's a good position to be in when you want something done. But, for the most part, I simply feed everyone and make blankets and other treasures."

"I don't think I have ever met a sewing bear."

Strongbear lifted a brow and stopped jogging. "I hope you're not judging my delight for crafting."

"No...of course not. I would never do such a thing. I apologize if it sounded that way." Gage thought to himself, *Whew, that was close. I have to watch what I say around this guy.*

"Apology accepted." Strongbear continued to jog down the path. "Don't judge this old bear by the fur that covers him. I have many skills other than sewing. I knit." He stopped in front of his diner, lowered Gage to the ground, then leaned over and whispered, "My other skills aside, I make my own special brew of ale and a wonderful corgan jerky. Are you a drinker?"

"I have been known to toss down a few on occasion." Gage winked. "You show me a full mug, and I'll show you the bottom of it."

Stongbear stood straight and grabbed the bottom of his chin with his paw. "I think I'm going to like you. What-da-ya-say...come on in and grab a bite. Are you with me, or against me?"

Gage shook his head. "Didn't we already determine that?"

Strongbear laughed, "I suppose we did." Again, the bear leaned down, "I'm already on my fifth ale this morning."

"So, that's what that smell is."

Strongbear stood and pointed at Gage. "I'm going to like you."

A Moment of Passion

Kiayasis held Joss at a steady pace. The krape lord's energy and desire to run made the task difficult. Shalee rode behind Kiayasis. As they followed the southern edge of the Mountains of Vesper to its furthest point west of their location, they planned to turn north. The goal was to be following the western shore of Lake Iple within 3 Peaks of Bailem.

"Tell me 'bout your family," Shalee said while holding onto Kiayasis as Joss rushed across the hilly terrain.

"My father is a good man. He's the leader of the Order. My mother, I'm sad to say, has passed."

"How awful. I'm so sorry."

"Don't be. She lived a good life. She was a gentle woman. Everyone loved her. She taught me how to treat a lady and how to be a good man. Her name was Gwen, and I remember her for her beauty."

"Ya make your momma sound like a goddess. I wish I could say the same thing 'bout my motha'. As much as I'd like ta, I can't think of anythin' ta say, other than she was a lil' irritatin'. Don't get me wrong, there were moments when we bonded, but it all seems ta be outweighed by her annoyin' ability ta ruin things. I did love her, though."

Kiayasis twisted just enough to see Shalee's eyes. "Despite your mother's shortcomings, a bit of perfection was born the day you came into the world." He winked, then faced forward.

Shalee was unsure how to respond. Instead of ruining the moment, she squeezed her arms about his waist. Kiayasis put his hand on her forearm and caressed its length with a single, soft stroke. Once done, he commanded Joss into a bouncing run. The beast sprang into the air with his hind legs and used his massive wings to cover a large distance before the weight forced him back to the ground.

As Joss bounced again, Shalee shouted her excitement. "Woo, hoo, hoo, hoo, hoo!"

Mary's Home

Brayson knocked on Mary's door. When she opened it, a bright smile crossed her face. She pulled him inside and threw herself into his arms. Their embrace was passionate. Brayson took the opportunity to steal his first kiss. Neither wanted the moment to end. After several moments, Mary drew back and found his eyes. "You're back. Does this mean Fisgig lives?"

Brayson kissed the top of her forehead. "He does. I left him with The Source. It will be a few days before he has gathered his memories, but my power has returned. You, my lady, were the first one I thought to visit once I could leave the cave."

Mary nestled into his arms. "You make everything sound so romantic. So, where are you taking me?"

"I'm afraid I must go to my office. By chance, has George returned?"

"No. Was he supposed to?"

"Not necessarily."

"Where is he?"

"It would be hard for me to explain. How about we say he's on a magical undertaking. There's nothing to worry about. You're welcome to come with me. I'll see to it you get home once I've completed my work."

"I would love that. Let me freshen up and we'll leave."

After arriving at Brayson's floating office, it wasn't long before Mieonus appeared next to Mary.

"You scared me," Mary squealed as she rushed behind Brayson. "I don't think I'll ever get used to the way people just appear on this world."

Brayson knew who stood in front of him. He knelt on one knee. "Goddess, this is an unexpected surprise." Keeping his eyes lowered, he tugged on Mary's arm to kneel with him. "How may I serve you?"

✦┼•┤┝✦

Now...fellow soul...as your spirited storyteller, I must interject. With all Brayson's knowledge and goodness, he has no idea his god is so wicked. Mieonus has misrepresented herself throughout the seasons and portrays herself as a goddess filled with compassion. The Head Master lives a fool's service. I find it humorous Mieonus has fed Brayson this crock of garesh. But, enough of my babbling. Let's get back to the story.

✦┼•┤┝✦

Mieonus sounded gentle and sweet as she spoke. "Hello Brayson. It's a pleasure to see you. Too long has it been since my eyes looked upon you. You look well. I have come seeking George. Is he still inside your book?"

"He is, Goddess."

Mieonus put her hand on top of Brayson and Mary's heads. She rejuvenated their spirits. "Accept this blessing." As a soothing current rushed through their bodies, she leaned down and whispered, "For the next 10 Peaks, the two of you will feel like children again. I trust you will use this gift to your advantage."

Though he kept his head lowered, Brayson smiled. "Thank you, Goddess. How may I be of service?"

"I would like to speak with George when he returns." Mieonus moved across the room and lowered a crystal to the top of Brayson's desk. "I will leave this with you. Have George use it to summon me when he has completed his task."

"I will, but I don't know when the task will be complete."

Mieonus turned her back to Brayson. A look of disgust appeared on her face, but her voice did not reveal her annoyance. "I understand. Please see to it that he gets the crystal." The goddess forced a pleasant smile, then turned around. "Look upon me, Brayson. Of all my subjects who live in service to me, I am most proud of you." Mieonus vanished.

Brayson assisted Mary to her feet. A look of awe appeared on Mary's face as she spoke. "Was that who I think it was?"

"You know her as Mieonus. She is the one I serve."

"I gathered that from the conversation. Why would a goddess come to see you? And, why would she be looking for George? She said something about a task. And, what did she mean by, 'is he still inside your book?'"

Brayson gathered his thoughts. "The mission George is on is a test to see if he is capable of bonding with Payne. If he's unable to complete this task, he could be lost in the book forever. He could perish."

"Forever! Perish! What about Athena and the baby? If he doesn't come home, she'll be left raising the child on her own. This is not good."

Brayson pulled her close. "I don't expect this will happen. George is a smart man. It's a necessary step for a mage of his caliber to take a goswig. A goswig of Payne's caliber will allow him to grow. George will become a wizard or warlock, depending on the path he chooses."

Brayson moved to his desk and rubbed his hand across the top of the Book of Bonding. "I'm not sure why the goddess would want to speak with him, but this is a conversation at which I intend to be present. It's intriguing to know my new Mystic Learner has a connection to the gods."

Mary shuddered. "I think it's unnerving."

"I'm sure George knows what he's doing. I wouldn't worry. Perhaps, you could help me with some of the organizing I need to do around here. It will help take your mind off George, and give me the chance to teach you some of the Elven language."

Mary smiled. "As long as you promise to say something beautiful to me." She leaned against Brayson. "I promise, the more beautiful their meaning, the more I will allow you to take advantage of the blessing we've been given."

A sinister look appeared on Brayson's face. "I like the sound of that."

Inside the Book of Bonding

George rolled over. His robes were charred and his forearms were burned. Payne lay next to him, face down and motionless. All George could do was watch as his alternate self moved to stand overtop his exhausted body. This being was far more powerful, but how, the mage did not know. The situation was hopeless.

George cried out, "You win! I can't fight any longer. My power has been drained. You're the better man. Just kill me, damn it, and get it over with."

With a cold voice, the duplicate self responded. "You're weak. I would've expected more, much more. You don't deserve to be bonded with such a powerful goswig. Payne has succeeded in beating his adversary, but he was unable to save you. He's close to death, as are you. I didn't wish to hurt him. He had the fighting spirit necessary to earn the right to leave this place. Unfortunately, your weakness has doomed you both.

"It is because of your failure, Payne will perish. I imagine he'll pass on not long after I'm finished with you. Too bad, the fairy-demon would have given you an incredible amount of power."

Tears flowed as George began to beg. "Please, allow me to die without the use of magic. I don't want to be left unrecognizable. Your magic will scar my face. I don't want my wife to see me that way. Please, just give me this request. It's the least you could do."

The duplicate George laughed. "I would not worry about your wife. She will never see your face again. She'll live a life without the satisfaction of saying goodbye."

George began to sob. "You can't do this...please...please!"

"Oh, but I can. It's funny how pathetic you are. You have failed and will die alone as a consequence of your weakness. Accept your fate and die with whatever dignity you can find from such a miserable life."

George couldn't argue. He had used and abused so many people throughout his life who had deserved better. "At least, allow me to die without the use of magic. Please, I beg you…just use my blade. Either way, I'll die, and you'll win."

"An interesting request. It's a good way to die, I suppose. I'm sure I can make it just as painful as the torture I could administer with my magic." The alternate George lifted his hands in the air and turned to look at the horizon. "What better way to die than to release your last breath to a setting sun? Your eyes will capture the glory of such wonderful colors before they close forever."

After a moment of allowing the sun to warm his face, the duplicate George turned to face his victim. A sharp cracking sound filled the evening air. The alternate's right eye exploded as the bullet passed through the tissue and into his brain.

George shouted, "I bet you didn't see that coming, did you, chump?" Watching his enemy fall to the ground, he scrambled to his feet. Blood flowed from the alternate's eye as George moved to stand above him. "You talk too much, moron! Everyone knows that's how you get yourself killed! You took the bait! Just look at you...you're freaking dead!"

The mage leaned over and spit on the duplicate's face. "Looks like some Earth magic just saved my ass. Kind of ironic, now that I think about it."

George moved to Payne and lifted the fairy-demon into his arms. Payne's body hung limp as he looked down. "This is bad...real bad." George closed his eyes, then teleported.

Brayson's Floating Office

George appeared with Payne hanging across his arms. He laid the fairy-demon on the floor. "Master Id, I need your help! He's not breathing!"

Brayson assisted Mary from his lap, then stood from the chair behind his desk. He teleported to the far side of the room, grabbed the vial filled with his special elixir from the bookcase, then teleported next to Payne. "George, open his mouth. I need to get the liquid below his tongue for it to work."

Once the light blue droplet had been administered, Brayson sighed. "There's nothing more that can be done. It's up to the gods whether he lives or dies."

George rubbed his hands across his face in disbelief. "He can't die! He saved my life. If he dies, it's my fault! I let him down!"

Brayson put his hand on George's shoulder. "It's not your fault, son." Mary watched as Brayson helped George to his feet. "We can't always control the outcome of things. Some things are bigger than we are."

"Is that supposed to make me feel better?" George snapped as he pulled away. "What kind of crappy logic is that?"

"It's just the way of things," Brayson responded, remaining calm.

"Garesh! I don't believe a word of that. I should've been there for him."

"You can't save everyone. If he dies...it was meant to be."

"Hell no, it wasn't. I don't believe that. You weren't there. It's my fault and I should've saved him. Your logic sucks. It's a pile of garesh."

Brayson was about to respond, but a faint voice filled the air.

"Yeah...garesh pile...crappy logic," Payne added as he struggled to sit up.

George pushed past Brayson and knelt at Payne's side. "You're alive. I thought you were a goner. That vial must have some vicious healing mojo in it."

The fairy-demon grinned. "Payne hungry."

"Ha! That sounds like the Payne I know. My hell, it really sucked where we were. I never want to go there again."

"Yeah...sucked," Payne affirmed.

Mary began to scold them both. "George, what have I told you about speaking that way? It's foul, and not something I wish my future grandchild to learn. Payne, you won't speak like that either. Do you understand me?"

George had been so caught up in the situation he did not realize Mary was in the room. "I'm sorry, mother. You're right." He turned to face Brayson. "Master Id, I was frightened. I owe you an apology. Thanks for saving him."

Again, Brayson put his hand on George's shoulder, only to pull away. "George, you need a bath. You smell something frightful. We have much to discuss, but first, go home and clean up. We can meet in the morning."

Mary interrupted before George could respond. "Aren't you going to tell him about the goddess' visit?"

Brayson moved close to Mary in an attempt to avoid George's nasty odor. "I will, but I think it can wait until morning. I'm sure we all have many questions, but I'm equally sure a good night's rest will give us the clarity we need for good conversation. We'll meet in the morning." He kissed the top of Mary's forehead. "Perhaps, you could make us some breakfast."

Mary enjoyed the tenderness of Brayson's arms as he put them around her. "I would love to make breakfast."

Before anyone could speak another word, Brayson teleported the group to the clearing in front of their community of homes. There was no more conversation beyond the normal goodbyes. George and Payne went inside, calling for Athena.

Mary took a moment to rub her hand through Brayson's short brown hair and played with the tips of his pointed ears. "You, Mr. Id, are a handsome man. I just love hair on a man's face. You may tickle my neck with it whenever you wish."

After giving Mary a long kiss goodbye, Brayson returned to his office.

The Northern Shore of Lake Floren
South of the Mountains of Vesper

Kiayasis and Shalee stopped for the night. They decided to camp at the base of the mountains. The Peak of Bailem had come and gone. The setting of opposing worlds to the north and south and the sun to the west was not far off.

Shalee's body was sore from riding on Joss' saddle. She fought through the pain and cooked their meal while the dark paladin set up camp.

"You've cooked outside before," Kiayasis said as he set the final pole holding a tarp above the ground where they intended to sleep.

Shalee looked up from a kettle filled with stew. "I did my fair share of campin' when I was younger. Any good Texan knows how ta cook a hot meal ova' a campfire."

Kiayasis tilted his head. "I do not know of this Texan."

Shalee laughed. "It's nothin' ta talk 'bout, really. What do ya say we get some sleep afta' dinna'?"

"Agreed. I could use the rest."

After their meal, Shalee used her bag to lay her head on and fell asleep. Once Kiayasis' eyes shut for the night, Lasidious and Celestria appeared, standing above Shalee. The gods remained invisible to the mortals as they took a knee next to Shalee's head. Celestria spoke. "Her sleep is peaceful. Do you find her beauty intoxicating, my pet?"

Lasidious looked up and found his goddess' eyes. "I only care to drink from the well of *your* beauty, my love. I have eyes for no other."

Celestria smiled. "Shall we begin?"

"By all means. You first."

Celestria lowered her mouth to Shalee's ear, then whispered, "You have affections for Kiayasis. He is strong. He is man. Your loins call to him."

Lasidious clapped his hands, "My turn." The Mischievous One lowered his mouth to Shalee's ear. "You were right, Sam looks at you with disgust. Only Kiayasis can remove this pain. Kiayasis is your destiny. He is the love you've always wanted."

Celestria thumped Lasidious on the head. "That was my line. Move back so I can finish this." Again, the goddess lowered her mouth to Shalee's ear. "You want to abandon your life on Grayham. Sam is a cancer. He wants to control you. You are a strong woman and deserve a man as strong as Kiayasis."

Lasidious stood and extended a hand to Celestria. The goddess took it, then stood and moved to his side. "How clever of us, my sweet. I wonder how many moments will pass before she acts on our suggestions."

Lasidious looked down at Shalee and grinned. "It didn't take long for her anger to manifest after you spoke to her on Grayham. The miscarriage was the perfect series of moments to manipulate her mind. She is susceptible while she sleeps. Her argument with Sam was brilliant. Perhaps, you should have been called the Mischievous One, and not I." The gods vanished.

Mary's Home
The Next Morning

Brayson knocked on Mary's door. She gave him a warm welcome and instructed him to take a seat at the kitchen table. Mary had put on her best dress—one of Brayson's many gifts. It was a yellow gown which hung low across her bosom. Her long hair and smooth skin complemented the ensemble. At 44 seasons, she looked radiant to Brayson's eyes of 730 seasons.

It wasn't long before George walked through the door and killed the mood. "Mother," he shouted from the front door, "what's for breakfast?"

Athena slapped him across the back of his arm. "Don't be rude. You don't have to yell."

"Yes, dear." He grinned. "You know...I think as the baby gets bigger inside your belly, you slap me harder and harder. That one stung."

"Then, start minding your manners."

"Yes, ma'am."

Payne was not far behind, but before they could get to the kitchen, George remembered they were missing someone important. "Athena, where's Kepler?"

She took him outside and pointed at the mound of rocks at the clearing's center. "Go to the other side of the stones. Kepler had a family of swassel gophers dig him a new lair. He's probably sleeping. All he's done since your departure is lie around and sulk. I think he misses you."

George gave Athena a quick kiss and made his way to the stones. He lowered himself into the large hole and used his power to clear the darkness. Sure enough, Kepler was lying with his head resting on his paws.

"Kep, wake up. I'm home."

As soon as the demon-jaguar heard George's voice, his spirit was lifted. Despite his excitement, Kepler downplayed his emotions. He stood, taking his own sweet moments and stretched his powerful body, then turned toward his friend. "I've been bored. Please, tell me we're going somewhere."

George moved toward the cat. He reached up to hug the demon's neck. As always, Kepler squirmed while inside the mage's embrace. "Must you do this? I keep telling you it's not natural for a cat of my stature to be close to a human. Perhaps, we should set boundaries."

George took a step back. "Not a chance. You'll just have to get use to it. Besides, I love ya, buddy." He reached up, grabbed hold of Kepler's massive cheeks, then shook them.

Kepler cringed. "Love is a strong word, don't you think?"

George smiled and changed the subject. "I bet you're dying to know what I've been up to."

"Not really."

"You just have to be coy, don't you? Anyway, I'm not sure what's going on, but Brayson said there is a god looking for me. You know what that means, something is about to happen. I bet Lasidious has something for us to do, though I don't know why he would approach Brayson about it."

"Perhaps, it's not Lasidious."

"I suppose we'll find out. Mary is making breakfast. Brayson is here and intends to speak with me about it. I'll come back and get you once I know more. It's good to see you."

Kepler growled. "You're not leaving me. If someone is making breakfast, I'd better be invited."

After breakfast, George took the crystal Mieonus left behind and met Brayson inside his floating office. Payne and Kepler tagged along. Brayson was the first to speak once everyone appeared. "George, use the crystal to summon the goddess."

The mage did as instructed. It wasn't long before Mieonus appeared. George recognized her as soon as he saw her. "I know your face."

"Yes, we've met. I see you're adjusting to life on Luvelles. I trust bonding with your goswig wasn't too difficult."

"I wish that was the case. We were almost eaten by a bunch of pissed-off plants. Then..."

Payne piped in. "Payne save Master!"

The goddess took a good look at Payne. She had no idea the fairy-demon existed. "And, what are you?"

Payne was about to answer, but George stopped him. "Don't get him started. Once he gets going, you'll regret it. Tell me what you want."

Brayson could not believe how direct George was with the goddess, but he stayed quiet as Mieonus took a seat behind his desk. She lifted her feet on top of it, then adjusted her gown. She acted as if she were one of them.

Brayson was shocked at how his Mystic Learner acted as if he was the goddess' equal—as if a friendship existed, or worse, as if George didn't care she was a deity. Never, would he have spoken to his goddess this way. Nevertheless, she seemed pleased to be speaking with George.

Mieonus looked through the Book of Bonding's pages while resting it on her curvy legs. "I wish to speak with George alone." She looked up from the book and found Brayson's eyes. "May we use your office? This conversation is to be between the two of us."

The Head Master wanted to object, but he could not fathom going against the wishes of the one he served. "By all means. I will leave." He vanished.

Mieonus waved her hands. Kepler and Payne also vanished, only to reappear outside the school of magic. Kepler let out an angry roar. "Garesh! This is no way to treat a Master of the Hunt. How can I help George dominate the territories of this world if I'm being left out? This is starting to piss me off."

"Kitty sound like Master. It okay, kitty." Payne hovered in front of Kepler. "Payne talk to kitty."

"Great! That's all I need. Just teleport us home, you little freak."

Back inside Brayson's office, Mieonus continued. "A piece of the Crystal Moon has been placed on Luvelles. I would like you to go after it, since you have the first two pieces. If you capture this piece, Lasidious will return the rest of the Crystal Moon to the Temple of the Gods on Grayham and everything will return to normal."

George began to laugh. "You can't be serious. What makes you think I care? Maybe you should talk to Lasidious. After all, he was the one who took the Crystal Moon from the Temple of the Gods in the first place. This isn't my problem...it's yours. I'm just a guy trying to learn the ways of magic."

Mieonus didn't like his response. She could see George was closed to the idea, at least for the moment. She decided to take another approach. "George, my dear, dear friend."

"Friend? Who in the hell are you calling a friend? Try using a different word."

Mieonus smiled, then removed the Book of Bonding from her lap. She stood and moved to the opposite side of the desk. After leaning against its surface, she responded. "George, my little mortal acquaintance. I think we both know you're the best man for the job. I would pay you well for your service. I only ask you to think about it. There's no one else who understands Shalee the way you do."

"Shalee is seeking the crystal? And, what about Sam?"

"She is, but Sam is on Grayham."

"Well, now! This changes things. I have a debt I would like to settle with her. She tried to kill me on Scorpion Island. If I had not been drained of my power, I would have settled the debt then. I have not forgotten how she sent her magic flying in my direction. I could have been killed if not for my ability to deflect it. I will think about your request. This may be something I want to do after all, but I don't work for free."

Mieonus' brows tightened. "Since when did you become so bold? How dare you speak to a god this way!"

George allowed a smug grin to cross his face. "I know there's nothing you can do about it. You may have your servants fooled...but, as for me, I couldn't care less about your status on Ancients Sovereign. I know you are bound by the laws within the Book of Immortality's pages. You'll need to pay me, and pay me well, or I won't go after the crystal."

Mieonus stood. "We shall see how confident you are when someone who serves me is breathing down your neck for the way you've spoken to me. Perhaps, then, you'll learn humility and beg for forgiveness once you've suffered blood loss." She tossed him another one of her crystals. "If you choose to perform the task, summon me with that. Think about it, George, accepting my proposal is the only way to save your life."

George sneered, then tossed the crystal back to the goddess. "You threaten me, then expect me to go after your damn crystal? Are you freaking nuts? Get the hell out of my face."

Mieonus sighed, then took George's hand and placed the crystal in it. With her finger pressed against George's chest, she backed the mage against one of the windows in Brayson's office. Her eyes were cold as she responded. "There's no threat implied, George. There is only a promise. If you don't rethink your choice, death will be delivered by those who command greater power than you. I don't need to touch you to abide by the rules in the Book. I have others who can do it for me. All it takes is a little promise and a simple suggestion. You're not a stupid man. You know I have the high ground. Don't allow your faith in Lasidious to give you unjustified confidence. It will get you killed. Summon me when you've made your final decision."

The goddess leaned in and kissed George's cheek. "The choice is simple. Your death, or retrieve the third piece of the Crystal Moon. Either way, I win. I always win. Make no mistake about that." Mieonus vanished.

George walked across the room and lowered into Brayson's chair. He began to think as he wiped the sweat from his brow. *Damn! That freaking sucked and didn't go how I imagined it would. I've got to be smarter than this. I need to get on her good side before she has me strung up. Damn it, George! Why did you have to go and be such an idiot? I mean, how stupid could you get?*

George's Home
Later that Night

George snuggled Athena while he lay sleeping. His dreams were of his Abbie. In this dream, Athena had already had the baby and Abbie was sitting on the porch of the home provided by Brayson. She was older now, maybe seven seasons, and holding her brother in her arms. Abbie's smile was gleaming, and her joy was evident.

But, as the Mischievous One had a tendency to do, Lasidious ruined a good dream and requested to be allowed inside. George opened his mind, and the god's projected image appeared next to Abbie on the porch. He removed the baby from her arms and began stroking the infant's face. Lasidious looked up and found George's dreaming eye. "You know this is not real, George. If we work together, we can make this dream a reality. It has been too long since our last conversation, old friend. It has been 140 Peaks since the last moment I visited in this manner."

From within his home on Ancients Sovereign, Lasidious watched the image of George as it flickered within the green flames of his fireplace. George rolled away from Athena into a more comfortable position. Lasidious reached into the fire and carried the vision of his pet creation to the table at the center of the room. After setting George's image on its surface, the god lowered to his chair, put his feet on the table, then spoke as he held his hand above the flame. "Did you miss me?"

As the dream continued, George responded. "Where in the hell have you been?" The vision of Abbie and the baby faded. It was replaced by Lasidious' face. "I thought you forgot about me."

"I'm sure you didn't feel too put out. You've been doing just fine without me. I see you've bonded with Payne. You're welcome, by the way."

"Then, I was right. It *was* you who sent Payne. I figured as much. I could only assume you were the one he called Friend."

"I am. Payne is strong, though he doesn't realize it. He has the potential to be the most powerful goswig a man could have. Even I don't know his full potential. He could become a dominant force while serving you. His mind is young. You can mold him into what you need him to be. Be good to him and he'll be loyal. Treat him with kindness and he'll never turn on you.

"You need to remember, if your goswig was to perish, your power would diminish. Listen carefully to what I'm saying. The death of a goswig weakens the power of its master, just as your power would weaken if Payne was to perish."

"Yeah, yeah, yeah, I get it. Your little hint is not so subtle. I'll remember that when the moment comes."

"As always, George, you don't disappoint. Now that you're bonded with Payne, you can draw from his power. You can do things you couldn't do before. Take the moments necessary to experiment. Learn how to channel his energy. Become one with Payne and use his energy to amplify your power as it flows through you."

George began to laugh.

"What's so funny?"

"Oh, nothing. You just sound like an old television show I used to watch on Earth. I feel like you should be calling me Grasshopper."

Lasidious had no idea what George was talking about. The god changed the subject. "I have something I need to tell you. It's about the piece of crystal hidden on Luvelles."

"Yes, I know. Mieonus wants me to go after it. She threatened to have me killed if I don't. She said she would have someone come after me."

Lasidious took a moment to ponder. "This is going to be tricky. We have plans to make. We need to make sure we do everything just right."

Mary's Home
The Next Morning

George walked through the door of his mother-in-law's home without knocking. "Mother, is Brayson here?" he shouted. "He's not at his office or his home."

There was no response. George headed up the stairs. "Mom, are you in there?" he said, speaking through Mary's bedroom door.

The door opened just enough for Brayson to slide through. He wore nothing but his undergarments. "What do you need, George? We're busy."

The mage grinned. "So, what are you doing in there?"

Brayson frowned. "That's none of your business."

George's grin widened. "That's okay, you don't need to tell me. I can fill in the details." He leaned close, tapped his temple with his finger, then whispered, "I can create pictures in my mind."

The seriousness of Brayson's frown magnified. "You forget with whom you speak."

"C'mon, man, where's the fun in being all serious? A master who doesn't play, is a master who's bored all day. Anyway, we need to talk. It's pretty important."

"What could be so important? And, why now?"

"Trust me. I wouldn't B.S. you. It can't wait. We need to have this conversation. I'll be out front."

Brayson sighed. "You do realize your moment of intrusion is terrible?"

"I feel you. But, I swear, I wouldn't bother you if it wasn't important."

Brayson turned to leave and started to push open the door. "Just give me a moment or two, then I'll come find you."

George winked, then patted Brayson on the shoulder. "Go get 'er, stud. I'll see you out front." The mage turned and bounded down the stairs.

Brayson whispered to himself as he shut the door behind him, "I'm sorry for the intrusion, Master. Oh, no, no, no, don't worry about it, George, I like my moments of passion being stolen. Anything for my new Mystic Learner, anything at all." The Head Master paused. "I wonder what B.S. means?"

George waited on the front steps. It wasn't long before Brayson appeared, seated beside him. "What could possibly be so important?"

"Master, Mieonus has given me an assignment."

"What? You said nothing of an assignment after your meeting with her."

George nodded. "I know. She appeared to me again last night. She has requested I undertake a task."

"A task? What task? When must you leave, and why?"

"I need to leave soon, but we have a problem. The task requires that I stand before The Source."

Brayson's eyes widened. "The Source? You're not ready to look into the Eye."

George shrugged, then threw up his hands. "Hell, I'm freaking out about it, too." The mage stood and walked down the remaining steps. He reached down and grabbed a blade of grass. "Look...I know this is unusual. But, for whatever reason, I have been led to Luvelles by the gods. They seem to have a plan for me."

Brayson pushed his right hand through his hair, then scratched the top of his head. "I have never had a Mystic Learner with such powerful friends. I don't know what to say."

George picked up a pebble, then drop-kicked it across the clearing. "I was told Amar was the vessel for our meeting. Mieonus said she sent him to speak with you."

"Really? I have often wondered why Amar would take an interest in the development of another's power. To do so is against his character. Having this knowledge explains his interest in you. But, why would the goddess use Amar as her vessel? He serves Lasidious."

George had to think fast. "Mieonus convinced Amar to abandon his service to Lasidious. Beyond that, you will need to speak with Amar to understand his reasons." George reclaimed his seat next to Brayson. "Regardless of Amar's reason, I still need to speak with The Source. The goddess told me there is war on the horizon."

"War? Everything on Luvelles is peaceful."

"Apparently, it's not as peaceful as you think."

Brayson had to think before responding. "Will Marcus have anything to do with this war? Is he planning something?"

George shrugged. "All I know...Mieonus said there is a deeper reason why this war will begin...a reason unseen by the eyes of mortals. When I asked her what the hell she meant, she told me the answer will be revealed when the proper moment arrives."

Brayson scowled. "Hmmm...a vague response."

"I agree, but what would you have me do? I couldn't force the answer out of her. Who am I to argue with a goddess?"

"Your point is valid."

"I know, right? Besides, it's what she said next that concerns me most. She said you won't be strong enough to survive the war. You're going to need my help. Mieonus wants me to look into the Eye to acquire the power necessary to stand by your side. She has forseen the war extending to your doorstep."

Brayson rubbed the back of his neck. "The Head Masters of the past have never chosen a side in war. We have always remained neutral...a voice of reason."

George rolled his eyes, but was careful not to let Brayson see. "Well, it looks like Mieonus knows something you don't. I don't know what to tell you, but I need to look into the Eye, so I can help you."

"But, you're not ready. The Eye will swallow your soul."

"I understand your concern, but the goddess thinks I am. You just don't realize it. Mieonus has prepared me for this day."

"George, if you only knew what happens when you meet with The Source. The Ancient One must allow you to look into the Eye. If he does, and the

Eye finds you unworthy, your soul could be lost forever. Mary would have my hide for letting you do something so foolish. You're not ready."

George patted Brayson on the shoulder. "I know all about the Eye. How many of your past Mystic Learners have gods as friends?"

Brayson stood and moved into the clearing beyond the porch. He crossed his arms in thought and looked toward the horizon. "I suppose I see your point. Mieonus is all-knowing. Who better to understand your ability? Perhaps, I worry over nothing."

"There you go. You have your answer. That's how you know I'm ready. You have nothing to worry about."

Brayson turned and found George's eyes. "This doesn't seem right. Why would the goddess wish to send a young boy of only 23 seasons to risk so much? Is there no other on Luvelles capable of this task?"

"Master...do you doubt your goddess?"

"No. I believe she is wise and knows what's best. But, this isn't something I would do without giving you proper training. Look at what happened when you bonded with Payne. You nearly perished. If you look into the Eye, you could very well finish what the bonding process was unable to. You would be sacrificing your life for nothing."

George shrugged. "I appreciate your concern, but how do we tell the goddess no? How many men could have lived through the bonding process with Payne in the first place? It was an impossible situation, but somehow, I pulled it off."

Again, Brayson rubbed his hands through his hair. His eyes seemed to carry the weight of Luvelles within them. "The way to The Source is filled with peril. You must go through the trials. I cannot allow you to pass by them. The Source won't speak with you unless you have passed the tests."

"Master, Mieonus knows something we don't. I have faith in my abilities. I don't doubt. With Payne and Kepler at my side, I'll pass the trials."

Brayson's smile was uneasy as he sat down to put his arm around his Mystic Learner. "I want you to remember something. I would never say this to anyone, but considering the circumstances, I will give you a hint. Don't forget...it is your belief in yourself that saves you. Belief is the key."

"I won't forget, Master. I'll make you proud, I promise."

"If there is a war coming, then I shall need you at my side. I'll just have to put my faith in the goddess' hands."

Brayson patted George on the back, then stood. "I need a few days to prepare the trials for your journey. I'll meet you in my office at the Peak of Bailem, 3 Peaks from now. You may want to gather the things you need. I cannot tell you what to take, so choose wisely."

"Thank you. I'll be there." George watched as Brayson walked back inside Mary's home. Once the door shut, a shallow grin appeared on George's face. "What a sucker."

An unexpected voice responded. "What's a sucker?" Athena inquired as she walked up and took a seat.

George put on an innocent face, stood, then pulled Athena into his arms. "A sucker is a good thing. It's just an Earth expression. How about we spend some quality moments together."

Athena put her head on George's chest, her favorite spot to be, "You're so adorable."

George put his chin on top of Athena's head and squeezed. He felt guilty for the lie. He was compromising his vows and hated himself for it. He thought, *Damn it, George. What's wrong with you? You need to keep your love sacred. You need to do better than this. Lying to Athena isn't acceptable. She deserves better from you. Find a way to be better. Don't mess this up.*

George lowered to her belly, then kissed it. "How's my little guy doing in there?" He looked up. "What do you say we have a picnic?"

"What a lovely idea," Athena giggled.

2 Peaks of Bailem have Passed
The Western Shoreline of Lake Iple

Since just before Early Bailem, Kiayasis and Shalee have been following the western bank of Lake Iple. Joss has been an effective means of transportation and the moment has come for them to set up camp for the night.

Now...fellow soul...let me bring you up to speed. The past few days have been enjoyable. Shalee has pushed her problems with the king of Southern Grayham to the back of her mind. Kiayasis' company has proven to be a wonderful diversion, providing the queen with a much needed distraction.

Shalee is feeling beautiful again. Her long blonde hair has been pinned up and she has used her magic to transform one of the dresses in her bag into a fitted pair of pants. The idea of using the dress' material to create such an item seemed unfashionable, but after putting on the finished garment, the queen was surprised at how great the pants looked. She could now straddle the krape lord's saddle without fear of being exposed.

The krape lord lowered its massive form to the ground to give the assistance necessary for Shalee to dismount. Kiayasis reached up as she slid from the top of Joss' saddle. The dark paladin caught the sorceress by the waist, then set her on the grass beyond the lake's shore.

Kiayasis emptied the krape lord's pouch. Once the leather saddle was removed, the beast spread its wings, then took flight toward the lake.

"Where is he goin'?" Shalee questioned as she marveled at Joss' graceful movements. "That's so incredible. When he flies, he looks like a dragon."

"He needs to feed. He'll be back by morning." Kiayasis took a seat and began to remove the hair from his armor which had attached itself while inside the krape lord's pouch.

Shalee moved next to the fire and held her hands near the flame to warm them. She watched Joss dive toward the water, then roll into a gliding position only feet above the lake's surface. "I neva' saw that in Texas. So, what does he eat?"

"I'm sure he'll find a large animal of some kind, or maybe a corgan from a farmer's field."

Shalee didn't respond. Instead, she enjoyed the setting sun as it cast an orange glow across the lake's surface. It was peaceful. She turned toward the west to allow what was left of the setting sun to warm her face before it disappeared below the horizon. The mood was magical.

The queen took a deep breath. With her eyes closed, she finally responded, "So, Joss eats meat. I don't know why I would've neva' guessed that. Maybe it's because, afta' bein' with him ova' the last few days, he just seems so gentle and sweet. I guess I assumed he ate somethin' else, since ya treat him like a pet."

Kiayasis chuckled. "Don't let your assumption mislead you. Joss is a killer. It's in his blood. But, don't worry...he's been trained not to attack unless given the order. He left the other night while you slept. You just didn't see him go."

"How do the farmers feel about him eatin' their livestock?"

"They don't say anything. The laws of Hyperia allow krape lords to feed whenever they want. The farmers are paid by my father, but I imagine it's not as much as they would be compensated on Merchant Island."

Shalee sat next to the fire and looked through the flames. As Kiayasis polished his armor, the light reflected off its metallic surface and flickered across his face. She took note of his long dark hair. Perfection. She desired him. And, in this man's eyes—she wasn't looked upon as a failure. Kiayasis knew nothing of her inability to carry her pregnancy to term. She could be herself, and he was enjoying her company. "Is there someone special in your life?"

Kiayasis looked up. "What? A woman shouldn't ask this question of a man."

Shalee looked away, embarrassed, and stared into the fire. "I'm sorry. I didn't mean ta offend ya. I was only tryin' ta get ta know ya betta'."

The dark paladin studied her reaction. "Perhaps, I overreacted. You are a queen, and special liberties should be extended because of your crown. I will answer your question."

Shalee felt stupid. "Please, if it's improper ta speak, maybe ya shouldn't talk 'bout it."

Kiayasis smiled, then lowered his breastplate to his side. "This is a question the men of our world initiate. Elven men do this in a subtle manner, and only if the male is interested in the female. However uncustomary, I shall answer your question. I would like you to know me."

Retrieving his bracers, Kiayasis continued polishing. "There is no one special in my life. I have dedicated my seasons to attaining my position of service within my father's army. I have only just attained the goal I set 20 seasons ago. I have longed to be with a woman, but I haven't had the moments to get to know one. I suppose I'm ready for something when the day comes that I should meet the right one." Kiayasis looked up and found the queen's eyes through the flames. "What about you? Is your king a great man?"

Shalee's mood changed. She withdrew within herself. Seeing her reaction, Kiayasis lowered his bracers to the ground and moved to take a seat beside her. He took her hands and placed them between his. "I didn't mean to upset you. Clearly, there's something wrong. You may have my ear if you need it."

The queen looked at the paladin's hands. They were strong, yet they held her own with tenderness. She looked up with tears in her eyes. "The king blames me for the loss of our child. He feels like I'm a disease. I don't think I can eva' go back ta Grayham. I should abandon my life there. I cannot live with a man who thinks I'm a failure and wants to control me. A controlling man is cancerous."

"Your king said these things?"

"Yes. It's in his every expression. I can hear it in his voice. He hates me. He loathes me."

Kiayasis pulled her next to him. His voice was soft, and his eyes carried a tenderness Shalee longed for. "I cannot imagine a woman with your beauty being a failure. Your grace alone should bring joy to the heart of your king. *Tula sinome, lle naa vanima, cormamin lindua ele lle.*"

"That sounded wonderful. What did ya say?"

Kiayasis made sure he held Shalee's gaze. "I said...you're beautiful and my heart would sing to be with a woman like you. Well...that's a rough translation anyway."

Shalee melted and allowed Kiayasis to nestle her in his arms. He held her close as she continued to weep. He did not let her go until the last tear fell.

When morning arrived, Joss landed and Kiayasis reloaded the krape lord's pouch. "Shall we get going? It will take us more than 4 Peaks to get to Bestep. There's something I must do before we head north to the swamplands. We will circle north of the Petrified Forest, then follow the coast to the northwest. Bestep is a less-than-desirable village. I will tell you about it along the way."

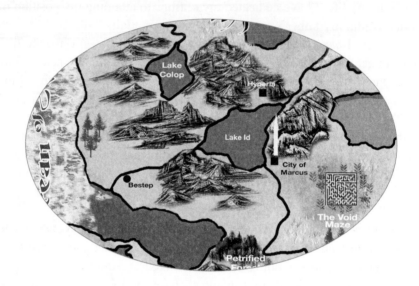

Shalee smiled as Kiayasis assisted her onto the krape lord's saddle. "Mornin', Joss," she said as she settled down on the padded surface. "I hope ya enjoyed your meal."

Joss' response was unexpected. He grunted as he released a pungent fart which vibrated the saddle. Gagging, the queen pinched her nose and yelled, "For heaven's sake! And, ta think I thought ya were growin' on me!"

Kiayasis could only laugh as he climbed up and took his seat. He grabbed hold of the beast's reins and commanded the krape lord into a powerful run across the lake's shoreline. With each extension of Joss' mighty legs, a wake of sand was thrown into the air.

The Dungeon of the Dark Order

As the sun reached the Peak of Bailem, the city of Marcus remained beneath a cloud covered sky. Despite the day being pleasant throughout the rest of Luvelles, the dungeon of the Order remained cold, damp, dark and miserable.

Four Paladins of Light wait in agony for the leader of the Order to arrive. They have been hanging by their arms since Early Bailem and have been beaten. Their flesh has been torn apart from being whipped, each receiving over twenty lashes. Once word spread there were spies within the Order's ranks, it didn't take long for Boyafed's commander to single out Lord Dowd's men.

When the leader of the Order made his descent down the dungeon steps, he commanded his men to leave. He stood in front of his enemies. They were weak and fading in and out of consciousness. Boyafed moved to the far side of the cell, then revived each one with a cold bucket of water. Once they were aware of his presence, he spoke. "I wish to know why you've come."

Seeing there would be no answer, Boyafed decided to start with the basics. "We are all military men. There's no harm in sharing our names. I am Boyafed...leader of the Order. Who among you is your superior?"

Spitting blood to the stones of the cold floor, a fit elf, with short blonde hair, lifted his head. Blood dripped from the end of his toes as he struggled to gather the air he needed to speak. "I am. I am called Tolas. There is nothing to be said. We will not answer your questions. We have been ordered to surrender our lives if need be. We're prepared to die for our gods. We're also prepared to die for Lord Dowd."

Boyafed admired Tolas' strength. He knew the elf would give his life to serve both his gods and his lord. He could only hope the others were not as strong. He moved to stand in front of another of his enemies. He reached up and grabbed the chin of an elf whose body was shaking. "Tolas is strong. He is a fine leader, to be sure. What's your name, boy?"

"I'm not a boy. You waste your breath." The elf pulled himself up against the chains to capture another breath. His muscles rippled as he did. "My name is Kollis. I will tell you nothing."

The Order leader pulled his bone-handled dagger from its sheath. He put the point of the blade against Kollis' chest. He could see the fear in the elf's brown eyes as he touched him with the blade's tip. "Your fear tells another tale."

Boyafed began to carve the symbol of the Order into Kollis' skin. The white paladin screamed. Tolas' men shouted for Boyafed to stop, but Tolas remained silent. Seeing Tolas' courage, Boyafed retracted his blade and smiled as blood flowed down Kollis' abdomen.

The dark paladin moved to stand in front of Tolas, then tapped the flat of his blade against the white paladin's chest. "If you won't allow your men to give me the answers I seek, then it appears I have no choice but to send them home with a reminder of their moments spent with me.

I'm sure Lord Dowd will be happy to welcome them with the symbol of Hosseff carved into their chests."

The elf hanging at the far end of the line spoke out. "We were sent to discover your plans to attack Inspiration. We..."

Tolas screamed, "Say nothing further! Respect your gods. Respect our lord." The white paladin superior turned to reclaim Boyafed's eyes. "You waste your moments. They will say nothing further."

Boyafed held Tolas' gaze, then smiled as he tapped the flat of his blade against Tolas' chest once again. "There's always a man who will speak. Perhaps, I should demonstrate my point."

As Boyafed walked to the end of the line, Tolas shouted, "Grolan, do not dishonor our lord further! Be strong!"

Grolan's red hair hung in front of his pale, freckled face as Boyafed stopped in front of him. The Order leader could smell his fear as he poked the tip of his blade into Grolan's chest. Grolan begged, "Please...I beg you. I don't wish to be scarred with your god's symbol. I don't wish to dishonor the gods I serve."

Tolas shouted. "Grolan, be quiet! You have already dishonored yourself! You have dishonored Lord Dowd, and you have dishonored our gods! Say nothing further, or I'll kill you myself!"

Boyafed chuckled. "Don't fret, Grolan. I'm going to let you live. I would not want your god's symbol carved into my skin either. Tell me everything you know, and I will let you go."

Tolas shouted again, commanding Grolan's silence, but Grolan didn't listen. His voice quaked as he spoke. "We have been sent for no other reason than what I have given. I swear. We were only sent to see if there were plans to attack Inspiration."

Boyafed stepped back and shook his head. "I believe you, Grolan. But, the task you described is a job for one man, not four."

Again, Tolas shouted and warned Grolan to say nothing, but the white paladin's terror superceded the order. Grolan pissed himself.

Watching the yellow liquid run down Grolan's right leg, Boyafed cupped his hands together, then lifted them in front of his mouth. "And, I thought today was going to be uneventful." The Order leader looked at Tolas. "I would wager this is Grolan's first assignment. He has never faced danger. I would wager further that, prior to this day, he has fought only his counterparts in training. His weakness provides for good entertainment. It is too bad I must break his spirit."

Grolan shouted at the top of his lungs, "I swear! I swear to the gods I serve! There is no other reason we're here!"

Tolas lowered his head. He knew Boyafed would not allow his men to leave without being punished. "Grolan is a boy, Lord Methelborn. He dishonors even you with his words. As for the rest of my men, they will say nothing."

Boyafed moved to Grolan and lifted his chin. His dark eyes burned through the paladin's soul. "You disgust me. There is no honor in betraying your lord. Dowd would kill you if he were here. But, I have other plans for you. I'll send you home with a reminder of your failure. I'm sure Dowd will deal with you. Why he would send someone so weak is beyond my imagination. If I were Tolas...you wouldn't leave this dungeon alive."

Boyafed carved the Order's symbol into Grolan's chest. He repeated the process on the others until he came to Tolas. He wiped the blood from his dagger across the hair on Tolas' chest, then sheathed the blade. He lowered the white paladin to the ground, then removed his bonds.

Boyafed extended his arm and pulled Tolas to his feet. "You're the only one worth respecting. You held to your oath and didn't waver. You spoke with courage. I respect this. Take your men and leave. Tell Lord Dowd that fighting one another would be a senseless loss of life. He should stay on his side of the Ebarna Strait, and keep his men away from the Order's ranks. If I find more of his spies, they won't be so fortunate as to arrive home in one piece."

Boyafed thought a moment, then handed his dagger to Tolas. "You have business which requires your attention. Leave the blade with the guards on your way out."

Tolas lowered his eyes to show respect. "Thank you. Lord Dowd will receive your message."

As the Order leader ascended the dungeon stairs, all that could be heard was Grolan's screams. Boyafed stopped at the top of the stairs. "Ah, the beautiful sound of death."

Three Little Words

Ancients Sovereign
The Hall of Judgment

The gods gathered and those able to sit around the large marble table, within Gabriel's hall, took a seat.

The Mischievous One stood and cleared his throat. "I've called you here to announce the location of the third piece of crystal. Each team has made a choice as to who will be seeking this piece. Mieonus' team has chosen George, and Mosley's, as we all know, has chosen Shalee."

Lasidious tossed two pieces of parchment on the table. "The crystal is hidden within these three words."

"Another riddle," Mieonus sneered as she stood, then reached across the table to snatch one. "This is ridiculous. Your last perplexity was practically impossible to understand." The Goddess of Hate unfolded the parchment. A look of disgust appeared on her face as she tossed it to the table in front of her. "How can a riddle be solved with only three words?"

Lasidious grinned. "There are only two possible answers. Both quests are filled with danger. The rules are simple. You will give the riddle to your choices. If anything is said to assist them in any way, I will destroy the Crystal Moon, and the worlds will follow. It is up to George and Shalee to determine which way they go."

Mosley jumped onto the table and read the words aloud. "A soul swallowed." The wolf looked up and found Lasidious' eyes. "Interesting. It seems simple enough. I'm sure Shalee will enjoy the challenge." He vanished.

Mieonus stomped her heel. "This is simply aggravating. I don't think the wolf knows anything. How could he? How could anyone understand what this means? How do you expect George to find something so small with a clue as useless as this?"

Keylom's hooves clapped against the polished floor as he moved to a position to see the words for himself. The centaur looked at Lasidious. "As always, your wit has provided entertainment."

"Oh, shut up," Mieonus barked. "He's toying with us again."

Ignoring Mieonus' comment, Lasidious took Celestria's hand. "Good luck." Both gods vanished.

Mieonus rolled her eyes. "He does this to appease his sick mind."

Hosseff stood and pulled his hood up. As the hood cast its shadow across his face, his features faded to nothingness. His wispy voice filled the room. "Just give the parchment to George, Mieonus. Stop complaining. I'm sure the others feel the same. I have better things to do than listen to your constant protests." Hosseff vanished and the others followed suit.

Mieonus and the Book were all that were left. "Gabriel, I think..."

"I don't care, Mieonus. I don't care." The Book disappeared.

The goddess stomped the lifted heel of her right shoe on the floor. "I hate when they do that!"

The Head Master's Island
George and Athena's Home

Mieonus appeared inside the kitchen of George and Athena's home. "George, we need to talk."

Athena was startled by her appearance. She moved behind George as he turned to face the goddess.

"Ever hear of knocking?" George snapped. "You should try it during one of your less rude moments."

Mieonus' eyes were cold as she responded. "Careful how you speak to me, George. I'm in no mood to deal with your sarcasm."

"My sarcasm? Who gives a garesh what you're in the mood for? I will act how I want to act in my home. Maybe you should leave, or better yet, go commission your friends to hunt me down. I have a little surprise for them, so bring it on."

Mieonus could not believe George's confidence. He was unshaken. She could have sworn she had left him with a sense of desperation when they last spoke.

The goddess was about to confront the mage when Athena tugged on the sleeve of his new royal-purple tunic. "George, where are your manners? I'm sorry for my husband's tone. I'm sure if you had knocked, this conversation would..."

Mieonus waved her hand and Athena's voice was silenced. "I'm in no mood to listen to you babble. I should destroy you both for your husband's arrogance."

"As if you could," George rebuffed. "I know something you don't. Spare me your threats, and get to the point of why you've come. I assume you have knowledge of the crystal's whereabouts and wish me to go after it. I have decided to go, but it has nothing to do with what you want. I hope you send your goons after me. I will use it to my advantage and ensure I steal their power from them. You have no idea how much power I can command. Give me the damn information, and take a hike?"

Mieonus wanted to destroy George, but instead, she remained calm. "It appears Lasidious has taught you something more than I'm aware of. No matter. I will find another way to torture you." She flipped the parchment at him. "Use this to help you find the crystal. I hope the journey kills you."

Athena was gripping George's arm. She knew he could feel her distress, but she also knew his personality wasn't about to back down. She was frightened, and Mieonus' power was not allowing her to express her feelings. Tears began to run down her cheeks as she waited for George's response.

After a moment of staring at the words on the parchment, George looked up and smiled. "This seems to fit what I've learned. Master Id is a better teacher than I thought. He said the Eye of Magic can swallow a man's soul if he isn't ready to take on the responsibility of handling great power. It seems your note couldn't have come at a better moment. I will go through the trials and speak with The Source. With a little luck, I'll pass the test. Maybe then, the crystal's location will be revealed."

Mieonus was stunned. "You got all that out of three words? How convenient it is that you find yourself in the position to be Brayson's new Mystic Learner. It appears we have an advantage. I can only assume your desire for power will strengthen your desire to go after the crystal for me?"

George could see the fear in Athena's eyes. He had to let Mieonus know he would go for the crystal, and find a way to make his wife feel better at the same moment. "I will go after your crystal, but I will do it only after you make the Promise of Sovereign. You will leave everyone I love alone. You must promise you won't send anyone to hurt them, or me, for that matter. You and I need to call a truce and start this relationship over. I'll give you the respect you deserve only after you make this promise."

"Lasidious has taught you well. I have one condition before I will agree to your terms."

Mieonus put her hand on George's shoulder, then pushed him aside. She looked Athena in the eye. "Your family will prostrate before me, George, whenever I appear. If they do this, I will enter the Promise of Sovereign and abide by your terms. Do we have a deal?"

George moved to stand between Mieonus and Athena. He made sure he had the goddess' attention. "I bet it took you all season to find a use for the word prostrate. I cannot tell you how strong my desire is to bash your head in. Athena will show reverence to no one, nor will her family. Either I bow alone or you can find someone else to go after the crystal." The mage tilted his head and gave a half-cocked smile. "Do we have a deal?"

Mieonus smiled. Again, she pushed George aside, then lifted Athena's head after placing her hand under her chin. She wiped the tears from her cheeks. "You should be proud to have a husband who will bow to a god he hates just to protect his wife. He has saved your family from a horrible death. It seems I won't have to come back to watch your family perish after all. Pity...I would've enjoyed that."

The deity wiped another tear from Athena's face. "It would have been fun to watch as the skin from your baby's body was peeled away."

George started to object, but Mieonus silenced him with a glance. After enjoying the irritation on the mage's face, she looked back into Athena's eyes and stroked her cheek with the backside of her fingers. "Perhaps, my anger has been misplaced. I hope your baby is every bit as beautiful as you are, my dear. I will take my leave." Mieonus vanished.

Once gone, George and Athena's voices returned. Athena didn't hesitate. She began to poke George on the chest. "You and I need to talk! You're coming with me! You're in more trouble than I can even express, mister! How dare you bring danger into this home!"

"Babe..."

"Don't even think about saying 'babe' right now! You don't say a word unless spoken to, you got it, Mr. Nailer?"

"Yes ma'am." George thought, *Damn, this is going to suck. She's pissed.*

As they walked out of the kitchen, a small bird with blue feathers was sitting on the window sill. The finch took flight, flapping its wings for a few strokes before vanishing.

Marcus Id's Dark Tower

Marcus' face was full of concern. He needed to speak with the Ultorian king and would have teleported into the king's throne room, but the magic necessary to protect him within the confines of the Ultorian's microscopic castle required more power than he could muster without the assistance of his goswig.

The Dark Chancellor has been pacing within the confines of his bedroom chambers for the last few days, waiting for the Ultorian king to return his request for a meeting. The smoke from his pipe has created a haze above his head. Just when he thought he was about to go insane, a crystal sphere, sitting on the stone table at the center of the room, lit up with the Ultorian's face inside. Marcus snatched his pipe from his mouth and moved to take a seat.

The Ultorian king spoke first. "How may I be of assistance, Chancellor?"

Marcus collected his thoughts. "I trust everything is well, Farun?"

"The reef continues to flourish. How may I be of assistance?"

Marcus watched Farun's face as he questioned, "Have you had any visitors I would have interest in? I'm sure you know of whom I speak."

"As we discussed many seasons ago, I would send such a visitor back to you if he made his presence known. If your goswig is missing, he must know you would seek him here."

Marcus leaned toward the crystal's image. "If you're protecting him, I'll destroy your kingdom. Are you sure you haven't seen Gage? Think hard before you answer."

"Your threats are unnecessary. I have not seen your goswig. Goodbye, Chancellor." The crystal's vision faded.

"Damn," Marcus shouted as he grabbed the sphere and threw it against the wall beyond the table. The ball exploded into hundreds of small pieces and scattered about the room. In desperation, he moved to the window and lifted his head toward the sky. "Lord Hosseff...hear your loyal servant! I beg you to deliver good news."

Moments later, Marcus' prayer was answered. "Tweet! Tweet!" The same blue bird which had been sitting on George's window sill appeared and was headed toward the tower. It flew through Marcus' window, then landed on the table.

Marcus took a seat. "Well, well. And, what news do you bring?" He leaned forward and looked into the bird's eyes. It wasn't long before a smile spread across his face. "This is good news. Thank you, Hosseff."

Ancients Sovereign
The Home of Mosley

Mosley called Alistar to his cabin home on top of Catalyst Mountain. The wolf looked down into the valleys as he waited for the God of the Harvest to arrive. He took a deep breath, then stretched. The air was refreshing. The wildflowers were in bloom all across the hillsides and appealed to the canine's senses.

It wasn't long before Alistar appeared on the ground at the base of the porch steps. "Have you given the parchment to Shalee?"

"I have not. It is not necessary. She knows where the crystal has been hidden, but the three words on the parchment will not give her its exact location. I plan to stay clear and allow her to continue her journey to Grogger's Swamp. I am sure the answer will present itself once she arrives. Beyond that, there is nothing we can do."

"Lasidious will not like your decision."

Mosley walked down the steps and began sniffing around their base. As he lifted his leg to relieve himself, he responded. "Lasidious trusts my judgment. He respects me. He will not have a problem with my decision. But, I have called you here for other reasons. Something is not right...something larger than the game we are playing with the Crystal Moon is happening. I want us to look deeper than what we see on the surface."

"What are we looking for?"

The wolf lowered his leg, then jumped up the steps to take a seat on the porch. He scratched the back of his neck as he responded. "I don't know. What I do know...Lasidious has been watching me. I'm going to need your help."

Alistar put his right foot on the second step, then leaned forward. "Do you have any suggestions as to where I should start, and what I should be looking for?"

"As I said, I don't know. Perhaps, you should start with George's family. You might discover something I have missed. It is hard for me to investigate when I'm being watched. You will be able to search without Lasidious' knowledge. There must be answers hidden under our snouts."

Alistar chuckled. "Our snouts. My nose has never been referred to as a dog's. But, I do enjoy our conversations, Mosley. I will find you once I know more." Alistar vanished.

The City of Inspiration
The Next Day, Early Bailem

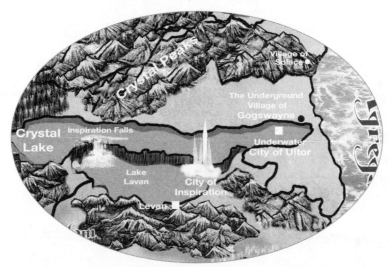

Lord Dowd entered Gregory's throne room. His face carried a look of agitation as he stopped in front of the White Chancellor's glass throne. Hepplesif was sitting on the arm of the royal chair next to Gregory as Dowd addressed the chancellor. "My men have returned from the city of Marcus. Boyafed has no plans to attack. In fact, Tolas informed me he desires peace. He believes a war would be a senseless loss of life."

Gregory relaxed his grip on the arm of the throne. "Then, it sounds as if Marcus has made an empty threat. This is good, but I'll keep the kedgles around for a while longer. I want to be sure the threat is behind us. Thank you, Lord Dowd."

"The news isn't all good. One of my men perished because of this mission. He dishonored himself and the gods. Despite this man's weakness, we should see to it his family is cared for."

Gregory nodded. "I will visit his family myself. Leave the information I need with Mykklyn, and I'll take the coin necessary to make the adjustment within their home easier. If need be, I will offer his woman a job within my palace to ensure they stay fed."

"As always, Chancellor, you lead by example." Dowd turned, then left the room.

The Luvelles Gazette

When you want an update about your favorite characters

Shalee and Kiayasis are approaching the Village of Bestep. They plan to stay at a local inn. Kiayasis has business he must attend to before continuing their journey to Grogger's Swamp.

George, Payne, and Kepler are making their way to the shrine located on the southern end of the Head Master's island. The shrine houses the key to The Source's temple located at the center of the Void Maze.

Marcus has been stalking George's group since their departure from Brayson's home the night before. He has been watching the group from the shadows of the forest on Brayson's island.

Athena, Mary, and Susanne have decided to take baby Garrin shopping. Brayson has given Mary a scroll of teleportation. She will use the scroll to take the girls on an adventure to the city of Inspiration. The women are excited to see Gregory's city of glass.

Boyafed is meeting with two of his finest dark paladin warriors.

Gregory Id spoke with Hepplesif after Lord Dowd left the chancellor's throne room. They have decided to leave a small group of kedgles behind to guard Gregory's palace. 20 kedgles will stay while the rest of the creatures of illusion return home to Brayson's island to be with their families.

Mieonus is looking for Mosley. She has questions for the wolf.

Thank you for reading the Luvelles Gazette

The Easy Way or the Hard Way

The World of Grayham
The City of Brandor, the King's Royal Garden

Sam placed his hands on one of the statues and shoved. The stone figure toppled and landed with a thud. As the king watched its head break off and roll across the garden, he shouted, "How could the queen just leave like this? How on Grayham could she allow our baby's death to come between us?"

The General Absolute responded from one knee. "Sire, may I speak?"

Sam motioned for his guards to leave the garden. "Stand up, Michael. We're alone. I need a friend, not a general. Forget about my position, and talk with me."

"As you wish." Michael stood. "The queen is acting like any other woman if she were to be thrown on an unfamiliar world and asked to do the impossible."

"Okay, okay...I'm listening. Keep going."

"Try to see your queen's point of view. Take a look at everything that's happened since your arrival from your Earth. You lost your families. You were asked by the gods to kill and fight your way into a position of power on a world you had no idea existed until you woke up inside the Temple of the Gods. The queen's best friend was taken from her. I heard the queen, with my own ears, describe Helga's loss as something she'd never heal from. She loved Helga as if she were her own mother. I'm sure you must've felt something similar when BJ took his life."

Sam sighed. "Sure, I felt terrible, but the loss was hard on both of us. I bet it was hard on you too, for that matter."

Michael sat on one of the many benches and took a moment to admire his surroundings.

Now...fellow soul...allow me to interject. In case you have not noticed, the theft of the crystal moon has created a unique situation. The flowers within the garden are still in bloom, just as they are across the rest of Southern Grayham. Under normal circumstances, this would not be the case. They should be lying dormant for the winter, but these are not normal circumstances. The theft of the Crystal Moon has had many side effects and one of these side effects has taken away each world's ability to flow through the seasons. This will not change until the pieces of the Crystal Moon have been reunited. Southern Grayham will continue to experience a mild summer.

Michael reached behind him, picked a carsoreign, then smelled its auburn petals. "You know the queen will come back when she's ready. She has lost her way, but she will remember how much you love her. The loss of your baby must've taken the last ounce of her strength. She has never been quite right after Helga's death. The added loss of your child was devastating."

Sam took a seat next to Michael. He removed the flower from the general's hand, then began to pluck its petals and drop them to the ground. "I know you're right...but, I'll be damned if I know how to solve this problem. This isn't something my intelligence can fix. I am out of my element. Okay, okay...what would you do if you were me?"

Michael put his arm around his king. "If I were you...I would take another approach. I will give you a suggestion, but it will require you to put a tremendous amount of faith in me."

Sam looked Michael dead in the eyes. "I trust you. I'm listening. Let me hear your idea."

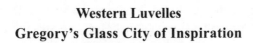

Western Luvelles
Gregory's Glass City of Inspiration

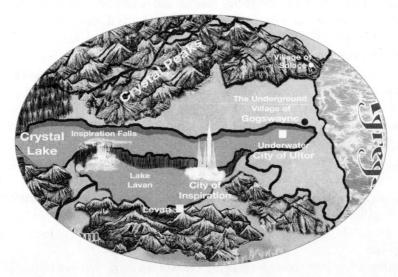

After listening to Brayson's instructions on how to use a scroll of teleportation, Mary collected her daughters. She put baby Garrin in his wagon, then ordered the girls to huddle together. After ensuring everyone was touching the baby, Mary read the scroll to release its magic. When the group reappeared, they were standing next to a river leading away from Gregory's city. The river's banks, like the rest of the chancellor's creations, were made of glass and were glorious to look upon.

The girls had come to Inspiration with a goal in mind: spend the day shopping and sightseeing while learning as much as they could. As they walked through the enormous gates, they marveled at how the glass had been altered. The gates appeared as if they were actual pieces of wood, but upon closer investigation, their secret was revealed. No matter where they looked, it was impossible to avoid the need to gasp at the next beautiful wonder. Cobblestone streets, merchants' carts, ornate lamp posts, and fountains which flowed outside almost every storefront—were all glass. Colors they had never seen before were used to give the structures definition and depth. Large prisms had been placed throughout the city. They cast rainbows which moved across the sides of Gregory's tower as the sun traveled across the sky.

Massive corannan trees lined the streets, casting shadows throughout the city. Smaller vegetation had also been given access to the earth, allowing their roots to retrieve the nutrients necessary to survive below the glass. After asking questions, the ladies learned the magic used to create the city also harvested the sun's excess heat. This excess was directed away from the plants to allow for abundant growth and further used as a source of power to replenish the magic's ability to maintain its function.

"Can you believe this?" Mary said while looking across the distance at Gregory's tower. "I would've never imagined that such a place could exist."

Athena took Mary by the arm and pulled her mother close. "I have to admit…I like your new man. This is going to replace our best day of shopping. How thoughtful of him to send us here."

"I agree," Susanne added, her voice full of excitement. "I have got to find me a magic man. It's not fair. You two can't have all the fun. Help me find a handsome one while we're here. I mean, how hard could it be? This is a city filled with them."

Mary and Athena laughed. Mary responded. "We'll add that to our shopping list."

After a few more pleasant giggles, the women came across a beautiful elven woman sitting on the edge of a fountain. The fountain was much larger than the others they had seen. The glass had been altered and held a canary yellow hue. The sign above the door was written in the language of the elves.

Mary reached into her handbag and produced a book. "Brayson said we could use this to translate what we don't understand. I guess this sign qualifies."

Susanne looked over Mary's shoulder while adjusting baby Garrin's weight to rest on her opposite hip. "Brayson thinks of everything. So, what's the translation?"

"Give me a moment. I'm working on it. I think it says…if I'm reading it right…it says, The Future's Vision." Mary looked up from the book, "Sounds mystical."

Athena tugged at Mary's dress. "It sounds interesting. Perhaps, we should check it out."

They nodded as they walked passed the woman. She was sitting on the edge of the fountain with a feathered mask which rested above her eyes and extended toward the top of her head. She stared at the women as they walked into the store.

Athena whispered to Mary, "How strange. That woman frightens me. I wonder why she's wearing a mask."

Mary nudged Athena. "Don't be rude. This is not our culture. Perhaps, staring is their way of acknowledging us."

"It's an odd tradition, if it is," Athena rebutted.

"I said, don't be rude. Let's look around."

The store was full of crystals, potions, and many jars filled with odd-looking creatures. A knee-high table sat at the center of the room. It had a circular top and a symbol engraved at its center.

Susanne looked at the symbol, then lowered Garrin back into the padded wagon. "What does it mean? Look it up, mother."

Athena took note of Garrin's heavy eyes. She crouched, then rubbed his head while waiting for Mary's response.

Susanne poked Mary on the arm. "Haven't you figured it out yet? What does it say?"

A voice from the store's entrance responded with the answer. "You look upon future's symbol."

Startled, everyone turned to look. It was the woman who had been sitting on the fountain's edge. As she entered, her movements were graceful. Her soft white bustier flowed against her figure while a red, patterned belt hung loose around her hips and swayed with each step.

Mary recovered from her surprise. "Hello, I am Mary. These are my girls, Athena and Susanne." She motioned toward the wagon. "This is my grandson, Garrin."

"Bryanna is my name." She lowered next to Garrin and rubbed her hand through his soft hair. "This is a glorious day. Fate has brought this little one to me." Bryanna stood, then looked at Mary. "I know you have many questions…questions of love…questions about your future. I can see all." She reached out and touched Mary's cheek. "I can see you. I can speak of things unknown. Do you wish to have revealed what is to be?"

Glances were exchanged, shoulders shrugged, and the desire to know more filled the ladies' eyes. "We would," Mary responded. She removed Bryanna's hand from her cheek, then patted the top of it. "How much will it cost?"

"Your coin matters not. Fate demands this of me. I shall speak of your destinies without compensation." Bryanna walked out the back of her store and onto a patio which overlooked the city. The view was breathtaking. The dome of Helmep's temple crested the trees as it lifted into the afternoon sky.

The seer lowered to her knees and leaned toward a second table which was similar to the one inside. Bryanna waved her hand over the symbol at its center. A mist appeared, and the face of Brayson formed within the haze as it lifted toward the ceiling.

Mary had to catch her breath. She could not believe her eyes as she backed away from Bryanna.

"Are you okay, mother?" Athena inquired as she moved close to Mary.

"What kind of trickery is this?" Susanne whispered, then moved to Mary's other side.

The green hue of Bryanna's eyes vanished and turned milky white. Her voice trembled as she began to chant. Soon, her chanting turned to a whisper. "Love. A true love. A union between elf and human. A union blessed," her voice amplified, "and doomed. Beware the danger."

Brayson's image faded and was replaced with George's face. "A heart cries for a soul's release. A young girl is trapped. A father desperately wants to witness her release, but evil stands in the way."

Bryanna began to shake. "Evil feeds off this family the way a child would suck its mother's teat. It guides its head and is testing a father's love." She began to scream, waking Garrin, who started to cry. "The worlds, death, destruction, sorrow...aahhhhhhhhhh...all is lost!"

Mary had had enough. She grabbed Garrin and ran from the store. Athena and Susanne grabbed the wagon and were not far behind. They did not stop until they were winded.

Mary tried to console the baby while Susanne and Athena caught their breath. She rocked Garrin in her arms. It took a while, but the motion pacified the child. He settled down, then fell back to sleep.

Mary lowered Garrin into his wagon. "I know I shouldn't speak as George does, but what the hell was that? What was she freaking talking about?"

"Mother," Athena said, covering her mouth. "How foul."

"Don't you 'mother' me. What did she mean when she said evil feeds off this family? She said it guides its head. What father's love is she talking about? Why did George's face appear when she began to shake? Does evil control him? She said Brayson and I were a union. Does this mean we're going to be married, and if it does, why is our union doomed? She said something about death, sorrow and destruction. That freaked me out."

Before the girls could answer, Mary pulled an emerald from her handbag. "Brayson said I could use this to summon one of Gregory's servants. They will take us to see him. Let's hope he can give us some answers. I have never been so scared in my life."

Susanne cut in, "Why don't we just go home and talk with Brayson? He could tell us everything we need to know. We can always come back."

"We can't use the scroll to teleport home until after Late Bailem. That's when Brayson said it would be safe to use it again."

Mary rubbed the gem. It was only a matter of moments before a glimmering carriage appeared. A tiny halfling, no taller than a few feet, jumped from his seat, then climbed up the side to open the door. *"Amin naa lle nai,"* was all he said.

Athena looked at Mary. "What did he say?"

Mary climbed into the carriage. "I don't know, but get in. We need to find Gregory."

Ancients Sovereign
Mosley's Cabin

Mieonus appeared on the front porch of Mosley's cabin. The wolf was lying in the sun and didn't bother to lift his head to acknowledge the goddess' presence. With his snout tucked beneath his front legs, Mosley spoke in a somber voice. "What do you want, Mieonus?"

"Is that the way you greet your guests, Mosley? I only wish to have a simple conversation."

"Again...what do you want? A guest is someone I wish to have around. You do not qualify as a wish of mine."

"Your words wound me, Mosley."

"Your drama is misdirected. What do you want?"

Mieonus turned away from the wolf and looked across the valley. "I've noticed Shalee is traveling near the Village of Bestep. She is with one of the Order's paladins."

"And?"

The goddess spun around. "And, I want to know why she's with him. The third piece of the Crystal Moon is nowhere near that part of Luvelles. I would like to know where she's going."

"As if I would tell you."

Mieonus walked up the steps and took a seat on the porch. She peeled back Mosley's legs, then reached under his snout to lift his head. After kissing the tip of his nose, she responded, "Must you always be like this, Mosley? I would like to start over. Let's try to be friends."

Mosley pulled away. "Your smell stings my snout." The wolf jumped off the porch. After walking a ways, he turned, squatted, then continued to talk amidst his grunts. "If you wish to be friends, then I am sure you are prepared to tell me where George is going."

"Must you do that while we talk, Mosley?"

"Do what?"

"What do you mean...'what?' Must you be so revolting?"

A look of understanding appeared on Mosley's face. "I apologize." The wolf pinched off what was left, then lowered his snout. Once satisfied the smell was as it should be, he jumped back onto the porch.

Mieonus stood and moved away. "As disgusting as you are, wolf, I would still like to create a friendship. I am willing to share everything I know about George. If we can't help the mortals find the crystal, then why not share information amongst ourselves?"

"Then, prove your sincerity. I am listening. Where is George going, and what conclusion did he come to after reading the three words on Lasidious' parchment?"

"George has decided to stand before The Source. He thinks the crystal will present itself once he has looked into the Eye of Magic. I think he's right. The parchment's words spoke of a soul being swallowed. The Eye does swallow souls."

Mosley lowered his head, then licked himself. He mumbled a response between licks, "Perhaps, he is right. But, we will never know if he does not survive, will we?"

"George is confident. I feel good about his chances." A smile appeared on the goddess' face. "It's your turn. Tell me about Shalee."

Mosley stood and stretched. "I am glad you were sincere, but I never said I wished to be your friend. You will have to wait and see where Shalee is going." Mosley vanished.

"Damn that wolf!" The goddess stomped her foot.

The Village of Bestep
The Peak of Bailem

Kiayasis assisted Shalee once again from the krape lord's back. He took a moment to put on his armor, then faced the queen.

Shalee took a cloth from her sack, then brushed the hair, which had accumulated while inside Joss' pouch, from his breastplate. "You look handsome in black. The gold accents have been well-placed."

Kiayasis winked. "Perhaps, you could help me out of it when I return."

Shalee could not hide her pleasure. "Are ya flirtin' with me?"

A feigned innocence crossed the dark paladin's face. "I wouldn't dare be so bold."

"Yeah, right. Well, if you're gonna flirt, then, ya best be willin' ta follow it up with a nice dinna'."

"Will this dinner be followed with a kiss?"

Shalee took his face into the palms of her hands. She leaned in and whispered in his ear. "You're bein' awfully presumptuous, don't ya think?"

Kiayasis blushed, then took Shalee by the hand. They began their walk into the village after tossing Joss' reigns to an Order's servant. The stable hand led the beast into a stall which had been prepared for the dark paladin's mount. A corgan was tied up inside. The beast screamed as the krape lord tore into his meal.

"Oh my goodness-gracious," Shalee said as she turned back to look. "That sounds absolutely dreadful. He must've been hungry."

"I told you, Joss is a killer." Kiayasis looked down the dirt road toward the village. "I have business to attend to. I will take you to the inn, then retrieve you for dinner once I'm done. I'll see to it our meal is special."

"I hope so." She winked.

Shalee's wink was so seductive, Kiayasis had to catch his breath. "Um... ahh...we'll need to leave in the morning. I think just after Early Bailem should give us the moments necessary to recover from a night of drink and fun. We still have a long journey ahead of us."

Now...fellow soul...allow me to tell you about the Village of Bestep. It is a rough place, full of hardened people. Many of the village's inhabitants are mercenaries—warriors, with magic for hire. Parts of Bestep lie in rubble. Hot tempers have destroyed many of the structures on the east side of the village filled with the less fortunate. There is a stone wall separating the classes. The wall has been scorched on the east side from killing those who commit crimes. Though the definition of a crime has a tendency to vary from one villager to the next, all sentences are given and carried out by one man, Tygrus, an ex-soldier of the Order, and owner of the village's best inn.

When Shalee and Kiayasis reached Tygrus' inn, *E Agar Kalpa* (The Blood Bucket), Kiayasis left Shalee under the retired soldier's care, then headed for his destination. Tygrus was well-known as a merciless killer and his inn was the safest place for the queen. All those who came to Bestep avoided confrontation while in his establishment.

It took most of the afternoon before Kiayasis arrived at his destination. As he crested the final hill, he stopped to look at an old, run down shack sitting on thick stilts above the Id River. He jumped from the back of his horse, then patted the animal's neck as it lowered its head and began chewing on some tall grass.

After securing the horse's reigns to a bush, the dark paladin walked down the hill toward the shack. The structure was rickety, and the wood planks of the boardwalk leading to it felt weak beneath his feet. The door to the structure was not solid. A fire burned inside and could be seen through the cracks in the wood. Kiayasis had to knock on four separate occasions before a brown eye peeked through one of the cracks.

A hermit of a man shouted, "No one's here, I claim! Go away, I say!"

Kiayasis' tone was cold. "Open in the name of the Order! Answer or die!"

"Open in the name of the Order, he says. Answer or die, he says. What else will the mean man threaten, I say?"

The bottom of the door scraped across the wooden floor. A little man with a bowed back and arms covered in sores, scurried away from Kiayasis. He took a seat next to the fire at the far side of the room, then pushed his long, matted hair clear of his face before pressing his tongue against the backside of a smile filled with rotted teeth.

Kiayasis could not hide his disgust. "How do you live like this, Gorne? It's not wise to have a fire in here."

"How does Gorne live like this, he says? Better than me, he thinks he is, I say. What does the mean man want from Gorne, I wonder? He wants something, he does. The fire isn't real, I say. A stupid man stands before me, I think."

Kiayasis ignored his comment and stepped into the room. His foot passed through the rotted wood.

"Hee, hee, ha, ha...heavy the mean man is, I say. Lose weight he should, I think. Fat, the Order has become, is the word I will spread."

Kiayasis gathered his thoughts, still ignoring the irritating mannerisms of the hermit. "I have business we need to discuss. I need you to sell me the knife."

"Eewww, hee, hee, ha, ha...the knife, he says. The Knife of Spirits he wants, I say. Why does the mean man think Gorne has the knife, I want to know, I say?"

"I'm in no mood for games. Sell me the knife so I can leave."

"Why, I say? The purpose...I want to know."

"Don't question my authority. I have the lawful right to take what I need. You can sell it to me or I will take it, but either way, I am leaving with it."

"Don't have the knife, I say. Go away, you should, I think. Shut the door, I command. Leave Gorne alone, you should."

Unsheathing his blessed sword of the Order, Kiayasis responded, "Give me the knife and do it now. I don't wish to kill you...but I will."

"Hee, hee, ha, ha, ho, ho, grrrrr...kill Gorne, he threatens, I say. Hate the mean man, I do. Give you the Knife of Spirits, I will. To kill something magical you need to do, I think. Strong this magic must be, I say."

Gorne scampered across the room, then reached under a mattress filled with holes. He tossed the sheathed blade and watched it land at Kiayasis' feet. "Go away, I say. Leave Gorne alone, I ask. I have given you what you want, I have. Hate you Gorne does, I say. Leave your coin on the table, I beg."

Kiayasis shook his head, then pulled the door shut after dropping a pouch filled with coin through a hole in the floor. He walked back across the board-walk and smiled as he heard Gorne dive into the water to retrieve the currency. Mounting his horse, he headed for the inn.

The dark paladin entered his room to make himself presentable before knocking on Shalee's door. His long black hair fell across his muscular shoulders covered by a fresh golden shirt. The blue of his eyes gleamed with anticipation as the queen's door opened.

Shalee had used her magic to create an elegant emerald gown. Her blonde hair had been pinned up to expose a thick gold necklace which closed tightly around her neck. Earrings, also made of gold, held an assortment of gems and shimmered as they dangled.

Kiayasis was the first to speak. "I have never seen anything so beautiful." He looked down at Shalee's feet. "Your shoes...they hold your heels high off the floor. Your face has color on it. I can't seem to take my eyes off you. How is this possible?"

Shalee grinned. "I will tell ya afta' dinna'."

Kiayasis' face showed a spirited pleasure. "It will be a shame to take such a wonderful gown off such a beautiful woman."

Shalee took a step back. "What?" Her hands moved up and down the front of her body as if she were putting herself on display. "You're not goin' ta see this dress fall so easily. Maybe...if you're lucky...I might allow ya ta kiss me goodnight...maybe."

"Then, a kiss it will be. I have ordered a special night. It is being prepared as we speak."

"Ahhh...so, you're gonna spoil me. But, we'll just have ta see 'bout that kiss, mister. Us Texans aren't floozies, ya know." Shalee took Kiayasis' arm, then squeezed. Not a single thought of Sam entered her mind as they headed out.

Brayson's Island
The Next Day
Just Before the Peak of Bailem

George, Payne and Kepler arrived at the shrine located on the southern tip of the Head Master's island. The key to The Source's temple was sealed inside.

"What kind of place is this?" George remarked as he scowled. "Sticking this thing out here in the middle of nowhere is freaking creepy. This is a stinking crypt, not a shrine. Brayson definitely has a flare for the dramatic."

George dropped his bag of supplies to the ground. He adjusted his purple tunic to a more comfortable position. It was split below his waist and a loose-fitting pair of pants covered his legs. His pistol was strapped under his right pant leg, loaded with his last bullet, and a short sword hung from his left hip. George was ready for the trials. They would begin as soon as the group entered the shrine to retrieve the key.

Payne flew above the shrine. He planted his small, red butt on top of it, then relaxed his wings before looking down and shouting, "I'm hungry!"

"Shut up, freak," Kepler growled. "Be quiet while we think."

"Ebbish nay...kitty," Payne snapped back.

Ignoring the fairy-demon, the jaguar began to sniff around the shrine's base. After a few moments had passed, the cat lifted his head. "George, what are you waiting for? You have the words to Brayson's spell. Use them and let's get going."

The mage was about to respond, but a voice from within the forest spoke out. "Well, well, well...the day has finally come!" Marcus emerged from the shadows, cupped his hands together, then held them in front of his chest.

Kepler was the first to react. The demon lowered into an attack position and prepared to spring into action. George remained calm and turned to find the source of the voice while Payne stayed put, hoping this new person would have food.

"I have been waiting for you," Marcus said, his brown eyes cold. "We have business to discuss, George."

Kepler growled. "How does he know your name? Who is this?"

George grinned. "His name is Marcus Id...Brayson's brother, also known as the Dark Chancellor. I hear he's a putz."

Again, Marcus clapped his hands. "I'm flattered. We'll be able to move past such useless introductions. They bore me."

Payne shouted, "Hey! You got food? Payne hungry!"

Marcus ignored the fairy-demon and continued to hold George's gaze. "You have something I need."

George leaned against the shrine and crossed his arms. Kepler waited for his response, but when one didn't come, he growled. "Aren't you going to say something?"

"Sure, when I'm good and ready. I'm still sorting out how little I care about what this chump needs. He's been watching us for a long while now. The bastard thinks he can just sneak up on us."

Kepler's eyes flashed. "What? When were you going to tell me he was stalking us?"

Marcus cleared his throat. "George, it seems you don't fully understand what I want."

Kepler's eyes continued to glow as he held them fixed on George and waited for the mage's response. George pushed clear of the shrine and found Marcus' stare. "I know what you want. I think you should leave. You're not going to get what you came for."

Marcus leaned forward, his voice filled with hate. "We can do this the easy way or the hard way. The easy way, you will live. The hard way...you will perish. Which will it be? Either way, I care not."

Kepler didn't wait to hear anymore. He lunged for Marcus, his massive claws outstretched. George had no chance to stop the demon's attack. He could only watch as Kepler's paw cut through the air, aimed at the chancellor's head. Instead of connecting with his target, Kepler's body lifted from the ground and was sent flying with a simple wave of Marcus' hand.

The force behind the chancellor's magic was severe. The collision the demon's body made as it wrapped around a tree, knocked the wind out of the cat. The branches broke beneath Kepler's weight as he fell limp toward the ground. Before he landed, an arrow of fire erupted from Marcus' right index finger and buried into Kepler's chest. The glow of the demon's eyes was lost as he landed, unconscious.

Upon seeing Kepler's fate, Payne reacted. He teleported behind Marcus and dug his claws into the back of the chancellor's legs. He ripped downward, opening gashes before he was also sent skyward into the trees. The fairy-demon tumbled through the branches and landed headfirst, not far from the cat.

George rushed in and punched Marcus on the side of his head. The Dark Chancellor fell to the ground. George followed his fall and threw his weight on top of him, straddling Marcus with a leg on each side.

The wizard waved his hand, but nothing happened. George smiled and smashed his fist into the chancellor's chest. Again, Marcus waved his hand, but still nothing. George delivered another shot to Marcus' face. The chancellor was forced to cover up to protect himself as George began to punch in waves. It was not long before a blow found Marcus' temple and knocked the chancellor out.

George stood and rushed to Kepler's side. He struggled while lifting the demon-cat's head into the necessary position to administer the elixir Brayson had given him. He reached inside the demon's mouth and lifted his tongue. He uncorked the top of the vial with his teeth, then allowed the drop to fall. After lowering the cat's head, he repeated the process with Payne. Once the fairy-demon's mouth was closed, he bound Marcus with his rope before the chancellor could awaken.

After dragging the Dark Chancellor's lanky body to a tree, George secured him to its trunk with a second rope. All he could do now was hope that Kepler and Payne would be alright.

As George paced, waiting for the elixir's power to heal their wounds, Marcus opened his eyes. Realizing he had been tied up, he spit the blood in his mouth to the ground. "Release me or I'll..."

"You'll what?" George screamed. "You won't do anything! You're going to sit there, and shut the hell up! Open your mouth again, and I'll finish killing you." George moved to Marcus, then crouched. He held the elixir in front of Marcus' face. "This better work. If they die...you're a dead man."

Noticing how severe the bleeding was on Marcus' legs, George sighed. His tone changed. "I can't have you bleeding to death before I know what's going on. The cuts on your legs look bad. Open your freaking mouth."

The chancellor did as he was told. The drop found its target and was swallowed. George moved to check on Payne. The fairy-demon was beginning to stir. George cradled the fairy-demon's body, then lifted him from the ground and carried him over to Kepler's motionless figure.

He propped Payne up against Kepler's belly. "I'll be right here, Payne. I need to check on Kep. Don't worry, I'm not going anywhere." George lifted the demon-cat's head and set as much of it as he could in his lap. "Kep... come on, wake up. Come on, Kep...we've come too far for you to die on me now."

Marcus' magic had struck Kepler's heart. George knew fire was the only thing that could stop Kepler. As George continued to encourage the jaguar, Payne finished gathering his senses, then moved to sit next to the mage. It only took a moment for his tiny mind to understand the severity of Kepler's condition.

With his claws outstretched, Payne stroked the demon-cat's neck. "Kepler," he whispered, leaning in to lie against the cat's black coat, "Live. Payne like kitty. Don't want kitty deader. Kitty Payne's friend. Kepler, Payne's favorite kitty."

The sentiment of Payne's words ripped into George's heart. Tears filled his eyes as he patted the fairy-demon on the head. Despite Payne's words, Kepler continued to lie motionless on the forest floor.

George reached into his pouch and administered another drop of the healing elixir. "Come on, Kep. I need you," he whispered. His mind continued to speak. *You're my best friend. I can't lose you, too. I've already lost too much. Fight this, Kep. Fight this, damn it.*

Payne watched as George lost hope. The mage began to shout as he stared at Kepler's closed eyes. "Get up, you big lug! Things just wouldn't be the same without you!"

George backed out from under Kepler's head and moved to the side of the demon's neck. He reached through the fur to feel for a pulse. It took a moment before he was able to find one. It was shallow, but there nonetheless. He held his fingers over this spot and waited for the elixir to strengthen the frequency in which he felt the next pump. But, this would not be the day for recoveries. Not long after—Kepler's heart stopped.

"No, no, no, no, no! Kep, you can't do this! Fight, damn it! Fight!" Seeing the demon was not going to respond, George fell across the cat's body. Unable to control his emotions, the mage wailed.

The sun lowered behind the horizon before Marcus decided it was an acceptable moment to break his silence. "George...I can help."

The sound of the Dark Chancellor's voice angered the mage. He pushed himself off the cat's body, them moved to stand in front of Marcus. He lifted his hands, and with all his hate, he sent his magic flying. Lightning enveloped Marcus, but failed to cause anything other than minor discomfort.

George closed his eyes and concentrated. He channeled Payne's power to amplify his own. A firestorm filled the afternoon air. The trees surrounding Marcus turned to ash, but the heat only managed to give the chancellor a slight tan.

George took a step back, his chest heaving. "How..."

Marcus cut him off. "Your magic isn't powerful enough to harm me."

The top of the tree behind the chancellor had disintegrated, leaving Marcus bound to a stump. George looked at the ropes. They remained intact. "Why didn't they burn?" George mumbled.

Marcus looked down at the rope running across his chest. "Because the ropes are touching my body. Everything I'm wearing is protected. These are things a Mystic Learner with your ability should know."

"Who in the hell are you to tell me what I should know?"

Marcus shook his head. The ash in his hair created a small cloud before settling on the ground. "Your skills are impressive. I was surprised to learn my brother was sending you to stand before The Source. When I learned of this, I was unable to fathom how a new student could be ready so soon. It appears I have underestimated you. You are far more powerful than his last one. I am sure you wouldn't hesitate to kill me if you could."

George spit on Marcus. "I don't need magic to kill you. I'll beat you to death with my bare hands."

Marcus grinned. "You could...but you won't."

"You don't know me!" George poked his own chest with his finger. "You don't freaking know me! Don't think I don't understand how to screw with someone's mind. You're not going to get into my head. I'm the master when it comes to that. Let me demonstrate how to kill someone." George began to walk toward Marcus and pulled his fist back into a striking position.

Marcus turned his head to prepare for the blow. "If you kill me, you won't be able to save Kepler," he blurted.

The mage stopped his swing. He grabbed the back of Marcus' head and forced the chancellor to look at him. "He's dead already! That's bad for you!"

"I can fix this!"

George thumped the back of Marcus' head against the stump, then lowered his hands. "What do you mean...you can fix this? He's dead! There's no saving him!"

Dazed, Marcus responded. "You're wrong. I can bring him back. I serve Hosseff. I command his Touch of Death."

George stood. "Tell me more about this touch!"

"If I tell you, you'll have the advantage."

"You still believe you have a card up your sleeve! Are you dense? What a fool you are. You must think I'm stupid." George took a knee next to the chancellor. "I should take your power from you. I should cut your ass open and eat your heart. I'll keep your power for myself."

Marcus started to laugh.

"So, you find this funny, do you? Only a fool would laugh." George stood and moved toward the shrine. "Or, maybe there's something you know that I don't."

Marcus nodded. "Indeed, I do. The power you need isn't mine to command at will. I know you could kill me and take my power. I have stolen more than one person's power myself. I'm surprised a human would have knowledge of how to do this. Somebody powerful must have shared this secret with you...someone worth my respect. But, it wasn't Brayson, was it? He wouldn't share this information with a student."

Marcus took a deep breath. "Unfortunately for you, the power you need wouldn't pass to you with my death. It doesn't work that way. The one power you would want to command most would be lost with my last breath. Your feline friend would remain cold."

"Explain!"

"You must be a servant of Hosseff, and not just any servant. You must be blessed by my lord himself before you can summon the power to raise the dead. The Touch of Death is only controlled by the chosen of the Order. With this single touch, we can take life or give it once per season."

George stood and looked into Marcus' eyes. "You're lying. I should kill you."

"You could, but what if you're wrong? Could you live with yourself, knowing you had the chance to save your friend?"

Payne walked over and stood next to George. He had heard everything Marcus said. He tugged at the bottom of George's tunic. "Umm...let help kitty."

George lowered to a height eye-level with Marcus. "I knew you would come here. Your brother warned me about his last Mystic Learner. He has known for many seasons that you were the one who killed him. Your power can't hurt me. I have been given something to protect me. This power is the same reason you have been unable to escape your bonds. It's why you have been unable to teleport home. If I set you free, what guarantee do I have you'll use your Touch of Death to save Kepler?"

Marcus adjusted within his bonds. The ropes were cutting into his wrists. "You have something I want. Since I can't take it from you, it appears I have no other option than to help you."

"Brayson told me you would try to force me to give you the words to his spell. He also said you would kill me if you had the chance. I'm not stupid. I understand your desire for power. I understand why you wish to speak with The Source and look into the Eye. Maybe, you're going about this the wrong way. Maybe, you should take a different approach."

Marcus thought a moment. "A curious comment. Your tone suggests your loyalty wavers."

George stood, then took a few steps back. "Loyalty is a funny thing. There are moments when unexpected alliances can be forged. My loyalty adapts as I do."

Marcus grinned. "I have never met a man like you. You speak with wisdom beyond your seasons. I wonder...what is it you have in mind? How do you suggest I attain the power I want?"

George moved next to Marcus, took a knee, then leaned in and whispered to keep Payne from hearing. Marcus' expression changed. After a long while of listening, the Dark Chancellor responded, "Ahhhh...I like it. I like it all. But, there is much we need to discuss if this is to work."

George nodded, then took a seat. "All the angles will need to be considered. I'm the man when it comes to covering angles."

Payne tilted his head. "What 'angles' mean? Tell Payne. Is Master talking food? Payne hungry."

Passionate Moments

Village of Solace

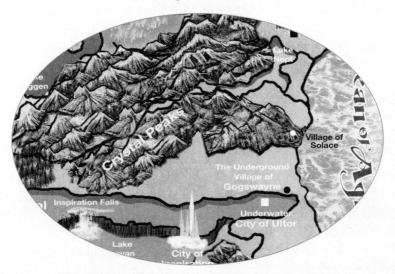

Brayson woke with Mary at his side. After propping his head on his pillow, he looked out across the ocean to watch the sun as it began to creep over the horizon. They had teleported to the village of Solace for an evening of dining and quiet relaxation. Dinner went well after a relaxing massage by torchlight set the mood. The feeling of romance led them into each other's arms.

Now...fellow soul...allow me to tell you about the village of Solace. It is a peaceful place, built into the tallest cliff overlooking the Ocean of Agregan to the east. The village was designed to be a seasonal escape, a place of relaxation and meditation. Everyone has the same view of the coastline far below the cliff's face, as each structure within this community has been built into the side of it. The east walls face the ocean and have been left open with nothing more than a stone railing to keep its inhabitants from falling. Thanks to the extended season, the weather has remained warm enough to bring Mary here for a quiet getaway—a getaway which has turned passionate.

Mary rolled over and put her chin on Brayson's chest. She reached up and played with his pointed ears and his goatee as she spoke. "Your ears are adorable. I can't stop playing with them."

"I'm glad you approve." Brayson rolled her over and brushed the hair from her face before kissing her soft lips. "I was hoping you would enjoy this place. Solace has only recently been created. The man responsible for this magical wonder nearly killed himself in the process, but the outcome was worth the risk, I would say. He has since recovered and maintains a residence here."

"I have never seen places as nice as the places I've seen on Luvelles. Even Kebble's inn makes the town I'm from seem less than desirable. You don't know this, but I still have a home in Lethwitch. My neighbors are keeping an eye on it for me. I'm from a rugged town...filled with farmers mostly, and magic is, well, it's not like it is here. As far as I know, there are only two men, or rather were two men, who could use it."

Brayson nodded, "Yes, I know them both."

Mary smiled. "Isn't Morre a good man? He's always been kind. I'll never forget the day I met him. He looked different than the rest of the townspeople. His gray beard and dirty robe gave me the creeps. Ha, that's something I learned from George...the creeps. He speaks so strange every now and then.

"Anyway, after I got to know Morre, I found a way to look past his foul smell. I guess he grew on me. I heard he had a brother, but I never met him, nor did I ask Morre about his family. I should have been more sensitive. I'm not sure why I didn't ask who his brother was. It was..."

"Amar," Brayson cut in. "His name is Amar. He studied on Luvelles under my supervision many seasons ago. He's a good man, but has a tendency to lean toward the darker side of magic. His power is limited because of his fear of failure. I wasn't able to allow him to meet with The Source. He never matured."

Brayson rolled to his back and put his hand behind his head. "Amar is still a friend of mine. In fact, he's the reason why I allowed George to come to Luvelles. I'm glad I made this decision. Ever since seeing you step onto Merchant Island, I've never been the same.

"George could be powerful someday. It seems he's been blessed by the gods. I was speaking with Amar about this the other day. He suggested I allow Payne to become George's goswig. I wasn't fond of the idea, but it just might work after all. I imagine Amar has gone back to Grayham by now."

Mary sat up. Concern filled her eyes as she pulled up the covers to hide her bosom. "That's impossible. Amar couldn't have been here. You must be mistaken."

Brayson sat up to match her position. "I wouldn't lie about something as trivial as Amar's visit. Why would you say this? Is there something I should know?"

"Amar is dead."

Brayson rebutted, "He's not dead. I just spoke with him."

Mary shook her head. "If you're saying Morre's brother was Amar...then he's not alive. There's no way he could've been in your office. Morre came into the inn one night while I was working. It was just prior to my family's departure. He was crying and drinking paradin whiskey. After a few drinks, he told me his brother's body had been found in a barn just outside of Champion."

Brayson's mind began to race. He stood, walked toward the stone railing without covering himself, then placed his hands on top of it. His muscles tightened. Mary could not help but notice the tension in Brayson's backside. It was impossible to ignore and was worth her admiration. She secretly enjoyed the moment while she waited for him to respond.

Brayson turned to face her. "Are you sure about this?"

"Of course, I'm sure."

"Then, if he's dead, I have been…" Brayson could see Mary wasn't hearing him. Her attention was elsewhere. He moved to the bed and pulled the cover around him. "Mary, this is serious. Pay attention to these eyes, not that one."

Embarrassed, Mary looked up. "You have my attention."

After a brief smile, the concern reappeared on Brayson's face. "If what you're saying is true, something is amiss. I need to speak with George."

"But how? You said he started the trials. I thought you couldn't speak with him until after he looks into the Eye. From the way it sounds, if the Eye swallows him, you may never have the chance to speak with him. I hate the sound of that."

"You're right. I can't speak with him, not now anyway. Besides, I need to investigate Amar's death first. I swear to you...he was just here."

"I believe you. I'm sure there's a good explanation."

"There must be. I'll search for the answer after I take you home."

Mary frowned. "But, I don't want to leave just yet. I like it here."

Brayson thought a moment. "One more day won't change anything. We can stay until tomorrow."

Mary smiled, then thought of her daughter. "What will I tell Athena if George doesn't return? I didn't have the heart to tell her he was going on such a dangerous journey. If he doesn't return, she'll be left to raise their baby on her own."

Brayson lowered beside her. "I'll be there. If he doesn't make it, I will help raise the baby with the rest of the family. After all...you and I would make good grandparents."

Mary gasped. "Do you hear what you're saying?"

"I do. I intend to make you my wife."

Mary grabbed his arm. "But, I will age and die long before you."

"I have knowledge of a way to extend your seasons. I haven't waited my whole life to have you come and leave so quickly. We will take a journey to Dragonia. The trip will be dangerous, but worth the risk. It will allow us to be together forever."

Mary grabbed Brayson, pulling him close. "Are you immortal?"

Brayson smirked, "I wish. I used the term forever loosely, or perhaps, you took me too literally. But, either way, we should live another 2,000 seasons if we drink from the Well of Covain."

"Oh my! There's a well that gives long life? Come here, you. I need to show you something. Tell me more about this magic while I make you smile."

"As you wish." Brayson pulled the covers over the top of them.

A short series of moments passed before Mary started to giggle. "Oh my. You're a naughty elf. Stop that. No, no, no...do it again. Stop that...eeeek! Ahhhhhhh. Brayson Id, you better...oh my. I dare you to do that again. I'm going to have to start loving you. Oh wow...again. Oh my...oh my...oh my!" Mary screamed, "I love you Brayson Id!"

Northwest of Bestep
The Beach of the Volton Ocean
Two Peaks of Bailem have Passed

The morning on the western shoreline of the Kingdom of Hyperia was brisk, yet comfortable with the assistance of a campfire Kiayasis had made the night before. Shalee sat close to the fire, holding her hot cup of jasin. She was impressed at how the roots of the scrawny bush Kiayasis ripped from the ground tasted after they were brewed. The beverage made a delicious replacement for the coffee she missed so much from Earth.

The sorceress could think of nothing better than to be sitting on a beautiful beach with the sand between her toes, looking out across the ocean. The only thing missing was the sun which would soon crest the mountains to the east and the warmth of Kiayasis' arms around her. Unfortunately, at the moment, there was nothing she could do about the sun, but she could do something about Kiayasis' arms since they were only a few feet away.

After cleaning up from their meal, Kiayasis lowered next to Shalee. He leaned in and gave her a soft kiss on the cheek. Aside from holding each other near the fire the night before, her cheek was as far as Shalee let him go. Even at the village of Bestep, she had held Kiayasis at bay.

Kiayasis smiled, "Still holding out, I see. I trust everything was to your satisfaction?"

Shalee caressed Kiayasis' forearm as he put his arms around her. "I think I've died and gone ta paradise."

"Paradise. I've never heard this word before. What does it mean?"

"It means, a place so beautiful you would be crazy ta wanna leave."

"Who says we have to leave?"

Shalee pressed into him, took another sip from her cup, then reached up to touch his face. "I've neva' snuggled on a beach before. Thank ya. It is a beautiful memory I'll cherish."

"As will I," Kiayasis responded. As all bone-headed men do, the dark paladin lost sight of the tenderness of the moment and changed the subject. "If we are to get you to Grogger's Swamp, we best get going."

"Goodness-gracious, you're definitely a man. Only a man would take the perfect moment ta talk about work. How 'bout we take a day off and stay here instead? I'm tired of ridin' Joss. My butt hurts. Let's take a mental health day for our bottoms." She kissed the top of his pointed ear. "I'm sure we could find plenty ta do."

Kiayasis stood, removed his clothes and headed for the water. He shouted as he ran, "I'll be waiting!"

"Are ya outta your mind? It's too chilly ta be goin' in there! I'm not gonna allow ya ta see me nekkid! Nice try, though!" Shalee continued to think, *Howeva', I have no problem lookin' at that cute butt of yours.*

Kiayasis reached down and splashed the water across his chest. "Awww, come on! I promise to warm you up! Come swim with me!"

Shalee giggled. "No! I told ya you're not gettin' my clothes off. We barely know each otha'!" She thought to herself, *But, I'll play, big boy. I'll play.* She hiked up her dress, then waded into the water, knee-deep. *Just not with my clothes off.*

Brayson's Island
The Shrine

Kepler struggled to open his glowing eyes. Marcus stepped back and allowed George to move in. The Dark Chancellor's Touch of Death had taken a full day to invoke before Hosseff answered his prayer and allowed the demon-jaguar's breath to return to his massive body.

Marcus collapsed from exhaustion. Payne rushed to his side and handed the wizard a pouch filled with water. The chancellor took a drink, then rolled to his back. "I need to sleep." It was instantaneous—Marcus was out cold.

After a period of grogginess, Kepler lifted his head from the forest floor. "What happened?"

George began to laugh and wiped the tears from his eyes. "You got your ass handed to you. Marcus knocked the garesh out of you. You died."

Kepler rose to his paws. After noticing Marcus' figure on the ground, he responded, "If I died, then why am I standing while he lies flat on his back? Did you revive me? Did I kill him before I perished?"

"Ha! If only that was the case," George chuckled while reaching up to give the cat a hug.

Kepler squirmed. "Great! I die and now you have the need to hug me. It's bad enough I have to put up with you, let alone allow your grimy paws to touch me. Can you let go now? George...this is awkward."

George continued to laugh as he released his hold on the jaguar. "You died, but you never touched him."

"So, how did he perish?"

Payne jumped into the conversation. "Not dead. Marcus sleep...and um, Payne glad kitty not deader no more."

Kepler rolled his eyes. "Ugggh, can someone put me out of my misery. George, kill me again. I can't keep hearing that word. The little freak is going to give me nightmares."

Payne laughed. "Kitty like Payne. I'm gooder freak...right, kitty?"

George gave Kepler a look. "Come on. Cut him some slack. He's trying to be nice."

Kepler moved to Payne and nudged him with the end of his snout. "If you're going to call me kitty, then I'm going to call you freak. We'll call it a fair trade."

George moved to stand over the Dark Chancellor's sleeping figure. "Marcus brought you back to life. He used a power given to him by his god."

"Why would he do this?"

George knelt next to Marcus and rifled through the pockets on the inside of his robe. "Let's just say we came to an understanding after I knocked him out with my fist."

"Now, I know you're full of garesh." Kepler sniffed the stale odor left behind by Marcus' tobacco.

"Seriously. No lie."

"Then, how did you avoid his magic? Tell me what happened."

"I'll tell you later." George removed a thin, round, polished tan stone from one of Marcus' pockets. "I wonder what the hell this is for?"

Kepler snorted, "You're asking me? How am I supposed to know?"

George shrugged. "I don't know." He put the stone inside his tunic. "We need to get going. We've lost too many moments and need to get started on the trials. We need to open the shrine's door and retrieve the key to The Source's temple."

Kepler nudged Marcus' head with his paw, then pressed the tip of one of his claws against the chancellor's temple. "What about him? Should I bury a claw into his brain? It's only fair after what he did to me."

"Naw. Just leave him be. I have plans for him. I told him we would be going once you woke. Besides, he has things to do…things which will stir the pot a bit."

"What kind of things? What pot are you referring to?"

"Let's go. We'll talk about it later. I'm sure you'll get a kick out of my little arrangement with Marcus. I think it will benefit us."

Payne tugged on the end of George's tunic. "What 'arrangement' mean?"

The Luvelles Gazette
When you want an update about your favorite characters

4 Peaks of Bailem have Passed.

Shalee and Kiayasis are now left to walk on foot. Joss has injured his leg and has had to fly back to the stables in Bestep to be cared for. They should have arrived at Grogger's Swamp by now, but with the loss of Joss' ability to travel, they are still 10 Peaks away.

Kiayasis was unable to carry his armor, their camp supplies and Shalee's bags at the same moment. As a result, he has been wearing his armor and carrying their camp supplies while Shalee has been carrying her bags and his clothes strapped to her back. She has used her magic to make their loads feel lighter.

George, Payne, and Kepler have set up camp. They can see the entrance to the Void Maze. It took most of the last four days to cross the Ebarna Strait. Other than the boat ride, they had to walk the distance to get to this spot. None of them knew the terrain well enough to teleport without fear for their safety.

Athena, Mary, and Susanne have decided to take another trip to Inspiration. They have agreed that, after having a small get together with Gregory and Brayson, the woman who scared them half to death was wrong and there was nothing to worry about. They plan to avoid her store and her prophecies of doom.

Boyafed is scheduled to meet with Lord Dowd. He has summoned the white paladin leader to meet with him just outside of Marcus' city, near the shoreline of Lake Id. The Order leader wants to assure Dowd the Order has no plans to attack his city.

Gregory plans to meet with the King of Lavan. There are issues which need to be addressed concerning the bridge connecting their cities.

Mieonus has been watching Shalee and Kiayasis. She now knows of their plan to head to Grogger's Swamp. She has sent word requesting to speak with Lasidious and Celestria.

Mosley has plans to meet again with Alistar.

Hosseff has been watching Marcus ever since the Dark Chancellor's prayer to invoke the Touch of Death. After watching Kepler's resurrection, the shade has been curious about the alliance Marcus made with George. He figures the events which should unfold as a result of this union will be worth watching.

Brayson is waiting for Morre to respond to his request to have a conversation. He has been in his office since the Peak of Bailem yesterday, waiting for his mirror to activate.

Thank you for reading the Luvelles Gazette

𝔓oorly 𝔄imed 𝔄rrows
2 Peaks of Bailem Later
Ancients Sovereign

After considering Mieonus' request to speak with them, Lasidious and Celestria appeared inside Mieonus' new home. Mieonus was drinking wine and watching Shalee and Kiayasis within the waterfall which fell like a sheet of glass into the large pool below the level where they stood.

Now...fellow soul...in case you don't remember, allow me to tell you about the home Yaloom created prior to Mieonus' occupancy. The foundation of the God of Greed's home was formed at the center of a 1,100 foot drop. The biggest waterfall on Ancients Sovereign plummets down this cliff and must pass through the home to get to the cliff's bottom.

As the water is directed throughout the structure, it forms the interior waterfall which once soothed Yaloom's restless mind. The water is gathered into the top of the home, then passes through six upper levels to reduce noise before falling past the main level where the living chambers were created.

After falling beyond this main level, the water continues past another seven levels before crashing into a pool filled with shimmering gems. From there, the water cascades over many smaller falls throughout two more levels before exiting the bottom of the structure. The base, or foundation of the home, built at the center of the drop, has a hole which remains open near the cliff. The hole forces the water to return to the cliff where it plummets the remaining 650 feet to a river which flows away from it.

Despite the massive amount of water which funnels through the structure, it is pleasant on the main level where the gods are standing. Mieonus enjoyed the serenity of Yaloom's loss as she turned to acknowledge her visitors.

"What did you want, Mieonus?" Lasidious questioned.

Mieonus walked across the room and made herself comfortable on a black settee upholstered with a plush cloth and thick cushions. She set her wine on a shaped stone, then lifted a bowl filled with grapes. "Would you care for one?"

Celestria rolled her eyes. "Just get to the point. Why have you called us here?"

"I thought you would find it interesting that I have figured out where Shalee is going. She thinks the crystal has been hidden in Grogger's Swamp. What I can't figure out is, why would one of the Order's paladins be escorting her? It doesn't make sense."

Celestria walked to the railing overlooking the pool and studied the images portrayed in the fall. Shalee and Kiayasis were walking hand-in-hand. "Lasidious...are you seeing this?"

The Mischievous One could only laugh. "I wish Sam was here to see this. How wonderful it would be to watch his reaction. Better yet, how fun would it be to watch a battle between Sam and Kiayasis? I would put my coin on Sam's blade."

Celestria purred as she leaned into Lasidious. "I would not be so sure. The Order's paladins are trained under the harshest circumstances. Kiayasis is Boyafed's son. I would not be surprised if he sent Sam's soul to find its place within the Book's pages."

Mieonus cut in. "Aren't you two the least bit curious as to why Kiayasis is with Shalee in the first place?"

Both gods answered as if sharing the same mind. "No. Should we be?"

Mieonus threw her leg off the side of the settee. The heel of her lifted shoe pounded against the floor. "Of course, you should! The Order exists to serve Hosseff. Shalee represents everything good. Why would she travel with someone like Kiayasis?"

Lasidious moved behind Celestria and put his arms around her. "Mieonus, perhaps you should consider Shalee's ignorance about the Order and their ways. Perhaps, she thinks Kiayasis is charming. Kiayasis may have found her beauty appealing and offered to assist her on her journey for this reason alone. Why are you so worried about trivial things? You should be more concerned about the missing piece of the Crystal Moon."

"The crystal is all but mine," Mieonus boasted as she stood to wave her hand in the direction of the waterfall. The image of Kiayasis and Shalee was replaced with an image of George sitting beyond the entrance to the Void Maze. Kepler was lying next to the mage and Payne was chasing the demon-cat's tail as it flopped back and forth. "George is on his way to speak with The Source. Once he looks into the Eye, the crystal will be under my team's control. Evil will rule the worlds as you have promised."

Lasidious and Celestria's laughter deflated Mieonus' confidence. "What's so funny?"

Lasidious was the first to respond. "The crystal isn't hidden in the Eye. George misunderstood the three words on the parchment. It appears Shalee is on the right path."

"What?" Mieonus shouted. "How could this be? The words spoke of a soul swallowed. The Eye of Magic does this when a person fails to portray belief in themselves. What else could it be?"

It was Celestria's turn to answer. "Look at it this way, Mieonus. If we were to put the crystal inside the Eye of Magic, and the Eye decided to swallow George, he would not be able to return the crystal to us, now would he? But, on the other hand, if we were to put the crystal in, ohhh, let's just say... somewhere inside Grogger's Swamp, more specifically, inside the toad's belly...a person with the power necessary to handle the job could retrieve the crystal and get out without being harmed. It appears Shalee is closer to finding the crystal than George."

Mieonus stomped her foot again. "Errrrrr...this is so irritating! By the moment George finishes the trials and figures out the crystal isn't there, he won't have the moments necessary to learn about Grogger's digestive traits. Shalee will beat him to the crystal."

Celestria reached out and adjusted the straps of Mieonus' gown. "I'm sorry, but it appears you will need to try for the next piece of the crystal once we have hidden it."

Mieonus pulled away. "Don't touch me! This is ridiculous! I have half a mind to stop playing your stupid game."

Lasidious smiled. "Ahhhh, but the game is fun. Think about it. You can keep yourself entertained while watching Shalee and Kiayasis. It seems their relationship could provide some wonderful confrontations. Not to mention, Celestria and I have been watching the three brothers. It looks like there's something brewing."

"What do you mean?"

Lasidious and Celestria vanished, leaving Mieonus standing in front of the images of George and his posse within the waterfall. She stomped her foot. "Damn! I hate when they do that! No one answers my questions anymore!"

The City of Inspiration
Lord Dowd's Home

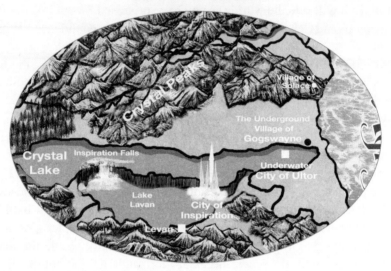

Lord Dowd stood next to his ghostly mount behind his home. He had worked hard to create his courtyard garden. This was his place of solitude, a relaxing escape where he sat on many nights to unwind after a day of intense training with his men.

Despite the abrupt nature his army had come to know so well, Dowd had a green thumb, and it was the simple things in life which he enjoyed most. Everywhere he looked something beautiful grew: roses, daisies, and other exotic flowers and bushes known only to Luvelles. His favorite within his self-planted world was the Sordandrian Sorgel, an intoxicating bush which, when fully grown, stood almost eye-level. The plant was covered with white, lacey leaves and orange blooms. It emitted a natural opiate which smelled like citrus and gave the person savoring its scent a short-lived buzz.

Dowd was a proud man. His silver and black armor had been polished to perfection and was fitted to his powerful frame. His hair had been cut, and he felt confident about his upcoming meeting with Boyafed on the shoreline of Lake Id.

As he attached his cape to a special set of snaps on top of his shoulders, he looked up. "The moment has come, boy," Dowd said, as he traced the hazy outline of his mount. "Let's hope this meeting has merit. There's no telling what Boyafed's thinking after releasing Tolas and his men."

Now...fellow soul...allow me to tell you about Lord Dowd's mount. He rides the same type of mount as the rest of his white army. There are no stables necessary to house these creatures. They are carefree and require no special provisions.

Shaban is a spirit-bull and his weight equals that of a bull from Earth, amplified by six. At almost 15,000 pounds when materialized, Shaban has been Dowd's mount for over 100 seasons. The bull has the ability to use defensive and offensive magic while Dowd remains mounted or touches him in any way. But, when Dowd dismounts or falls from his saddle, the spirit-bull dematerializes and becomes weightless, appearing as nothing more than a smoky object. Shaban stays in this form until Dowd touches him or his tack again.

Now, how Lord Dowd bonded with his mount is a whole other story. I shall save this tale for another series of moments.

Dowd pulled on the spirit-bull's reins and watched as the beast materialized. The ground crushed beneath the animal's hooves as the weight of Shaban's 15,000 pound frame created four large impressions. "Come here. Let's have a look at you before we go, shall we?"

Shaban responded and lowered his head, allowing his master to rub his snout. This simple exchange of affection was yet another pleasantry in life Dowd enjoyed, but this moment was to be short-lived.

From an unknown location, a bolt flew past Dowd's head and pierced Shaban's left eye. The spirit-bull exploded. The shock wave sent Dowd flying backward into the opening of a well's mouth at the garden's center. His armor filled with water, and the weight of the metal sucked him under the surface with relative quickness.

From the far side of the courtyard, Marcus lowered the crossbow to his side. "That was unexpected. Hmmm...they blow up. I would've never guessed he would have ended up in the well. I suppose an adjustment to our plan is in order." After a few moments passed, the Dark Chancellor vanished.

Deep below the well's water level, Dowd worked to remove his armor. Every strap fought against his survival. He could not move fast enough. He felt helpless and his air was in short supply. His mind began to cloud as he fought the need to gasp.

Just as his last bit of oxygen escaped his lips, something hit his shoulder. Dowd turned and located a rope with a small stone attached to its end. He tugged. It was secure. Without hesitation, he pulled himself to the surface. As he emerged, the air was like a drug when it filled his lungs.

After catching his breath, he struggled to remove each piece of armor while draping his arm through a lasso he created to free both hands. It took all of his strength to climb up and over the top of the well's glass mouth.

Dowd collapsed on the ground, but only rested for a moment before pulling his armor to the surface. With his chest heaving, he scanned the area, but no one could be seen. *Who would throw a rope in to save me and leave,* he thought.

As he tossed his armor to the ground, something caught his eye. He put his hands on top of his head to finish catching his breath, then moved to the area where the spirit-bull had been standing. The bolt killing Shaban was lying inside one of the spirit-bull's hoofprints. Upon further investigation, Dowd realized the bolt had come from one of the Order's crossbows. He rolled the projectile in his hand and said only one word, "Boyafed."

As Dowd tapped the bolt against the palm of his hand, the God of Death was standing near him—invisible—not more than five feet away. Hosseff smiled as he watched the white paladin leader retrieve his armor, then walk inside his home. "This should provide good entertainment. With war, comes death."

The shade waved his hand over the top of the rope he used to save Dowd. It lifted from the ground, then floated to the spot where the god had found it. As it hung itself up, the deity envisioned his haunted garden on Ancients Sovereign, then vanished.

The Underground Village of Gogswayne

It did not take long for Gage to realize that living with the goswigs was not going to be easy. Strongbear keeps everyone busy and over the last few days, he has decided to expand their underground world. The badger cannot fathom where Strongbear finds his energy. He runs his diner, makes blankets for the other goswigs, and if that's not enough, the bear plans to find the the moments necessary to supervise the village's growth.

"Good morning, Gage," Strongbear said from behind the counter of his diner as he tossed a new blanket in the badger's direction. "Are you with me today...or are you against me?"

Gage rolled his eyes and responded in a half-hearted tone. "I'm with you." He was sick of hearing the bear's stupid statement. It was always the same old thing whenever he wanted something. Gage took a seat and began to rub the sleep from his eyes. "What are you going to make us do today?"

Strongbear smiled as a brown bear would. "I think we're going to continue working on the area south of the village. We have a lot of dirt to move before we'll have our new lake."

Gallrum shouted from across the dining room. "Let him wake up, will you? No one is with you when they're half-asleep!" The Serwin flew across the room to join Gage at his table. "The poor guy hasn't even had the chance to breathe this morning and you're already barking orders."

Gallrum's tail coiled as he lowered his body to the seat. "How are you this morning, Gage?"

Gage pulled his paws away from his eyes and looked around before answering. The diner was pleasant, but rugged-looking, and was similar in style to Strongbear's cave which sat just behind the diner. Many of the goswigs Gage had met at the city meeting were having breakfast and enjoying a good chat.

Strongbear was known for his ability to serve each goswig what they enjoyed most. There were beavers who feasted on bark, chickens eating grain, eagles ripping apart raw fish, billy goats gnawing on straw, lions devouring corgan meat, fairies nibbling on fruit, bats drinking the blood drained from the corgan, wolves, boars, and many other forms of animals and other mythical creatures.

"I'm fine, thank you," Gage responded. "Doesn't Strongbear ever take a day off? Why does everyone listen to him anyway? It's not like the village will fall apart if he has fun every now and then. We should find a way to get him to relax."

Gallrum laughed. "Normally, Strongbear would be hibernating by now, but for some odd reason, summer has continued to drag on. We usually enjoy ourselves while he sleeps."

"I heard that," Strongbear shouted from the far side of the room. "You're all going to need your strength today. I would eat up if I were you." As if instructed to do so, every goswig moaned and started complaining at the same moment.

"Hey! Knock it off and eat!" The bear turned and went into his kitchen cave.

They lowered their heads as instructed and began eating. As usual, Gallrum ate his quaggle, but Gage didn't have an appetite for fish eyes. The badger had adapted many seasons ago and enjoyed normal everyday elven food. He ate strips of ham, which irritated the boars, eggs which made the chickens nervous, and followed them up with a small loaf of freshly baked bread which seemed to sit better with everyone.

After breakfast, Strongbear ordered the group to report to the dig site. "I want that lake to be finished before I die. That's one big hole we need to dig, so we can't afford to waste the day. There are just too many projects to be done in this village before we're finished. Let's get moving! Are you with me...or are you against me?"

Gage rolled his eyes.

The Void Maze

After a long conversation, George and the demon-cat decided Kepler would lead the group into the maze after sitting down for a meal. Between bites, George looked across the field to the entrance of the maze and studied the tall, leaf-covered bushes which shaped its walls.

Since their arrival, something had been bothering the mage, but he couldn't figure out what it was or why he had such a sick feeling in his stomach. George tossed the spoon onto his plate, then lowered it to the ground. "Kep, that place gives me the creeps. Even from here, it freaks me out."

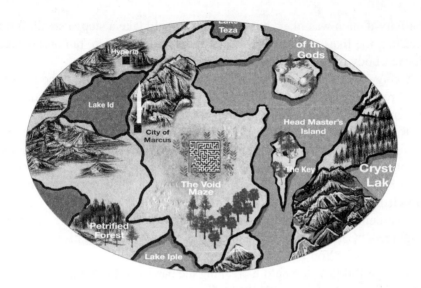

Kepler swallowed a mouthful of the corgan he had killed the night before. "I don't know. It doesn't look bad to me. I can prowl that territory just as I can any other."

Payne looked up from his seated position next to George. "Why go in, Master?"

"Because, we need to get to the temple at its center."

"Um...but why?"

"I have told you already. We need to see The Source. Going through the maze is the only way to get to him."

"No...um...no...no, it not."

Kepler growled. "Look, freak, it is the only way. You're wasting our moments by arguing."

"No, kitty...Payne show you."

The fairy-demon spread his wings and flew toward the maze. George watched. Once he understood what Payne was going to do, he turned to Kepler. "He just might have a good idea. He's going to fly over the top and find the temple. We'll be able to teleport right to it once I look into his mind to see what he saw."

Kepler snarled, "The little freak is brilliant. Who would've ever guessed?"

"I know. Can you believe that garesh?"

Their moment of excitement was short-lived. Payne smashed into an invisible barrier high above the maze's entrance, then fell to the ground beside it. George and Kepler jumped to their feet. They started to rush in to see if the fairy-demon was okay, but before they could take a step, a small, furry creature, the likes of which neither of them had ever seen, ran out, picked Payne's body off the ground, then darted toward the entrance.

George raised his hand, a single arrow shot from his palm. The missile cut through the air with tremendous speed, but missed its target by a narrow margin as the creature turned the first corner inside the maze.

Kepler covered the distance. His paws thumped against the field every 40 feet of so before launching into his next stride. The demon-cat passed through the maze's entrance and turned the corner in pursuit. He stopped, crouched in a guarded position and stared down the empty corridor. He growled, then shouted. "There's no one here! He's gone!"

The demon's eyes had changed from their normal glow to an intense, bright red. "George, don't come in here," he shouted, raising his voice louder than before. "You won't be able to see!"

George slid to a stop before breaking the barrier of the entrance. He took a moment to catch his breath. "Why?"

Kepler tried to return to the entrance, but as he rounded the corner, it was gone. All he could see was a brick wall made of large gray stones. The cat snarled, "Where are you? Can you hear me?"

From outside the maze, George shook his head, confused. "What do you mean? Yes, I can hear you. You're standing right there yelling at me. Why are you acting so damn strange?"

Kepler sniffed the base of the walls. "I can't smell your scent. Everything has changed."

"What the hell are you talking about? You're right freaking there. What do you mean, everything has changed. Are you losing it?"

Kepler growled. "You know me better than that. Of course not. The Master of the Hunt would not lose it. Everything has changed, I tell you. I can't see you from where I'm standing. It's as if you've disappeared."

George thought a moment. "Then, why can you hear me?"

Kepler sat back on his haunches. His eyes flashed. "Why do you ask me such stupid questions? How should I know? You're the magic user! You tell me!"

George lifted his right hand in front of his face and moved his fingers as if the hand was talking. He whispered, "Blah, blah, blah...how should I know? You're the magic user." After appeasing his need to mock the cat, he shouted, "Okay...start by telling me what you're seeing!"

"It's pitch black in here. Your eyes aren't made for this. You will need to use your magic on them before you come in."

"I'm not coming in there until I know what you're talking about. What do you mean, it's pitch black? It's morning. There's plenty of daylight left."

Again, Kepler growled his frustration. "When I passed the entrance, everything went dark. There must be powerful magic being used as you pass the barrier."

"What freaking barrier? I swear, I'm looking right at you!"

"That may be, but the entrance isn't normal."

"Explain!"

"It must be some sort of barrier. From out there...from where you're standing...I saw a maze with leaf-covered walls. But now, I see heavy stones stacked on top of one another, and I'm standing in a dark corridor. I'm in some kind of underground dungeon."

"What the hell are you talking about? Can't you see the sky?"

Kepler's eyes flashed. "If I could see the sky, then I wouldn't have said the word underground, now would I...dumbass!"

George smiled at the cat's insult. "Point made. So, tell me what else you're seeing."

"Just use your magic on your eyes and come look for yourself."

"Why would I do that? We need to get you out of there."

Kepler shook his head and sighed, "Am I the only one with a brain? Didn't you tell Payne this was the only way to get to The Source's temple? You need to come in so we can get through the maze. Have you become dense?"

"Bah! Okay, smart ass, I'm coming in." George waved his hands across his eyes and stepped through the entrance. The light changed to darkness as he passed the invisible barrier. Just as Kepler said, the sky could not be seen.

The magic assisting George's vision allowed him to study his surroundings. The corridors of the maze were cold. The gray stones were stacked like giant bricks. The walls were covered with moss, and water seeped from the ceiling, feeding its growth. Vines emerged through the floor, then snaked up the walls and across the ceiling.

George stood next to the demon-cat. "Damn, Kep...this place is dreadful."

The jaguar's eyes burned red hot as he looked down the corridor. "I don't have a good feeling about this place."

George slapped his own forehead. "Ya think? Maybe now, you'll trust me when we're sitting around a campfire and I say, Kep, this place gives me the creeps."

Kepler ignored George's tone and moved ahead. "It's easy to see how that thing disappeared with Payne."

George nodded. "This is going to suck. Just watch where you're walking. I've seen places like this on Earth."

Kepler stopped dead in his tracks. He looked at the mage. "You've been in places like this? Then, you should be the one leading the way."

"Um...not exactly. But, I have seen movies like this."

"Hmpf! You're just as lost as I am. The movies you've told me about aren't even real."

"Oh...I forgot...you're right...*this* seems *so* real." After listening to the cat growl, George continued. "Anyway, they were good movies. I don't care what anyone says. Let me tell you more about them. It'll keep our minds off the creepiness of this place." As they pressed forward, George continued. "There was this one movie. It was about this powerful mummy. You know... the kind that curses everyone..."

Brayson's Floating Office

Brayson is pacing within his office high above Floren and has been since the Peak of Bailem yesterday. Three days have passed since Brayson sent word through Brandor's mirror, requesting a conversation with Morre. Michael was the one who received the request. The General Absolute assured the Head Master that Morre would be allowed access to the king's mirror.

Brayson's personal mirror, framed with the same wood his desk had been made from, filled with Morre's image. Morre had prepared for their conversation and had taken the moments necessary to clean up. His long gray beard had been trimmed, hair brushed, and his charcoal-colored robe was new. The only thing he had forgotten to do was clean what was left of his teeth. The image of Morre's body fit within the mirror's surface, yet the wrinkles around his eyes could still be seen.

Upon seeing Brayson's image, Morre lowered his head and bowed to one knee. "Head Master, I came as soon as I received word of your request to speak with me. I'm sorry it has taken so long. The general has seen to it that our conversation will remain private."

"Please, stand. It's been too long since last we spoke. I trust things are well for you and your brother?"

Brayson made a mental note as he watched Morre's reaction. He could see the pain as it appeared on the mage's face. "You haven't heard? My apologies. I should've found a way to contact you, Master Id."

"Please, call me Brayson. I am your brother's friend. We should also talk as friends."

"I would like that, but I fear my news is grim."

Brayson swallowed hard. "Tell me what I haven't been told."

A single tear fell from Morre's right eye. "My brother was murdered by someone who left him lying in his own blood. They found him mutilated in a smith's barn, not far from Champion's gates. A chisel and a hammer were used to pry his chest open."

Brayson moved closer to the mirror and waved his hand. The heavy wooden chair behind his desk floated to him. Once seated, Brayson responded, "His chest was ripped open?"

"Yes."

"What of his heart?"

"It was missing."

"Missing?"

"Yes, it was, but..."

Brayson interrupted. "Who on Grayham would have this knowledge?"

Morre looked confused. "What knowledge are you referring to?"

"I'm sorry, my friend, but I cannot answer your question. How long has it been since Amar's death?"

The mage lifted his hand to his chin in thought. "I have lost track of the days, but if I was to guess, it has been nearly half a season."

Brayson knew he had been deceived. His mind filled with rage as he thought about the imposter who had visited him in this very room not long ago. He stood from his chair and with an aggressive whip of his hand, sent the chair flying across the room. The object busted through one of the windows, then began its long fall to the land below.

An awkward series of moments passed before Morre broke the silence. "I'm also angry about my brother's death. I had no idea you cared so much for him."

Brayson took a few deep breaths. "I'm sorry, my friend. I'm going to find the person responsible for his death. I'll bring him to you myself and allow you to have your vengeance. Someone came to my office just the other day claiming to be your brother. He looked just like him. He even spoke as Amar would. I have been lied to. I have made many decisions thinking it was your brother who requested these favors. I'll find this impostor, and he'll regret the day he met me."

Morre nodded. "I would cherish the chance to meet my brother's killer. I want to know what kind of man would do such a thing. I hope I have the power necessary to punish him when the moment arrives."

"Don't worry. You will. You will." Brayson waved his hand, and the mirror's image faded. He vanished.

Far below Brayson's office, just outside the school of magic's entrance, two male elves, both students, were having a conversation about the day's lesson. Brayson's chair slammed into the dirt behind them and splintered into many pieces which went flying in all directions. The elves grabbed hold of one another, frightened. Once they realized how their embrace looked, they released their grip, straightened their robes, then turned to walk in opposite directions as if nothing happened, stepping over the debris as they went.

West of the City of Inspiration
The Coastline of Lake Lavan

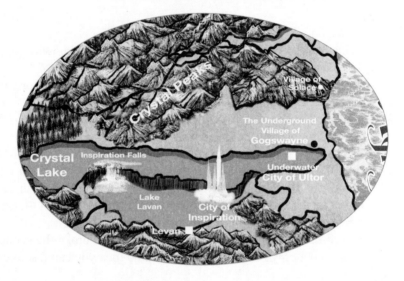

The White Chancellor appeared with the King of Lavan on the shoreline of Lake Lavan, west of Inspiration. It is from this spot the two leaders intend to begin construction on their bridge of glass which will extend southwest across the lake to the shoreline north of Lavan. Many workers are standing around, waiting for a decision to be made.

As the two leaders move toward the beach, the workers part to let them through. Gregory started the conversation as he acknowledged the men as they passed. "So, what seems to be the problem, Heltgone?"

The overweight, halfling king pointed his chubby finger toward a boat floating off shore. "The workers have run into a problem. Their magic isn't strong enough to hold back the water. It's stopping them from moving forward with the construction of the first support."

Gregory played with the yellow rope holding his green robe shut as he responded. "Have they tried combining their power?"

Heltgone lifted his jeweled crown, with a sordan sparrow resting at its center, then scratched the top of his head. "They have on many occasions, but the magic necessary to hold the water aside is more than they can summon. They are able to push it back, but cannot hold it long enough to set the stones."

Gregory's brow furrowed. "Well, we can't build a bridge without proper support, now can we? Let me think on this a moment."

Heltgone leaned over to grab a few pebbles laying on the shore. To do so, he had to spread his legs wide to allow his belly to roll between them. After putting his free hand on his knee, he grunted while pushing himself up. As he tossed the pebbles into the crystal clear water of the lake, his right arm had to move around his body to allow for the heft of it to pass. "Whatever solution you come up with needs to be safer than what we've tried. Six men lost their lives in the last attempt. The weight of the water crushed them when the magic failed."

"Have their families been compensated for their loss?"

"They have. I saw to it myself."

"Perhaps, we're going about this the wrong way. I know of a way to increase the magic needed to finish the job. I will speak with the Ultorian King and ask him to offer assistance. Their kind has more than enough power."

Heltgone reached up to play with his goatee. He was about to respond, but before he could, Gregory's goswig, the lioness, Mykklyn, appeared with Lord Dowd at her side. The Paladin of Light leader held the bolt which killed Shaban in the palm of his hand. Dowd didn't waste any of his moments. He tossed the bolt at Gregory's feet.

With a simple motion of Gregory's hand, the projectile lifted from the ground and into his palm. "What's this?"

"It's a bolt from an Order crossbow. They tried to kill me."

"What? Where?"

"In my garden. They missed, but killed my spirit-bull."

"Shaban is dead?" the King of Lavan added.

Dowd looked at Heltgone. His eyes were cold. "Yes! Shaban is dead. I was supposed to meet Boyafed earlier today, but found myself at the bottom of my well fighting for my life."

"During what moments did this happen?" Gregory queried.

"This morning, before Early Bailem."

Gregory rolled the bolt in his palm. "Then, my brother does intend to go to war."

Dowd shook his head. "The attempt on my life wasn't the work of your brother. Marcus wouldn't wield a weapon. He would use his magic. This was an order given by Boyafed."

Mykklyn moved between them as she spoke. "If the Order wants you dead, then they must've been planning this for a while. An attack of this nature isn't something Boyafed would order unless he intends to weaken the army. With you out of the way, he must feel they would have an advantage."

Heltgone cleared his throat. "It appears there are larger problems to worry about than the construction of our bridge. I'll return home and have my Argont Commander put the city on notice. I'll wait for your call. If my army is needed, we'll be ready."

Lord Dowd lowered his head. "I appreciate your willingness to fight, Sire. I'll be sure to let you know if this is, indeed, a sign that war approaches. I missed my meeting with Boyafed. I must try to figure out what his true intentions are before I react."

The king patted Dowd on the arm. "I'm sure as long as you're around, we'll all be in…" Before the king could finish, another bolt flew past Dowd's shoulder and pierced Heltgone's right eye. Death was instantaneous as he fell to the ground with a thud. Dowd unsheathed his blessed sword and took a defensive position. He pushed Gregory behind him as he searched for the projectile's origin. Gregory crouched and put an invisible wall of force around himself and the king's body.

The workers were shouting from a location not far away. Dowd and Mykklyn rushed to see what the commotion was about. It was clear they had seen what happened.

The bridge project leader, a large male elf, made sure he had Dowd's attention. "Lord Dowd! Lord Dowd! I saw him! I saw him!"

"Speak, man! Who did this?" Mykklyn snarled.

"I saw a warrior, dressed in the Order's armor. He appeared right over there." The elf pointed to an area near a mound of stone which had been stacked on the shoreline. "It all happened so fast. He appeared, shot his bow, then disappeared just as fast." The elf lifted his hand and presented a weapon. "He dropped this before he left."

Dowd took the crossbow and examined it. The symbol of a high ranking officer within the Order had been engraved on its stock. Angry, he moved back to where the king's body lay. "This makes twice they've tried to kill me today." Dowd pulled the bolt from the king's eye. "This was meant for me."

Mykklyn interjected. "If this was an attempt against your life, Boyafed sent an amateur."

"What do you mean?" Dowd snapped.

The lioness sat on her haunches. "Boyafed's men are trained better than this. They wouldn't miss, nor would they leave their weapon behind. I find it odd they failed to hit you on two occasions, but somehow, they managed to hit the same spot on both victims."

Dowd tossed the bolt to the ground. "You're right. They hit the eye. Could this be some kind of warning? Is Boyafed toying with us?"

Gregory removed his barrier, then stood. "I don't know, but the king needs to be taken home for a proper Passing Ceremony." The White Chancellor commanded the king's body to be moved. A large number of halfling men rushed in and lifted Heltgone's figure above their heads. "Take him to my palace, and prepare his body. I'll take him to Lavan and light the fire myself."

The City of Marcus
The Dark Order's Temple

Boyafed tossed his black leather gloves onto the golden altar sitting at the feet of Hosseff's statue. His voice echoed throughout the great hall as he looked up past the demons hanging from the god's fingers and lifted his hands into the air. "Hosseff, give me guidance!"

Boyafed's second-in-command entered the hall and rushed to Boyafed's side. He lowered his head in respect for Boyafed's position. "My Liege."

The Order leader lowered his hands. "Dayden, my friend, you have come at the perfect moment. My mind is in turmoil. I would like your opinion on a matter of importance."

"You may not wish to have my guidance once you hear what I have to say." Dayden was a larger man, strong, fit, confident, and wielded magic almost as powerful as Boyafed's. He wore black, except for a gold shirt, and his cape bore the Order's symbol at its center. Just as every other member within the dark army, Dayden's rank had been engraved into his belt buckle, and then again on each of his weapons.

Boyafed had been friends with Dayden since childhood. As Boyafed studied his Argont Commander's face, he put his hand on Dayden's shoulder. "What is it? Your eyes carry the weight of Luvelles within them."

"Three of our men lay dead as we speak."

"How? Where?"

Dayden produced three arrows with the white army's markings and handed them to Boyafed. "Dowd wishes war."

"Damn him! I was supposed to meet with him this morning, but he never showed. My message must have fallen on deaf ears. I should've killed his men when I had the chance. What more can you tell me?"

"I have the bow used in the attack. The killer must have dropped it when making his escape."

"Did anyone see his face?"

"No, but they saw enough of him to give chase. The men who pursued him said he wore the colors of light."

"And, the rank on the bow?"

"It is the same rank as Tolas'."

"Are you saying the man I let go is responsible for the attacks?"

"No. All I am saying is the rank on the bow is the same as the man you allowed to return to Dowd."

Boyafed leaned against the altar. He unsheathed his sword's polished blade, then tapped the flat of it against the sole of his boot. "Dowd has issued a challenge. Do you think we should answer it with war, Dayden?"

"My Liege, with all due respect, this isn't a decision I should be asked to make. It isn't my place to question your command."

Boyafed pushed free of the altar, then secured his blade. "I'm not asking for a decision, my old friend. I'm asking for an opinion."

"Then, it is my opinion that three men aren't worth killing thousands over. I think we should try to resolve this another way. Our army relies on you to have a full understanding of events before you send its men to war. If I were you, I would send spies to investigate Dowd's intentions before making a final decision."

Boyafed pulled Dayden close. After a brief hug, he kissed his forehead. "You are wise, my friend. This must be the reason our friendship has lasted so long."

As Boyafed turned to grab his gloves from the altar, Dayden jabbed him in the ribs. "I love you as well."

As both men left the hall, Marcus stepped from the shadows behind Hosseff's statue. His eyes were cold as the torchlight flickered across his face. He lifted another of the white army's arrows and spun it in his hand. "It seems a little more persuasion is in order." He looked toward the door Boyafed and Dayden had exited. "War will come, Boyafed. It will knock on your door. Soon, I will have the power to force you to kneel at my feet."

A Heavy Heart

2 Peaks of Bailem have Passed
Ancients Sovereign

Mosley and Alistar are sitting on the porch of Mosley's cabin on top of Catalyst Mountain. They have been enjoying the view of the valleys below while conversing.

Alistar rolled the cuff of his robe up his arm. "I have been watching George's family for signs that would suggest Lasidious and Celestria are up to something."

Mosley lifted his head from the wooden planks. "And, did you find anything?"

"I did not." Alistar continued to fidget with the cuff of his robe. "I found nothing suspicious, but I still share your concern. They are up to something. The game they have us playing feels as if it is a masquerade. How could it not be? All we do is watch and wait to see who'll capture the crystal's pieces."

Mosley closed his eyes and turned his snout into the sunlight. "It is beautiful up here. There are days when I cannot bring myself to move from this porch. Do you think Bassorine would have cared if I decided to stay in this spot forever?"

Alistar leaned forward in his chair and unrolled his sleeve. "Bassorine was fond of you for more than 300 seasons. If he hadn't cared for you, he wouldn't have left the Book with instructions for you to take his place as God of War. If he were to have a problem with anything you have or have not done, he would say you have not acted as a God of War should."

Mosley's ears lifted. "How so? I have done nothing against the gods."

"It's not the gods you're failing. You're failing the people of the worlds. You don't seem to care that it's your job to create war. It's your job to act as a form of population control. With nothing more than a few simple suggestions, you have the power to make kings fight for lands, take each other's food, and force the faith of their gods on the people they conquer."

The God of the Harvest stood and moved to the porch railing. "Look at what I've done on Harvestom. Why do you think I initiated a famine across the Kingdom of Kless? I did this to set up a desperate situation so you can place the desire for war in their hearts. The King of Kless believes the Tadreens have stolen their Seeds of Plenty. With your help, war would consume the centaurs' forests. Souls would rise and room would be made for the Book to release the souls of those who wait to live again."

Mosley lifted from the porch and stretched. He walked next to Alistar, then lifted his front paws onto the railing. "I see your point. I need to move beyond my own issues with death. I know I must do my job. I just hate to see the beings of the worlds perish. I realize it is necessary to create wars to maintain the cycle of life. I have been trying to avoid this issue, but I understand I cannot avoid my duties any longer. I have been failing as the leader of the new pack I have been given."

Hosseff appeared on the ground amidst the flowers. The shade had left his hood down and the light of the sun passed through his shadowy head. Once the effect of his appearance had been felt, his face materialized. He looked human. His eyes were golden brown and his hair was long and dark. The gold robe he had decided to wear was trimmed in black and hung to the ground, covering his feet. His windy voice sounded like a whisper as he spoke. "Mosley, there are matters on Luvelles which require your attention."

The wolf lowered from the railing and moved to stand at the top of the steps. "What matters are you referring to?"

"The Light and the Darkness on Luvelles are in distress. The moments are ripe for your suggestions of war."

Alistar laughed at the irony of Hosseff's comments. "How interesting is it you would appear at this very moment, and with news of war no less? Mosley and I were just discussing his responsibilities."

Hosseff lifted his hood from his back. His face dissipated and returned to its shadowy form as the light failed to penetrate the robe's heavy cloth. "Then such news should give the wolf enjoyment. Mosley, you need to ensure this war happens. I will savor walking through the battlefields. I shall collect the souls who perish and return them to the Book's pages. I'll do my job, once you've done yours." The shade vanished.

Mosley jumped from the porch, then turned to face Alistar. "It is moments like these which make being a god seem less desirable." The wolf disappeared.

Alistar sat in his chair, put his feet up on the railing, threw his hands behind his head, then lifted his face toward the sun's warmth. He spoke aloud, despite being alone. "But, it is moments like this, when I'm alone, surrounded by such beauty that I can enjoy how well the plan is coming together." He chuckled. "They're all fools, my brother."

The Void Maze
The Dungeon Catacombs

George was sick of being attacked. He turned, pushed past Kepler, then lifted his hands. Fire erupted from his fingertips, filled the corridor, and enveloped a creature no larger than Payne. As a result, the werebear fell to the floor, burnt and unrecognizable. The moss surrounding its corpse was charred and the vines which had not disintegrated, fell to the dungeon floor in a heap.

Kepler growled and his eyes flashed. "Good work, George."

The mage moved to stand over the sizzling heap. A small patch of brown fur on the creature's back was all that was recognizable as he kicked what was left of the werebear's body to the side of the corridor. One of its legs broke on impact and as its arm fell toward the floor, a nail from one of its claws scraped against the surface of the stone, making an eerie noise.

"Damn, I hate that sound. Kep, I'm starting to lose track of our moments. I have no idea how long we've been walking through this stinking place. If I have to kill anymore of these turds...I'm going to go crazy."

Kepler sniffed the creature's remains. The smell of burnt fur filled his nostrils. He snorted his displeasure. "It's not like they're hard for you to kill. Quit complaining. I'm the one with all the scratches."

"I hear you. I'm just sick of wandering aimlessly through this place."

"You cry too much. If it will stop your sniveling, I have good news."

"Really? And, what would that be? No wait...don't tell me. I bet there's another corner just ahead. We'll be able to make that turn and get lost down that corridor, just like we have all the rest."

"Well, you can continue to pout, but I can smell Payne's scent. I'm going to check it out. He's around the next corner."

"Don't garesh me. Are you serious?"

The demon-cat nodded.

"Ya know, Kep, there are moments when you really know how to lift a guy's spirits. Come here, you big lug."

"Don't get amorous with me. I don't need another hug. You're too sensitive."

George reached up and tussled the fur on the side of Kepler's neck. "Let's get moving."

"Yes, let's, and keep your hands to yourself."

George took a knee at the corner, then peeked around it with Kepler above his head. To his surprise, the area opened into a field. George pulled back. "We've made it through. The temple is sitting on the far side of the clearing."

Kepler also pulled back, then looked down at George. "I'm not blind. I can see, you know." The demon peeked around the corner again. "We need to get Payne out of that cage."

Payne had been suspended above a large bonfire at the field's center. His metal cage was glowing due to the length of moments he had been held above the flames. Hundreds of creatures, similar to the werebears they had been killing for the last couple of days, danced around the fire. Most of them seemed agitated, perhaps because the fairy-demon wouldn't cook.

Payne was singing. He appeared to be happy and unable to comprehend the seriousness of his situation. He acted grateful, as if he appreciated the flaming bath.

Kepler shook his head as he pulled back. "What a freak. Only Payne would sing in captivity."

George rolled back against the wall and covered his mouth to muffle his laugh. "He's too young to get it. I don't think he knows his life is in jeopardy."

Kepler grinned as a jaguar would and peeked around the corner. "Look, George."

The mage peered around the corner and watched as Payne extended his arms toward the thick iron bars of his cage. One of the creatures dancing by the fire lifted from the ground and flew through the air. The werebear slammed against the bars and was pinned. The screams it made as the fire consumed its flesh were hellish. Even Kepler was bothered by the sound as Payne continued to hold his arms steady.

One by one, the werebear's bones began to break and double over. Payne's magic remained strong until the creature's form was sucked through the cage's narrow gap. Once it was in his claws, the fairy-demon tore into the creature and ate what was left of its flesh before the heat burnt the flavor from it.

George rolled back against the wall and whispered. "Holy garesh. Payne is a freak of nature. I think the fire is feeding his power."

Kepler thought a moment. "At least we know why he's happy. His belly is full. I think his hunger allowed him to use power he didn't know he had. Perhaps, his power is instinctive. Think about it. When he saved you inside the Book of Bonding, you said he let his body burn. He did it without thinking. All he knew was that he wanted to save you. He knew you needed light to teleport. Who knows how powerful Payne is, or how powerful you are since you're bonded."

"Do you really think so? If this is true, then who knows what we can accomplish?"

"I agree. Your power must be growing. This must be the benefit of having Payne as your goswig."

"I think you're right. I bet that was hard for you to admit. Payne is growing on you, isn't he?"

"Bah! He's still a freak."

George smiled, then looked around the corner. "Maybe, Payne will eat them all if we give him the moments to do so."

"I don't doubt it. But, I'm hungry myself and we're out of food. I wouldn't mind eating a few myself."

George looked up and winked. "You need to stay behind me when we go out there."

"Why?"

"Just trust me. Stay behind me." George took a deep breath, then stood to walk out. Kepler stayed on his heels, and as they passed the end of the dungeon's exit, they could see the dark clouds lining the sky.

With the sun getting ready to set, George's steps were filled with purpose. He focused on Payne as he approached the hundreds of werebears surrounding the fire. He stopped when he felt Payne's magic surround him and shouted, "Hey you little pieces of garesh...come and get me! Daddy brought dinner!"

Kepler lowered to the ground, ready to pounce. "How clever you have become, George. You sound like an idiot. Which reminds me...do you want me to tell them something once they get here? Should I tell them you don't know what you're doing? I could tell them you told me to tell them we're both crazy."

"Shut up! I'm concentrating. Tease me later, damn it."

Seeing George, Payne became excited and shouted from his cage. "Master came for Payne!"

The sounds the werebears' claws made as they pounded against the earth were intimidating, but George held strong. He closed his eyes and focused on Payne to channel the fairy-demon's power. George raised his hands.

Thousands of needles shot from his fingertips. He moved his arms back and forth to ensure he covered the spread of bodies as they began to tumble to the ground.

When George opened his eyes, they were filled with blood. Kepler moved beside the mage. "George, are you okay? Your eyes."

George's body began to sway. He fell toward the ground. Kepler reacted and used the backside of his paw to soften his fall. He watched as his friend's eyes shut, and his body relaxed. The mage fell into unconsciousness.

Kepler knew he did not have the moments to waste. The power George used was too much for his body to handle. The demon tried to retrieve the vial from the mage's robe, but his paws weren't built for such tasks. *I have to get Payne out of that cage*, he thought.

The demon-jaguar ran toward Payne's prison. He launched into the air. "Hold on," he shouted. Payne grabbed the bars just as the demon-cat smashed into the cage. Kepler's body consumed the structure as his momentum carried them beyond the flames. The chain holding the cage snapped as they fell to the ground.

Kepler rolled off the bars and roared. The heat of the metal had burnt through the fur covering his belly and seared his skin. As he settled down, he noticed the bars of the cage had collapsed, leaving Payne pinned inside. "Are you hurt?"

"No, not hurt, kitty."

"Can you teleport out of there?"

"No...um...can't."

"We have to get you out. I need you to give George a drop of the potion Brayson gave him."

"Payne can't get out. Bite hand off."

"What?"

"Bite hand off. Payne help Master."

"How will biting your hand off help?'

Payne shouted, "Bite!"

Kepler lowered his mouth toward the fairy-demon's hand. "Uggh, you stink."

"Bite, kitty, bite!"

"Oh, how I've longed to hear those words. I consider this a pleasure."

Kepler chomped and severed the hand with ease. Payne screamed in agony as the jaguar spit it to the ground and questioned. "Now what do I do, freak?"

With tears in his eyes, the fairy demon responded. "Payne help Master."

The hand began to morph. It wasn't long before a tiny likeness of the fairy-demon began to fly toward George. Kepler followed and hovered over the mage's figure as the morphed Payne retrieved the vial and set it on the ground with the lid up.

Morphed Payne looked up at the jaguar and shouted, "Kepler, I need your help! Use your teeth to open the vial. I am not strong enough."

Kepler shook his head. "You're a lot smarter than he is." He looked across the field. Payne was still stuck between the bars and crying. "Why do you speak differently?"

Morphed Payne bore his teeth. "Why does it matter? We don't have the moments to discuss this. Now, remove the cork."

Kepler growled, covered the cork with the tips of his teeth, then twisted. The cork slid out. Reaching inside the bottle, the morphed Payne cupped the liquid with the palm of his claw, then flew above George's mouth. He crawled in, slid under the mage's tongue, then emptied his hand beneath it. He repeated the process to ensure enough of the elixir had been used. After administering a drop under Kepler's tongue, the morphed Payne rejoined the fairy-demon's body.

South of Grogger's Swamp
1 Peak of Bailem Later

Kiayasis finished setting up camp. They had followed the shoreline of the Volton Ocean as they headed north. After eating, he gathered enough wood to ensure the fire would continue to burn strong through the night, then sat next to Shalee and pulled her close. This would be their final night together before Shalee entered the swamp. The weather was peaceful as the sun approached the horizon.

"This is hard."

"What's hard?" Shalee asked with a soft voice.

"I have been with you for the last 31 Peaks. We've spent so many moments together. I've never done anything like this before."

"Is my company so bad? Are ya tired of me?"

"That's not what I mean. I'm saying it's hard because when this is over, you'll be leaving. You'll return to your king and your duties as queen. I don't think I can bear the thought of being apart from you. You've captured my heart, and I wish I could be with you."

Shalee grinned. "Well, aren't ya just sexier than a lightnin' bug's butt." She stroked his face. "I don't know that I wish ta go back ta Grayham. I'm happy where I am. I'm happy with you, Mr. Methelborn."

Kiayasis wrapped his arms around Shalee and watched as the sun disappeared behind the horizon. The waves of the ocean crashed against the shoreline, amplifying the mood. "I hope you stay. I would cherish you. *Manka lle merna amin merna quen mela en' coiamin.*"

"Goodness-gracious, what did ya say?"

"I said, I would make you the love of my life, if you wish it."

Shalee couldn't believe her ears. "Ya think ya could care for me that much?"

"I don't think. I know. I would love you. I do love you."

Fear rushed through Shalee's mind as it went wild with thought. *What will Sam think? How will he feel when I tell him I'm not comin' home? How will I tell him? Will he use his authority ta force me ta come home?*

A moment later, a whole new, fresh set of thoughts ran through her brain. *What's Sam gonna do 'bout it? He can't do anythin'. My power is strong enough ta fight any demand he'll make for me ta come home. I'll use my magic ta stay here where I'm loved and not looked at as if I'm a failure. He doesn't want me, anyway.*

"Shalee. Shalee. Hey, are you okay? You look like you've seen a spirit."

The sorceress refocused. "I'm sorry. I was just thinkin' 'bout how I'm gonna tell Sam I'm not comin' home. I want ta stay here and be with you."

"Are you genuine?"

"I'm serious as a heart attack. I can't believe this is happenin' ta me."

Kiayasis grinned. "I must work harder to understand the meaning of your words. Does the seriousness of this heart attack mean you have no doubt?"

Shalee giggled. "It means, I want ta stay. But, only if you'll love me."

"I already do...and always will."

Shalee pressed into him. "Then, show me how much."

Kiayasis stood, lifted her in his arms, then walked across the beach to a small pile of furs he had laid out. He kissed her while respecting the boundaries she had set. He rubbed her shoulders and the small of her back until she was sound asleep.

Kiayasis gently pulled away, put on his shirt, then began walking along the beach. When enough moments had passed to put a considerable distance between himself and the camp, he removed a small mirror about the size of his palm. He spoke to it as if it was alive. "Find my father."

It was not long before the mirror lit and an image of Boyafed appeared. "Kiayasis, my son, how is your journey?"

"I fair well, but Joss was injured."

"I have received word. He will heal. I wouldn't be concerned about his recovery. He's one of the finest krape lords in my army."

Boyafed could see an estranged look on Kiayasis' face. "What bothers you, my boy?"

"Father...the woman I travel with is a good woman. She's done nothing to deserve the end you've ordered. She is kind, and this isn't an order I wish to execute."

Boyafed frowned. "If you were any other man, I would have you beaten. This wasn't a casual order I gave. This was a request from Hosseff. Who are we to question his wishes?"

"But, I love her."

Boyafed took a step back from his mirror. "You what? How could you fall in love with a woman you intend to kill? How could you allow yourself to become so blind, so gullible? What's wrong with you, boy?"

"Father, I know you're angry, but..."

"But, nothing! She's a queen! Her king would not allow her to stay with you even if it was possible for you to be with her. She doesn't even have elven blood. The Head Master would not allow her to stay. You must honor Hosseff and fulfill your order. Our lord requested you for this mission. You should feel honored."

"Please! Can't you speak with Hosseff? Perhaps..."

Boyafed shouted over the top of him. "Kiayasis! You have a job to do! I won't bother Hosseff with my son's inability to follow orders."

Kiayasis lowered his head. "I don't wish to shame you, father. I will carry out my order and ensure Hosseff is pleased with my actions."

"That's better. I knew you would come to your senses. I'm proud of you. I'll be sure to reward you once you've finished your task. Did you retrieve the Knife of Spirits?"

"I did."

"So, Gorne had the knife as I said he would?"

"He did, father."

"Did you kill him?"

"No. I felt his pathetic existence was enough punishment."

"Then, you are more compassionate than I. This was a trait passed from your mother. When the queen has finished her task inside the swamp, use the knife to steal her power, as we discussed. You know what to do from there."

"I won't fail, father."

"I know. You're the son of a Methelborn. I couldn't be more proud of how you turned out."

"Thank you, father."

"We'll speak again soon. I'm going to grab some ale with Dayden. Good-bye, my son."

The mirror went dark. Kiayasis fell to his knees and began to cry.

The Luvelles Gazette

When you want an update about your favorite characters

The Next Day, Just Before Late Bailem

Shalee and Kiayasis have arrived at the entrance to Grogger's Swamp. The sorceress plans to make her entrance tomorrow morning. Kiayasis has set up camp and will wait for her return. As they sit beside the fire, Shalee calls Kiayasis, baby.

Kepler and Payne are still waiting for George to come out of his unconscious state. Payne has used his magic to move George against Kepler. The cat has been acting as a cushion and has allowed his friend to rest against him without complaint. A few wandering werebears emerged from inside the maze and attacked, but Payne slew them with little trouble.

Athena, Mary, and Susanne are at home, but plan to use the Scroll of Teleportation to visit the city of Nept in the morning.

Boyafed is inside the Order's temple. He plans to meet with Marcus. The Dark Chancellor has requested his presence.

Gregory Id has returned home from the King of Lavan's Passing Ceremony. He plans to attend the meeting Lord Dowd has called with his military leaders. It will be held at Late Bailem tomorrow. With the slaying of the king, Gregory feels Lord Dowd will have no choice but to call for war.

Mosley plans to secretly attend Lord Dowd's meeting.

Mieonus is inside her home on Ancients Sovereign. She has been watching Shalee and Kiayasis' relationship develop. The goddess also enjoyed watching Boyafed and Kiayasis talk through the mirror. When Mieonus learned about Hosseff's request to kill Shalee, she danced throughout her home. She was looking forward to the sorceress' misery, but something unexpected has happened, and now the goddess is anticipating a larger confrontation.

A new player has joined the game and has learned of Shalee and Kiayasis' location. This bold figure has tracked them and is watching from a distance, but remains close enough to hear Shalee and Kiayasis' conversations. Mieonus smiled at the stalker's reaction when Shalee called Kiayasis, 'baby.'

Brayson plans to travel to Mogg's Village. He needs to speak with the visionary about many of the current events which have transpired. He is anxious. Dealing with the sprite is no easy task.

Gage and the other goswigs within the underground village of Goswayne are hard at work. Strongbear has been relentless with his order to finish their new lake. Everyone is with the brown bear and not against him.

Marcus is standing over another dead body. This is the last person he thinks he must kill. He believes war is sure to follow once Boyafed hears the news.

Lasidious and Celestria are inside their home beneath the Peaks of Angels. Celestria is nervous about Mosley and Alistar's investigation to discover evidence that they are up to something larger than running a game to collect the pieces of the Crystal Moon.

Thank you for reading the Luvelles Gazette

A Secret Revealed

Lasidious and Celestria's Home
Beneath the Peaks of Angels

Celestria stared into the green flames of their fireplace. "They are going to figure it out. Alistar has been snooping around and Mosley is too smart. It is just a matter of moments before they find out about our son."

Lasidious stood from his chair next to the table, then moved behind his lover. With a hand on each shoulder, he turned her to face him, then looked into her eyes and spoke with a soft, relaxed voice. "Take a deep breath."

"How can I?" the goddess snapped. "We are going to be made mortal. Once they discover Garrin's existence, they will kill him. Our end will be no less dreadful than Yaloom's."

Lasidious pulled her close. "I have things under control. You worry too much. There's nothing for them to find. There's no reason for them to look for Garrin. Mosley doesn't believe we're willing to go against the Book's law to have a child."

"How can you be so sure? The wolf is clever, and Alistar is just as smart. If Mosley does not figure it out, Alistar will."

"Alistar and Mosley are looking for something sinister, not something which cries and soils its diaper."

"But..."

"But, nothing. Everything is under control. Mosley's attention is focused on Luvelles. With the dark and white armies on the brink of war, he has no choice but to focus on his duties. He must ensure the leaders of the armies choose war over diplomacy."

Celestria frowned. "What about Alistar? He has the moments to look for a problem."

Lasidious began to laugh.

Celestria pulled away. "What is so funny?"

"Alistar isn't a threat."

"What do you mean? How can you be so sure he will not find anything? He is every bit as smart as Mosley, and we have already danced around that wolf's snout being stuck in places we do not want it."

Lasidious reclaimed his seat. He tossed his feet up and leaned back. "There's something you don't know about Alistar."

"I know plenty. I have known him for over 13,000 seasons. Or, maybe it has been 14,000 seasons now."

"Yes, you know him alright. But, who was he with when you met him?"

"He was with you. Why?"

Lasidious gestured for his lover to take a seat. As she did, Celestria tucked her cherry-red gown under her legs. The Mischievous One lowered his own, then leaned forward. "When the Farendrite Collective was formed, it was Alistar and I who started it."

"Why do you talk to me as if I do not know this? What are you getting at?"

"There's a secret Alistar and I have kept from the Collective." Lasidious reached out and took Celestria's hands. "We have also kept this secret from you."

The goddess' brow furrowed. "Why me? We share everything."

Lasidious grinned. "No, my love. We share almost everything."

Celestria pulled her hands away, then stood and moved to the far side of the table. "You better have a good explanation."

Lasidious leaned back in his chair. "You won't be mad for long. I'm sure you'll find everything I have to say intriguing."

"Spit it out already."

Lasidious held up his hands. "Just relax."

"Do not tell me to relax. Spit it out."

"Okay. But, what I'm about to tell you will need to be said under the Rule of Fromalla."

Celestria's eyes filled with rage. "Why would I need to enter into the pact of Fromalla with you? I'm your lover, not your enemy!"

Lasidious stood, then moved behind his chair. He remained calm. "I'll explain everything once you've agreed."

Celestria reached out and passed her right hand over a vase filled with fresh roses. The flowers wilted as the light emanating from within the walls turned red, casting a glow to match her mood. "This better be good. I agree to Fromalla. This better be the explanation above all other explanations or you will be spending the rest of your existence without me in your bed."

Lasidious smiled, "Your beauty becomes more intoxicating when you're vexed."

Celestria knocked the vase from the table and held Lasidious' eyes as it flew across the room and smashed against the wall beneath the tapestry. "I would speak now, if I was you!"

Lasidious threw up his hands. "Just breathe for a moment. There's no need for threats. I assure you...you'll be quite happy when I'm finished."

"So, get on with it!"

Lasidious took a deep breath, then sat on the edge of the table. "Alistar and I have known each other since birth." He paused to put a slight grin on his face. "We're brothers."

Celestria gasped. With a wave of her hand, the chair at the end of the table pulled back. She fell into the seat, then looked across the room into the green flames. She watched the fire dance for many moments before responding. "This is an enormous secret. I am not sure what to say."

Lasidious pushed clear of the table, then took the seat next to her. "Allow me to explain."

"Please do. I feel betrayed."

"I understand how you could feel that way, but I assure you there was a reason. You see, after Alistar and I thought of the idea of the Collective, we realized it would be easier to get others to join if we were selling a perfect balance of good and evil. This balance was not only necessary for the survival of those who fought together, but it was also necessary for the creation of a new set of worlds. With the destruction of Heaven and Hell, it was more important than ever to create a group to represent both paths. Good and evil had to be part of the Collective...and it was necessary to make the others join.

"Alistar and I knew we weren't powerful enough to live through the wars if we fought alone. We needed help. One of us had to take on the role of goodness. We agreed never to tell anyone. We couldn't allow this secret to get out. It would ruin our chances for any kind of advantage over those we intended to recruit."

Celestria stood. "Have I been a pawn in your game all these seasons?"

"No, no, no. You're wrong to think that way. Alistar and I never intended to recruit you. In fact, we never knew you existed until we found you in what was left of your father's heavenly kingdom. We went to Challic seeking him. We intended to recruit Dograin, but he was destroyed before our arrival. All we found floating amongst the debris was your unconscious figure. Your father must have been powerful to keep you from perishing."

Celestria wiped the moisture from her eyes. "My father was powerful. He could have defeated his attackers if it was not for his desire to protect me. I am the reason he was destroyed. I miss him so much. I only had the chance to spend 100 seasons with him after my ascension. My poor mother was distraught when he came to her home to collect me."

Lasidious gave Celestria a moment to gather herself. "The strength of your father's power was the reason we planned to recruit him. It was only after I laid eyes on you that I convinced my brother to allow me to bring you into our group. If you remember, Bassorine and Mieonus had already joined. I was taken by your beauty. I approached only because I wanted to know you and learn more about who you were. The fact we followed the same path was a bonus."

Celestria finished wiping the tears from her face. "So, how does this fit into our plans? How does this get us to where we are now?"

"Great questions. You see, Alistar and I knew Bassorine was powerful... so powerful that, with the assistance of a small group at his side, we could handle anything which threatened us while the God Wars continued. All we had to do was assemble a team which could handle the creation of the new worlds.

"But, Alistar and I agreed we had a problem to overcome. We knew Bassorine would be strong enough to rule the new worlds after they were created. We had to manipulate the others of the Collective into thinking the creation of the Book of Immortality was necessary. As you know, we convinced them to glorify Bassorine throughout the worlds. In exchange, Bassorine would succumb to the Book's governance."

"I still don't understand why Bassorine did this?" Celestria questioned while crossing her arms.

Lasidious moved to stand above the broken vase. He waved his hand across the mess and watched as it vanished. After snapping his fingers, a new vase filled with fresh flora appeared on the table. "If Bassorine was to fight against the Book's creation, there would have been consequences. Perhaps, the grief of your father's loss has affected your memory. Alistar and I convinced the rest of the Collective to abandon Bassorine if he chose not to allow the Collective to be governed by the Book. He would have been left alone within the vast expanse of an empty universe with no one to talk to, no one to love, and no one to serve him. He would have been miserable.

"Alistar and I convinced the Collective to give Bassorine the confidence that his sword could destroy the Book if ever he needed to reclaim his dominance. We did this for two reasons. The first was to give him peace of mind about the Book's creation. The second was to protect us from the Book if the moment ever came when the Book chose a path of its own."

Celestria stood from the table and spoke in a tone Lasidious had not heard for over 3,000 seasons. "You lie! I was there when the others had the conversation about the weaknesses the Book of Immortality would have. Do you think I am stupid?"

"No, of course not. Do you think I would be foolish enough to lie to you after all we've done? Look how far we've come. You know I can't lie to you. You made sure of that. We are close to having complete control over the others. Just think about it. What happened to Bassorine?"

Lasidious watched her expression change. "Are you telling me you and Alistar knew you were going to use the Book against Bassorine before its creation?"

"I am."

"But, why convince the Collective to create a book filled with laws that even you were required to live by? We created something stronger than Bassorine."

"Yes, but we also created something with a limited amount of power. We created a neutral being with no alignment to either path. We created a being whose only desire is to do the job assigned by the gods. Gabriel is the balance Alistar and I needed to put our plans into effect."

Lasidious put his hands on Celestria's shoulders, then stroked the length of her arms. "Thanks to you, our baby's power will grow. Soon, he will be strong enough to take control of the Book. With Alistar working with us, we'll be able to keep the others from learning of our deception. Garrin can continue to grow without fear of death."

Lasidious pulled Celestria to him, but she held up her hand against his chest and pushed away. "How could you have known I would be willing to have your child?"

"I didn't know how you would react. Our baby was a backup plan, and you were the only piece of the puzzle I had to figure out in order to implement it. All I knew was I wanted you. I knew you had a piece of my heart, and I was willing to do anything to be with you. I took an enormous risk drinking the potion you gave me so many seasons ago. I knew it would stop me from lying to you, but you were worth it. Alistar and I felt that my desire to love you would win your affections. We hoped you would avoid asking me anything which would reveal our relationship as brothers. We hoped you would grow to love me, and you did. Together, you and I have given birth to the baby who will take control of the Book. The other plan Alistar and I created has also been implemented and will soon become known to the Collective."

Again, Lasidious tried to pull Celestria close, but the goddess backed up. Lasidious smiled, then continued to work his way out of trouble. "You know your potion keeps me from lying to you. You know I'm telling the truth. Now, you can relax and know our son is going to be okay. There's nothing to worry about. Alistar is going to keep Mosley busy. The wolf won't have the moments necessary to figure anything out."

Celestria stared into Lasidious' eyes. "I want to know...do you and Alistar have plans to dispose of me after our child has taken control of the Book?"

Lasidious laughed. "Of course not. I have told you how I feel on a million different occasions. You know what the plan is. I will explain the details of our backup plan, as well."

"Then, you really love me."

"Yes, of course I do. How could you doubt that."

"Then, why are we talking when we should be making up?" The goddess cupped his face in her hands and kissed him. "You can explain the details after you have apologized properly." She opened the front of Lasidious' tunic and rubbed her hands through the hair on his chest. "I want you to take me on an outing. I want you to be clever and surprise me. Make me smile."

The City of Marcus
The Dark Chancellor's Tower-palace

Marcus appeared inside his bedroom chamber. He was in a hurry and needed to meet with Boyafed in the dining hall. His servants had prepared a bath. The blood covering his body needed to be removed, and he had to change into a clean robe before joining the Order leader for dinner.

When Marcus appeared, he headed for his seat, but Boyafed had already taken it upon himself to sit at the head of the table. Boyafed smiled, knowing full well his choice of seats would irritate Marcus, but the chancellor handled the situation with humility. He had come with an agenda. "Good evening, Boyafed."

"What do you want, Marcus? Why am I having dinner with you? I have better things to do with my evening."

Marcus lifted his pipe and lit it. He took a long drag and allowed the smoke to escape as he spoke. "Boyafed, must we always fight? You and I have irritated one another for too many seasons. I wish to call a truce. I wish to apologize for speaking to you without the respect you deserve. I understand you're the backbone of this city, and without you, the strength of the army would pale in comparison. I should give you the same respect your men do. I owe you this much. I intend to do so from here on out."

Boyafed pondered Marcus' words. "I never expected an apology to leave your lips. What has caused this change of heart?"

"I have recently realized that if I am to achieve my full potential as a leader, I need to better myself. I see how the men treat you. I see how powerful you are. I want to receive the same respect from those I command, as you do."

Boyafed lowered his knife onto his plate. He stood and carried his meal to another seat. "Your goal is admirable. I accept your apology. Please take your seat at the table's head. Consider this my first act of respect."

Marcus smiled and feigned his appreciation. As he moved to take his seat, he thought, *News is coming your way, Boyafed. I will enjoy the pain on your face when your men find the body.*

Mogg's Village

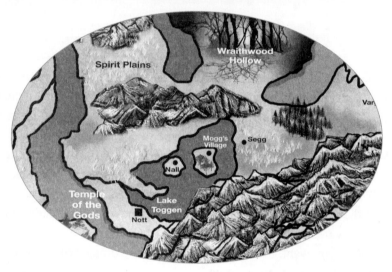

Brayson is standing in front of an ancient tree with a thick trunk. Much of the tree has been hollowed, and a tiny hole rests above his head. The hole acts as the entrance to Mogg's home, and he is waiting for the sprite's return.

The rest of Mogg's kind has lived for 300 seasons inside this community of hasspellyan spruces surrounding her own. They are hiding amongst the branches and are agitated by Brayson's presence.

The Head Master knows his presence is a threat to this tiny race, but his reason for coming outweighs his concern about their anxiety. Mogg is the only creature on Luvelles to master the magic of the past and Brayson needs her help to gather the knowledge he desires.

Late Bailem passed before Mogg returned from her outing to gather the village's dinner. She was with two companions, and the trio struggled to carry a single blushel berry through the trees.

It took a significant amount of moments before they managed to place the berry on the ground. Their breathing was labored as they lowered to their backsides to catch their breath. They had spent most of the day picking this one piece of fruit from a nearby bush.

Mogg recognized their large elven visitor and lifted to a hovering position only feet in front of Brayson's face. Her wings hummed as many dazzling colors fell as a shimmering glitter which dissipated prior to reaching the ground. It wasn't long before Brayson had hundreds of these tiny beings hovering all about him.

"For what when have you come, Head Master?" Mogg said, her voice small and high-pitched.

"I need your help."

"I didn't say *why*, wizard. I said...*when*."

"I don't understand."

"I know you seek knowledge of the past. I know you desire my help. When are the moments from which you seek answers?"

Brayson put his hand to his goatee and stroked it. "I seek to know the truth of a friend's death. The moments when this happened are unknown to me. It happened nearly a half season ago."

Mogg crossed her tiny arms across her bosom. "What can you offer for my help, wizard?"

"I don't know. What would you ask of me?"

Brayson watched as Mogg's eyes moved away from his and began to follow a beautiful red and yellow butterfly. Though night was approaching, the butterfly glowed as if it had been placed under a black light. The entire village began to follow it as if hypnotized by the fluttering of its wings. Brayson had to snap his fingers to capture their attention. He knew the sprites were notorious for their short attention spans and their insatiable love of butterflies.

"Mogg, please focus. I need your help."

The sprite kept her eyes on the butterfly. "They are beautiful, yes?"

"They are." Brayson snapped his fingers again to capture her full attention. "Now, what can I offer to help your village?"

Mogg refocused. "We need berries. You could gather them for us. Your magic is strong and could protect them from rotting. My family would be spared this labor. If you do this once a season, I will help you."

Brayson shifted his weight and put his hand on his hips. "You want me to pick berries?"

"Yes, wizard. It is a hard task for us. But, you are large and it will be easy for you."

"I'll pick your berries, but only this once. I'll pick enough to fill a single tree. I'll protect this tree with my magic to keep them from rotting. If you don't agree, say so, and I'll leave."

Mogg knew a treeful would feed their village for at least two seasons. "These terms are acceptable. I'll help you acquire the answer you seek... once the task has been completed."

Brayson bent over and picked up the berry off the ground. He held it between two fingers, then dropped it into the tiny hole of Mogg's tree. "I'll return in the morning and begin filling the tree of your choice. I hope you enjoy your dinner." Brayson vanished.

The Next Morning
Grogger's Swamp

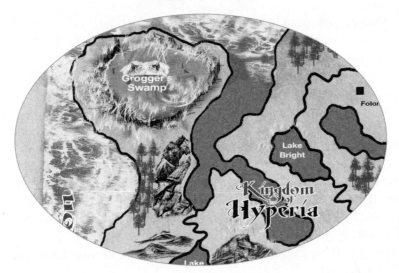

Shalee and Kiayasis had stopped the night before and set up camp within view of Grogger's Swamp. Once camp was set, they embraced while lying next to the campfire. Kiayasis' advances are becoming harder for Shalee to resist, and her desire to satisfy him is growing.

With the sun cresting the mountains to the east, Shalee is smiling as she finishes her breakfast. The morning air carries a chill, and the sky is growing angry, as if it is threatening to stop Shalee's entrance into the swamp.

As Kiayasis tossed another log onto the fire, lightning filled the sky in the distance. He sat on the edge of a boulder, unsheathed his knife, then began to run it across his whetstone. "I've been thinking about making a few changes in my life." He looked across the fire and watched the queen dip her biscuit into her soup. "I get tired of sharpening this dagger." He stroked the blade of his bone-handled knife across the stone. "I'm tired of living by the rules of my father's army. He always says: 'You can't carry a dull blade, my son.' Perhaps, the moment has come for me to create a path of my own."

Shalee didn't respond. Her attention was elsewhere.

"Shalee. Did you hear me?"

"It looks so dark...so dreary...so ugly."

"What does?"

"The swamp. It feels like I'm 'bout ta go into some kinda cemetery. It looks haunted."

"What do you mean, 'some kind of cemetery.' What's that?"

"Oh, for heaven's sake. I apologize. Sometimes, I forget I'm not at home anymore."

"What do you mean by 'sometimes?'"

"Goodness-gracious, I did it again. I just keep doin' it, don't I?"

Kiayasis shrugged. "Apparently. Please explain."

"I know ya burn the dead ta celebrate their passin', but where I'm from, a cemetery is a place where we bury the bodies of the people who've died. We put 'em in the ground and cover 'em with dirt."

"Why would you do that? Doesn't this dishonor the dead? I did not know Grayham's customs were so different from our own."

"I'm not originally from Grayham. The place I'm from was called Earth. Many of us had a belief that a person's body would rise again when our god returned to collect his faithful. We laid the dead facin' east so when they rose again, the first thing they would see was our lord's face as he came for us. I can only imagine what that would've been like."

Kiayasis set his dagger down. "I'm not familiar with your Earth. Do you still have this belief?"

"No. Now, I find my beliefs are lost ta me. I had faith once...a strong faith...or at least as strong as it could be, considerin' my upbringin'."

"What do you mean, 'upbringing?'"

"I mean how I was raised. The problem is, after comin' ta these worlds and seein' the things I've seen, I'm not so sure I believe in much of anythin' any longer. I find it strange ta believe in gods who are so flawed, so imper-fect, so opposite of the concept of the god I used to believe in. A god is sup-posed ta be perfect. In my mind, they should be all-knowin', a figurehead worth praisin'. I suppose I think it's all a big crock of garesh now."

Kiayasis shook his head in disappointment. "Then, you haven't served the one true god. Hosseff is powerful and all-knowing...just as you said a god should be. He possesses power beyond our comprehension, and you would be wise to serve him."

Shalee began to laugh. Kiayasis lifted his eyes to the sky, worried Hosseff would strike her down. The dark paladin questioned why she would find his statements humorous.

After a moment, Shalee calmed herself, then responded, "I'm sorry, but I think it would be best if we changed the subject. I don't wish ta offend ya 'bout your beliefs."

"Fair enough. I feel the same way. Why don't you tell me why you left this Earth of yours?"

Shalee looked at the swamp's entrance, and again, her mind began to wander.

"Shalee, I asked you a question. Shalee...Shalee. Where's your mind?" Kiayasis waved his hand to capture her attention. "I'm over here."

Shalee struggled to pull her eyes from the fog. "It just hangs there, threatenin' ta suck me in." A chill ran down her spine before she forced herself to find Kiayasis' glare. "I'm sorry. It just looks so evil."

Kiayasis tossed another log onto the fire. "I wouldn't worry about it. The swamp always looks angry. I would be more worried about what's inside if I was you. I would go in with you, but my orders are to allow you to go in alone. I can't go any further."

"Is this your way of cheerin' me up? How could someone be so cute and so ignorant durin' the same moment?"

Kiayasis smiled. "You're right. I wasn't thinking. Let's talk of other things. Tell me why you left your Earth."

"I left because I had no choice. I was..."

Kiayasis interrupted. "We always have a choice. Choices are what make us who we are. Choices give us character."

"Yeah, right! If only that were true. Ya think ya know, but ya don't. We don't always have a..."

Again, Kiayasis stopped her. "We always have a choice. I recently had to make one of the hardest choices of my life. I think you'll like what I have to tell you. The..."

Shalee returned the favor and cut him off. "Ya don't even know what a hard choice is. Everythin' was taken from me. And, no...we don't always have a choice in what happens ta us. Things just happen. They get forced down our doggone throats. Don't go playin' all self-righteous on me like ya understand."

Kiayasis tilted his head, confused. "I'm not playing anything."

"Hmph! Men! Just forget 'bout it. Like I was sayin' before ya so rudely interrupted me...I had no choice." She cocked her head. "I was taken from my home by the gods. Did ya hear that, Mr. Smartypants? I said...*the gods*. They gave me no choice in the matta'."

Kiayasis crossed his arms. "I'm sorry. Please, continue. I would love to hear how the gods took you away from your Earth."

"Love? You would love ta hear 'bout my pain? Do ya enjoy otha' peoples' misery or somethin'?"

"That's not what I meant. I'll just be quiet."

"Good! That would be the best thing for ya ta do right now." After a long, awkward moment of silence, Shalee continued. "Talkin' 'bout this just makes me mad. As I was sayin'...I had no choice in the matta'. I was stolen from my home. Hell, all of us were stolen from our homes. I was put on Grayham with Sam...and a jerk named George. Sam and I were asked ta do so many horrible things. I still have nightmares because of 'em. I have killed so much...and so has Sam. Life here has been stressful for us. I would've never chosen ta leave my family and neitha' would Sam...no matta' what we were offered. I neva' wanted ta be put in a position where I had to kill anyone. I can only imagine how Sam must have felt."

Shalee lifted her hands and covered her mouth. "Oh, my goodness! How Sam must be feelin'." Shalee lowered her eyes and stared at the hot coals feeding the fire. A tear rolled down her cheek.

Seeing Shalee's distress, Kiayasis moved to sit beside her. He lifted his arm to put it around her. "It will be okay."

Shalee pulled back and stood to escape Kiayasis' embrace. "What am I doin'? How could I be so selfish?"

"What are you talking about? You're not being selfish."

Shalee looked toward the mountains. "I have not been fair ta Sam."

Kiayasis' heart sunk. He could feel Shalee's love pulling away. "Stop this. You said yourself...your king treated you poorly. You have only done what was right for..."

"Right for who?" Shalee shouted. "Is this truly what's right for me?"

Kiayasis stood and moved to her. "Of course this is what's right for you. It's what's right for us. I have decided to leave my father's army for you. My father's army isn't the best way to begin a life together. I can build us a home. I love you."

Shalee shook her head and moved further away. "No, Kiayasis! Don't say that." Tears ran freely down her face. Her voice trembled. "Sam...oh my heavens, Sam has done nothin' wrong. I've betrayed him. How could I be so awful...so selfish? This is not how a queen should act. How can I lead others if I cannot lead myself?"

Kiayasis moved to her, grabbed her by the arms, then turned her to face him. "You won't need to lead others. This is about you and me. We can build an amazing life together. Besides, you said your king loathes you. You said he doesn't love you. You said he looks at you as a failure."

"I know what I said," Shalee snapped as she pulled free of his grip. "He neva' actually said any of that. I was insecure. I went bonkers for a bit. This is all my fault."

Shalee shoved past Kiayasis and walked to her bag. She put on a pair of pants, hiked them up beneath her dress, then retrieved a sweater. She began walking in the direction opposite the swamp.

Kiayasis pursued and grabbed her by the arm. With a yank, he forced her to face him. "What about us?"

Shalee's eyes filled with a fire Kiayasis had never seen. She looked down at her arm. "If ya know what's best for ya, you'll remove your hand, sir."

Kiayasis released his grip. Shalee continued to speak as she rubbed away the pain. "Weren't ya listenin' ta me? How can there be an us? I need ta think. I need ta be left alone so I can gatha' my thoughts."

The dark warrior exploded. "Leave you alone? I won't do that! You have said things you can't take back! You have allowed me to hold you in my arms! I respected your boundaries! You can't just tell a man you love him, then walk away! What kind of a woman does that make you?"

Shalee lifted a finger and held it in front of Kiayasis' face, then rocked it back and forth. "Why don't ya tell me what kinda woman it makes me, mister? I've already done it once. I left Sam, and I told him I loved him during many moments."

Shalee extended her hand toward the campsite. Precious lifted from the side of her bag and flew across the distance into her hand. She tapped the staff's butt end on the ground as it started to rain. "Let me tell ya somethin'. Do ya wanna know what Sam said ta me before I left? His final words were: 'I'll always love ya, no matta' what, no matta' how hard it is ta do.'"

Shalee wiped a raindrop off the end of her nose. So, tell me, Kiayasis, do ya think Sam could've been anymore lovin'? I am wrong for doin' what we've been doin'."

Kiayasis stood in silence. Shalee could see he was at a loss for words. She continued. "This problem you and I are havin' is self-created. I was too self-absorbed. I felt guilty for losin' the child Sam gave me, and now...I've thrown everythin' away...and for what? I..."

Kiayasis shouted. "Go ahead...say it! You would be throwing away your life for someone like me! You don't think I'm good enough!"

Shalee took a step back and matched the strength of Kiayasis' voice. "It's not that you're not good enough...you're just not a replacement for Sam!" Seeing the look on Kiayasis' face, Shalee realized how harsh she sounded. She sighed, "This is all my fault. If I wouldn't have been so selfish, I would neva'..."

"You would have never what, Shalee? You would have never cared for me? You would have never said the things you have? How should I react to this?"

"I don't know! What I do know...we can't continue this relationship. It's wrong and both of us know it."

Kiayasis fell to his knees and grabbed the top of his head. He squeezed his hair inside his fists. Seeing his pain, Shalee moved to stand over him. She put her left hand on his right shoulder and tried to speak in her softest voice. "Listen ta me. I believe we could've been a good couple. I do love ya. But, I must return home once I'm done here, and beg for Sam's forgiveness."

Kiayasis mumbled something beneath his breath.

"I didn't understand ya. Kiayasis, please don't make this harder than it has ta be. What did ya say? Come on...let's not be like this with one anotha'."

With a swift motion, the dark paladin grasped the Knife of Spirits from his hip and slashed Shalee across her abdomen. He jumped to his feet, grabbed her by the ears, then head-butted her. With his left hand full of hair, he reached back and slugged Shalee just above the wound. As Shalee doubled over, Kiayasis reared back, then kicked her to the ground with the sole of his boot. The sorceress rolled to a stop.

Kiayasis shouted as he watched Shalee raise a bloody hand to invoke her magic, but her power failed. "You made this decision easy for me! You're a fool! You should've never turned your back on me!"

The sorceress began to scoot away. Pain shot through her body with each movement. She continued to hold her hand extended, but the magic wouldn't come.

Kiayasis taunted his prey. "Ahhhhhhh...your magic has left you." The dark paladin looked toward the forest and nodded his head in its direction. "I'll give you a headstart. There's no fun in killing without good sport."

Shalee pushed against the wound to ease the pain. "Why? Why would ya do this?" she screamed.

"You know the answer. You're a tease. I would have expected this from a wench, not a queen. You have hurt me deeper than any other. I'm going to show you the meaning of pain. I'm going to string your bowels through the trees, then hang you upside down and let the animals feast on your flesh." Kiayasis leaned over Shalee, then hissed, "I suggest you run."

Kiayasis turned and walked toward the campfire. He wiped Shalee's blood from the Knife of Spirits, sheathed it, then sat on the boulder. He lifted his bone-handled dagger from the ground and continued to sharpen it.

Shalee struggled to stand. She had to hunch over in order to keep the wound from ripping further. Her white pants absorbed the blood as it ran down her legs. She tried to use her magic again, but the power failed to flow through her. She had no choice. She needed to run.

Kiayasis' eyes followed Shalee as she hobbled toward the forest. He threw his dagger across the fire and watched it penetrate one of the logs he had collected the night before. He reached into his bag and removed the mirror Boyafed gave him. He placed the mirror flat on his knee, then bashed his fist against its surface. Lifting the mirror in front of his face, he spoke to his shattered image, "You will have your way, father. Praise Hosseff."

Traitor

The Void Maze
The Source's Temple

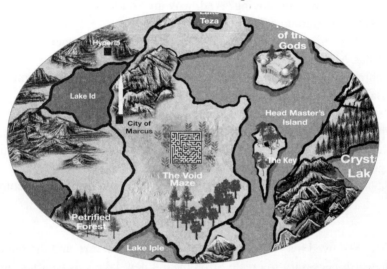

Kepler was sound asleep when George woke in the field just outside The Source's temple. Payne was the first to see the color of George's eyes. He flew over and held up a piece of werebear George had killed just over a day and a half ago.

"Master hungry? Payne cook it like kitty say to cook. It meat."

Kepler opened his eyes and rolled his head over the top of his shoulder. "Well, look who's awake? How are you feeling?"

George took a moment to gather his thoughts. He pushed against Kepler and stretched. "I feel like I've been hit by a train."

"What 'train' mean?" Payne plopped down on George's lap.

"Don't start, freak," Kepler growled. "Let him breathe. Get off of him."

"Fine...ebbish nay." The fairy-demon began to pout.

George rolled to his feet. He reached down and took the piece of meat from Payne's claw, then took a bite. "I'm starved. I could eat a horse. Thanks for being a pillow, Kep."

Kepler stood and stretched. Payne's eyes followed the tip of the cat's tail as it extended. The fairy-demon licked his lips. Kepler snarled, "Don't get any ideas, freak." He looked at George. "I'm glad you're okay, and you're welcome, but don't start hugging me. You don't need to show me your appreciation."

"How long was I asleep?"

Kepler yawned. "Not long enough."

George had to laugh. "I feel rested."

"Good. Can we get moving? And, why are you looking at me that way? What are you grinning at?"

George's smile grew. He looked at the fairy-demon. "Payne."

"What, Master?"

George gave Kepler an evil grin. "I want you to hug Kepler for me."

"Bah! Dang it, George, keep that freak away from me."

Payne put his tiny claws together and rubbed them back and forth as a sharp-toothed grin appeared on his face. "Come to Payne, kitty."

Kepler's eyes flashed. "George...you better stop him. This isn't funny. I'm going to have to kill someone in a moment."

Payne began to chase Kepler around the clearing in front of the temple.

Village of Gogswayne

Gage removed his harness. His fur was covered in dirt, and the removal of the earth necessary to create Strongbear's new lake was wearing on his patience. He was tired of hearing the brown bear shout his favorite phrase, "So are you with me...or are you against me?" Gage was now against him.

The badger had been working with Gallrum at his side, along with many of the other goswigs. They were all as irritated as he was, and it was the perfect moment for a break.

Gage climbed to the top of a large boulder and plopped down by his basket of food. He brushed aside the colorful cloth which Strongbear had placed over the top of it and reached in. The bear had provided every goswig with a lunch holding their favorite flavors. After a few bites of cooked corgan, Gage lifted his head and motioned for Gallrum to join him.

The serwin flapped his wings and made his way over to the top of the rock. Once he had lowered into a coiled position, Gallrum spoke as he reached into his basket to retrieve a bowl of fresh fish eyes. "I can't be sure, but I think every scale on my body is sore." He lifted the bowl to his mouth. His long, thin, snake-like tongue shot out, scooped up one of the eyes, then pulled it in. "Would you like some?" he mumbled with his mouth full.

Gage turned up his nose. "I'd rather not."

"Okay, but you don't know what you're missing."

Gage secured a tin filled with water between his paws and took a drink. "I've been doing some thinking."

Gallrum slurped up another eye and hissed a response. "What about?"

"The other day you said something about Strongbear hibernating when the season changes."

"Mmmmmm...you've got to try one of these."

Gage's brow furrowed as a badger's would. "Gallrum! Pay attention. I have an idea that will benefit us all."

The serwin swallowed an eye, then burped it back up. "Oops. Guess I didn't chew that one enough."

The badger fought the need to gag. Gallrum looked at Gage like his reaction was uncalled for. The badger pushed his disgust aside. "Anyway, I was thinking Strongbear has accumulated enough fat. He is ready to hibernate."

"I agree. But, the season hasn't changed. It isn't cold enough for him to sleep."

"I know. But, I have a solution. There are enough of us living in Gogswayne to do something about it. I bet if we all combined our magic, we could create a change of season."

Gallrum adjusted his coils. "You expect us to change the season on all of Luvelles? Only the gods can do such a thing."

"No. Not on Luvelles. I want to change the season in Gogswayne."

The serwin scratched the top of his head. "You mean change the weather of the village?"

"Yes. That's exactly what I mean. If we cool it down around here, Strongbear will hibernate. He won't be able to boss everyone around."

"This is brilliant!" Gallrum's wings began to flap. He lifted from the stone and hovered to a position eye-level with Gage. "How do we inform the others without Strongbear finding out? I would hate to see a bear of that size become angry."

The badger took another bite of corgan. "How often do you go topside to speak with Swill?"

Gallrum lifted his eyes and counted in his head. "Every seventh day I must be standing on the shore of the lake after sunset. Swill swims up and takes a report back to King Ultor. It's my job to inform him of significant changes which transpire within the village."

"Who goes in your place when you're sick?"

"Strongbear, of course." Gallrum began to grin. "Aahhhh...you want to have our meeting while he's reporting to Swill."

Gage chuckled. "I think you're catching on. When's your next report?"

"Tomorrow night. But, there's going to be a problem with tomorrow."

"And, that problem is?"

"I don't feel sick. How can Strongbear go if I'm not sick?"

Gage growled and thumped the top of the serwin's forehead with the backside of his paw. "Are you truly this thick? You pretend. You fake it. You act sick. Do I have to spell it out for you?"

"Aahhhh. I can do that. That could be fun. You know..." The serwin straightened into a regal posture, then put his right claw on his chest. "I've always pictured myself as a thespian."

Gage grinned. "I'm going to enjoy the thought of Strongbear's slumber." He mocked, "So, are you with me...or are you against me?"

Gallrum winked. "Oh, I'm with you."

Both goswigs laughed.

Mogg's Village in the Trees

Brayson made his way back from the blushel berry bushes not far from Mogg's village. The sprite had chosen a tree just behind her personal residence for Brayson to fill with the fruit. He had filled two baskets with over 2,000 berries, and judging by the size of the hole within the tree, a single trip would be more than sufficient to fill the hollowed area within its trunk.

Many of Mogg's family flew all about Brayson as he sauntered into the village carrying a basket in each hand. Their excitement could be heard as their voices cried out in song. Many glorious showers filled with sparkling colors fell from their wings.

Brayson stopped in front of the tree and waved his hand across its surface. The hole opened and allowed the Head Master to pour the berries inside. Once the task was complete and the spell had been cast to protect the fruit, the hole reduced to its normal size.

Brayson returned to Mogg's tree. The sprite emerged and hovered in front of him. "You have kept your word. I will keep mine. Follow me, wizard."

"Where?"

"Not where, wizard. When. Follow me to your when."

"How do I follow you to the past?"

Mogg shook her small head. "You ask many questions, wizard. How is it you talk so much and still manage to learn? Just follow me. You'll see. Your when is about to become your now."

"But, how do you know what when I seek?"

"I always know, wizard. Stop talking and follow."

The other fairies disappeared into their hollowed homes. Brayson followed as Mogg began to fly through the trees. He watched as the scenery changed before his eyes. When the images slowed, the daylight had faded and a barn, or rather a large shed, now stood in front of them. Its outline was lit by a single torch on the side of the road.

"This is your when, Head Master."

"How can you be so sure? Where are we? When are we?"

"Your when is the night of your friend's death. Your where is on Grayham. This place is a smith's barn outside of a city filled with champions. The answer you seek is walking this way."

Brayson turned and looked down the gravel road. The gates of Champion were well lit in the distance. It was too dark to make out the figures at first, but as they grew closer, the torches lighting the road showed their silhouettes. "Mogg, can they see us?"

"No, wizard. We aren't a part of this when. We can only observe."

As the silhouettes came into focus, Brayson smiled as he saw Amar's face. Yet, someone unexpected was with him—someone he would have never imagined to see at this particular moment. It was George. "Mogg, are you sure this is the when I'm seeking? The other man shouldn't be here."

"Yes, wizard, I'm sure. Just watch. See, instead of talk. My magic to seek out moments is strong. I have brought you to the right when."

"Can they see us?"

Mogg giggled. An increase of sparkling colors fell from her wings as she did. "You have already asked me this, wizard. You lack much intelligence for such a powerful elf."

Brayson ignored the sprite's tone and moved in to listen to George and Amar's conversation. He followed them to the door of the smith's barn.

George fumbled with the lock on the door. "I need a hammer from inside. Amar, use some of your hocus pocus to manipulate the lock."

Brayson watched as Amar held up his staff. He spoke the simple command, and the lock released. Both men entered, and Brayson was quick to follow.

George took a seat on a wooden bench near the forge. "Sometimes, I feel like I'm going crazy. I miss my family, Amar. I want to tell you something. When I first met you, I didn't like you much, but I've grown fond of you over the last few days. You remind me of my uncle back home. I really need someone I can trust in my life. I was wondering if you needed a friend? How would you feel about that? If you don't want to, I'll understand. I'm sorry I've bothered you if this is the case."

Brayson watched as George began to cry. He moved to a better position and waited for Amar's response. Amar sat next to George. "I don't have any problems being your friend. I would prefer to travel this way. I also want this, but I've had my doubts, just as you have. I didn't think you cared for my companionship. I must say I'm surprised at your request. What made you decide this?"

Brayson knew something wasn't right, but he could only watch as George hugged Amar. "I've been so alone since my arrival. I can't tell you how grateful I am we'll be friends. It warms my heart to know that I've found companionship worth keeping on this world. I have news which will make you happy, my new friend."

"What kind of news?"

"Well...it's like this. I know where you can gain a significant amount of power above what you already command." Brayson watched closely as George enjoyed the surprise on Amar's face. George continued. "That's right, I know of your power, Amar. I also know of a woman who has substantial power. Her abilities would increase your own if you seek her out and take them from her before her soul leaves her body."

Brayson was floored. His elven ears couldn't believe what he was hearing as he focused on Amar's reaction. "How do you know of my power? I have said nothing of it. And, how do you know the secret of the ancient elves?"

"I'm a smart man, Amar. Your knowledge of this secret comes from the same source as my own. Now that we're friends, I'll tell you her name if you want to know it. This is my way of showing you it is my true desire to be your buddy."

"George, this is valuable information. I would like to know her name."

"Friends for life, right?" Brayson watched as George smiled. He could feel the deception as George added, "Let's take this friendship to new heights until we rule this world."

"I agree. We will dominate,"

This is a trap, Brayson thought. He stood close enough to look into George's eyes and though the mage could not hear, he spoke anyway. "What are you up to, George? I can see through your smile." He turned to look at his friend. "Amar, don't fall for this." Brayson grit his teeth, knowing his plea had fallen on ears from another when.

Brayson stood and began to pace as George spit in his hand and extended it. He cringed with every sentence his Mystic Learner uttered. "Where I'm from, this is how we become friends. You spit in your hand, and I spit in mine. Once we shake, we become brothers. We'll become true buddies. You do still want to be my friend, right?"

Brayson shouted. "Stop smiling, Amar! This is a trap! Can't you see it? You're a fool!" He turned to face the sprite. "Mogg, allow me to say something to him."

"We cannot change the past, wizard. You know this. Perhaps, you should finish what you came for, or we could return to the when from which we came."

"No. I need to see what happens. I wish to stay. I need to know the truth."

"As you wish, wizard. But, the truth from this when is not the truth you wish it to be."

Brayson frowned as Amar took George's hand. He could see George's eyes change as the darkness appeared within them. "Amar, I'm so glad you fell for this line of garesh."

Brayson saw the change. It was instantaneous. Amar's eyes widened as he started to speak, but it was too late. His tongue and lips had turned to stone. Amar ripped his hand away and tried to move, but his feet were heavy. They were also stone, and both of his hands were beginning to change.

Brayson could see the pain was severe as he watched the grayness spread. Amar tried to take a step back, but the weight of his feet caused him to become unbalanced. He fell backward to his butt.

Brayson tried to pull George back, but his hand passed right through the mage's shoulder. George touched Amar's nose. Amar's pain stopped as George pushed him to his back.

Again, Brayson looked at Mogg. "He's killing him. I need to help. You must allow me to help."

"I cannot, wizard. As I have said, you can only watch the things which happen during this when. We cannot change another's when for reasons of our own. If we do, our own now, the now from which we came, will not be as it was. You can only watch, wizard."

Brayson's eyes narrowed. "This is wrong. How can you just stand by like this?"

"I do nothing because my nothing is somebody else's something in our now. You don't wish to take someone else's now from them, do you?"

Brayson stopped arguing with the sprite. He turned and listened to George say, "Ha! Cat got your tongue? Just relax a little bit. Don't be so bitchy. Your eyes are cussing at me. That's not very nice. And, you seem so tense. You must be eating wrong."

George peeled back the sleeves of Amar's robe. "You know what, I didn't do a very good job. What was I thinking? How could I be so rude. Turning your hands to stone isn't very giving. After all, we are friends. You deserve more. Allow me to fix it for you."

Brayson watched George touch the mage's flesh over and over. Small spots of Amar's arm turned with each touch. George leaned over and looked into Amar's eyes. "Hey, I wish I had a marker. I'm curious. I wonder if all these dots have a pattern. Oh man! How am I going to know which dot is first? Wait. I know. Check this out." Again, George placed his finger on Amar's flesh. Tiny numbers appeared by each dot. "That's better. Hey, Amar, I'll tell you a secret. If anybody figures this out, it's going to spell your name...Gullible."

Brayson paced as Amar's torture continued. He watched George pry open Amar's chest. Brayson vomited as George ripped out Amar's heart and took the first bite. Brayson stumbled out of the barn with Mogg following as the smith's shed filled with a storm of flashing light.

What Brayson saw next was unexpected. A man dressed in a hooded tunic stood in the failing torchlight at the center of the gravel road. His face was hidden within the shadow of his hood, but it was clear he knew what was happening and appeared disinterested in doing anything to stop it.

Brayson was taken aback by the thought that someone could care so little about a murder. The figure vanished a few moments later.

"Mogg, I wish to follow that man, the one who disappeared. I want to know the next thing that happens in his when."

The sprite hovered in front of him. "We cannot follow his when. I cannot find his trail."

"What do you mean? His trail begins over there."

"I'm sorry, wizard. His trail is too powerful. I would perish if I were to attempt to take you there. His when is untraceable."

"Then, let's follow George. I wish to know more about his when."

Mogg closed her eyes and after a moment of silence, she responded. "George's trail beyond this when has been blocked and is no longer one I can follow."

"What? Why?"

"I sense the man who stood on the road knows we're here to learn about George's when. He must have hidden the trail from me. He's made George's trail from this when forward untraceable. He has hidden it somehow. I fear it isn't safe here any longer. We best leave."

"Mogg, how can a man from our now block another man's trail from this when...especially when that trail is a part of his own when? How could he have known we were here?"

"I don't know this answer, wizard."

Brayson thought a moment. "You said his when from here forward has been blocked. What about his when farther back? Is George's past beyond this when also blocked?"

Mogg closed her eyes again. After a moment, she opened them. "The when further into George's past is still an active trail which I can follow."

"Mogg, I need you to take me to the most significant event in George's past, the past prior to this when we're visiting."

"Follow me, wizard." Once again, the scenery changed, but now there was nothing familiar to his eyes. They now stood in an old, rundown home of some sort. The furniture was nothing like he had ever seen. There was a box sitting on top of a small table with pictures moving inside it. Brayson moved to touch it. He expected to be able to reach inside, but found he could not.

"Mogg, what sort of magic is this? I cannot touch the objects inside." He tapped the glass. "What sort of barrier protects the..." Brayson stopped talking and moved back. He watched as a man ran toward the screen and dove in his direction as an explosion blew up a building in the background. The flames appeared to travel beyond the box's picture, but when Brayson moved to see if it had escaped, he could not understand how the box still felt cold to the touch. Brayson lowered back in front of the box and tried to reach through the glass again.

His voice was filled with frustration as he shouted, "Mogg, we need to save this man! He could be dying! The building behind him burns and... and..." He could not believe his eyes as the man stood as if nothing had happened and dusted off his clothes. "He lives! How is this possible?"

"Shut up, you fat cow!"

Brayson turned as a grumpy man with a pot belly entered the room. He lifted a thin paper full of tobacco to his mouth and sucked on it. The way its red cherry lit up on the end reminded the Head Master of his brother's pipe.

"I told you to have that little mistake take out the trash. And, get me another beer while you're at it!"

Brayson watched as the dark-haired man plopped into a worn-out chair. He leaned back and forced a lever to lift a cushion-covered surface to hold his feet. After setting his metallic container on a circular side table, the man shouted again. "Woman! Tell George to get his little ass in here. I need to handle some business!"

Brayson watched as a woman ran into the room. She had an unhealthy face. It was filled with panic. She screamed, "You said you wouldn't touch him again! He's your son, Nathan! You can't do this. You shouldn't make him do these awful things. He's still recovering from the beating you gave him last night. I'll call the cops on ya! I'll do it!"

Brayson rolled his hands together in a nervous fashion as Nathan stood from his chair. He grabbed the woman's frail frame and slammed her into the doorway leading into another room. Nathan hit her across the face with his fist. For a brief moment, her brown eyes rolled up into her head.

Nathan continued his abuse. "Look at you!" He looked her body up and down. "You're a complete waste of good air. If I wanted an opinion, I would give it to you. Do you want me to call your probation officer? I could always tell her where your stash is hidden. Do you really want to go back to jail?"

The woman fell to the floor and began to cry. Brayson desperately wanted to help her. He knelt next to her and listened. "Please! You don't have to do this. I'll do whatever you tell me. He's just a child. Please don't do this to my baby."

"Your baby? He's an irritating piece of crap. He's ruined our lives. Look at you. You're pathetic. You're just a crack whore. Why would I want you? Go find your stash, and leave me alone. I'll send the little mistake crying to you once I'm done with him. Now, get out of my face before I decide to kill him."

Brayson moved to stand beside Nathan and looked into his eyes. They were cold, full of hate, and his breath reeked of an ale smelling substance on top of his tobacco. Brayson looked at the sprite. "Mogg, I cannot allow this man to do this. How could he do such things?"

The sprite flew over and lowered into a seated position on Brayson's shoulder. "I understand your frustration, wizard, but we cannot change George's when. You can only watch."

Brayson took a deep breath as Nathan lowered back into his chair. "George, get your butt in here and bring a hot towel! I need to get this over with! My favorite show is on in an hour!"

Brayson watched as the frail woman lifted from the floor and left the room. He could see the pain in her walk and after some moments passed, a young George entered.

"Oh, no, no, no. Mogg, he's just a child."

"Yes he is, wizard. You said to bring you to the most significant event in George's when. I did as you requested? Just watch."

Brayson did as instructed. George spoke. "What do you want?"

Nathan's back was to the boy. He did not bother to turn his head from the box of pictures as he responded. He held up the container which he had referred to as lotion. "Watch your tongue, boy! Get in here, I ain't got all day."

Brayson was surprised at how strong George sounded. "I don't want to. I hate doing that. It hurts. It makes me bleed...and you stink. You freaking disgust me."

Nathan kept his eyes focused on the box of pictures. "Look, you little bastard...get in here or I'll kill ya!"

Brayson could see the fight in the child's eyes. "Mogg, I think he is going to make a stand. I can see it in his face."

George darted across the room and struck Nathan against the temple. It was as if he was berserk, swinging wildly without hesitation. Nathan cried out and shouted for help as George's punches connected again and again.

George screamed. "You're a piece of crap! You're nothing but an abusive loser! I hate you! I'll make sure you never touch me again or anybody else! I'm not your toy! Who do you think you are? I hate you!"

The fight continued for a long while. Many of the items scattered throughout the home had been thrown and windows were broken. George lifted a metal object with a light at its end and hit Nathan across the face. Nathan fell to the floor and balled up.

Eventually, the door burst open and four men in blue clothing, with shiny metal objects pinned to their chest, rushed in and subdued George. They pulled him off Nathan's body which still lay in a fetal position covering his face. The whole way out the door, George screamed. "Let me kill him! That scum deserves it! Let me put him six feet under! Let me kill him! Let me kill him!"

Brayson stood in silence and scratched the sides of his head just above his pointed ears. He passed through the door leading outside and watched as the men put George into a metal beast with wheels. Lights illuminated from the beast's back, and it cried a horrific noise as it rolled away through a wall of people who had gathered to see what the disturbance was about.

Mogg lifted from Brayson's shoulder and flew to the far side of the yard as the Head Master followed. "Do you wish to know anything else, wizard?"

"I do. What is the name of this place where we stand?"

"It is called Orlando, Florida. This is a world not like ours. We have traveled over 14,900 seasons to see this when known to George."

Brayson was speechless as Mogg continued. "Your Mystic Learner is very old...much older than you are, wizard."

A while passed before Brayson spoke again. "I wish to visit another part of George's past. I wish to see the when of his arrival on Grayham. I wish to know when George came to our now."

Mogg's wings fluttered. The sky darkened, and the normal shower of colors which fell from them increased. The scenery began to change, and after a considerable amount of moments passed, their journey stopped at a place Brayson knew all too well. "Mogg, I asked to see George's arrival on Grayham. I didn't want to come to the temple on Luvelles. We need to go to Grayham."

"Yes, wizard, I know. You're standing inside the Temple of the Gods on Grayham. I have brought you to the when which happened nearly a season ago."

"What? What about the last 14,000 seasons? Are you telling me George only recently came to our worlds?"

"I'm telling you nothing other than this is the when you requested to see."

Brayson began to look around. Not far away, standing just behind a large pillar, three people were moving around the statue of Bassorine and Mosley. After looking a while longer, Brayson moved closer. "Mogg, this is the King of Brandor and his queen. Why are they dressed in such ridiculous attire? Why is George with them? I need to know why they are together."

The sprite closed her eyes and began to concentrate. As she did, Brayson listened to every word Sam was saying and learned of the prophecy which had been written on the statue's base. When the sprite opened her eyes, George was standing on top of it. Brayson watched as George leaned over and took a piece of the Crystal Moon. The rest of the pieces vanished.

George reacted. "Holy crap, man! Did you see that? The damn thing just disappeared. What do we do now?"

The statue began to shake. Brayson watched Sam move his queen to a safer position. The floor beneath the statue opened and George fell through a large hole with the statue's base. He listened to the king scream George's name, but nothing could be done to save him.

All of a sudden, the temple went dark. All Brayson could see was the shower of colors falling from Mogg's wings toward the polished marble beneath his feet. The darkness only intensified the shower's descent. Rather than dissipate, the colors burst into quiet, miniature explosions of intense light as the sparkles hit the floor.

Mogg was scared. Brayson could hear it in her voice. "It's not good to mess with the gods. We must return to our now. We must leave before we perish in this when."

"What do you mean? How are we messing with the gods?"

"We don't have many moments left. You must follow me, wizard."

Brayson wanted to argue, but knew it was pointless. "Lead the way."

The scenery changed again. Soon, they were standing in their own now from which they had departed. Mogg stopped and hovered in front of the entrance to her tree. Her anxiety was clear as the colors of her sparkle showered the forest floor.

"Mogg, you said something about the gods."

"I don't wish to talk further, wizard. I fear for our lives. George's when is the reason that our now will end if we investigate your curiosities."

"How?"

"You're not very smart for an elf of your seasons. If you wish to tempt fate by challenging a god's warning, then do it without my help. I will not utter another word about this night. I wish you to leave."

"But..."

"No! I said leave my village or I shall be forced to trap you within another when from which you cannot escape."

Brayson took a long look at the sprite's tiny face. He could see she was serious. "Very well, then. Goodbye, Mogg." Brayson vanished.

The City of Marcus
Inside the Temple of the Dark Order

Boyafed looked down at his best friend's mutilated body. Dayden had been found on the outskirts of the city. The Argont Commander's head had been severed, along with his arms and legs. His privates had been shoved inside his mouth and his lips sewn shut. It was all the leader of the Order could do to control himself and keep from killing the messenger who delivered Dayden's body to the Great Hall of Sacrifice.

Boyafed had been best friends with Dayden since childhood. He laid Dayden's body on Hosseff's altar. He could not fathom a reason for the killing. After clearing everyone from the hall, Boyafed lowered to his knees and dropped his head into his palms.

Now...fellow soul...as Boyafed kneeled next to the altar, memories of his childhood flooded his mind. He recalled many of the fond moments he and Dayden had shared. He thought of the homes where they grew up. They were located on the southern shore of Lake Teza. The homes were quaint, provided by the Order for families with sons who commanded magic, and had the potential to join the ranks of the dark paladins.

Lake Teza

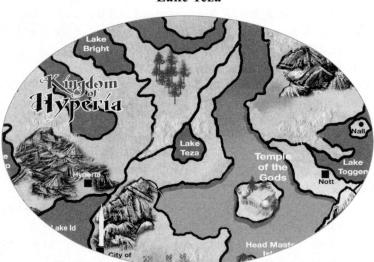

But...fellow soul...these memories are not about the army. They are about friendship and bonding.

"You two boys best dress to charm," Dayden's mother shouted from the kitchen of their home as she opened the food closet to put away the corgan milk. "You cannot expect a young lady to attend a ball with the likes of you if you cannot dress appropriately!"

"Yes, Mother," Dayden responded after cracking the door to his room to poke his head out. "We'll be sure to make you proud!"

"You better! I'm telling you, no proper young lady wishes to be escorted by a pair of mongrels!"

"Yes, mama!" Dayden pulled his head back into the room, looked at Boyafed, grinned, then poked his head back out the door. "We even managed to bathe! I bet you're proud!"

As Dayden's mother cracked open a vestlechick egg, she smiled. "You jest, Dayden, but the dirt on your hands speaks the truth! You best wash them before you go! A lady does not wish to hold a filthy hand!"

"Yes, mama!" Dayden shut the door. At only 71 seasons, he turned to face Boyafed. "Did you find it? I swear it's there. I put it under there last night. My dad has been searching for it all day."

Boyafed, also the same age, pushed back from beneath the bed. "I got it!"

"Shhhh! Be quiet, she'll hear you. We need to get it out of here. How are we going to do it without her knowing? She has extra eyes, you know."

Boyafed tossed the bottle on the bed. "Let's just get dressed. I'll put it under my pant leg, and we'll walk out of here as if all is normal. She'll never suspect a thing."

After being inspected by the pretty, petite elven woman, the boys hugged Dayden's mother before walking out the door. They hurried down the long pathway leading away from the estate, then cut through the woods. Boyafed leapt over the top of a fallen tree trunk. As he landed, the bottle fell from under his pant leg and onto the ground. The boys stopped as they heard the bottle tumble through the twigs.

Dayden bent over and snatched the bottle. Winded, he wiped its label off as if it was some sort of treasure. "Be careful! We can't replace it."

Boyafed frowned and ripped the bottle out of Dayden's hands. "Shut up! I'm not thick. It was not my intent to drop it. Let's hurry. I'll hold it the rest of the way."

After running the remaining distance, the boys stopped at the edge of the tree line and looked across the field. Twilight was approaching, and the ball was being held in the barn on farmer Bedgess' estate. Boyafed punched Dayden on the shoulder, "Race ya." He began to run across the field.

The boys looked through the cracks on the southside of the barn. Glow spirits, a bug found only in Wraithwood Hollow, had been captured, transported, then released to fly around the structure's ceiling amongst the decorations. Individually, these bugs released soft bursts of blue light which lasted only a short series of moments, but when they were placed in a large group, the frequency in which the bursts appeared increased, creating a romantic mood.

Boyafed nudged Dayden. "This is perfect. The girls will love this. Come on."

Boyafed peeked his head around the corner of the barn and whispered from the shadows. "Pssst! Jennikas...come here and bring Corissa. She's in the barn."

Jennikas' keen elven eyes looked into the shadows and responded. "Where's Dayden?"

Dayden peeked his head around the corner above Boyafed. "Shhhh, don't tell her I'm here. Just get Corissa, and meet us by farmer Bedgess' stump."

Jennikas shifted her weight, put her hand on her hips, rolled her eyes, then sighed. "I don't know why Corissa likes the games you play." Without saying another word, she walked into the barn with attitude. She was dressed in a beautiful red gown. Her elf ears were exposed, and her hair had been pulled back and pinned to the top of her head.

When the girls arrived at the farmer's stump, Jennikas and Boyafed embraced. Corissa and Dayden kissed, then Dayden lifted Corissa to the top of the stump. She loved green and her eyes, also green, complemented her gown's color. Corissa pushed back her blonde hair, then adjusted the gown's straps.

Farmer Bedgess' stump was the remains of a massive jedsolip tree, the godfather of all trees on Luvelles. It rested on the banks of the canal feeding his lands. Twelve men could easily sit on top of the stump and still have plenty of room.

Boyafed removed the bottle of Mesolliff wine from the inside of his shirt. He placed the sweet-tasting, silky-smooth vintage, made from the vineyards of Nept, in the palm of his hand.

"Ahhh, you got it," Jennikas said, her voice filled with excitement.

Boyafed winked. "We did. And, you lucky ladies are going to share it with us. Are you ready for what will happen if we drink this?"

The girls huddled. After a moment of whispering, they turned to face the boys. "We're ready."

Dayden clapped his hands. "Tonight, we drink to the sweetness of love. Tomorrow, we will be men and you will be women."

Corissa giggled. "Don't be silly. We will still be girls and you will still be boys, but we won't be virgins."

Now...fellow soul...I am sure you would like to know more about Boyafed and Dayden's night with the ladies, but we cannot spend all of our moments reliving their past. Allow me to take you back to Boyafed's current situation.

The Order leader lifted from his knees and stood at the side of the altar. He looked down at Dayden's body. "Goodbye, my friend. I will miss you." He took a step back and lifted his hands toward the statue of Hosseff. "Lord

Hosseff, please accept your servant's empty vessel. His soul no longer fills it with life. He has served you well. I ask you to honor him. Take his body from this world. Give him a place of honor amongst the loyal who have died before him."

Boyafed took another step back from the altar and watched as the demons, hanging from Hosseff's fingers, animated. Their clawed feet released their grip. They fell with wings spread and landed on the floor at the altar's ends. Their sharp toenails scratched the floor as they began to circle the altar while passing their dark red hands over Dayden's body.

Boyafed cringed as his friend's corpse erupted in flames. As the tears rolled down his cheeks, he stayed silent as Dayden's body reduced to a pile of ash.

The demons lowered their mouths and ingested Dayden's remains. After licking the stone clean, they lifted from the altar and returned to the ends of Hosseff's fingers. Once their clawed feet had reclaimed their grip, they lowered into an upside down position and stretched their arms toward the altar. A moment later, they solidified.

Boyafed lifted his hands toward Hosseff. "Thank you, My Lord. I will serve forever."

A high ranking officer rushed into the hall. The man was next in line to replace the fallen Argont Commander. "My Liege, I have news of the commander's murder."

"Speak, Christopher, or must I cut the news from you?"

Christopher was dressed as Boyafed, wearing all black, except for a golden shirt. His cape also bore the Order's symbol. His bone-handled dagger was sheathed on his left hip and his blessed long sword hung on his right. His hair was long and pure white and his eyes looked as if they were made of a fogged crystal with a gray pupil. Christopher's voice was strong and his skill with the Order's blade was well-respected throughout Boyafed's army.

"A runner has returned from the spot where Dayden's body was found." Christopher tossed Boyafed a dagger used by the white army.

Boyafed unsheathed the ivory-handled blade and lifted it to get a closer look. The mark on the blade was the same as the marks on the arrows. Boyafed's scream filled the hall. "Dowd!"

Christopher waited only a moment. "What are your orders?"

"Call for the council! I want them to be seated and ready for my arrival by Late Bailem!"

"Will that be all, My Liege?"

Boyafed's eyes sent chills down the future Argont Commander's spine. "Unless you wish to be offered to Hosseff, I would get out of my sight."

Christopher fled the room. Boyafed vanished. Marcus emerged from the shadows, smiling. "How interesting. Both councils shall meet tonight." The Dark Chancellor disappeared.

Just South of Grogger's Swamp

The morning has been unkind to the lands of Northwestern Luvelles. Pebble-sized hail and earth-scarring strikes of electrical fury have punished the terrain. The forest has taken the brunt of the storm. The high winds have abused the evergreens, and the weakest of their branches have broken and fallen to the ground. Countless mud puddles are scattered along the dirt road following the tree line.

Shalee grit her teeth and moaned as she crawled along the road. The wound across her abdomen has left a trail for Kiayasis to follow. The once sporadic, speckled drops of blood are beginning to turn into smaller coin-shaped pools of saturated earth as her escape slows. She has used her sweater to try to pack the wound, but nothing seems to help. She is tired, and the loss of blood is making her sleepy. Her desire to live is beginning to be replaced by her desire to end her pain.

Kiayasis grinned as he stalked Shalee from a distance. He knew she was approaching the end of a valiant effort to run. He rubbed his hand across the blood-stained earth. "You can't flea forever," he whispered, "Your blood gives you away. It didn't have to end this way. I will miss you." He rubbed the essence of her life between his fingertips, then tasted it.

Shalee pulled herself off the road and into the forest. Her forearms were torn from the gravel embedded in her skin. Her teeth chattered as her body continued to lose heat. She managed to force herself into an upright position against a large stone. The Knife of Spirits had made a clean cut. Again, she tried to use her magic to cauterize the wound, but failed.

She thought, *Why can't I use my power?* Her mind screamed for answers, but none could be found. She closed her eyes and tried to teleport—nothing—there was no escape. *I've gotta get outta here. He's gonna kill me.*

It wasn't long before Kiayasis stood above Shalee, looking down with eyes filled with evil intent. He had changed and was now dressed in the Order's armor. "You betrayed me. You tossed me aside as if I were no better than the slop trudgeboars eat."

Shalee's voice was weak. "I'm so sorry. Please, I beg ya ta stop. I don't wanna die. What can I do ta make ya stop?"

"The moments for talking are over. You could have had a wonderful life with me. I was prepared to give up everything for you. I was sent here to kill you, but as we went along, I fell in love with you. I was going to let you live and start a life together. We could have moved far away from my father's army."

"I'm sorry, Kiayasis. Please, don't do this ta me."

Kiayasis unsheathed his long sword. He lifted it toward the sky and shouted, "Hosseff, accept this sacrifice as a token of my faithful service! Her blood shall cover the blessed blade of the Order's faithful! We are your children and as your child, I wish to please you! You are wise and an almighty god!" He stomped his foot. "Blessed are the children of Hosseff!"

As Kiayasis lowered his blade, a voice from the side of the road called out. "If it's a sacrifice you're seeking, come and claim it!"

Shalee couldn't believe her eyes. "Sam. Oh my goodness, Sam, help me."

The King of Grayham was dressed in leather hunting clothes. He wore no armor, but Kael hung from his hip. His crown was missing and his hair was a mess from the high winds. The front of his shirt was only tied halfway up and his broad shoulders pulled the material apart, exposing his muscular chest.

Kiayasis began to laugh and shouted, "How poetic! The King of Brandor has come to retrieve his whore. There's much you don't know about your wench. She has been quite the naughty girl. Do you wish to know..."

Sam spoke over him as he entered the trees. "Why does everyone talk when the moment comes to fight? Ready your weapon and pick on someone your own size!"

"What honor is there in fighting with blessed blades?" Kiayasis watched Sam's surprise. "You didn't think I would know of such things. I have been informed of your skills. We will fight with daggers...if you're man enough to accept the challenge."

As Sam lowered Kael to the ground, Kiayasis tossed his sword aside. They pulled their daggers from their sheaths and engaged. An exchange of metal clanks and grunt-filled lunges filled the air. It wasn't long before Kiayasis' fist found its mark, leaving the king's lip split open.

Sam didn't allow the punch to faze him. He grabbed Kiayasis with his free hand and yanked him to the ground. Sam's knee followed, smashing into the dirt beside Kiayasis' body as the dark warrior rolled to his feet to avoid the paralyzing effect of Sam's failed attempt.

Kiayasis nodded. "Solid moves for a king. I'm going to enjoy this."

"Again...more talk. Not enough fighting."

Shalee managed to shout out a few words. "Sam, he has..."

Kiayasis attacked before Shalee could finish. The dark paladin's stab was defended, but Kiayasis rolled to the side and buried his knee into Sam's kidney. The blow sent Sam falling forward, but the king rolled to his feet fast enough to defend a downward strike from the paladin's dagger meant for his head.

Sam secured Kiayasis' arms and rolled backward, pulling the paladin with him. He pushed with his legs and threw the dark warrior into the side of a tree. His plate armor made a loud thud against the bark as he fell in an awkward position on his shoulder. Kiayasis dropped his dagger. Sam followed and stomped on the blade with his foot. The king brought his fist down across the side of Kiayasis' face. Blood began to fill Kiayasis' mouth as his two front teeth fell to the forest floor.

Sam grabbed Kiayasis' dagger, stuck it into the side of a tree and pushed sideways to snap the blade. He threw the bone handle to the ground and shouted, "Get up and fight!"

Kiayasis stood and wiped the blood from his chin. Again, Shalee tried to speak, but the dark warrior shouted above her. "Shut up, woman!" He faced Sam. "Does your queen always run her mouth so?"

Sam ignored Kiayasis' snide remark and began to untie his shirt. He took it off. With the shirt clenched in one hand and the dagger in the other, the sky opened and the rain began to fall. The water ran down Sam's chest. Shalee had never seen her husband look so intimidating.

Sam studied Kiayasis' face as he threw both the knife and his shirt to the ground. "Now it's a fair fight," Sam mocked as he cracked his neck. "I have no blade and no armor. Maybe you'll stand a chance."

Without waiting for a response, Sam lunged toward Kiayasis, motioning as if he was going to bring up a left knee. Kiayasis reacted and lowered his arms, but the king's knee was a ruse. Instead of following it through, Sam pulled his knee back and delivered a right hand above the paladin's lowered arms. His knuckles landed flush against the bridge of Kiayasis' nose.

The dark warrior fell backward to the forest floor. Sam stopped his attack and allowed Kiayasis the moments necessary to recover. The king's voice was cold. "You're not much of a warrior. I bet Boyafed is sick to his stomach."

Kiayasis stood and removed his hand from his nose. The blood poured down his face as he responded. Every emphasized word sent a spray flying through the air. "You don't know me! You don't know anything about my father! You know nothing of the Order...or my father's feelings for me!"

The paladin lifted his arms. Fire erupted from the palms of his hands. Flames enveloped Sam's body. For a period of moments the king could not be seen. Sam's screams filled the forest, but as the flames dissipated, his screams were replaced by hysterical laughter. Sam pointed at Kiayasis, then grabbed his belly. The heat had not affected him. Even the hair covering his head had escaped harm.

Kiayasis was stunned. "How?"

Sam straightened. "Does how really matter?" Sam rushed in and threw a series of punches and kicks which Kiayasis struggled to defend. The king kept at it, pushing forward, trying to overwhelm the dark warrior until Kiayasis made a critical mistake. The paladin failed to block a right hook. The impact broke his jaw on the left side of his face. Kiayasis fell to the ground.

Sam followed, rolling his enemy to his back. He mounted Kiayasis with a leg on either side and pinned him to the ground. He continued to punch Kiayasis until the dark warrior was knocked into unconsiousness. The king continued to punch over and over again and would have continued until Kiayasis' life left his body, but Shalee called out to Sam.

It took the last ounce of strength Shalee had to get Sam's attention. "Sam! Ya have ta stop!"

After one more solid punch, Sam stood. He looked down at Kiayasis' bloodied face. He spit on him, then moved to stand above Shalee. Realizing her condition, the king ran to the road, grabbed his bag and produced a vial.

He crouched next to the queen. "Open your mouth and lift your tongue. I need to put a drop of this under it. It'll stop the bleeding and you'll begin to heal."

Shalee did as she was told. Sam's eyes failed to show his love for her. His movements were tense and his actions were cold and precise. Her heart dropped. Shalee knew Sam was aware of her unfaithfulness.

Shalee watched Sam bind Kiayasis' arms and legs. He pulled the dark warrior by his feet across the forest floor. Sam stopped near a tree, threw Kiayasis' feet to the ground, then grabbed hold of Kiayasis' breastplate. He slammed the paladin into a seated position against the tree trunk, then tied him up.

Shalee found the nerve to speak. Her voice was shallow. "How did ya find me?"

As Sam bent down to check the progress Brayson's healing elixir had made on Shalee's wounds, he responded. "I tracked you down after meeting with the Head Master."

"Since when do ya know how ta track someone? And, how did ya protect yourself against Kiayasis' magic?"

"I made a few requests prior to my arrival. I'm wearing rings which protect me from the elements. As for tracking, I don't know how to do it, but the tracker I hired did. Once I had you in my sight a few days ago, I told him he could leave. I've been watching you ever since. I wanted to wait until you were alone. I didn't want to confront you while you were curled up with your 'baby' over there. I was going to return home without speaking with you after hearing your pet name, but as it turns out, changing my mind has saved your ass. How could you call him 'baby'...especially after everything we've been through?"

Shalee lowered her eyes. "Ya heard that?" She looked up, "Then, ya know I didn't sleep with him."

"Okay, okay, hold on just a moment. From what I saw, you slept with him. You just didn't have sex with him, but you slept with him. In my mind, one is just as bad as the other. You allowed him to hold you. I saw you kiss him. How could you be so selfish?"

"Sam, I'm so sorry."

"Don't apologize, Shalee. Your regret isn't something I care to hear right now. I'm leaving for Grayham. You'll have to continue your search for the crystal without me. I want you to know something before I go. I'm going to kill the man whose arms comforted you. You make me sick. Did your parents forget to teach you what faithfulness is?"

"Sam, ya don't have ta kill him. I told him I wasn't gonna continue with the relationship. That's why he tried ta kill me. I was so messed up in the head. I felt like ya hated me. I know I was selfish. I wish I could fix it all and make it go away. Ya don't need ta kill him. He isn't a threat ta us any longer."

Sam stood. Without saying a word, he moved to untie Kiayasis. He pulled him clear of the trees, woke him, then lifted the dark warrior to his feet. Once Sam was sure he had Kiayasis' full attention, he said, "You should leave. Tell your father that no man will be killing my queen...not today, or any other. Don't let me see your face again. The chances of you finding me in a forgiving mood when next we meet are highly unlikely. Now, go."

Sam watched as Kiayasis turned to leave. Once confident the dark warrior would not return, Sam turned to face Shalee. He lowered to his knee to take one final look at the queen's wounds. The bleeding had stopped and the pebbles in her forearms had been pushed out of her skin, but it would be a while longer before the cut across her abdomen would heal. Her condition was stable. He could leave.

Suddenly, Shalee cried out. Sam was barely able to spin fast enough to stop the downward force of a large stone meant for his head. With both hands open, Sam caught the stone and used his strength to repel the stone's intended path. With a thud, the forest floor took the damage, the stone landed next to Sam's right knee.

As quick as the attack happened, Sam's right fist was now on a collision course with Kiayasis' groin. The blow stopped Kiayasis' advance. The paladin stumbled backward and fell to his knees. Sam stood and kicked. The muddy sole of his right boot left a nasty imprint and broke the socket around Kiayasis' left eye. Kiayasis was thrown to the forest floor.

After sitting the dark warrior up, the king knelt behind Kiayasis' limp figure. He tapped the paladin on the cheek until he woke up. "What am I going to do with you? Do you have a death wish?"

Kiayasis forced his words through clenched teeth. "I live to serve Hosseff." As blood continued to pour from his nose, he professed. "I cannot return to my father's good graces until your queen is dead. I will not stop hunting her."

Sam shook his head and with a powerful strike to Kiayasis' temple, he sent the dark warrior back into unconsciousness and tossed him to the ground. He stood and ran his hands through his hair. "This guy is leaving me no choice."

Shalee knew what was coming. She wanted to say something, but the words were no longer available. She knew Kiayasis had sealed his own fate.

Sam sat Kiayasis up and knelt behind him. He looked at the queen. "Shalee, I tried to give him his life. I have no choice. You heard it yourself. I want you to watch this. Your actions have consequences."

Shalee cringed as the bones in the dark paladin's neck filled the air with a horrid crackling. Sam's eyes were cold as he moved to stand above his queen. "I told you, you could come home when you're ready. I also told you I would always love you. I'll be there when you get back. I suggest you try to be faithful from here on out."

Shalee tried to say something, but Sam stopped her. "I don't care right now, Shalee. I don't care."

Sam reached into his bag and tossed her a package. "You should eat. You're going to need your strength." He put his shirt on and took a deep breath as he tied it. "I do still love you. The problem is...I'm not sure I can trust you." Sam pulled a scroll from his pack and after a few words were spoken, he vanished.

Shalee began to cry. She was left to sit only feet away from Kiayasis' lifeless body. As the rain began to pour, she was too weak to move and would have to suffer the agony of Sam's disappointment, the sight of Kiayasis' body, and the cold, alone.

City of Inspiration
The Circle of the High Council

Lord Dowd walked toward the head of a chamber located at the center of a large circular structure. He had always been fond of this building and admired the many shades of color which had been applied to the glass throughout various areas of this domed meeting hall. Created at the far end of a garden courtyard opposite Gregory's tower, the design was official, governmental, if you will, and had been created for the White Paladin Council.

Lord Dowd took his position as the rightful head of the council with Gregory at his side. He shut the gate to a waist-high enclosure and motioned for Gregory to ascend a short staircase. Surrounding their seats was a stage which allowed a significant amount of freedom while addressing the council members.

The council took their seats. Numbering 120, each man had served and retired as an officer in the white army. They are dressed in black with silver accents. Their shirts bear the symbol of the army, the Turtle Elf of Healing, across their chests. These men are responsible for making the decision of how the Kingdom of Lavan will handle the threat of war. On this day, the council has gathered to address Lord Dowd's declaration.

⭑⭑⭑

Mosley, Alistar, and Hosseff have taken positions behind the council and are looking down at Lord Dowd and the White Chancellor. The deities are unable to be seen by all present and have come for the same reason.

⭑⭑⭑

Now...fellow soul...Gregory Id has found himself in a unique situation. Not only must he perform his duties as the Chancellor of White Magic, he must also assume the duties of the dead king, Heltgone Lavan, until the Head Master meets with Lavan's white republic leaders to appoint another king.

Because of his weight, the King of Lavan was impotent and had no sons or daughters. His wife died a few seasons ago, and his only living relative is a sister, but she is deaf and dumb, and her many personalities are incapable of running a kingdom. Brayson is required to determine who the five most powerful families are within the Kingdom of Lavan, and with the republic's help, he will choose the one which best fits the role of the royal family. The head of this family will be named king.

Fellow soul...in case you don't understand the hierarchies of the Kingdom of Lavan and the Kingdom of Hyperia, let me explain. Both are similar, each having a king to represent the halflings. These kings are not powerful men, despite being treated as such. They act as figureheads for the halflings living throughout the Lands of Kerkinn. Since the halflings' magic is inferior to the magic of the elves, the Head Masters throughout the ages have required two councils to govern the masses. They have done this in an effort to keep halflings from being enslaved by elves commanding dark magic, no matter where they live. The kings' voices are the only voices the halflings are given when their respective councils convene.

The most powerful position within each council is held by the man who leads their respective army, yet this position is not the position the people of Luvelles consider the most esteemed. Gregory and Marcus' positions are the most prestigious throughout the world of Luvelles, second only to Brayson's position as Head Master.

To maintain the balance of power, the Head Masters throughout the seasons have required the chancellors of magic to abide by their respective council's rulings. Just as the leaders of the white army before him, Lord Dowd must also abide by the council's rulings after the council adjourns.

<hr />

Lord Dowd lifted from his throne and looked beyond the stage toward the bleachers which ascended in front of him. "Councilmen, thank you for coming. I've summoned you here to answer my call for war. In the past few days there have been two attacks on my life. During one of these attacks, the King of Lavan perished, as you all know. The weapon responsible for his death was a crossbow crafted by the Order."

The members of the council began to murmur. Dowd continued. "I wish to gather our forces and call the dark army to the Battlegrounds of Olis."

An older elf who once held Dowd's position, stood. His belly was now rounded from his lack of training and the five pints of ale he consumed each night. His nose looked like cauliflower, with a strawberry hue, and he had allowed his graying beard to lengthen, but when he spoke, all on the council listened.

Dowd recognized Heflon's presence and surrendered the floor. Heflon nodded and cleared his throat. "Lord Dowd, I understand the death of a king is tragic, but to call for war would kill thousands of elves. Is war necesary over the loss of one halfling? Is there a way to settle this dispute between the two armies without confrontation? Have you tried to contact Boyafed? Have you tried to find out what he knows of the attack which took the king's life?"

Dowd took a deep breath. He didn't like the passive sound of Heflon's questions. The white army leader respected Heflon by bowing his head to satisfy the politics of the situation. "Councilor, I was scheduled to meet with Boyafed five days ago. It was at this moment the first attempt on my life was made. Instead of killing me, the attacker missed. My spirit-bull of 100 seasons perished from a bolt to the eye from an Order crossbow."

Heflon nodded his understanding. "I was told the bolt responsible for killing the king pierced Heltgone's eye as well. Is this correct?"

"It is. Each bolt missed my person by only inches and killed an unexpected target."

Heflon folded his hands and placed them on top of his belly. "Lord Dowd, don't you find it odd that a man trained by the Order would fail to hit a stationary target on two occasions, yet he was able to hit the eye of the beings standing nearest you? The dark army doesn't make mistakes of this nature. These were intentional misses, and the bolts killed their intended targets."

Dowd's face tightened. "I would argue that whoever this man was, he missed on both occasions. I would also argue that, if the bolts did find their intended targets, then the Order is toying with this council. I say this is an act of war no matter how you try to explain it. This is the Order's way of spitting in our faces, and this disrespect requires action. If the King of Lavan was your brother, I doubt you would feel the need to object."

Heflon looked around the room and started laughing. "If the king was my brother, I would be no better than any other halfling." The chamber filled with laughter, but Gregory and Dowd failed to see Heflon's humor. Once the hall settled, Heflon continued his rebuttal. "War will kill many. We don't have proof the Order is responsible. For all we know, this man who attacked could have nothing to do with the Order and simply laid his hands on one of their weapons. I don't believe an elf trained by Boyafed would miss. I believe this to be the trickery of a mere marksman and nothing more."

Most in the room seemed to agree with Heflon, but there were some who agreed with the white paladin leader. Lord Dowd began to argue against Heflon's logic. The room became angry as the men started to shout at one another.

The gods began to converse as they watched the proceedings grow out of hand. Alistar addressed Mosley. "The moments have come for you to do your job. It looks as if Heflon will talk the council out of an aggressive action. They will look for a diplomatic resolution. He has a point. This doesn't seem like the work of the Order. The council is sure to agree with his logic. You must make them feel the proper course of action is war."

Mosley lowered his head. "I have been dreading the day this moment would come."

Hosseff responded as Mosley looked into the emptiness beneath the shade's hood. His wispy words found their way out of the shadowy darkness. "Mosley, take solace in the knowledge that war is necessary to control the worlds' populations. The souls waiting within the Book will be given a chance to live again. When you perform your craft, you're creating a new cycle of life. This is a good thing. It isn't evil to do what's necessary."

Mosley snorted, "Well, it does not feel like a good thing, though I understand your reasoning." Mosley began his descent down the bleachers. He had to pass through the members of the council to reach Heflon. As he did, the wolf's body penetrated those who were in his way. The men who experienced the chill of the god's presence, looked to one another for an explanation as they rubbed themselves for warmth.

Once standing next to Heflon, the invisible God of War lifted onto his hind legs and whispered into Heflon's ear. "War is necessary. The Order has played a trick on this council. Boyafed wants you to think the attacks are the work of a marksman. Heflon, you are too clever to allow this deception to fall on this council's ears. Lord Dowd is right. His call for war is necessary. Only you can make these men see that war is a proper course of action. You must rid Luvelles of the darkness which plagues this world."

Once finished, Mosley moved up the bleachers to stand beside Alistar. Again, the men warmed themselves as he passed through them. "Let us see how my manipulation worked."

Alistar nodded. "That was a fine bit of suggesting, Mosley. I never tire of seeing how the people react as we pass through them. I'm sure they will feel feverish tomorrow."

"How could you be so blind, Heflon?" Dowd shouted over the council as the men continued to argue their points of view.

After a moment, Heflon raised his hand. It was as if he commanded their voices without saying a word. The room quieted. "My fellow councilmen, there may be another side to consider. Let us assume the Order wanted to kill Heltgone. Let us assume the Order wanted us to think a marksman was responsible for the attacks. Perhaps, they wanted us to believe they were not responsible because their assassin missed Lord Dowd. It would be a fine deception if this council were to believe another man stole the Order's property and wore its colors to kill the king. The Order would get away with murder without fear of retaliation. To attack the king, though a mere halfling, is to attack every member of this council. Despite his polluted blood, he was appointed as one of us. The moment for war...is now!"

The room erupted with calls for war. Lord Dowd seized the moment and lifted his blessed blade of the white army high above his head. He shouted with all his might. "I call for war! What say you, councilmen?"

The decision was unanimous.

Mosley turned away from the frenzied cries. The wolf looked at Hosseff. "It appears we have our war. It will not be long before you will be collecting souls and returning them to the Book's pages."

The shade pulled back his hood and a smoky image of his face appeared. "You have done your job well, Mosley. But, there's another matter on Harvestom which needs your attention. Perhaps, you should see to it that war encompasses the centaurs' forests as well."

Mosley looked at Alistar. "Shall we go?"

Alistar put his hand on the wolf's head. "Mosley, I understand how this makes you feel, but I assure you, you're doing what's necessary to ensure a continuous cycle of life. I'll stay with you until the job is complete."

"Thank you. It will take a while for me to adjust. I am not sure how to deal with the sick feeling in the pit of my stomach."

Hosseff laughed as he lifted his hood and the emptiness returned. Alistar and Mosley stared into the nothingness as the god spoke. "Mosley, you will learn to deal with such emotions as the seasons pass. I like you, and I know your heart is breaking." The shade vanished.

Alistar looked at Mosley. "I don't think it's necessary to visit Boyafed. I'm sure his council will call for war considering recent events."

Mosley sat on his haunches and scratched the back of his neck. "What events are you referring to?"

Alistar fidgeted with the sleeve of his robe as he responded. "Hosseff told me Boyafed's Argent Commander was murdered. Boyafed thinks Dayden was killed by the white army."

Mosley shook his head. "None of this makes sense. How could the leaders of both packs be manipulated this way?"

"I don't know, my hairy friend, but this is the case, and Hosseff knows more than he's willing to reveal. The Order will accept Dowd's challenge to meet on the Battlegrounds of Olis. This will be a war worth watching."

Mosley watched as the last councilman teleported away from the hall. "I must find a way to understand how Hosseff thinks."

"That could take many seasons. I doubt I'll ever adapt to the eerie feeling I get when I look into the emptiness beneath his hood. It's unnerving, don't you think?"

After a mutual agreement, the gods left for Harvestom.

The Luvelles Gazette

When you want an update about your favorite characters

Shalee has worked her way back to the camp Kiayasis abandoned outside Grogger's Swamp. She removed the Knife of Spirits from the dark paladin's body and now carries it high on her right thigh beneath her dress.

Sam's disappointment and the pain on his face have been haunting her thoughts. She plans to find the missing piece of the Crystal Moon and hurry back to Grayham to beg for forgiveness.

Kepler and Payne are waiting outside The Source's Temple. George opened the temple doors with the key they retrieved from Brayson's shrine. The key vanished after opening the lock. Once inside, George stood on the teleportation platform located at the temple's center.

Kepler and Payne tried to walk through the entryway of the temple, but George was the only one who could pass. Payne teleported with the demon-cat back to Kepler's lair.

Mary, Athena, Susanne and Garrin woke early. They have eaten a hearty breakfast and have gathered in Mary's kitchen to read from the Scroll of Teleportation.

Though the Head Master stayed the night, he avoided talking about George. He did, however, help the girls devise a plan. The ladies are going to visit Nept, a city surrounded by vineyards. Brayson kissed Mary goodbye and left after breakfast.

Athena is only 36 Peaks from giving birth.

Boyafed and Lord Dowd are speaking via mirror. Dowd has delivered the Kingdom of Lavan's call for war, and as expected, Boyafed has accepted. Their conversation was short. The dark and white armies will meet on the Battlefields of Olis. The battle will begin in 50 Peaks of Bailem.

Gregory Id has been asked by Lord Dowd to go to Lavan. The chancellor is to issue the call for Lavan's army to meet up with the white army, north of Lake Tepp, in 20 Peaks. From there, it will be a 28 Peak march to the battlegrounds. The armies will then rest and prepare for battle over the next two days.

Dowd has also asked Gregory to travel to three other places in search of support for the war. First, Gregory is to go to the shore of Crystal Lake. He is to call on the Ultorian King for any assistance he may be able to offer.

Second, Gregory will go to the enchanted woods of Wraithwood Hollow. He will ask the Wraith Hound Prince, Wisslewine, to call his pack of canine warriors out of the Under Eye and bring them to the Battlegrounds of Olis.

Third, Gregory is to visit the Spirit Plains. The chancellor is to find the king of a race of spirits called the Lost Ones. Gregory will need to capture Shesolaywen, their king, so Dowd can use the king's Call of Canair.

Mieonus watched as Sam saved Shalee's life. The event was seen through her waterfall. The goddess enjoyed the pain on Sam's face as he confronted Shalee about her unfaithfulness. She also enjoyed Kiayasis' death. The dark paladin's demise has given the Goddess of Hate a wonderful idea.

Mosley and Alistar are on Harvestom. The famine created by the God of the Harvest is spreading across the Kingdom of Kless and desperate moments are beginning to turn the centaurs against one another. There have been four cases of cannibalism reported amongst the browncoats. Neighbors are afraid to open their stable doors and live in fear for their lives.

The King of Kless is convinced, now more than ever, that the King of Tagdrendlia ordered his kingdom's Seeds of Plenty stolen. Without the seeds to produce crops for his lands, Lasolias' browncoat race will starve. Lasolias also believes his centaurs are no longer strong enough to fight the blackcoats. He feels the Seeds of Plenty may be lost for good.

On the other side of Southern Harvestom, in the Kingdom of Tagdrendlia, Boseth has collected a bountiful harvest, and his blackcoat army is healthy and strong. Boseth believes his race can withstand an advance by Lasolias. Boseth has tried on three occasions to tell Lasolias he does not have his bag filled with the Seeds of Plenty, but Lasolias will not listen.

The browncoat and blackcoat kingdoms have enough abhorrence over one another's appearance without the missing Seeds of Plenty being an issue. This tension has existed between the races of centaurs since the creation of the new worlds.

Brayson has arrived at his floating office and is waiting to meet with the King of Southern Grayham. Sam is expected to arrive soon.

Gage and the other goswigs are free of Strongbear's constant barking of orders. Once they voted to pool their magic and bring winter to their underground village, the large brown bear retired to his cave and is now hibernating.

Marcus is watching Gregory. The moment is approaching to carry out another step of the plan he created with George at the Head Master's shrine.

Lasidious and Celestria are inside their home beneath the Peaks of Angels. Lasidious plans to visit George during the mage's next dream. George will need to work at a rapid pace to avoid the problems which may arise as a result of the Head Master's journey to visit George's when while traveling through the past with Mogg.

Thank you for reading the Luvelles Gazette

A Very Old Dragon

The Mountains of Oraness
Just Outside The Source's Cave

After stepping on the teleportation platform inside The Source's temple, George appeared in the same alcove the Head Master had appeared in with Mary. He is now looking at the flames above the pool surrounding Fisgig's perch.

Holy crap, that's hot, George thought as he stood with his hand in front of his face. He looked up. *Damn, these cliffs are tall. What the...? You got to be freaking kidding me. Is that...? The damn water's on fire. What the hell...it's not even boiling? Okay, something's freaking wrong with this place. Where the hell am I?*

Okay, Georgie boy, focus. Think, man, think. Pull your head out of your ass and let's figure out what the dealio is. Looks like there's no way around the fire, so now what?

George could see the cave's entrance on the far side of the pool. He closed his eyes and tried to teleport, but nothing happened. *Okay, well that didn't freaking work. The Head Master has probably got some wicked mojo cast on this joint.*

Damn it, George, think. I can't go back, but if I walk any further, the flames will burn my ass to a crisp. There's got to be some way I can get across. Hmmmm, what do I have in my bag of tricks? What kind of garesh will mess with fire? Let's try some ice.

George lifted his hands and a blizzard erupted from his palms. The ice covered the pool's surface, and for a brief moment, the flames subsided. While they were down, George saw some sort of bird sitting on a perch at the pool's center.

Now, we're getting somewhere. I wonder what's causing the fire to burn on the water? And, why is a damn bird sitting in the flames? Wait! Oh man, oh man, oh man! What if it's...no way...you've got to be kidding me. Have I just seen my first phoenix? That's Brayson's freaking goswig!

Okay Georgie boy, let's think. If that's a phoenix, then why isn't it attacking? I did just cover it with ice. Wonder why it's not all pissed off? Shouldn't the ice have pissed it off at least a little bit? Maybe, the intensity of the magic wasn't strong enough for it to give a garesh. Maybe, it's not supposed to attack. Maybe, this is some sort of mental game for me to figure out. Maybe, I need to hit it with something a little stronger...something a little more harmful to fire. What's fire's worst enemy? Water...yeah, water...but not just any water. Let's show this little bastard a tidal wave. I bet that will rile his ass.

Wait, what if this doesn't work? What if I only manage to piss it off? What if it kills me and pecks my eyes out with its beak?

George...come on, you've got to stop this. You're standing here talking to yourself like a bleeding idiot. I bet the phoenix is sitting over there thinking he's spotted his first moron. You can't let this feathered freak psych you out. Oh my hell...I am a moron. I'm sitting here talking with myself, about myself, about what a damn bird thinks about me. I must be insane.

Damn it, pull your head out. If I don't do something, I won't get to the other side. And, why does it have to be so freaking hot around here anyway? Was the phoenix the only goswig he could've picked? Criminey! George wiped the sweat from his forehead with his sleeve and fanned the front of his shirt.

Okay...sack up...grab 'em like ya got a pair, and let's put it all on the line. Let's see what this little freak is made of. George lifted his hands. "Try this on for size, you little piece of garesh."

Instead of ice, a huge wave of water filled the area and extinguished the flames. Brayson's goswig was drenched. The force of the wave left the phoenix with no choice, but to use its talons to cling to the perch. It took all of the goswig's might and concentration to do it.

George followed the wave with a quick bolt of lightning. It hit the base of Fisgig's perch. The shock traveled up the wet surface and surged through the bird's crimson body. The phoenix fell to the ground and started convulsing.

George watched as the tidal wave reached the far side of the clearing. The water rebounded off the cliff walls and headed back in the mage's direction.

George's eyes widened. *Oh crap! I didn't think of that.* George had to throw up a wall of force to keep from being swept away. He chastised himself. *Way to go, idiot. You could have killed yourself. I mean...where else would that much water go? You're standing in a damn toilet bowl made of cliffs. Use your head, George. Geesh!*

A long series of moments passed before the water finished funneling into the cave's mouth. Heavy steam billowed out of the cave and crept up the side of the cliff. Again, George began to think. *Looks like it's going to be hot in there. I wonder what's causing the steam?*

George lowered his wall of force and moved toward the entrance. As he did, he saw the phoenix lying next to the base of the cliff near the cave's opening. The bird was not moving.

George trudged through the pool and knelt next to the goswig. He plucked one of its feathers, then put it inside his tunic. Fisgig winced when the feather was pulled, but remained unconscious. George didn't wait to see if the bird would finish dying. Instead, he made his way into the mouth of the cave.

It took a while, but Fisgig began to move. He managed to lift himself off the ground. He shook his head to collect his bearings, then whispered, "This Mystic Learner is far more advanced than any other. I must speak with Brayson."

The cave was dark for the most part, but still navigable with the naked eye. Small streams of lava surfaced and ran along the floor before disappearing into the mountain. The glow from the molten liquid created an eerie feeling, and the air was pungent. Steam billowed along the stalactite covered ceiling, and the condensation was dripping off their ends. Each moment a droplet hit the lava, it created a puff of steam which lifted toward the ceiling.

Again, George's thoughts ran wild. *I would've been afraid of this not too long ago. But, now something this creepy seems almost like a second home. Hell...living on these worlds has really screwed with my head. Could I really be this brave, or am I just a dumbass with no common sense? I can't be insane. Insane people don't know they're insane...do they?*

After working his way deep into the mountain, George came to an area which opened into an enormous cavern. It almost felt as if the mountain had become hollow. The top of the cavern could not be seen. The walls to either side were hundreds of feet away and were visible only because of the glow from the lava which flowed down their surfaces, then across the floor as a river before disappearing back into the wall.

A booming voice filled the cavern. "I've been expecting you, George."

George lifted his hands and prepared to use his magic, but he was unable to see a target. Again, the booming voice spoke, but during this particular series of moments, the sound echoed off the stone. George had to cover his ears to stop the pain. "Do not be frightened, Mystic Learner. I am the one you seek."

George didn't waste any of his moments. "Show yourself," he commanded. "I want to see my first dragon."

The dragon laughed, the rumble of his chuckle forced George to cover his ears again. Once the laughter subsided, George spoke, "Do you always greet those who wish to speak with you with such rudeness? Not the kind of manners I would've expected from an ancient."

From within his veil of invisibility, The Source lowered his head to a position just above George and snorted. The wind nearly knocked George to the ground and covered his face with moisture. "You're a confident one, aren't you? I can see you're not afraid. A good quality to have, but this is also your weakness."

George finished wiping his face, then straightened his hair. "Confidence is only a weakness if backed by ignorance. I know what your purpose is. I know you're not here to harm me. You're also not the main reason why I've come. I have questions. Show yourself so we can have a decent conversation."

Again, The Source chuckled, and again, the mage grabbed his ears. "Apparently, young Mystic Learner, you are under the same belief the others were who stood before me. You think the Eye of Magic is the only being responsible for swallowing souls. Perhaps, I have used my position as an opportunity to sample a few misguided morsels. Perhaps...I too...have consumed a few."

George swallowed hard, then gasped as the dragon appeared, filling the cavern. The Source rose to stretch. His tail and neck elongated. The muscles in his legs tightened as he balanced his weight to extend his wings. Their tips touched the walls on either side with an impressive span of over 500 feet. As the ancient folded them, wind filled the cavern. George was blown to the ground. He tumbled head over heels, more than once, before stopping at the edge of a lava stream. He scooted back from the heat and remained seated.

Again, The Source spoke as he lowered his head. "You know of me, George. I only jest about eating those who seek the Eye's ultimate power."

George looked up and wiped the sweat off his brow with the sleeve of his tunic. He shouted, "Well, that's a freaking relief! You almost knocked me into the lava! You could've killed me!"

"You fret over naught. If your life would have been lost, I would have returned it."

George's eyes squinted. "You can give life?"

The Source chuckled and grinned as George covered his ears. "Of course. You do not realize it, but you looked upon me during much of your wretched life on Earth."

George struggled to collect his thoughts. "How would I not remember looking at you? Were you invisible or something when I looked in your direction? How did you know I was from Earth?"

"I was not invisible. In fact, I was in plain sight. I am older than your Earth. I am over 29,000,000 years old."

"Did you just say years? I haven't heard anyone say that word since my arrival on Grayham."

"As I have said, I know your Earth, and I watched as the God Wars destroyed your planet. Granted, there wasn't much left after the humans unleashed their weapons of mass destruction, but I saw it explode nonetheless. It was sad to see such advanced races destroy themselves. Knowledge can be deadly. I never did understand why your gods allowed their creations to treat each other so. But, I suppose their struggle wasn't much different than the way the beings living on the new worlds fight for dominance of their own. It's as if the Collective doesn't care, or perhaps, they desire war. I don't care much one way or the other. I simply fail to comprehend the gods' logic."

George crossed his arms and set them on top of his knees. "So, then, you're not a god?"

"No. I am not a god. I choose to live a simple existence."

"What do you mean?"

The dragon cleared his throat. George had to grab his ears as the sound echoed off the cavern's walls. "I had taken my place amongst the stars with my ancestors. The light you came to know as the North Star was how you once knew me. I was beautiful, and my glory captured the attention of your galaxy. But, when the gods began their wars, many of my kind had to surrender their place within the heavens. We were forced to return to our solid forms. This mere vessel you see before you is all that's left of my being."

George was blown away. "Well, from where I'm sitting, what you call a 'mere vessel' is what I call majestic."

"Your flattery is received with open wings."

George could only stare as he responded. "The idea you were a star trips me out. I can't imagine how you must feel. I mean, holy garesh, you were not just any star...you were the freaking star everyone on Earth knew about. Do you realize the role you played in our ways of navigation? I have to tell you, I did more than one report about you when I was a kid."

Again, the dragon chuckled, and again, George covered his ears. Once the noise subsided, The Source spoke. "I know of your daughter. I also know of your desire to see her again. I can hear your thoughts. I know you will do whatever it takes to retrieve her soul from the Book's pages. I believe you're strong, but you have many weaknesses. Do you not fear these weaknesses?"

George lifted to his feet. "It's hard to fear something I can't pinpoint. I appreciate your concern, but all I care about is getting my daughter out of the Book. You're right...I'll do whatever it takes. I'm sure you would do the same for a child of your own, or dragon cub, or whatever you call it."

The dragon snorted. The force blew George to his backside. "You presume much, mage. I am dragon. I would find it easier to release my offspring's soul than you would. One tooth piercing the Book's binding would do the trick." The dragon winked his massive left eye.

George wiped the moisture from his face. "Ha! Humor. I wouldn't have expected humor to come from a dragon's mouth."

The Source pulled his head back. "You must be careful. Do not allow the hate in your heart to cloud your judgment. The iniquity running through your veins could be your undoing. You're stronger than the others who have come before you, but strength is nothing without wit. If you allow your anger to control your mind, all will be lost.

"There is much in your past running through the depths of your mind. I can feel the pain these moments have caused your spirit. I understand why you resent those who hurt you. You have allowed your pain to turn you into a killer. I would ask you to re-evaluate what's important. I can hear your daughter's soul. She would not want her father to kill those he came in contact with to release her."

George lowered to the flat of his back and put his hands behind his head. "I hope you don't mind, but it's easier to look at you this way."

The dragon nodded. "Understood."

"Anyway, it kind of freaks me out that you can hear my daughter's soul. Can you speak with her as well?"

"I can hear her, but I cannot speak with her."

"Is she happy? Does she have good dreams? Does she think I come home to her every night?"

The dragon tilted his massive head, then lowered it to a position only feet above George's body. "How do you know such things? How could a mortal have any idea of what..." The dragon hesitated, then continued. "Ahhhh...I hear your mind. It seems someone has given you information beyond what the gods would normally share with mortals. You have found favor with this god. Perhaps, I will speak with him on this matter."

"But, does she think I come home to her every night?"

The dragon pulled back his head. "Alas, our conversation must come to an end. The moment approaches for you to look into the Eye."

Frustrated the dragon ignored his question, George sat up. "How do you suggest I retrieve Abbie's soul without killing the folks who stand in my way? I'm open to suggestions."

The Source's large figure began to dissolve. "Only you can decide how to handle your issues of morality. I can sense the good in you. I can also sense you will struggle to find your way. I do hope the Eye finds you worthy of its gift. You may want to get some sleep before entering the Eye's chamber. You will want to have your wits about you."

The last bit of the dragon's form vanished. "Remember this George, if you allow your past to victimize you, you will never find true happiness. You must forgive."

George called out, "Wait, don't go. Who am I supposed to forgive?"

After a long, agonizing silence, George sighed. He moved past the ancient dragon's lair and came to a heavy metal door at the end of a long corridor. *This must be the place,* he thought. *I'll sleep here before I go inside.* He lowered to the ground and put his hands behind his head.

Once asleep, Lasidious made his presence known inside his dream. "George...we need to talk."

"Holy garesh, man, where have you been? I have a million questions."

"I'm sure you do, George. I have a few things to tell you first. But, you're going to have to think quick."

"Nothing new with that concept. What's up?"

"Brayson knows you killed Amar."

"How in the hell did he find out?"

"Celestria was spying on Brayson. Your mother-in-law told him. Apparently, Mary spoke with Morre before you left Lethwitch. She knew of Amar's death, and when Brayson mentioned Amar had visited his office, Mary told him his friend was dead."

"This is bad. So, how did Brayson figure out it was me who killed him? Has he said anything to Athena or Mary?"

"Brayson visited a sprite who has the ability to bend moments. He saw you kill Amar after the sprite took him to the past. I don't think Brayson will say anything to Mary until he understands your reasoning. You need a plan."

"Ya think?" George snapped. "This is a nice pile of garesh you've gotten me into, Lasidious."

Brayson's Floating Office

Brayson watched through one of the windows of his office as Sam made his way into Floren. The wizard had posted one of the students outside the school of magic's invisible tower to greet the King of Brandor and show him the way inside.

Like the many others who had entered before him, Sam marveled at how the spiral staircase shot up into the distance for what seemed to be forever. The fairies moved between the walls of bookcases, and as always, they were rearranging the books from one shelf to another in an organized fashion. Sam moved to stand beside the table where Kepler had injured his neck when fighting the silver sphere. He moved his hands across the etched markings of magic.

It wasn't long before Sam found a symbol he recognized. It was the symbol which had been etched into one of the rings Brayson had given him after arriving on Merchant Island. He moved to one of the bookcases and began to search for a reference in which to study the symbol's meaning. Though his knowledge of the elven language was minimal, it was not long before his genius mind was lost in thought.

The Head Master appeared at Sam's side. "Sam...it's good to see you again. I trust you and your queen will be returning to Grayham?"

Sam's mood went from one of extreme interest to one of enormous irritation upon hearing the reference to Shalee. "She will continue her journey to find the missing piece of the Crystal Moon."

"You do not appear to be satisfied with your visit. When I teleported you south of her position, you seemed anxious to catch up to her. The window showed she was with someone. Who was her guide? Did your journey to catch her give you the moments you requested to think?"

Sam found Brayson's eyes. "The answers to your questions are not something I wish to discuss. I'm ready to go home."

Brayson nodded. "Fair enough. I do hope your queen is right about the crystal's location. I have recently uncovered grave news...news which has left me with many questions. I ask you to indulge me."

Sam grimaced. "Where shall we talk? Somewhere comfortable, I hope?"

"Of course." Brayson waved his hand and before Sam knew it, both of them appeared inside his office. Brayson pulled back his new chair and motioned for Sam to sit. Once Sam was comfortable, Brayson leaned against the edge of his desk and crossed his legs in front of him. "I would like to know how you came to Grayham."

"Why do you ask?"

"My new Mystic Learner is traveling to meet with The Source. Although you never said anything, I think you may know him."

Sam crossed his arms. "Let me guess. George is the one you're talking about."

"He is. So, you do know him?"

"I know him alright. I'll tell you everything I know. But first, what is The Source and why would George meet with it?"

Brayson sighed. He explained The Source's function and what would happen if George looked into the Eye of Magic and survived.

Sam stood from the chair and moved to the far side of the room. "This isn't good. George is a manipulative bastard. He is a liar and a thief. Before he left for Luvelles, he managed to start the largest war Grayham has ever seen. Many died and almost as many will spend the rest of their lives as sad reminders of the men they used to be."

Brayson had to find the courage to ask his next question. "Are you from the same world George is from?"

"You know of Earth?" Sam questioned, caught off guard. "Who gave you this information?"

"It doesn't matter. I suppose whether you came from this Earth or not tells me nothing other than you are alien."

"Alien? I've never been called that before."

"I mean no offense. What else can you tell me of George?"

Sam's brow furrowed. "Why are you asking me so many questions about him? What has George done now? Has he screwed you over, too?"

"He has done nothing to harm me, or anyone else I know, since his arrival on Luvelles. I'm more concerned about the person he killed on Grayham. This person was a friend of mine...an old Mystic Learner to be precise. It is the way George killed him which has me concerned."

Sam reclaimed Brayson's chair. "You say that as if there is a way to kill someone that wouldn't cause you concern."

Brayson gave a shallow smile. "I see your point. I assure you, I'm not a fan of death. The way George killed this man requires answers. Only the most ancient elves know this secret. It is forbidden to speak of it."

"Forbidden? What secret? It isn't forbidden for you and I to share information. My position as King of Southern Grayham allows us to speak of secrets which may prevent war. I studied your laws before I came, and I know this to be true."

"Impressive. You are correct. But, George has done nothing to cause a war on Luvelles. The two kingdoms below are at odds with one another, but this has nothing to do with George."

Sam moved to look out one of the office windows. "Your lands are beautiful. I wouldn't be so sure George isn't involved. He's a man who looks for every angle. I studied his tactics after he went missing on Grayham. After gathering the full story, George used those around him to do his dirty work. He did it without lifting a finger. He managed to create a war he never fought in."

Sam turned from the window. "Brayson, I assure you...if George is on this world, he is looking to gain as much power as he can. I would bet my crown that, if your kingdoms are at odds with one another, it is because George has established the odds."

Brayson took a seat in his chair. "If what you say is true, then I need to stop him before he speaks with The Source. Come with me, Sam."

Brayson began to reach for the king's shoulder, but before they could teleport, Brayson's phoenix appeared. "Your Mystic Learner gave me quite the shock. He has been visiting with The Source for a while now. His power is stronger than the others. He is even stronger than you were before you received your gift so many seasons ago."

Brayson lowered to his chair beneath the weight of the news. "Then, we are too late. It is up to the Eye to determine whether George will receive its gift."

Sam looked past the phoenix's presence. "What do you mean, it's too late? Let's barge in there and kill him before he has the chance to finish his visit with this Eye. What is the Eye anyway?"

Brayson leaned forward. "The Eye isn't something you can barge in on. Once The Source has initiated his conversation with George, no one can enter the ancient's cave. The dragon's magic is too powerful. I cannot pass through it."

Sam slapped the side of the bookcase. "Damn! We need to level the playing field." He put his hand to his chin and played with the scruff. "I think I know a way to do it. Brayson, take me to the swamp of the beast you call Grogger. I'll go in after the crystal's missing piece. You can send Shalee to meet with this Source. She's powerful. She'll be able to kill George once she has looked into this Eye and receives the same gift."

Brayson stood. "Your queen is not ready for a task of this magnitude..." Brayson paused in thought, "...unless she has also eaten the heart of another."

"What are you talking about? Why would Shalee eat another person's heart? Her power is growing because of a god's blessing which was placed on her spirit before being sent to Earth. She also carries the memories of Yaloom within that irritating brain of hers."

Fisgig spoke. "How are such things possible?"

Sam continued to look out the window. "When I was on Earth, if a bird began to question me the way you have, I would have said, how are such things possible? I have come to understand that it doesn't matter how. It just is. So...shall we go get my wife?"

Brayson waved his hand and the trio vanished. Once gone, Hosseff removed his hood and appeared. He had been listening to their conversation. As the light in the room penetrated the haze of his face, his appearance changed into his human form. He thought, *Bassorine must've been the one to bless Shalee's spirit. If he didn't do it, then he's responsible for initiating it.*

The shade walked around Brayson's desk and waved his hand across the window. He watched as it zoomed in on Grogger's Swamp. The image of Shalee came into focus. *So, Yaloom's memories are now yours to call upon. How intriguing. I wonder how long it will be before you're capable of summoning the memory to teleport to Ancients Sovereign. It was clever of Yaloom to make you his tool. I would have expected far less from him. Using your son's death to find a way to live again was brilliant. He may find his way back to godliness.*

Grogger's Swamp

Shalee entered the swamp the night before. She had used her magic to adjust her clothes to keep the leeches away from her skin. As she waded through the marsh, many mutated creatures fell dead as a consequence for their attacks. Some of these creatures had teeth the size of her fingers.

On one occasion, a large, bird-like, catfish-spearfish looking whatever-in-the-heck it was, swooped out of the fog and tried to stab her with its point.

Now...fellow soul...you'll have to bear with me on this one. This bird-fish thing was so messed up, Shalee was unable to describe it to me with great detail during my interview with her. Based on our conversation, no description of its grotesque nature could show the detail of its deformities. Anyway, the thing flew, it looked creepy, and it was dangerous. Enough babbling, back to the story.

Shalee managed to avoid the bird-fish's attack. She ducked as the creature flew past her position and stuck into another beast which had been stalking her from behind.

Shalee was walking within a protective barrier of magic when Brayson appeared with Sam and Fisgig at his side. The trio stood within a protective barrier of their own, and had appeared close enough to give Sam the chance to speak with Shalee.

"What are ya doin' here, Sam?" Shalee said as she studied his companions.

Sam's voice was cold. "You need to go with the Head Master. Your skills are needed elsewhere. I will go after the missing piece of crystal."

"What? Why?"

"Just go with Brayson and he'll explain."

"Are ya still angry with me?"

"Look...this isn't the moment to play, 'Let's Make Shalee Feel Better.' You're in trouble and you know it. Just go. Save me the irritation. We'll speak once I've had the chance to calm down."

Brayson spoke up. "Shalee, I am Head Master, Brayson. This is Fisgig. Come into my magic. It'll keep you safe."

Shalee did as instructed. Sam turned to look at Brayson. "Is there anything I should know about Grogger?"

Fisgig answered. "The creature will try to swallow you if he finds you. I'm not sure where your crystal could be, but if you were to be swallowed by the toad, the acid inside its stomach will digest you over 10 seasons. It will be torturous."

"That's disgustin'," Shalee said, staring at the phoenix. "So, you can talk?"

Sam was irritated by Shalee's surprise that a bird could speak after all they had gone through since their arrival on Grayham. He ignored the queen and turned to Brayson. "Okay, okay, the acid is no problem." He lifted his sword of the gods. "Right, Kael?"

The blade responded. "This is correct, Sam." Kael lifted from the king's hand and floated over to Brayson. "Head Master...I may be able to feel the crystal's presence if you were to magnify Sam's senses. I should be able to draw from this power and use it to rule out large areas of the swamp and narrow our search."

Brayson waved his hand over Sam's head. "It's done. Will there be anything else?"

Sam thought a moment as Kael returned to his sheath. "Something more suitable to wear while trudging through the swamp would be nice. I don't care for leeches."

Shalee snapped her fingers. "I got this." She moved to stand in front of her king. She leaned in and motioned for Sam to bend down. She whispered in his ear. "I'm sorry. I do love you."

Standing back, Shalee lifted her hand and passed the top of Precious across Sam's clothes. The cloth altered its appearance and sealed, protecting Sam's skin. "The leeches won't be able ta get ta ya now. But, the water will seep in like a wetsuit. It should keep ya warm."

Sam wanted to say something kind, but his anger would not let him. Instead, he barked out an order, "Get out of here. You need to get started on the trials."

The Underwater Kingdom of Ultor

The leader of the Ultorians stood in front of a watery likeness of Gregory. The White Chancellor's image had taken form at the base of the steps leading to Ultor's throne. Except for the spot where Gregory's image stood, the Ultorian King's coral castle remained clear of the element and was dry inside. A magical barrier had been used to keep the water out.

The colors of Ultor's flesh were marvelous to look upon as the White Chancellor used his personal mirror from inside his tower to look through the watery eyes of his likeness. Ultor bowed to show his respect for Gregory as did the chancellor from the other side of the mirror. As Gregory bowed, so did his likeness.

"What cause may I assist you with, Chancellor?"

"Thank you for visiting with me. War is approaching. I need your help to keep the Order from spreading darkness across the land. There is no telling what my brother will do if he is allowed to take control of Luvelles."

Ultor nodded. "I understand, but we are a peaceful race. We are unable to fight a battle which remains on land. Unless you bring the battle to the shores of Crystal Lake, there is no way to help you."

Gregory thought a moment. "Perhaps, the goswigs could help. Would you speak with them, and ask them to join Lord Dowd's men north of Lake Tepp? Their combined magic would bring a powerful force. They can march with Dowd to the Battlefields of Olis."

The pressure of Ultor's hand displaced the colors of his chin as it pressed against his face. As he removed it, the colors returned. "I will speak with Strongbear. If he chooses to go to war, the goswigs will join the fight. But, if he chooses not to fight, I won't make him go."

"Understood," Gregory said as he bowed in front of his mirror. "This is all I could ask. I will hope my answer arrives, ready for battle."

The king bowed in return. "Let's hope."

Gregory watched as the mirror sitting in the center of his bedroom chamber went dark. The White Chancellor had no idea he was being watched. A sinister smile crossed Marcus' face as he peeked around and stared at his younger brother from behind Gregory's mirror. The Dark Chancellor stood within a spell of invisibility and was about to strike his brother down when Brayson appeared with Shalee and Fisgig. Without offering Gregory an explanation, Brayson teleported them away from the White Chancellor's tower of glass and reappeared in an area where Marcus couldn't follow.

Marcus shouted. "Damn you, Brayson!" After a long series of moments filled with agitated swearing, the Dark Chancellor began to laugh. "What irony...Brayson saved your miserable life, little brother."

Brayson appeared with the group inside the shrine on the southern end of his island, which once again held the key to The Source's temple. He motioned for the darkness to dissipate, and it was replaced with a soothing light.

"What's going on, brother?" Gregory said as he took note of his company. "Why have you brought me here? I have much to do and very few moments in which to do it."

Brayson introduced Shalee, then explained, "I'm sending the two of you to speak with The Source. I'm going to teleport ahead of you to let the Ancient One know you are coming. I'm going to need assistance and each of you needs to look into the Eye. Let's hope you are able to do this and live."

"Why would you do this?"

Brayson put his hand on Gregory's shoulder. "I need you to trust me. We are going to need the power to fight the forces which will come out of the Kingdom of Hyperia. Boyafed will send his new Argont Commander to rally the forces of the mercenaries of Bestep. He'll continue to the forest of Shade Hollow and ask the Serwin King to follow him into battle. I imagine Boyafed will meet with Kassel, and we both know the numbers of the Hyperian King's army. The one thing I fear most is Boyafed will call upon the debt Balecut owes him."

"No! Not Balecut."

Shalee spoke up. "Who is Balecut?"

Fisgig responded. "He's a powerful wizard who lives within the Petrified Forest. He can summon the power to bend the moments in which we live. Even though this power will not work against another wizard, or even another warlock who commands magic equal to his ability, he is feared by most everyone on this world."

"So, you're sayin' this Balecut character can manipulate time?"

Fisgig's feathered face appeared confused as he responded, "I'm not familiar with this term, 'time,' Shalee. Please explain."

"It means the same thing as the moments ya just referred ta as bein' bendable, but it will be easier ta explain when we have enough time or ratha', enough moments in which ta explain it."

"I think I understand. As I was saying...Balecut can slow down the moments in which we live. This could give the dark army an advantage in battle. This is why it's so important for one of you to successfully look into the Eye of Magic. Brayson will be able to teach you how to summon this cherished power once you have received the Eye's gift."

"I understand," Gregory responded.

Shalee was deep in thought. Brayson moved to get her attention. "What has your mind tied up, Shalee?"

Shalee took a deep breath. "Is it safe ta say one of us may neva' return from this lil' outin'?"

Brayson lifted her chin and looked into her eyes. "Both of you may never return from this journey. You can have no doubt in your abilities, Shalee. You must find the courage to go before the Eye and look into the gem's light.

The Source won't stop you once you arrive, I'll see to that. But, you'll still need to find your way through the Void Maze in order to get there."

Gregory nudged Shalee. "This will be easy. I've done this before. I'm far more powerful than I was the first series of moments I went through the maze. We will be standing before The Source's cave within a respectable series of moments. Just stay close to me."

Shalee lowered to a stone bench inside the shrine. "Head Master, Sam told me ya possess the strongest magic on Luvelles. Why don't ya just stop this Boyafed fella' from recruitin' this Balecut character in the first place?"

"My position as Head Master, though powerful, does not allow me to choose a side in war. I do not wish this war to happen, but if I were to force those on Luvelles to stop, it would be an abuse of my power. All I can do is try to act as peacemaker. You are not bound by the same rules. You will be able to use your new power to help stop this war. I will try to find what is causing the tension between the armies. I plan to start by speaking with your friend, George."

Shalee cringed. "George is no friend of mine. Is he behind all this?"

"I can't be sure, but if what Sam has told me is true, and George was indeed responsible for your war on Grayham, then I think he would be the best choice to begin my investigation."

"Oh, it's true alright." Shalee said, then stood. She looked at Gregory. "Shall we go?"

Gregory looked at Brayson. "I need you to deliver a message to Lord Dowd. He must finish gathering the forces for battle. I already spoke with Ultor. Dowd will need to do the rest of what he has requested of me."

Gregory took Shalee by the hand after securing the key to The Source's temple and placing it inside his robe. The next thing Shalee knew, she was standing outside the entrance to the Void Maze.

𝕴'𝖒 𝕯𝖗𝖚𝖓𝖐 𝖆𝖘 𝖆 𝕾𝖐𝖚𝖓𝖐 𝖆𝖓𝖉 𝕹𝖊𝖊𝖉 𝕾𝖔𝖒𝖊 𝕷𝖔𝖛𝖎𝖓'

The Dark Order's Temple

Boyafed was preparing to leave to go to the Petrified Forest. He was standing, without his shirt, in front of a mirror located inside his bedroom chamber inside the Order's temple when the goddess, Mieonus, appeared before him. He jumped back with lightning reflexes, grabbed his blessed long sword and took a defensive position, ready to strike.

The goddess smiled. "Relax, Boyafed. I'm not here to harm you. Do you know who I am?"

Boyafed pointed the tip of his blade in Mieonus' direction. "You should tell me before I decide to cut this conversation short."

Mieonus put her finger on the point of Boyafed's blade and pushed it aside. "How clever you must consider yourself. I'm Mieonus. You may kneel before me."

The Order leader knew the name. He took a knee and bowed his head. "Has Hosseff sent you, goddess? What must I do to serve My Lord?"

Mieonus hated the way his statement sounded. The thought of being the shade god's personal errand girl made her want to vomit. Dismissing her irritation, she moved across the room. Her red gown flowed curvaceously as she moved. Her black, lifted heels clicked against the white marble of Boyafed's bedroom floor as she sauntered to the side of his bed. She sat, then maneuvered into a seductive position and studied the warrior before responding. She was amused at how trained Hosseff's followers were. He had kept his head lowered and waited for her to speak.

"Hosseff didn't send me. Come to me and relax."

Boyafed did as instructed. She watched him as he walked across the room, then she patted the bed beside her for him to sit. He did so without question and kept his head bowed once seated.

The goddess enjoyed his strong elven features and found him attractive. His eyes were dark brown, his hair soft and he had a defined jaw which complemented the masterpiece which served as his frame. She reached over and lifted his chin until his eyes found hers. She could feel him tremble as his skin covered with goosebumps.

With her sweetest smile, Mieonus spoke, "Have you ever touched a goddess, Boyafed? Would you enjoy being with a woman of my beauty?"

Boyafed was unsure how to respond. He remained quiet while trying to find a way to gather his thoughts. The goddess leaned in and kissed his lips, but Boyafed didn't kiss back. She kept at it until he responded. After a few moments, he found the courage to reach in and pull her to him. She was intoxicating, and Boyafed could feel his heart pounding.

The Order leader stood, lifted Mieonus from the bed, then took control. The goddess received his aggression for a long series of moments before the mood subsided and both lay satisfied.

The goddess smiled as she prepared to deliver bad news while lying in his arms. "Boyafed...I wish with everything in me I could say my visit was solely for the benefit you have so graciously blessed me with. But, I cannot say this without it being a lie. I hate to tell you...but, something awful has happened. I do not wish to hurt you, but I have come to deliver bad news... news I'm sure will make you wish to seek vengeance. I assure you, I truly do not wish to deliver such grave news."

The Order leader rolled toward her, kissed her, and with a rejuvenated attitude, replied, "I am a man. I can handle it."

"I do not doubt your ability to handle any situation. I have no doubts in you at all. I wouldn't be lying here beside you if I did."

"Tell me...why is it you've come?"

"You must first promise to hear me out before getting upset."

"I promise." Boyafed stroked Mieonus' hair. "Please, continue."

"Your son, Kiayasis, has been killed by the King of Southern Grayham. I have come to tell you he broke your son's neck and left him lying in the forest southeast of Grogger's Swamp. I have always admired you, and a man of your stature deserves better."

Boyafed rolled clear of the bed and stood, failing to cover himself. "What would make the king decide to kill him? He would have had no knowledge of Kiayasis' order to kill his queen."

Mieonus enjoyed Boyafed's pain, though her facial expression did not show it. "The king saw his queen lying in Kiayasis' arms. I'm sorry for your loss. I wouldn't want any child of mine rotting on the forest floor."

Boyafed's face hardened. "And, where is the king now?"

"He's inside the swamp. If you hurry, you can catch him. If you wish, I'll return to comfort you when you have collected the payment for your loss."

The goddess watched as Boyafed donned the black plate of the Order. He sheathed his sword and helped Mieonus out of the bed. He took one last glance at her body before kissing her goodbye. "I must go. I have a king to kill and a sacrifice to give Hosseff. I would enjoy your company when I'm finished." Boyafed vanished.

Mieonus smiled as she put on her dress. She whispered to the empty room and pretended Boyafed was still standing in front of her. "My attraction to you is fictitious, Boyafed. You're an idiot. How could you believe that I, a goddess with my beauty, would want to be with someone like you? You'll finish grieving without me." Mieonus hesitated. "However, I must give credit. Your movements were a delightful satisfaction. Perhaps, I shall use you on some other occasion."

Boyafed appeared outside the stable which held his krape lord. Before the dark warrior had the chance to enter, Hosseff appeared. Boyafed dropped to one knee. "My Lord, how may I serve you?"

From within the nothingness beneath the god's hood, Lasidious altered his voice to match Hosseff's wispy tone. "Be careful, Boyafed. Do not allow yourself to be deceived. What Mieonus told you about your son is true. Kiayasis is dead. Your desire to avenge his death is acceptable, but Mieonus has desires of her own far beyond lying with you. Her desire is to manipulate you for purposes of her own. I don't wish to see you turned into the goddess' puppet. You're far too strong for this."

Boyafed sighed, "I shouldn't have laid with her, My Lord. I beg your forgiveness. It won't happen again."

"Nonsense. I understand the desires of a man. You did what any man would have done, considering the situation. I applaud you for taking advantage of the opportunity while it existed. The goddess is indeed a beautiful woman, is she not?"

"Yes, My Lord. She was a good lover, to be sure. I'll avoid her in the future."

"There's no need to avoid her. Use her how you will. Turn her into a plaything of your own. Just remember the god you serve when the moment comes that she tries to manipulate you further. We have many things to discuss. Your desire to avenge your son's death can be harnessed to glorify me. I have a task for you, Boyafed. Are you ready?"

"I live to serve, My Lord. What would you ask of me?"

The City of Nept
Just after Late Bailem

Now...fellow soul...Nept is a city with a large population, but it is not the city the inhabitants on the rest of Luvelles come to see. It is the outskirts of the city which calls many to its beauty. The countryside of Nept is the home to the finest vineyards on all the worlds. The grapes grow naturally and are used to produce many different forms of wines, but one special wine is made from a vine which grows not far from an inn called *Lisse Fion,* which means, sweet wine. This is the only inn on Luvelles, or better yet, the only inn on all the worlds, with a wine called Mesolliff. The amount of coin it takes to buy a single bottle is steep.

Mary, Athena and Susanne are sitting in this old, country inn. This is the first place the ladies have seen on Luvelles which reminds them of their farming community in Lethwitch. Athena and Susanne are glad to get off their feet after chasing Mary around the countryside in her drunken state.

For the most part, Susanne has been taking care of baby Garrin while she watches Athena help Mary walk between farms. There isn't a lot of fancy magic being used around these parts. In fact, it is quite the opposite. Most of the locals are unable to command the arts at all.

Mary has taken a liking to Mesolliff. It only took one sip for her to become intolerable.

Mary opened her bag and retrieved the coin Brayson gave her and slammed it on the bar. She looked at the sommelier who was at the far side of the bar and shouted, "Bring another bottle!"

Athena and Susanne refused the drink. "Mother, stop this. You're embarrassing us. The things you're saying are awful."

Mary took another sip of Mesolliff. She lifted her head and shouted, "I'm drunk as a skunk and need some lovin'!" She said it over and over, announcing to everyone in the establishment that she was anxious for some specific attention. She leaned up against Athena. "I need some lovin'! I need some lovin'!"

Athena snapped, "Mother, shut up, will you? You're embarrassing us." She looked at Susanne. "Let's take her home so Brayson can shut her up."

Susanne wanted to die as she watched the owner of the inn walk over to speak with them. "This must be her first series of moments tasting Mesolliff. It's easy to spot a woman who has just had her first taste of nature's seduction. I suggest you take her home before she starts to fondle the furniture. It'll get worse before it gets better. I would hurry if I were you."

Mary lifted the bottle and took a swig. The man behind the counter smiled. "I hope you don't have pets. She's going to have an active night. She might find them attractive."

The girls' faces showed their disgust. They gathered around Mary. After

Susanne lifted Garrin into her arms, Athena read the spell from the Scroll of Teleportation. In an instant, they were home and standing in Mary's bedroom next to the mirror Brayson had given their mother.

Mary didn't waste any of her moments. She tossed the corked bottle to the floor, stumbled up to the mirror, and evoked its power. Athena grabbed the bottle from the floor and headed for the door. The girls didn't even have a chance to leave before Brayson's image appeared. As they shut the door behind them, all they heard Brayson say, in an excited voice, was, "I'll be right there!"

Mary threw open her window to the outside world, tore off her clothes, and flopped onto the bed. Athena and Susanne felt as if they were in the house of a woman they didn't know as Mary's screams of passion filled the night once Brayson began to satisfy her needs.

Kepler and Payne poked their heads out of Kepler's den beneath the rocks. The demon-jaguar shouted as Athena shut the door to Mary's house, "Athena, why the noise?"

The fairy-demon responded, "Payne go see, kitty."

Athena screamed at Payne. "You move, and I'll skin you alive! You go back into that hole, or I will beat the both of you! I'm embarrassed enough! Now, get some sleep! Do you understand me?"

Kepler lowered back into the hole without saying another word, but Payne waited until Athena and Susanne went inside Susanne's home before teleporting to a hovering position just outside the window. Seeing what was happening inside, the fairy-demon's head poked above the window sill. He tilted it back and forth in many different directions as he became confused. After many, many moments passed, and Mary's screams continued to fill the night, all he said after teleporting back into Kepler's lair was, "Kitty, why they do that? It's yuck."

Kepler didn't look up, but a grin crossed his furry face, which was covered by his front legs. "You will understand someday, freak. Get some sleep."

Athena left Susanne's home and walked across the clearing to her own. Once inside, she shut the door and leaned against the back of it. She thought, *I'm glad Brayson likes mother's adventurous side. But, how can I be expected to look her in the eyes tomorrow?*

The Source's Cave
The Eye of Magic's Chamber

George began to stir. He felt rested, and his visit with Lasidious during his dream had been informative, very informative. He grabbed a quick bite to eat out of his pack, then stood to face the heavy, metal door. Behind it, the Eye of Magic waited.

He reached out, but the door opened before he could touch it. A chill ran down his spine as the heavy hinges squealed from many seasons without proper maintenance. Beyond the door, sitting attached to the top of a thick wooden staff at the center of a cubed-shaped room was a ruby-red gem. It looked like a fire burned within, and it was large, about the size of his fist. Nothing else occupied the room.

That's it? George thought to himself. *How anticlimactic is this? It's just a stone on a piece of wood. I was expecting something...well, something more, I suppose.*

He walked into the room. The door slammed behind him, the heavy metal making a thunderous noise. He rubbed his ears, trying to stop the ringing as the room filled with a blinding red light. He had to cover his eyes to protect them, and before he knew it, he was standing in front of an angelic being. The red light softened and was replaced with a soft white, everywhere, except for one spot.

The being's face could not be seen due to the light which took its place. A ghostly body shimmered while large, feathered wings extended on either side. George had no idea what to say or do.

Many moments passed before the silence broke. "I have been waiting for you, George."

George watched as the light of the illuminated face began to fade and was replaced by a large eye. There was no mouth, no lips, nothing to go along with it. It was just a big eye sitting on top of the shoulders of an angel's body.

"Does looking at me displease you?"

George swallowed. "I wouldn't say I'm displeased. I would say I'm unsure of what I think."

"Your first honest answer. I trust you're prepared to look into my eye? Do you feel you're ready? Do you worry I will steal your soul and swallow it?"

"I'm not worried about anything. I do have questions, though."

The eye blinked. "I have never had a Mystic Learner come before me and request questions answered. Do you not fear for your soul? I have taken the lives of many who were not ready."

George shrugged. "Garesh...I have nothing to lose. If I die, you're just doing me a favor. I won't have to deal with this damn place any longer. Other than that, I feel pretty good about my chances. I can handle whatever it is you're going to throw at me."

"Your confidence is intriguing. I will allow one question."

George had many, but needed to narrow it to the most important. After a short while, he spoke, "I have listened to Master Id speak of using his power to become god-like. He said no one has ever been able to obtain this ultimate power, though your gift will allow this to happen. I would like to know why they have not been able to take your gift and use it to accomplish godhood. I guess what I'm asking, what's holding them all back?"

Again, the eye blinked. There was a long silence before its voice filled the room. "Even the most confident have failed to realize they have no limitations to their power. It is their own inability to believe in the magnitude of the gift which keeps them from moving to a heightened level of exaltation. You are the first to stand before me and have the confidence to pursue a higher level of knowledge. The others simply looked into my eye when asked, and because of their blind ambition, most surrendered their lives."

"What about Brayson?"

The Eye blinked. "That would be another question, but there is no harm in answering it. Even your master didn't bear the presence of mind when he looked into my eye. Step forward, George Nailer. Receive your gift."

George did as instructed. As he looked into the massive pupil, he began to feel light, as if floating away from the floor. Images appeared before him and his mind was filled with the knowledge of the most ancient of mystics. 427 expansions of his chest passed before he lowered to the floor and closed his eyes.

The Eye looked down at George's motionless figure. "Sleep, warlock. You need to rest. Your confidence has made you extraordinarily powerful."

Grogger's Swamp
The Next Morning

With Kael in his hand, the trail of death the King of Southern Grayham left as he and the sword moved through the murky water of the swamp was long. They had come to a good-sized hill and were able to crawl clear of the water for the first moment since their entrance.

Walking up the steep embankment, Kael whispered, "Stop climbing, Sam."

"Why?" Sam whispered back.

The blade responded. "It's the crystal. I sense its power. If I'm right, it is beyond this hill. I suggest greater caution. We have no idea what we could be facing."

"Agreed." Sam lowered to the ground and finished climbing the hill on his belly. At the top, he peeked over, but there was nothing but a large mossy mound in the middle of more swamp. The king rolled over and lifted Kael close to his mouth. "I see nothing. It looks the same as everything else we've seen."

"Trust me. The crystal is here. Look again. Perhaps, you're missing something."

Sam rolled back to his belly and peeked over the hill. Nothing was there. After thinking it through, he picked up a small stone which laid nearby. He rolled to one side and chucked it. Moving to his belly once again, he waited for the pebble to disturb the water around the mossy mound. What he saw next gave him great concern.

The large mound was not a mound at all—it was a creature. It turned and opened its mouth. A freakishly large tongue lashed out in the direction of the pebble's disturbance. The tongue's mass displaced much of the swamp's water as it tore into its surface.

Sam rolled to his back, then whispered, "Okay, okay! They said Grogger was big, but what an understatement that was. I wouldn't call him big. I'd call him enormous."

Kael responded. "I have news, but it won't make you happy."

"And, what would that be? Wait, let me guess. The crystal is inside the toad."

"Yes, it is, and you need to get it out."

"Damn, you could have said no."

For the first series of moments, Sam heard the blade laugh at his humor before responding. "So, what is the plan?"

"Beats the heck out of me," Sam shrugged. "It's not like I go charging into the belly of a toad every day. Let me think a bit." Sam rolled over to take another look. Grogger was gone. He looked up. To his surprise, the shapple toad was falling from the sky. The beast intended to land on the back side of their position.

Sam commanded Kael to bring forth his fire, and further, commanded the blade to protect his skin from the toad's acid. He tucked Kael tight to his body to ensure he didn't drop him and kept the point of the blade toward the ground. He closed his eyes, balled up tight, and waited. He could hear the screams of the souls wailing from inside the toad's stomach as its mouth opened. The force with which Grogger pulled them inside nearly knocked Sam unconscious, but somehow he avoided any broken bones. In fact, the toad swallowed them so quickly, the flame of Kael's blade didn't have a chance to burn the creature until they were inside.

As the burning began to sizzle the lining of the toad's stomach, Grogger began to stir as his guts took the brunt of Kael's heat. The motion helped Sam regain his composure. When he opened his eyes, he found himself in a pocket of protection. A man dressed as a hunter, and holding the crystal's missing piece, was staring at him. They were thrown about as Grogger hopped in pain. Sam managed to discard his surprise and fought through the pain inflicted by Grogger's tongue. He buried Kael deep into the base of the beast's stomach and hung on.

They could hear Grogger's horrific cry. Suddenly, the pile of bodies beyond the protective barrier began to shift. The toad was going to barf. Sam reached over and pulled the hunter close.

"Hang on! This is going to get messy!" Sam screamed for Kael to extend his blade.

Like projectiles, every creature and being inside Grogger's belly was thrown out and into the open, all of them landing on the side of the hill. Sam held tight to Kael as they were pushed out. His command for the sword to extend its length had provided the effect Sam had been after. Kael sliced the toad from its belly all the way out of the beast's mouth. The size of Grogger shrank once the mound of bodies filling him had been expelled. The brutal cut left the toad lifeless and split in half throughout the lower portion of his body.

Sam stood and commanded Kael's flame to dissipate. He wiped the blade clean as best he could under the circumstances and extended his hand toward the hunter.

Once on his feet, Sam spoke while looking around the hillside at all the partially digested bodies. "What's your name?" he questioned as he reached down to pick up the piece of Crystal Moon from the ground. "This is what I came for. I hope you don't mind. I need to take this bad boy with me."

Geylyn nodded. "Yes, yes, please, take it. My name is Geylyn Jesthrene, from Hyperia."

"Well, Geylyn, it looks like this is your lucky day. How long were you inside the toad's belly, and how did you protect yourself from the acid?"

"I have no answer. I have been asked to hold my tongue. The crystal is yours. I must return home without speaking further. Thank you for saving me, sir." Geylyn pulled a small scroll from beneath his shirt, read the words from it, then vanished. Sam watched Geylyn's invisible body make tracks along the hillside as he worked his way to the water of the swamp.

Sam lifted Kael to his face. "Well, how's that for gratitude? Let's find my pack and help as many of these people as we can. Let's get them out of here."

Before a step could be taken, Mosley appeared. The wolf-god said nothing and gave the king a moment to think.

Sam swallowed his pride. "Mosley, I owe you an apology for how I spoke to you in my throne room. I was out of line, and I'm sorry for speaking to you in that tone. Are we still friends?"

"Of course we are, Sam. I told you you would calm down." Mosley stopped and sniffed the air. He lowered his snout to the ground and began exploring his surroundings. After the third half-digested body, the wolf looked up, then snorted to clear his nostrils. "A brush with death will make anyone think about what is important. Sam, I know you are struggling with Shalee's unfaithfulness. I want you to know, I understand your pain. With enough moments, this pain shall pass, and your anger will be replaced with love. Everything will turn out as it should. Once you leave the swamp, you may want to return to Grayham. War is coming to Luvelles, and it will not be safe here much longer."

"What about Shalee? I can't leave her."

Mosley tilted his furry head. "Where is Shalee?"

"Shalee has started the trials to meet with The Source. Brayson has sent her to look into the Eye of Magic." Sam could see Mosley knew something he didn't. "What are you not telling me?"

"I wish I could tell you, Sam. I cannot speak of all I know. It was Bassorine's wish I stay silent."

"What does that mean?"

"I must go, Sam. I will come to you at a later moment. I must join this piece of the crystal with the others." The wolf vanished.

"Damn the gods," Sam snapped. After a moment, he redirected his attention. He removed the small vial Brayson had given him, and after a close inspection of all the motionless figures, he decided he could save only ten. He would lead them to safety once they recovered and had been fed.

The Village of Gogswayne

That night, the goswigs could not believe their eyes as King Ultor made his way onto the banks of Crystal Lake. He had sent Swill and Syse ahead to summon the goswigs to a meeting. Everyone was present, except for Strongbear, the one Ultor wanted to speak with most.

The king's skin finished changing as he stood in front of nearly 1,000 creatures which held the title, goswig. Ultor looked at Gage. "Where is Strongbear?"

Gage swallowed hard. "He's hibernating, Your Majesty."

"Why would the bear be hibernating when the season has not yet changed?"

The entire goswig population began to murmur, all of them unsure how the badger would explain the situation. They had agreed that Gallrum would avoid telling the king about the uniting of their magic to bring winter to their underground village.

Gage decided to tell the truth. "Your Majesty, Strongbear was driving us mad. We were tired of listening to his orders, so we pooled our magic to bring in the new season to our village."

The reaction they received was not the one they expected. Ultor began to laugh. Gage held his stomach as the gagging motion of the Ultorian's laugh made him sick.

Eventually, the king settled down. "Who organized this use of power?"

Every goswig pointed at Gage. Again, the king began to laugh. The badger watched, and on every occasion the king lunged forward, he did too. He found his stomach cramping as a result of the tension he felt from the king's reaction.

Ultor's laughter subsided. "You will need to wake Strongbear. The white army needs you to fight beside them in the upcoming war. Strongbear's power will be needed. I will be back tomorrow night." Ultor moved into the water and disappeared beneath the surface. His skin once again changed to an iridescent blue as his large water wings propelled him through the water.

Gage tapped his staff against the ground. "Great! We've got to wake him." The badger turned and looked at the mass of goswigs. "Are you with me...or against me?" he mocked.

All the goswigs grumbled as they headed home.

The Luvelles Gazette

When you want an update about your favorite characters

The Next Day, Early Bailem

Shalee and Gregory are working their way through the Void Maze. Since George killed most of the creatures inside the dungeon's corridors, they are left with the task of just finding their way through it.

Kepler and Payne are still waiting for George. Kepler has been teaching Payne to speak correctly. Something strange is happening. Payne is learning at a rapid pace.

The demon-cat has decided to embrace the little freak and accept his company as permanent. Kepler hates to admit it, but Payne is growing on him.

Mary, Athena, Susanne and baby Garrin are inside Mary's home having breakfast. The events of the night before last are fresh in Mary's mind, despite the hangover she still has from the effects of the Mesolliff wine.

Boyafed has set up camp. The Dark Order leader is waiting for Sam to exit the swamp.

Brayson has given Lord Dowd the message that Gregory will not be able to finish gathering the forces necessary for the upcoming war.

Dowd has sent Krasous, his Argont Commander, to meet with Wisslewine in the enchanted woods of Wraithwood Hollow. Krasous is to ask the Wraith Hound Prince to call his pack of ferocious canine warriors out of the Under Eye and bring them to the Battlegrounds of Olis.

Krasous will also go to the Spirit Plains to find the king of a race of spirits called the Lost Ones. Krasous must capture Shesolaywen so Dowd can use the spirit's Call of Canair.

Brayson is sitting outside the entrance to The Source's cave. He is waiting for George to exit.

Mieonus is watching as Sam guides those he saved from Grogger's belly out of the swamp. The magic inside the swamp will not allow for teleportation. Once they make their exit they will be able to teleport home. She is looking forward to the confrontation between Sam and Boyafed.

Mosley and Alistar have returned to Ancients Sovereign. They have called for a meeting of the gods to be held inside the Hall of Judgment.

Mosley has managed to successfully leave an impression on the minds of the leaders of Harvestom. They believe war is the only course of action. The King of Kless has called for war, a decision made because of the theft of the Seeds of Plenty. He ordered the commander of his Brown Coat army of centaurs to march against the King of Tagdrendlia's Black Coats by Early Bailem tomorrow. What is left of the food supply in Kless will be used to feed the army as they march into battle.

Many souls will be returned to the Book of Immortality's pages from the devastation. Hosseff will be busy collecting souls and returning them to the Book.

Gage and the other goswigs are waiting for Strongbear to exit his cave. They have used their magic to reverse the change of season and the bear has been slow to wake. The badger and Gallrum are expecting a grumpy brown bear to emerge.

Marcus is waiting inside his dark tower-palace. He is hoping George will return soon so they can implement the last part of their plan. Soon, Marcus will be able to stand before the Eye of Magic.

Lasidious and Celestria are inside their home beneath the Peaks of Angels. Both are getting ready and plan to teleport to the Hall of Judgment for Mosley's meeting. Despite this being the wolf's meeting, Lasidious is about to deliver some heavy news which will change the course of everything.

Lasidious' meeting with Boyafed, outside the Order's stables, was everything he hoped it would be. The Mischievous One will no longer need to take the form of a shade to manipulate the Dark Order's leader. The last thing Boyafed said to him when ending their conversation was, "I live to serve you, My Lord."

Lasidious then returned home to Ancients Sovereign to celebrate the deception with his lover, Celestria.

Thank you for reading the Luvelles Gazette

A Pair of Eyes Closed Forever
Ancients Sovereign

The gods assembled inside Gabriel's Hall of Judgment. As always, Keylom's hooves clapped against the marble floor as he entered the room. Lictina's ugly face, which hardly complemented her elegant robe laced with gems, followed as her tail swished across the floor while taking her normal seat. Bailem appeared behind his chair, adjusted his robe covering his portly belly, then spread his wings just enough to allow him to sit. The rest of the Collective either appeared or walked into the room one after another, and as always, Lasidious and Celestria were the last to bless everyone with their presence.

Mosley opened the meeting once Gabriel lowered to a comfortable position on the heavy stone table. The wolf announced, "I have the third piece of the Crystal Moon. Lasidious, the moment has come to join it with the others."

Lasidious shrugged. "Then, do it. No one's stopping you." Lasidious' tone was snide. "We didn't need to come to a meeting for you to join it with the others. Go to the temple on Grayham and place it with the other two."

The room filled with questions. Mosley spoke over the top of them all. "I thought George had the crystals. When did you place them in the temple?"

"They have been there for nearly 20 Peaks." Lasidious smirked, "I suppose I forgot to mention it."

Mieonus stood and shouted. "How could you forget to mention something like that?"

"Shut up, Mieonus," Mosley snapped. "Your anger will solve nothing. When will you figure it out? He does this to irritate you, yet you allow him under your skin? Sit down."

Mieonus stomped her lifted heel. "I will sit when I wish to sit." The goddess looked around the room. When every eye looked at her as if she was an idiot, she stomped her heel again, then sat in a huff.

Mosley could not help but enjoy Mieonus' irritation. After a moment, he turned his attention back to Lasidious. "I assume you have protected the crystals from being taken. All we can do is add to the pieces, is this correct?"

Lasidious stood, then took Celestria's hand as she stood from her chair. "Mosley is correct. The pieces can be added to the new statue they now rest upon."

Hosseff leaned forward. His wispy voice filled the room. "What new statue are you referring to?"

Lasidious' grin widened. "I suggest you take a look for yourself. The statue will be the new resting place for the Crystal Moon." The Mischievous One and his lover vanished, headed for their home.

Without further discussion, the rest of the Collective also vanished, only to reappear in front of the new placeholder for the Crystal Moon. The statue was made of the most precious gem which could only be found in the mines of Trollcom. It was called Diamante. The statue was clear with a slight yellow hue. The light within the temple reflected from it, producing a glorious glimmer.

The image portrayed was that of Lasidious. He stood with his hood down. His head and hands were extended toward the paintings on the temple's ceiling. His hands had been placed together, and the golden dragon, which cradled the first two pieces of the Crystal Moon, stood in his palms.

Including the black marble base, the total height of the Mischievous One's new image was more than 20 feet. Forever, would Lasidious' vanity stand where the statue of Bassorine had rested for more than 10,000 seasons.

Mieonus was the first to speak, sneering. "I say we destroy it! Who does he think he is? This is an outrage."

Alistar stepped forward. "He doesn't need our approval. We cannot destroy it. If we do, he will destroy the Crystal Moon. He doesn't need to ask how we feel. Lasidious is the strongest of us all. He holds the power to govern the worlds in the palms of his hands...no pun intended, of course. We can do nothing, but allow him to glorify himself. He has found a way to capture the eyes of the worlds without taking their free will. I hate to say it...his plan is brilliant." Alistar looked at Mosley. "It's safe to say we now understand what the bigger picture is."

"What picture are you referring to?" Keylom questioned. His hooves clacked against the floor as he moved to a better speaking position. "How does a statue explain a bigger picture?"

Mosley spoke out, ignoring the centaur. "Alistar, you may be right. This makes perfect sense. Lasidious stole the Crystal Moon to implement his plan to get rid of Bassorine. He knew, with Bassorine's destruction, he would be powerful enough to keep the Collective away from the Crystal Moon."

The wolf turned to Gabriel who hovered next to Bailem. "Lasidious also knew you would be unable to take the Crystal Moon from him after its pieces were put back together. He will use his free will to hold the threat of the Crystal Moon's destruction over our heads as a way to manipulate us. He knows the Collective does not have the power to recreate the worlds, if destroyed."

Lictina added, "Lasidious also knows that, without Bassorine, the Collective doesn't have the power to create another Crystal Moon. He never had any intention of destroying anything. The game he has us playing is a diversion. He simply wishes to be the centerpiece for all the worlds to see. He has kept us busy so he can achieve this objective."

Mosley looked up from licking himself. "I think Lasidious has a bigger plan than being the figurehead for the worlds. I would wager he hopes to increase the number of his followers. I believe the game with the Crystal Moon has been about his desire to get the masses to stop worshipping us. He wants them to worship him so he can gain the power to take control of the Book."

Alistar spoke out. "I agree with Mosley. But, if I know Lasidious, he is prepared to destroy the Crystal Moon if we don't continue to play his game." The gods watched as Alistar leaned forward and motioned for them to come close. He whispered, "Everyone, touch one another. We need to combine our power to protect what I'm about to say. We can't afford to have Lasidious listening in. This is critical and I'm invoking the Rule of Fromalla."

The gods did as requested. Alistar put one hand on Bailem's shoulder and the other on Mosley's back. He continued, "Clearly, we didn't take everything into account when we created Gabriel. We overlooked many important details."

The Book of Immortality responded. "Many of your laws aren't written to completion, but there is no flawed law which would pertain to this conversation."

The others agreed while Alistar remained patient. "I'm not referring to a law which has been written. I'm not referring to a law at all. I didn't think of it until now, and even then, I didn't put it together until Mosley said Lasidious plans to take control of the Book. Gabriel, you don't have the ability to grow in strength."

Hosseff's voice emanated from the emptiness beneath his hood. "Why would it be necessary for the Book to grow? The Book is stronger than us all. I'm not following your logic."

Alistar nodded. "The Book is powerful to be sure, but Gabriel's power is limited to what each of us has given him when we poured a part of our being into his pages."

"What are you getting at?" Mieonus snapped in an irritated manner.

Alistar looked at her a moment, shook his head, then continued. "All of us know we seek followers to increase our power. Just look at what Lasidious has accomplished thus far. His power has grown over the last 10,000 seasons. He has surpassed us all, and the one he was unable to surpass, he used the Book to destroy. We know there were many who served Bassorine, and those who served him on worlds other than Grayham, no longer have a god to worship, and they don't even know it."

Alistar leaned into the huddle further. "Think about it. Mosley is right. We have watched Lasidious grow because of the sheer number who choose to worship him. Much of Dragonia bows to him. The trolls on Trollcom, and even the vampires worship him, and we all know how significant their numbers are.

"Lasidious must be planning to gain the followers necessary to obtain the power to make Gabriel subservient. Clearly, he's doing this by making himself a figurehead in each world's Temple of the Gods." Alistar looked up. "Just look at his statue. He's glorifying himself, and he will continue to glorify himself until every being kneels before him."

The wolf growled. "This is frustrating." Mosley snorted his disdain. "How could the Collective have been so shortsighted?" The wolf scanned the group. "Lasidious is using the laws you created against us. His plan is brilliant. It is not nice, but brilliant, nonetheless. There is nothing we can do to stop him. He will become the leader of the grandest pack of all."

"Now, hang on just a moment," Bailem interjected. He straightened to adjust his robe to a better position. Before adding further to the conversation, he once again touched the back of Keylom and the shoulder of Alistar. "This is very disturbing. How should we proceed? It doesn't appear there are options. If we fight, we'll be destroyed. If we don't, Lasidious will eventually destroy us. I see no other solution. We should surrender the Book to Lasidious, and allow him to govern Gabriel while we still can. All we can do is hope he will allow us to continue to exist."

"I agree with Bailem," Alistar urged. "I have no desire to be destroyed. We should vote on this. Right now."

Those present erupted into an argument over the different ways they could foil Lasidious' plans, but none of their ideas had merit. Eventually, Mosley managed to get their attention. He did so by lifting his head and howling. The temple walls reverberated his call. With their full attention, the wolf spoke. "I may have a solution."

Mieonus snapped, "Oh, here we go!" She put her hands on her hips. "As if you could be our savior!"

Almost as if everyone shared the same mind, the group shouted, "Shut up, Mieonus!"

Mosley smiled as Mieonus stomped her foot and crossed her arms. He waited for her to calm down. After watching her place her hands on the centaur's back and Lictina's shoulder, the wolf continued. "As I said, I may have a solution."

With stealth, Alistar lifted his hand just off Bailem's shoulder, careful not to let the others see his movement. Bailem was so intent on listening to what the wolf had to say, he did not realize Alistar had removed his hand.

Now...fellow soul...the Rule of Fromalla is allowed to be broken only by the one who initates the pact. With Alistar's hand removed, Lasidious can now listen in on the conversation. The Book of Immortality cannot sense this action since no law has been broken.

Lasidious and Celestria watched the image of the gods from within their home as the group stood in the temple, huddled together. The green flames of their fireplace projected each deity with perfect clarity. Lasidious smiled as he watched Alistar lift his hand. The voices of the gods could now be heard through the fire.

"As I said, I may have a solution." Mosley cleared his throat as he studied the group's faces. "It is clear we have a job in front of us. All of us...and I do mean all of us...will need to work together to save ourselves. If Lasidious' intention is to gain followers to increase his power, and take control of Gabriel, then we must act to counter his efforts.

"We must keep the populations on each world from abandoning the gods they serve. I doubt we will be able to convert those who worship Lasidious, but we should try. He is far too cunning to allow something like this to happen. But, we can stop those who are able to be manipulated from serving him. We need to become a part of their everyday lives. We will appear to them as often as Lasidious appears to his followers or Hosseff does to his. This way, they will be less likely to be persuaded to serve him."

Without thinking, Owain removed his hat with his right hand and used it to point at the wolf. "Perhaps, you should be doing a better job. Those who followed Bassorine should already be aware of his destruction. They should have been serving you by now."

The wolf growled as he watched the others agree. Frustrated, he sat on his haunches and scratched the back of his neck. "Your point has been made. There is something else I should bring up. I should not share this information, but in light of current events, I feel it necessary to do so."

Lasidious and Celestria leaned toward the flames, anticipating what the wolf had to say. "This is going to be good. I can feel it," Lasidious said as he pulled Celestria close.

Mosley had everyone's attention. "As we all know, when Gabriel was created, Bassorine allowed his creation."

Gabriel stopped Mosley. "Are you sure it's wise to reveal Bassorine's plan?"

The emptiness beneath Hosseff's hood whispered, "Intriguing. How is it the two of you share the knowledge of Bassorine's scheming, yet the rest of us have no knowledge of his plotting?"

Alistar added, "We should know Bassorine's secrets, Gabriel. The sanctity of the Collective is in jeopardy. If we cannot find a way to stop Lasidious, everything will be lost to his control."

"I agree," Keylom added, stomping his right-front hoof against the temple floor.

Seeing the Book's hesitation, Mosley contemplated his delivery of Bassorine's secret. "I have a better way of saying this. What you all do not know is...Bassorine developed a plan to regain control of the Book if one of us was able to abuse its power. He called this plan his failsafe. After all, tactics were what he did best. As of this moment, the backup plan is not powerful enough to stop Lasidious from controlling Gabriel, but with the proper allocation of moments, it will be able to."

Alistar broke into the conversation. "You use the word 'it' as if 'it' isn't a being. What, or who are you referring to when you say, 'it?'"

Mosley looked into Alistar's eyes. "I will not answer your question. All I will say is...'it' needs the moments necessary to mature, and until 'it' does, we need to keep Lasidious from gaining the power necessary to control the Book. This will keep us busy."

Alistar's brow furrowed. "I wish to know more about this 'it.' Is 'it' a being, or not? It would make sense if it was. Share with us so we can help this plan acquire the power to stop Lasidious. I would like 'it' to save us all."

Mosley thought long and hard about his answer. The wolf decided to lie to Alistar. "The plan does not involve a being. It is something much larger. I'll say nothing further."

The room erupted with angry voices. Mosley looked at Gabriel and winked. The Book smiled, then vanished. A moment later, Mosley turned to face the others. "I know you do not approve of what I have chosen to divulge, but there is planning to do. Let us return to the Hall of Judgment."

Lasidious walked away from the fireplace and took his seat at the table. Celestria sat on his lap as Alistar appeared at the other end. There was fear in the God of the Harvest's voice. "Did you hear what Mosley said? I have to get to the Hall of Judgment. What plan could this be?"

Lasidious smiled. "Go to the meeting, brother. There's nothing to worry about. We will speak later." The Mischievous One watched as Alistar vanished.

Lasidious chuckled. "If it wasn't for Mosley, the Collective would have taken the bait. They would have surrendered the Book to me. It was worth the effort. Mosley is a worthy opponent. I'm enjoying our game. I imagine the others will be busy running between worlds to stop me from gaining the followers I need to dominate Gabriel."

Celestria stood, agitated, and began to adjust the vases throughout the room. "What about Bassorine's plan? Does this not bother you? It bothers me. How are we going to deal with something we cannot control? If it is not a being, then what could it be? What could grow to have the power to take back your dominance over Gabriel once you have it? You need to find out what that wolf is talking about."

Lasidious chuckled again.

"What's so funny? I fail to see the humor."

"Don't you see? 'It' is a being. It's Shalee. There's no one else it could be. Mosley must have sensed it wasn't safe to reveal Bassorine's secret. I think he knows I was able to hear him, though I don't think he knew it was because of Alistar's deception. I'll encourage Alistar to keep the gods busy while I prepare George for his new role."

"How do you know it is Shalee? You seem sure of it."

"How else do you explain the growth of her power? She's grown faster than any sorceress before her. She possesses the power of a woman who has commanded magic for over 200 seasons. She has done it without the help of the gods. I laugh because Mosley feels he has a secret. But, I have everything under control."

"I would love to know how you have it under control. You cannot touch Shalee. She is protected by the Book, and we do not have power over Gabriel yet. How are you going to get rid of her?"

Lasidious stood and enveloped Celestria within his arms. He kissed her forehead. "Who said anything about me getting rid of her? That's what George is for. After his visit with the Eye, he should be powerful. He'll be able to teleport between the lower three worlds. Shalee's power isn't strong enough to match George's. I can only hope George understands what to do with his new power."

Celestria smiled and positioned her mouth near Lasidious' ear. She whispered in her most seductive voice, "I suggest we celebrate the development of your pet. George is becoming everything you wanted him to be. Your cunning makes me hot."

Just Outside the Source's Cave
The Peak of Bailem

Brayson was standing next to Fisgig's perch waiting for the new warlock to make his exit. When George strolled out of the cave, he stopped and looked across the pool.

After seeing George's past, the Head Master called out in a diplomatic manner. "I see the Eye has spared your soul. This is good."

George didn't respond. Instead, he backed into the cave. He reached under his tunic and removed the feather he had plucked from the phoenix prior to entering The Source's cave. He lifted the feather close to his mouth, cupping it in his palms, then began to whisper a chant in the Elven language—a language learned as part of the Eye's gift.

"What are you doing?" Brayson questioned, trying to sound positive and upbeat. He knew what he had to say would cause tension. He cared for

George, despite what he had learned. He wanted to help his Mystic Learner find peace. "Come out of there. Let's chat. I have questions for you."

George lowered his hands from his mouth, then opened them. A single arrow made of water, cursed with the essence of the phoenix's feather, shot from his hands and skewered Fisgig's crimson body.

Brayson watched as his goswig fell to the ground at the base of his stone perch. The Head Master reacted by waving his hand to slow George's moments, but the power to do this died with Fisgig. George did not hesitate. He sent a wave of force into Brayson. The magic knocked the Head Master into the opposite wall of the cliff beyond the pool. For good measure, George sent two other waves of force in his direction to ensure Brayson would be knocked unconscious. The Head Master's head sunk beneath the pool's surface.

George trudged through the water, and pulled Brayson clear to keep him from drowning. Once out of the pool, he lowered Brayson to the ground, then grabbed him by the feet. He dragged the Head Master into the alcove where he first appeared prior to entering the cave. He bound Brayson with a rope from his pack, then leaned down next to the heavy weave it was made of and whispered another chant, but during this series of moments, it wasn't the language of the elves—the language spoken was that of the Ancient Mystics. *"Tolamea susayan, cun noble spolasemos papaya ress."*

The rope tightened. The tension woke Brayson. He cried out in pain. George casually took a step away from Brayson, and with a wave of his hand, commanded the water in the pool to create a shimmering throne on which to sit.

Brayson's eyes widened as the young warlock took a seat. The two stared at one another for a long series of moments before a word was uttered. "I know you know about Amar's death, Brayson. Do you deny it?"

Brayson nodded. "I witnessed the murder with my own eyes."

George sighed. "Then, we have a problem, don't you agree?"

Again, Brayson nodded, but said nothing.

"What should I do with you? Mary knows Amar is dead. Have you told her I was the one who killed him?"

Brayson shook his head. "I have said nothing. I wanted to speak with you to understand your mind."

George tilted his head. "Isn't it obvious? I ate his heart to steal his power. But, you know this."

"Do you intend to eat my heart?"

George had to laugh. "Why would I want to eat a heart with less power than my own? Eating your heart would only screw things up. It would cause me to lose the power I have over you. Now that your goswig is dead, you can't touch me."

Brayson wasn't sure how to respond. He fumbled through his next statement. "Wh...why are you doing this? Wh...what do you want?"

George laughed again as he stood and trudged through what was left of the water. He lifted the phoenix's body by its claws. Once standing back in front of Brayson, he threw Fisgig's corpse at Brayson's feet. "You can't give me anything I don't have the power to take."

Brayson knew his situation was grim. "Do you intend to kill me?"

George reclaimed his seat on his watery throne. "You know what? That's a good question. You see...I have been asking myself that very thing ever since I met you at your school. I have to admit, I intended to kill you as soon as I could, but then you became an important part of Mary's life. Now, the question I have to ask myself is, do I love my wife? And, the answer...I do. My next question: do I love her family? And, my answer...I do, very much. So, if that's the case, should I find a way to spare your life and treat you as the father-in-law you're bound to become, and not my enemy? Should I give you the love I have given them? Should I find a way to accomplish my goals and work around you? Do you love my mother-in-law enough that it would matter if I killed you, or better yet, does she love you enough to miss you once you're gone?"

Brayson cleared his throat and tried to find a more comfortable position within his bonds. "Your decision?"

George looked Brayson dead in the eyes. He leaned forward and, with a cold stare, responded. "My decision: I will spare your life. I don't wish to hurt Mary. I believe you love her. I also believe she loves you. I hate to say it, but your old ass is growing on me. But, there are a few things you will need to change if I let you live."

Brayson sighed. "It appears I have no choice. What changes need to be made?"

"I will take over your position as Head Master. You will retire. I'll do everything you would have done. I will figure out a way to stop the war that's coming. I'm tired of killing. I'm equally as tired of hurting others."

The young warlock pushed his hands through his hair. "The dragon told me he saw something good in me. Maybe, I have a chance to change my life. Maybe, I should take advantage of this opportunity."

George looked at the phoenix. "I'm sorry I killed your friends. I didn't even know Amar all that well."

Brayson looked up from Fisgig's corpse. "How am I to respond?"

George leaned back. "I know. That's some heavy garesh you've got to deal with. But, somehow, you have to move past this. If you're willing to work with me to change things, we can fix the problems on Luvelles. We can live peaceful lives with the ones we love. What do you say?"

Brayson sat in silence for a long series of moments. As he watched the crimson color of Fisgig's feathers fade to a pale white, he exhaled in defeat. He knew he had to cooperate. "Do you truly intend to stop the war?"

"I do."

"Do you plan to make Luvelles a peaceful place?"

"I do."

Brayson fought off the tears as he looked again at Fisgig's body. "Without my goswig, I won't be able to perform my duties as Head Master. I could help you move into this position without objection from the people. Once they understand you command the power required, they won't argue. Elf or not, you would be accepted. They respect the power, not the man. You may run into a problem with the gods, however. Humans are not allowed to live on this world unless permission is granted. The gods may not allow you to take this position."

George smiled. "If you knew what I know about the gods, you wouldn't worry about such things. They're useless. They'll do nothing to stop me."

"If what you say is the truth, then I have one more concern. This concern is for my safety. It also involves the safety of Mary and your family."

"I'm listening."

"My brother, Marcus, will kill everyone I love once he realizes I don't have the power to stop him. He'll do it as a way of appeasing his sick desire to torture me. He will make me watch. It would be best to kill me now to spare their lives. Once the people know you're their new Head Master, word will spread. Once it reaches Marcus' ears, he'll come for me."

George stood from his shimmering throne. With a wave of his hand, he removed Brayson's bonds. He stepped forward, extended his hand, then pulled Brayson to his feet. The water from the throne crashed back into the pool as George put his arm around Brayson. "So, if I told you I have a plan to deal with Marcus, would you allow me to call you dad after you take Mary as your wife?"

Brayson reached up and played with his goatee. "I'm angry with you. You killed my friends. You do everything you promised, then we will revisit your request. You must stop this war."

George chuckled, "I've got to love a man with the balls to negotiate in your situation."

Brayson removed George's arm. "I am not finished with my negotiation. I want you to allow Fisgig to live. He won't be able to use his power any longer, but I wish to enjoy his company. He was more than a goswig. He was my friend. I loved him. As the Head Master, you will be able to restore his life once you receive the secrets of the position. He'll live a long life, without power, and I can enjoy our friendship."

George thought a moment. "What do you mean? How?"

"Throughout history, the gods have given the Head Masters this power. The power resides within the Stone of Life. We are allowed to use the stone once per solstice season. This is similar to the power the Order calls upon when using their Touch of Death. But, they are limited to using the touch once per season."

"I know of this Touch of Death. Are you saying when the power is used, the person or beast it's used on loses their power?"

"That's what I'm saying."

"Does it strip this person or beast of their natural abilities as well?"

"No, it doesn't take anything natural from them."

George touched Brayson's shoulder and teleported them onto the porch of Mary's house. "I need to think about your request regarding Fisgig. I don't understand everything, but I think you've given me enough to ponder. As of this moment, I don't see a problem letting the phoenix live. But, like I said...I want to think about it."

George leaned in and whispered in Brayson's ear. "As far as your brother goes...I wouldn't worry about Marcus. I have plans for him. Maybe, you should go inside and work on creating a happy family. Okay, dad?"

Brayson moved to the bottom of the steps. "You can use that word after Fisgig lives, and not before. Show me the things you've promised are truthful."

"Don't worry. I've got it all under control."

"Then, I will say good night. I have no choice but to trust you. I hope my trust isn't misplaced."

George jumped down the steps. "I forgive you for getting on my good side and for being such an old fart. Maybe, we should avoid discussing this with the girls. I'm still not sure I've made all the right decisions. I want to ensure I do the right things, not only for Luvelles, but our family as well."

Brayson reluctantly nodded. "Perhaps, there is hope for you. I hope the Ancient One was right. I hope there is good in you. I have been told many terrible things about you since last we spoke, but I trust the dragon's judgment. I will see you in the morning."

As soon as Brayson closed the door, George teleported inside Kepler's lair beneath the stones and waved his hand. The darkness dissipated. Kepler and Payne had to cover their eyes to keep the brightness from hurting them.

"What do you want?" Kepler growled. "I was sleeping."

"Master, get out of here and let us get some sleep!" Payne shouted.

George was floored as he looked at Payne. The fairy-demon had grown over six inches since the last moment he saw him. He had also used a complete sentence which, somehow, made perfect sense.

"Did I just hear him right, Kep? Did he actually make sense?"

"Yes. I've been working with the little freak."

"Stop calling me freak. I have stopped calling you kitty, haven't I?"

George took a seat. "Wow! I leave you guys for a few days and when I return, I run into Captain Sentence over here. What's gotten into you, Payne?"

Kepler interrupted. "Don't get him started. He'll go all night and won't shut up. He's on this whole, 'I can talk better than you' kick. Though irritating, at least he makes sense. He has been eating everything he can get his hands on. I've never seen anything grow the way he has over the last few days. So, why did you wake us up?"

George shook off his surprise. "I need to know if you have any abilities which would be considered a power, and not a natural ability."

"Why?"

"I'll explain, but be honest...this is crucial."

"I have one power. Everything else I do is natural. I can hide within the shadows naturally. I can see in the dark naturally, but the ability to control my skeleton army is a power given to me by Celestria. Why?"

George thought for a bit, then responded. "I don't think you can control your skeletons any longer."

"Ha! Why would you think such nonsense?"

"When Marcus returned your life, you may have lost it. I want you to go out tonight and test your power. Payne will go with you. If you cannot control the corpse, then I'll know what Brayson has told me about Marcus' Touch of Death is true. This will tell me how I should proceed with my relationship with him."

"What are you talking about?"

"Just trust me. Do it, okay?"

"I can kill someone if you want, but it seems like a bother to prove something I know I can do. A Master of the Hunt knows his abilities."

"Just go check. I'm sure you'll enjoy yourself and it'll make me feel better to know your power is intact. Payne, I want you to teleport Kepler to the city of Marcus. I'm sure it won't be hard to find a soul worth killing there."

Payne stood and stretched his wings. "I would be happy to do this for you, Master. Will there be anything else?"

Kepler growled. "Just stop already, freak. He's already impressed."

Grogger's Swamp
Just Before Late Bailem

Boyafed waited for Sam to exit the swamp. He had set up camp just outside its entrance. He was dressed in his black plate with gold accents. The Order leader had a debt to settle and hoped to confront the King of Southern Grayham—providing the king managed to survive the swamp.

It was just before Late Bailem when Sam made his way out. Boyafed waved to capture Sam's attention, then waited for the king to say goodbye to those he had saved.

Meanwhile, on Ancients Sovereign, Mieonus called the others to her home. She had been waiting for this confrontation and wanted to share her manipulations of the event. She had informed the Collective that something big was about to happen, and most of the gods came out of sheer curiosity. Lasidious and Celestria chose not to attend.

Standing in front of Mieonus' waterfall, those present watched the image of Sam as he said goodbye to the people while Boyafed waited. Mieonus took the opportunity to brag about her handiwork while Mosley stared into the image of the falls without saying a word. The wolf was sick to his stomach, and worry could be seen in his eyes.

Once the group surrounding Sam had thanked him, they teleported and went their separate ways. Sam turned to face Boyafed's camp and took a deep breath. He gathered his nerve, then moved to join the dark paladin.

Boyafed motioned for Sam to take a seat. He had prepared a comfortable spot for him to sit, placing a stack of furs on top of a stone. A nice meal was cooking over the open fire.

After watching Sam take his seat, Boyafed spoke. "Do you know who I am, King of Brandor?"

"I do." Sam looked into the pot which hung above the flames. "What's for dinner?"

"I hope you like it. I have prepared jackram stew. I took the moments necessary to hunt a few. They're quick little critters. If it wasn't for their clumsiness and the fact they trip over their ears, I don't imagine I would've been able to shoot them with my bow. They make a fine meal."

Sam leaned forward and scooped a ladle full into a wooden bowl which Boyafed tossed to him. "I know why you've come." Sam pulled his eyes away from the iron pot to look at Boyafed. "I'm asking myself...why the meal? Why the idle chatter? Why would you do this when you have come to avenge your son's life?"

Boyafed filled his bowl. After sitting back and taking a bite, he replied. "I have heard of your skills. I know of your war on Grayham and the victory you claimed. News of such victories finds its way between worlds. Both of us are men of war, but this doesn't mean we can't be civil. I prefer to get to know the man I intend to kill."

Sam nodded. "I like your style." He pushed the stew around in his bowl, then looked up. "You should be proud. Your son fought well. You should know this as his father. He served you until his dying breath." Sam smelled the delicacy. "I know you gave him the order to kill my queen."

Boyafed took another bite, then pointed his spoon at Sam. "I appreciate the sentiment, but my son failed his orders. If he were any other man, I would not be here." He took another bite. "This is good, no?"

Sam swallowed a bite of his own. "I suppose you cook alright."

Boyafed grinned. "You jest. I like that." The Order leader leaned forward. His face turned serious. "You are correct. I gave the order to kill your queen, but my son fell in love with her. As a father, I wish I could say my son was a good soldier, but he was weak...both at following instruction and in battle. I should tell you, it was Hosseff who requested your queen's death. I had nothing against her."

Sam shrugged. "What's a guy to do? You must obey your god. And, all men must love their children no matter how often they disappoint them. It's clear you loved Kiayasis."

Boyafed nodded, then chuckled. "I also love my mongrel mutt who waits for me at home."

Sam smiled. After a few more bites of stew, he lowered the bowl to the ground. "I would imagine we could talk all night about many things, but I think we should dispense with these pleasantries and get this fight of ours over with. Besides, I'm not that hungry, and your stew needs seasoning."

The gods were fixated on Mieonus' waterfall as they made comments of who they felt had better skills. Mosley, on the other hand, was in a world of his own. He stared into the image and tuned out the others. Sam was his friend, and this was the king's toughest opponent yet.

You can do this, Sam, he thought. *You must fight ferociously.* The thought ran through the wolf's mind over and over.

Sam and Boyafed stood and moved away from the camp. Sam pulled Kael from his sheath and commanded the blade to bring forth its fire. Boyafed shouted in the language of the elves, and his sword also burst into flames.

Sam smiled. "You're the first person I've met with a blessed weapon. I suppose that commanding their power won't be necessary. I'm sure we both know how to avoid damage of this nature."

Boyafed nodded. "Agreed. This will be a fight without the power of our blades. I can see the rings on your fingers. I know you're well protected from the affects of magic. The markings are those of the Head Master. I will fight with a cold blade."

As they began to circle, Sam's curiosity got the best of him. He remembered what Bassorine had told him. His blade was to be the only one with the ability to summon the truth from others. He questioned Boyafed to test the god's truthfulness. "Can your blade seek the truth in others as mine can?"

Boyafed stopped moving. He lowered his sword to his side. "Your blade can do this? Most impressive. What an incredible power to have at your disposal. I can't tell you on how many occasions I could've used a power like that." The Order leader hesitated, then continued. "Just the other day, I tortured a small group of men in my dungeon. I wish I would have had your sword during those moments. It would have saved me a lot of trouble."

"Yes-siree-bob, it would've. I have had to use it twice, myself. Bassorine gave this sword to me. I call him, Kael." Sam spun the blade in his hands, then pointed its tip at Boyafed's sword. "What about yours?"

The Dark Order leader tossed his blade in Sam's direction, handle first. "Take a few swipes with him. Feel how light he is in your hand. I call him Quel Kaima."

"Aahhhh...an elven name. A blade called, 'Sleep Well' is rather appropriate for the death you must've dealt throughout your seasons. I think this is a clever name, for sure."

Boyafed paused. "You know elvish. I'm impressed."

"Not all of it. Just enough to get by. Give me a few days, and I'll have the hang of it." Sam moved Boyafed's sword back and forth, then tossed the blade back to Boyafed. "Nice. It is balanced well. What is his special power?"

Boyafed grinned. "I hate cowards, don't you?"

"Most definitely. Why?"

"Quel Kaima will allow me to throw him for quite a distance to strike men down who would choose to run from me in battle. I have killed many cowards this way. The blade hates a man without a spine as much as I do. He returns to me with a simple wave of my hand. Hosseff, himself, gave this blade to me. Beyond that, Quel Kaima will do anything your blade can do... minus your weapon's Call of Truth, of course."

Sam tilted his head in thought. "I never thought to name Kael's power. May I use this name, Call of Truth? It has a ring to it, don't you agree?"

Both warriors had to stop speaking while Kael and Quel Kaima took the moments necessary to introduce themselves to one another. After the swords finished their chat, Sam turned to look at Boyafed. "Well, that was a first for me. Never thought I would see the day when two swords had a conversation."

Boyafed had to smile. "For me, also. To answer your question regarding your sword's power, you may use this name, but I doubt you will have the chance. I promise to make your death a quick one."

"Again, very clever. We'll see about that." Sam decided he had done enough chatting. "We best get this over with. Let's find out who'll be returning home in a casket."

Boyafed bowed. "Agreed. No matter the outcome, King of Grayham, I consider you a worthy opponent."

Sam bowed in return. "And, I you."

Without further conversation, Boyafed moved in. The metal of each blade seared against each other as they clashed in a barrage of upward, downward and side-to-side strikes—all of which were defended by both men.

They stopped and backed away. Boyafed took the opportunity to speak. "Your skill is impressive. May I call you, Sam?"

"Why not? If I don't like the way you say it, I can always kill you."

"And, you say I'm clever. I'm going to enjoy this battle far more than any other. I have never had a man stand before me who used humor while anticipating his death. Most men run."

"Who said anything about anticipating my death? There will be no running."

Without further delay, Sam lunged and delivered one swift strike after another. Again, each of these deadly advances was defended.

Boyafed returned Sam's attack, pushing Sam backward. Swipes, lunges, elbows, headbutts, leg sweeps and a series of attempted stabs were delivered, but everything was defended.

Once again, both men began to circle. Not more than six breaths passed before Boyafed attacked. He kept coming until a small opening presented itself. Boyafed's blade slashed across Sam's left arm, just below his shoulder. The Order leader followed the cut with a right foot to the side of the king's leg. Sam fell, but managed to defend a downward stab, then pushed Boyafed back before rolling to his feet while sending an arching slash toward Boyafed's stomach. The dark paladin blocked the attack, then stepped back to give Sam the moments necessary to regain his composure.

Boyafed spoke. "You are the finest opponent I have faced. There is only one man I will look forward to battling after this day. Lord Dowd is also our equal."

Sam spit on the ground. "You have to get past this day first." Sam searched deep within his soul. He knew he had to call upon his inner demon. He opened the monster's cage and allowed the beast to rush to the forefront of his mind. He lifted Kael and attacked. During this series of moments, he would do the pushing. Strike after strike, lunge after lunge, elbow after elbow, punch after punch—all defended, until finally, Sam managed to find an opening of his own. He lunged forward. Kael penetrated Boyafed's left shoulder just below the collarbone and emerged from the other side.

Boyafed's training allowed him to ignore the pain as if nothing had happened. With Sam's blade stuck in his shoulder, he used his right hand to send his sword arching toward Sam's head.

As Sam reached out and caught Boyafed's right forearm with his left hand to stop the deadly strike, he failed to account for Boyafed's left hand, which Boyafed had used to secure his bone-handled dagger. With Sam's right hand still on Kael's grip, the Order's dagger pierced Sam's ribs on his right side. Boyafed released the implanted dagger, then grabbed Sam's right arm with his left hand to keep the king from pulling Kael free from his shoulder and doing further damage.

The pain Sam felt was excruciating. Boyafed had laced the blade with poison and the king could feel the burn as it began to make its way through his body.

Sam released Kael and reached in to take Boyafed's throat in his hand, but this last effort was defended with one quick motion to pull his arm free. With every movement, the Order's dagger did further damage as blood rushed from the wound.

Boyafed felt the fight was over. Sam dropped his arms and Boyafed allowed the king to step back. The Order leader left Kael buried in his shoulder until he was certain Sam would not be able to make further advances.

Boyafed grunted as he forced himself to reach into his boot. He tossed Sam a small vial full of a red potion. "Drink, King of Brandor. It will dull the pain and allow you to die in peace. I'll make sure your body finds its way back to your General Absolute. You'll be given a proper passing as per your custom. You have my word."

Sam looked at Boyafed after swallowing the liquid. With blood running down his chin, he lowered to his back. "Please. Tell my queen I love her. Tell her I always have." With that, Sam looked to the sky for his final thought, *I wish my father was here. I wish I could apologize. I should've been a better son.*

Boyafed watched as the king's chest stopped rising and the last bit of air inside Sam's body, escaped forever. The Order leader drank a vial filled with a blue potion, then pulled Kael from his shoulder. His cry filled the twilit sky as the anguish overwhelmed him. Falling to his knees, he removed another vial and poured a few drops of the healing liquid into the open wound.

He crawled next to Sam's body and took a seat. "I shall always remember you, Sam. You were the first to wound me. You were a worthy adversary.

You were worthy of being a king. I shall tell tales of your greatness as I show the scar. What a tale it shall be."

Boyafed lay back on the ground after putting several more drops under his tongue, then enjoyed the high as he began to hallucinate. He would not be able to stand until morning.

Mieonus jumped up and down and clapped her hands as she turned away from the waterfall. "Oh, how delicious Boyafed's victory must taste! I'm going to enjoy Shalee's pain once she learns of Sam's demise."

Without responding, the gods vanished, except for one. Alistar took the opportunity to express his feelings. "Mieonus...you often wonder why the others ignore you. I know you also wonder why they treat you with disdain. Allow me to enlighten you. You have no tact. You don't understand when to stop hating and show respect. You look foolish, as a jester does before a king."

Mieonus crossed her arms. "I suppose you're going to explain how. I set up this confrontation. The fight *you* enjoyed, *I* manipulated."

"It wasn't the battle which made you look inferior. It was your comments afterward. The fight was honorable, one between two honorable men. But, you found a way to take the honor out of Boyafed's victory. You tainted it by dishonoring the fallen. You should have kept your comments to yourself. You allow your hate to cloud your judgment. You fail to show dignity." Alistar vanished.

Mieonus stomped her lifted heel. "I hate him!"

Mosley fell onto the porch of his cabin home high atop Catalyst Mountain. He looked across the valleys below as tears filled his eyes. He lifted his head and began to howl. He would not dishonor Sam's death by using his godly power to hide the pain.

A False Prophet
George's Home

After sending Payne with Kepler to test Brayson's revelation about how the Touch of Death works, George went inside his home. The evening was pleasant, and the family, including Brayson and Mary, had gathered for a meal. When night came, the warlock removed his tunic, draped it across the chest of drawers, then took his position next to Athena in their bed.

It wasn't long before George was dreaming. Lasidious interrupted his visions. "George, we need to speak. There are plans we need to discuss...plans which are urgent and need to be implemented."

George's dream had been good until now. Abbie, Athena, and their new baby were having lunch on a hillside. George had made Abbie a kite and was watching her fly it while Athena prepared their plates. The baby was sleeping at the center of a large cloth Athena had spread for them. It was a pleasant dream, but now it had been shot to garesh. All he could do was speak with Lasidious since the Mischievous One's face had replaced his visions of happiness.

"You know, Lasidious...the moment of your arrival sucks. Maybe, you could let me finish my dream before you barge in from now on. It's the least you could do."

⊷⊱•⊰⊶

Lasidious smiled as he stared into the green flames of his fireplace and watched as George shifted in his sleep. He leaned down and spoke into the fire. "George, this is important. We need to plan."

⊷⊱•⊰⊶

"Are you freaking kidding me? Now, what? Can't you see I'm trying to get some sleep? I've got everything under control. I've got Brayson right where we need him. Kepler is on his way to find out if he still has the power to control his skeletons. If he can't, then I'll allow Brayson's phoenix to live again. If he can use his power, then I'll know Brayson lies, and I'll just have to kill him and be done with him. No one else can touch me. We have everything you wanted to accomplish on this world under control. War is coming, and the gods are watching. What could possibly be so important that I can't get one night's sleep?"

Lasidious shook his head, then leaned back from the fire. He pulled a chair close, then took a seat. "Don't you get it, George? You have been groomed for greater things than being the Head Master of Luvelles. It would be best to let the population of Luvelles believe Brayson still has his power. Besides, you have not accomplished all our goals on this world."

"What do you mean? Other than killing Shalee, everything else will be a walk in the park. I just need to put the finishing touches on the war with Marcus, and..."

Lasidious stopped him. "About the war...let it develop on its own. Don't worry about Marcus for now. Your moments need to be spent elsewhere. You need to go to Harvestom."

"What? How in the hell do you expect me to explain that to Athena? I can't move us to another world. She would freak. She would hit every stinking wall in our house. I don't wish to live with a pissed-off, pregnant woman. It's a dangerous thing to do, even with all the power I've got. What will I tell Mary? How will I explain that she has to leave Brayson?

"Normally, I like your ideas, Lasidious, but this one sucks garesh. If I have to choose Athena, her family, and my unborn baby over getting Abbie's soul out of the Book...I'll do it. I can't lose Athena's love. She means everything to me...so does her damn family."

The Mischievous One listened to George rant as he scooped the warlock's image out of the fire and set it on the table. After putting his feet up, he leaned back and put his hands behind his head. "I'm not asking you to leave Luvelles, George. I have seen to it that you have the ability to call upon the power of the Ancient Mystics for a reason. I built your confidence so the Eye would grant you the power you need for this task. Now, you have the ability to teleport between the lower three worlds."

"What do you mean, 'lower three worlds?'"

"I mean you can teleport to Harvestom, Luvelles, and Grayham. You can move freely between them. As you know, as long as you're familiar with where you're going, you can travel to your destination within a matter of moments. You're the only mortal on the lower three worlds with this ability."

"Yeah, yeah, yeah, blah, blah, blah, whatever. I don't have any knowledge of Harvestom. How do you expect me to go there? And, why can't I teleport to the other two worlds, as well?"

Lasidious took a deep breath. "To answer your question: you cannot teleport between the other two worlds because you're not powerful enough to pass through the magic which fills their atmospheres. It's that simple."

"Okay, but that doesn't help me get to Harvestom."

Lasidious leaned forward in his chair. He reached into the flame with his finger and touched the image of George on the head. "I'll give you a vision of a key location on Harvestom, but beyond that, you'll need to learn its lands on your own. The power necessary to give you more locations could alert the others of the Collective as to what we're doing. We cannot allow this. You don't have to fight with Athena to save Abbie. Your family can stay on Luvelles.

George rolled to a more comfortable position. "So, this leaves me with a question. Am I still weak compared to the other two worlds? That's pretty hard to imagine, if I am."

Lasidious smiled as he leaned back in his chair again. "I understand the limitations of your mind. It wasn't so long ago you felt magic and talking jaguars to be unimaginable. I'm sure you don't believe you're all-powerful. You are far from powerful, I assure you. There has never been a man or an elf, for that matter, since the creation of the new worlds, who has been able to summon even the most basic power of the mystics before Brayson Id found a way to rise to this level throughout his seasons. But, even he is considered powerless compared to the Ancient Mystics on Trollcom. Trollcom is heavily populated by the Ancient Mystics, and the trolls also wield a power similar in strength. Don't be a fool. You are not ready to stand against them. You would be considered a meager irritation against their power...a bug they would simply swat."

George responded, "But, once I find a way to match their power, I'll be considered powerful, right?"

Lasidious laughed. "No, George. Even the Ancient Mystics are considered powerless to those who dwell on Dragonia. The dragons have power which rivals the weakest of the gods'. Their power gives them the title, Swayne Enserad. This is the final level you must master before becoming enlightened. Even the Swayne Enserad have trouble mastering their power. In the last 10,000 seasons, not one has managed to become enlightened and become strong enough to be given godhood. I intend to see to it that you're the first."

"Holy garesh, Lasidious! So, you're grooming me to become a god? Athena's going to want a much better house if I get that kind of power."

Lasidious smirked. "There is no place more beautiful than the hidden god world. Once I control the Book of Immortality, you will have your daughter's soul and your family can move to Ancients Sovereign."

Lasidious dropped his feet to the floor and leaned forward. "You're the most powerful being on the lower three worlds. I think your growth would be considered solid since your arrival on Grayham, don't you think?"

The warlock thought a moment. "I guess you're right. So, I will need to become an Ancient Mystic, then Swayne Enserad, before becoming a god. Am I understanding you right?"

Lasidious smiled. "Yes."

"Does this mean you're going to need my help getting Abbie's soul out of the Book, because that wasn't a part of the plan?"

Lasidious pulled back his hood. "Getting Abbie released is something we can accomplish before you become enlightened, providing you live long enough."

"What do you mean, providing I live long enough? What the hell?"

"It means you have to avoid getting killed when on the other worlds, just like you have avoided this outcome on Grayham and Luvelles. I wouldn't worry. Aside from a small task we need to accomplish on Trollcom, a task you won't need stronger power for, you won't see the upper two worlds for nearly a season. You have work to do on the lower three. A prophet's work is never done." Lasidious winked.

George rolled onto the flat of his back. "Oh, hell no! You've got to be freaking kidding me! You want me to become your damn prophet? Are you out of your stinking mind?"

George waited for a response, but when one never came he continued his rant. "I can see it now. You want me to run around praising your supposed good name. What a damn joke that is. I'm going to laugh my ass off for days."

Lasidious had to grin. "It's all part of the plan to get your daughter back, George. You don't have to believe, to preach. You learned that on Earth. All you have to do is share the good word, and allow the people to decide what they believe. Do you want your daughter back, or not? It's your choice."

The warlock thought long and hard before responding. "Make no mistake, Lasidious, I don't like this idea one bit. It makes me sick to my stomach. But, if this what it takes to get my Abbie back, then I'm on board with your pile of garesh. And, by the way, I think you mean you want me to be your false prophet." A grin appeared on George's sleeping face. "A false prophet's work is never done."

Lasidious laughed within the warlock's dream. "George, you wound my pride with such cutting words. I thought we were better friends than this. Do you really dislike this idea as much as you claim?"

"No doubt! I hate this idea. I hate it a lot, in fact. But, like I already said, if this gets my Abbie back, then so be it. We both know you're just as full of garesh as I am, so stop playing wounded. You couldn't care less if I like the idea, so let's just be honest for a moment. You and I get along because we have something in common. I have something you need, and you have something I want. This relationship is based on our desire to accomplish selfish goals which happen to benefit each other. And, as I've already said twice, as long as this gets my Abbie back, I'll do whatever it takes, even be your false prophet, *providing*...and, I do mean providing...it doesn't affect my ability to keep Athena and her family safe. I won't sacrifice my love for Athena to retrieve my daughter's soul from the Book. I would let the idea of seeing my daughter again go before I fail Athena in our marriage. It's bad enough I've had to lie to her already. I can't allow deceiving her to continue. You and I need to be careful with how we treat my relationship with her... and the rest of her family. I hope you are on the same playing field with me on this."

Lasidious grabbed hold of his chin in thought, then responded. "It seems we each appreciate the other's position."

"Good," George responded. His tone changed to something happier. "I'm sure Brayson will be thrilled to keep his position as Head Master. I'll have to do a little creative thinking, but I'm sure I can pull this off. So, what's my role on Harvestom, and when can I get a little more of this Ancient Mystic power?"

"Slow down, George. First things first. I have things to tell you. We have plans to make. I also have something to say about Brayson's phoenix and the hidden god world."

The Underground Village of Gogswayne

Gage stood beside the entrance to Strongbear's cave. He was using the tip of his cane to draw pictures in the dirt as he waited. The brown bear had gone into such a deep hibernation he was struggling to come out of it. The goswigs' power to bring back the change of seasons had worked, and now, it was a matter of waiting for the big guy to emerge.

Gallrum had left to report Strongbear's condition to Ultor, and Gage was dreading how angry the bear would be once he realized the village had conspired to put him to sleep. Gage was considering the idea of having Gallrum deliver the news to the bear upon his return, justifying his decision on the fact he didn't have the seniority to deliver such news.

The Next Morning
Just Before the Peak of Bailem

The family gathered at Mary's home for breakfast. George sat next to Brayson as they watched over 30 people, along with Payne, move throughout the house. Kepler had come and gone. He had reported that his power to control his skeleton army was no longer his to command, then left George to entertain. The demon-cat retired to his lair beneath the rocks to sulk.

Payne was showing off, flying from one family member to the next, doing his best to impress them with his newfound ability to form complete sentences.

As George studied his surroundings, all he could do was marvel at how his life had turned into one big fantasy. Never, in his wildest imagination, would he have believed that many of the things he had seen in the movies he loved on Earth could have been founded on potential facts. He could only assume there had been beings on Earth who had understood the reality of what the gods were. They must have known what was on other worlds, scattered throughout the galaxy, before the God Wars. He was not sure if any new concept could be given the title, fiction, any longer.

Brayson looked up from his plate of greggle hash. "George, I'm sure you have much on your mind, but have you made any decisions?"

George finished chewing a piece of his chicken-fried corgan steak, and swallowed it before responding. "This is a conversation best left for your office. What do you say we say our goodbyes and go there?"

It was not long before the two men appeared inside Brayson's floating office. George moved to the window and looked out. After Brayson showed him how it functioned, George commanded the window to find Shalee. The window zoomed in across the world and settled on the entrance to the Void Maze, but it could not penetrate the magic surrounding the maze to produce her image.

George turned from the window. "How long has she been inside the maze with your brother?"

Brayson looked confused. "How did you know she's with my brother? Did the goddess tell you this?"

"I will explain, but first, tell me how long they have been in the maze."

Brayson moved to take a seat. "I would imagine that with my brother's past knowledge of the dungeon, and considering the fact you killed most everything inside it, they should be arriving at the Source's Temple at any moment."

George nodded. "This is good, but there are a few problems we need to chat about. I've got some things to say that aren't going to sit well with you. I need you to hear me out before you respond. This is going to sound bad. This is going to require you to have an open mind."

Brayson frowned. "I'm listening."

"First...I've decided the god we serve isn't worth my service any longer. Mieonus was the one who commanded me to do so many hurtful things. And, one of these things was what caused the death of your friend, Amar."

Brayson stood and put his hands flat on the top of his desk. "What?" His stare was piercing. "The goddess would never!"

George held up his hand to curb Brayson's protest. "Like I said...hear me out." The new warlock teleported to the top of a bookcase and sat on its edge. Looking down at Brayson, he continued. "Mieonus asked me to do things which go against my nature." He pointed at Brayson. "This included killing you. I only obeyed her commands because she said she would retrieve my daughter's soul from the Book of Immortality."

Brayson motioned to speak. George stopped talking. "Why would your daughter's soul be in a book? Why isn't her soul in the heavens with the god she served?"

George crossed his legs and tightened the lace of his left boot. "All souls are placed inside a book. You have been deceived if you believe your soul will live in the presence of Mieonus. My daughter has been trapped inside this book for over 14,000 seasons."

The Head Master scowled. "I don't believe you."

George shrugged. "Whether you believe me or not, it doesn't change the fact that your god is evil. Like I said, she commanded me to kill Amar."

"Why would she do that?"

"I don't understand the goddess' reasoning. I cannot explain why. All I know is, I am tired of hurting people. I refused to kill you to satisfy her."

"Why would the goddess want me dead, and why would she choose you to do it?

George hopped to the floor. "Mieonus said she wanted a stronger leader to govern Luvelles. She said you have failed to choose a side and she despises your neutrality. She wanted me to get rid of you so I could bring darkness over all of Luvelles. She wants evil to thrive."

"Mieonus isn't evil, George. Why do you try to deceive me?"

The new warlock took a seat on the edge of the desk. He looked Brayson dead in the eyes. "I'm not deceiving you. I could've killed you already, and you know it. I spared your life because I'm tired of killing. I'm tired of living in hate and causing others misery. Whether you know it or not, your goddess despises you. I wouldn't lie about such things, and soon, you will be getting confirmation of your own from the one I now serve. But for now, I ask you to listen.

"There's only one god strong enough to maintain a heaven for his followers. I was visited by him last night after returning home. Many truths have been revealed to me. I..."

Brayson interrupted. "None of this makes sense. What do you mean there's only one god powerful enough to maintain a heaven?"

George remained patient. "Look, you will get confirmation. Like I said, Mieonus has used your faith in her to get you to allow me to meet with The Source. I knew everything I needed to know about the Eye long before you gave me advice about believing in myself. You should be dead right now, but I cannot keep killing. Because of my choice, there will be repercussions. I can only hope my new god will protect me."

Brayson thought a moment. "What of this god? Tell me more."

"Lasidious came to me in a glorious light and spoke with me while Athena lay sleeping next to me. At first, I was frightened, but then Lasidious assured me he had not come to harm me. He said he loved me. He said he knew my mind, and he was proud of me for going against Mieonus' command to kill you." George picked up the Book of Bonding and set it on his lap. He used the book to prop up his crossed arms. "Brayson, Lasidious told me to leave you in your position as Head Master."

Brayson lowered to the edge of his chair as George continued. "Lasidious told me the others keep their followers' souls inside a book called the Book of Immortality."

Brayson stopped him. "When you say others, do you mean the gods?"

"Yes. Lasidious also said Mieonus lied to me, and she doesn't have the power to retrieve my daughter's soul from this book unless the others on the hidden god world agree to release her."

Brayson sat back. "Wait a moment. What hidden god world are you talking about? I know nothing about it."

George scratched the top of his head. "I'm not sure about that part. But, it was clear Lasidious wanted me to know the truth. He told me he knew about the deaths I've caused and the murders I've committed while serving Mieonus. He said they would never be glorified, no matter how pure my intentions were to retrieve my daughter's soul."

George traced the name on the Book of Bonding as he continued. "If it wouldn't have been for The Source reminding me of the goodness within me, I would've killed you. I would've never had the chance to have Lasidious come to me. I would have never been given the chance to spread his words of love and kindness...his words of peace.

"Death and destruction isn't a proper way for Mieonus to control her followers. I've been asked to bring peace to the worlds. Lasidious has asked me to be his prophet. He wants me, of all people, to spread his words of love and keep those who would go to war with each other from doing so. Lasidious said you would be my greatest ally. I am to work with you to bring peace to this world.

"I hate to say this, Brayson, but given everything I have learned, you serve the wrong god. She has deceived us both. We need to do what's best for our family. Mary and Athena's happiness is resting on whether you and I make the right choices. I'm asking you to act as my father. I need your guidance. Do you feel my change in service to Lasidious is appropriate?"

Brayson lowered his head in thought. There was a long period of silence. For every moment that went by, George remembered his training on Earth. He had given his sales pitch, and the first rule of sales was: the first one to speak—loses.

It felt like an eternity before Brayson lifted his head. "I find it hard to concentrate. It's not everyday my Mystic Learner takes away my power by killing my goswig, then spares my life. To know you were asked to kill me and take my position as Head Master is disheartening."

George nodded. "I feel you. Maybe, you should talk to Athena. She was in the kitchen of our home when Mieonus threatened to have me killed. I won't serve a goddess who threatens her own children."

"Perhaps, I will speak with her. I don't wish to serve one who would spread evil. I can see it in your eyes. I believe you're sincere and want to become a better person. I also want the best for our family. I just wish I knew why Lasidious would choose you. Why would he want you to be his prophet when you have done so many terrible things?"

George scratched the top of his head again and acted confused. "I wish I had the answer. To tell you I understand a god's mind would be a lie. All I know...The Source was able to see something good in me, and I've been given the chance to spread Lasidious' words of peace and love throughout the worlds. I just need a bit of fatherly advice. Should I do this, or should I be doing something else with my life?"

Brayson stood and moved across the room. He looked out the window and waved his hand in front of it. It wasn't long before the window zoomed in on Mary's house. Susanne and Athena were walking up the front porch steps. He could see how rounded Athena's belly was becoming.

Eventually, Brayson turned around. "I believe you should spread the word of Lasidious. I will serve Lasidious just as you have chosen. I'll do what's necessary to help. I'll keep an eye on our loved ones while you spread our new lord's vision of tranquility."

George moved across the room and pulled Brayson close. He held the embrace for many moments. "For now, Lasidious has asked us to do nothing about the war on Luvelles. When the moment is right, he will tell us what to do. His love must reach all who are willing to listen. You should expect a visit from our lord. He wishes to speak with you."

"Me? He wishes to speak with me? Why?"

"I told you...you're going to be my greatest ally and a critical part of spreading his word. You should stay at your own home tonight. Our lord has a surprise for you. I think you'll be pleased with his visit."

From deep within the Peaks of Angels, Lasidious passed his hand across the green flames of his fireplace as the vision of George and Brayson faded. He turned to look at his lover. "It appears George is quite the salesman. When I took him from Earth, his talents were being so wasted. I think we've found a much better use for his skills."

Celestria reached down and pinched Lasidious' left butt cheek, then headed for a chair near the table. "Continue to gloat, my love. What other surprises do you have in store for me, my sweet?"

Lasidious grinned. "I was there when Brayson decided to confront George outside The Source's cave. It gave me the chance to capture Fisgig's soul before it left for the Book. George couldn't have picked a finer moment to kill the phoenix. With the gods unable to see inside the Mountains of Oraness, thanks to the Ancient One's magic, I had the opportunity to snatch Fisgig's soul as it left for Gabriel's pages. The Book doesn't even know he's dead. This is brilliant. It was an opportunity I couldn't pass up. If there's any doubt in Brayson's mind about my love for the beings on the worlds, or my desire to have peace on Luvelles, this doubt will soon be abolished."

Celestria leaned back in her chair. She looked across the room at the vases filled with day-old flowers. She reached out and snapped her fingers. Each vase filled with fresh flora of assorted colors. She looked at Lasidious. "Your mind is delightfully cunning. With your brother working to confuse the Collective, and their lack of knowledge about George's ability to tele-port between the lower three worlds, they'll always be a step behind as our plans move forward. I must admit, my pet, you impress me more with each passing day. Your pride looks as if it tastes delicious. Allow me to nibble on you while you bask in the brilliance of your deceptions."

The thought of Celestria touching him gave Lasidious goosebumps as he watched her stand from her chair and seductively walk toward him.

Brayson's Home
Later that Night

Brayson did as George suggested and spent the night at his home within his pile of boulders. He woke in the middle of the night to a glorious light with a heavenly glow. The illusion provided by the kedgles, to make his hol-lowed mound of rocks seem as if he was living in the outdoors, amplified the mood as he gazed upon an image of his new lord. He could not see a face. All he could see was a silhouette outlined by magnificence.

"Brayson," the voice said in a deep, soothing tone, "I am Lasidious. I have come to ask you to be a disciple of peace and love. I ask you to follow the words of my prophet. For doing so, I will reward you and your family with a peaceful existence. There will be many trials in the near future, but with your strength, my son, peace can be brought to this world. You'll be my shining light on Luvelles. You can make the leaders of this world understand that the words of the prophet are true. Are you ready to do what your god is asking of you?"

Brayson climbed out of bed and lowered to his knees. "I live to serve, My Lord."

"I have a gift for you, my son." The silhouette extended its hand. Fisgig flew from it and landed on the headboard of Brayson's bed. "I have decided to return your friend to you. No longer will you hide him within the mountains. He's to be a symbol of power given to you by your loving god. I have restored the power he commanded before George took his life. No longer will he need to burn and rise from the ashes. Consider this gift a gesture of my love and appreciation for your service. You are whole once again, Head Master Brayson Id. Your power is stronger than it ever was. Obey your prophet, Brayson, and I will reward you in the afterlife."

Tears rolled down Brayson's cheeks. "I will, My Lord. I will serve you until my dying breath. Thank you for returning Fisgig to me."

Lasidious allowed his silhouette to take form. He was wearing a pure white robe with a white woven rope tied around his waist. He removed his hood, then lifted Brayson to his feet. Once he held Brayson's eyes within his own, he continued. "The prophet will come to you when the moment is right to act. For now, it is best to do nothing. Go...enjoy your family. Enjoy your friend. Give your vows to the woman you love. Soon, you will be living on a world blanketed in peace...warmed by my love. There is no better moment than now to begin a family."

Lasidious' glorious image faded, then vanished in a burst of light. Brayson dropped to his knees and began to sob.

The Luvelles Gazette

When you want an update about your favorite characters

The Next Day, Early Bailem

Shalee and Gregory are standing outside the entrance to The Source's cave. Shalee will not be allowed to go inside until Gregory has returned from looking into the Eye.

Kepler and Payne are waiting for George to give them instruction on what is to happen next. Payne's appearance is changing fast, and as a result, he has been sleeping more than usual. Something is about to happen to Payne.

Kepler, on the other hand, is still dealing with the fact he has lost his power.

Mary and Brayson have spent the day together after his visit from Lasidious. He has given Mary the good news about his new god, and how Lasidious wishes him to help George bring peace to the worlds.

Brayson avoided telling Mary that George had been commanded to kill him. With Fisgig's return, Brayson is convinced Lasidious is the one true god, especially after receiving confirmation from Athena that Mieonus threatened George.

George, Athena, Susanne and baby Garrin are inside George's home having dinner. George is explaining to the ladies that he will be in and out of the home doing the work of Lasidious. He has avoided telling them he has the ability to teleport between the lower three worlds.

He has assured Athena he will be there to help raise their child. This seems to be everything Athena needs to hear. George only needs to wait for the sign that Shalee has made it to the entrance of The Source's cave.

Boyafed has brought Sam's body to the Dark Order's temple. He will order one of his paladins to take the king's body to the Merchant Island on Luvelles. With every last resource preparing for the upcoming war, it is a challenge to figure out the details of Sam's return to Grayham, but the king earned Boyafed's respect and Boyafed plans to keep his word to honor Sam.

Boyafed will place Sam in the Order's finest casket before sending his body to Merchant Island. Boyafed will send word through his mirror to Michael, Sam's General Absolute, that the king will arrive on Southern Grayham's Merchant

Island within the next 4 Peaks of Bailem. Michael will thank Boyafed before his mirror goes dark.

Boyafed will then go to the Petrified Forest to solicit the help of Balecut, a powerful wizard, who can bend moments.

Christopher, Boyafed's new Argont Commander, the man who replaced Dayden, Boyafed's childhood friend, as his second-in-command, is preparing to meet with Tygrus—the retired soldier of the Dark Order who lives in Bestep. Tygrus is the same man Kiayasis entrusted with Shalee while retrieving the Knife of Spirits from Gorne, the hermit.

Christopher is hoping that Tygrus' reputation as a merciless killer will help rally the mercenaries of Bestep. He will ask the mercenaries to join the Order on the Battlefields of Olis. He is prepared to give them the coin necessary to accomplish this goal.

Christopher also plans to meet with the Serwin King in Shade Hollow.

Lord Dowd is waiting to hear from Krasous, his Argont Commander. Krasous is about to meet with Wisslewine inside the enchanted woods of Wraithwood Hollow. Krasous has taken a knee and is waiting for the Wraith Hound Prince to emerge from the center of the Under Eye.

Krasous will also visit the Spirit Plains. He will have to find the king of a race of spirits called the Lost Ones. He must capture Shesolaywen inside the Scroll of Canair.

Mieonus was watching Shalee and Gregory until they stepped onto The Source's teleportation platform inside his temple at the center of the Void Maze. The visions within her waterfall went dark as soon as this happened. The ancient dragon's magic is far too powerful to watch the events while inside his mountains.

The goddess plans to go with Keylom and Mosley, once the wolf returns from Harvestom, to the world of Grayham. The trio will appear to the people in an effort to gain followers, but something is about to happen on Grayham which will make this task difficult.

Mosley, Calla, Hosseff and Alistar are on Harvestom. The wolf will leave for Grayham once they have ensured the war between the kingdoms of Kless and Tagdrendlia is moving forward. The group has agreed to leave Alistar behind to begin their work to foil Lasidious' attempt to gain followers on Harvestom. Calla and Hosseff will go to Luvelles to begin the Collective's work to gain followers there.

Helmep and Jervaise are headed to the World of Dragonia. Most of the demons on this world worship Lasidious. Making a dent here is going to be nearly impossible. The only creatures who do not worship Lasidious are the dragons. They worship no deity, but have a fondness for Celestria.

Bailem, Owain, Lictina and Keylom have been assigned to the world of Trollcom. Bailem and Keylom will meet with the trolls while Lictina and Owain meet with the lizardians and the dwarves.

The trolls will not do anything without the approval of their king. Kesdelain is highly respected amongst the races of trolls for his masterful role in enslaving the races of lizardians and dwarves.

Though the lizardians and dwarves have succumbed to slavery, a bitter war thrives between the trolls and the vampires. Their fight has lasted since the creation of the new worlds. They fight for bloodroot.

In total, four races of trolls make up 33 percent of this world's population. The Ancient Mystics, also known as the souless immortals called vampires, make up another 35 percent. The lizardians and the dwarves make up the final 32 percent.

The Ancient Mystics, dwarves and lizardians scatter their beliefs among many deities, but the trolls only worship Lasidious. If Bailem and Keylom can convince the King of Troltloss to change who he worships, the rest of the trolls will follow his lead. Once the news spreads, Lasidious would lose over 2,350,477 beings who pray to him twice daily.

Gage and the other goswigs have listened to Strongbear yell since he emerged from his cave. After hearing what Gallrum had to say, he became—for the lack of a better description—really pissed off. It bothers Strongbear to know he is not as appreciated as he thought he was in Gogswayne. Since the bear's fit, the goswigs have gathered on the shore of Crystal Lake. They are waiting for King Ultor.

Marcus has gone into seclusion inside his dark tower-palace. He is beginning to wonder if George will return.

Lasidious and Celestria are inside their home beneath the Peaks of Angels. They plan to separate to visit the leaders of many different kingdoms who serve them on each world.

Celestria also has plans of her own to help her lover increase the number of his followers.

The lovers have a special surprise they are itching to stick under the noses of the Collective.

Thank you for reading the Luvelles Gazette

A Pile of Ash

**The Enchanted Woods of
Wraithwood Hollow**

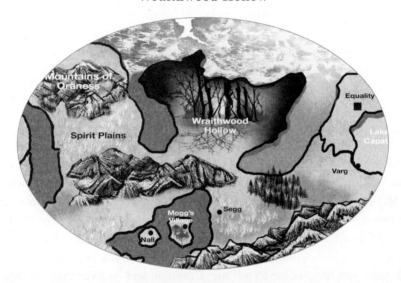

Krasous, the Argont Commander of the white army, took a knee before the Under Eye within the enchanted woods of Wraithwood Hollow. He is waiting for Wisslewine, the Wraith Hound Prince, to emerge from his plane of existence after summoning him with the Orb of Spirits.

When, finally, the wraith stepped out of the darkness, a chill ran down the commander's spine. Despite the fact Krasous knew Wisslewine was an ally, he had never seen the Wraith Hound Prince in person. The wraith's appearance was far more frightening than the stories he had heard as a child.

Krasous' light blue eyes filled with anxiety. Every muscle trembled beneath his silver armor as he looked into the hound's pitch black eyes. The size of the prince made the Argont Commander feel small, despite being a good-sized man of over six feet. The way the wraith's muscles rippled beneath his ghost-white coat as he moved, sent a message to Krasous that he was the inferior race of the two.

The prince snarled as he walked down the gray, stone steps leading away from the Under Eye. As the wind wisped through the branches of the hollows, his claws scraped the stones with the placement of each hoof. The beast sounded angry as the hound's saliva dripped from the end of his teeth.

Wisselwine spoke in a language unknown to Krasous. A scroll given by the White Chancellor to Lord Dowd, then passed to Krasous to read before summoning the wraith, carried a spell which allowed the Argent Commander to understand and speak in the creature's tongue.

"What do you want with me, paladin?" Wisselwine snarled. "Why have you summoned me from my slumber? This plane of existence is miserable. I consider my moments here less than desirable. I wish to return to my territories within the darkness."

Krasous' teeth chattered as he spoke. "It is under dire circumstances I have been asked to disturb your rest, Your Grace. War threatens our lands and..."

Wisslewine growled as if he was going to attack. "Why would I care about a war which threatens your lands? Has the dark army decided to threaten your way of life, yet again? Are you going to tell me it is to my benefit to protect your kingdom so they do not destroy the Under Eye and, ultimately, my home within it? Are you going to say I'll no longer be able to sleep peacefully within my plane of existence?" The wraith prince growled and snapped his ghost-white teeth together. He shouted in a booming voice, "Is this what you have come to tell me, Commander? Answer me!" Wisslewine watched as a yellow liquid seeped out of the bottom of Krasous' armor while waiting for the urine covered commander to reply.

Krasous' voice was weak. "Your Grace...uh, ummm...these are, indeed, the things I have come to convey." Krasous lowered his head. "Please, don't eat me."

The wraith hound moved close to Krasous and put his snout inches from the commander's ear. Krasous could feel the warmth of the wraith's breath as he growled while baring his teeth. Once the Argent Commander finished losing what was left of the color in his face, he was as white as a ghost himself.

Enjoying the commander's fear, Wisslewine decided to lighten the mood.

The hound began to smile as he pranced back up the steps toward the darkness of the Under Eye. "Are we fighting on the usual battlefield?"

It took a moment for Krasous to answer. "Yes...Your Grace."

"Good! Then, tell Lord Dowd I have finished toying with you. I shall meet him for battle. My hounds shall number 1,000 strong." Wisselwine turned to step through the Under Eye, then stopped. His head twisted over his shoulder. "Commander...you may want to bathe before you speak with Dowd. You smell as if you had fish for dinner." With that, the prince chuckled and walked into the darkness.

Krasous exhaled as the wraith disappeared, "I hate this job!" He reached down and rubbed his hand across the wet dirt, then lifted it to his nose. "Ugggh...it does smell like fish."

The Shore of Crystal Lake

The goswigs watched, while standing in columed ranks, as Ultor finished his transformation after emerging from the water to stand before them. The king addressed Strongbear, explaining the upcoming war. Gregory's request for the goswigs to join Lord Dowd's white army, north of Lake Tepp, was delivered. Further, Ultor asked Strongbear to march to the Battlegrounds of Olis.

"The decision is yours, Strongbear," Ultor said while scanning the goswigs' formations. "Whether or not the goswigs join the fight is a decision I will allow you to make, my friend."

Strongbear thought long and hard before responding. "We will join, Lord Dowd. Our presence could be the key to victory."

A sigh of disappointment filled the air. Ultor smiled as he studied the goswigs' faces, then looked at Strongbear. "It doesn't appear your decision is favorable. Are you sure this is what is best? You may decline if it pleases the others."

Strongbear pushed out his mighty chest. "If we don't fight, and the dark army takes over, there is a chance our masters will find us. Many of us would be pulled away from Gogswayne forever. I cannot allow this to happen. If we go to battle and make a stand, we may be able to defeat the dark army and never have to worry about the secret of our village being learned. This decision is for the best. They may not see it now, but they will as their moments pass. We will fight."

Ultor nodded, then turned to make his way into the water. Strongbear watched as the Ultorian's iridescent glow returned as the king's large angelic wings began to emerge from his back.

After watching Ultor disappear beneath the lake's surface, Strongbear turned and looked at the population of Gogswayne. He shouted his favorite phrase. "So, are you with me...or are you against me?" The bear never got a reply as the rest of the goswigs turned and headed home to prepare for war.

The Mountains of Oraness
Entrance to The Source's Cave
The Following Morning

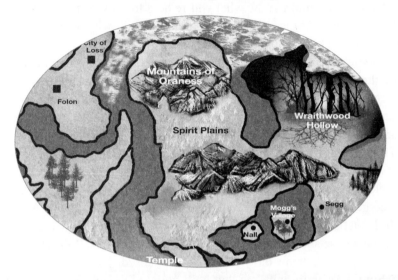

George appeared inside the mouth of The Source's cave. He looked across the pool to where Shalee sat. She was sitting with her back to him and was leaning against Fisgig's stone perch. He lifted his hands in front of his right eye and rolled them into the shape of a scope. He looked through the tunnel and smiled. "She looks like a target," he whispered.

It was only moments ago that George had been asleep. Lasidious had disturbed his dreams, but during this series of moments, the Mischievous One had not interrupted a dream of Abbie.

Instead, Lasidious brought news which had intrigued the warlock. Shalee was alone and waiting outside The Source's cave for her chance to enter. Gregory had gone inside, and this was George's opportunity to make his move. The Collective would be unable to see his handiwork, and because of his newfound power, George was now able to teleport directly into the Mountains of Oraness.

As George stared across the pool, he rubbed his hands together and thought, *She has no clue I'm here. Let's shake her up a bit.* The warlock teleported.

Shalee was startled when George appeared. She lifted her hand and sent her magic flying. The warlock smiled while thousands of tiny needles bounced off him.

George crouched in front of Shalee. She couldn't believe her eyes. She felt helpless. All she could do was wait for George to kill her. After a long period of silence and George doing nothing but staring at her, she shouted, "Quit toyin' with me! I know what you're here for...so get it ova' with!"

With a peaceful voice, George responded. "Chill, will you? I'm not here to kill you. I'm here to explain my actions."

Shalee crossed her arms. "Yeah, right! Ya can't explain actions which cause the death of many people. How could ya possibly justify that?"

George lowered to sit, pulled his knees to his chest, then crossed his arms around them. "We have been lied to, Shalee. The things the gods have told us are untrue."

The sorceress' lips curled. "Goodness-gracious, George, ya know I can't believe anythin' ya say. I mean, how could I trust ya? You've made so many horrible decisions?"

George shook his head and held Shalee's eyes within his own. "And, how could I trust someone who has cheated on her husband? How could I trust someone whose adulterous actions got the man she loves...killed?"

Shalee gasped. "How did ya know?" She paused. "Sam is not dead. He's fine. Sure, he's angry with me, but he'll get ova' it. He's in the swamp retrieving the..." Again, she hesitated, unsure if she should continue.

George grinned. "Yes, I know what Sam was doing. I know he was after the crystal, and he got it, by the way."

"He did? How do ya know?"

"Oh, I know more than you could imagine. I know Sam was killed by Boyafed after he retrieved the crystal. Apparently, the man you chose to have an affair with was the son of the man who commands the strongest army on Luvelles. Boyafed waited for Sam to exit the swamp. He killed Sam to get vengeance for Kiayasis' death. The next person Boyafed intends to kill...is you. After all, you're the one responsible for Sam's decision to kill his son."

Shalee remained silent. She had no idea how to respond. George took the opportunity to continue. "Shalee, do you remember the day we all had dinner in Lethwitch? You know...the day I found out my daughter was dead. I was with you inside your room at the inn. Do you remember?"

The queen managed a response as tears began to flow. "I rememba', but what does that have ta do with Boyafed and Sam?"

George sighed. "It has nothing to do with them. Just hear me out. You said you remembered the day you told me my daughter was dead. Do you also remember asking if I had been contacted by Lasidious? Do you remember I had no clue what you were talking about?"

"I do, but I wanna know 'bout Sam and Boyafed. What's goin' on? If Sam's dead, where's his body?"

"Don't worry about Sam, for now. He won't be dead long."

Confusion spread across Shalee's face. "What in tarnation are ya talkin' 'bout, George?"

"Everything will make sense. Just relax. I plan to take you to Grayham so you can watch the one true god return Sam's life. Lasidious has promised he will return Sam's soul."

"That's impossible, George," Shalee snapped as she wiped the tears from her chin. "Lasidious is evil. There's no way he can command someone's soul ta leave the Book of Immortality. I don't believe ya. This isn't how things work here."

"Yeah, yeah, yeah. I'm getting to the explanation. Just chill, and allow me to explain. If I'm right, the gods told you Lasidious was a mischievous being. They told you they thought Lasidious was the one who brought me from Earth. How am I doing so far?"

Shalee's eyes narrowed. "So far, everythin' you've said is what we were told."

George straightened his legs, then leaned back and supported himself with his arms. "Did they also tell you Lasidious planned to use me to do his dirty work?"

"They did. Doggone it, George, what are ya gettin' at?"

"Well...what I'm trying to say is...it wasn't Lasidious who brought me here. It was the goddess, Mieonus. She was the one who asked me to do all those hurtful things."

Shalee rebutted. "Hold on a cotton-pickin' moment. For argument's sake, let's say this is true...just for argument's sake, mind ya. Why would ya do these terrible things in the first place? Why would ya hurt so many, even if the goddess did ask ya to? The gods can't force us ta do anythin'."

George leaned forward, pulled his right knee up, then crossed his arms around it. "Let me ask you this. When you lost your baby, how did you feel?"

"What does that matta'?"

"Just tell me. Then, I'll explain."

"For heaven's sake, I felt like I wanted him back, of course."

George snapped his fingers at Shalee. "Exactly! That's the same way

I felt when Mieonus told me she could get my daughter's soul out of the Book. She told me if I helped her create a diversion on Grayham to keep the attention of the gods off her while she worked on a plan to take control of the Book of Immortality, she would return Abbie to me."

"For the love of God, George. The love of your daughta' doesn't give ya the right to kill so many."

"I agree. I agree with you 100 percent. I was really screwed up for a while. You knew I was hurting inside...didn't you?"

"I did. But, still."

George lowered his head and feigned his shame. "Look, I feel bad about the things I've done. But, I'm not the only one who has done them. Let me ask you something. How many people have you and Sam killed in order to fulfill that freaking prophecy about setting an example on the worlds? Take a hard look at everything that's happened. Even if you didn't have to fight in the war I caused, Sam still had to kill in the arenas of Grayham to gain the glory the gods asked you guys to obtain. You both had to kill to lead. How sick and freaking disturbing is that concept? How can it be okay to kill in order to create an empire for the races to emulate? What makes you taking life acceptable and me taking life...unacceptable?"

Shalee sat in silence for a long series of moments. "I hate ta admit it, but I see your point. But, you're still killin' folks, aren't ya? Why are ya doin' it if ya feel so bad? Has Mieonus brought ya here ta start anotha' war?"

George nodded. "Yes, that's exactly what she brought me here to do."

Shalee barked, "I knew it! You are up ta somethin'!"

George held up his hands. "Whoa! Take it easy, cowgirl. Holster that Texas spirit so I can explain. It's not what you're thinking. I have no intention of doing what Mieonus wants me to do."

"Really? And, why is that? Why turn a new leaf now?"

George picked up a pebble from Fisgig's little island, then tossed it into the water. "Fair question. The reason is...I found the truth. I found out there is a heaven, one where the souls of Lasidious' followers are kept. The gods are jealous. They loathe Lasidious and have created many lies to get the beings of the worlds to turn their backs on his path of righteousness."

"George, what in tarnation are ya talkin' 'bout? Sam has said nothin' about Lasidious havin' this kinda power. In fact, Sam said everythin' ta the contrary. He read everythin' in the royal library in Brandor about the gods. He said Lasidious is dastardly."

George shook his head. "Don't you see, Shalee, Lasidious doesn't have many followers on Grayham. Bassorine had most of the followers on that world. I'm sure Sam told you this. He had a statue of himself erected there, for hell's sake. You remember the damn statue, right?"

Shalee recounted. "I rememba' Sam was irritated because Bassorine's destruction left a lot of people without anyone ta believe in. Sam said it seemed like a joke ta have gods who are so limited in power...so limited in their knowledge of so many things."

Again, George snapped his fingers at Shalee. "That's what I'm trying to tell you. The gods are limited in power, except for Lasidious. After I started the war on Grayham, Lasidious, the one true god the others fear, came to me. He was pissed because of my actions. But, despite his anger, he took me to see his heaven. I saw so many glorious angels. I saw the most magnificent creations I could've never imagined. Shalee, I saw things that would have blown your mind."

"I'm listenin'. Tell me more."

"Lasidious told me I was to go back into the world and change my ways. He said he saw something good in me. Don't ask me how, but he did. Anyway, he asked me to become his prophet of peace."

Shalee rolled her eyes. "Was Lasidious drunk or somethin'? Does he not realize the kinda person ya really are? Or, does he have an affection for screw-ups?"

George smiled. "Look, I feel you. But, who am I to tell a god that he's wrong. Lasidious gave me a chance to become something better. If you were me, wouldn't you be thrilled if you had the opportunity to do something great? I'm sick of being an asshole."

Shalee stood and walked to the edge of Fisgig's island. She looked down and saw her reflection in the pool. After a fair amount of moments passed, she turned, then responded. "I suppose I see your point. Keep talkin'."

George stood and wiped the dirt from his backside. "Lasidious wants me to spread his words of peace and love. I am to do everything I can to bring harmony to the worlds. He said the other gods are constantly manipulating to bring war and heartache to the masses. The gods want war so the souls who perish can be replaced by the souls living, trapped inside the Book. Apparently, this is their sick way of allowing the souls waiting inside the Book to be reborn. It's a vicious cycle of death. It's the most ridiculous thing I've ever heard."

Shalee stood in silence. It wasn't until after George cleared his throat that she responded. "If you're lyin', I'll know it eventually. I drank a potion which will give me the memories of the gods. It may take a while before I can recall them, but I'll know."

George had to think fast. He had no idea what Shalee was talking about. An idea popped into his brain. "Shalee...think about it. The fact you drank a potion which gives you the memories of the gods causes me to have concern for you. I think you need to consider the source of where the potion came from. You may eventually know many, many things, but with the way the gods have concocted so many lies, how are you going to know what's really true? I don't envy you at all. I can only imagine how confused you will be. Is this really how things should work? Shouldn't there be a better way?"

Shalee pushed her hands through her long blonde hair, her blue eyes revealing her stress. "This is terrible. If what you've told me is the truth, then Mosley is keeping terrible company. I can't fathom the idea that Mosley could be as misled as we've been. That poor wolf."

As Shalee turned her back to George to look into the pool, a sinister grin appeared across George's face. "I hate to break it to you, Shalee, but Mosley is part of the gods' deceptions. He never really ascended. He was a god when you met him. He only pretended to be Bassorine's pet. You should ask Mosley what his job as the God of War entails."

Shalee turned to face George. "What do ya mean?"

"I mean, I have been told Mosley's job is to make sure the beings of the worlds choose war over peaceful solutions. He does this willingly to ensure the souls within the Book of Immortality are rotating through its pages. Mosley knows he is on the wrong side. He also knows he has deceived you, the same way the others have. Once you have spoken with Mosley, you'll know the truth about his character. But, be careful how you ask questions. If you anger Mosley, he will bring war to your kingdom. I would hate to see this happen again."

Shalee shook her head in disbelief. "So, you're sayin' Lasidious isn't a michievous god. Everythin' is a big lie told by the others? This is bogglin' my mind. It's hard ta believe."

George moved to Shalee and put his hands on her shoulders. "Lasidious is quite the opposite of everything you have been told. Lasidious is a loving god. He saved me from a life of hate and deceit. Mosley is every bit as evil as Mieonus."

George lifted his hands toward the sky. "I am a prophet of peace and love." He lowered his hands and looked into Shalee's eyes. "I have come to share this love with you. I'm here to allow you to say goodbye to Sam before you look into the Eye of Magic. If your soul is swallowed, I want you to know Sam will live again, and Lasidious intends to return his soul in front of the people of Brandor before they have the chance to light the fire of his passing."

Shalee sighed. "Then, take me ta Sam. I want ta see his body."

"I'll take you, then bring you back once you've said goodbye. If you wish to put off looking into the Eye until you've had the chance to witness his resurrection, I'll allow you to stay with my family until the moment arrives to take you to Brandor.

"You will like my wife. Athena will treat you well. Besides, there's nothing for you to do on Grayham. Sam's passing celebration has already been scheduled. You'll be able to witness the true power of the god I serve."

Shalee's brow furrowed. "How dare Michael schedule the lighting of Sam's fire without me. I'm his queen, for heaven's sake."

"This is something you'll have to take up with your General Absolute. Close your eyes and I'll take you to Sam's body."

Meanwhile, Lasidious was standing next to Sam's coffin. The casket had been placed inside a heavy iron crate, which had been scheduled for the Merchant Angels to transport to Grayham. The Mischievous One opened the lid, then reached inside. He laid his right hand on Kael's blade which had been placed on Sam's chest. The blade's handle sat at the base of Sam's chin and extended toward his feet.

The Mischievous One addressed the blade. "How have you been, old friend? It won't be long before your master realizes who he is. Do you look forward to that day?"

Kael's blade began to pulsate. "I long for that day. It has been too long since our last conversation, Lasidious. Soon, everything will be as it should have been. The reuniting of the fallen will be a blessed event, and my master will finally return to his glory. I long to speak with him and grow tired of waiting."

Lasidious lowered across Sam's body and kissed his forehead. Then, he took Sam's hands and folded them across the top of Kael's handle. As George and Shalee appeared outside the crate, Lasidious whispered, "The moments are approaching to remind my brother of who he is, old friend. Remember, you must do this subtly, or his mind will crumble beneath the weight of his memories. Until we speak again, protect him." Lasidious lowered the lid, then disappeared as the door of the crate opened. The Mischievous One circled to the back side of the casket and watched as Shalee's face became tormented.

As the door opened, Shalee covered her mouth with both hands. Tears began to run down her face. She hated herself. She knew her infidelity had been the cause of Sam's death.

George entered, and though he could not see Lasidious, he winked to the emptiness of the crate beyond the coffin. With his back to Shalee, the warlock smiled as he lifted the casket's lid. Sam was lying inside with Boyafed's dagger still buried in his side.

"Oh, my heavens," Shalee said as she stopped next to the coffin. "How could Boyafed be so cruel? He just left his dagger in Sam's side." She reached in and tried to pull it out, but was unable to. She tried to use her magic, but still, the dagger would not budge. She tried again and again, but no matter how hard she fought, the blade would not pry free. She gave up and leaned over the side of the casket, then kissed Sam on the lips. She tried to talk to Kael to learn what happened, but the sword was unresponsive.

George waited without saying a word. He allowed the queen to grieve. He would remain silent until her last tear fell. It seemed like forever before Shalee kissed Sam for the last moment. She turned away from the casket. "I'm ready ta go."

George put his left hand on Shalee's right shoulder, then teleported them outside the entrance to The Source's cave. "I'm sorry for your loss, Shalee. Why don't you come with me and meet Athena? She'll take care of you."

Shalee lowered to the ground. "I prefer ta be alone. Is there someplace else ya could take me 'til we head ta Brandor?"

George thought a moment. "I could take you to Floren. The innkeeper there is a delightful elf named Kebble. He will ensure everything you need is taken care of. Will that work?"

Shalee shrugged. "I suppose. I can't think of any otha' place ta go. I would ask ya ta take me ta Brandor, but I don't think I'd be able ta find a moment ta myself once I'm there. The people would be all ova' me."

George extended his hand to help her up. "Then, it's settled. Floren it is." He touched her shoulder. When they reappeared, they were standing outside Kebble's Kettle. "Let me introduce you. You should be okay here until I return. I'll be back in eight days. This should give you ample moments to mourn. Then, if you decide to witness the power of the one true god, I'll be happy to take you to Brandor. Don't worry, Shalee...my god gives me the power to teleport between worlds. If you decide to go, you'll see your husband rise again, I assure you."

As they walked through the swinging doors, Kebble's smile widened as he saw George. He hurried over and waddled up his booster steps behind the counter. "And, who would this beauty be, George?" He looked at Shalee. "How can Kebble help you today, my dear?" The elf lifted his pipe to his mouth and took a puff of his cherry-smelling tobacco.

Shalee's voice sounded defeated. "I just need a room, please."

George spoke up. "Kebble, this is the Queen of Southern Grayham. She has come to escape the pressures of life. Her ears have recently heard tragic news. Will you see to her safety, and ensure she has everything she needs? I will pay you upon my return."

Kebble removed his pipe. A larger than life smile crossed his face as he leaned across the counter to lift Shalee's chin. "Any friend of George, is a friend of Kebble's, My Lady. Kebble will see to it that you are well taken care of." The short elf winked. "He has a fond affection for beauty."

Despite Shalee's despair, a slight grin appeared on her face.

Marcus Id's Dark Tower-palace

After leaving Kebble's inn, George appeared in Marcus' throne room. As soon as Marcus saw him, he rushed up to the warlock. "You live! I was beginning to think the Eye had swallowed your soul."

George nodded as he put his hand on Marcus' shoulder. "It's good to see you, Marcus. Everything is going as planned. Have you accomplished everything we discussed while I was gone?"

"It is done, and then some. The armies are gathering forces. They'll meet on the Battlegrounds of Olis. Now, you can send me to meet with The Source. I wish to look into the Eye as soon as possible."

George took a step back, then moved to the window of the tower. As he looked at the gloomy sky, he responded. "Soon, you will meet The Source. For now, there are two people going through the trials as we speak. Brayson has sent your brother to look into the Eye."

Marcus' face tightened. Rage filled his eyes as he threw his pipe across the room. The tobacco filling it dispersed as the bowl of the pipe shattered. "This is an outrage! Why would Brayson send Gregory when..."

George held up his hand and used his power to silence Marcus. "Does why really matter? I told you you'll look into the Eye...and you will...as soon as I can get you in. I will see to it that you're the Head Master of Luvelles before I leave this world."

George walked away from the window, moved up the steps leading to Marcus' throne, then took a seat. "Maybe, you should learn to control your anger. You need to find a way to make those around you enjoy your company, not despise you. What good will your power be if no one respects you? I'll tell you when the moment is right to stand before The Source. Until then, there's something I want you to do for me."

George released his power so Marcus could speak. "Am I to be your errand boy?"

George had to smile.

"What's so funny?" Marcus snapped.

George shook his head. "Look, this is a favor. You don't have to do anything you don't want to. This will help me get you the position you've always wanted...a position we both know you deserve far more than Brayson. If you want to be the Head Master, then I need your help. I need you to go to Grayham and find a rat named Maldwin. I need you to bring him to me."

"A rat? What could you possibly want with a rat?"

"Just get him, Marcus. I don't have the moments to explain. I'll set everything up. The Merchant Angels will take you to Grayham three nights from now. I..."

Marcus cut him off. "Brayson will never allow me to leave Luvelles, let alone, allow a rat to return. Only Brayson can make the request to travel between worlds."

George frowned. "You leave Brayson to me. I'll make sure you're allowed to catch a ride with the Merchant Angels. He trusts me. I'll come up with a clever deception. The rat is important, and I need you in the Head Master's position before I can move my family to Harvestom.

"You'll find the rat south of a city called City View. He lives in a cave which sits at the edge of the Mountains of Latasef where the cliffs drop into the Ocean of Utopia."

George tossed a rolled parchment across the room. "Use this scroll before you call the rat out of the cave. It will protect you if he gets scared. Once you've read it, you'll have two days to find him before the spell's effect will no longer protect you. This should be sufficient."

Marcus stopped him from continuing. After reading the scroll, he looked up. "Why do I need to protect my mind? Is this the power the rat possesses?"

"No. It's not a power," George replied to protect Maldwin. "The rat's ability is natural. He has had this ability since birth. You won't be able to eat his heart and steal the ability from him."

Marcus couldn't believe his elven ears. "How could you know about such things? Eating the heart of another is a secret only the most ancient of elves know."

George shrugged. "How I know is my business. I know many other things only the most ancient of the elves know. You won't be able to surprise me, Marcus."

George stood from the throne. "Don't forget to read the scroll before you call for the rat. When you see Maldwin, I want you to give him this note. It's written in the rat's language. Once his claw touches the parchment, it will speak with him."

Marcus tilted his head as a dog would. "You cast a spell which makes the parchment talk? I've never thought of doing that."

George began to laugh. "I know, huh…doesn't that just crack you up? I stole the idea from a movie I saw on Earth. You should've seen this sick flick. Their packages spoke when they were delivered to the kids. Since my home has been destroyed, they won't mind me using their idea, will they?"

Marcus just stood in silence, looking at George with a blank stare. George had to chuckle at the Dark Chancellor's confusion. "I imagine that when..."

Marcus stopped him again. "What will the note tell this Maldwin to do? I should know if the parchment will be speaking in a language I cannot understand. You should tell me what you plan to do with the rat's ability. And, how did you learn to speak the language of this beast? I feel as if you are not telling me everything."

George took a deep breath. "Look, man...I don't speak Ratanese. Somebody I know speaks the rat's language. I don't have to tell you anything other than what's necessary to get you into the Head Master's position. All I've got to do is fulfill my promise. Do you get my drift?"

George could see the agitation on Marcus' face. "Look, trust me. I can convince the rat to use this natural ability to get the people of Luvelles to accept you as their Head Master."

The new warlock extended his hand toward the wall. The broken pipe lifted from the floor, then flew across the room. After mending itself, while hovering in front of Marcus' face, the Dark Chancellor reached out and plucked it from the air.

George smiled. "I could've killed you if I had wanted to. You know this. So, maybe, you should allow me to finish giving you what you want. Stop being an obstacle. Damn, Marcus...you can be annoying. Like I said, once you're the Head Master, you're going to have to chill out."

"What does this 'chill out' mean?"

"It means you're going to need to stop being such an ass. If you don't, the people will hate you. I can get you into the Head Master's chair. I can even get them to accept your position, but I can't make the people respect you once I'm gone. You're going to have to do that on your own. Why do you think your brother is so beloved? He doesn't act like a piece of garesh."

Marcus clinched the stem of his pipe. "I see your point. I will try to do this chilling you've suggested."

"Good. I imagine once Maldwin listens to the note's message, and understands you're there to bring him to me, he'll want to come. You'll need to know how to shout out his name when you're calling for him. This should make things much smoother. Hopefully, your use of the scroll to protect your mind will be for nothing. This is how you say his name...Mal-a-*quay*-o.

"Once Maldwin finds you, I want you to ball your fist, then lift your thumb like this, and say, 'Everything is A-okay, man.' The rat will know I've sent you. He will listen to the note without objection. Do you understand?"

"I do. If going after this beast will..."

George vanished before Marcus could finish. The chancellor's eyes grew dark after watching the warlock disappear. "I'll retrieve your rat, but your life will end once I've looked into the Eye."

The Village of Bestep

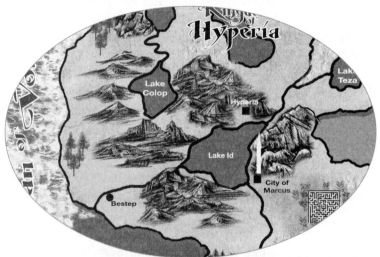

Christopher, Boyafed's Argont Commander, looked across the bar inside Tygrus' inn and admired the curves of the halfling woman who had served his ale. His long, pure white hair fell across his shoulders, and his eyes were without color, looking as if they were made of a fogged crystal.

Christopher's voice was strong as he made an advance. "Girl...do you have the moments to lie with an officer of the Order tonight?"

A much heavier voice replied from behind the bar as he walked out of the door leading to the kitchen. "My daughter isn't a whore, Commander. I suggest you sow your seed elsewhere. You should find a different vessel in which to put your manhood...or, I could just kill you."

Christopher felt foolish as he watched Tygrus walk around the bar to take a seat next to him. Tygrus' brown eyes, which matched his long hair, carried within them a confidence few men possessed. As Tygrus spun on his stool to face Christopher, the Argont Commander studied the much older elf. Tygrus had retired from his commission over 60 seasons ago. Despite his retirement, he was still one of the most feared men on Luvelles, and his magic was as strong as ever. He was the only man who had served in the Order whom Boyafed considered an equal when holding a blessed blade.

Tygrus slapped his hand on top of the bar, shouting at a human woman who was his wife and his daughter's mother. "Woman, bring my pipe, and be quick about it." Tygrus' wife was only 15 seasons old when her family visited Luvelles 30 seasons ago. After returning home, her father, a senator of Brandor, realized she was pregnant. After speaking with Brayson Id, it was agreed she would return to Luvelles to spend the rest of her life with Tygrus. As the retired paladin watched his wife carry his pipe across the room, he motioned to Christopher. "What do you want, Commander?"

Christopher took a drink of his ale. "I have been ordered to request the presence of your mercenaries on the Battlegrounds of Olis."

Tygrus took the pipe from his wife, then kissed the top of her hand. He bowed his head. "As always, my love, I cherish you."

The woman smiled, then walked away. Tygrus lit his pipe. He took a drag and admired her beauty as she continued her chores. He turned and blew the smoke in Christopher's direction, then enjoyed the commander's displeasure. "You best have brought coin. My mercenaries will cost Boyafed."

The World of Trollcom
The Kingdom of Troltloss

The gods, Bailem, Owain, Lictina and Keylom are on Trollcom. Trollcom is a dark world, with an even darker way of life—but, the story of this way of life is best left for later—it is a story of an unexpected sacrifice.

Lictina and Owain have gone to meet with the lizardians and dwarves. Bailem and Keylom are waiting for the King of the Trolls to return to his throne room after an evening with his 400th queen. When Bailem and Keylom had first approached Kesdelain, the troll was sitting on the riverbank of Greslowfem feeding his queen, Sholifenda, the brains of a slaved dwarf miner—waiting for fish to strike at a special bait which had been cast using a carved pole made of whipple wood—a wood known for its flexibility and durability.

Kesdelain is a mastermind at controlling the different races of trolls—a mastermind thanks to two gifts given by Lasidious many seasons ago. As a result, all trolls serve one king and hold Kesdelain in highest regard. Kesdelain was born of a dominant bloodline, a race of troll called the Tradesmeal, (Tra-des-*meal*) or when translated, Deadly Ones. His mother and father were nobles and had a strong set of family values—as strong as family values could be, considering they often ate their young for disobeying.

Kesdelain's black and red-orange skin is vibrant. His features are considered handsome by troll standards. His blood is acidic and can burn through many forms of light armor. His ability to regenerate at a rate much faster than other trolls is respected throughout his kingdom. He is the first and only king to have the respect of every race of trolls.

Eventually, Kesdelain sauntered into his cave and made his way to a special cavern which holds his throne. The cavern is dark, except for light cast by two torches which sit on either side of his throne. The wall on the south side of the cavern holds back a body of water called Lake Shovain. Because of the moisture which seeps through the wall, the room is cold and carries a nip.

The torches flanking Kesdelain's throne were not placed because light is needed for the king to see. In fact, his eyes prefer the darkness. They are for shedding light on his majestic form, and the slaves who serve him need the light to perform their service.

Kesdelain knew who Bailem and Keylom were as he took a seat on his throne. He cared nothing about the gods and ignored their presence as he made himself comfortable. His service to Lasidious was given only because of the Mischievous One's gifts many, many seasons ago. In return for the god's gifts, Kesdelain agreed to decree that all races of trolls would live in service to Lasidious, and pray to him twice a day.

Because of Lasidious' gifts, a law was added to the Book of Immortality. A god could no longer give any being on any world anything which would change the balance of power on their world. Lasidious' act of generosity gave the Mischievous One what he was ultimately after. His power increased because of the trolls' service.

Now…fellow soul…just like many of the laws within the Book of Immortality, the law created because of Lasidious' generosity has flaws. Though the law states: no member of the Collective may give a gift, or blessing, which will give a being on any world the ability to control or manipulate the free will of others, it does not state a god may not give a gift which would glorify or increase the influence of someone who is already in power and has the ability to control or manipulate the free will of others. This is the loophole Bailem and Keylom intend to use when approaching Kesdelain to acquire his service.

Fellow soul…for those of you who are saying, "Well, didn't Lasidious give George his abilities, and because of this, doesn't George have the ability to control the free will of others?"

My answer to your question would be: Lasidious never gave George anything. There was no gift or blessing bestowed on George. The Mischievous One simply told George where he could find power if he chose to go after it. In every case, George has had to seek out and take the power he has acquired. Lasidious' use of information has not broken any laws.

But, enough of George. Let us speak more of the Troll King. I will translate into common tongue and spare your soul the aggravation of reading the troll's language.

As Kesdelain looked down the steps leading away from his throne, the troll spoke. "I care not about speaking with gods." He sniffed the air, then scowled. "Your stench pollutes my cave."

Bailem allowed a glow to appear around him as he stretched his wings. Once folded, he stepped forward. "We bring a gift. We wish to have every race of troll live in service to us. Their prayers will magnify our names in the heavens, and for doing so, we shall reward you and make you the envy of every world."

Kesdelain laughed. "Everything I need, I have. There's nothing to give that I cannot take. Spare my nostrils. Be gone with you!"

Bailem stood firm. "I said nothing of need. I said we shall make you the envy of every world. We wish to glorify you, and in return for your faithful service, we wish to make your name immortal. You shall be as esteemed as the gods."

The troll leaned forward and placed his clawed-hands on his knees. "What kind of gift would do this?"

Before another word could be uttered, a blinding light filled the darkness of the cavern. Kesdelain had to cover his eyes. As the light dissipated, Lasidious stood at its center with George at his side.

The Mischievous One wasted no moments, speaking before Bailem or Keylom could. "Kesdelain, why do you entertain these fools? These creatures do not have the power to give you such a gift. They are not gods. They're nothing more than mystics. They deceive you. They are liars."

Bailem was outraged. The angel-god's anger was amplified by the clacking of Keylom's hooves as he confronted Lasidious. "You treat us as if we're mere mortals. How dare you. Do you have no shame, Lasidious?"

Lasidious didn't respond. Instead, he stood silent while George walked up the first few steps toward Kesdelain. The Troll King watched as the warlock knelt on the shaped stones.

George's voice was filled with reverence. "Great King...I have heard powerful stories about you. Lasidious speaks of you as if you are a god in your own right. The service of your kind pleases him. The stories of your beautiful queens, and your greatness amongst the races of trolls are stories of legend."

The muscles of Keylom's flanks rippled as he moved to stand next to George. He looked over his shoulder at Lasidious. "Do you have a new pet? Does George travel with you as a dog would? Why would you bring a mortal to do the job of a god?"

Again, Lasidious didn't answer. George ignored Keylom and continued. "As I was saying…Great King of..."

"Hold your tongue," Bailem shouted. He looked at Lasidious. "Send your puppet home."

Again, George continued and again, Lasidious allowed him to do so. "As I was saying..."

"I said hold your tongue!"

Lasidious began to smile while George turned up the heat. The warlock walked down the stairs and stopped in front of Bailem. "Why would a king such as Kesdelain wish to serve a fat man with wings? You are weak. You are a step away from pathetic. You have no power over me. I will not hold my tongue."

Bailem remained calm. He spread his wings in an attempt to show his glory. "I find it humorous you have the nerve to speak to me in this manner. I think the moment has come for you to..."

Lasidious lifted his voice to a level which made every mortal within the king's cave cover their ears. "Enough!" Once he had everyone's attention, he addressed Bailem and Keylom. "If you have the ability to strike down my so-called puppet, I'll allow your gift to be given to the king."

Keylom responded, "You don't have the authority to stop us. We have no desire to kill this mortal. You're wasting our moments."

Again, Lasidious shouted and again, he commanded everyone's attention. "You say mortal as if you are not mortal yourself. I say you don't have the power, or you would have done it already."

Bailem was unsure how to respond. He knew George was protected by the Book of Immortality's laws. If he struck him down, he would be made mortal.

Lasidious used the gods' silence to his advantage. "Just as I expected. You don't have it in you."

Keylom had had enough. He decided to turn Lasidious' game against him. "If he's just a mortal, then you have the power to kill him yourself. If you cannot, then there's no reason why Kesdelain should serve you. If you're unable to destroy him, then Kesdelain's loyalty has been misplaced."

Lasidious walked up the steps and stopped beside Kesdelain. "He uses the word loyalty as if he understands its meaning." The Mischievous One pointed down the stairs. "Kesdelain, you have witnessed their failure to provide proof of godhood. Allow your eyes to behold the power of a true god."

The Mischievous One lifted his hands and pointed them in George's direction. George took a step back. "Hold on a moment. This isn't what we agreed on. You can't do this, Lasidious. I'm not a damn sacrifice!"

Lasidious nodded. "Your service is no longer necessary. I will reward you in the afterlife."

George lifted his hands in front of his face and screamed, "No," as lightning erupted from Lasidious' hands.

Bailem and Keylom watched as George combusted. A moment later, his ashes fell to the floor. They could not believe what they had seen. They waited for the Book to appear and pass judgment, but Gabriel never came.

Lasidious smiled at his handiwork as he walked down the steps away from Kesdelain's throne. He stopped in front of Bailem. "My point has been made." He looked up the steps. "I trust the prayers of those who live in service to your crown shall remain steadfast for the seasons to come. I don't need to remind you who gave you your position as king. It's just as easy to take this position from you and give it to another. I'm sure your prayers will reflect your gratitude. I am to remain exalted on this world." Lasidious vanished.

A Very Happy Kitty

Kepler's Lair Beneath the Rocks

"Damn," George shouted after appearing with Lasidious in the darkness of Kepler's lair. The warlock commanded the darkness to dissipate. George's tunic was smoldering. He turned to speak with Lasidious as he brushed himself off, but Lasidious had already departed. "Garesh! I barely made it out."

"What are you talking about?" Kepler questioned as he stood to stretch.

George frowned. "Oh, nothing. It's just a little coordinating issue which can be fixed with practice."

"Are you here to stay, or are you going to run off and leave me behind again?"

George finished brushing himself off. "You sound like you've missed me, Kep? Do I need to give you a hug?"

Payne sat up. "Do it! Give him a hug, Master," the fairy-demon chided. "I wish to see him squirm."

George whirled around. He couldn't believe what he saw. Payne was an additional five inches taller than the last moment he had laid his eyes on him. "Holy garesh, Payne. You've grown at least a foot in a matter of days. Your voice is deeper, too."

Kepler cut in. "But, he's still a freak. All he talks about is the hair on his privates. I think he's hit puberty."

George couldn't believe his ears. "How does anyone hit puberty at three seasons? Maybe, you are a freak, Payne."

The fairy-demon picked up a fish he had caught earlier that day and chucked it across the lair. It hit Kepler upside the head. "Now, look at what you've gone and done. Even Master is calling me a freak. I should teleport you to a frightful height, then drop you."

George shook his head. "Payne, do you realize you're speaking as if you're educated?"

Kepler growled. "Don't give him that much credit. I figured out what's going on. Once I began showing him how to speak, he figured out he could look into your mind. He knows everything you know. I've had to explain many things, and on more than one occasion, I've had to stop him from saying things to Mary and Athena that he shouldn't. I convinced him to wait until you got back before he does what he says he's going to do."

George turned to Payne. "And, what do you plan to do?"

Payne stood. He still had the mind of a young boy, despite having George's knowledge. He had no real idea of what to do with it. "I don't like how your mind makes me feel. I don't want to lie to Athena. I want her to know everything."

George lifted his hand. It only took a moment for Payne to realize he could no longer move. "I'm sorry, Payne, but I can't have you telling Athena anything. Look into my mind. What will I do to you?"

Payne's face showed his surprise as he listened to George's thoughts. "You would kill me? Why?" Again, Payne read his master's mind for the answer. "You think if I say anything, it will stop you from getting Abbie's soul out of the Book. You're willing to sacrifice me to save her."

George kneeled beside the fairy-demon. He cradled Payne, then lowered him to his back. "What am I thinking now, Payne?"

Fear spread across Payne's red face as he answered. "You're going to give me a choice. I can surrender my power and the memories I have of your deceptions, and you'll let me live. If I don't, you'll turn part of my spine to stone. You'll cut my chest open and allow Kepler to eat my heart. You're willing to allow him to steal my power. You're willing to send my soul to the Book. You would give my abilities to Kepler because you know he won't say anything about the lies you've told. You trust him more than you trust me."

George leaned over the fairy-demon, exposed his palm, and a knife appeared. His eyes turned cold. "What will it be, Payne? Live or die? You choose."

Payne began to speak in the language of the Ancient Mystics. George knew what was happening and allowed him to continue. Eventually, the warlock watched as a ball of energy emerged from within Payne's chest and moved across the lair. The ball passed through Kepler's fur, penetrated his body, then engulfed his heart.

The color of Kepler's heart and the blood coursing through his veins changed from black to red. The transformation was more than the demon-cat could withstand. He fell to the ground and sunk into a deep sleep.

George watched in amazement as the fairy-demon's body began to shrink. It wasn't more than a few moments before Payne was once again his normal size and smiling like a child. Payne looked up and said, "Master, got food for Payne? Why Kitty sleep? Payne go to Athena? Athena feed Payne gooder."

George smiled and rubbed the top of the fairy-demon's bald head. "You don't have to call me Master anymore, little guy. Call me George or even dad if you want to. You can call Athena whatever works best for her. Why don't you go into the house, and let her know you're hungry."

"Payne go now." The fairy-demon closed his eyes to teleport, but nothing happened. He tried again, and still, nothing happened.

George picked Payne off the floor. "Why don't you fly, buddy?"

"Okay, George." Payne fluttered out.

George took a seat next to Kepler and rubbed the cat's head. "Sleep it off, big guy." He lowered his forehead against the bridge of the cat's snout. "There's no way I could've killed Payne. He's like family to us, for hell's sake. What's the matter with me, Kep? Payne didn't do anything wrong. This garesh is getting way too deep. I've got to get us out of this mess."

The warlock leaned back. "I wish you were awake, big guy. We need to talk." George stood, moved to the side of Kepler, and rubbed his back. "Let's just stick to the plan for now. We'll find a way out sooner or later. Let's just take care of the family, and stay the course until an opportunity presents itself. We need to know more before we can make a change. We need the upper hand, Kep."

The Spirit Plains

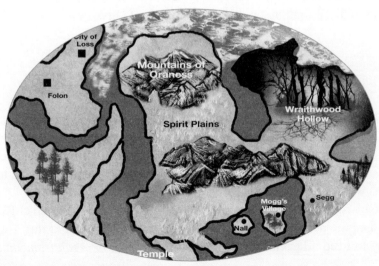

Krasous took a deep breath. He adjusted his breastplate, then tied his spirit-bull to a tree. As soon as he finished petting his mount, the bull dematerialized and became a ghostly figure.

"I'll be back, Hellzgat," Krasous said as he turned to look across the rolling plains filled with vibrant colors. "I'm not sure how long this is going to take, but I'll be back."

After his visit with the Wraith Hound Prince, the Argont Commander dreaded the idea of meeting another spirit. The problem was, he wasn't sure where he should go. The Spirit Plains spanned a large area, and he was seeking a specific spirit—one which could be anywhere.

To his knowledge, or anyone else's knowledge within the army, Shesolaywen, the Spirit King of a race of souls called The Lost Ones, wandered aimlessly across the plains. Shesolaywen had no castle or any kind of a home to speak of. The spirit simply wandered, and the bad part about it was, the Spirit King wouldn't show himself unless Krasous was alone, and worse still—naked and vulnerable.

The ghostly spirit-bull snorted as he watched Krasous undress. "Hey! Keep your eyes to yourself. This is bad enough without you eyeing me," Krasous grumbled as he gave Hellzgat's shadowy form a slight grin.

Somehow, the Argont Commander had to find Shesolaywen and manage to keep the spirit from possessing him long enough to read from the Scroll of Canair. The scroll would capture the Spirit King's essence inside its parchment. Krasous would then need to take the scroll to Lord Dowd. Dowd would then read from the scroll once the moment arrived for the armies to begin fighting on the Battlegrounds of Olis.

The Following Morning
The Mountains of Oraness
The Entrance to The Source's Cave

The morning was crisp and frigid. Since his arrival on Grayham, George had not seen a significant change in the weather, but today was different. The air felt as if a new season was approaching, and all the warlock could do was guess it was the third piece of the Crystal Moon being added to the others which caused the change in climate.

To his surprise, frost had buried its chilly claws into the steep cliffs surrounding the pool where Fisgig's perch rested on its island of dirt. He was going to need a heavier tunic. *I suppose I'll have to create something to handle the cold,* he thought, *but it's going to need to make a statement to complement the power I have now.*

George could only laugh as he lifted his right hand and allowed a flame to burn within his palm to provide warmth. After a few moments of allowing his mind to wander, he pulled his head out of the clouds to the task at hand. He needed to finish what he came for, then hurry home before anyone realized he was missing. He knew his little white lie about going outside to check on Kepler wouldn't buy him more than a few moments.

Scanning the cliff walls surrounding the pool, he chose a spot above the entrance to The Source's cave. He lifted his hands and concentrated. His magic reached inside his mind to retrieve the effect he was after. A portion of the cliff pulled away from the rest and remained suspended above the entrance. The rest of his thought commanded the magic to release the stone as soon as Gregory Id exited the cave.

With a wry smile, George vanished. When he reappeared, he looked down at the giant jaguar. Kepler was still sleeping. George thought, *I wonder how long you'll be asleep. Receiving Payne's power must have been a shock.* "Sleep it off, big guy."

George climbed out of the lair and made his way inside the house. As it turned out, Athena had fallen back to sleep. He took off his clothes, crawled in beside her, and snuggled his way into a comfortable position. After kissing the nape of her neck for many long moments, he rolled her onto her back, then positioned his head on her shoulder, just above her bosom. He allowed the beat of her heart to be his lullaby as he drifted off to sleep.

Later that afternoon, Athena, Mary, Brayson and George worked together to finish packing for an evening George would ordinarily call, Hell.

George rolled his eyes. "I hate camping."

"What's bothering you, George?" Athena said as she put a few corgan sandwiches inside a sealed wooden container Brayson had created for such outings. As she opened the lid a slight chill could be felt on her hand. She enjoyed the magical cooler as she looked up to listen to her husband's response.

George was trying to put on a happy face, but he knew Athena could see through his façade. "Nothing I can't handle, babe. Are you sure we should be doing this? You're getting close to having the baby, and sleeping on the ground might not be a wise thing to do."

Brayson gave George a look and watched as Athena put a finger on George's chest to push him back against the kitchen table. She maneuvered as best she could to accommodate her belly's roundness, then leaned in to give George a kiss. "I know you don't like doing this kind of thing. You can always stay home if you'd like. I won't be angry if you do. But, I'm going because I enjoy it."

"Nonsense," Mary said while walking past Brayson and pinching his backside on her way to the pantry, her bare feet gliding across the hardwood floor. "George, you listen to me. You'll just have to...um...how do the people from your old Earth say it again? I think you said it was, suck it up and stop acting like a wimp."

Everyone laughed at George's expense. A few moments later, Mary continued. "Besides, this will be our last chance to do this kind of thing before the baby arrives. Put on a happy face, and let's have some fun."

Mary had to open the pantry more than once to get the effect she was after as she waited for George's response. The environment inside changed to the atmosphere necessary to keep items chilled. She walked in and retrieved a dozen eggs and a large tub of greggle hash. Upon shutting the door, she turned to look at George. "I don't see that frown turning upside down, Mr. Nailer."

Brayson had to laugh as he watched the warlock continue about his business without responding. "Do you despise calling nature that much, George? I may have a better idea. Instead of calling nature, why don't we go to the Foot and stay with the giants. At least there, you'll be able to keep your mind on so many other things, you'll forget you're roughing it. The giants have interesting homes. I'm certain we will be able to stay with their leader. I'm sure you would find it educational to meet Grosalom. He's an enormous man and carries a massive presence about him."

The thought of meeting a giant reminded George of Kroger. He still regretted the day he turned the gentle ogre to stone. After a moment, he continued to fill a jar with a milk-like substance and responded. "I guess it wouldn't be so bad to meet the giants. I think I would enjoy doing that."

Athena smiled and moved to pull her husband's hands about her waist. With her back to him, she turned her head. "Thank you, honey. Imagine how big their mattresses will be. We'll be able to roll over and over and over before we find an end."

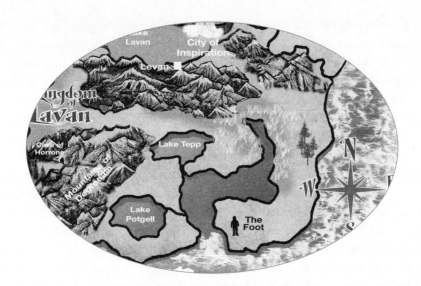

That evening, after teleporting to the Foot, Brayson made their introductions. The group had to sit over 40 feet away from a massive bonfire while seven, 60 foot tall giant indian-looking figures danced around it. Their weight caused the ground to quake.

Noticing the environment was dangerous, due to the size of their hosts, Brayson used his magic to protect the group from being smashed by a large foot.

As George watched Grosalom's giant tribe of feather-covered rainseekers move about the fire with paint-covered faces and rattles cut from the tales of giant serpents, he could only marvel. Everything in this part of Luvelles was enormous. Even the remnants of the serpents, draped across a large wooden tripod—the top of which had to be seventy feet at its highest point—made the structure seem miniscule. Both the snakes' tails and their heads rested on the ground on opposite sides.

Holy garesh! Those things have to be over 150 feet long. I bet their bodies are at least four feet thick, George thought as he continued to scan his surroundings.

George's eyes settled on Grosalom's home which reflected the bonfire's light in the distance. *Damn! They live in giant teepees. I bet that thing has to be at least 200 feet tall and twice as wide at its base. This is fascinating. Seeing this is worth roughing it.*

Grosalom looked down at his tiny visitors and spoke in a booming voice. He ordered the dancers to stop. The ground stopped quaking as the heavy footsteps subsided.

Once everyone had taken a seat around the fire, the giant leader continued to speak in a whisper—a voice which still seemed commanding to his small visitors. Only Brayson could understand. When the conversation ceased, Brayson turned to the others to translate. "Grosalom has had a place prepared for us to sleep. He said it would be best for us to ride with his daughter or it will take us all night to get there. She will return in the morning to bring us to breakfast."

Once agreed, they climbed into the female giant's palms. The ground beneath them moved swiftly as she walked. With each footstep, they marveled at the sound. Arriving at their destination, she lowered them to the ground. Brayson shouted as loud as he could to thank Sheswyn for her generosity. After watching her go, the group turned to look up at their teepee.

George used his power to lift the group onto the wooden platform on which the structure rested. As they walked inside, they noticed how thick the hides were which covered the teepee. They marveled as they imagined how large the animal must have been to carry such a remarkable skin.

The mattresses which had been scattered across the floor were made of the same hides and had been stuffed with some sort of wool. As if the fact that one of these beds would sleep two of these giants wasn't impressive enough, they had to marvel further at how thick the mattresses were. Beginning at the floor, they stretched to a height nearly fourteen to fifteen feet.

George looked at Brayson. "I have only one question for you."

Brayson smiled. "You like this place, don't you?"

"I do, but that has nothing to do with my question. What I'm wondering... if everything is so big here, what about the bugs that can crawl onto the mattresses? How big do you think they are, and how do you think we should handle this so we can get a good night's sleep?"

Kepler's Lair
The Next Night

George appeared inside Kepler's lair after spending the day with Brayson and the girls. "Wake up, Kep," George said as he waved his hand to remove the darkness.

Kepler covered his eyes with both front legs as he buried his head beneath them. "George, you have got to stop doing that," he moaned. After a moment, he pulled back one of his legs and looked up at George with one eye. "What do you want?"

The warlock shook his head in disbelief. He closed his eyes, then re-opened them. Sure enough, Kepler's black coat had changed color. His fur was white, and his burgundy-red eyes were vibrant. His new look was captivating. "Holy garesh, Kep. What happened to your coat?"

"Not now, George, I'm tired. I've been out all night learning what my new power can do."

"Sit your big ass up. I want to look at you."

The demon-cat lifted from the floor and posed. "I know, I look amazing, right? I'm pleased with my new look. Now, I am a refined Master of the Hunt."

"You look better than amazing. Athena is going to freak when she sees you. How do we explain this?"

Kepler licked his chops. "I don't know, but when I awoke, yesterday, I looked like this. Where have you been? I looked for you."

"I thought it was best to let you sleep. You were out of it. When I left, you were still black. Brayson took me and the girls on a calling nature trip."

The demon-cat chuckled. "I bet you hated every moment of it."

"It wasn't as bad as I thought it would be. Brayson took us to a place called the Foot. There are enormous giants there. Apparently, the white army has requested their assistance during the upcoming war. Their leader is a massive man named Grosalom. You and I should go there sometime. Everything is so stinking huge.

"Anyway, I bet your new power caused the change to your fur. Just tell the family you used your new power to make the change."

Kepler was shocked. "Are you saying they know I have Payne's abilities?"

"Yeah, I told them last night."

"Do you think that was wise?"

"I had to say something. I told Athena I made Payne give you his power because I wanted to make sure he didn't accidentally do something to hurt Garrin while he was playing with him."

Kepler thought a moment. "You best not forget, Payne still has natural abilities. So, you're now okay with lying to Athena? "

"No, I'm not okay with lying to Athena, but how else was I going to explain it? I didn't see any other choice."

Kepler pondered what George said. "I want you to know I have access to your thoughts. I understand how you feel about lying to Athena, and I know you're telling the truth. I understand how much love you have for her and this family. I have to admit, I was surprised when I learned Brayson was growing on you. But, the thing I find most puzzling, is your love for my companionship."

George smiled. "See...I told you I loved you, big guy."

Kepler swallowed and forced a response. "I suppose I want you to know I may feel the same way on some minor level. Don't get too excited. I would still rather eat you, then let you hug me."

George chuckled. "Well, I guess that's a starting point." He elbowed the cat. "Come on, Kep, you like me more than that, don't you?"

The demon stretched. George watched his muscles ripple beneath his new coat. Once finished, the giant cat said, "Let's change the subject. I want you to know I understand everything that's going on. I like what you're planning on Harvestom. I think..."

George stopped him before he could continue. "We should save this conversation for later. You never know who's listening. Besides, I have something to show you. I have been working on mastering it for the last few days."

George looked into Kepler's eyes. After a moment, the giant cat understood what was happening. He returned George's thoughts with a few well-placed thoughts of his own. *This is intriguing. We can speak telepathically now. I like this, George. We will never need to watch what we say. Imagine the messages we can exchange while standing amongst the family, or any other group.*"

George answered back with his thoughts. *About Harvestom...I'm going to take you with me when the moment is right. Your new look will make quite the impression. We should use this to our advantage. I'll create a new tunic. It will be white with burgundy trim to match your eyes. I'll create a black chain to go around your neck. It'll have a pendant attached to it with a large gem at its center. The gem will also match your eyes, of course. I'm going to need a staff made of black wood to complement your chain. I think that would look tasteful. Oh, oh, oh...and let's create a black saddle for you to wear and lace it with more of these burgundy gems. No matter where we go, we'll look sick.*

Kepler cringed. *Why would you want us to look sick?*

George rolled his eyes and grinned. *Ha! Sick means good, Kep.*

Kepler thought a moment. *You say the strangest things. I like this idea of looking sick. It'll be a powerful statement while dominating territories.*

Agreed. You'll be the most disgusting looking kitty in all the land.

Kepler growled and stopped their mental conversation. "You just had to go and ruin the moment, didn't you? You just had to say kitty."

George held up his hands. "You're right, my bad. I'm sorry. Look, we have a lot to talk about." George began to communicate telepathically again. *So, I think we need to...*

The Source's Cave
The Next Morning

Brayson and George appeared outside The Source's cave. It took only a moment for Brayson to notice the large mound of rocks which had fallen from the cliffs above the cave's entrance. Both men headed for the scene. Brayson used his magic to lift the stones and push them clear of the entrance.

To George's surprise, Gregory was nowhere to be found beneath the trap he had set only days earlier. Somehow, the White Chancellor managed to avoid being killed, and this changed everything.

Realizing a new plan was necessary, George reacted. "I wonder what happened. We should go inside and see if Gregory's in there. Do you think he survived his encounter with the Eye? We should ask The Source if he came out of the Eye's chamber."

Brayson was still studying the cliff's face. "This is strange. I must come back to take a closer look. Someone powerful is responsible for this. These walls are protected by magic. For them to break apart like this doesn't make sense."

"It makes sense to me," George replied without hesitation. "I bet it's more of Mieonus' handiwork. I'm sure she's angry since I told her I won't do her dirty work. But, why would she care about making rocks fall like this? Now that I think about it, you're right...this doesn't make sense."

Brayson touched George on the shoulder. When they reappeared, they were standing in Gregory's throne room. Brayson located one of the handmaidens and asked if the chancellor had returned. Once confirmed, he sent the elderly woman to retrieve him, then faced George. "At least we know he's alive. With the Eye's gift, he'll be able to help us spread the word of our lord. We should sit with him so you can explain everything. I'm sure he will want to help."

George thought to himself, *Maybe, the rocks missing Gregory won't be such a bad thing after all. I should be able to manipulate this inconvenience into something beneficial.* George smiled. "You're right, Brayson. Your brother will make a fine addition to our cause. If he sees things as we do, I will ask Lasidious to make him a disciple."

Brayson nodded. "First, let's find out how strong his power has become. This way, you can tell Lasidious how effective Gregory will be while spreading the word of the one true god."

Kebble's Kettle
The Next Evening

George and Kepler appeared outside Kebble's Kettle after spending much of the day preparing their new look. The moment had come for the warlock to take Shalee to Brandor. George was sitting in the black saddle lined with garnet-colored gems. Kepler's white fur accented the saddle which was a snug fit. George's new tunic was elegant. His dark staff matched Kepler's black chain and had a gem at its top which matched the gem at the center of Kepler's pendant.

As soon as Shalee saw the pair, she stood from her seat, then took a step forward on the porch of the inn. Her voice was tentative as she spoke. "Is that...?"

George answered. "Yes, it is. Kepler understands the truth. He also serves Lasidious. He sees the importance of bringing peace to the worlds after his visit with my lord."

"This is unnervin', George. Kepler is a soulless demon. How could he be a part of bringin' peace ta the worlds?"

Kepler decided to speak. "I am standing right here, Queen of Brandor. I am no longer souless, and you may ask me your questions."

Shalee walked down the steps. "Okay, then. Consider yourself asked."

The demon had rehearsed a response for this confrontation. "Our lord has given me a soul. He is mighty and has the power to bestow this blessing. He has found a soul within his heaven who was willing to share my being. We live together as one and serve Lasidious in unison. I know now what I need to do to atone for the pain I have caused. I must spread the word of love. I must make my lord proud and help his prophet to make those who call for war see there is a better way."

Shalee shook her head, confused. "So, there's like two of ya in that body of yours? Can ya hear the otha' one talkin' ta ya? Isn't that kinda discombobulatin', or somethin'?"

"There is no confusion in my mind. I wish I had an answer which would make sense, Shalee. If you were to ask our god, he could explain it far better than I. He wishes to speak with you after your husband's resurrection."

"Good! I have a few million questions for him."

George decided to bring the conversation back on track. "The moment has come. We need to go, Shalee."

Shalee tapped Precious on the porch step. "Thank goodness. Ya have no idea how stir-crazy I've been sittin' here. I've considered teleportin' outta here on a hundred occasions ta catch a ride with the Merchant Angels. I've neva' felt so torn about so many things. I'm unable ta cry anymore. I swear ta ya, if it wouldn't have been for Kebble, I may have lost my mind." The sorceress' expression changed. She looked George in the eyes. "I won't lie ta ya, I'm still tryin' ta decide if everythin' you've told me is the truth."

George nodded his understanding. "Close your eyes, Shalee. I'll teleport us to Brandor. You won't doubt me after you've seen your husband rise from the dead. His Passing Ceremony is being held inside the arena. The king has ordered the Senate to attend, even the barbarian senators."

"King? How could there be a new king when I'm still alive?"

"Michael has temporarily taken Sam's place until you return. This is per your laws. Are you ready?"

"Please."

George reached down from his saddle. He had a special treat in store for the people sitting inside Brandor's arena. He touched Shalee on the shoulder. They reappeared within a bright light. The darkness of night amplified its magnificence. As the light faded, they were standing on top of the wooden tower which would burn during Sam's passing.

Mosley was on the far side of the platform. The wolf was visible to the mortals and listened as the crowd chastised their queen for the company she was keeping.

Michael jumped from the king's box and rushed to the top of the platform. He silenced the crowd, then turned to face Shalee. "What is the meaning of this?"

Shalee held up her hand. "I'll explain later. Stand down. Go back to your box."

From below the platform, standing unseen on the sand of the arena floor, Mieonus and Keylom looked up. They had agreed to allow Mosley to represent the gods during this event since the beings living in Brandor were already acquainted with the wolf.

Keylom spoke with Mieonus. "This is unexpected. What would Shalee be doing with George? I thought you were watching her?"

"I was. After she went into The Source's mountains, I could no longer see past the Ancient One's magic. My waterfall went dark."

Keylom shifted his weight. His hooves failed to leave an impression in the sand to keep the mortals from discovering his presence. "This will be interesting. The last appearance George made was devastating to our cause. We should call the others to witness this. Perhaps, Lasidious plans to make an appearance as well."

"Agreed, but you better call them, instead of me," Mieonus confided. "They won't come if I summon them."

The centaur lifted his head toward the sky, then shouted in a voice only the Book of Immortality could hear. When Gabriel appeared, Keylom asked the Book to summon the Collective. Gabriel did as requested and every god appeared, with the exception of Lasidious.

Seeing the gathering, Gabriel addressed Celestria. "Why isn't Lasidious with you?"

The goddess grinned. "You'll see. This night is about to become an event which will change lives on this world."

The Book's heavy brows furrowed. "What are you up to?"

Celestria's grin turned to a seductive smile. She reached out and caressed the Book's left cheek. "Watch and see."

Mosley moved across the wooden platform to speak with Shalee. "Why would you allow yourself to be seen with George? The people know of his treason. His company is beneath you."

Shalee knelt next to the wolf. "Mosley, if everythin' George has told me happens tonight, I'm afraid you and I will no longer be on speakin' terms. I can only hope you have not lied ta me."

"What? How could you possibly think I have lied?" Mosley looked up at George. He growled as he spoke. "What kind of deception is this?"

George began to methodically pick pieces of lint from his tunic. "Save your questions for someone who doesn't know the truth. Tonight, the one true god will grace Brandor with his presence and return life to their king. Sam will live again, and Grayham will know of Lasidious' generosity."

Mosley was taken aback. "Sam is dead. There is nothing the gods can do about it. Not even Lasidious has the power to retrieve a soul from the Book's pages."

The warlock dismissed the wolf, dismounted, then brushed past Mosley as he motioned for Kepler to join him next to Sam's casket. With each step George and the giant cat took toward the king's coffin, the crowd shouted curses.

Mosley looked at Shalee. "Why are you with George? He represents everything you loathe. How could you possibly be fooled by him? There is no way for Lasidious to return Sam's life."

Shalee sighed. "We'll know soon enough. If George is tellin' the truth, then I want ya ta leave me alone. Sam will feel the same way once I've explained everythin'."

"Why would I do that, Shalee? You are more than a queen speaking to a god. You are my friend. Have you forgotten?"

Shalee looked at the coffin. "We shall see if we're truly friends. If you've lied ta me, then there never was a friendship ta begin with, was there?"

Before anything else could be said, the air began to stir. The arena became a whirlwind of blowing sand, causing the spectators to cover their eyes. The platform and those on it were spared the current's effects as Lasidious appeared in a white robe.

When the atmosphere settled, the Mischievous One lowered his hood, then moved to the front of Sam's casket. Without a word, he lifted the lid, then reached inside. He pulled the dagger free from Sam's side—a task Mosley and Mieonus were unable to accomplish. Once finished, Lasidious leaned over and whispered into Sam's ear, "You didn't think I would allow you to perish again, my brother. Search your mind. Remember. Remember the moments of your past. Soon, we shall reclaim glory."

Lasidious lifted the dagger toward the sky and shouted in a voice which captivated every soul present. "Beings of Brandor! Witness the power of the one true god! I have breathed life into your king. Enjoy this blessing which only I can bestow!" Lasidious vanished.

Much of the crowd exploded with shouts of disbelief, others with shouts of joy, and yet others with a thousand questions. It was an emotional frenzy.

From the sand below, Mieonus screamed at Mosley from within her veil of invisibility. She spoke in a voice only the gods could hear. "Say something, wolf! The people need to hear you speak!"

Mosley looked down from the platform. "What would you have me say, Mieonus? Anything I say will make us look foolish. The people will wonder why I did not return Sam's life. I told them Sam would be well-received in the heavens. I told them Michael would make a fine king until the Senate could elect another. Again, I ask, what would you have me say?"

Mosley looked at Gabriel. He continued to speak in a voice only the gods could hear. "How was Lasidious able to retrieve Sam's soul from your pages?"

The Book replied, "I have been looking through my pages since our arrival. I am as shocked as you are. I did not know Sam was dead."

Hosseff added to their conversation. "I was unable to collect it to bring it to you. I have been searching for his soul since his death. Something is amiss."

"This looks bad for us," the wolf responded, shaking his head. "I have no idea what to say or how to turn this to our favor." Mosley redirected his attention as Shalee leaned over Sam's casket.

The queen witnessed the stab wound on Sam's side begin to close as the poison was forced from the king's body in a black puss. Tears filled her eyes as she realized George had spoken the truth. She would need to face the people of her kingdom, and let them know everything she had learned. She lifted Sam's hand and placed his palm across her face. She closed her eyes and enjoyed the warmth as it returned to his body. "Oh, Sam...I thought I had lost ya foreva'."

George mounted Kepler and took the opportunity to address the crowd. As he moved across the platform, he looked at Mosley and winked. He spoke to the wolf telepathically. *I hope you enjoy this pile of garesh I'm about to spew as much as I will. The people will no longer believe in you once I'm done. They'll believe in Lasidious. They will believe he is the one true god. They will glorify him and there's nothing the gods can do about it. Face it...you're screwed.*

Without waiting for Mosley to respond, George lifted his head and shouted to the audience. He used his magic to amplify his voice. "Beings of Southern Grayham...your king lives again! He lives because Lasidious loves him. The gods have lied to you. They have treated you like fools. They have no real power. Lasidious is the deity Grayham should worship."

Mosley shouted above him. "He lies! The gods love the beings of Grayham! You all know I am the god who has blessed this city. I blessed the union of your king and your queen. This man is a threat to you all."

Shalee had something to shout of her own. She also used her magic to amplify her voice. "Hear me, now! What the prophet of Lasidious speaks is the truth. The gods have lied ta us. Our king lives and his soul has been returned. When your king emerges from his casket, know this...there's no otha' with the power ta give life. I know this ta be true. I will no longer listen ta Lord Mosley."

The queen turned to face George. "I can't tell ya how much I appreciate ya openin' my eyes. I'm glad ya found your way and decided ta live a moral life." Without acknowledging the wolf, Shalee turned her attention back to Sam.

Mosley stood in astonishment as he listened to the crowd shout their questions. He couldn't believe Shalee's announcement. The people were confused, and many were now questioning their faith.

George looked at Mosley. Again, he spoke to the wolf without opening his mouth. *Even Shalee has bought into my line of garesh. I think the moment has come for you to go lick yourself someplace.*

Mosley responded with a few thoughts of his own. *I give you my word, George. I will find a way to destroy you before this is over.*

George rolled his eyes. *Yeah, yeah, yeah. Blah, blah, blah. You'll never find a way. You have too many rules. Your Book is your crutch. When I'm through, every soul on Grayham will worship Lasidious. Face it, Mosley... you've lost. The beings of this world will soon worship the one who couldn't care less if they live or die.*

Mosley replied with a forceful thought. *Do not be so sure! I will be coming for you soon. There will be no place you can hide."*

George shook his head. *Get out of my sight.*

Mosley sent a thought which echoed inside George's head. *I would watch my back if I were you.* The wolf vanished.

George felt a chill run down his spine. He had to gather his thoughts as he turned to look at the crowd. After a moment, he took a deep breath, then shouted for all to hear, "Only Lasidious loves his followers! It is this love which has given Southern Grayham their king. I am the prophet of Lasidious. Together, we can bring peace to all of Grayham. You can live your lives without fear of losing the ones you love to the ravages of war. Lasidious loves you...and I, the prophet of Lasidious, love you. I bid you all...goodnight!" Kepler roared, then they vanished.

The people erupted with cheers as Sam sat up inside his coffin. He grabbed his head and looked at Shalee. "What's going on? What's everyone screaming about?" He took a look at his environment. "Holy garesh! Were you going to burn me?"

Shalee started to laugh. "It's not as bad as it looks. I'll explain when we get home." After instructing Michael to see to it that the crowd dispersed, Shalee touched Sam on the shoulder, then teleported.

From below the platform, Celestria turned to the gods who remained invisible on the arena sand. "This has been a delightful event. I hope you have enjoyed your moments tonight." The goddess vanished.

Alistar spoke out after watching her depart. "Everyone, touch one another. This meeting needs to be protected from Lasidious' ears. There's nothing minor about what Lasidious has done...we all know this."

Once sure the circle was complete, Alistar continued. "Somehow, we need to stop Lasidious from gathering followers. We need to have a meeting of the gods. Gabriel, I request you summon everyone to this meeting. Have them come to the hall in the morning. I want to know how Lasidious gave

Sam his life back. I want to implement a new rule within your pages and vote on it. If what I'm thinking is correct, you need to make sure Lasidious and Celestria come to this meeting. We cannot vote to stop Lasidious from gaining more followers, but there's one rule we need to add to your pages."

Keylom responded, "What's on your mind, Alistar? And, how do you intend to make them come? They won't care about this meeting."

Bailem added, "I agree. Lasidious won't come. He has bigger plans."

Alistar pretended to think. "I'll explain everything in the morning. But, for now, Gabriel, let Lasidious' curiosity about this new rule be the reason he and Celestria attend the meeting. Make Lasidious feel as if there's mystery behind it. Make Lasidious think I have found a way to add a rule to your pages without using the Call to Order. All you have to do is give the Call to Order as soon as they arrive. They will be forced to stay for the meeting once the law governing the call is in effect. Let's manipulate Lasidious the way he has manipulated us." Alistar vanished.

Keylom looked at the others. "I'm impressed. Who would've guessed Alistar had a bit of mischief in him? Whatever he is planning, it is bound to make Lasidious angry. I say this is worth having a meeting for. I will tell Mosley about it." All the gods disappeared.

The Luvelles Gazette

When you want an update about your favorite characters

George and Kepler are standing outside the entrance to The Source's cave. They are waiting for Alistar. There are important matters to discuss.

Prior to leaving Grayham, George met with RJ, the Leather Guy, in Lethwitch. He asked RJ to make Athena another gift.

Athena is working with Payne to teach him table manners. Payne has been calling Athena, mother, despite being asked to call her by her first name. Athena plans to speak with George about his comment while in Kepler's lair that it was somehow okay for Payne to call him, dad. She is not happy about it.

Mary and Brayson have spent the day together after teleporting to Nept to retrieve more Mesolliff wine. They fell asleep, but only after Brayson enjoyed the benefits of Mary's intoxication.

Susanne and baby Garrin are inside Susanne's home. Garrin has just done something which frightened her. Susanne is about to go over to Mary's house to wake her mother and Brayson to talk about this latest development.

Boyafed plans to meet with the king of Hyperia, Kassel Hyperia, in the morning. Boyafed expects to add another 6,200 men to the dark army's numbers. He is also expecting resistance from Kassel.

Christopher, Boyafed's Argont Commander, has met with the Serwin King. The meeting went well. They will join the Order in battle.

Boyafed has ordered 400 scribes to create 10,400 Scrolls of Teleportation. They will be used to bring the mercenaries of Bestep and the army of Hyperia to the Battlegrounds of Olis. Many of the mercenaries command strong, defensive magic, but do not have the ability to teleport. This will allow the entire force supporting the dark army to arrive as a single unit instead of taking countless boats across the Ebarna Strait.

In total, just over 21,000 souls will fight for the dark army. This includes the army of Hyperia, the mercenaries of Bestep, the serwins of Shade Hollow, and the wizard, Balecut.

Lord Dowd is waiting for Krasous to return from the Spirit Plains. The army is ready to begin their march to the northern shore of Lake Tepp. They will make camp there and wait for the goswigs, the giants of the

Foot, the army of Lavan, and the wraith hounds of the Under Eye to arrive before continuing their march to the Battlegrounds of Olis. In total, the white army will number just over 19,800.

Krasous, Lord Dowd's Argont Commander, has found the Spirit King, Shesolaywen.

Strongbear has once again taken charge of the underground village of Gogswayne. Each goswig has been ordered to report to the surface and line up on the shore of Crystal Lake for inspection in the morning.

Marcus has arrived on Grayham. Brayson set up Marcus' trip with the Merchant Angels as George requested.

Lasidious and Celestria are inside their home beneath the Peaks of Angels. Gabriel has requested to speak with them.

Keylom is standing in front of Mosley's cabin high atop Catalyst Mountain. The wolf is distraught.

Thank you for reading the Luvelles Gazette

A Sacrifice of Immortality

Alistar appeared outside The Source's cave where George and Kepler were waiting. The warlock was leaning against Fisgig's perch when Lasidious' brother showed up. He appeared with his back to them and did not acknowledge either of them. Instead, he lifted his head to take a deep breath.

George gave Kepler a look and without opening his mouth, spoke to the cat. *Great. Just what we need...another pain in the ass to deal with. He thinks we're beneath him.*

Kepler returned a thought of his own. *Watch what you say. We have no idea if he can listen to our thoughts.*

Garesh. I should've thought of that.

George tapped Alistar on the shoulder. "It looks like the moment has come for us to get to know one another. I have to admit, I hated not being able to speak with all the players of this game of ours."

Alistar turned around after looking the area over. "It has been many seasons since the last moment I came to these mountains. I should speak with The Source while I'm here."

Kepler growled, "Hello to you, too."

"Yeah," George added. "Holy garesh, Alistar. Is that how you greet everyone? You didn't even say hi, kiss my ass, pack sand, shove it, or anything remotely close to a damn greeting. Come on, man, you can do better than that. I don't want to work with you if you're going to be a jerk."

Alistar had to smile. "My brother said he enjoys your humor. I can see why he likes you, George. You are direct."

George nodded. "Would you have it any other way?"

"I suppose not." Alistar walked over to Kepler, grabbed a handful of fur, then shook it. "Amazing. The power surging through your veins has even improved your appearance. Are you pleased?"

A look of disgust appeared on Kepler's face. "You say it as if I was repulsive before. You're not good at dealing with the beings on the worlds, are you?"

Alistar released his grip. "Nonsense." He looked at George. "The moments have come to finish what has been started. Lasidious will no longer be able to communicate with you in your dreams. In his absence, I will deliver his messages. The gods are watching him now, more than ever. They don't know of our kinship, so this gives us the advantage."

"You've got to love an advantage," George responded. "So, were things nuts after I left Brandor?"

"Yes. You've done a remarkable job. The beings on Southern Grayham will be questioning their loyalty to the gods they serve. Mosley will be the one who is affected most. With the way Keldwin embraced the wolf before his death, and with the way Sam exalted Mosley during his wedding, the people naturally began to worship him. It was a smooth transition. But, now that the people believe Lasidious has returned life to their king, their beliefs will falter once word of this miracle has spread. A few more visits by Lasidious' prophet should do the trick."

George began to laugh. "I think you mean Lasidious' false prophet."

"False or not, the people will listen to you."

George thought a moment. "I have an idea. Athena and I will visit Grayham. I'll implement the rest of Lasidious' plan while we're there and take her on a trip down memory lane."

"I'm sure Athena will enjoy herself." Alistar began to pace. "There are plans to make. We need to speak of your future visit to Harvestom."

Ancients Sovereign

Gabriel was able to appear inside Lasidious and Celestria's home once Celestria agreed to allow the Book to enter. After lowering his heavy binding to the table within their cave-like home, Gabriel spent a few moments talking with Celestria about the pleasant feel of her decor while they waited for Lasidious to join them.

Eventually, the Mischievous One walked out of the bedroom and took a seat at the table. "Welcome to our home, Gabriel. I'm sure you have questions. But, before you ask them, let me save you the breath it takes to utter the words. I won't answer them. My secrets are mine to keep."

The Book allowed a smile to appear across his face. "I am not here to ask questions, Lasidious. You have broken no laws. Whether I have an understanding of your accomplishments or not, doesn't matter. You have the free will to do what you wish...as long as the laws of the Collective are not violated."

Celestria decided to respond. "Then, this is a social visit. I should create something to drink. Would you like some cold ale?"

"Or, perhaps some nasha," Lasidious added.

The Book lifted his right hand and waved off the offer. "I'm not here for pleasantries. I have come to let you know the others intend to call a meeting of the gods. It will be held in the morning."

Lasidious chuckled. "We will not be attending this meeting. It doesn't pertain to something I can manipulate. I have no desire to listen to the Collective babble."

The Book lifted from the table, then floated closer to Lasidious before lowering back to the table's surface. "I knew you would feel this way. This is why I have come to tell you that Alistar has informed me of a loophole he claims to have found within my laws. He believes he won't need you to be present to invoke the Call to Order."

"What? I know of no such loophole. How's this possible, Gabriel? Have you searched your pages to find this oversight?"

"I have done nothing other than come to you. If Alistar says he intends to vote, then you might want to figure out how he intends to do this."

Lasidious leaned forward and looked the Book in the eyes. "This is a trick. Why would you help them?"

Gabriel floated from the table. After creating a comfortable distance, he responded. "Everything I have said is what Alistar told the Collective. You can do as you wish. You have been warned." The Book vanished.

Mosley's Cabin
Late Bailem has Come and Gone

Night had swallowed the opulent valleys below Mosley's home. Keylom appeared in the darkness near the cabin. A crystal orb, mounted to the right of the door, shed enough light for Keylom to view the structure. The centaur could see the wolf sleeping in his usual spot at the top of the porch steps.

Even from where he stood, Keylom could hear Mosley's distress as the wolf whimpered in his sleep. Mosley was reliving his confrontation with George.

Keylom approached in silence to avoid startling his sleeping friend. The closer he got, the more he noticed the mess surrounding Mosley's body. The wolf's shedding had clung to the wooden planks, and his prized spot at the top of the steps was covered to the point it was almost as black as his coat.

Keylom cleared his throat to capture the wolf's attention. "Mosley, perhaps, you should tidy this porch. It's a mess."

Mosley lifted to his feet, stretched, then sat on his haunches. He used his back right paw to scratch his neck. Fur fell to the porch and added to the accumulation. When finished, he looked around. "What mess are you referring to? I see nothing to tidy."

Keylom chuckled. "I suppose you wouldn't." Seeing it was pointless to argue, the centaur changed the subject. "You were bound to be the brunt of one of Lasidious' schemes. All of us have been on one occasion or another. But, the Collective needs you to have a clear head if we're going to stop Lasidious from recruiting the followers necessary to control the Book."

Mosley jumped from the porch and began to pace. His thoughts took him away from the cabin and into the darkness before returning to the light cast by the orb. Keylom said nothing as he waited for Mosley to work through his anxiety.

Eventually, Mosley stopped in front of the centaur. "I cannot express the depth of my anger. I see no way for the gods to fight Lasidious. We are bound by ridiculous rules. We have lost the power to act as gods. Prior to Bassorine's destruction, I believed him to be the grandest pack leader of all, but now, I see the truth. The gods forfeited all that sets them apart from mortals."

Keylom scuffed the earth beneath his right front hoof. "You simplify the gods' importance. You cannot lose heart."

Mosley growled. "I should have killed George while I had the chance."

"You know the consequences of breaking this law," Keylom rebutted.

"Being a god is not worth my immortality."

"You don't mean that, Mosley. Things may seem difficult at the moment, but they will get better. Of all the gods, you have the wit to outsmart Lasidious. Bassorine had to know this when he planned for you to take his spot within the Collective. He wasn't stupid, no matter how Lasidious made him look. Perhaps, you should think like Lasidious. You can beat him at his own game."

Mosley walked away from the cabin. He crouched to relieve himself. As he did, he responded. "Thinking like Lasidious is why I have come to an important conclusion." He turned, sniffed the pile, then returned to the cabin and plopped onto the porch. "George is able to use telepathy now. He said something while projecting his thoughts." Mosley balled up and began to gnaw at the fur on the inside of his left rear leg.

"Mosley, clearly you're out of sorts. Your actions are unpleasant and your thoughts are scattered. Focus. What does George have to do with your conclusion?" Keylom's hooves scuffed the grass as he shuffled to a better position. "What are you thinking?"

"George's words echo inside my head. His words were, 'Face it, Mosley…you've lost. The beings of this world will soon worship the one who couldn't care less if they live or die.'" Mosley lowered his head to the porch. "Those words haunt me. If those who worship me withdraw their service and offer it to Lasidious, then there is no reason for me to stay on Ancients Sovereign. My position within the Collective would be pointless."

Without waiting for a response, the wolf lifted his head toward the sky and called for Gabriel. When the Book arrived, he continued. "Gabriel, I need you to protect our conversation. Everything discussed shall be under the Rule of Fromalla."

The Book nodded and looked at the centaur. "Do you wish for Keylom to hear?"

"I do."

The Book waited for Keylom to acknowledge the rule, then waved his arm to create an environment of privacy. "We may speak without worry."

Mosley stood from his hair-covered place of comfort, then paced along the length of the porch. "I want to know how I can return to my mortal life, and keep the power necessary to go after George."

"What?" Keylom was flabbergasted. "You're willing to give up your immortality to seek vengeance on a mortal? You can't do this. It's against our laws."

Mosley stopped pacing. "The laws are the problem. They are the reason I wish to return to my old life."

Keylom admonished Mosley. "Your question has no solution. You must cleanse your mind of such foolishness."

Mosley held the centaur's stare for a long series of moments, then addressed Gabriel. "The laws written on your pages have loopholes. Lasidious manages to find them. I intend to find one. If I do not do something, George will turn the people of the worlds into a massive congregation of Lasidious' followers. Someone must stop him. Shalee's power is not growing fast enough. I will kill George, and you will be forced to return me to my mortal life."

The Book's heavy eyebrows furrowed. "There is a problem with your conclusion. If you break the rule of the gods which speaks of killing mortals, you know I would be forced to destroy your spirit. As a god, killing George would sacrifice not only your existence, but your soul. You would not find your way onto my pages."

The Book lifted his hand to his chin in thought. "As you know, there are many rules which prohibit a god from choosing a mortal life."

Mosley howled. "There must be a way. We just need to find it. Gabriel, find the loophole."

Keylom insisted, "There is no way. The gods voted on this long ago. We were careful to ensure every angle was covered. The laws pertaining to this matter had to be specific."

"Not every angle," Gabriel retorted. "There may be a way."

Keylom couldn't believe his ears. "Gabriel, you're unable to choose a side. How can you do this? We were careful when we voted these laws into effect. You're bound by them just as we are."

"Yes, but there is one law which supersedes them all. This law requires me to ensure the gods' laws remain superior to the desires of a single deity. This means, I'm to assume any role necessary to keep them sacred. I only need to be mindful of free will. This is the only law which I cannot supersede. Mosley's desire to become mortal could help the Collective protect the laws from Lasidious' manipulations."

The Book floated over to the porch and lowered onto the railing to avoid Mosley's hair. "I am no fool. I know Lasidious seeks to control me."

Keylom cut in. "But, this doesn't mean you can make Mosley mortal. Not even you can assume that Mosley's mortality would stop Lasidious."

The Book frowned. "Perhaps, you're right. But, there is another way."

Keylom tugged at the vest covering his torso. "I'm listening."

The Book looked down at Mosley. "The gods were careful how they voted to restrict the members of the Collective from choosing mortality. But, they were not so diligent when voting on what is to happen when a god is punished. They voted to give the punished a last request. They even implemented a law to keep the punished from requesting a return to immortality. They assumed the members of the Collective were old enough the consequences of being made mortal would cause the punished to die within days. They assumed further governing wasn't necessary since the punished would not have the moments to retaliate. The Collective's failure to restrict my judgment when administering punishment is the loophole you are looking for. You could use this to your advantage."

The Book hesitated, then continued. "Before I explain further, I must request one thing. This is something to which I will hold you accountable."

Mosley tilted his furry head. "What would this request be?"

"You can never speak of your knowledge of the gods to anyone who doesn't already possess this knowledge. If you do, I'll be forced to extinguish your existence. I want you to give this promise, or I won't divulge anything further. As you know, a god's promise...if broken...is enforceable by death. You'll make this promise to me before you become mortal. I will kill you if you break it. Mortal or not...I'll torture your soul for lying to me before I devour your spirit and spit it into the darkness of space. You will wander the darkness in misery, cursed. No one will find you for all eternity. Do we have an agreement?"

Mosley and Keylom were stunned by the Book's harshness. The tone Gabriel used was something far more serious than Keylom had ever heard the Book use before.

The wolf thought for a fair amount of moments before responding. "I will strike this accord. Can you grant my mortality and salvage my power?"

Gabriel's face filled with regret. "I cannot allow you to return with the power necessary to kill George. To do so would affect the balance of power on not only the worlds, but also Ancients Sovereign. You must seek the power to destroy him. I must also limit your memories. What is true about the gods will remain, but your memories which would allow you to affect the free will of others must be removed. This power must be earned, not given.

"Since Bassorine gave you an extended life before your ascension, I will restore this blessing. You won't age as the others of the Collective would."

Mosley spoke up, "Will I have any power at all, or will I be restricted to my natural abilities?"

Gabriel searched for the answer. "You will possess your natural abilities. You will also possess power, but to what extent, I cannot be certain. Messing with one's magical foundation is tricky...even for the gods. Magic is bigger than we are. It's far easier to build upon one's foundation, than to tear it down."

Mosley's head tilted as a wolf's would. "I do not understand. How can magic be bigger than the gods?"

The Book grabbed his chin again, in thought. "I will not answer your question."

Keylom rebutted, "You will not, or cannot?"

The Book frowned. "I did not mispeak. I will not answer his question. I will not speak more of this." Gabriel looked at Mosley. "I only know the power you will possess will not be enough to defeat George. It will be up to you to rebuild your foundation while acquiring the power necessary to face him. Are you certain you want to do this?"

Mosley thought of the consequences. There would be no coming back if he changed his mind. After a long series of moments, he responded. "I am sure. This is what I want. I want you to make sure Lasidious does not have knowledge of my mortality. I want to seek the power I need to defeat George without Lasidious sending his puppet after me before I am ready to face him. I want you to send me to the Siren's Song. I will start my journey there." The wolf paused. "Gabriel, will you allow me to save my last request for a moment in which I wish to use it?"

Keylom stomped his right, front hoof on the ground. "This is insane! Mosley, you're making a big mistake! What happens when the gods gather in the morning? When Gabriel gives the Call to Order, and you're not present, they'll know something is up."

"You're right, my absence will be an issue. My presence is necessary for Gabriel to give the call." Mosley looked at the Book. "Gabriel, you may have my vote to do as you please. This will allow you to give the call, and excuse my absence." He looked at Keylom. "You could help me on my journey."

Keylom reared onto his hind legs. "I have no desire to become mortal. I won't go with you, nor will I help you when trouble finds you."

Mosley grinned. "I do not need you to go with me. I need you to be my eyes and ears on Ancients Sovereign. I want you to give me guidance, the same way Lasidious has given George guidance. We shall fight fire with fire."

Keylom pondered the wolf's proposal as he stared into the light of the orb. "This would provide entertainment. I would enjoy seeing George's downfall. I can also imagine the surprise on Lasidous' face. I will help you."

The Book took control of the conversation. "Mosley, you must break one of the god's laws. I'll do the rest. With your absence on Ancients Sovereign, there will be two gods I need to replace. Yaloom was so full of himself he failed to give me the name of the one who was to take his place. Mosley, you have also failed to speak of the one who will replace you. Do you have a name?"

Without hesitation, the wolf responded. "Shalee."

"I cannot. Nor, can I give it to Sam. Lasidious had the foresight to see to it this would not be allowed. Lasidious felt Bassorine was up to something. A Call to Order was given and the Collective voted against their ascension."

"Damn!" Mosley chuckled. "Lasidious is truly clever. Gabriel, you may choose for me. Choose someone you trust to do a good job. How long can you wait before you must introduce my replacement to the others?"

Gabriel lifted from the porch and hovered eye level with the wolf. "This is not for you to worry about. I see no urgency in finding your replacement."

Mosley jumped from the porch. "When Lasidious asks where I am, tell him I have decided to go away for a while. Say I do not care about his game, and I will not be back until I find myself. It would be best to let him think you have no idea where I went. Tell Lasidious I said this: I do not want him or the others looking for me. I have gone to look for the elements necessary to create my own world. This should throw him off."

The Book thought long and hard for many moments. "I will explain what you have said. For now, I want you to attack Keylom. Then, I will do my job to make you mortal."

"No!" Keylom snapped as he backed up. "I don't want the wolf attacking me."

Gabriel smiled. "That's why it will work. It's not wanted. You can take Mosley to Grayham and leave him at the entrance to Siren's Song. The wisp will find him when the moment is right. Just make sure Lasidious isn't paying attention when you leave."

Gabriel floated down the steps, then lowered next to the wolf. He reached out and put his hand on top of the wolf's head. "I hope you succeed, Mosley. You'll be vulnerable to the people of the worlds, and we won't be able to protect you."

The wolf nodded, then took one last look at the cabin. After taking a final breath of the clean air surrounding the peak of Catalyst Mountain, he attacked Keylom without saying a word.

The Head Master's Island
Susanne's Home
That Same Night

Susanne hurried out the front door of her home with Garrin in her arms. She was pale, nervous and scared half to death. She pounded on Mary's door and didn't stop until Brayson answered.

When the door opened, Brayson's eyes looked exhausted. He wasn't wearing a shirt. The evening had been quite the affair, and the affects of the Mesolliff wine had left him begging for sleep. "What is it, Susanne? What's so urgent?"

Susanne pushed past Brayson, then set Garrin on the living room floor. He's got the magic in him!"

Brayson queried, "What do you mean?"

Susanne continued to shout, "He's got the magic! He made my goblet float around the kitchen! The boy isn't normal!"

Garrin began to cry at the sound of his mother's tone. Brayson laughed.
"What's so funny?" Susanne barked.

Mary was making her way down the steps after putting on her robe.
"What on Luvelles is all the commotion about?"

Brayson picked up the baby. "It's nothing. Nothing's wrong. Susanne's
just scared because she doesn't understand why Garrin has the ability to
command magic. This is quite the gift, if you ask me. To be showing signs
of power so soon after birth is rare."

Mary moved to stand next to Brayson. She played with Garrin's cheeks
to encourage the child to smile. She wasn't bothered by the revelation of the
baby's power. "This is good. I think a man with magic is sexy. My grandson
will grow up to be as dashing as you are."

Susanne was floored at their lack of concern. She continued to shout,
"How could a child of mine have the ability to use magic? I don't have it!"
She pointed to Garrin. "So, how could he have it? This doesn't make sense!"

Brayson put his hand on Garrin's pointed ears. "I imagine the power
comes from the elf you were with. I wanted to ask you about it, but I felt it
improper. What was the elf's name you pleasured during the baby's conception? Perhaps, he was one of the men who escorted the Order's council to
Grayham."

Susanne was taken aback. "I cannot remember pleasuring any man."

Brayson placed his hand under Garrin's chin, then lifted his head to kiss
his forehead. He responded while smiling at Garrin. "Clearly, your mother's
memory of your father is not necessary for your birth." He gave Mary the
baby. "You know, now that I think about it, there were two other groups who
visited the kingdoms of the ice kings on Northern Grayham during the period of his conception. Perhaps, someone took liberty on their way back and
ended up in your town. It could only be one of 30 men, though it would be
hard to imagine it being a member of the white army. It is, after all, against
elven custom to leave a woman in this condition without taking care of their
responsibility. Perhaps, he did not know he left you with child."

Susanne sat on one of the chairs in the room. "How could I have forgotten something like this? I know I didn't lie with thirty elves, that's for sure.
I am not a whore."

Mary touched the points of Garrin's ears. "I want to know why we never
noticed his ears were pointed until now. How is this possible?"

Susanne added, "I have not even thought about his father. How could
I not remember who he is? How could I be so awful? I wonder if George
knows who he is. Are there any elves living on Grayham?"

Brayson shook his head. "There are none that I know of. George will be back soon. I will tell Athena to have George come to us when he arrives."

Susanne

Mary spoke. "Why look for the father. We're doing fine without him. If he doesn't care to keep in touch, then he's not worth the hassle."

Susanne gasped, "Mother. I need to know. How can I go through life without allowing Garrin to know his father? We must make the effort to do what's right."

Mary handed Brayson the baby, then took a seat beside Susanne. She placed her hand on her daughter's knee. "What if the answer is something you don't wish to hear? What if he doesn't want to be a part of the baby's life?"

Susanne rebutted. "But, what if he doesn't know he left a baby behind? If he doesn't want to be with us, then at least we've done what's right. I'll be able to tell Garrin the truth. I'll have a clear conscience."

Brayson sat Garrin on the floor. "Until we figure this out, we should celebrate. My future grandson is going to command strong magic. I've never known a child to show power this early."

A moment later, George walked through the door. He put his staff in the corner, then turned to face everyone. "Sup, guys? Why are you up so late? Where's Athena?" Kepler poked his head in, then took a seat in the entryway. The cat's body consumed the foyer.

Susanne rushed across the room and gave George a hug. "I'm glad you're here."

The warlock looked at Mary with questioning eyes. Brayson motioned for George to sit. He pried Susanne's arms off of him, then took a seat. "So, what's the deal?"

Brayson responded. "Susanne cannot remember who Garrin's father is. I assume he must be from Luvelles."

George hung his head.

Now...fellow soul...George knew this day would come. Knowing the name of Garrin's father was the only incomplete part of the vision Maldwin gave to the family. Before traveling to Luvelles, George had no knowledge of its inhabitants, so picking a name was impossible. Because of this, he had to wait to address the problem with Lasidious. A solution was provided during his last dream. He now knew the name of an elf who had journeyed to Grayham, and as luck would have it, this person recently perished.

George kept his head lowered and waited for someone to pry.

Susanne could see George had bad news. "What is it? Tell me."

George sighed. "I don't know if it's bad or good. Maybe Brayson can tell us the answer. Dayden is the name of the man who impregnated you."

Brayson walked across the room and lowered onto the couch. "George, how do you know this?"

"Lasidious told me."

Brayson lowered his head into the palms of his hands. Mary could see the disappointment in his eyes. She moved to take a seat next to him.

As Mary walked across the room, George looked at Kepler and communicated telepathically. *Can you believe this pile of garesh? I'm glad we got here when we did.*

You're evil, George. That's why I like you.

Awwww...thanks, big guy. I'm touched. Remind me to give you a hug later.
Don't start that again. Keep your hands off me or I'll tell them the truth.
Ha! You love me, and you know it. George looked away and waited for Brayson to tell the girls what was on his mind.

Brayson looked up. "Dayden was Boyafed's Argont Commander. He was one of the men who went to Grayham to visit the ice kings. He was a powerful elf."

"What do you mean, 'was?'" Mary said as she looked at Susanne's distraught face.

"News of Dayden's death reached my office. This was one of the reasons why Boyafed called for war."

George took a moment to act as if he didn't know who Boyafed was. "Are you referring to the dark army leader?"

"Yes. Dayden was also Boyafed's friend. If Dayden was the father of your baby, Susanne, then there is nothing we can do to include him in Garrin's life."

Susanne began to cry. Garrin watched as his mother's tears fell. He lifted from the floor and floated over to sit next to her. Mary and Susanne became nervous as they watched the baby lower to the tile-covered surface.

George pushed clear of his seat. "Since when did Garrin start using magic?" Without waiting for an answer, he motioned for Brayson to follow him outside, then walked toward the door. As the warlock squeezed past Kepler, he grabbed his staff, then sent the cat a thought. *Stay here and keep the ladies busy. This is bad, Kep. This is not the best moment for Garrin to start showing his power.*

Kepler returned a thought. *You don't want to talk where they can hear you.*

Agreed.

Mary looked at Brayson after watching George leave. "What's wrong with him?"

Brayson stood to follow. "I don't know. I will let you know upon my return."

George waited for Brayson to exit. As the Head Master shut the door, George reached out and touched his shoulder. When they reappeared, they were outside The Source's cave. George tapped the butt of his staff on the ground. Light began to emanate from the gem resting at its top and provided warmth for the shirtless Brayson.

"George, why are you acting so strange?"

After taking a deep breath, the warlock replied. "We can't do the things we need to if we are constantly worrying about Garrin. The magic he used is powerful, and we both know it. He has not even reached his first season."

George moved to the edge of the water surrounding Fisgig's island. "We cannot concentrate on bringing peace to Luvelles if we are spending our moments watching the baby. He could unintentionally hurt the family."

Believing George to be correct, Brayson nodded. "What should we do about it? He's a baby. We can't tell him not to use his power."

George pondered. "Can't we use our power to put up some kind of magical barrier or something? We just need to buy the moments to do the things our lord has asked us to."

Brayson pulled at his goatee. "I suppose you're right. It would be hard to monitor the baby. And, the women are unable to defend against his magic. I do have a potion we could use. It will restrict his ability to use his power for nearly a season."

"Damn!"

"What's wrong?"

"A season is too long. What else can we do?"

Confused, Brayson responded, "Why would a season be considered too long?"

George thought to himself, *Because I need Garrin to be ready when Lasidious decides to take control of the Book. I want my Abbie back.* A moment later, George responded. "I think to bind his power for so many moments seems a bit excessive, that's all."

Brayson, still not understanding, shrugged. "I could always lower the dosage to cut the days by half. But, he's young, and a season is a short series of moments to bind his power."

George moved away from the water and leaned against Fisgig's perch. "I hear what you're saying, but I think we should have more control over Garrin's growth. I think half a season should work. We can always give him more if we need to. Where's the potion?"

"My office. I will go get it. I'll give it to the child tonight."

George smiled, then put his hand on Brayson's shoulder. "This is good. We must bring peace to Luvelles before we can deal with Garrin's power. I will explain everything to the ladies while you grab the potion. How much crazier can things get around here?"

Brayson started to laugh. "I don't know. Since I've met you, there hasn't been a dull moment. I can only imagine what's next." Brayson vanished.

Later that night, after Garrin's power was bound, and everyone was in bed and sound asleep, Lasidious appeared to Brayson. All the Head Master could see was the god's silhouette since Lasidious was surrounded by a bright light. Brayson crawled out of bed and took a knee. "My Lord, how may I serve you?"

Mary began to stir. As she opened her eyes, she screamed. Lasidious allowed her to shout until Brayson could calm her. Once she too was kneeling, the Mischievous One spoke. "Mary, I am the god your future husband serves. I have come to speak of your union. I will bless it when the day comes to take his hand and declare your vows. I shall give you a gift…one which will give you long-lived happiness."

Brayson responded. "Thank you, My Lord, but what do you mean by 'long-lived?'"

The silhouette disappeared as Lasidious allowed himself to be seen. He spoke to the room, "Illuminate." He reached out and touched Mary on the head. "I am here to bless you. You shall live a life equal to the length of your husband, and your womb shall be restored."

Neither Brayson nor Mary could believe their ears as the Head Master touched his forehead to Lasidious' feet. "This is truly a blessing we both shall cherish."

Lasidious lifted Brayson from the floor. He cupped the back of Brayson's neck and pulled him close. "Are you ready to live in service?"

"I am, My Lord."

"You will know when the moment is right to perform this next task. What you will need to do is…"

The Spirit Plains

Krasous, Lord Dowd's Argent Commander, has found the Spirit King, Shesolaywen. Krasous is near exhaustion from running naked through the plains to avoid being possessed. He has had to use his magic to see in the darkness.

After putting some distance between himself and the spirit, Krasous jumped on top of a boulder and began shouting the spell's words he memorized from the Scroll of Conair. He finished without a moment to spare, saving himself from being devoured. He watched as Shesolaywen disappeared into the parchment of the scroll.

Krasous fell to the ground, shaken. He spoke to himself while he fought to steady his hands. "I do not wish to see another angry spirit." He rubbed his arms to remove the goosebumps. "Only one more season until I can retire my commission." He closed his eyes. When he reappeared, he was standing next to the tree where he had tethered his spirit-bull.

After putting on his clothes, Krasous grabbed Hellzgat's reigns. The spirit-bull materialized, allowing the commander to put the scroll into the saddle's pouch. "I hope Lord Dowd appreciates this, old boy." Hellzgat snorted as Krasous teleported onto his back.

Southern Grayham
Sam and Shalee's Bedroom Chamber
That Same Night

Sam was irritated as he paced across the stones of his bedroom floor as Shalee lay in bed watching him. Sam refused to take his spot next to her. "Look! I hear what you're saying, but I don't believe it. I don't believe Lasidious is the one you should serve...especially with George involved. I can't believe you would tell the people you knew George was speaking the truth. What's wrong with you? First, you cheat on me, and now, you want to serve a god you know nothing about. Have you become dense?"

"That's not fair," Shalee snapped. "Ya didn't see what I saw. I saw Lasidious return your soul, even afta' Mosley said it couldn't be done. You, mister, were a goner. I felt your skin. It was like ice in my hands. The people watched Lasidious give ya your life back...just like I did, mind ya. Ya would've done the same thing if ya had been in my situation."

Sam plopped into a chair across the room. "Believe me, I'm glad to be alive. But, I don't believe for a moment Lasidious has the power to return someone's soul. He has tricked the people."

Shalee grunted her frustration. "Well, if it's a trick...then it's a purdy good one."

"So, you keep saying." Sam stood from the chair, walked across the room and sat on the hearth of the fireplace to warm his back. "What about the potion Yaloom gave you? Have you been able to recall any of his memories?"

"No. I don't think it worked. I don't feel anythin' has changed. Maybe, he was wrong."

Sam slapped his hand on his knee. "Or, maybe, you're too stupid to handle it. Maybe, you're not smart enough to retrieve his memories."

Shalee sat up and found Sam's eyes. "I have already apologized for hurtin' ya. Stop bein' such a jerk. I was wrong, and I hate m'self for it. If ya want me ta leave, then just say so. I don't have ta sit here and keep bein' chastised. Make your choice, and do it now. Do I stay, and ya forgive me, or do I go? If I go, I will neva' talk ta ya again? I won't live like this."

Sam stood and moved to the window. After taking a deep breath, he turned to find his queen waiting. "You should go. The thought of what you did makes me sick."

"Fine!" Shalee threw back the covers, crawled out of bed, grabbed Precious, then stormed out of the room. Her bare feet slapped against the stones of the floor with exclamation marks as she went.

After watching her leave, Sam moved across the room. He opened a chest at the foot of their bed, then lifted the other half of Yaloom's potion. He allowed the light of the torch, hanging on the wall, to pass through its pale blue liquid. His thoughts ran wild. *What secrets are hidden inside you? Why isn't Shalee remembering the things Yaloom said she would? I need to know the truth. I need to know his mind now, not later. Does your potion hold the answers?*

Sam removed the lid and put the vial under his nose to see if it had an odor. Kael's blade began to pulsate as it hung on Sam's hip. "Drink it, Sam. Drink it. The answers are a swallow away."

Sam lowered the potion, secured the lid, then unsheathed Kael. He lifted the blade in front of his face. "I promised I would save it for Yaloom. To drink it would be wrong."

Kael responded. "His memories will give you the answers you seek. He doesn't need them to live again. You can keep your promise. Once you have the nasha, you can use it on Yaloom's corpse, but drink what you have. Keep the memories of the fallen and his power for yourself. You deserve it."

Sam shook his head. "I can't go back on my word." He lowered the blade to the bed, then took a seat. "How did we get here, Kael?"

Again, Kael's blade pulsated, "Drink the potion, and you'll know."

Sam's face grew stern. "I won't hear another word of it. Now, be quiet."

The sword did as instructed. Sam's eyes began to trace the spaces between the stones of the floor. *Okay, okay. Think, Sam. Do you really want to save your marriage? Can you look at Shalee and feel the same love you did before she betrayed you?*

But, you want to see Sam Jr. live again. You want to see him smile when she holds him. She was going through a lot when she cheated. But, so were you. What gives her the right? How would she react if you did the same thing? Would she forgive you? You should be allowed to walk away without feeling guilty.

The king clenched his fists and looked up at the ceiling. *Come on, Sam! You're better than this. Mom and dad raised you to be better. Carrying around this anger isn't going to help. It'll eat you up inside. It doesn't matter how Shalee would react. It doesn't matter if she would forgive you or not. It only matters how you react. You're the one who's been put in this position. If you don't forgive her, how could you expect her to forgive you when you do something stupid? Granted, you wouldn't do this to anyone, but...damn it, Sam...pull your head out. Are you going to forgive her or not? It's simple... YES or NO.*

After many long moments, Sam stood from the side of the bed and left the room. When he found Shalee, his voice was filled with the softness the queen longed to hear. "I thought I would find you here. To your beauty, the garden pales in comparison."

The queen recognized the difference in his tone. "Why did ya come? Ya just booted me outta your life. Ya sent me packin'."

Sam shook his head. "I don't want to talk. I want to forgive."

Shalee turned her back to him. "Ya can't just take it back. I wanna be left alone. I'll be gone in the mornin'."

The king reached out and pulled the queen into his arms. With her back against his chest and the light of her staff setting the mood, he whispered into her ear, "I love you, Shalee."

Shalee pretended to struggle, but Sam's arms kept her close. The king spun her around. "I said I love you, Shalee."

Seeing the look in his eyes, she melted. "I love you too, Sammy-kins. I'm so sorry."

Sam put a finger across Shalee's lips. "Shhhh. You don't need to say anything. The fight is over. Let's move forward, and never talk about it again." He took her by the hand and led her to one of the benches scattered throughout the garden. Once seated, he cupped her face. "I will always love you."

Their lips met. It didn't take long before Sam felt his passion return. The intensity grew with each kiss. He lifted her from the bench to carry her inside. The kissing continued as he began to walk. Only four steps were taken before they vanished to their bedroom.

Titans

Ancients Sovereign
The Hall of Judgment

The next morning, the gods were beginning to gather inside Gabriel's hall. Jervaise was the first to arrive. She entered in her spherical form. Once near her seat, she transformed into an apparition before taking her normal position at the marble table.

It wasn't long before the others began to arrive. As usual, Keylom's hooves clapped against the floor while Bailem walked through the doors with his wings folded behind his portly body. Lictina's tail swished across the floor until she reached her seat. The lizardian lifted her tail, then tucked it through a special opening which had been cut into her chair to allow her to sit in a comfortable position. As always, Lasidious was the last to arrive with Celestria on his arm.

The Mischievous One noticed right away there was someone missing. "Gabriel, where's Mosley?"

The Book lifted from the table and floated to a position eye level with Lasidious. "Mosley has grown tired of your games. He left and won't be back. Your theatrics on Grayham have caused him to seek solitude."

Lasidious frowned. "Where did he go? I should apologize."

Gabriel's thick brows furrowed. "He doesn't want you to know."

"He's up to something, and you're covering for him."

Gabriel floated back to his spot. As he did, he responded, "You could always track him when he decides to use his power."

Lasidious flopped in his chair. "Well, this is unexpected. I would not have thought the wolf to be a quitter. If he doesn't want to be found, I'm sure he knows not to use his power."

Keylom interjected. "Mosley did say he intends to create his own world. He intends to gather the elements necessary to create a world of beings to worship him. There is, after all, nothing in our laws to prohibit this."

"Now, that sounds more like my Mosley." Lasidious chuckled and looked at Celestria. "I knew the wolf was up to something. I love that wolf. Nothing is going to bring him down...not even me."

Bailem stood from his chair. "I would like to know how you returned Sam's soul? How could you manipulate such an event? You do not possess the power."

"Sam's name was never added to my pages," Gabriel responded.

Bailem replied, confused. "Explain."

Gabriel shrugged. His little shoulders protruded from the sides of his covers. He pointed at Lasidious. "Ask him, not me."

Lasidious leaned over to kiss Celestria on the cheek before standing. "I trapped Sam's soul within the blade of an Order dagger. I visited with Boyafed and asked him to kill Sam."

Hosseff lifted from his chair. The shade's wispy voice emanated from the nothingness beneath his hood. "Boyafed would not do this. He serves me and no other."

Lasidious allowed himself to fall back into his chair. "You're right. But, Boyafed thought he was doing your will...not mine. I appeared to him in your image. I requested he use this special dagger to deliver the killing blow. The blade trapped Sam's soul and didn't allow it to ascend onto Gabriel's pages. Mieonus' affair with Boyafed could not have come at a better moment." Lasidious turned to the Goddess of Hate. "Once you were done with him, his mind was made up to kill Sam. I knew you would want to witness Boyafed's misery. I used your manipulation to accomplish one more part of my plan."

Mieonus shouted. "You knew? How? I was careful to pick the perfect moment."

Celestria decided to answer. "You have no understanding of careful. I watched you lie with Boyafed. I am sure Boyafed would agree he could have had a better lover than you. Your moves were that of an amateur while pleasuring him. You are not worthy of being a goddess. You are pathetic."

Mieonus stomped the lifted heel of her right shoe on the marble floor. "Careful, Celestria, you're not powerful enough to speak to me this way."

The Goddess of Beasts pushed her seat back from the table. Her flowing hair and gentle curves captured her lover's eyes as she stood. She addressed the Collective without acknowledging Mieonus' threat. "Mieonus' intent to orchestrate Sam's demise only managed to strengthen our position." Celestria moved behind the Mischievous One's chair, pulled back his hood, then stroked his hair as she continued. "Mieonus, you gave my sweet the opportunity to use the dagger he created so many seasons ago."

Alistar stood and leaned forward. "You had no right to create such a dagger without the approval of the Collective. It's against our laws." The God of the Harvest turned to Gabriel. "Why haven't you stripped him of his immortality?"

Gabriel lifted from the table once again. "He must've created the dagger before the law was added to my pages. I had no knowledge of the blade's existence until I saw him pull it from Sam's side. Even then, I had no idea what its purpose was, other than killing the king. He has broken no law."

Lasidious looked Alistar in the eyes. "You're as pathetic as Mieonus. Do you believe I'm stupid? Do you think I would create something against the Book's laws? I have no desire to be made mortal. Gabriel is right. I created the dagger before the law existed. I've been waiting for the perfect moment to use it, and thanks to Mieonus, the opportunity presented itself."

Mieonus wanted to object, but she knew her objection would make her look more foolish.

Alistar chuckled.

Lasidious responded. "I fail to see what's so funny."

Alistar gave the Book a nod. Gabriel gave the Call to Order.

Lasidious screamed. "You tricked me, Gabriel! Our laws do not allow you to choose a side. But, no matter, you cannot give the call without Mosley present."

Gabriel hovered over to Lasidious. "I can make the call if Mosley has surrendered his vote. My laws allow me to do whatever is necessary to protect the sanctity of this Collective...as long as my actions do not affect free will. Your campaign to gain the followers needed to control me isn't something I can allow. You have come to this meeting because you have chosen to attend. This means, I can give the Call to Order without taking your free will."

Lasidious thought for a moment. "You cannot vote to take my dagger from me. That would be to take my free will."

Alistar cut into the conversation. "You can have your knife. There are other matters we intend to vote on."

Lasidious smirked. "What can you vote on that I would possibly care about?"

Alistar turned to the others. "It would benefit us all to vote that we can no longer appear in the likeness of another within the Collective. This kind of manipulation is far too powerful. Also, I further say we should vote that we can no longer take the form of the people on the worlds to increase our flocks. No other rules are necessary at this moment."

Alistar looked at Lasidious. "These laws would not affect your free will. We're free to vote, and the Call to Order has been given. You have no choice. You must vote as the law states."

Lasidious scanned the faces surrounding the table. "This is an outrage! You cannot vote to take this away from me. I have plans."

Celestria looked at Lasidious. "They are our plans, not just yours. They cannot do this to *us*."

Lasidious rolled his eyes. "That's what I meant."

As Lasidious and Celestria continued to fight, Helmep lifted from his seat and assumed a perfect posture. "It appears this is the proper moment to implement these laws." He looked at Lasidious. "I'm sorry, but your ambitions are far too dangerous to remain unleashed. You cannot be allowed to run around, stealing the loyalty of our followers."

The room exploded with mixed emotions. It was four against eight as the gods cursed one another, each with a strong opinion. The Book of Immortality floated to the center of the table. "I call this meeting to order! We will vote. Mosley's vote will remain neutral.

"The first matter: the gods will no longer be able to take the form of any other deity for any reason whatsoever. Those in favor, raise your hand."

Four hands in the room did not go up. Lasidious, Celestria, Lictina, and Hosseff, despite the shade being the one Lasidious had chosen to impersonate, refused to raise their hands in support of the law. Hosseff and Lictina tried to express their objections, but Gabriel reminded them their chance to voice an opinion had passed once the vote had been called.

After counting the hands, the Book continued. "Then it's settled. The first law is decreed. Gabriel opened his binding and allowed the gods to watch as the rule appeared on his pages. He uttered the words as they were scribed. "The members of the Farendrite Collective will no longer be allowed to take on the form of another without penalty of being made mortal." He closed his binding.

"Now, for the second matter presented: the gods can no longer impersonate the people of the worlds in an attempt to gain additional followers. Those in favor of adding this law to my pages, raise your hand."

The same four hands stayed lowered while the others lifted theirs.

"Then, this law is also decreed." Again, Gabriel opened his pages and allowed the gods to watch it appear as it was scribed. "The members of the Farendrite Collective can no longer impersonate the people of the worlds in order to gain additional followers." He closed his cover. "The Call to Order has concluded."

Lasidious stood and took Celestria's hand. "You are fools!" They vanished.

Alistar laughed and slapped the top of the table. "We beat him at his own game! This should minimize any future advantage he has over us."

Hosseff shook his head. "The ratification of these laws was a mistake. We could have used such manipulations to fight Lasidious at his own game. We could have confused the people and kept them from worshipping him. We could have used his own tactics."

Alistar moved to the head of the table where Lasidious had sat. "The laws are in our favor. I must take my leave. There are matters of famine I must see to on Harvestom. Now that Mosley has sought solitude, it appears it's up to me to keep the war brewing." The god disappeared.

Moments later, Alistar appeared inside Lasidious and Celestria's home beneath the Peaks of Angels. The brothers embraced, and after Alistar greeted Celestria, they sat around the table.

"I think that went rather well," Lasidious said. "Don't you agree, brother?"

"I do. They do not realize this is what we wanted to happen. I would love to see their faces if they knew I was the one who created the dagger you used to capture Sam's soul. It's nice to watch our plan piece together. It won't be long before you rule the others."

Celestria sat in silence. Lasidious saw her hesitation. He pulled his chair beside her. "What's wrong?"

A moment of silence passed. "As I sit here listening to the two of you gloat, I realize there is much I do not know. Allow me to tell you what is going to happen next. You will level with me. You will tell me everything. Once you are finished, I am going to look at you, my pet, and ask you if there is anything you have not disclosed. You best not have omitted even one detail, because if you do, the potion I gave you will reveal your lie. If this happens, my love, you will never touch this body again. I will have no more secrets kept from me. Look me in the eyes, Lasidious. Do you understand?"

Lasidious looked at Alistar, then back at Celestria. "I do. I'm sorry you're feeling left out."

"Do not apologize. Just answer this. Do you and Alistar intend to rid yourselves of me once you have control of the Book, or is it your intent to love me forever?"

A smile crossed Lasidious' face. "My love for you is genuine. I would never do anything to intentionally hurt you. I would never betray you. You, our son, and my brother are all I care about. You have asked me this question before, and my answer has always been the same. You are everything to me."

Celestria took a deep breath. "Then, I suggest the two of you start talking. I want to know everything. I refuse to be the one who is uninformed. Do you two understand me?"

Alistar chuckled. "Yes, ma'am."

Western Luvelles
City of Hyperia

Hyperia, located north of Lake Id, is filled with halflings and elves with limited magic. The city is split into two sections. Half remains inland, surrounded by mountains while the other half is comprised of anchored structures which float on the lake. This half of Hyperia would remind someone from Earth of a medieval Venice. The people of the city move freely through waterways. They row from storefront to storefront and home to home. The most important structure in this section of the city is the king's castle.

To the east and west, the mountains do not touch the shore. In each case, massive walls have been constructed. At over 70 feet wide and 75 feet high, the walls extend into the water beyond the shoreline.

There are only two points of entry into Hyperia. Both entrances are guarded by the king's finest. These men are the strongest warriors in the city and also command dark magic, though their skills in the art pale in comparison to the magic of the Order.

Boyafed appeared in front of the king's throne. He took a seat on Kassel's chair, then sent one of the guards to fetch him. There would be no kneeling to show respect on this chilly morning. With a motion of his hand, every servant in the throne room vacated. The Order leader intended to have a direct conversation with Kassel once he arrived.

Eventually, the king entered. Boyafed stood from the throne. He did not offer Kassel a proper greeting. Instead, he chastised the king. "Why do you keep me waiting? I do not intend to spend my day wasting my moments on you."

The king took his seat. "I know why you've come. This war you intend to fight is not the problem of my people. There is nothing to be gained by fighting a war which cannot be won by either side. The last war my ancestors followed the Order into nearly killed every man in Hyperia. They were used as shields. Our magic isn't strong enough to withstand the forces of the white army. I will not order good men into battle."

Boyafed shook his head, then moved toward the window. His breath billowed in front of him as he looked down at the canal. A halfling woman was carrying a bag of grain toward her boat. She slipped and fell head first into the water. The bag of grain hit the corner of her boat which she had docked in front of the store. It burst open and spread across the canal.

Boyafed enjoyed the woman's shrieks as she flailed in the frigid water. She reached up and grabbed the boat's edge. She tried to pull her rounded, grain covered frame into the craft. As she struggled, her weight caused the boat to flip on top of her.

The men standing outside the store reacted. They grabbed a rope and tossed the woman an end to fish her out. It took three of them to pull her onto the dock. After a few blankets had been retrieved to protect her from the cold morning air, Boyafed turned to face the king. He walked toward Kassel and stopped only inches from his throne. He leaned over and allowed the warmth of his breath to find Kassel's face. "I am not asking you to order your men into battle. I'm telling you. If you don't, there are others who want to be king. Perhaps, someone who sits on the council...someone who despises you as much as I do."

Kassel stood and reclaimed his personal space before responding. "This is against my agreement with Marcus. You cannot override his authority. What will he say about this?"

Again, Boyafed closed the gap between himself and the king. He grabbed the halfling's throat and pushed him against the stone wall behind the throne. He pressed until Kassel began to choke. "I doubt Marcus would say anything."

Boyafed tightened his grip. "Have your men open their homes to the mercenaries of Bestep. They are headed this way. Give them anything they request. I will send word when the moment is right. Your army will meet me on the Battlegrounds of Olis. You will be used as shields."

Boyafed leaned in and allowed his forehead to find the king's. "Do I make myself clear, Kassel?"

The king nodded. The Order leader vanished. Kassel collapsed, gasping and trembling from the exchange.

Southern Grayham
The Village of Lethwitch
Mary's Old Cottage Home

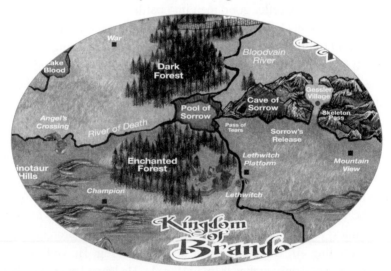

George and Athena appeared outside Mary's home. Athena was surprised at how her feelings for her mother's cottage had changed. Mary's neighbors had maintained the property, but Athena felt the home was primitive, now that she had a taste for the finer things on Luvelles.

Athena reflected. "I used to think this place was so adorable. It seems barbaric now. I bet Mother and Susanne would just die if they knew I was here."

George pulled her close. "I don't know. I find this place charming." He touched her rounded belly. "Lethwitch is where our baby was conceived." He lowered to one knee and spoke to the baby. "This house is where my new life began. I found your mother in this town, and as far as I'm concerned, your grandma's cottage will always be beautiful to me."

Athena's smile widened. "You can be so romantic."

George stood. "I'll show you romantic." He extended his hand. A small, leather, jewelry armoire appeared in his palm. "I had RJ, the leather guy, make this for you." As Athena gasped, he snapped his fingers. "I also got you this necklace."

"Oh, honey, they're beautiful. You spoil me. I can't wait to show mother. Susanne will love this." Athena's mood changed as she thought of Susanne. "I'm worried about Garrin. Susanne is upset about the baby's father. Garrin can feel her sadness."

George opened the door to the jewelry box and hung the necklace inside. "I'll just send these home for now." He snapped his fingers. The armoire disappeared.

Athena reached out and adjusted the collar of George's tunic. "I'm sorry. They were beautiful. I wasn't trying to ruin the moment. I'm just worried. You know Susanne is my only sister. I just feel like I should be there to take care of her. I..."

"Shhh, shhh, shhh. Don't get yourself so worked up." George pushed a single strand of hair clear of Athena's face. "I'll just tell RJ you couldn't contain your excitement." He lifted her chin. "Garrin will be fine...so will your sister. Brayson and your mother are keeping an eye on them. They plan to keep them so busy, Susanne won't have the moments to sulk."

After a moment of silence, Athena responded, "Perhaps, you're right. Do you think Payne will be okay with Brayson and mother?"

"Sure, he will."

"Good. That's a relief. Oh, and why did you tell Payne it was okay to call me, mother?"

"Ummm...I didn't actually say that, if I remember right, but I should be punished." George gave Athena a cute puppy dog look, then waited for her forgiveness.

Athena slapped his arm and grinned.

George rubbed the sting from his arm. "Payne does need to be loved. Letting him call you mother will give him the feeling he belongs with us. Don't you agree?"

Athena frowned. "I agree he needs us to be there for him, but you should be more careful about what you say to him."

George leaned in and kissed her. "If you'll forgive me, I'll promise to try harder. You know I love you."

As always, Athena melted when he touched her. "I forgive you, but you better start consulting me from now on, Mr. Nailer."

"Yes, babe. Maybe you should go into town and thank RJ. I have things to do for the next little while. But, I do have a surprise for you before we head back to Luvelles. You'll love it. I'll meet you at your mother's inn at Late Bailem."

After pulling Athena into his arms, George gave her a kiss goodbye, then vanished. Athena grinned as she stared at the empty spot her husband left behind. "You're just lucky I think you're adorable, Mr. Nailer."

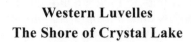

Western Luvelles
The Shore of Crystal Lake

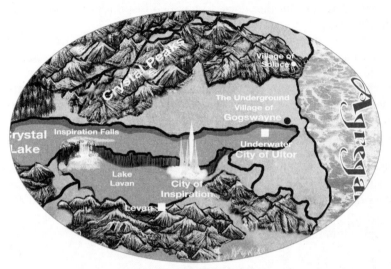

Strongbear stood in front of 733 goswigs as he inspected them one-by-one. He refused to have untidy formations. The brown bear had already sent 265 goswigs home. Some were instructed to clean their armor while the rest were sent for other appearance-related infractions. Each moment someone was asked to leave, Strongbear shouted, "Clearly, you are against me!"

Gage was wearing a new robe he had created for the inspection. It was white with green trim. The ensemble accented his fur and his cane.

Gallrum's appearance remained unchanged. His magic was fickle. He had to remain unclothed for his power to work. But, his scales were tough—so tough, in fact, he did not need armor. However, the serwin was able to place a few rings on his talons to increase his resistance against the dark army's magic.

Strongbear looked imposing. His heavy plate covered the majority of his body. He looked born to kill. The apron he normally wore while strolling around Gogswayne had been folded and placed inside his cave. There would be no needlework for the big brown bear for the foreseeable future.

After the others returned from fixing their infractions, Strongbear gave the order to teleport to Inspiration. Once there, each goswig would be allowed to go their own way until the call to gather was given. They would join Lord Dowd and march to the Battlegrounds of Olis.

Gage took the opportunity to look around the city. It was a cloudy day, so Gregory's masterpiece could not show its reflective appeal. The badger looked toward the White Chancellor's tower. "It appears you don't toy with the weather as your brother does. I imagined Inspiration would sit only beneath clear skies."

The badger stopped beside a wagon loaded with jugs filled with corgan milk. He tapped the wagon's side with his cane. Despite being made of glass, it sounded like wood. At the head of the wagon, a black, miniature horse, graying from its seasons, turned its head to find the cause of the disturbance. A boy elf walked out of the nearby store, grabbed the horse's reigns, nodded in the badger's direction, then led the horse to their next delivery.

Gage marveled at how the wagon looked like any other, as its glass wheels rumbled across the placed stones of the roadway. As the badger continued his tour, it did not take long for Gage to develop an affection for the city. At one point, the sun poked through the clouds. Its rays penetrated one of the prisms scattered throughout the city. A rainbow was cast on the side of Gregory's tower. Gage smiled. "This place is magnificent and peaceful. I now understand Marcus' jealousy."

Southern Grayham
Brandor's Arena

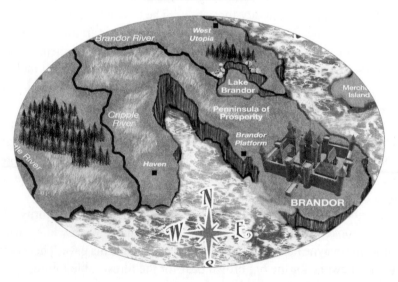

George appeared at the center of Brandor's arena after leaving Athena. Three guards rushed toward him with the intent to arrest him. The warlock's actions would have normally left him sitting in a cold dungeon, but not on this day.

As the prophet watched them approach, he lifted his hands and shouted, "Go into the city, and announce to the people that the prophet of Lasidious, the savior of your king, has come to speak with them! I have come to spread the word of the one true god!"

The guards stopped in front of George as he continued to speak. "Make haste. Bring the masses to me. No being should miss hearing what I have to say."

George tossed each man a single Yaloom coin, then spoke to the man with the highest rank. "You, sergeant, what is your name?"

"My name is Cholis." He bowed on one knee. "Prophet, please tell Lasidious I pray to him now. Tell him my family desires to be in his favor."

George smiled inside. *Like putty in my hands.* George responded. "I was looking for you, Cholis."

The sergeant looked up. "You were looking for me? Why, prophet?"

George reached out and put his hand on top of Cholis' head. "Our lord has heard your prayers. He favors your family. I am here to bless you." George reached inside his tunic to retrieve another Yaloom. He placed it in Cholis' hand. "Lasidious knows your heart. He knows you're a good man. Go home, and spoil your family."

George turned to the next man. "Corporal, what is your name?"

"My name is Diayasis."

"Diayasis, go to your king, and announce my arrival. Let your king and queen know I have come to spread my lord's good word."

Diayasis lowered his head. "Yes, prophet." He hesitated. "My family also prays to Lasidious."

Being the master of deception, George heard the lie hidden in Diayasis' comment. He reached out and lifted the corporal's head until their eyes met. "Are you sure you speak the truth, Diayasis? If I hand you a coin, and you have lied to me, Lasidious would be displeased. The last man who lied to me lies unrecognizable, frozen in the tundra of the north."

Diayasis fell to his knees and grabbed George's feet. He begged, "Please, prophet, forgive my transgression."

George assisted the corporal to his feet. "You are forgiven. Now, go."

"Yes, prophet." Diayasis rushed off.

It was late morning before the people of Grayham began to file into the arena in large numbers to take their seats. George did not wait for the crowd to settle before he started to speak. He only needed to get the message to a few before leaving. He would then lead Sam and Shalee away from the arena so the people could move into the city to spread the word.

He lifted his voice to address 300 souls. "Lasidious has seen to it that Southern Grayham has a king. He wants you to know he intends to bring peace and prosperity to your kingdom. He will do whatever it takes to ensure a higher quality of life. No longer will Lasidious allow war to consume your lands. No longer will any man's family want for food. Your needs will be provided."

A voice from the crowd responded. His appearance was well-groomed. "How does Lasidious intend to ensure the people want for nothing? How does he intend to ensure peace on Southern Grayham? If you can answer these questions, I will serve Lasidious."

George lifted his voice. "What is your name, friend?"

"I am Kolton, Senator of Brandor...voice of the Fourth and Fifth Marks."

George had no idea what Kolton meant, but he had hoped someone of importance would come to this meeting. "Kolton, Senator of Brandor, voice of the Fourth and Fifth Marks, I have a gift for the Senate. Lift your hands to the sky, and open your palms so I may leave it with you. You, Kolton, will be the one I trust with the responsibility for the safekeeping of Lasidious' Promise."

George reached into a small pack and pulled out a crystal orb. It had a green hue and bore markings which resembled Grayham's topography. The crystal was supported by a dragon's base which was similar to the one which cradled the Crystal Moon. George lifted the statue above his head. Once he saw Kolton's arms had been extended, he used his power to send the orb floating across the arena. Some in the arena were frightened, while others watched in awe.

Once The Promise rested in Kolton's palms, George continued to speak, but now, he stood in front of a much larger crowd. "Beings of Brandor, hear me. I am Lasidious' prophet. This orb will allow Kolton, Senator of Brandor, voice of the Fourth and Fifth Marks, to call for my assistance when Southern Grayham is in need. Hold out your hands. Cup your palms together. I have a gift for you all."

George thought to himself as he watched the people do as instructed, *Let the greed of the people win their loyalty.*

Yaloom coins, the highest currency in the land—3,425 in total—were dispersed throughout the crowd. Each set of hands was filled filled with five coins. George listened to their exclamations as they realized the wealth they had been given.

"Lasidious desires that you share this gift with your loved ones. Those given this privilege will pass four of your coins to others in your family. You are only to keep one coin for yourself. This act of kindness is Lasidious' way of ensuring your understanding that giving and loving is the only way to true happiness."

George listened to the cheers of the crowd as he began walking toward the arena's exit. He no sooner passed beneath the arches when Sam and Michael approached, riding their mist mares.

Sam shouted at George. "Who do you think you are to come into my city and speak to the people without speaking to me first?" The king dismounted, then unsheathed Kael. He motioned for Michael and the rest of his personal guard to surround George.

George smiled and held up his hands in submission. "You're right, Sam. I owe you an apology. I'm not here to fight, or cause problems. I'm here for other reasons."

Sam placed Kael's tip against George's chest. "I don't care what you're here for. You're a dead man."

With a quick gesture of his hand, George used his power to hold Sam and his entourage in place. The warlock took a step back. He scanned their faces. "None of you have power over me. I am not here to fight. I am here to speak with your king."

Sam rebutted. "And, you think binding me is going to get you the conversation you're after?"

George grinned and bound everyone's ability to speak. "18 vs. 1 is not what I call fair odds. Binding you is my way of saving my ass."

One by one, George approached each man and released his hold over him. As he did, he handed them a handful of Yaloom coins, then instructed them to go home. "Return to the castle in the morning. There will be no consequences for abandoning your post. Now, go."

Each man looked at their king. George used his power to force Sam's head to nod his approval.

George then moved to stand in front of Michael. He released the general's unseen bonds. "Your king will be safe. No harm will come to him." He reached inside his tunic and removed a ring. He placed it in Michael's hand.

"Lasidious knows of your daughter's sickness. Place this ring on her finger. Her body will be whole by morning. Now, go to her."

Michael looked at Sam. "My King?"

Again, George used his power to force Sam's head to nod. Once the general was gone, George released his control over Sam's mouth.

Sam sneered. "Do you think undermining my authority is going to get you what you want? Why are you here? Have you misplaced the rock you crawled out from under?"

George sighed. "Walk with me, Sam. Calm down so we can talk." The warlock turned and headed toward Sam's castle.

Realizing he could move, Sam grabbed the reigns of his mist mare and began to walk. As he did, Shalee arrived on a mare of her own.

George turned and began to walk backward. "I'm glad you could make it, Shalee. I have come to keep my promise to you." He looked at Sam. "I promised her I would make sure she had the chance to look into the Eye of Magic. She will need the additional power to help you defend this kingdom."

Sam grunted. "I don't believe anything you say."

George stopped. "Then, use your sword to see if I'm telling the truth." The warlock took a knee and lowered his head. "Go ahead, ask your questions."

Sam looked at Shalee. The queen nodded. "Go on, Sam. Here's your chance ta see I'm right."

Sam stared at George. He studied the warlock for a long series of moments before raising Kael and placing the blade on George's shoulder. "Shalee has told me Lasidious has a heaven. Is this true?"

Kael's blade began to pulsate and he searched for the answer. A moment later, the blade responded. "He speaks the truth. Lasidious has a heaven."

Sam was taken aback. He lifted the blade in front of his face. "Are you sure?"

"Of course. Ask your next question."

Sam lowered the blade back onto George's shoulder. "You told Shalee Lasidious has the power to return souls. My questions: does Lasidious have this power? Have the gods been lying to us?"

Again, Kael's blade began to pulsate, and again, it was only a moment before the blade responded. "George spoke the truth, Sam."

Sam pulled the blade away from George's shoulder. "I'm still not convinced."

George stood and found Sam's eyes. "If you cannot trust your sword, who can you trust?"

Sam glared. "Once a tyrant, always a tyrant. I don't trust what I've heard."

Kael pulled away from Sam's hand and rose to a hovering position in front of the king's face. "Sam, if you cannot trust yourself, trust me. George speaks the truth."

George smiled. "Hell...I don't think I would believe me either if I was you. I guess only time will tell if I'm being sincere. You know, I've got the power to kill you if I want to, but this isn't why I've come. All I ask is that you give me a chance to show you I want to change."

With lightning reflexes, Sam grabbed Kael's handle and placed the blade against George's throat. "Do not speak with the people again without my knowledge. I want to be informed when you decide to make your little appearances. If you're serious about being trustworthy, then this won't be a problem. Do I make myself clear?"

The warlock allowed the blade to press against his throat. As he spoke, its sharp edge drew blood. "I agree to your terms. But, I have already given the Senate a way to call on me when they need help. I have brought you something as well. You will need my help in the near future. Allow me to help you save Southern Grayham from a tyrant far worse than I ever was."

Sam pressed the blade just a little harder. "Why would I need your help?"

Before Sam knew it, his blade had been turned against him and the handle of Kael rested in George's hand. George leaned forward, keeping Sam bound with his power. "Because you are weak. My power can save your ass. Are you going to forgive me, or not?"

Sam's eyes narrowed. The demon in the back of his mind was throwing buckets of hate to the forefront of his eyes. "It appears I have no choice," he hissed.

Shalee cut in. "Y'all need ta lower the testosterone level a notch or two. People are watchin'."

George lowered the sword. He released his hold on Sam. "She's right." George turned and continued walking down the road toward the castle. He waved to the people, smiling, as Sam mounted his mist mare to follow. He could feel Sam's stare burning into the back of his head as they moved through the crowd.

Eventually, the warlock stopped to face the royal couple. "Shalee, maybe there's someplace private where we could continue this conversation. Take us there, and I will tell you more."

Shalee teleported the group into the royal garden behind the castle. George took a look around and admired the beauty, but his enjoyment of the moment was disrupted as Sam barked, "Why don't you get on with it? I can't wait to hear this pile of garesh."

George shook his head, then took a seat on one of the benches. "I know you have no faith in me, Sam. I deserve your hatred."

Sam rebutted. "I don't hate you. I pity you. You're easily manipulated. I will save my hate for Lasidious and the others."

Shalee remained quiet. She didn't want to contradict Sam when their relationship was still rocky. She figured George would have to find his way over the walls Sam was putting up.

George moved to stand beside the king. He produced a picture of Abbie, then grabbed hold of the reigns of Sam's mist mare. He lifted the picture. "Go ahead...take a look. She's the reason I caused the war on Grayham. I lied, murdered, and cheated, all because Mieonus filled my head with a lie. She promised to give me Abbie back. I have since learned of the gods' deceptions. I know everything Bassorine wrote on his statue, and everything Mosley told you, were lies. I have seen Lasidious' heaven. I want to go there when I die. I have to live a better life to get there."

Sam dismounted, then helped Shalee down. He tethered their mist mares to one of the statues spread throughout the garden. "I don't believe you have decided to live a good life. This seems sudden. It seems too convenient that Lasidious is some kind of almighty force the others relish. There must be other reasons why you're here. What haven't you told us?"

George smiled. "You're right. There is something else we need to discuss...something important. There is a powerful threat which will come to Brandor. I have the ability to help you fight him. Your sword will not be able to defeat this person."

Shalee jumped into the conversation. "What threat are ya referrin' ta?"

"The Dark Chancellor on Luvelles has made his way to Grayham, as you know. Lasidious has informed me that Marcus intends to take control of Southern Grayham."

Sam grabbed his head in disbelief. "Okay, okay, hold on a moment. We just finished fighting a war. We're not healthy enough to fight another one. We took heavy losses in the last massacre you led us into. I could've died, and you could've cared less. How can I believe anything you say?"

"I'm not here to justify my actions, Sam. I have admitted I was wrong, and my excuses for doing the things I did are not justifiable. I had no right to manipulate this world because of a goddess' promise to return my daughter's soul."

George turned and walked a few paces away. He spun back around. "I mean...who am I to put my life above others? I was wrong, Sam. All I can do is try to make up for my actions."

Sam thought a moment. "You expect me to believe Lasidious is omnipotent, and the others fall short. Why is it that he is the only god with a heaven...and, if he is so all-powerful, why doesn't he allow the souls within the Book to live in his heaven?"

George shrugged. "Look, Sam. I don't pretend to have all the answers. But, I have seen his heaven, and I want to go there. I want to go there with everything in me. All I know about the others who call themselves gods is this: Lasidious called them Titans. He said they are not gods."

Sam cut in. "Titans? Like the Titans of Greek mythology? Titans were gods."

George rubbed his head in thought. "Beats the hell out of me. I don't know anything about Greek mythology. I didn't study it when I was in school. I know this: a guy with your intelligence could sit with Lasidious and have everything figured out in no moments at all."

Sam took a seat on a bench. Shalee remained quiet. She also had limited knowledge of mythology. After many moments passed, Sam lifted his head and looked across the garden. "None of this makes sense. In Greek mythology, Titans were considered gods, but you say they are not. Then, why isn't Lasidious powerful enough to get rid of them?"

George shrugged again. "Beats me. Ask him when you get the chance."

The warlock needed to redirect the conversation. "Look, all I know is this: Lasidious asked me to come to Grayham and warn you of the threat Marcus is about to become. Lasidious wants me to make sure Shalee receives the power she deserves by looking into the Eye of Magic. In doing so, she'll be able to help you fight against the army Marcus intends to bring to Brandor."

Sam turned to find George's eyes. "What army could he find on Grayham to fight for him? The barbarians won't lift a finger to help after the way we took control of the northern territories. Who else could he possibly command?"

George took a seat on the grass. "Marcus isn't your normal wizard. He has the ability to control the minds of those he comes in contact with. He could walk into your city all alone, and the people will turn on one another.

Your own army will come for you. You will need to find Marcus before he sets foot in Brandor. You have the moments to prepare." George looked up at the sky. The sun was approaching Late Bailem. "It's getting late, and I have a date with my wife. I'll come back as soon as I can."

Sam crossed his arms. "You're leaving? What do you expect me to do with this information?"

George moved to take a seat next to Sam on the bench. "You need to talk with your queen. She needs to look into the Eye. You also need to speak with the Senate to decide whether or not you want my help. I'll be back when the moment is right. Lasidious will tell me what to do next."

With that, George teleported away from the garden. Shalee lowered to her knees in front of Sam. "Maybe, we should talk 'bout this ova' dinna'. I'm sure your head hurts as much as mine does."

Sam shook his head. "I need an ale. Is there anything on this world that is as it seems to be? I don't know how to tell what the truth is anymore."

Southern Grayham
Gessler Village

It has been five days since Marcus set foot on the Merchant Island of Grayham. Since that moment, he has been unable to teleport because he has no knowledge of Grayham's topography. He has been forced to travel by boat, then on horseback, and if that was not bad enough, he is now traveling by hippogriff.

Marcus looked forward to a good night's sleep as the hippogriff began its decent to the landing platform in Gessler Village. Without saying a word, he dismounted and walked down the steps.

After questioning a few shady characters who tried to rob him—a robbery he foiled by using his magic to throw the thieves high onto a steep hillside, he watched as they tumbled to the ground. One of the thieves struck his head on a rock and perished while the others were not so fortunate. Marcus used his power to peel the skin from their bodies, then left them hanging upside down in a nearby tree. The rest of his trip was uneventful as he made his way to the Bloody Trough.

As he looked the place over while standing on the street, he noticed a stone statue which had been placed to the right of the entrance. The man was large. He looked as if he was wearing furs and leather.

As the Dark Chancellor walked inside, he could see the patrons were different than the patrons inside the inns located on the outskirts of the three other cities he had stayed near while traveling. The crowd exuded darkness and, for a moment—though a brief moment—he felt as if he belonged.

Many of the men were sitting at larger than normal tables. They were dressed the same as the statue standing outside. They were over a foot taller and much bigger than he was. He felt their eyes watching him as he headed for the bar to take a seat. He tried to order a drink, but the man behind the counter didn't seem to be in a hurry to stop his conversation with the other patrons.

Marcus chose not to wait. With a wave of his hand, a mug lifted from the counter, floated to the tap and remained suspended beneath its spout. The handle toggled. Once full, the mug floated toward Marcus and lowered onto the bar in front of him. The tap remained open as the ale continued to pour onto the floor.

The barkeep stopped his conversation. He rushed to the tap to shut it off. He stared at the handle for a long series of moments before turning to face Marcus. He had seen magic like this before, and he knew what magic of this nature was capable of. He was working the night George turned the barbarian on the front porch to stone.

The barkeep approached Marcus with caution. "Hello, friend. Will there be anything else tonight? I see you found the ale without trouble."

Marcus wasn't in the mood for idle chatter, but he needed information. He decided to answer the barkeep's question. "I could use a meal and some answers. Perhaps, you could tell me when the next hippogriff leaves for Latasef. That is my next stop if I have read my map correctly."

While using a rag to clean the counter, the barkeep responded, "Food I can help you with, but the hippogriffs cannot take you to Latasef. If this is where you are going, you will need to travel by foot, or perhaps horseback, if you intend to go further."

Marcus shook his head in disgust and whispered under his breath, "I hate you, George. The rat better be worth the trip."

"I'm sorry, friend, I did not hear you."

Marcus clenched his mug. "Nothing. I'll need a room. Do you know anyone who could guide me to my destination? I can pay well."

After pondering the question, the barkeep threw Marcus a key, "Your room is up the stairs and down the hall to your right. I'll have a guide waiting in the morning to take you anywhere you want to go."

Marcus flipped the barbarian a coin. "I'll see your guide in the morning."

The Luvelles Gazette
When you want an update about your favorite characters

The Next Day, Early Bailem

George had just finished breakfast when Athena's water broke. He had planned to go to Harvestom, but Athena had other plans. The family is beginning to gather for the event. Mary and Brayson have the situation under control.

Because of the baby's birth, Gregory will become an essential part of spreading the word of Lasidious much sooner than George anticipated. The proud papa is glad his attempt to kill Gregory failed.

Hosseff and Mieonus are inside the goddess' home watching her waterfall. The images portrayed are of George and his family as they rush to do anything they can to help with the baby's birth. In the midst of the confusion, the gods will learn a secret.

Alistar has arrived on Harvestom. He is watching as the centaur armies close in on one another. He intends to watch Gregory make an appearance to the browncoated King of Kless.

Boyafed plans to go to the Petrified Forest to call in a debt. But, something unexpected is about to happen to Boyafed.

Lord Dowd will order the white army to march once the hounds of Wraithwood Hollow appear. With the Scroll of Conair in hand, Dowd can now command the Call of Conair.

The goswigs have fallen into formation with the white army. They will meet up with the army of Lavan and the giants of the Foot just north of Lake Tepp, then continue west to the Battlegrounds of Olis.

After the wraith hounds arrived, Strongbear started a conversation with Wisslewine, the Wraith Hound Prince. It didn't take long for the ghostly hound to become tired of hearing, "So, are you with me...or are you against me?"

Marcus has arrived at the home of Maldwin. He has killed his guide after searching his memories of Grayham's topography. He will read from the scroll and begin calling the rat's name.

Lasidious and Celestria are inside their home beneath the Peaks of Angels. Lasidious visited with Brayson once again in the middle of the night. Lasidious asked Brayson to deliver a message to George. The message will reveal the location of something which has been hidden on Grayham since its creation.

Keylom is about to take Mosley to the Siren's Song. The wolf will begin his search for the wisp hidden inside the mist.

Gabriel has decided who he will approach to replace Yaloom. This creature will become the new God of Greed, providing he accepts. Gabriel anticipates his selection will cause tension on Ancients Sovereign.

Thank you for reading the Luvelles Gazette

Dragon World
Western Luvelles
George and Athena's Home

"Holy cow, this is stressful," George said as he pushed his hands through his hair while facing Brayson. "I've never heard a woman scream so loud. Are you sure Mary knows what she's doing?"

Brayson laughed as he opened the door and allowed the healers he had sent for to come in. He pointed to the teleportation platform which would take them to Athena's room. Once the last healer vanished, Brayson turned to George. "Like I've already said on three occasions, everything is under control."

George led Brayson onto the front porch. "Look...I know you're busy tonight, but I need you to do me a favor."

"And, that would be?"

"I need you to take Gregory to the Kingdom of Kless on Harvestom... more specifically, the throne room, or I guess the king's barn would be more accurate, if I wanted to label it. You know...I bet he has a really cool stall, and it's probably full of the freshest hay since he's the king and all. Or, do centaurs even eat hay? Do you know what they eat?"

Brayson had to reel him in. "George, you're letting your mind wander, but yes, Lasolias does have a unique throne. I have also spoken with the centaur on a few occasions over the seasons through my mirror. Now, finish what you were going to say, so I can go."

George refocused. "Gregory will need to tell Lasolias that his bag holding his kingdom's Seeds of Plenty hasn't been stolen by Boseth. Lasidious told me the Titans intend to start a war on Harvestom. They have lied to both kings. The reason for this war doesn't exist. Lasolias' bag has been hidden, not stolen."

Meanwhile, on Ancients Sovereign, Hosseff and Mieonus could not believe their good fortune as they listened in on George and Brayson's conversation.

Mieonus smiled as her eyes studied George's image. "Finally, his pet has made a mistake."

Hosseff's wispy voice added, "With this knowledge, we can defeat Lasidious at his own game."

"Agreed."

They turned their attention back to the waterfall.

"So, then, you understand everything," George confirmed.

"I do," Brayson replied.

"Good." George reached out and put his hand on Brayson's shoulder. "Hurry back. I need you here. This is stressful." George telepathically communicated the rest of what he had to say. *I will go to Harvestom and get your brother tonight while you handle the business our lord has asked you to.*

Brayson nodded, then continued aloud. "I will hurry. Once I explain everything to Gregory, he'll stop this war on Harvestom. The word of peace and love shall be shared today."

"This is the break we've been waiting for," Hosseff said as the image within the waterfall faded. "We need to find Keylom. He is the best one of us to appear to Lasolias."

Mieonus frowned. "I hate the idea of giving that centaur anything…especially when it involves handing him followers. But, you're right…he is our best chance to use this information to our advantage. We best hurry. Keylom needs to arrive before Gregory."

The gods vanished.

Once Brayson left, George rushed up the stairs to check on Athena. He was surprised by his greeting. Athena screamed from the bed. "Oohhh...so, you've decided to be a part of this after all! How nice of you to take a moment to stop by, Mr. Nailer!"

With a smile hidden inside, George moved to take her hand. "I'm sorry, babe. I thought you were in good hands up here."

"You're not allowed to think while I'm in this much pain! Do you understand me?"

"Yes, dear. But, you better pay attention to what the healers tell you."

Again, Athena snapped. "Don't you tell me what to do! Listening to you is what got me in this situation! You don't look so charming when I'm in pain! Just shut up, and hold my hand!"

Mary gave George a quick grin to let him know everything would be okay. "Give her something to squeeze."

As Athena pulverized George's fingers, Payne hung outside the window with his claws grasping the sill. His eyes were peeking over the edge, just enough to satisfy his curiosity. He had never seen a birth. With each yell, the fairy-demon cringed.

Kepler looked up and shouted while lying on the pile of boulders above his lair, "Get down here, freak. Leave them alone."

Southern Grayham
Maldwin's Home

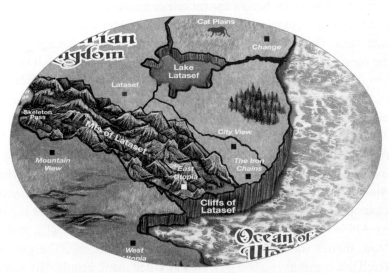

Marcus read from the scroll George gave him. With his mind protected, he was sitting outside a hole leading into Maldwin's cave, shouting the rat's name. Every now and then, he would emphasize the phrase, "Everything is A-okay, man!"

Not far from the exit, Maldwin sat, hidden in the shadows. For many moments, he listened, trying to decide what to do. He was conflicted. On one claw, he wanted to use his ability to project a vision, and send his un-expected visitor walking off the edge of the cliffs of Latasef. On the other claw, he heard the man shouting the phrase George used while they traveled together. Eventually, he decided to exit the cave.

Once in the open, Maldwin spoke. *"All quay alla foot uswayya doy."*

Not understanding, Marcus lifted his thumb into the air. "Everything is A-okay, man." The Dark Chancellor reached into his robe and removed the letter.

Maldwin took a step back and readied a vision. His nose twitched as Marcus set the paper on the ground and slid it toward him. Once he felt the parchment was close enough, he looked up and shouted, *"Yaway astoot,"* which meant, "That's far enough."

Marcus could only smile. He held up his hands. "It's okay. I'm not here to harm you. I'll back up and give you some room."

Maldwin did his best to appear threatening as Marcus moved clear. Many more moments went by before the rat felt comfortable enough to drop his guard. He moved in to take a look. He poked the paper with his claw. It was instantaneous. The parchment began to speak in his own language.

The message, when translated, said, "Hey, Maldwin, it's me, George. I hope my message has found you and your family in good health. I have to admit, I miss traveling with you. Anyway, I'm living on a new world called Luvelles, and Kepler is with me. I would like you to visit for a while, if you wouldn't mind, of course. I have made special arrangements for you to find your way to my home, and I have plenty of cheese waiting for you.

"You will need to catch a ride with the Merchant Angels on Grayham. Use your visions on this man sitting in front of you to make him take you to Merchant Island. After you arrive, you'll need to find a man named Hesston Bangs. Allow Hesston to see a vision of my face. He'll know what to do.

"Now, there's something else I'd like you to do for me. The guy who delivered this message is a bad guy. He has killed many people. His name is Marcus Id, and he's the Chancellor of Darkness on Luvelles. He has no idea that this parchment is casting a spell to counter the effects of a scroll he read to protect his mind from your visions before calling you out of your home. This spell will reopen his mind.

"I have sent him to you so you can use your ability to make him stay on Grayham. Give him another vision which explains that he needs to go to the city of Brandor. I want him to be punished for the crimes he has committed. He needs to be put away for good.

"I do hope you come to Luvelles to visit. I imagine by the moment of your arrival, my new baby will be here. Once you arrive on Luvelles, a man named Brayson will come get you. Don't forget, I have cheese waiting for you, and everything is A-okay, man."

The parchment went on to explain other details about what Marcus needed to do while on Grayham. After listening to the parchment list the details more than once, Maldwin went back into his cave to think.

It was not long before he heard Marcus shout the words, "Everything is A-okay, man!"

Maldwin moved back into the open. He lifted his head, twitched his nose, then used his vision on Marcus' mind.

Southern Grayham
The Siren's Song

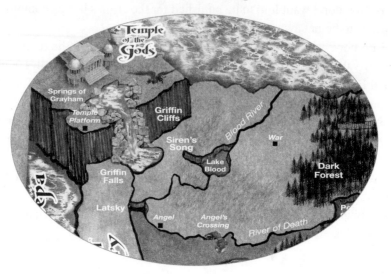

Keylom and Mosley appeared in the mist of Siren's Song. With the change of season caused by the third piece of the Crystal Moon, the moisture in the air carried a slight chill, but this did not bother Mosley. With the thickness of the wolf's coat, the moisture was a minor inconvenience.

"Mosley," Keylom said, "I will miss you on Ancients Sovereign. I hope you succeed on this journey. I further hope you find a way to rejoin the Collective."

Mosley nodded. "Just be my eyes on Ancients Sovereign. I want to know everything Lasidious is up to. I best get moving if I am to stop him from commanding the largest pack of all."

Before another word could be spoken, Gabriel appeared beside Keylom. The Book's voice sounded urgent as he hovered eye level with the centaur. "Keylom, go now to the Hall of Judgment. There isn't a moment to lose. You'll understand upon your arrival."

Without hesitation, Keylom did as instructed.

Gabriel looked at Mosley. "I wish you well. Remember, you may call upon me when you wish me to grant your last request. Good journey, my friend. I'll be watching your progress."

"I am comforted...even if you can offer no further help. I will see you again."

"Let's hope you're right. You've grown on me." The Book vanished.

Mosley turned and looked at the thick brush covered by the mist. He lowered his nose to the ground, sniffed for the perfect spot, then lifted his leg to mark the beginning of his trail. Once finished, he took a deep breath, then pressed forward, singing:

> *One big wolf just trottin' through the jungle.*
> *Don't mess with me...don't mess with me.*
>
> *Who has white teeth and the breath to make you slumber.*
> *Don't mess with me...don't mess with me.*
>
> *I will hunt George down and make him tremble.*
> *Don't mess with me...don't mess with me.*
>
> *This night terror wolf is comin' for you.*

When Keylom arrived inside Gabriel's hall, he was greeted by Hosseff and Mieonus. The centaur's hooves clapped against the marble floor as he moved into a better position for good conversation.

"Where have you been?" Mieonus inquired. "We've been looking for you."

Keylom whipped his tail. "If only you were a fly, Mieonus. I was busy. Since when do I answer to you?" He turned to find the nothingness within Hosseff's hood. "For what reason have you summoned me? What business could I possibly have with the two of you?"

The shade responded. "As you know, the centaurs on Harvestom are about to go to war. We have knowledge that Lasidious plans to use this opportunity to convince them to serve him."

"How?"

Mieonus answered. "Lasidious plans to send his new disciple to stop the war. He has convinced Gregory Id to worship him. You need to speak with the King of Kless before Gregory arrives. Explain that his Seeds of Plenty were hidden, not stolen. You need to be the one who stops this war. We cannot afford to have them serve Lasidious."

Keylom crossed his arms. "This could be the loophole in Lasidious' plan we've been looking for. I will go now." The centaur vanished.

Mieonus stomped her lifted heel against the marble. "Doesn't he want our assistance?"

Hosseff laughed. "I think he would rather allow Lasidious to have his followers than be assisted by you."

Mieonus gave the shade a nasty look.

Hosseff shrugged. "What? You know I'm right. Besides, Alistar is already there."

"Hmpf! Let's go to my waterfall and watch what happens."

* * *

Keylom appeared next to Alistar inside Lasolias' throne room. The gods remained invisible to the mortals.

"What are you doing here, Keylom?"

"I intend to appear to Lasolias to inform the king that his army does not need to attack Boseth. I will tell him where his Seeds of Plenty have been hidden. I will make him believe I have spared his kind. In return, I will allow his browncoats to worship me."

Alistar smiled. "I can only see one problem with your plan, my friend."

"Please, explain."

"Even if you stop the centaurs from going to war, they'll never serve you. Their hatred for the blackcoats runs deep within their souls, and you, my blackcoated friend, are a representation of what they hate most. I think a different plan is in order."

Keylom looked at the black hair on the stallion portion of his body. He sighed. "What do you suggest?"

* * *

Meanwhile, Mieonus and Hosseff watched from her waterfall as Alistar explained that Keylom should go to the Kingdom of Tagdrendlia and speak with the blackcoats. He suggested a blessing be given to Boseth, as well as a promise of peace. Alistar agreed to stay behind and appear to the King of Kless to deliver the news about his kingdom's Seeds of Plenty. He would promise Lasolias a bountiful harvest, and abolish the hunger his people were experiencing.

Mieonus waved her hand across the waterfall. The images faded.

"What did you do that for?" Hosseff snapped, irritated that Mieonus would dismiss his desire to watch.

"We should've thought about the color of Keylom's coat. One of us should have tried to convince the browncoats to serve us. I hate the fact that Alistar is going to gain this benefit."

Hosseff once again began to laugh.

"What's so funny, shade?"

"You don't want a bunch of fly-covered centaurs worshipping you. They are beneath you. Your anger is misplaced."

"I suppose you're right. But, the idea Alistar will benefit from this makes me sick."

A moment later, Lasidious appeared. "Mieonus...Hosseff...meet me in the Hall of Judgment, and be quick about it. This matter concerns both of you." Lasidous vanished, leaving Hosseff and Mieonus to ponder his demand.

A moment later, Lasidious appeared again, but now he was standing in front of the Book of Immortality. "Gabriel, I wish to speak with you. Mieonus, Hosseff and the others are on their way."

Before another word could be said, Celestria appeared beside him. She looked at her lover. "The others are on their way, my pet. But, I have been unable to find Mosley, Alistar, or Keylom."

"What's the meaning of this meeting, Lasidious?" Gabriel snapped. "I have no desire to speak with you at the moment. Leave my hall."

"Then, don't speak with us," Lasidious snapped back. "I will take the others outside onto the grass."

Gabriel gave Celestria and Lasidious a feigned look of frustration. "I will stay out of curiosity. I hope this isn't another waste of my moments."

One by one, the gods began to appear.

Meanwhile, back on Harvestom, Keylom left to speak with Boseth. With the others of the Collective occupied, Alistar appeared undisguised to Lasolias.

Lasolias' throne was like a large swing which hung suspended from the rafters of a gigantic barn within the Woods of Cornoth. The swing was made of strong leather and was padded for comfort. Further, it was designed to hold the king beneath his horse belly and allow him to lower into a rested position. Fresh hay was scattered about the floor, and a large basket filled with assorted grains sat within reach.

Lasolias' guards attacked as soon as they saw Alistar appear, not knowing the being before them was a deity. Alistar held up his hand and froze them in place while he began his deception, or rather, his campaign to increase the number of his brother's worshippers. "Lasolias, I am Lasidious, God of Peace and Love. I have come to deliver good news. Your Seeds of Plenty have not been stolen. I have come to return them to your people."

Alistar tossed the bag at the hooves of the king who remained suspended as he hung in his swing. "The war your army intends to fight is unnecessary. It is my desire you stop your course of action. For doing so, I will replenish your kingdom's food supply. Your kind will never know hunger again."

Alistar stopped talking and waited for Lasolias to gather his thoughts. It was easy to see he had never seen a god. The centaur stared at his guards, who remained motionless. Their faces were frozen with the look of battle on them.

After many moments, Lasolias responded. "My army is many, many days from here. Word would not reach them before they begin their attack. Your request is impossible."

Alistar smiled within himself. "Soon, my disciple will make his presence known to you. I want you to give him this crystal." He tossed a red-colored stone and watched as Lasolias caught it in his right hand.

"This stone will show my disciple where to go. He will see to it that this war is stopped. Your brown coated army will be spared a senseless death.

"In return for my generosity, I want you to speak with your subjects. Tell them of my name. Tell them Lasidious has brought peace to your world, and he promises to replenish your lands with enough food to feed your kingdom for seasons to come.

"If they agree to worship me, your hunger will cease before tomorrow's end. They must speak my name twice daily in their prayers. If they do, I will forever bless your kind.

"I leave you now so that you may decide what your answer will be. Inform my disciple of your decision when he stands before your throne. If you choose to accept my grace, then shout my name to the heavens as soon as my disciple arrives. Do not wait for him to utter a single word. Shout my name, and hand him the gem I have given you. If you do this, you will never know hunger again." Alistar vanished.

Meanwhile, back on Ancients Sovereign, Lasidious held the gods' attention. "Celestria and I have found enough matter to create a new world for the dragons to call their own. As promised by this Collective, the dragons will be rewarded. We have also gathered enough material to give each of the existing worlds their own moon."

Lictina stood from her seat. "Why was I unaware of this harvest?"

Lasidious smiled. "You should know by now, my secrets are my own. 1000 seasons ago, I sent for this matter to be retrieved after word of its existence came to my ears. My Salvage Angels have since returned. They are only days from being within range for us to take advantage of this opportunity. I have known of this surprise for many seasons, and now I find it gratifying to share this secret with you."

Gabriel lifted from the table. He floated to a position in front of Lasidious. "You cannot create this world without enough matter to birth a star to warm it."

Lasidious thought a moment. "The matter to create a new star is not available. But, a new sun is not necessary."

The Book reached up to rub his chin. "Then, how do you intend to make the new world habitable? Without a sun, there's no way to sustain life."

Hosseff stood to add to the conversation. "Perhaps, there's another way, Gabriel." Lowering his hood, the shade took his human form. "I have been looking forward to this day. Lasidious, is there enough matter to add to the current sun's size?"

The God of Mischief grinned. "There is more than enough to accomplish this. We share the same idea. Please...explain it to the others."

As usual, Mieonus had to add her scoffing remarks. "Yes...please inform those of us who are challenged and unable to understand that a larger sun will allow us to move the planets back. Perhaps, we don't understand that more room is necessary to place this new world in an orbit of its own. Perhaps, we do not understand room is necessary for the moons to orbit their worlds. Please, wise and all-knowing Hosseff...explain how we could control this new world. Perhaps, you are forgetting that Lasidious still possesses two pieces of the Crystal Moon. How will we keep the worlds and their moons from colliding?"

As Hosseff glared at Mieonus, Lasidious and Celestria began to laugh.

Gabriel was the first to speak. "I fail to see the humor."

Lasidious leaned forward and calmed himself enough to respond. "Despite Mieonus' rude way of addressing the situation, she has made a valid point." For a brief moment, Lasidious allowed Mieonus to enjoy his compliment.

The Mischievous One continued. "Let us talk candidly for a moment, shall we? It seems we all know, especially in light of current events, my game with the Crystal Moon is about gaining the followers I need to capture the power necessary to control Gabriel. We also know I will continue to do whatever is necessary, within the Book's laws, of course, to gain the power to rule this Collective. You have learned enough about my plans, and this game with the Crystal Moon is no longer necessary. I say we stop the game to create the new dragon world."

Lasidious pushed back his chair and began to stroll around the table as he continued. "Regarding the Crystal Moon, I'm willing to surrender the final two pieces. I am willing to place them on my statue inside the Temple of the Gods on Grayham. I am willing to release my control over the Crystal Moon to Gabriel under three conditions."

Again, Mieonus entered the conversation. "I find it entertaining that you would have the nerve to make enemies of us all. You boast about your plans to control us as if you have no fear of what we will do to stop you."

Lasidious chuckled. "I don't fear you, Mieonus." An evil grin spread across his face. "I feel sorry for you all. But, how I feel is irrelevant. Shall we continue with my three conditions?"

Before another word could be said, Alistar appeared. "What did I miss?"

It did not take long for Gabriel to bring Alistar up to speed.

Alistar looked at Lasidious and rubbed his hands together. "Great. So, about these conditions...I would love to hear them. You never seem to bore us, Lasidious."

The Mischievous One took his chair. "My conditions are: first...I will surrender the Crystal Moon in its entirety to Gabriel, but only if it is written into the laws within his pages that my statues will always hold the Crystal Moon and its replicas within the temples on each world. Gabriel is to be the protector over the Crystal Moon. He is to keep its pieces from being taken. It will be a law that no deity, not even Gabriel, can touch them...this includes me.

"Second...whenever the gods need to add an additional piece to the Crystal Moon to allow for the expansion of the worlds, or the creation of another solar system, the additional pieces necessary to govern these creations will fall under the law of my first condition. Each additional piece of crystal must be added to the Crystal Moon's overall size and left to rest in my statues' hands.

"My third and final condition...when we create the dragons' new world, it will be my statue that is erected inside the new temple. Beyond this new world having a shimmering image of me within its temple, and the statues I have already placed within the existing temples on the other worlds, I will no longer require other statues be erected to honor me."

Alistar plopped into his chair. "Wow!" He looked at the faces around the table. "Now that, my friends, is what I call a heavy set of conditions." He looked at Lasidious. "If we agree to these conditions, when would the creation of the dragon world begin?"

Mieonus stood and stomped her foot. She began to study the others' faces. "We cannot allow him to manipulate us like this! This is outrageous. I say we finish the game Lasidious has started. We should settle this once and for all as to whether good or evil prevails. We don't need to agree to his list of terms in order to take the crystal from him. He cannot back out of the game if we don't let him."

Lasidious cleared his throat to get everyone's attention. "Mieonus is right. I am bound to the game I started, and if this Collective wishes to continue this meaningless course of action, then so be it. But, I would hate to see the uprising of the dragons. Can you imagine what the winged Titans will do once I tell them this Collective intends to postpone the creation of their world until the completion of a game."

"You wouldn't dare," Mieonus shouted. "The dragons would kill everything. They would no longer respect the boundaries we set for them. They would abandon Dragonia. Even you must see this as madness."

Lasidious leaned back in his chair, put his feet on the table, then crossed his legs while leaning back with his arms folded behind his head. "You use the word 'madness' as if madness is a substandard emotion. I say let the Titans run free. Allow them to pick their teeth with the bones of those who serve you."

"If the beings of the worlds perish, so does your power." Hosseff responded, remaining remarkably calm. "You would fail in your quest to control the Book."

Lasidious began to laugh.

"What's so funny now?" Mieonus snapped while pushing her brunette hair clear of her face.

Lasidious leaned forward. His voice was filled with an evil the others had never heard. "With the loss of your followers, the Book will also weaken. You see, the Book's power is limited. When we created it, we never did anything to ensure it couldn't be drained of its power. If I allow the worlds to collide, or use the dragons to kill the beings on the worlds, then its power will dwindle. The dragons will spare those who worship me. Eventually, I would be able to control the Book to use it against you. I'll be able to control you as a result of your failure to fulfill our promise."

Jervaise decided to make her opinion known. She lifted her ghostly form from her chair. As she did, all the gods turned to face her. "For as many seasons as I have known you, Lasidious, I have understood your mind to be cunning. These manipulations are far beyond your normal mischief. I don't doubt for a moment, after watching recent events, that you would be willing to mislead the dragons in this manner...or destroy the Crystal Moon. I also feel you may want us to continue your game for reasons we may not understand or see at this moment. I find it difficult to know which path is right to follow. I find myself resenting you."

Now, it was Hosseff's turn to laugh. The others surrounding the massive table watched him as he stood and pulled his hood over his head.

Mieonus barked, "What's so funny, shade? How could you possibly find humor in this?"

Hosseff collected his thoughts, and after a couple of long deep breaths, he replied. "Lasidious is failing to mention that I was more powerful than he was before the worlds were created. The dead will increase my power. If he allows the Crystal Moon to be destroyed, then I will once again be his superior. Once those who serve the rest of you perish, I will feed on their souls. This much death will leave me in a position to destroy Lasidious, so I doubt he would do something so foolish."

Alistar spoke out to help his brother. "Neither of you are correct in your assessments. I would be the one to command the power to control the gods, and I would not allow us to destroy one another if this was to happen.

"What you failed to mention, Hosseff, is that I was more powerful than you prior to the creation of the new worlds. You failed to mention that it wasn't just Bassorine who commanded the power to rule the gods. I would be the one to fear."

Alistar turned to face Lasidious. "I would punish you far beyond all imagination if you were to allow the Crystal Moon to be destroyed. So, I feel this option isn't the one you will choose to pursue." Alistar finished his act by sitting down and leaning back in his chair.

Lasidious began to chuckle. He stood from the table and moved behind the shade. With his hand placed on Hosseff's shoulder, he said, "Now, that's the real reason I have no plans to destroy the Crystal Moon. You're not the one I fear, Hosseff. Alistar's power is the reason I have seduced the dragons. My relationship with the winged Titans is stronger than ever. Once the people realize that serving me will save them from the dragon's wrath, they will pray harder to me than they ever have to the likes of any of you. Eventually, I will have the followers I need to control the Book...and Alistar."

Lasidious watched as the gods looked at each other. He could see they were floored at how devious he had become. He continued, "I suppose I should level with you. I will tell you the whole truth. I have already spoken to the dragon council. I told them of the expected arrival of the matter necessary to create their new world. I have also told them I intend to approach this Collective and demand we fulfill our promise. They know I campaign for them. Their loyalty is strong. They know I will give them their world once I command the Book."

Gabriel lifted his voice to a level the gods had never heard. The sound was so deafening each world could hear his screams as thunder. "ENOUGH! Lasidious, you will stop speaking about me as if I'm not in this room. Have the respect to use my name if I am to be plotted against. Speak of me in this way again, and I shall sacrifice everything I am to strike you down. The quadrillions of souls whose names rest on my pages will once again be scattered into the darkness, and I shall perish with the satisfaction of knowing I took you with me."

Everyone present was at a loss. They didn't know how to respond. Eventually, Lasidious managed to regain his composure. "You have my sincerest apologies, Gabriel. I will no longer speak of you as just a Book. I will use your name from here on out. My scheming doesn't have to be done with disrespect. Please forgive my thoughtlessness."

Gabriel's face tightened. "If only you meant what your words suggest. Make no mistake, Lasidious. If I hear you speak of me as if I'm not in the room again, I will strike you down."

Lasidious nodded. "I will remember that, Gabriel. I shall continue my scheming without disrespect." He turned and faced Hosseff again. "As I was saying, I can give the dragons their world once I control..." Lasidious looked at the Book and bowed, "...once I control you, Gabriel. But, I will say this...I would much rather abandon our game and surrender the final pieces of the Crystal Moon. We can work together to give the dragons their new world."

"This is outrageous!" Mieonus said, stomping the lifted heel of her right shoe into the hall's polished floor. "I hate you, Lasidious. You too, Celestria."

Bailem slapped his hand against the table to get everyone's attention. His face showed his distress as he looked about the room to find the eyes of each deity. "I have no idea how to proceed. There appears to be no option which will provide me with peace. I will choose to follow the same path Gabriel follows."

Calla, Jervaise, Owain, Helmep and Alistar agreed to do the same. Mieonus, on the other hand, plopped into her chair. "I hate all of you."

Gabriel ignored the goddess' animated mood. He floated over to Lasidious and hovered in front of the Mischievous One's face. "If we choose to accept your three conditions and, in doing so, agree to create the world for the dragons, I want you to surrender your control over the Crystal Moon immediately. I want you to promise you'll never use the power of the dragons as a weapon against the worlds under any circumstances. I want you to make this promise to us now so there will be consequences for your actions if you fail to live by your word. I also want Celestria to make this same promise, and every other god in this hall shall also make this agreement. The dragons are never to be used as a weapon against the worlds to kill the followers of any god or assist in any campaign which would change the balance of power amongst the gods. If you will agree to this, Lasidious, then I'll support your desire to create this new world. I will support the creation of the new piece of the Crystal Moon which is necessary to govern this world. I will add this piece to the others and create new replicas for your statues to hold. Do you agree to my list of terms, Lasidious?"

With a sly smile, the God of Mischief responded. "I agree. I see no harm in giving everyone peace of mind."

Gabriel looked at Celestria. "And, you?"

In all her beauty, the goddess replied. "I also agree to the terms."

Once the others had agreed, Lasidious released his control over the Crystal Moon with a wave of his hand, then thought, *I love loopholes.* The final two pieces appeared on the table for the gods to see.

The new dragon world would be created. The other five worlds would be moved away from the sun and put at a distance in which they could continue to support life as they revolved around this expanded star. The new dragon world would be placed at this same distance and given an orbit of its own.

Now, this new solar system would consist of six worlds, one hidden god world, a single sun, and each world would be given its own moon. The beings of the worlds would be put in stasis for the moments necessary for all of this to take place.

Gabriel looked at Lasidious. "I imagine the dragons have plans to worship you once this world has been created. I assume Celestria is going to surrender her power to ensure you are able to gain the power over me you seek. I just have one thing to say before I take my leave."

Each deity's ears were now focused on Gabriel's every word. They waited as the Book floated around the room preparing his thoughts. "Now that I have your promise regarding the Titans, I will share a bit of my own scheming with you, Lasidious. You're not the only one with secrets. Even if you manage to collect your following of dragons, don't be fooled into thinking this will give you the power needed to control me. I will relish your misery once I'm finished with you. You will be a reminder of the god you wanted to be. I will be calling for another meeting soon. I suggest you all come so you can watch Lasidious' face."

The Book began to float out of the hall. The others watched as the Mischievous One gave chase. "Gabriel! What do you have planned? Gabriel! Gabriel! Come back! Gabriel! Don't be like that! Come back!"

𝕷𝖎𝖙𝖙𝖑𝖊 𝕵𝖔𝖘𝖍𝖚𝖆 𝕶. 𝕹𝖆𝖎𝖑𝖊𝖗

Western Luvelles
George and Athena's Home

Joshua K. Nailer emerged as the healer lifted his tiny body onto his mother's belly. He screamed as he was pulled free of the warmth of his mother's womb, the chill of the room needling his sensitive skin. The umbilical cord was severed, and after a magical circumcision, he was wiped off just enough to allow his proud parents to dote.

Joshua was beautiful. He had blue eyes, his mother's hair, and his father's—well, they weren't really sure what he had of his father's looks, since his skin was so shriveled. He looked like a pink prune.

George leaned over and gave Athena a kiss while Mary took the child to clean him up. "You did good, baby. I love you so much."

A tear rolled down Athena's cheek. "I love you, too. I'm sorry for being so nasty."

"Nonsense. You had every right to react the way you did." George turned his head toward the window. "I think we have a little guest hovering outside. He's dying to see what's going on. Should I let him in?"

Athena peeked over George's shoulder. "Yes, let him in. But, you better explain that Joshua doesn't have the ability to rip his fingers off like he does. I don't want any test morphing happening with the baby. Oh, and make sure he knows Joshua cannot burst into flames either. He needs to understand the baby doesn't have the ability to do the things he can. Make sure he..."

"Babe. I get it already. I will speak with Payne. How about this? We'll tell Payne he is his brother's protector. I think it's important that Payne doesn't feel we love him less than Joshua. He needs to know he's loved unconditionally."

Athena sighed. "Let him in. Maybe you should show Payne his new bedroom. Let him know he will be sleeping inside from now on."

George waved his hand, and the window opened. He motioned for the fairy-demon to come inside and allowed the window to shut behind him.

"Payne, come here a moment. I want you to meet your brother." He pointed to Mary who positioned the baby for a better view. "That's Joshua K. Nailer."

Payne scratched the top of his head. "It look funny."

George smiled. "He is not an 'it.' Joshua is a baby, and his looks will change as our moments pass."

"What K for?" Payne questioned as he flew over to Mary and hovered above her shoulder while she finished cleaning Joshua.

"Well," George responded, "Athena and I decided that since we're going to allow you to sleep inside with us from now on, we should do something so Kepler doesn't feel left out. The initial K means, Kepler, but we aren't going to say his full name. So, when you say his name, you will say, Joshua. Do you understand?"

True to form, Payne's mind had moved past his curiosity about the baby. "Payne hungry. Mother feed Payne?"

George had to laugh. "Come with me, buddy, and I'll feed you. How about I make you some pancakes?"

Southern Grayham
Sam's Throne Room

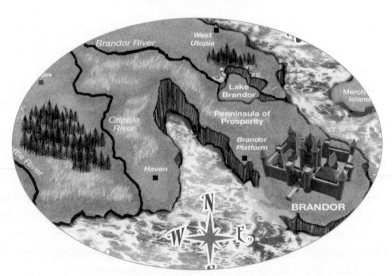

Shalee smiled as she watched the sun touch the horizon through one of the throne room windows. The people below moved about the cobblestone streets of Brandor with joyful hearts. It was easy to see the happiness in their gaits, and it appeared as if everyone had a new sense of respect for one another.

Sam had allowed word to spread about the army's findings inside the Serpent King's underground city. Now that the army was bringing this surplus of coin back to Brandor, new word was begining to spread that the treasure was bountiful enough to strengthen the kingdom's economy for many lives over. As a result of this great news, celebrations had followed. But, the coin of the serpents wasn't the only reason the people celebrated.

Despite Sam's encouragement to keep Lasidious' Promise quiet, the Senate believed in Lasidious' desire to see Southern Grayham flourish. They voted to overrule the king's wishes, and as a result, runners had been sent throughout the kingdom to spread word of Lasidious' gift, which George had given the Senate.

The people were now in a giving mood, and the coin George left behind was the talk of Brandor. With the Senate's newfound sense of faith, how could Shalee—or even Sam for that matter—contradict the facts of what was happening?

Shalee knew there was another reason the people were joyful, and this reason didn't involve a god, or a prophet. It involved the greatness of her husband. Before returning the kingdom to the Senate, Sam had made many changes and implemented many new laws.

First, Sam freed the slaves across Southern Grayham. He declared these hard-working beings were to be treated as equals. They would be allowed to choose their employer.

Second, Sam decreed that each master of the freed slaves would receive ample compensation for the abrupt change in their lives. Sam further decreed that each master be given the coin necessary to pay for services equal to those lost for a period of one full season.

Third, ten new barbarian members of the Senate had been named, and homes were ordered to be built within the walls of Brandor to accommodate the senators when visiting the city.

Fourth, every member of this reformed Senate was required to swear an oath that no man or barbarian, no matter how wealthy or strong, would be seen as anything other than equal under Brandor's laws.

Fifth, Sam established laws for the kingdom's newfound wealth. He implemented a banking system and, more specifically, created protocol on how this wealth was to be distributed as loans to the people.

Sixth, each member of the army who had fallen in battle was to be compensated. Their family's debts would be wiped clean and the Senate would see to it their creditors were paid in full. Families with no creditors were to be given a lump sum of coin for their loss.

Seventh, the members of the army who had survived were also to be given a lump sum of coin to help return to everyday life. For those disabled in battle, Sam ordered schools built and temporary compensation be given on top of their lump sum until they could be trained to earn another living.

Eighth, Sam declared that any Senator who failed to uphold the new laws would find themselves facing the Sword of Truth. They would answer questions regarding their transgressions. If found to be a liar, this senator would face a possible prison sentence on Dragonia, of no less than one season, or other term deemed fit. Sam also reserved the right to sentence a senator to a punishment as strong as death if the betrayal was considered traitorous.

Finally, and quite possibly Sam's finest moment as king, he changed the name of Southern Grayham. All lands would be unified under one title. This kingdom would be called, The United Kingdom of Southern Grayham. The old kingdoms would now be referred to as territories: the Territory of Brandor, the Territory of Bloodvain, the Territory of Serpents, and the Neutral Territory. The bears and the minotaur were also given territories with names reflective of their kind.

Shalee turned from the window and looked at Sam who sat on his throne. Her relationship with her king felt stronger than before, and she wasn't about to let anything come between them again. She requested that everyone leave the room.

Once the room was clear, Shalee walked toward the thrones and plopped onto Sam's lap. She waited for him to cradle her in his arms. After lowering her head to his chest, she began her praises. "The people love ya, Sam. I've neva' been so proud of someone in my entire life."

Sam tried to put on a happy face, but failed to project the joy to go along with the smile.

"What is it, Sam? What's got ya boggled?"

"I can't get George and Lasidious out of my head. I have asked the Senate to call me before using Lasidious' Promise. I want to know everything that's going on. I gave the Senate the scroll you gave me. I'm glad they'll be able to teleport into the throne room to solicit my presence."

Sam stood and lowered Shalee to her feet. "But, something isn't right. This whole thing isn't sitting well with me. I don't care what Kael says."

Sam unsheathed the blade and held it in front of his face. "Kael, answer this: what if George is being manipulated? What if he's a victim of Lasidi-ous?"

Kael's blade began to pulsate. "Your moments will divulge the truth. What George professed during his visit was truthful. Perhaps, you worry over nothing."

Sam's brow furrowed. "Perhaps. And, what of this new threat George spoke of? I have read everything in the royal library about the Dark Chancellor. The writings speak of his power as if he's some kind of magical badass. How do you suggest I proceed?"

Kael pulled away from Sam's hand and floated toward Shalee. "You should allow George to take Shalee to look into the Eye. You will need this power to save Southern Grayham."

"Agreed," Sam responded. He looked at Shalee. "The writings make me think your magic will be useless against the Dark Chancellor. If I hadn't seen how easily you could've been killed on Luvelles, I wouldn't give this concept a second thought. I hate to say it, but George is our only option."

Shalee smiled. "I have a good feelin' 'bout George now. I'm sure we'll get past this last threat...just like we have the others. But, somethin' else is botherin' ya, isn't it? I can see it on your face."

Sam moved to look out the window. The last bit of light faded from the sky as the sun ducked behind the horizon. Children were running through the streets, lighting the torches to fight the darkness. He leaned against the sill. "What if you look into the Eye and it swallows your soul? What if you don't come back? I don't think I can handle losing you. We've lost too much already. That would be the end of me for sure."

"I wish I knew what ta say ta make ya feel betta', Sam. But, the Eye won't swallow my soul. I give ya my word on that. When I return, I'll be powerful enough ta defend the kingdom from the chancellor."

Western Luvelles
The Petrified Forest
Near Balecut's Home

The night was a miserable collection of moments in which to visit the forest. The sounds of anything that moved echoed between the trees, their petrified trunks acted as sounding boards. It was impossible to tell the direction from which the sounds reflected. The slightest flap of a wing, skitter of a beetle, snap of a twig—all heightened the tension inside the warrior's mind.

With each step, Boyafed pushed forward, looking for the tree of Balecut. With his elven eyes, he searched the shadows for the beasts he knew were hidden in the darkness.

Tricksters—devious creatures with the ability to teleport so fast it was almost impossible to bury a sword deep enough to kill one. They were hideous game players with the features of gremlins, only taller than their cousins by a foot or so. They toy with their victims before administering a gruesome death.

The wizard, Balecut, lived somewhere inside one of these massive trees which had been hollowed at its center, and Boyafed knew the closer he came to Balecut's front door, the more likely it was that the tricksters would attack.

To Boyafed's knowledge, there were only two men who commanded the ability to control these killers. The first was Balecut, and the second was Brayson Id. Each of these wizards had found a way to command the ability to bend moments, and it took this kind of power to manipulate the tricksters to do Balecut's will—although Boyafed didn't understand how the magic worked. But, what the Dark Order leader did know was this same power would come in handy for the upcoming war, and having Balecut at his side would ensure victory. All he had to do was find the wizard before the tricksters found him. But, this was easier said than done.

It seemed as if every other footstep prompted a new bead of sweat to roll off Boyafed's brow. His heart pounded. He knew he was getting close, and he wanted to avoid teleporting home to evade a confrontation with the gremlins, only to return to start over. He wanted no part of these creatures. A confrontation would be a sure death. But tonight, Boyafed wouldn't be given the chance to teleport—tonight he was too slow.

Four vines shot out of the darkness and secured to each of Boyafed's limbs. The Dark Order leader closed his eyes to teleport, but when he opened them, he found his magic had failed to carry him to safety. The vines securing his arms lifted him into the night, suspending him high above the ground while the vines which had attached to his legs pulled them back toward the forest floor. He was helpless, without the ability to retrieve his blessed blade.

Four tricksters began to pop in and out about him, shouting curses in a language he couldn't understand as they poked him with needles. Their games had begun, and now, all Boyafed could do was call out. "Balecut! Balecut!"

One of the tricksters appeared before him, and with his claw balled tight, he punched Boyafed in the throat to stop his calls. The gremlin enjoyed the Dark Order leader's struggle to breathe and to add insult to injury, the trickster poked Boyafed with a needle in the side of his neck, only to vanish and reappear behind him to poke him on the other side.

The tricksters grew bored with this game, and a different game began. They took turns appearing before Boyafed, only to slug the Order leader as hard as they could in his gut for four different rotations. On sixteen occasions Boyafed suffered their blows, and on each occasion, he struggled to gather what he could of the air surrounding him.

Two tricksters began to remove his armored boots while the other two levitated behind Boyafed's head and took turns pulling out one hair at a moment. They giggled as the elf tried to move his head from side to side to keep them from securing another strand.

With boots falling to the ground and socks wrapped about the tricksters' necks as scarves, the pair below began to poke needles into the bottoms of Boyafed's feet. He screamed as the nerves were struck with each puncture. On 41 separate occasions they buried the length of the two inch needle. On more than one occasion, the needle entered the bottom of his foot only to emerge through the top. Soon, they also became tired of this game, then moved on to the next round of sadistic pleasure.

Each trickster began to appear one by one in front of him. They levitated long enough to briefly urinate in Boyafed's face. They did it over and over again as if they were dogs able to control the release of their streams. Boyafed tried to turn his face and avoid the foul liquid, but his efforts were pointless. The wretched liquid began to burn inside of his mouth, his eyes, the inside of his ears, and even his nostrils.

Once the taste of the tricksters' piss found his tongue, Boyafed began to gag. His reaction amplified their desire to pee longer and harder. Now, they began to urinate from four angles and would have kept at it until all bladders were emptied, but a loud, penetrating howl filled the night.

The call pierced the darkness as if it came from an angry beast. The warning sent fear into the tricksters' hearts. They vanished, leaving Boyafed suspended and vomiting.

Boyafed fought to gather his wits. He looked through the fog in his eyes, but the burning persisted. He shook his head to shed what was left of the urine from his hair. As the moments passed, his eyes began to clear. To his delight, Balecut stood on the ground, looking up.

The wizard looked tired, too old for his seasons, and barely able to stand. His back was doubled over, and he used a cane to keep from toppling. His hair was long, gray, and gnarled while his beard, also poorly groomed, was patchy and short. Even his robe lacked the luster of the man Boyafed once knew.

"Get me down," Boyafed pleaded.

With a simple motion of his hand, Balecut released Boyafed's restraints, then turned up his palm to keep the Order leader from falling. Once Boyafed's bare feet rested on the ground, Balecut released his hold. Boyafed crumbled to the ground and pulled his feet toward him. He reached inside his pouch to retrieve an elixir. After pouring two drops under his tongue, he watched as the puncture holes began to seal.

Boyafed stood, lifted his boots and scoffed at the idea that his socks had vanished with his attackers. He moved with a limp to thank Balecut, but the wizard lifted his hand to ward him off.

"Stay where you are," Balecut warned. "I have no desire to shake the hand of a urine-covered idiot."

After looking himself over, Boyafed responded, "I see your point. So much for a pleasant greeting."

Balecut chuckled, then turned to walk. "Follow me."

Boyafed did as instructed. He had to remain patient while Balecut hobbled toward his hollowed tree. Upon their arrival, the home seemed like any other of the petrified giants, with two exceptions. There was a door made of a wood which wasn't petrified, and a small window located high on the trunk. A faint light escaped through it.

Balecut passed his hand over the vegetation of the forest floor. A tub full of hot water appeared. With another wave of his hand, a bar of soap also appeared, which he tossed to Boyafed.

"Bathe before you come inside. You're foul," is all he said before shutting the door of his tree behind him and leaving Boyafed standing alone again in the darkness.

As the Order leader removed his armor, he looked into the night. He could see the tricksters. Their eyes were glowing in the darkness, threatening to cross the boundary they feared to pass. They wanted to finish the job they had started. This would be the most uncomfortable bath of Boyafed's life.

Once finished, Boyafed left his armor and most of his underclothes in a pile. He put on just enough to cover his privates, then went inside. "I'm sorry for the way I'm dressed," he shouted as he ascended the steps, littered with ancient tomes, toward the room filled with light. "Maybe, I should teleport home and come back once I have changed."

Balecut responded. His voice echoed off the home's petrified walls. "Since when did you become so modest, Boyafed? I don't remember you being so bashful when we were children. Just stay a while. I'm sure your underpants will suffice. How about an ale?"

"That would be nice," Boyafed responded as he reached the top of the stairs. He studied his surroundings. Balecut lived like a swine. Clothes, scrolls, unclean dishes covered with rot, and half-full mugs laid scattered about. Boyafed said nothing as he moved toward the table near the window.

As Balecut poured the drink, he thought back to their childhood. "Boyafed, do you remember when you, Dayden and I went swimming bare skinned in Farmer Perryman's pond? You weren't so bashful then." Balecut began to laugh as he continued. "Do you remember Dayden screaming when the fish bit his manhood?"

Boyafed chuckled, "I remember. He was scared it had been bitten off."

Balecut lowered both ales onto the table. "I never did have the heart to tell Dayden that I had used my power to make him feel like he had been bitten. I have enjoyed the memory of my jesting for more seasons than I can remember."

Boyafed took a seat on a rickety chair which was heavily padded and positioned near the table. It wobbled beneath his weight as he leaned back. "Then, it was you who did that. I cannot tell you how many different occasions Dayden and I have laughed about that day. It was a fine deception, my friend."

From his spot, Boyafed could see out the window. To his surprise, the tricksters still loomed in the darkness. He took the opportunity to lift his feet for inspection. They were killing him, despite the elixir's magic.

The taste in his mouth still loomed, despite using the water from his bath to wash it out. He took a large swig of his ale, swashed it around, opened the window, then spit it to the ground. "Damn, those gremlins."

Boyafed shut the window. "Perhaps, you could freeze a few for me so I can gut them. A little vengeance would be sweet."

Balecut lowered his mug. "If only I could. As of late, I find my power is diminishing. Without my goswig, I am deteriorating."

Boyafed leaned forward. "You look worse than the backside of a krape lord taking a garesh."

Balecut frowned. "I still have feelings, you know."

"I apologize."

"I find it hard to accept that you and I are nearly the same age, and yet, I look as if I'm ready to pass. Ever since Gallrum abandoned me, I have been withering. I have lost my ability to control much of my power. The tricksters only flee from the man I once was."

Boyafed put his elbows on the table and placed his head in his hands. "This is terrible news. I came seeking your help. I intended to ask you to fulfill the debt you owe me for saving your life. The rest of what I came for is pointless, considering your current state. I wanted you to stand by my side and slow the white army's moments. Perhaps, a new plan is in order."

Balecut stroked his beard. "The moment of your arrival is intriguing. Brayson plans to visit me tonight. He sent word that he wishes to speak with me, although I don't know why. He said something about his new god telling him the moments were right for a visit. I'm beginning to think he may be right, considering you're here."

Boyafed looked puzzled. "Why would Brayson want anything to do with you? He must know my intent to solicit your help."

"I suspect this may be the reason." Balecut tapped his cane against the edge of the table. "Brayson has no idea my health or my power has diminished. We can use this to our advantage."

"Explain."

"If I were to have some help, perhaps, from someone such as yourself, our power combined could overwhelm him. I could steal his power."

"Are you insane? Brayson has the power to destroy us both. If we try to bully him, he would swat us as he would a fly. We would perish from our efforts. Besides, in your current condition, I doubt you could finish eating his heart without throwing up."

Balecut stood, hobbled over to a shelf, then reached for a vial filled with a black liquid. "With this, I can handle the taste. Don't you worry about that. I also would not worry about our ability to defeat him. I have something I can slip in his drink. We can bind him once he sleeps."

"You've gone mad. The loss of your goswig has taken more than your power."

"Perhaps. But, I expect Brayson to arrive shortly. If I can regain my youth by eating his heart, I will help you win your war."

Boyafed looked out the window toward the menacing eyes scattered throughout the darkness. He shook his head. "If we do this, we make it look as if the tricksters got him. Agreed?"

Balecut smiled. "Agreed."

George and Athena's Home

George stood next to the kitchen table with Joshua nestled in his arms. He was listening to Brayson's account about leaving Gregory on Harvestom.

George looked at Brayson and whispered. "So, you just showed up to drop Gregory off and the king began shouting Lasidious' name. Well, that's a tad bit strange, don't you think? Tell me more about this gem the centaur handed Gregory."

Brayson leaned in and adjusted the blanket around Joshua's face. Once satisfied the child was cozy, he responded with a whisper of his own. "The gem was left behind by our lord. Lasolias told Gregory he was to use it to teleport to the location where the armies intended to battle. Lasidious must be a gracious god. Lasolias was anxious to worship him. As I said, he began shouting before Gregory could introduce himself."

George smiled, then looked down at Joshua. His heart was full of joy as he played with the soft blond hair on the child's head. "I told you, Lasidious wants nothing but the best for us. Maybe, you should prepare for your outing tonight. I want you to be ready for anything. Convincing Boyafed and Balecut they need to stop pursuing this war won't be an easy task."

Brayson took a seat at the table. "I doubt either of them will want to hear what I have to say."

"You'll do fine. Lasidious didn't choose you to be one of his disciples without a good reason. The right words will come to you, I'm sure." George shifted the baby to a different position to free his right hand. He looked at Brayson. "I need you to face me, and lean forward. Allow me to touch your head. I want you to open your mind to me. I need to go somewhere after I get your brother, and I know you know the area. I need to see what it looks like. Do you mind if I familiarize myself with your vision of this place?"

Brayson could only marvel. "So, you have the ability to see inside the willing mind? And, I thought your ability to speak tele..."

George cut him off. "Hey, hey, hey...now that's a secret you and I need to keep between us. We never talk about that out loud."

With an odd look, Brayson leaned forward. "Okay, but I cannot imagine why it's such a secret. It doesn't seem any worse to talk about that than it does your ability to retrieve a memory from my mind." Brayson lowered his head. "Go ahead. Find your memory. I only wish I could see the memories inside your mind."

George laughed. "Believe me when I say this, you wouldn't want to see the nasty things I have done. I would rather forget them. As I have told you before, I was a..."

"...a jerk," Kepler added while finishing George's sentence. As he walked into the kitchen, the room became cramped. The cat was careful to keep his voice low to respect the child's sleep.

George pointed at Kepler, and whispered, "Ding, ding, ding...we have a winner." George shook his head in amazement as the giant cat lowered to a comfortable position on the floor. "Damn, Kep, you take up most of the room. Good thing we pushed the table to the side or you wouldn't fit in here." George continued telepathically. *You're one majestic creature, buddy.*

George turned his attention back to Brayson. "Let me touch your head, this will only take a moment."

Brayson leaned forward. George placed his hand on his head and closed his eyes. A moment later, George opened them. "You best get ready. You need to leave."

After Brayson vanished, George turned to Kepler. He broadcast his thoughts into the cat's mind. *Stand up a moment, Kep. Let me touch the top of your head. This is the information you needed. It won't be long before Brayson arrives. Be careful tonight. I don't want to lose you.*

Kepler responded with a thought of his own. *I'm going to enjoy killing him.*

Like I said...be careful...you're my favorite kitty.

Kepler sent a growl into George's mind. The warlock smiled and reached down to adjust Joshua's blanket. He moved so Kepler could get a good look and whispered. "Isn't he cute?"

Kepler leaned in and sniffed the child. As he pulled back, he snorted, then responded. "He's cute if you like the way he smells. He needs to be changed."

After the two had a good chuckle, Kepler vanished.

The Petrified Forest
Balecut's Home

Brayson appeared outside Balecut's tree. He knocked on the door, then waited as he took note of the tub full of dirty water sitting on the forest floor. It wasn't long before Boyafed answered. The Order leader acted surprised to see him, and after greeting the Head Master with the respect he deserved, they ascended the stairs to the windowed room.

Balecut didn't bother to stand as he greeted Brayson. "Ahhh, Head Master. I never imagined that you, of all the elves on Luvelles, would come to my humble home. Why do you grace us with your presence?"

"I have business to discuss," Brayson said as he looked at the mess scattered about. Taking note of the wizard's withered body, he took a seat beside Boyafed. "I would like to have a conversation with the two of you." He looked at Boyafed. "My lord said you would be here."

Boyafed became nervous. "What business would your god have with me?"

Balecut decided to speak before Brayson had the chance. "You have come to request that Boyafed stop his advance against the white army, haven't you?"

"I have."

"I knew it." Balecut stood. He used his cane to balance himself. "I have a fresh jar of ale around here...someplace. Allow me to get you a mug full."

Brayson gestured. "I won't be here long enough for you to waste fresh ale on me. Thank you, but I'll pass."

"No, no, no. I insist," Balecut responded without hesitation. "It's not everyday the Head Master visits my home. Please, allow me one drink so I may have a proper story to tell when sitting in the company of others. Would you like it served warm or chilled?"

Brayson smiled. "Chilled would be fine." He watched Balecut use his power to cool the drink before setting it down in front of him.

With a simple nod to give thanks, Brayson continued their conversation. "Boyafed, the war you intend to have with Lord Dowd is unnecessary, and although I cannot stop you from taking this course of action, I am here just the same. I have been assured by the god whom I now serve that peace is coming to Luvelles. Loss of life is not necessary to find a solution to the problems between the armies."

Boyafed adjusted to a more comfortable position in his seat as he watched Brayson take a drink of the chilled beverage. He smiled within himself as he watched Brayson's Adam's apple bob. "As much as I respect your opinion, Head Master, it wasn't you who had to deal with the loss of your best friend when the white army killed him. It wasn't you who had to set his remains on Hosseff's altar and watch as his body burned. I know nothing of the god you serve, nor do I care to know him. Lord Dowd will pay for what he's done."

"As well he should pay for his actions," Balecut added. "But, perhaps, we should speak of other things. I find it fascinating that a god would approach the only man on Luvelles who is required to remain neutral in the ways of war. Why would a god ask you to get involved in matters which you should stay clear of? Isn't it your job to act as an advisor in matters pertaining to unexplained magical happenings which the kingdoms are ill-prepared to handle?"

Brayson set his empty cup on the table. "You're correct. As I have stated, I cannot stop Boyafed from pursuing his course of action. I simply do not wish to witness the death of thousands because of a situation which can be settled between two men."

Boyafed leaned forward in his chair and put his hand on Brayson's shoulder. "I wouldn't consider Dayden's death...my best friend's death...to be a situation two men can discuss."

Boyafed and Balecut could see the effect the drugged ale was beginning to take on Brayson. But, Boyafed continued to talk as if he noticed nothing. "Dayden was a good man. His death is inexcusable. I will have vengeance."

Boyafed stood and moved to stand behind Balecut. "Head Master, you look as if you don't feel well. Can I get you another mug of ale? You look as if you need a drink. Your skin is flushed and your brow is covered with sweat. Allow me to fetch you a wet cloth."

Brayson reached up and wiped the moisture from his forehead. "Why am I sweating so? I feel sick and a bit lightheaded."

Balecut was quick to respond. "It's hot inside my humble tree. I have taken precaution to ensure the cold stays outside these petrified walls. I find my body doesn't respond to the cold the way it used to. Boyafed is right...a wet cloth would do you wonders. Allow me to get you another drink while he fetches it for you. I'm sure it will make you feel better."

Brayson stood from the table. "I don't know that I should…should… drink…"

Boyafed moved to catch the Head Master as he fell face forward toward the table. After lying him on the floor, he looked at Brayson's face. The dark warrior was now conflicted after listening to his own words. Speaking of Dayden's death reminded him of honor and how he cherished it. To kill the Head Master in this way was wrong, and he would have no part of it.

Boyafed stood. "There's no honor in killing him this way." He looked into Balecut's eyes. "There must be another way to recover the power you've lost without losing our honor. I don't wish to dishonor the Head Master in a way that is no better than how Dayden was disgraced by Lord Dowd."

Balecut's face was cold as he responded. "There is no other way. You wish to win your war, do you not? Without his power, I cannot ensure your victory. I cannot help you avenge Dayden's death."

Boyafed moved clear of Brayson's motionless figure. "Taking the Head Master's life in this manner isn't an acceptable way to gain justice for my loss. Only Hosseff has the right to command that a man's life be taken without reason. I will not dishonor Brayson."

"Ugggh! We've been friends for far too long to allow something so trivial to come between us. If you cannot watch him die, then leave. I'll finish the job without you."

Boyafed shook his head. "You're not hearing me. I said this isn't honorable. I cannot allow you to do this."

Balecut struck his cane against the floor. "It seems you and I are about to have our first disagreement. I have been loyal to you over the seasons, but now…well, now the circumstances have changed. I need his power to keep from rotting away. I won't stop what we've started, and you don't have the power to stop me."

Boyafed didn't hesitate. He lifted his hands and sent a wave of force into Balecut. The wizard flew backward, passing over Brayson's motionless form. He slammed into the wall above the staircase, then rolled head over heels as he descended to the bottom before coming to rest near the door.

The dark warrior jumped over Brayson and hurried toward the stairs to finish the job. His feet were light, despite the needles which had penetrated them earlier, and his movements were crisp and strong. As he bound down the staircase, he was forced to stop mid-stride.

A giant cat loomed over Balecut. Blood saturated the white fur around its mouth. Boyafed watched the beast spit Balecut's head to the floor. Realizing the significance of this new threat, Boyafed closed his eyes to teleport.

When he reopened them, his magic had failed, and the beast was stalking him, ascending the stairs with fiery, burgundy-red eyes.

The dark warrior drew his blessed blade and began to match the predator's advance as he backed up. Step by step, they ascended the stairs toward the windowed room. Step by step, Boyafed held the glowing eyes of the jaguar. Never in his life had he seen a cat this large. The width of the staircase was filled with the beast's mass. The only way to retreat was up.

Boyafed's mind raced as he looked for a way out. *The window. I could escape through the window. He's too large to follow me.* With the window in sight, Boyafed rushed for it, but Kepler responded with a nod, freezing Boyafed in place.

The room above was tight due to Balecut's clutter. The demon's size filled what space there was. In order to move past the Order leader, Kepler pushed Boyafed aside with a flip of his head. Each paw thumped against the petrified floor as he moved to stand above Brayson. After ensuring the Head Master was alive, Kepler began to chuckle.

Boyafed felt a chill as the cat turned to face him. The beast spoke. "Hello, Boyafed." Kepler licked his massive chops to clean the blood. "My name is Kepler. You don't need to fear me." Kepler stopped talking and began to sniff the air. He released his magical hold on the dark warrior. "Get behind me. Pull Brayson with you. We have visitors."

The tricksters could be heard below as they began to pick through Balecut's remains. Their howls, chuckles, and verbals reverberated inside the tree's trunk. It would only be a matter of moments before they began their ascent toward the windowed room.

"What would you have me do?" Boyafed whispered. "I don't have the power to fight them."

Kepler responded in a low growl, "Stay put and don't move."

"You don't understand. They will kill us."

Kepler twisted his head over his shoulder and gave the Order leader a look of warning. "Do not say another word. Allow me to show you how a refined Master of the Hunt fights."

The first of the tricksters crested the top of the stairs, his gremlin eyes were filled with malice as he stared down the giant feline. Once the group of four had assembled, they began their advance.

With a heavy growl, Kepler said, "You may want to pay attention, Boyafed. Allow me to show you how to kill."

The demon-cat sprang into action, using the ancient power of the mystics to accelerate his movements. Even within the confined space, he was lightning quick, and the tricksters were no longer able to teleport fast enough to avoid being hit. His heavy paws clubbed the sides of the gremlins' heads. One by one they perished, falling lifeless to the floor after hitting the petrified walls with a thud. In one case, the trickster fell without a head attached.

Kepler smiled and thought, *Hmph...two heads in one night.*

Boyafed remained quiet as he watched the cat stand motionless in the center of the room. After many moments passed, Kepler turned to face the Order leader. "I want you to listen to me. Your god has deceived you. He isn't worth your service."

Boyafed began to speak, but Kepler silenced him. "Your desire to defend your god is admirable. But, he is nothing more than a Titan. Your service is wasted on the weakest Titan of them all. Your war, the same war you're so eager to rush into, is a creation of Hosseff. He was the one who had Dayden killed. He was also the one who ordered your men to be struck down in cold blood. Hosseff is a Titan of Death for a reason. He is not a god. Gods do not need to survive on the souls of those who perish to command power which appears god-like. This war is exactly what Hosseff wants. He will devour the souls of the dead just as he has devoured Dayden's."

Kepler freed Boyafed's tongue. "How do I know you speak the truth?"

The jaguar lowered to the floor. "Allow me to explain." A long conversation followed. Kepler concluded by saying, "This will give you the chance to see for yourself that your god has deceived you."

Boyafed shook his head. "And, if I refuse?"

Kepler laughed. "I don't believe I have given you a choice. This is non-negotiable. Besides, you will enjoy the task."

Boyafed's disgust was evident. "It seems arguing with you will get me nowhere. What must I do?"

"Then, it's settled. You will need to stop your army from traveling to Olis until you have completed the task. Once you have retrieved your truth, and see I have not lied, you will be glad you saved the lives of innocent men. You may even decide to serve a new lord."

Boyafed crossed his arms. "I will do your deed. But, my service to Hosseff will remain unchanged. I promise this much."

Kepler sighed. "I'll come to you when the moment is right. Stay near your temple. I don't want to search for you."

Kepler put his paw on Brayson's leg. They vanished, leaving Boyafed bewildered.

The Luvelles Gazette

When you want an update about your favorite characters

Two Days Later, Early Bailem

George and Athena are awake and sitting with Payne at the kitchen table. They are working with the fairy-demon to improve his table manners. George has created clothes for Payne to wear, and the couple has explained he will be required to bathe on a regular basis. Payne isn't happy about the new rules.

George plans to take Joshua and Kepler on a trip to give Athena a few moments to herself. The warlock and the demon-jaguar have two stops on this outing.

The Collective is meeting to think of other ways to keep Lasidious from gaining followers. Gabriel is not at this meeting, and the others are now aware that both centaur kings have decided to spread Lasidious' word.

Keylom took the moments to explain how Gregory's appearance on the centaurs' battlefield was devastating to his campaign to solicit the blackcoats' service. Gregory had shown up at an inconvenient moment, and after acknowledging Keylom's presence, the White Chancellor moved past Keylom to speak with Boseth.

The chancellor knew all the right things to say and had used his reputation from previous visits with Boseth to gain favor.

Gregory, although careful to show Keylom respect, told Boseth Keylom was a Titan, and Keylom regretted his reaction to the insult. The god's anger at Gregory's comments solicited an unwanted validation that his power was, in fact, limited. Gregory used this opportunity to explain how Lasidious was the only god capable of commanding the power necessary to offer his followers a heaven. He explained how Lasidious had sent him to create peace on Harvestom.

Alistar put on a show of frustration while he ranted to the Collective. He feigned his surprise about Gregory's ability to sway the kings' hearts. He continued the masquerade, informing the Collective that when he left Lasolias, he felt confident the centaur would command his kingdom to serve him.

Alistar's theatrical reaction to Keylom's revelation seemed to solidify the Collective's belief that Lasidious had masterfully manipulated the events on Harvestom.

Lasidious and Celestria avoided the Collective's meeting. They are chatting inside their home deep beneath the Peaks of Angels. Everything planned until now has fallen into place, and more planning is in order to grant George and Kepler more access to power.

Boyafed has returned to the city of Marcus. He's going stir crazy as he paces the polished floor of the Order's temple. He has sent word with his runner that he wishes to meet with Lord Dowd to call off the war. He has further ordered his Argont Commander to have his army wait for additional instructions.

The words Kepler used to define Hosseff bothered him. He had called his lord a Titan, and further said, his god was not worthy of his service. The jaguar had said many other blasphemies during the rest of their conversation, yet Hosseff had done nothing to stop him.

As the Order leader ponders Kepler's words, he admits it is strange that Hosseff would want the souls of his fallen paladins to be offered to him by laying them on his altar. He wonders if the cat is right. What if the souls are being devoured and used for the purpose the cat said? He needed to learn more before speaking with his lord again.

Gregory is with Lord Dowd and the rest of the army doing more of his lord's work. The White Chancellor has stopped their march to the Battlegrounds of Olis. He is explaining the situation while standing in a massive field. Gregory's goal is to convince Lord Dowd that a meeting with the Dark Order leader is necessary.

Marcus is wandering Southern Grayham. After teleporting Maldwin to Merchant Island, for some reason, he feels the need to stay. Something is telling him he needs to go to Brandor, but the specifics are not yet clear. All he knows is he has a desire to be at an inn just outside the city of West Utopia's gates before the Peak of Bailem.

Maldwin is in a container which has been carried between worlds by the Merchant Angels. He plans to stay put on Luvelles' Merchant Island until a man named Brayson Id comes to take him to George. He looks forward to his visit with his old friends, even the cat, Kepler, though he often feels like a meal around him.

Mosley has found the Wisp of Song within the mist below the cliffs of Griffin Falls.

Gabriel has decided to replace Yaloom and Mosley. He is speaking with the future gods who will take their place. The Book intends to introduce them to the Collective, soon. Gabriel plans to enjoy the anger on Lasidious' face when the Mischievous One sees his choices.

Mary took care of Brayson after Kepler brought him home. Brayson was ill after his run-in with Balecut.

The family united to help with his recovery. Now that the Head Master is back on his feet, he has work to do. He needs to go to Merchant Island to retrieve the rat while George and Kepler are on their outing.

Susanne and baby Garrin are doing fine. The potion to keep the child's power from manifesting is holding strong.

Susanne is nervous. Brayson has invited Gregory to dinner. The Head Master has taken it upon himself to play matchmaker. If things go well, she too could have herself a magic man. Susanne considers the White Chancellor to be a handsome elf.

Thank you for reading the Luvelles Gazette

𝕲𝖔𝖉𝖑𝖞 𝕿𝖍𝖗𝖊𝖆𝖙𝖘

Southern Grayham
The Siren's Song
Beneath Griffin Falls

After searching for the wisp within the mist, Mosley found the elusive ball of energy. He now stood less than 200 feet from where George listened to Cadromel's song not more than half a season ago. The air was chilled, and the wolf knew winter would soon shower Southern Grayham with its white rain.

As Mosley stared at the wisp, his breath billowed in front of him. The steam rising from the pool illuminated as the sphere ascended from the water's depths. The water cascaded from its smooth surface in sheets as the ball hung suspended only inches above the pool's surface. Mosley admired how the steam enveloped the sphere's mythical form.

A long period of silence passed before the wolf began to sing to the wisp in its own language—a benefit of having served Bassorine. The wolf howled with what he felt was all the passion he could muster. Despite his best effort, his ability to carry a tune approached horrifying, and he sounded like garesh.

Cadromel stopped Mosley before the wolf could finish his song. He begged Mosley to spare him the torture. After a few moments of silence, the sphere began a song of its own. The fog filled with a glorious melody, a song which would have melted the heart of the most evil being.

Mosley could understand the song's lyrics as they rang true to his core. They spoke of loving someone so unconditionally they become just as important as air is to breathing. They spoke of trials, and staying true to this love, treating this bond as unbreakable—cherished above all else—so it would stand the test of a never-ending continuation of moments. They spoke of a promise of an everlasting eternity with this love in a heaven for a life well-lived.

By the end of Cadromel's last note, Mosley was left to clear the tears from his eyes. His love for Luvera resurfaced as a result of the song's power, and without his godly power to protect his heart, he was unable to hide from the pain. His wife's soul was stuck inside a book. She was not living a beautiful existence within a heaven. She was not waiting for him to come to her as the song promised.

"Why have you come, wolf?" Cadromel inquired in a rhythmical manner, after allowing Mosley the moments necessary to collect his emotions. "I see my song has touched you."

Fighting to push back the pain, the wolf forced a reply. "Thank you for your gift. It has been too long since you last sang to me. Your words reminded me of how beautiful my...my...my wife..."

Mosley began to wail. He fell to the pool's bank. He lifted his snout to the sky and howled, trying to release the burden of his agony.

Cadromel composed a melodic collection of words. "I know of your loss. My song was meant to be uplifting and spiritual. It was not meant to sadden your soul. I long to take your pain."

Again, Mosley fought back the heartache. "You are not at fault. The one who murdered my wife is the one who administered my pain. Kepler is the one responsible. You have done nothing for which to be sorry."

The mentioning of Kepler's name gave Mosley new focus. It was as if a switch had been toggled. It gave the wolf's mind direction as he focused on his hatred for George and the demon cat. He would now be able to speak with Cadromel without crying.

After shaking off the water which saturated his coat, Mosley spoke with a stronger voice. "I have come seeking power, but not just any power. I want to know where I can find the secrets of the Swayne Enserad. Is there any place on Grayham I can find this?"

The wisp floated back a few feet as if somehow caught off guard. A moment passed before his melodious speech once again filled the mist. "Why would a god seek the secrets of the Swayne Enserad?"

"Vengeance," Mosley replied. "I seek vengeance. I have sacrificed what I was to become what I wish to be. I no longer possess the power of the gods."

Cadromel shimmered as a plethora of electrical charges ricocheted throughout his sphere. "To sacrifice one's godliness for the sake of vengeance seems desperate. I cannot pretend to understand your reasons."

Mosley snorted. "My sacrifice was necessary. This is all I can say. Please, tell me...can I find the secrets of the Swayne Enserad on Grayham?"

"No. You cannot find their secrets on Grayham. But, there is a way to get to the catacombs of Morsarasala by finding the gate of Gormasala which has been hidden on Grayham. The journey to the gate is perilous. Beyond that, I have no knowledge of the catacombs, or where the swayne have hidden their secrets within them. But first, are you prepared to journey to find the answer to my questions in exchange for the location of the gate?"

A strength appeared behind Mosley's eyes. "I am more than ready to begin this journey. What would you have me do?"

The sphere began to spin at a remarkable velocity. Within the wisp's body, an image of the frozen lands of Northern Grayham appeared. Many moments passed as the visions took the wolf on a flight across the tundra. It was not long before the vision took them beneath the ice and stopped inside a throne room of made of the element.

The wisp began to sing. "You shall travel to the Kingdoms of the Ice Kings. Once there, you must find the Tear of Gramal, and return it to its rightful owner. Her name is Clandestiny, and only she can tell you the secret of the Tear. She has been without her crystal for more than 285 seasons. Once you have returned the Tear, ask her this question. What fuels the Tear's power?"

Mosley thought a moment. To clarify, he reiterated the song's message. "So, I must travel to the lands of the ice kings and find this Tear of Gramal. Once I have it, I am to return it to this woman named Clandestiny. I am to retrieve the answer to your question, and in return, you will give me the information I seek. Is this correct?"

The wisp began to lower into the pool, but before the sphere submerged, it stopped. "You must also ask her why the Tear was stolen. If you gather this information and return to me, I will divulge the way to the gate."

The Wisp of Song submerged. Its light faded.

Mosley searched his mind. He found he had no knowledge of Northern Grayham. Not only that, but his godly memories about the other worlds' topographies no longer existed. Other than his vast knowledge of Southern Grayham, the only thing he could remember about their landscapes was what each Merchant Island looked like.

He now knew Gabriel was being cautious. Mosley sighed as he remembered one more thing which angered him. While living his life on Southern Grayham, he had never traveled beyond the northern shoreline of Lake Latasef. He would not be able to teleport beyond this area. He would have to cross the plains of the giant cats by paw in order to get to the Isthmus of Change.

The Isthmus was the only way to get to the Kingdom of the Ice Kings from Southern Grayham. The journey was long, and there would be perils while crossing it. But first, he could only hope he had the power necessary to survive the plains.

George and Athena's Home

George placed a parchment on Athena's pillow for her to find when she awoke. She was exhausted and needed rest. He had taken the moments necessary to write a poem. It read:

My Athena

Your beauty is the sun, fiery and untouchable
Your eyes are as the sea; graceful, undeniable
Your voice is like the birds, sweet and unrestrained
Your smile is like diamonds; shining, unadorned

Your hands are more gentle than the softest breeze
Your laugh sweeter to the ears than the finest song
Your embrace is warmer than a summer day
Your hair more lovely than a full-blown rose in bloom

Your eyes twinkle in the sun
In the dark they are lit by the beauty within
Your beauty sets your skin aglow
Like the flowers at midnight

Sweeter than the finest music
Your laughter fills the air
Warmer than the sun
I am caught in your embrace

You are my light
You are my heart
You are my warmth
You are my soul

George walked out of the room, then took Payne by the hand. He led the fairy-demon to Susanne's house with Joshua cradled in his left arm. Payne was still fighting his new rules. He did not want anything to do with learning table manners, bathing, or wearing clothes. Since George was going to be gone for most of the day, he wanted to leave Payne with someone who would see to it that he obeyed. George felt confident Susanne would keep Payne in his place. To keep the fairy-demon from burning anything, Brayson used another one of his potions to block Payne's ability to burst into flames.

All in all, Payne's fits were to be expected since he was so young. George was learning his patience for the demon-child's antics was more than sufficient to raise him.

After dropping Payne off, George called to Kepler who lay sleeping inside his lair. It was not long before Kepler appeared on top of the rocks. George waved his hand, and his saddle appeared on the jaguar's back. The cat's white fur contrasted well against its black, gem-covered leather, and George's staff was secured to its side.

Kepler jumped to the ground, then lowered to his belly. He waited for George to mount and announce he was strapped in place. He turned his head to look over his shoulder. "Is the baby secure?"

George nodded. With a wave of his hand, the warlock teleported the trio to Southern Grayham.

George rode Kepler up to the base of the cliffs while the cat studied his surroundings. "Where are we, George?"

"We are at the base of Griffin Cliffs, on the northeast side of the Temple of the Gods, on the shore of the Blood Sea."

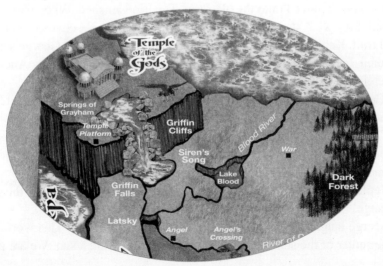

Without further conversation, George used his free hand to secure his staff. He pointed the gem at the base of the cliffs, then shouted in the language of the Ancient Mystics. *"Tormay consoladifo! Mejasimadoma ys ne tepa!"*

The rock began to crack and rumble. The stone peeled away, creating an opening and exposing the way inside. "Lead the way, Kep," George instructed.

As Kepler walked into the cave, George waved his hand to command the darkness to dissipate. The rock once again began to rumble, causing Joshua to stir in George's arms as the mouth of the cave sealed behind them. George caressed the baby's head to soothe him back to sleep.

After appeasing his own desire to see if the baby was comfortable, Kepler turned to focus on the path ahead. "Something isn't right with this place. I can sense it. This territory is dangerous."

George lowered his staff across the front of the saddle, then reached forward to pat the demon-cat on the shoulder. "It's only dangerous if you continue down the path you see before you. We are taking another less-traveled path."

Before Kepler could respond, George began to whisper in the language of the Ancient Mystics. *"Tormay jesolomondo mequa."* The path ahead began to change. The walls of the cave pushed back and formed a perfect circle. At the center of this cavern, a platform rose from beneath the floor. A yellow portal appeared, creating a gate.

George smiled. "You know what to do, Kep."

The jaguar moved onto the platform. The trio vanished. When they reappeared, they were standing in an orchard filled with trees covered with ripened fruit. Kepler looked over his shoulder. He looked inside George's mind for their location. The demon-cat's eyes widened. "Is this truly Ancients Sovereign?"

George nodded. "I know, this is freaking nuts. Can you believe it? It's beautiful, right?"

"It's beyond beautiful. It's glorious."

George adjusted Joshua to a more comfortable position as he looked around. "What else do you notice?"

Kepler looked to the mountains beyond the orchard, then to the sky. "Strange. I can look upon the sun. It is not as intense."

George laughed. "You're going to freak when I tell you. This world sits at the center of the sun. You are looking at a sun within a sun. We are literally inside the sun which warms the worlds." George looked around. "And, if that's not freaky enough, we're in a flourishing orchard. The mountains look normal, the clouds fill the sky, and still, I know in my mind...we are inside the sun. It doesn't even feel hot in here. Is that some crazy-ass garesh, or what?"

Kepler lifted his nose in the air and sniffed. "I'm thankful nothing smells like it's burning. I guess that's a good thing. What are we here for?"

George pointed to one of the trees. "Take us under it."

The cat did as he was told. George reached up and plucked a single piece of fruit, shaped like a pear, from a branch. He placed it inside his tunic, then reached up to pluck another. "These should come in handy."

"What are they?"

George smiled. "They are life." Before another word could be said, the trio vanished again only to reappear on the cobblestone streets of Brandor.

Kepler held his head high as he walked through the city toward the castle. The people moved to the far side of the street as they approached, unsure if it was safe. It didn't take long before someone recognized George. The man was rounded and aged for his seasons. His hair was long and pulled into a ponytail. He ran toward them, shouting, "Prophet! Prophet! Have you come to bless us?"

George commanded Kepler to stop. "What is your name, sir?"

"My name is Modain. I now serve Lasidious."

George lifted his staff. He touched the gem to Modain's forehead. As he did, he whispered, *"Psolema ente ne wano, orsay."* The gem began to glow. The light enveloped Modain. Kepler was forced to look away. As the light faded, the people who had gathered could see the transformation. Modain no longer looked old. His youthfulness had returned.

The crowd shouted praises as they closed in. The prophet showered them with Lasidious' words of love and lifted Joshua for all to see.

Kepler was enjoying the attention, right up to the moment when the children began to touch him, pulling at his fur, and shouting out their calls of "Kitty! Kitty! Mommy, look, it's a pretty kitty!" Despite his hatred for this kind of attention, he allowed the children their enjoyment. For vengeance, he licked their faces with his massive, extra slobbery tongue, pushing them to the ground.

They led the crowd toward the castle. As they approached, the gate opened. Waiting on the other side were Sam and Shalee.

George waved. "Hey guys! I want to share something with you."

Sam could only stare as he watched Kepler approach. Shalee had told him of Kepler's new look, but he had not been able to imagine how beautiful the demon-cat looked until now.

The king shook off his surprise. "I'm glad you're here. I have questions." Sam took note that George was carrying the baby. "And, who do you have with you?"

Kepler came to a stop and lowered to the ground for the warlock to dismount. Once his feet were planted, he pulled the blanket clear of Joshua's face. "I wasn't sure if I should bring him, considering everything you have gone through, but I wanted you to meet my son, Joshua. He is the main reason I decided to make a fresh start. If you want me to leave, I can come back without him."

Shalee moved to George's side. "Don't ya be gettin' all silly-like on us. Life must move on, right? Besides, Sam and I would love ta share this moment with ya." She took the baby into her arms. "Goodness-gracious, Sam, look at him. His hair is so soft, and he's as cute as a button."

George moved to stand next to Sam. "I know you are wary, but I wanted to share my happiness. I hate the fact I acted like a jack-ass."

Sam frowned. "It's what you do best, George. I expect nothing less."

George grinned. "I figured you would say something like that. So, to show you I'm sincere about patching things up, I brought you something. I would be willing to bet my life on it that this gift will make you very happy."

Sam looked George in the eyes. He was unsure where to go with the conversation. His contempt for George, and Kepler for that matter, was still at the forefront of his mind.

Eventually, the king responded. "You'll have to forgive me. I doubt there is anything you could do to make me happy. You're up to something. Get to the point of why you're here."

George patted Sam on the shoulder as he moved to stand beside Shalee. "He's adorable, isn't he?"

Sam spoke over Shalee's response. "You're stalling. Do you have something to say, or did you come here to rub his birth in our faces?"

George sighed, then reached inside his tunic. He removed a piece of the fruit he had plucked from the tree on Ancients Sovereign, then tossed it to Sam.

The king caught the fruit and looked it over. "You brought me a pear. What the hell do you expect me to do with this?"

George looked up and found Sam's eyes. "I think the best name for what your holding would be called…nasha."

The look on Sam and Shalee's faces was priceless. George took the opportunity to take Joshua and move beside Kepler. He placed the baby in a cloth. Once cradled, he reached up and tied the ends to Kepler's saddle. To ensure the knots would not come loose, George used his power to bind the cloth at its ends. He lowered Joshua into a hanging position, then propped a bottle in his mouth.

George circled to the front of the demon-jaguar. "Keep an eye on him for me, Kep. I'll be back."

Kepler grunted. "Great, babysitting again. But, I refuse to lick the garesh from his backside."

As George chuckled, Michael, Sam's General Absolute, rushed into the courtyard riding his mist mare. Seeing George, he dismounted and looked to Sam for his orders.

Sam was preoccupied with thought, so George addressed Michael. "General, have your men stand guard while you come with us. I have brought something for your king and queen which I think you need to see for yourself. This will be the happiest day this kingdom has ever seen, and the celebration you shall have tonight will be one to remember."

George led the group into the castle's kitchen and found a mug. He used his magic to force the fruit's juices to flow until the last drop fell into the wooden container.

Michael looked at George. "How will the juice from a piece of fruit bring joy to this kingdom?"

Shalee lifted her hand to shush the general as she waited for what was next.

The warlock lifted the mug from the table. "Where's your son's body? Let's go give him his life back. You deserve to be parents."

Sam's legs felt weak as he led the group toward the crypt. Sam had ordered a mausoleum to be made out of a room not far from their bedroom chamber. A guard remained outside the door during each moment of every day.

The king's hands trembled as he fought with the lock securing the door. Tears began to run down Sam's cheeks while Shalee found it almost impossible to breathe. Her heart beat against the front of her chest as the door swung open, revealing the casket at the far end of the room.

George tried to hand Sam the cup, but seeing the king's hands were unsteady, he thought better of it and moved into the room to stand beside the coffin. The warlock passed his hand across the lock. It popped open. After lifting the lid, he leaned in to pull back the cloth which had been used to cover Sam Junior's body. Slowly, he poured the liquid over the infant's tiny parts.

The walls of the crypt began to shake. The coffin began to vibrate and shift toward the edge of the dais on which it was resting. Sam reacted and steadied the container. Several moments passed before the quaking stopped. A light emerged from the ceiling and lowered to a position just above the child's body.

Sam and Shalee gasped as they watched Sam Junior's spirit merge with his corpse. Now, an even brighter light filled the room. Everyone had to close their eyes. When the light faded, all that was left was a healthy new-born crying for his parents.

Michael stood in absolute silence as he watched his king remove the child from the coffin to cradle him in his massive arms. He watched as Shalee summoned a blanket with a wave of her hand. She moved to Sam's side and wrapped Sam Junior in it.

George looked at Sam. "I will leave you alone to become better acquaint-ed. I wouldn't worry about the threat to Brandor which we spoke of the other day. Lasidious has asked that I keep you safe. I want you to know one thing before I leave. The return of your son's life is a gift from Lasidious. He wishes you nothing but happiness."

Sam handed the baby to Shalee. He grabbed George and lifted him from the floor, embracing him. "I now believe. Make sure you come back tonight. This city is going to celebrate. This is the happiest day of my life."

George chuckled the best he could from within Sam's grasp. "I will come back if you promise to put me down so I can breathe."

Lowering the warlock to the floor, Sam adjusted George's tunic. "How about we forget the past?"

With a nod, George turned to leave. "Enjoy your day with your son."

Shalee handed the baby to Sam, then gave George a kiss on the cheek. "Maybe, we could wait a bit before I look into the Eye. I should make sure Sam knows what he's doin' first."

"I agree one hundred percent. I'll see you tonight. I intend to bring my family with me, so make sure you have places set for thirty-seven and one giant cat. I may also bring two others with me, but I'm not sure just yet."

Shalee smiled. "Bring as many as ya like. We'll be ready for ya all. The moment has come for some hoopin' and hollerin'."

The World of Dragonia
The Home of the Demon Queen, Sharvesa

When the nasha fruit was used, Gabriel was caught off-guard. His binding was forced open, and despite the Book's best effort to close his cover, his pages fanned to the page holding Sam Junior's name. Without his consent, the infant's spirit emerged from the script in which it had been written and ascended toward the roof of the demon queen's palace.

Seeing the Book's distraction, Sharvesa leaned forward from her throne made from the tusks of the beragamore. "Gabriel, why do you fan yourself? Is my palace uncomfortable?"

The Book's heavy brows lifted as he watched Sam Junior's soul penetrate the roof to begin its journey to Brandor. He closed his binding. "Your Highness, please excuse me. I will return in a short series of moments." He turned to look at the demon council who had gathered. "Please be patient." Gabriel vanished.

The Book followed Sam Junior's spirit to the crypt inside Sam's castle. When he arrived, he remained invisible to the mortals. He watched as the infant's spirit reunited with his body.

Upon hearing George say, "The return of your son's life is a gift from Lasidious. He wishes you nothing but happiness," the Book spoke to himself in the language of his former being before becoming the protector of the gods' laws. *"רוציל וחילצה אל מילאה קוח דוע,"* which meant, "Yet, another law the gods have failed to create." After sighing his disgust, he teleported back to the demon queen's palace.

Gabriel looked at Sharvesa. "As I was saying...upon your ascension, it is my desire for your kind to worship you, not Lasidious."

Sharvesa stood from her throne and walked down the steps. She scanned the faces of the council who remained on one knee. "Does this gathering believe that all demons, red, white, and green would worship me if I accept Gabriel's proposal?"

A strong white demon stood. The horns protruding from his forehead were long, symbolizing his seasons. He took a step forward, placed his claws together, then bowed. "As our queen, all demons respect you, Your Highness. We would worship you. I, the leader of this council, would abandon my service to Lasidious to worship you."

Upon hearing Shadrowayne's pledge, and seeing the nods of the other council members, Sharvesa turned to Gabriel. "Then, it is settled. I accept your proposal."

Gabriel floated to a position in front of Sharvesa. "Then, kneel, and accept your gift of enlightenment. You are now the Collective's new God of War."

Southern Grayham
The City of West Utopia
The Peak of Bailem

George returned to Luvelles long enough to leave Joshua with Mary. Kepler retired to his lair, and Brayson left to retrieve Maldwin. George then teleported back to Southern Grayham. He is now standing in front of an inn located above the cliffs, east of the gates of West Utopia.

What a dive, George thought as he looked up at the inn's sign which hung crooked on a set of chains. *Who would freaking sleep here?*

The inn was called The Utopian Queen, but nothing about its appearance resembled anything royal. Even the wood the porch was made of looked abused. Some of the nails securing the planks had backed out, and as he walked across it, the wood rocked beneath his feet.

Once inside, George scanned the room full of rickety, defaced, wooden tables which were surrounded by unmatching chairs. Throughout the seasons, patrons had carved everything from slanderous comments to pictures of animals into their tops. He looked beyond the hodgepodge, filled with undesirables, for Marcus, but the Dark Chancellor was nowhere to be found.

George took a seat and waited for the bartender to approach. "Excuse me, have you seen a man..."

"A man like me?" a voice responded from behind.

George turned to look. Sure enough, Marcus had made it this far.

George took hold of Marcus' forearm. "The rat told me you decided to stay on Grayham when I spoke with him this morning. Do you realize how hard it is to find someone who doesn't want to be found?"

Marcus took a seat beside George. "Two ales," he commanded, raising his hand to summon the barkeep. "See to it that they're cold."

The bartender scoffed, then pulled his rag off his shoulder. The hair beneath his shirt stuck out from under the edge of his collar. He tossed the rag onto a hook hanging on the wall beside the tap. "You'll get the ale as it's always served. Cold ale. Whoever heard of cold ale?"

George reached out and grabbed Marcus' arms to keep him from using his magic. "Hey, hey, hey...you can't go around killing folks for not having cold ale. This place isn't like Luvelles. It's a primitive world."

"What a waste of a race."

George tapped the edge of the bar with his knuckles. "So, what made you decide to stay? Don't you want to be the Head Master?"

The Dark Chancellor stood from his stool and pushed his long hair clear of his face. "I don't know why I stayed. For some reason, I feel the need to go to Brandor."

"That's odd," George replied. He stood from his stool, chugged his ale, then slapped Marcus on the back. "Walk with me. We need to talk."

George tossed a Yaloom on the counter and headed for the door with Marcus in tow. The bartender lifted the coin from the counter. His eyes widened. He bit the coin to be sure it was real. As the doors swung shut, he called after them, "Come back often!"

George led Marcus north along a dirt road following the cliffs above the coastline east of the city. Once he was sure they were by themselves, George began to talk. "I bet your subconscious is guiding you."

"My sub-what?"

George put his arm around Marcus' shoulder. "The back of your mind is what I'm talking about. You know, that voice in your head that guides you. You already know what you want to do. I think it's brilliant."

Marcus' brows furrowed. "What are you talking about? What's brilliant?"

"Come on, man, you know. If you go to Brandor to kill their king, you would be the ruler of Southern Grayham. You could rule two worlds and teleport between them...after you've looked into the Eye, of course. But, I bet you knew that. Hell, all you would have to do is put someone in a key advisory position in Brandor who answers directly to you. I bet you even know who this person would be."

Marcus shook his head. "I never considered these things. My mind...or this subconscious you speak of has not led me in that direction."

George removed his arm. "Hmmm. Maybe, I've given you too much credit. Maybe, you're not as cunning as I had hoped. That's too bad. You could've accomplished so much more than just being the ruler of one world. You could have controlled the lower three. Maybe, I need to find someone with loftier goals."

Marcus stopped walking and turned to find George's eyes. "I didn't say my goals couldn't be adjusted, but wouldn't this be a conflict of interest? Why would you hand this power to me when you could have it for yourself?"

Without responding, George changed direction. He descended a long staircase which had been attached to the side of the cliff to get to the shoreline. The warlock removed his boots, rolled up his pant legs, then waded into the water. He watched as the waves crashed against the beach, and for that moment, everything felt peaceful.

George closed his eyes to smell the ocean breeze. A long series of moments passed before he turned to face Marcus. "What are you waiting for? Come out here!"

Marcus grunted, then took off his boots. Once he was standing next to George, the warlock answered his previous question. "I have bigger plans than ruling the lower three worlds. I intend to become a god. When that day comes, I will expect your loyalty."

Marcus began to laugh. "You're mad! You've gone insane. I will not worship you."

Without hesitating, George used the back of his hand to slap Marcus across the face. "You'll do as I say!"

The Dark Chancellor reacted with lightning reflexes. He reached into his cloak, drew his blessed blade, then with a fluid motion, stabbed George in the stomach.

The tip of the blade failed to penetrate. George smiled as he looked down. Even his tunic remained unscathed. The warlock grabbed the weapon, pulled it free from Marcus' hand, then tossed it onto the beach.

Marcus tried to react. He turned to command the weapon's return, but found he was unable to move.

George chuckled. He circled to stand in front of Marcus. His blue eyes turned cold, as if hate overwhelmed him. He reached up and stroked Marcus' face. "Did you truly believe you could kill me?"

Again, George backhanded Marcus. He allowed the chancellor to topple into the waves. George turned his hand over and extended his palm. He used his power to hold Marcus beneath the water. Many moments passed before he allowed Marcus his first gasp of air. George dunked Marcus again and again, until the chancellor slipped into unconsciousness. The warlock whipped his hand in the direction of the beach. Marcus flew through the air and landed on the sand with a thud.

George followed. He used his foot to roll Marcus to his side, then straddled the chancellor. He cupped his right hand under Marcus' chin, then used his power to shock the wizard into consciousness.

The warlock waited for the chancellor to spit up the water he had swallowed. After pushing Marcus to his back, George leaned over and placed his face only inches away from the chancellor's. He relished the fear filling Marcus' brown eyes as he tightened his grip on his chin.

The warlock hissed, "Do I appear insane, Marcus? Do not doubt me. I am capable of accomplishing anything I set my mind to. This includes killing you. I am only 23 seasons, yet I have found the power you have failed to find in over 700."

Marcus managed a weak response. "Please, forgive me."

George stood, then pulled Marcus to his feet. He had to use his power to keep the chancellor from falling. Once he was sure Marcus was strong enough to remain erect, he put his arm around the chancellor's shoulder. "It sounds as if you and I will be able to work together after all."

Still shaken, Marcus nodded. "I will do as you command."

"Perfect. That's just what I wanted to hear." George took a seat beside his boots. As he brushed the sand off his feet with his socks, he continued. "This is what I want you to do. You are going to kill the King of Brandor. You will need..." The conversation continued.

Western Luvelles
Later That Day
Before Late Bailem

George appeared outside his home. To his delight, the family had gathered. Brayson had returned with Maldwin, and a large bonfire was blazing near the mound of rocks at the clearing's center. The air was crisp, and the clouds were threatening to storm. Despite the threat, everyone was bundled up and had gathered to enjoy each other's company.

As expected, Gregory was present. His curiosity about Susanne had been piqued by Brayson. But, Gregory was not the only guest. George had also asked Brayson to invite Boyafed and Lord Dowd. They were standing near the fire, each holding a mug of ale.

George addressed them as he approached, "Lord Boyafed, Lord Dowd." The warlock reached for their forearms.

Each army leader responded, "Prophet."

Dowd continued, "Thank you for the invitation."

Boyafed added, "Agreed. It is a fine evening."

George smiled. "I'm glad you could set your differences aside for the moments necessary to enjoy a meal. Tonight will be a night of games, fun and good conversation. In a moment, I plan to take our little gathering some-place special. For now, is there anything I can get you?"

Lord Dowd responded. "No, nothing, thank you."

Boyafed redirected the conversation. "The Head Master told us you wish to speak with us."

George motioned for both leaders to take a seat on one of the benches the family had placed around the fire. "We will speak later. For now, let's enjoy each other's company. I have a surprise for everyone."

Athena's voice filled the air as she approached. Joshua was wrapped in a bundle of blankets, sleeping in her arms.

George kissed Athena on the forehead, then took the baby. "Give me a moment, please. I need to speak with these gentlemen."

After Athena left, George handed the baby to Lord Dowd. Sensing the white army leader's hesitation, he assured Dowd he wouldn't break him. It was easy to see that Dowd had never held a baby before.

Boyafed chuckled. "I remember that feeling. The first moment I held Kiayasis, I thought I would break him in half. I thought he was too fragile." Boyafed patted Dowd on the back. "Take the child, Henry. I assure you, he will grow on you."

George released Joshua. "So, your name is Henry? I would have never guessed that."

Dowd cradled Joshua in his arms. "There aren't many men who know my name. I prefer this to stay between us, if it's all the same to you. My given name is Henry Frolond Dowd."

Boyafed laughed as he reached over and put his hand on Dowd's shoulder. "It's good you're holding the child so you can't strike me. Frolond? I, too, would have kept that name a secret. It's a travesty."

The mood between the three men was light. George reached in and removed the blanket from Joshua's face. "Gentlemen, this little guy is the reason I search for peace. Many of your men have families, sons and daughters, of their own. We owe it to them to find a peaceful solution to your disagreements."

A frown appeared on Boyafed's face. "Our problems cannot be solved through diplomacy."

Dowd nodded. "The moments for negotiating have passed. We will dine tonight, respecting each other as honorable men should, and tomorrow, I will bury my blade into his stomach."

Boyafed lifted his mug. "I'll drink to that. But, let us hope it is your stomach my blade finds."

George could only marvel at their candor. "Gentlemen, I have knowledge that neither of you did anything to provoke this war. You have been deceived by the gods, and because of this deception, I asked you to come. But, as I have said, let's enjoy each other's company."

George no sooner finished his statement when Brayson walked up to call for everyone's attention. "I have something I wish to say before we depart." Once the atmosphere had settled, Brayson lowered to one knee near the fire. He took Mary's hand.

Mary's eyes widened as she held Brayson's gaze. She was wearing a new, black dress which covered her feet. Over this, she wore a thick, knitted, yellow sweater and had shoes to match. Her outfit had been given to her by Brayson that morning.

Athena grabbed hold of Susanne's arm and began to squeeze. Susanne was standing next to Gregory who wore a white and green tunic with white pants, which Mykklyn had convinced him to wear for his first date. Gregory smiled as Brayson gathered his nerve to continue.

Brayson cleared his throat. "Mary...I have watched your elegance ever since the moment you stepped foot onto Merchant Island. Luvelles has never been the same for me since your arrival. I have never wished to spend my life with any other before you. Will you accept me as your mate?"

Everyone was silent as they waited for Mary's response. The first snowflake of winter landed on Mary's nose as tears filled her eyes. She looked up and followed another flake, and as if it was meant to be, it landed on Brayson's nose.

Mary gasped. "It seems the mood of winter's white rain would be ruined if I was to decline. My answer is yes. I will be your mate."

The crowd erupted as the family gathered to congratulate them. George turned to Boyafed and Dowd. "It is moments like this which prove peace is far better than war. Shall we go to Southern Grayham and dine with the King of Brandor and his family? Something has happened there which will make you question your beliefs."

Before they could answer, George felt something scratch the left leg of his pants. When the warlock looked down, he could only smile as he lowered to lift Maldwin from the ground.

Maldwin was excited to see his old friend. All he could think of to say was, "Everything is A-Okay, man!"

George gave the rat a thumbs-up. "Everything is A-Okay, man!" He turned to excuse himself from the two army leaders. "I better get this little guy some cheese. His name is Maldwin."

Dowd and Boyafed shrugged. Boyafed asked, "You have a pet rat?"

George smiled. "Doesn't everybody?" He turned his attention to Lord Dowd. "Will you please give my son to my wife when you're done holding him? I think you're getting the hang of it. You'll be a fine father someday. I'll be back in a bit, then we'll go."

George lifted his voice and called to the far side of the fire. "Kep, come with me for a moment. Susanne, please keep Payne with you until I return from the house."

Dowd looked at Payne, then Kepler, then the rat. "George, you keep diverse company. I don't think I've ever seen a man with such companions."

Boyafed put his hand on Dowd's shoulder. "I watched that cat kill four tricksters."

Dowd looked across the fire at Kepler. "He is glorious."

"You will get no argument from me."

Kepler heard their comments. He looked at Dowd, then winked. He teleported onto the porch of George's home.

George and Maldwin caught up with the jaguar. As he shut the door behind them, George spoke. "Kep, do me a favor. Tell Maldwin I'm happy to see him. Tell him there are things we need to accomplish while he's on Luvelles. Tell him if he wants me to, I can give him and his family a better home than the one they have. Tell him..."

Kepler interrupted. "Great. Here we go again with the tell him, to tell you, to tell him, to tell you thing. Have you gone dense again?"

George shook his head. "Would you just shut up and listen so we can get going?"

Maldwin chimed in. "I like cheese, George!"

Kepler rolled his eyes. "I'm reliving a nightmare."

Ancients Sovereign
The Hall of Judgment

Gabriel had lowered his binding to the top of the large marble table within his hall and was waiting for the gods to arrive. The moments had come to deliver his news. The deities he had chosen to replace Yaloom and Mosley would be introduced. The Book had sent word to ensure the Mischievous One would attend.

One by one, the gods made their appearance and as always, Keylom's hooves clapped against the floor as they waited for the fashionably late couple. Eventually, Lasidious appeared with Celestria at his side. The goddess was wearing a bright red gown which hung low across her bosom. Her hair was pinned up to expose her gem-covered neck and dangling earrings. She was radiant and greeted everyone with a smile.

Once everyone was settled, Gabriel rose from the table. "As we all know, Yaloom failed to provide a name as to who would replace him. Because of this failure, our laws command me to choose."

Gabriel floated to a position directly above the table's center. "There is another matter I wish to discuss." Gabriel took a deep breath, then continued. "Mosley has broken a law. He has been stripped of his right to remain on Ancients Sovereign and must also be replaced."

Lasidious was the first to react as he stood from his chair. "What could he have done to deserve such a consequence?"

Keylom responded, thumping a heavy hoof on the floor to get everyone's attention. "Mosley attacked me. We had a confrontation, and he failed to control his anger. Gabriel had no choice."

The others began to shout questions as Lasidious sat in his chair. He looked at Celestria. "Too bad. Mosley was my favorite. I wonder...what could have caused him to do something so drastic?"

Celestria responded. "Perhaps, his reasoning was not drastic at all. Perhaps, it was for other reasons which we do not know, reasons which we can find out if we find him. He is not stupid."

Gabriel floated over to the couple. "You're right. The wolf isn't stupid. He broke the law intentionally. He used Keylom as a way to regain his mortality.

"Mosley didn't enjoy the games we play. This is what made him choose a mortal life. His final request was that I place him on Trollcom, but his reasons were not divulged."

Alistar lifted from his seat. "Why all the secrecy about the wolf? And, why have you waited until now to choose Yaloom's replacement? You could have chosen this being sooner."

"That's a great question," Mieonus added as she pushed her brunette hair clear of her face.

Bailem stood and adjusted his robe as he always did. "Get on with the announcement, Gabriel."

The Book moved clear of the table and stood at the far side of the hall. He motioned for Sharvesa to enter. Everyone in the room gasped. Lasidious looked at Alistar, then Celestria. The Book's decision would threaten their plans on many levels.

The demon queen was tall, nearly eight feet. After addressing the Collective, she looked at Lasidious and spoke in the language of the demons. A rough translation was, "With respect to your greatness, My Lord." She hesitated. "Perhaps, I should address you in a less formal manner, now that I've ascended. It is good to see you."

Sharvesa thought a moment. She reconsidered her position and decided to stay with what she knew best. "My Lord. The council has met. All demons will worship me as soon as my daughter, Teshava, has succeeded me as queen. However, I enjoyed serving you while living on Dragonia. I'm sure you can understand my desire to rule my own kind."

Everyone in the room watched for Lasidious' reaction, but the Mischievous One refused to give Gabriel the satisfaction. He respected the demon queen for her tact. He stood from his chair and smiled. "You will make a fine goddess. I must compliment Gabriel on his choice." Lasidious turned and found the Book's eyes. "She is worthy of replacing the wolf. Who's next?"

Gabriel's heavy brows furrowed as he studied the Mischievous One's face. He was unsure how he felt about Lasidious' reaction. He motioned for the other being, waiting outside, to enter. As Kesdelain appeared, the room once again filled with gasps.

Lasidious had to fight back his emotions to keep a straight face. Alistar and Celestria also felt the threat of the Book's choice. They, too, had to work to keep their anger hidden.

Now...fellow soul...I must interject. Between the demon queen and the troll king, the loss of worshippers serving Lasidious will drastically effect his plan to control the Book. This was not the best series of moments for this to happen. Lasidious was so close to seizing control.

Even though the centaurs on Harvestom, the beings on Southern Grayham, and the elves and the halflings on Luvelles are all questioning their faith, Gabriel's choices will keep the addition of the dragons' service from giving the Mischievous One absolute power. It looks as if Celestria, Alistar, and Lasidious will need to work harder to find replacement followers in other places.

Lasidious once again smiled as he spoke to the troll king. "So, Gabriel has made you the new God of Greed, Kesdelain. I doubt you have what it takes to handle a job of this magnitude." He looked at the Book. "I would have expected a wiser decision, Gabriel."

The troll responded in his own language before the Book could say anything. "I have despised you for too many seasons, Lasidious. To think I was foolish enough to believe your charade in my throne room. I will lay claim to the prayers of every troll. I will enjoy watching you lose the power their prayers provide. It feels good to crawl out from under the burden you held over me. It is my turn to reign as god over the races of trolls."

Lasidious moved close and stood face-to-face with Kesdelain. "I wouldn't be so quick to glorify yourself. You aren't nearly as clever as those I have manipulated into throwing away their immortality. I have made much smarter minds than yours crack."

Alistar stood and added, "Kesdelain, listen to me for a moment. Lasidious speaks the truth. He will tear at your mind until you make a mistake. I would tread with caution if I were you."

Mieonus shouted at Alistar. "You act as if you're on Lasidious' side. Why do you care if he tortures the troll?"

With a calm demeanor, Alistar responded. "Because...we need Kesdelain. Without him, Lasidious will convince the trolls to continue worshipping him. Must I explain a concept as simple as this to you, Mieonus? Does every detail need to be drawn out for you as I would for a child? Perhaps, you should spare us your babbling. Sit down and salvage what is left of our misplaced perception of your intelligence."

Celestria laughed as she watched Mieonus sit in a huff. She stood from her chair, then sauntered toward Kesdelain. "Do you really know what you have gotten yourself into? You will not last a season before Lasidious convinces you to destroy yourself. Be careful who you disrespect from now on. I pity you."

Gabriel decided he had had enough. "There shall be no more discussion within my hall. Everyone leave."

Lasidious decided to take a new approach. He moved to stand before Gabriel. "And, what will you do if we don't, Book? Will you sacrifice yourself to shut me up? Will you allow the laws within your pages to destroy you if I continue to torture this troll's mind? I dare you to destroy me. Allow your hatred to employ you to do something so foolish. Do you really think I haven't prepared a way to survive if you strike me down? Do you truly think your decisions will stop me from controlling you?" Lasidious raised his voice. "Go ahead! Strike me down! Or, are you afraid?"

The hall went silent as they waited to see what Gabriel would do. Many long moments went by before Lasidious made a scoffing sound. "As it is with all the gods, even you speak with words filled with empty threats."

Lasidious moved to stand before the troll. "Make no mistake, Kesdelain. I will find a way to destroy you. Your days are numbered. I would hate to be you. Ask anyone in this room. You won't last a season."

Lasidious turned his attention to the demon queen. "Sharvesa...as always, it was nice seeing you again. It is a pleasure to have someone so brilliant living on Ancients Sovereign. When you are ready to choose a home, find me. There are places beyond the horizon to the south which I'm sure you'll enjoy."

Lasidious turned to face the Collective. He spoke with a calm voice. "I'm sure this has been entertaining for each of you. I bid you all good night." He looked over his shoulder and found Gabriel's eyes. "I will speak with you later...Book!" After taking Celestria's hand, Lasidious teleported.

Gabriel floated toward the table and lowered his binding onto it. "Have I made poor choices?" he said for all to hear. "Perhaps, I have awakened a sleeping giant."

Alistar looked at Gabriel. "I'm not sure what to think. I doubt the troll will last." He looked at Kesdelain. "If I were you, I would look for a way to find favor with Lasidious. I, too, pity you." Alistar vanished.

Hosseff stood from his chair and vanished, leaving a wispy laugh echoing throughout the hall.

Mieonus moved to stand before the two new gods. "I wouldn't worry about Lasidious. You can always speak with me if you need anything."

Sharvesa laughed. "If you don't mind, I must go." The demon queen disappeared.

Mieonus hid her anger, then turned to Kesdelain. "And, what do you have to say on the matter?"

Kesdelain sighed. "To befriend you would serve no purpose." The troll teleported from the hall.

Mieonus stomped her high heels on the marble. "Damn them!" When she turned around, the only one left in the room was the Book. "I think you made fine choices, Gabriel. This will set Lasidious back in his planning. He never saw it coming. You quite possibly saved us all."

Without responding, the Book vanished.

Another high heel found the floor. "Damn, damn, damn," she screamed.

Brother vs. Brother

Southern Grayham
Brandor's Dining Hall
After Late Bailem

The dinner celebrating Sam Junior's resurrection was delicious. Shalee had worked with the castle's chef to prepare a delectable meal for their guests while Sam cared for Sam Junior. The king was learning his skills as a warrior paled in comparison to the skill required to change an infant's diaper—especially one made of cloth.

Sam had invited the heads of the legions, the members of the Senate who lived in the city, and a number of other families Shalee had befriended since becoming queen to attend. With George's family, Lord Dowd, and Boyafed, 187 people have been sitting around a massive table in a dining hall which stretches more than 200 feet and spans a width of 70 feet. Everyone is enjoying each other's company.

During many moments over dinner, Sam made a point of showing George his gratitude. Mary, Athena, Susanne, and Shalee have been spending their moments discussing the features of the babies. Sam Junior has the hair of his father and the eyes of his mother. Joshua is showing signs of George's chin and nose. Yet, Susanne and Mary have been struggling to find any resemblance to Susanne in Garrin. Seeing this, George convinced Boyafed the baby's features resemble Dayden's. Hearing Boyafed's confirmation, Susanne's anxiety subsided.

Lord Dowd and Boyafed returned to sharing stories of Luvelles' past with the members of Sam's military and the Senate. George watched as Payne sat next to Athena in his high chair, a chair the warlock used his power to create, one which took into account the space needed for the fairy-demon's wings. He used his power on the buckle to ensure Payne could not get loose.

Kepler was also mingling. He had a large pile of rare meat stacked in the corner. On occasion, he strolled over to take a bite, then returned to his conversation. The jaguar is interested in the stories Dowd and Boyafed are telling.

Maldwin decided to take up his own place of comfort on the floor beneath George's chair. He was in rat heaven, his nose twitching as he savored the flavors of ten cheeses which Shalee requested from the chef once she realized the rodent was present.

George reveled inside as he watched his plan come together. He would wait until after dessert to speak with everyone in the room. Tonight would be a productive night.

Southern Grayham
The Cat Plains

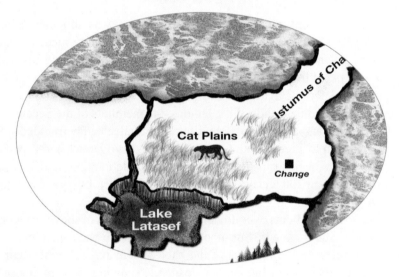

After teleporting just north of the shoreline of Lake Latasef, Mosley began his journey around the Cat Plains. The weather on Grayham was changing throughout the day, and all across the plains it had been snowing. It was now ankle-deep.

The wolf was unsure what the extent of his power was as a mortal. He had been doing little things along the way to experiment. He could still command fire, ice, water, and even the earth to do small, useful things, but his power was not strong enough to be used on a large scale. The good news, he did not need to use words to command the elements. The downside, he now knew his skills were equal to that of a weak mage. This made him nervous—extremely nervous—considering the area he was skirting.

He knew the cats of the plains hunted in packs, similar to the way he had hunted with his father when he was a pup. On many occasions, his father allowed him to hunt small game with his brothers. He could still remember his first outing.

A young Mosley was standing beside his father, waiting for his brothers to chase a horned rabbit through a ditch. Mosley's father had whispered something special to him that day. "When the rabbit rounds the bend, you'll be the only thing standing between its freedom and becoming our meal. Today, my son, you become a night terror wolf. No longer will the others call you, pup."

Mosley smiled as he remembered what happened next. His brothers funneled the animal into the ditch where he stood at the opposite end. The ditch's sides were steep, and the only way for the rabbit to free itself was to get past him. His father stood at the top of the embankment looking down while he waited for Mosley to face their meal head-on.

The rabbit rounded the bend. Seeing the wolf in front of him, he lowered his horns. Mosley crouched and prepared to tackle his prey, but unfortunately, the rabbit proved too much to handle. Mosley was run over by the rabbit, then by his seven brothers as they continued to give chase.

His father jumped into the ditch and moved to stand over him. Mosley remembered the wolfish grin on his father's face. "Now that you're a wolf and no longer a pup, perhaps you should pick yourself up, and help your brothers catch our meal. Make the pack proud."

A warm-hearted soul, Mosley's father always knew the right thing to say. On that day, he grabbed the back of Mosley's neck and lifted him to his paws before rushing off to bring down the oversized, horned rabbit. Even though Mosley was still a pup, his father had made him feel so much bigger.

As the sun disappeared below the horizon, Mosley's senses warned him of danger. He knew he was being watched by something in the darkness, but by how many sets of eyes, he did not know. He had been following the river which flowed north from Lake Latasef to ensure he could not be surrounded. He knew cats hated water, and if he had to, he could jump in. But, the current was swift, and he did not know if he would be able to swim back to shore.

With his back to the river, he used his magic to create fires to his left and his right, allowing a group of bushes to burn in hopes of discouraging an attack. The magic fought the snow and refused to extinguish. The fire's hiss reminded him of George. An idea popped into his head. He decided to call out to the ones stalking him. He would be as cunning as George in this situation.

He shouted in the language of the giant sabertooth, the dominant language of the cats roaming the plains. When translated, his deep-throated growl meant, "I have come by order of Lord Kepler!"

Upon hearing no response, Mosley growled in a deeper tone, "I have come by order of Lord Kepler! Show yourself!"

Now, he could hear the snarls of the figures hidden in the darkness. He knew his assumption was right. They spoke sabertooth, and by the sound of their snarls, they were confused.

Again, he growled, "I have come by order of Lord Kepler! I require an escort through the plains! I come with orders given by your lord for five of your finest to travel with me into the lands of the ice kings! I demand you serve me as you would if your lord was present! Show yourselves, so I may tell Kepler of your loyalty! He has promised a reward for those brave enough to act as my guard!"

An enormous figure crept from the shadows. Two of his top teeth were long and sharp. They acted as beacons as the fire lit them. The color of his fur appeared as shades of gray until he was close enough for Mosley to see the browns, yellows, and blacks which covered his form. His eyes reflected the firelight, and with each calculated placement of his heavy paws, imprints larger than Mosley's head, were left in the snow.

The saber spoke in an irritated snarl, "Why would Lord Kepler wish us to travel the territories of the north with a wolf? What is your relationship with him to command our escort?"

Mosley took a deep breath, then came up with a new plan. He looked at the base of the cat's paws. Without saying a word, he commanded the snow surrounding the beast to melt while sparing the cat the heat's intensity. The water hissed as it evaporated, causing the sabertooth to jump backward.

Seeing the fear in the cat's eyes, Mosley took the advantage. "Perhaps, Kepler knows of my power. Do you mean to deny me the company of your warriors, and risk the wrath of your lord? Kepler would tear you apart for your disobedience."

The beast snorted, then lifted his head into the night. A deafening roar covered a great area surrounding their location before he lowered his head and allowed his yellow eyes to find the wolf's. "I am Rash, ormesh of my clan. I will travel with you. We will need to pass my lair to collect the others as you have requested. You will not speak with them until I deem you trustworthy. If this does not work for you, then speak, so I may be on my way."

Mosley walked onto the patch where the snow had melted and stood before the cat. He lifted his head to find the saber's eyes, which were a good three feet above his own. "My name is Mosley. Your terms are acceptable. Your reward upon our return will be grand. Shall we go?"

Rash growled. Seven other cats emerged from the darkness. Mosley felt helpless as he watched them surround him.

Rash ordered, "Follow me, wolf."

Western Luvelles
6 Peaks East of the Battlegrounds of Olis

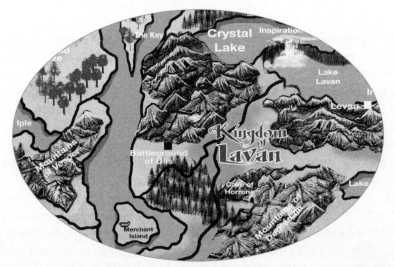

The white army has set up camp. Their orders: stop marching, and hold tight until word has been sent from Lord Dowd about how to proceed.

Strongbear ordered the goswigs to set up their own section of camp to keep their sense of community. Unfortunately, there was a problem which no one knew how to fix. Winter slapped Strongbear upside the head, causing the brown bear to lie down in his tent. He fell into a deep slumber and began to snore. His snoring was so loud, the Wraith Hound Prince, Wisslewine, entered their section of camp and made a threat to devour Strongbear if the goswigs did not find a way to shut him up.

Gage and Gallrum discussed their options. Eventually, the decision was made to teleport the bear back to his cave. When the deed was done, Gage looked at the bear after covering him with four of his homemade blankets. Smiling, the badger turned to Gallrum. "Well, we may not be with him... but, we certainly aren't against him." Both goswigs chuckled before they vanished.

Later that night, it was discovered that sleep was still going to be impossible for everyone. The leader of the giants had a nasty snoring habit of his own. When Wisslewine went to investigate the cause, the wraith hound just took one look at the size of the beast-man, then shook his head. He growled as he returned to his pack.

Southern Grayham
Brandor's Castle
That Same Night

George decided the proper moment had come to address everyone present. He stood from his chair, and after moving to stand on top of the massive dining table, said, "I want to thank everyone for coming to celebrate the gift Lasidious has given to the king and queen of Southern Grayham. We all know this kingdom has seen too much sorrow, and many lives have been affected."

George looked down at Sam who had leaned back in his chair and was holding Sam Junior. "I have been promised this pain will be replaced by happiness, love, and prosperity." He pointed at the baby. "We see an example of this happiness by gazing upon the blessing Lasidious has given.

"Sam Junior's life is one of many blessings Lasidious will bestow upon this unified kingdom. He has promised ongoing peace which will be delivered before the end of the day tomorrow. The final threat to Brandor is making his way to the city's gates, and there are few present with the power to stop him."

George looked down at Dowd and Boyafed. "I have much to say to the two of you. I request you allow me to speak before I answer your questions.

"I find it interesting that my lord has chosen two men, who fight on opposing sides, to come together to defeat an evil which threatens a kingdom for which you have no responsibility to protect. You are leaders among elves, and you have chosen to be the example others strive to follow. My lord has asked me to encourage you to work together to destroy the evil which threatens to bring war to your homeworld."

George concentrated on Boyafed. "You, Lord Boyafed, are the leader of the Order. You serve a god who commanded your chancellor to kill Lord Dowd's spirit-bull. Hosseff also ordered Marcus to kill Heltgone. He even ordered you to kill Sam, yet, the King of Southern Grayham sits here before you, alive and well. You saw him die with your own eyes, and you have made seven comments during dinner confirming your disbelief of this fact, despite the king sitting in front of you."

The warlock then turned to Dowd. "You, Lord Dowd, are also a great leader. This same man who deceived Boyafed, also plotted against you. Marcus Id killed Dayden, and the others of the Order. Do not allow this deception to kill thousands.

"Both of you are going to be given the opportunity to avenge the lives of the lost when Marcus enters Brandor. The chancellor's intent is to kill this royal family."

George listened to the murmurs as they filled the hall. He watched as Sam stood and handed the baby to Shalee. "Marcus will be here tomorrow? How should we prepare? There's no one in my army who commands this kind of power."

George held up his hand and motioned for everyone to listen. "It is no coincidence Lord Dowd and Lord Boyafed sit with us tonight. Lasidious knows justice needs to be delivered to these men. My lord has requested that I protect your families. He has made me responsible to keep you safe while these warriors, who cherish honor, defeat Marcus inside Brandor's arena. He wants the beings of Southern Grayham to see the final threat to this kingdom fall before their eyes."

Boyafed stood from his chair and motioned for Dowd to do the same. He extended his hand and grasped Dowd's forearm. "Knowing Marcus Id the way I do, I do not doubt for a moment that he is the one responsible for our conflict." The Order leader looked at Kepler. "I have done much thinking since our encounter in the Petrified Forest."

Boyafed scanned the faces surrounding the table, then stood on his chair. "Tonight, when I saw your king walk into this room, my eyes could not fathom his ability to walk through those doors. Hosseff would not have given this kingdom such a gift. Not only does your king live, but his son lives. I no longer will serve a god who is without honor." Boyafed found Dowd's eyes. "I would be honored to fight by your side to defend the lives of these people."

Dowd studied many of the faces surrounding the table. He saw the emotion in their eyes. He could see their desperation as they waited for his response. Facing Boyafed, Dowd extended his hand and reclaimed Boyafed's forearm. "I will fight with you at my side under one condition."

Boyafed smiled. He knew what was coming as Dowd continued. "Once this fight is over, and Marcus lies dead, you and I shall see who the best warrior is between us. I know this answer, but I can think of nothing finer than for us to meet in an honorable battle."

Sam began to clap his hands. He stood and shouted. "If only Pay-Per-View existed on this world! Now, this is going to be a fight worth watching!" He looked at both warriors. "I have a suggestion, gentlemen."

Dowd and Boyafed waited for Sam to continue. "To kill each other would be a shame. Your influence will be necessary as your world makes the changes needed to ensure peace. I may have a solution which will allow you to settle your desire to know who is the best, without killing one another. On my homeworld..."

Sam paused to allow a huge smile to cross his face. "On my old homeworld, we had a style of fighting called Mixed Martial Arts. If you would allow me to teach you, I will show you how this form of battle could become a great way to settle differences."

George began to laugh. Everyone turned to look at him. Sam was the one to speak. "What's so funny, George?"

George jumped down from the table and moved to stand beside Sam. "Nothing. I was just thinking, you'll probably use that brilliant mind of yours to bring these fights into the homes of the people. We just may see a form of Pay-Per-View on this world soon enough. Heck...I bet it isn't long before you have HD piped into their homes."

Boyafed turned to face Sam. "What is HD?"

Southern Grayham
The Peak of Bailem
The Following Day

Snow covered the streets of Brandor as Marcus made his way into the city. It was as if everyone had been told he was coming. Footprints were scattered everywhere, many leading into homes or storefronts. Even the guards who should have been on patrol were absent, leaving the streets unprotected. Something was amiss, but Marcus knew his power was greater than any on Grayham. He continued to make his way to the castle.

The only place which appeared to have any semblance of normal activity was a gigantic structure which formed an oval. The people inside were shouting and laughing as if something exciting was happening.

Drawn to the noise, Marcus lowered his pipe as he passed beneath the arches leading into the arena. He had not taken more than fifteen steps before the people inside went silent. A chill ran down his spine as he hesitated. The iron gates attached to the arches slammed behind him, and the massive locks resting at their centers clanked shut.

Marcus tossed his pipe to the ground, lifted his hands, then sent a wave of force into the gates, but nothing happened. He sent a stronger wave, and still, nothing happened. Something was wrong. He closed his eyes and thought of the Merchant Island on Grayham, but when he opened them, he had gone nowhere.

A voice shouted from inside the stadium. The voice was faint, but familiar nonetheless. Marcus turned to make his way through the tunnel which led to the sand of the arena floor. What he saw as he placed his feet on the fighting surface was thousands of people sitting side-by-side, and at the center of the arena, a man stood on a pedestal. Marcus recognized his face. It was Boyafed, dressed in the Order's black and gold plate. The Dark Chancellor now knew, George was no longer his ally.

Marcus walked toward Boyafed as he scanned the crowd for the warlock's face. With each step, his irritation grew, and as if Boyafed's presence was not bad enough, a second pedestal was beginning to emerge from beneath the arena floor. Marcus' heart sank as Lord Dowd stood dressed in his black and silver armor bearing the white army's symbol on his chest. Each man had his blessed blade drawn. They lifted them in Marcus' direction to formalize their challenge.

Marcus tried again to teleport, but failed. He knew George was somewhere. The warlock was using his power to keep him from escaping. Marcus wondered if he could teleport within the arena. He tested his theory by closing his eyes. When he reappeared, he was only feet from where he had been standing.

Marcus screamed, "You will regret your betrayal!"

From his seat within Sam's box, George snickered as he looked at Brayson. "Looks like he's pissed."

Sam was sitting next to Brayson. He leaned forward to look past the Head Master. "George, are you sure this is a good idea? Allowing the people to watch is dangerous. They have no way of protecting themselves from wayward magic."

Gregory was sitting behind George. He leaned forward and put his hand on George's shoulder, then responded to Sam. "The Prophet has the power to protect them. Just watch the fight."

Athena tugged on the arm of George's tunic. She lifted three bottles filled with corgan milk. "Do you mind?"

George smiled. He placed his hands on each bottle and used his power to warm the milk. "There you go. That should keep them happy."

Athena turned to Mary who sat next to her, holding Garrin. She gave her mother one of the bottles, then offered the third bottle to Shalee.

Shalee smiled. "Well, aren't ya just a peach. Thank you."

Meanwhile, back on the arena floor, Marcus stared down his challengers as he stopped a fair distance from their pedestals. He shouted across the sand. "I will not fight you both! There is no honor in unfair odds."

Boyafed shouted in response. "Honor? Where was your honor when you killed Dayden? Where was your honor when you killed Heltgone and Dowd's spirit-bull? There was no honor in the senseless killing of my men! You will fight us both! You will fight us now!"

Boyafed leapt from his pedestal with Dowd behind him. The people within the arena began to cheer as both men lifted their blades to charge. Marcus reached beneath his robe and drew a blessed sword of his own. He lifted his hand and sent a bolt of lightning into Dowd. The charge slammed into the white army leader's chest and threw him across the arena where he rolled to his feet.

Boyafed's blade met Marcus'. A frenzied exchange of steel followed before the dark warrior was struck by a well-placed burst of wind. The blast lifted him from the arena floor and threw Boyafed into the wall beneath the crowd.

Dowd closed the gap between Marcus and himself. The white army leader lifted his free hand and sent a wave of force barreling toward Marcus. The Dark Chancellor captured Dowd's magic within his palms, then returned it three-fold. The power plowed into the white army leader, sending him flying into the wall opposite Boyafed.

Marcus redirected his attention at the perfect moment, deflecting a wall of fire Boyafed sent his direction. The fire continued toward the people in the stands, but George stopped the power from killing the spectators with a wave of his hand from the king's box.

He leaned forward and looked at Sam. "Damn, that was close. Maybe, I should keep everyone protected." He moved to the far side of the box where Kepler was standing and motioned for Shalee to join them. "Stand beside me. I need to feed from your power." George placed one hand on Kepler's back and the other on Shalee's shoulder. With a nod, he created an invisible wall to protect the people.

Boyafed and Marcus once again met with blades slamming into one another. Lunge after lunge, stab after stab, slice after slice, were defended until the Order leader found a small opening. He sent a magic arrow into Marcus. The chancellor flew across the arena. Marcus rolled to his feet, unfazed, then teleported behind Boyafed. The Order leader spun to block Marcus' blade from slicing him in two.

Again, Marcus teleported, but during this series of moments, he appeared on the far side of the arena. The chancellor sent his strongest bolts of lightning hurling in two directions. Dowd and Boyafed were forced to dive out of the way. As Dowd rolled to his feet, he teleported next to Marcus and began a masterful series of metal on metal clashes before finding a small opening.

A wave of force carried Marcus toward the wall behind him, but before the chancellor slammed into it, his body vanished, only to reappear behind Dowd. With blade ready, Marcus lunged. He savored the penetration as the blade buried into the small of Dowd's back. He could feel the white army leader's spine sever. Marcus pulled his blade free and watched as Dowd fell to the sand.

Boyafed reacted. A series of metal clashes and blocked magical strikes continued for a long series of moments before Marcus found the opening which would send the Order leader to the sand. Boyafed suffered a slash across his abdomen, followed by a downward strike to his shoulder, ending the fight.

Blood from both men saturated the earth as Marcus moved to stand over Boyafed to deliver the killing blow. His blade began his descent as it arched toward Boyafed's head. But, the weapon only made contact with the sand as the bodies of the wounded vanished.

George motioned for Sam to come close while he listened to Marcus shout his curses. "Sam, I hope your healers have the vial Brayson gave you. They are going to need it if they are to survive."

Sam nodded. "I have something far better than that. I have given it to Jaress."

George turned to face Brayson. "You're going to have to be the one who kills him. I would do it myself, but I cannot be perceived as a killer."

Mary grabbed Brayson's arm. "You're not going out there. Neither of you are. Do you hear me, George?"

Athena cradled Joshua in her arms. "I don't want the grandfather of my child falling. Don't you dare go out there."

George smiled as he found Brayson's eyes. "Well, this is one of those moments where you're going to have to beg for forgiveness. Settle this once and for all."

Brayson reached beneath his robe and unsheathed the blade of the Head Master. He was about to teleport to the arena's surface when Sam spoke out. "The rings...wait a moment. What about the rings you gave me when I visited Luvelles? Are they strong enough to protect me against his magic?"

Brayson thought a moment and confirmed they were more than sufficient.

Sam removed Kael from his sheath. "I can rip this guy apart if his magic is removed from the fight. I'm sure of it."

Shalee handed Sam Junior to the handmaiden. "Don't ya even think 'bout goin' out there."

Marcus shouted from the arena, "Are you afraid to face me, brother? Do you fear me now that you have seen my ability?"

George turned. With a wave of his hand, he knocked Marcus across the arena. The crowd laughed, but quieted as Marcus sent a wall of flame toward the spectators nearest him. They lifted their arms in front of them as they watched the firestorm approach. They screamed as the explosion hit George's protective wall. Shaken, it took a moment before the crowd began to laugh again.

George faced Sam. "What an ass he is. If you go out there, he'll kill you. You don't stand a chance."

Before another word could be said, Brayson teleported from the king's box and appeared on the arena floor. The people cheered as they prepared for the next fight.

Marcus brushed the sand off his robe. Seeing Brayson standing with sword drawn, the Dark Chancellor lifted his sword to his mouth. He spoke to the blade in the language of the elves. *"Entula en' templa."*

The brothers ran toward each other. Sharpened steel once again filled the arena with its wicked sounds. Slices, lunges, spins, stabs, and sweeps were all used in a barrage of calculated movements to find the upper hand.

Many, many moments passed before Brayson found the first opening. He kicked Marcus in the chest with his right boot.

Falling to the ground, the chancellor scrambled to his feet only to find a right hand, filled with the butt end of Brayson's sword, clubbing him upside his face. Again, Marcus fell, but now he was unable to stand without falling forward to his knees.

Brayson's right boot found his brother's ribs as Marcus lifted from the sand due to the force of the impact. Marcus' ribs cracked. The sound was heard by the people nearest the exchange. Again, the crowd's cheers filled the air.

Brayson moved in to finish the job, but Marcus managed to collect himself enough to lunge blade first. The attempt was blocked and followed with a left foot to the side of Marcus' face. The chancellor spun and fell flat to the sand.

With Marcus' back to Brayson, the Head Master saw his opportunity to finish the fight. He thrust his free hand forward to deliver a powerful storm of iced needles. The magic plowed into Marcus, but the result wasn't what Brayson expected. The Head Master's power was redirected. He became the target. There was not the moments necessary to react as the force of his magic impaled him. The force of the impact sent Brayson flying across the arena, crashing into the wall below the king's box. His head hit the stone, and he fell to the ground unconscious.

As the iced needles began to melt under Brayson's skin, Marcus gathered his wits. He stood and limped across the arena to stand above his brother. A smile crossed his face as he tightened his grip on his blessed blade, appreciative of its special power. His blade's ability had allowed him to redirect Brayson's magic. Marcus watched the blood flow from the holes the iced needles left behind. He enjoyed how saturated Brayson's robe was becoming.

Mary's cries could be heard as she begged Marcus for mercy, but the chancellor's ears were deaf to her pain.

Marcus scoffed, "You disappoint me, brother. Of all the men I have killed, I will enjoy your death the most."

Marcus lifted his sword with the intent to plunge it into Brayson's chest. But, before the chancellor's blade could begin its strike, Boyafed appeared behind Marcus and thrust his sword into the chancellor's back. The blade pierced Marcus' heart and emerged from the front of his chest.

The Order leader fell unconscious as Marcus fell dead. Boyafed had teleported from the healer's table. Once he saw Marcus' back was to him, he had teleported again to deliver the killing blow.

George waved his hand, sending Brayson and Boyafed to the healers' vestry. Seeing the stress in his mother-in-law's eyes, he touched Mary on the shoulder. When they reappeared, they were standing next to BJ's brother.

Jaress turned to face George to give his prognosis. "They will live once the griffin's essence has been administered, but Dowd may never walk again."

George nodded, then left Mary at Brayson's side. He reappeared inside the king's box.

Athena was the first to speak. "Are they okay?"

Again, George nodded. "Brayson and Boyafed should be fine in a day or so, but it will be a while before we know if Dowd will walk again."

George looked at Sam. "The final threat to your kingdom has been eliminated. My family will need a place to stay. Mary is going to need her daughters to be with her while Brayson heals. She's a mess."

Shalee responded. "I was fixin' ta have rooms assigned ta everyone in the castle. Y'all can stay as long as ya like. I'll see to it that someone helps with the babies."

"Thank you, Shalee," George replied. "Sam, you can dispose of Marcus however you see fit."

The warlock turned to Gregory. "We have work to do tomorrow. We will be gone for most of the day. Check on Brayson, then get a good night's rest."

Sam put his hand on George's shoulder. "You have proven to be a good man. I'll do whatever I can to help."

"And, so will I," Shalee added, giving George a hug.

George motioned for Athena to stand beside him. He looked at Shalee. "Once things settle down, I'll take you to the Eye. For now, let's take the moments to gather a sense of where our lives are headed. Let's set the groundwork for peace and ensure our families are taken care of." George and Athena vanished.

Ancients Sovereign
Lasidious and Celestria's Home

Lasidious threw a candle made of red wax into the fireplace. "I hate that troll," he shouted as he continued to storm around the table. "How dare that piece of garesh speak to me that way! To me...of all the gods...he should fear me most! I will torture his pathetic little mind! I will make it my mission to destroy him! Kesdelain's soul will find the inside of the Book's pages soon enough! Mark my words!"

Most everything Celestria had done to accent their home had been ripped from its normal resting spot and thrown in every direction. Lasidious had not taken a moment to rest since Gabriel's announcement the day before.

Alistar and Celestria sat at the table without saying a word and waited for Lasidious to calm himself. It wasn't until after Late Bailem, and a full day of continuous shouting, that the Mischievous One stopped. Lasidious took a long deep breath, then plopped into the chair next to Celestria, across from Alistar.

The Mischievous One spoke as if nothing was wrong, as if he had never thrown a fit. "It appears a new plan is in order...don't you think?"

Alistar responded with a sly smile. "Only if you're finished venting."

Lasidious looked at the mess he made. "I am."

"Good," Celestria responded. The goddess went to work. She waved her hand across the room. The mess was replaced with fresh decor. New place settings appeared on the table along with vases filled with fresh flora. The stains on the throw rug beneath the table vanished and a new chair to replace the one Lasidious broke apart and tossed into the fire also appeared. Even the tapestries the Mischievous One had taken a knife to, mended.

Seeing that everything was in order, Alistar summoned three cold mugs of ale. He looked at Lasidious. "I have a concern which does not involve the troll you hate so much. My concern is Sharvesa."

Lasidious shook his head as if confused. "Sharvesa? Why would she be a problem?"

Celestria pushed her hair clear of her face. "Sharvesa is Payne's mother. What will happen when she finds out her son is being cared for by a human and not Defondel? Worse still, what will happen when she realizes this human is your prophet? I know she respects you, but does she respect you enough to allow her son to continue to stay with George?"

Lasidious thought a moment. "Even if she doesn't want Payne to stay with George, what would it matter? Payne has served his purpose, and Kepler has his power. Even if Payne leaves, it won't stop George from accomplishing his goals to get his daughter's soul out of the Book."

Alistar stood from the table, then leaned toward Lasidious. "I don't think you're seeing the full picture, brother. Payne has become much more to George than just a fairy-demon."

Alistar took a drink of his ale. "Haven't you seen how George and Athena treat Payne? They make him take baths, wear clothes, and George created a high chair for him. The entire family treats Payne as if he is one of their own. They gave him his own room. Even Kepler has accepted his role in protecting him."

Alistar reclaimed his chair. "Granted, the relationship the family has with the fairy-demon is strange, but it is strong. George has become attached, and despite our failure to understand this attachment, George will remain loyal to Payne."

"Agreed," Celestria added. She put her hand on Lasidious' knee. "I know you remember what George told you. He said he would sacrifice retrieving his daughter's soul to protect his family. This means, he would do the same to keep Payne."

"She's right." Alistar summoned a bowl of fruit. He continued to speak as he peeled a banana. "If Sharvesa was to take Payne from the family, who knows what George would do? This whole prophet plan of ours could backfire. I hope you're seeing the bigger picture now."

Lasidious stood from the table, grabbed the bowl of fruit and threw it across the room. The fruit hit the wall with such force, chunks were sent flying in all directions. "Damn that Book," he screamed. "We were so close to having everything!" The Mischievous One's temper took over as pieces of furniture began to fly.

Western Luvelles
The Camp of the White Army
The Next Day, the Peak of Bailem

George and Gregory appeared at the center of the white army's camp, just outside the tent meant to house the Argont Commander. They lowered a heavy chest to the ground and waited for Krasous to make his exit.

Once the warrior stood before them, Gregory began the conversation. "Krasous, I would like you to meet the Prophet of Lasidious. He has seen to it that there will be no war fought on the fields of Olis. Your men can go home to their families."

The Argont Commander lowered his head to symbolize his respect. "Please forgive me, Prophet, but I serve the gods of the white army. I am sure you are a great man to carry such a title, but I know nothing of your god. I fail to see why your lord would bother himself with a war whose combatants do not serve him."

George put his hand on the commander's shoulder. "When Lord Dowd returns, you shall feel differently. For now, I give you my word that you can break camp. Allow your men to go home to their families."

Krasous' brow furrowed. "If it's all the same to you, I will keep my men in place until Dowd gives the order."

Gregory answered. "Lord Dowd is on Grayham, recovering in the city of Brandor. Dowd fought the evil which threatened our world. He fought side-by-side with Lord Boyafed to put an end to our struggle."

Krasous stroked his chin. "Why would Dowd fight with Boyafed at his side? He is a sworn enemy of the army."

Gregory nodded. "I'll allow Lord Dowd to explain when he returns. Your men owe him their lives for his sacrifice. He may never walk again. When he returns, he will profess his loyalty to Lasidious."

George jumped back into the conversation, "Order your men to return home." The warlock reached down and patted the top of the chest. "Give each of your men two of these for their inconvenience."

George waved his hand and the lid opened. It was full of Yaloom. "This is a gift from Lasidious. He wishes for Luvelles to see prosperity. When the moment is right, I will return to share his message of love. Allow your men to be rewarded, and return to their families."

George placed his hand on Gregory's shoulder. They vanished. Krasous was left standing in the snow, staring at the chest full of wealth.

George took Gregory to the camp of the Order. With a similar speech and a second chest full of coin, Christopher was given a parchment containing an order from Boyafed to send his men home to their families.

George saw to it that the mercenaries were paid far greater than they would have imagined. He explained to Tygrus that peace was coming to Luvelles. His warriors would no longer be allowed to find employment hurting others. The prophet also suggested the mercenaries find new jobs, and become productive members of society. George and Gregory left Tygrus standing in the snow with the third and final chest.

A Cracked Gem

Southern Grayham
The Isthmus of Change
Five Days Later, Late Bailem

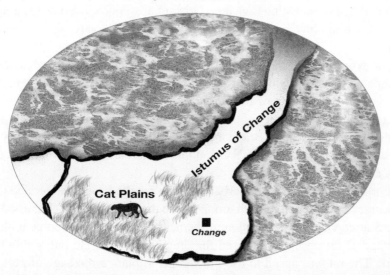

Mosley stood with his feline companions at the edge of the world he knew as Southern Grayham. They looked north across the Isthmus which extended beyond the horizon. The night terror wolf knew the perils ahead would be great. Never had the Wisp of Song given any man, or beast, a journey free from tragedy.

Mosley also knew his sabertooth companions might not be enough protection to survive. Despite his fear, he had to go. North was the answer to the wisp's questions, and this was the only way he could acquire the knowledge it was after. With this knowledge, the sphere would reveal the way to the gate which would take him to the catacombs holding the secrets of the Swayne Enserad.

130 Peaks of Bailem have Passed

Now...fellow soul...much has happened over the last 130 Peaks. Peace has settled across Southern Grayham, Harvestom, and Luvelles. Alistar visited George and gave the warlock the news of the Crystal Moon's return to the Temple of the Gods. George delivered this news to Sam and Shalee, telling them Lasidious forced Mieonus to return the crystal's pieces. Since the threat to the worlds is over, the king and queen can focus on making life better for their kingdom.

Lasidious has made many appearances to the beings on Southern Grayham to deliver his life-changing message of peace and love. Lasidious is now known to most everyone across the land as a peaceful god.

Lasidious opened the doors of the temple and allowed the beings to return to the plateau resting high atop Griffin Falls. Since that day, the prayers uttered inside Grayham's temple have, for the most part, worshipped his name.

As expected, the vast majority of Southern Grayham has decided to change who they worship after hearing about Lasidious' gift of life to their king's son. Even many of the barbarians have begun to pray to Lasidious after seeing the generosity of the reformed Senate. The same race who once hated the swine living in Brandor now approve of their new king. They understand it is because of Sam's vision that all barbarians have found a better way of life.

For the scattered sects of barbarians who rebelled, George corraled them in secrecy and teleported each group inside the Mountains of Oraness. With The Source visiting the location of the new dragon world, George took advantage of his absence and used the dragon's cavern. He put Maldwin to work. The rat was asked to use his visions to plant a message of peace in the dissenters' minds. By the moment the barbarians were teleported back to their homeworld, they no longer felt the need to rebel.

Over 925,000 souls are now praying to Lasidious on Southern Grayham. This number is expected to rise.

Now...fellow soul...much has also changed on Luvelles. Once healed, Boyafed returned to the city of Marcus and assumed his new position as chancellor. He made many changes and declared the army would no longer be called the Order. Instead, their name would be changed to the elven phrase, *Bragol Thalion*, which means, strength.

Christopher was promoted from his position as Argont Commander to the new leader of the army once he accepted Lasidious as his new lord.

Christopher was ordered by Boyafed to change the army's policies. They would no longer govern the lands of Hyperia by force. Because of this order, many rules have been implemented to ensure there are peaceful resolutions to the kingdom's problems.

For those soliders who wish to remain enlisted, or commissioned, within the new army, these men are expected to pray to Lasidious twice daily and ensure they work hand-in-hand with the white army to maintain peace throughout all Western Luvelles, not just Hyperia.

Further, Christopher was ordered to gather the darkest magic users, and give them the chance to stop their use of the art. Those who refused to accept peace as a way of life were thrown into the swamp they had polluted with so many deadly, deformed creatures. Brayson helped Boyafed find a magic strong enough to ensure none of them would escape their marshy prison.

Boyafed also decided to change the city of Marcus. As a way of poking fun at his new friend, Lord Dowd, he renamed the city, Frolond. Every statue, token, idol and altar meant to glorify Hosseff, has been destroyed. The perpetual clouds hovering over Frolond have been removed. No longer will the city be shadowed by gloom.

The walls surrounding Frolond are no longer considered a barrier for the less fortunate. The people living beyond the city's walls have been told the army will recreate their homes to bring them up to the standard of living which is enjoyed inside the city. No longer will there be a separation of class. Any man who wishes to earn a living inside the walls—whether they command strong magic or not—is welcome to try.

Fellow soul...the Kingdom of Lavan has also made many changes. After healing to the point he could use his arms to move his wheelchair, Lord Dowd began his work with Gregory to spread the word of Lasidious. Dowd moved to Lavan and took over as their new king.

Once Krasous accepted Lasidious as his new lord and swore to put off retirement, the Argont Commander accepted the position as the leader of the white army. The men who refused to accept Lasidious' word were removed from their positions within the army and given estates to show the kingdom's appreciation for their service. These men were not punished for their beliefs, but were retired and allowed to worship who they chose. Of the thousands who served in the white army, only 2,793 men chose to accept retirement.

The number of those who chose to accept retirement in Boyafed's reformed army was much higher. 8,764 men chose to continue serving

Hosseff. Due to the nature of their beliefs, a secret guard was implemented to ensure there would be no problems.

In total, between the two armies on Luvelles, over 34,200 are now praying to Lasidious twice daily. Including the members of their families, 123,472 souls serve the "so-called" God of Peace and Love. The rest of Western Luvelles is starting to take note of the changes.

Fellow soul...there was one other significant change the armies implemented—a change Kepler's scheming mind manipulated with Maldwin's help. Kepler convinced Maldwin to implant the desire to glorify him in Boyafed and Lord Dowd's minds. Thanks to Maldwin's specific visions, both men approached their respective councils with the rat in their arms.

By the moment Maldwin was finished, both councils agreed to meet with Kepler. Once they understood the cat's power, they agreed his abilities, size, strength, white fur, and red glowing eyes would make the cat the perfect choice for the newly created position, Protector of the Realm. The jaguar is now viewed as a unified symbol which both armies have adopted and placed on their armor.

A new palace is under construction for Kepler. It is being built at the center of the Battlegrounds of Olis. An enormous statue of the jaguar will be erected to honor his position. This area of Luvelles will be Kepler's to begin a family. All the jaguar needs is a mate, and thanks to Lasidious, Kepler knows where to find her.

Now...fellow soul...the centaurs on Harvestom have spent a considerable amount of their moments with Gregory. They have come to accept Lasidious' disciple as a great man. Susanne and Garrin have accompanied Gregory to Harvestom on many occasions, and the relationship between the chancellor and his new love is blossoming into something wonderful.

The Blackcoats and Browncoats have agreed to set aside their differences. Thanks to George's secret visits with Maldwin, the centaur councils are talking about creating a unified kingdom. Over 121,000 centaurs have begun to worship Lasidious.

Fellow soul...allow me to get back to the story.

The City of Inspiration
The Peak of Bailem
Today is a Day to be Celebrated

Brayson and Mary are standing at the top of the steps leading to the entrance of Gregory's glass palace. A rainbow of color rests against the walls of the chancellor's tower as the sun passes through the prisms throughout the city. Spring has arrived, and it is a wonderful day for a wedding.

Many beings have traveled to Inspiration from the lower three worlds in support of the Head Master. The streets surrounding the palace are filled as far as the eye can see. In total, over 80,000 beings are waiting to see the couple.

George teleported to Brandor and brought the royal family back to celebrate the event. Shalee's fashion expertise has been solicited. After speaking with Brayson and Mary, the couple decided to go with her recommendations. Shalee used her magic to create dresses, tuxedos, and floral arrangements for over 5,000 souls.

Sam and Shalee have taken their positions as honored guests while Sam Junior is sleeping in his mother's arms. Gregory has taken his position as Brayson's *Ho Mellon* (Best Man) while Susanne is standing beside Mary as her *He Mellon* (Maid of Honor).

George and Athena are standing beside Sam and Shalee, with the rest of the family behind them. Joshua is also asleep in his mother's arms while Payne is holding George's hand, fidgeting something fierce while wearing his first tuxedo. Approaching his first season, Garrin is sitting on George's other arm, looking down the palace steps at the movement of the crowd.

Lord Dowd has been provided a platform for his wheelchair next to Boyafed, and behind them, the esteemed members of both armies and their families are standing.

The one sight no one expected, and perhaps, the most memorable sight no one will ever see again, is the position Kepler has been given. The jaguar has worked with the scholars of Luvelles for the last 30 Peaks and will marry the couple speaking in the language of the elves.

Standing at the top of the long flight of stairs, Kepler lifted his head toward the sky. The Protector of the Realm let out a mighty roar which commanded everyone's attention. Knowing this was going to happen, George used his power to ensure every child present would not hear the fearsome sound.

After addressing the crowd and thanking them for coming, Kepler turned his attention to Brayson and Mary.

"Brayson...*Lle naa belegohtar, Cormlle naa tanya tel'raa.*"

"Mary...*Vanimle sila tiri, Lle naa vanima, Oio naa elealla alasse.*"

Mary motioned for Kepler to pause so Brayson could tell her what he said.

Brayson smiled. "The cat said I'm a mighty warrior, and I have the heart of a lion. He also said your beauty shines bright, and to see you gives him joy."

Mary winked at Kepler. "Keep up the good work."

Kepler returned the wink and continued to speak in the elvish language. Fellow soul...I shall translate to make it simple.

"Today is a day to celebrate. Peace has come to Luvelles, and your Head Master has chosen a bride. This union will break the boundaries of race. It will show the beings of this world that we all are created equal. This couple sets the standard for all to emulate. If there is anyone here who knows of a reason why this couple should not be joined...speak now."

"Doomed! This union is doomed!" The woman commanding the voice emerged from the crowd and began to float up the stairs as she continued to shout, "Doomed! Doomed! This union is doomed!"

It was Bryanna, the visionary who scared Mary and the girls during their first visit to the city. She was dressed in black, ash covering her body. "The head of this family is surrounded by evil! He is cursed! This union will perish because of it! I have forseen it! Death will come to those who follow Lasidious' Prophet!"

George ascended the steps and handed Garrin to Brayson. After commanding Payne to sit next to Mary, the warlock vanished. He reappeared next to Bryanna. With a wave of his hand, he silenced her. He used his power to lift Bryanna above the crowd. With the visionary on display, George addressed the gathering.

The warlock used his magic to amplify his voice. "There are those who would have this world live in fear! Luvelles deserves better! There are those who would seek to destroy a union as blessed as the one we see before us. I ask you now, are there any others besides this crazed woman who would object to this world having a Head Master who seeks his own happiness? Is there any other who can say one bad thing about Brayson? I see no evil in this man. Since my arrival on Luvelles, I have seen his honor, his integrity, and his loyalty to every being. If you wish to witness this union, shout your approval!"

Thousands of people lifted their voices to the sky as if it had been rehearsed. George lowered Bryanna to the ground, then released his power over her. He commanded four guards to carry her away, and throw her in the dungeon.

As they dragged her through the streets, Bryanna continued to shout, "Doomed...doomed...this union is doomed!"

George shook his head and gave everyone around him a big, bright smile. "I can't tell you how happy I am she isn't my mother-in-law!" He listened to the crowd laugh, then teleported next to Brayson. After taking Garrin into his arm and Payne's hand, he took his position next to Athena. "Wow. What a nut job that lady was. Shall we continue?"

Kepler smirked. "Other than the crazy lady, is there anyone else who wishes to object?"

Once the laughter subsided, the street quieted. It felt as if everyone was waiting for a voice to cry out, but when one never came, Kepler moved forward with the ceremony. He concluded by saying, "By the authority given to me by Lasidious, I pronounce this couple united. Brayson, you may lick your bride's face."

Brayson and Mary shook their heads and stared at the jaguar.

Susanne leaned forward and spoke in a whisper. "Kepler, he needs to kiss her. We don't lick one another."

"Oohhh. My apologies. Brayson, you may kiss your bride's face."

Again, Susanne spoke in a whisper. "No, Kepler. We kiss on the lips."

Kepler growled his frustration. "Just kiss whatever it is you feel like kissing. I hear the lips work good for this."

Lord Dowd and Boyafed led the laughter as the crowd enjoyed the awkwardness of the moment.

Later that night, Sam caught up with George inside Gregory's ballroom. "George, you handled the crazy woman rather well. I have to admit, she freaked me out. It wasn't that long ago I would've believed her, but after watching the way you've handled yourself, I believe you've become a good man."

George put his hands on Sam's shoulders. "Thanks, man. You know, since you and Shalee are on Luvelles, why don't you let Shalee take her look into the Eye so the two of you can teleport between worlds? She has already passed the trials, so it wouldn't take long. There are so many amazing places we could go if Shalee had this power. We could visit anywhere we wanted on Harvestom, Luvelles and Grayham. It would be a lot of fun. We could call it...our moments to bond."

"I don't know, George. The baby needs..."

"I think that idea sounds swell," Shalee blurted as she joined in. "Goodness-gracious, Sam, you know how ta handle the baby. You'll be okay 'til I get back. I could go tomorrow night."

Sam took the baby from her arms. "What about the soul swallowing? I would rather have my son's mother around. I don't want to lose you."

George looked at Shalee. "He does have a point. It is possible the Eye could swallow your soul."

Shalee pushed Sam Junior's hair clear of his forehead. "If I had any doubts, I wouldn't do it. My power is progressin' at a rapid pace. I have no worries 'bout my soul. I am 100,000 percent sure I won't leave ya without a wife. Besides, travelin' wherever we want would be fun."

"Then, I shall take you tomorrow night...that is, if you're okay with it, Sam."

Sam shrugged. "If there is one thing I've learned about being married to this woman, she's too stubborn to tell her no. If I don't agree, she'll torture me until I do. The baby and I will wait here in the palace."

George clapped his hands. "Then, tomorrow night it is. We should celebrate."

Ancients Sovereign
Lasidious and Celestria's Home

With his feet on the table, Lasidious leaned back in his chair. He watched the vision of Sam, George, and Shalee fade within the flames of his fireplace. He turned to Alistar who sat on the opposite side of the table. "This is what we have been waiting for. Tomorrow night we'll have our meeting with the dragons to discuss further adjustments to the land masses of their new world. Finally, we'll be rid of the biggest threat to our plans."

Alistar stood from his chair, "Things are once again beginning to go our way. I've convinced the Collective to concentrate their efforts on perfecting the dragon world. They want it to be our most beautiful creation yet. The Source will be in attendance. The dragon wants his new home to be perfect before he moves from Luvelles."

"Can you blame him?" Celestria responded as she stood from her chair. "You two talk too much." She reached out and pushed Lasidious' feet from the table. With a flip of her wrist, she used her power to move Lasidious' chair into a better position. Facing him, the goddess straddled his legs and lowered onto his lap.

Seeing the moments were about to become awkward, Alistar vanished.

Celestria purred, "You see, my love, my pet, my sweet, my cute little devil-god, we shall control the Book soon enough." She leaned into Lasidious and kissed the top of his ear. The Mischievous One trembled. He placed his hands on her hips and listened while she continued to whisper. "Soon, our son will be old enough. We will draw from his power to take control of Gabriel. You, my pet, will be a king among gods. Perhaps, you should show your future queen the passion her king has for her. She longs for you." She leaned in and licked his lips.

Fellow soul...the rest of what happened I will leave to your imagination. For those of you who will take a moment to ponder what may have transpired...STOP...BE GOOD...keep reading.

Western Luvelles
The Shoreline of Crystal Lake

Gage and Gallrum stood on the shoreline of Crystal Lake as they watched Luvelles' new moon rise above the horizon opposing the sun to begin its journey across the sky. The sun's rays were beginning to peek over the mountains and glimmer off the water. Neither goswig could have asked for a more perfect spring morning in which to begin their adventures.

"I'm nervous," Gage said while using his cane to carve his name in the pebbles covering the shoreline. "I have never left Luvelles. We are free to do whatever we wish, now that our masters are dead. Where should we go?"

The serwin reached up and scratched his head. "I can't say I know. It feels strange to know I no longer need to stay hidden."

Gage pondered a bit before responding. "We can go to any world we choose since there are no restrictions on our races. I want to expand my knowledge of the other worlds."

"Where do you suggest we do this?"

The badger stopped pushing his cane through the pebbles. "I had a dream last night about the ice of Northern Grayham. I have to admit, I felt like I was being called to it. I feel as if someone is in trouble. He needs our help. Perhaps, we should head to Merchant Island. Let's find warmer attire, then catch a ride with the Merchant Angels. Let's go see what has called to me."

Gallrum smiled. "What could it hurt? Let's see what your dream is all about."

Without further conversation, Gage took Gallrum's talon. Both goswigs vanished.

Ancients Sovereign

From inside the Hall of Judgment, the Book of Immortality sighed as the images of the goswigs faded from within the marble table. Gabriel reached up and scratched the chin protruding from his binding. "Help is coming, Mosley. Help is coming. Just hang in there. You must fight for survival. Help is coming."

Western Luvelles
The Next Day
Late Bailem

George and Shalee appeared inside The Source's cave. George knew the Ancient One would be with the gods discussing the changes to the new dragon world. He escorted Shalee to the heavy iron door of the Eye's chamber, then stopped. He reached out and took Precious from Shalee, then leaned the staff against the wall before slapping his hand against the door. "The Eye of Magic is on the other side."

Shalee embraced herself. "Tarnation. Chills just ran through my body. I'm a bit nervous. Did ya feel the same way?"

"Of course." George's face turned serious. "Let me give you a piece of advice Brayson gave me. The key to looking in the Eye is your belief in yourself. You must have no doubt you deserve its power. Go in there and show the Eye who's boss."

"You're right. That Eye hasn't ever met a genuine Texan before. I can do this." She leaned in and gave him a hug. "Ya didn't turn out so bad after all, George. Thank ya for everythin'."

George smiled and put his forehead against Shalee's. "You can thank me once you get your blessing from the Eye. Now, get in there, and know you deserve what's coming to you."

Shalee opened the door and walked inside. She walked only a few feet before the door slammed behind her. The deafening sound sent a chill through her as she stared at the gem sitting atop a wooden staff at the center of a cubed-shaped room. The gem was beautiful and larger than her fist. Its fiery-red color called to her fashion sense. Nothing else occupied the room.

Suddenly, a blinding light emerged from the gem, and before she knew it, Shalee was standing in front of an angelic being. The light softened and was replaced with a soft glow surrounding a face which could not be seen. A ghostly body hung suspended while feathered wings extended to either side. Shalee felt as if she was in the presence of a god as the large eye sitting on the being's shoulders came into focus.

George waited until the bright light caused by the Eye's presence faded from beneath the door. He knew the Eye had finished pulling Shalee inside its gem to question her. The moment had come to act.

The warlock used his power to push the door open. He looked across the room. The gem, sitting atop the staff, held a soft glow. Without entering the chamber, he lifted his hands. A single bolt of his most powerful lightning struck the gem's polished surface. The gem cracked—trapping Shalee inside as the power filling the stone faded.

George grinned from ear to ear as he spoke in a soft voice filled with wickedness. "You'll never get the chance to thank me, Shalee. Your husband will learn to adapt without you...that is, if I don't kill him. But, I have business to attend to on Eastern Luvelles first. I have a heart to eat. They have shapeshifting wood elves there."

George hesitated. "I don't know that I can bear the thought of leaving your son without a parent, despite the hatred I have for your husband. I will contemplate Sam's fate as I travel." The warlock retrieved Shalee's staff. He walked into The Source's cavern, then tossed Precious into the lava. He laughed, then teleported home.

The next day, The Source returned. He lowered his massive form across the rivers of lava which flowed across the cave's floor. He lifted his nostrils into the air and sniffed. He could smell the scorch mark left behind on the gem's surface. He shut his eyes and used his power to look into the Eye's chamber. Seeing the crack, the Ancient One pulled back within himself, then opened his eyes. Anger erupted from the depths of The Source's being as he filled the cavern with fire.

Outside the cave, Alistar leaned against Fisgig's old perch. He watched as the cliffs surrounding the pool began to crumble as the sound of the Ancient One's anger filled the Mountains of Oraness. The mighty dragon burst through the top of the mountain. Before vanishing, the Ancient One made sure every being within a two day ride on a krape lord's back could hear his anguish.

Inside the Cracked Gem
Two Days Later

Shalee continues to wander through the red haze. The angelic form of the Eye is nowhere to be found, and her heart is racing as she frantically looks in every direction.

Has somethin' gone wrong? she thought. *Am I supposed ta just wait? Is this the same thing George saw? Has my soul been swallowed?*

Shalee continued to wander for many long moments before three blinding lights appeared. Forced to cover her eyes, she tried to look through her fingers, but the lights were too strong. She was forced to turn her head away.

As the illuminations faded. Three figures were left behind. Shalee's eyes fought to adjust as she faced her unexpected company. As the beings came into focus, she gasped, "Oh my heavens!" It took a moment to peel her hand from her mouth. Stepping forward, she reached out to touch one of the figures. Sure enough, her friend was standing before her.

Shalee squeezed the woman's shoulders. They felt familiar. She fell to her knees and embraced the woman's waist and placed her head on Helga's abdomen. "Goodness-gracious...Helga...is it really you?"

Helga's smile widened, "Hello, child. Did you miss me?"

A grumpy voice added, "Did you miss me, too?"

Shalee removed her head from Helga's stomach. She stood, faced BJ, then rushed into his arms. "Of course, I missed ya, grumpy guss. Don't be silly. Sam is gonna be so happy ta know you're alive."

The third figure placed his right hand on Shalee's shoulder. Once the sorceress was facing him, he spoke. "The moments have come, Shalee. You must build a new heaven. Only then can you return to the worlds."

The End

Keep reading for a
SNEAK PEEK
inside the pages of
Book 3
Crystal Moon
The Kingdoms of the Ice Kings

The Kingdoms of the Ice Kings

"Run, Mosley! You must run, my love," Luvera shouted as she looked up the cliff's icy face. Her haunches trembled beneath her dark fur as she limped toward the path ascending the most treacherous mountain in Northern Grayham.

From high above, Mosley kept his gaze fixed on his enemy. He cried out his response. "I cannot! It is too late for that! I will not lose you again!"

With the placement of each paw, the weight of the snow hounds crunched into the crusty layer of snow covering the path. Their eyes gleamed with anticipation as they closed in on their next meal.

Mosley backed up, looking for the best opportunity to act. He was running out of path. It was now or never. Crouching into an attack position, he sized up his foes for one final moment. These hounds were nearly twice his size. The white fur covering their rippling muscles had been stained by Luvera's blood, and the drool dangling from their loosened lips dripped to the snow.

Mosley growled. The steam from his breath rose in a fog. His legs extended as he launched head-on into the first of three attackers.

Yelping, Mosley's eyes snapped open, jarring him back into reality. It took a moment, but he soon realized he was still lying on his prison floor made of ice. It was hard to keep his eyes open. They were so swollen. The last five days had been filled with suffering during his waking moments. Beaten, tortured, and questioned for answers he would not disclose, he found the strength to rise to his feet as another enemy, a real enemy, approached.

The Frigid Commander of Hydroth grabbed the bars of the cell, opened the door and stepped inside. Ensuring the door was locked, his blue hand, covered with a glove made from the hide of a slagone, released the ice.

Mosley watched as the light of a glowing orb glimmered off the crystallizations embedded in the commander's skin. The orb's light was soft, and the heat cast from it did not soften the cell's integrity. The cell had been shaped into the ice, and like the rest of Hydroth, it had been chiseled into the shelves covering the frozen tundra of Northern Grayham.

The commander's feet were bare. His body remained uncovered, except for a hooded cloak and a dangling cloth covering his groin and two tribal bands encircling the width of his biceps.

As the powerful Isorian turned to face Mosley, he moved to stand over over the wolf, then motioned for his guards to turn away. A cruel smile stretched his lips as he looked down and watched as the wolf hobbled into a corner. The wrinkles around the commander's milky eyes tightened as he crossed his arms. "It pleases me you are up, Wolf. You are resilient. I will relish this day's trobletting."

Mosley snarled, exposing his teeth. "I will not speak with you."

Fellow soul...if you want to know more, read Book 3.
I just stuck my soulful tongue out at you.

Enjoy the next few pages of concept art for Book 3

The Kingdoms of the Ice Kings

Clandestiny and Medolas
(Clanny)

Shamand
(Bumps)

Salvasen
(Slips)

Northern Grayham
Mountain Range of Tedfer

World of Dragonia
Mount Moragamain – The Source's New Home

**Books, apparel and other
Crystal Moon products:**

www.worldsofthecrystalmoon.com

Facebook:

www.facebook.com/worldsofthecrystalmoon

You can email Big Dog at:

phillip.jones@hotmail.com